ALL WE HOLD DEAR

"Kathryn Lynn Davis will hold you spellbound with this exquisite evocation of a unique time and memorable people."

—*Romantic Times*

"Readers who loved the bestselling *Too Deep for Tears* will also be ensnared by this ambitious sequel. . . . Davis' nineteenth-century characters are so richly drawn that it's difficult to leave them."

—*Publishers Weekly*

"I couldn't put it down. . . . *All We Hold Dear* is beautiful, passionate, and wild like the rugged Scottish Highlands. Excellent reading adventure."

—*Rendezvous*

"*All We Hold Dear* displays Davis' growing power as a storyteller who can capture the imagination and hold it until the final page."

—*The San Bernardino County Sun* (CA)

"Deftly crafted. . . . The loves, lives, and tragedies of the family are sensitive and heartbreaking. The outstanding setting portrayal breathes life into this poignant story."

—*Affaire de Coeur*

"A very pleasurable read. . . . The author's descriptive powers are as skilled as her ability to tell a good story."

—*Chattanooga Times* (TN)

TOO DEEP FOR TEARS

"Populated with unforgettable characters, *Too Deep for Tears* sweeps the reader around the world and back. . . . [A] compelling story of loss, betrayal, love, and discovery."
—*Affaire de Coeur*

"Complex, beautiful, and sensitive. . . . Lyrical and lovely."
—*Roanoke Times & World News* (VA)

"Engrossing . . . moving . . . Every woman will find a part of herself in *Too Deep for Tears*."
—*Rave Reviews*

"Her characters are richly drawn, and the relationships between lovers, friends, parents, and children are beautifully portrayed."
—*Inside Books*

"Get out your handkerchiefs. . . ."
—*Dallas News*

"Captivating. . . . A major novel."
—*The San Bernardino County Sun* (CA)

Books by Kathryn Lynn Davis

Somewhere Lies the Moon
All We Hold Dear
Too Deep for Tears
Child of Awe
Sing to Me of Dreams

Published by POCKET BOOKS

KATHRYN LYNN DAVIS

SOMEWHERE LIES THE MOON

POCKET STAR BOOKS

New York   London   Toronto   Sydney   Singapore

This book is a work of fiction. Names, characters, places and incidents are products of the author's imagination or are used fictitiously. Any resemblance to actual events or locales or persons, living or dead, is entirely coincidental.

 A Pocket Star Book published by
POCKET BOOKS, a division of Simon & Schuster Inc.
1230 Avenue of the Americas, New York, NY 10020

Copyright © 1999 by Kathryn Lynn Davis

Originally published in hardcover in 1999 by Pocket Books

All rights reserved, including the right to reproduce
this book or portions thereof in any form whatsoever.
For information address Pocket Books, 1230 Avenue
of the Americas, New York, NY 10020

ISBN: 0-671-73606-X

First Pocket Books paperback printing August 2000

10 9 8 7 6 5 4 3 2 1

POCKET STAR BOOKS and colophon are registered
trademarks of Simon & Schuster Inc.

Cover illustration by Brian Bailey

Printed in the U.S.A.

Grateful acknowledgment to Heather Sullivan & Ron Alan
Cohen for the lyrics from "Somewhere There Lies the Moon" by
Heather Sullivan and Ron Alan Cohen. Copyright © 1998 by
MAYDAYBLU Music/BMI and Ron Alan Cohen/ASCAP. All
rights reserved. Used by permission.

To my husband Michael:
"Had we but world enough, and time," I would tell you everything I feel. But I'll say only this: I'm here; we are together; we have hope; I'm looking forward now instead of back. As Andrew Marvel wrote long ago: "Thus, though we cannot make our sun stand still, yet we will make him run." And so we will.

And to my sister, Annie:
Because, I thought it was complete surrender, but she insisted it was a declaration of war. And though she was fighting her own battles, she nevertheless helped me retain my faith and determination; refused to let me give up or in. Fighting side by side, and making peace with our separate causes, we've come to understand the bond between sisters, which is much more than friendship—an intuitive sensitivity of thought and feeling that is unique and priceless. I've waited too long to express my deep gratitude for her tenacity, and my admiration for her incredible compassion, strength, and kindness.

Acknowledgments

This book has been a challenge and a triumph in ways I could never have imagined. The process has not always been easy, but the lessons I learned are extraordinarily powerful and exhilarating. I learned that I am stubborn; it's hard to stop me once I've made a decision. I am stronger than I knew and my creativity is not reserved for those moments of euphoria when all things seem possible. Even when, occasionally, the conditions are less than perfect, once I touch a pen or the keys, inspiration is waiting, smoldering within. Most important, I learned that I *can do anything*—the greater the risk, the better. I will not be conquered; my obstinance and love of writing are too great.

I did not learn all this alone. I had the help of friends and family, who maintained an unshakable faith in my perseverance, my ability and my compulsion to tell a story once it's taken root in my heart.

My friend Jillian Hunter, who read the manuscript so often and so quickly—she didn't want to leave me in suspense. That's only one example of her boundless compassion.

As always, my sister, Annie, and my mother, Anna, read the manuscript and gave suggestions, helping me perceive, and therefore, I hope, to write a better book.

Kim Feazell, surely a kindred spirit from long ago, also read, and wept, touching me deeply, making me determined that one day she should hold *Somewhere Lies the Moon* in her hands and know she's made a difference.

My assistant, Cheri, who protects me like a wildcat her cub, while making me laugh or cry, whichever is more necessary at the time. I'm very glad she's in my life.

Phyllis Lovell and Gary Sheets, acupuncturists and friends who kept me functioning through it all. If I needed them, they were always available, no matter the day or time. I am keenly aware of their generosity and genuine kindness. Thank you, not only for your care, but for being attentive enough to ask questions, for listening to my wordy answers and for helping me keep my creative fire burning.

Many thanks to Hazel Carney, who enthusiastically conveyed her intimate understanding of, and, I suspect, passion for wildcats living in the hills and forests, their habits and weaknesses and amazing strengths. Because of her, what might have been merely an injured animal became a symbol of the vitality and frailty in the people who live in my world—the wild Scottish Highlands.

My deep gratitude to Martha Eaton, not only for her amazing skill, but also for her generosity, her wisdom, and, most of all, her extraordinary sense of empathy.

Theda Shapiro, who offered to share her thorough knowledge of France just when I was ready to despair. With her help and her numerous stories of the world outside Paris, I built a town and peopled it with characters of whom I've grown quite fond.

Heather Sullivan, a talented musician who wrote a song that struck a chord in me, gave me the title of this book, and verbalized the themes. Thanks to Heather's graciousness in allowing me to use the lyrics, the song, "Somewhere There Lies the Moon," has become an integral part of the novel. And David, with his innovative, exciting and generous ideas for helping to fuse song and book. I admire your ingenuity. Thank you.

Everyone at the Jane Rotrosen agency, who made me feel like part of their family, buoying me up when necessary, rejoicing with me, sometimes sympathizing, sometimes pointing out the truth even when I might not want to hear it, and generally being there—always welcoming and willing to help. Thank you all for making me feel I was never alone. And though these last few years have been a challenge to her as well, my agent, Andrea, kept her faith in me alive. It's a blustery sea out there, AC, but when the wind dies down, the view is amazing. I intend to keep my eyes open, waiting for the glow of the moon across the water.

My editor, Linda Marrow, who taught me I can do anything if only I'm determined enough.

From the bottom of my heart, I thank my new friend and collaborator, Virginia Blumenthal, who has given me so much in such a short time. She taught me (and will, no doubt, be reminding me frequently) how to be positive, even when I want to be morose. She forced me to find and feed my faith in myself, to make it stronger. She brought back the enthusiasm, the thrill of inspiration, and my true love of writing. We were meant to meet; I'm sure of that. Meant to become close friends, and meant to go on and create new and different stories. Meant, perhaps, to make miracles now and then. I'm ready.

There are two more I must mention here, because both changed my life, and both died this past year, when I could not grieve for them properly. Esther Gobrecht, friend and high school English teacher, who loved words as much as I do, and never failed to come to a book signing, lecture, or celebration. She thought she died having accomplished nothing. Many, many students, including and especially me, say she couldn't have been more wrong. We remember how many lives she touched, and we will never forget.

The second is John Phillips, my history professor in college; I'd known him for over twenty years. Like Esther, he was also my friend. He was a man who did not give in to adversity, but bashed it soundly on the head and went on his way. He was still young, vibrant, full of energy and kindness for those who needed it. He was a brilliant teacher, and to him that did not mean simply giving lectures in the classroom. He helped me get my first grant to go to Scotland and research *Child of Awe*, and several grants after that. He helped me gain confidence and applauded my success, almost reveled in it. He respected me in a way few teachers have, and I can find no words of thanks for all he did and all he was. Words would never be enough (which for me is saying a very great deal).

SOMEWHERE
LIES THE MOON

The Dream

"MARRY ME."

For an instant, Eva Crawford hesitated, facing Rory Dey across the room. "I can't," she said, mystified by her refusal. She did not know where the words had come from. A book lay open in one hand; unconsciously, she ran her fingers over the faded words on the brittle yellowed pages. She was only dimly aware of the smell of the past, of old leather and dust and ink long dried. Trying to avoid Rory's questioning gaze and her own confusion, she stared down at her great-great-grandmother's journal—a compelling voice that bound Eva to a family, a history, a past.

"It's five years now I've been waiting," Rory reminded her. "Five years of having just so much of you and then no more. I want it all, Eva. You know that well enough."

"I want it too," she said vehemently, but once more her gaze was drawn to the journal in her hands. *To Ena*, the frontispiece read. *Flame, Hope, Miracle.*

Rory had been her lover for a long time and knew her as no one else could. He sensed the barrier the journal represented. "Put that book down and talk to me."

Eva flushed with remorse. Feeling the inexplicable pull

of the past, which had begun to draw her in, despite her own inclinations, away from this man and this moment, she did as he asked. He deserved her full attention. He deserved so much more. Carefully, so she would not harm its cracked, fragile binding, Eva placed the journal on the nightstand then turned back to Rory. "I can be with you, love you, make love to you, talk endlessly, as you know all too well. But I can't do something so—" She hesitated again, "so permanent. Not yet. Don't ask me why, Rory. I don't know. Honestly, I don't." She was not aware that with one hand she caressed the old leather delicately.

Perplexed by her response, Rory nevertheless refused to give in. It was one of the reasons they'd been together for so long. He crossed the room and pulled her down to the edge of the bed beside him. "You're always staying over at my flat, or I at yours. I'm just thinking of practicality, is all." He smiled at the obvious lie and spread her long thin fingers out on his knee. "What's troubling you?"

Shaking her head in frustration, Eva mused, "I've got you, this lovely flat, the scholarship at university, my music and my friends. But still, I feel . . ." she glanced at the journal, "restless . . . or confused. Perhaps both." In agitation, she ran her fingers through her shoulder-length chestnut hair. "I don't know why."

He regarded her thoughtfully, blue eyes intent, sun-browned skin striped with the last of the dying light through the blinds. "Because you're stubborn? Because you think you'll never fulfill your dream?" His voice was touched equally with whimsy and with worry. "Come live with me and let me show you otherwise."

Attempting, as always, to understand the odd moods that shaped Eva's music and, in the last few days, her reticence, he was intensely aware of the stillness in the room. For once there was no music on the cassette player and the television was switched off. It was rarely silent around Eva;

even in the absence of tape or record, melodies seemed to cling about her like a finely woven, invisible shawl.

At his concerned expression, Eva leaned forward, hands outstretched. "I'm really trying to say yes, to make myself take the risk. I'm trying."

Rory touched her cheek affectionately. "Very trying."

Eva laughed; she couldn't help it. "I know," she agreed. "And you're so patient I begin to fear you're a saint."

Grasping her around the waist, Rory pushed her down on the rumpled bed, knocking the lamp over as they fell onto the mattress. "Aye? Then let me disabuse you of that notion here and now." He kissed her forehead, her nose, her cheeks, as his black hair brushed her skin. Fiercely, he drew her closer till their lips met in a long, deep kiss. He looked up, eyebrow quirked in a question. "Do you see my point?"

Eva smiled when he leaned down to kiss her again, and they breathed together, laughter and desire mingled.

When she caught her breath, she whispered against his lips, "Why am I lucky enough to have you? Why haven't you given up in despair?"

He buried his fingers deeply in her hair. "Because I'm a stubborn bastard who can't resist a challenge." His grin turned serious and sensual. "Nor can I resist you. You can be as miserable as you like and I won't be made to go away. And if you want to weep, well," he drew out the word in a heavy Scottish brogue, then made an "x" on his shoulder with his index finger, "I've a broad shoulder ready and waiting, and an excellent laundress to clean my shirts."

Tears came to Eva's eyes as she smiled. "So you do." She kissed him again, hungrily. "Perhaps I'm only trying too hard."

Rory grinned. "No such thing, lass. Allow me to demonstrate."

He held her close, seeking the place inside that released her from the pressure of distracting thoughts and allowed passion to overwhelm reason. Clinging together, they made love, losing themselves in the warm reality of their pleasure.

Afterward, they fell asleep, her cheek buried in the crook of his neck.

Eva awoke with a start. Rory slept soundly beside her, yet the darkness rang with the sound of his eagerness and devotion. *Marry me.*

She wanted to, so much, but some instinct held her back. She felt a wariness, a waiting for something she could not imagine. Something she suspected had nothing to do with Rory. That was what disturbed her most of all. She did not want to lose him, could not imagine her life without him. She would give anything to push aside her reluctance, to ignore it and throw herself willingly and forever into her lover's waiting arms. She reached for him, but her hand froze, hovering above his bare shoulder as if stopped by an invisible pane of glass.

Perhaps it was because she was not being totally honest, even with herself. She felt incomplete, somehow, inadequate. Three years ago she'd written and recorded a song that had unexpectedly been a hit. She'd been rejected so many times since that she'd lost count. She just couldn't seem to find success again. She'd become more and more frustrated; she felt she had to prove herself, to prove she was worth something.

One thing she didn't want was to lean on Rory as she had been doing recently, to depend on him so much. Yet she felt that if she tried to stand on her own two feet, she'd surely stumble. She had to be certain she could hold her own before she made a commitment to Rory. Otherwise it would be unfair to them both. She watched him longingly, wanting more than anything for him to take her in his arms and comfort her.

Feeling deeply alone despite his presence, she turned to the journal on the nightstand, the letters beside it, bound in a faded purple ribbon and written by her ancestor Ailsa Rose Sinclair. The carved Chinese chest from which the papers had come sat in the place of honor at the foot of the bed. The journal lay open in a pool of lamplight, the familiar handwriting calling to Eva. She glanced at the page and read: *We ran far and forever that night in our fear, and in escaping, found our way home*.

Eva heard the words as clearly as if someone had spoken in her ear. Unnerved, she turned away. In the dim light, she stared at the painting on the opposite wall, hung in a simple wooden frame. Though it was across the room, draped in night shadows, to Eva the image was perfectly clear, glowing with color and light. At the left was a young girl with blue-violet eyes and chestnut hair falling loose to her waist. She was kneeling beside a burn, looking at a reflection in the still golden water. In the center stood an exotic Chinese girl with a thick black braid and almond shaped eyes that were startlingly sky blue in her bronzed face. She wore an intricate Chinese robe and held a moon-shaped mirror in her hands, gazing at the lovely Oriental face caught in the silver glass. At the right was a slight young blonde, her hair tumbling from its pins, staring pensively at the portrait she was painting of a fragile woman with her own flyaway hair and mysterious blue-gray eyes. The three were half-sisters borne of a man named Charles Kittridge, who had wandered the world, leaving each daughter behind, until in the end, he had painted this portrait as a gift and an apology to them all.

"Ailsa," Eva murmured, naming the girl on the left, knees sunken in soft loam. "Lian." She looked into the Chinese girl's blue eyes and her exotic mirror. "And Genevra." Eva examined the girl's dreamy face, the portrait she was painting, as if to memorize details she had memorized long since. Every night Eva stood before the painting and repeated this little ritual, trying to know, through sight, through aged and mellow paint, these women who were her ancestors. Usually, it gave her comfort, made her feel that she belonged. But not tonight.

She rose precipitously. She could not stay still with the sound of Rory's even breathing so close. He was sleeping deeply, undisturbed. Why couldn't she find that kind of peace, that elusive contentment anymore?

Because you're not enough, might never be enough, a voice inside her head answered. Trying to shut it out, she flung her robe about her shoulders and slipped out the door of the small flat. She headed for the stairs, too impatient to wait for the lift.

Once out in the misted air of the garden, with the soft give of the turf beneath her feet, she sniffed the fragrance of blooming roses and honeysuckle and waited for the pulse of the earth to take her.

But tonight there were no fleeting songs among the heavy, overblown flowers. Usually Eva found a rhythmic line of verse in the dew on a petal or a bit of a tune among the soft, swaying branches. Tonight the moon was hidden by clouds and the darkness was heavy with a silence no lilting melody could break.

As chilled and melancholy as she was confused, she looked up at a sky full of stars masked by clouds and felt bereft. There was no respite for her here, no music in her head to soothe her. She stumbled back inside and pushed the button for the lift, exhausted and full of misgivings. She would go back to her dreams: there was nowhere else.

She slipped inside the flat and into bed without waking Rory and fell uneasily into sleep.

The dream quickly became a nightmare. She was running toward the sound of a rushing burn, but when she found the still pool ringed in ferns, she could not see her reflection in the water. She turned and was swathed in silks and satin, holding an ornate mirror, but the glass was empty of her image. She shook with fear, and each time she moved, her chest ached with the painful rasp of her breath. Sometimes the effort seemed too great, until at last she sat on a folding stool and held her aching sides. She did not know what she was running from, but each time she looked where her face should have been and found emptiness, her heartbeat raced and her palms grew damp.

She found she was holding a paintbrush in her hand, poised before a canvas with the half-painted willowy figure of a woman taking shape. Eva worked on her features, darkening, shadowing, shaping the pale cheekbones and wide eyes, but when she looked closer, the face was blank—a wash of white paint without definition.

She dropped the brush and ran as her shadow faded and disappeared. Where it should have touched her feet, reaching out and away from the light to make the shape of her tall body on the spongy ground, there was nothing. She felt naked, alone in a way that made her throat raw with dread. She had to get back to the flat where Rory waited. He would hold and comfort her, make her forget. She needed the weight of his arms around her, his breath in her disheveled hair.

When she flung open the door, he did not stir at the crashing noise. Eva noticed with dismay that her ancestor's journal and letters were gone. The chest was gone, the painting, all traces of the past that was her lifeline. She froze. Then she saw the bed where she'd lain in restless sleep. The sheets were smooth, cold, unwrinkled, as if it had not been slept in.

Rory lay sprawled half across her side of the bed, arm outstretched, but she knew he was not reaching for her. Then he opened his eyes and glanced at the spot where she stood shuddering.

He did not see her. Eva did not have to look into his eyes to know that she would find there no memory of her face. She had no more substance than vapor, a draught that had crept under the door, uninvited and unremarked.

Eva felt a terror so cold it stopped her heart. She felt herself dissolving, staring into Rory Dey's blank blue eyes. It was not only that he did not know her.

It was as if she had never been at all.

Book One

❧

There's a great big world
outside your little window;
Like Christopher Columbus
We're sailing through space.

Book One

1

Glen Affric, Scotland, 1879

THERE WERE NIGHT SOUNDS BEYOND THE RING OF LANTERN light that caught within it streams of rushing water, divided and fused again, tumbling over huge striped boulders in the swift summer burn. In the darkness beyond the circle, the nightingale sang, a white owl hooted, a wildcat called to her missing mate. The breeze ruffled the treetops—a promise, a threat, a faint caress—the cool summer child of the harsh winter wind. There was no mist, yet shapes and hues and textures blurred together—a dark background for the luminous sphere of light.

Mairi Rose Kittridge, Ailsa Rose Sinclair, Wan Lian, and Genevra Townsend reclined in the radiance on smooth flat rocks, contemplating low, stairstep waterfalls descending gently from level to level. Where the falls did not turn it to swirling foam, the water was clear golden, and lush ferns grew in hollows that followed the curve of the river.

Ailsa, Lian and Genevra had stripped down to their shifts to luxuriate in the mild summer air. But Mairi Rose was fifty-six, and though she enjoyed seeing the young women take off their clothes and release their inhibitions, she remained fully dressed, regarding them with tenderness and concern. She had contented herself with removing her brogues and raising her skirts to wade in the large pool where the waterfalls dissolved into stillness. She'd unpinned her silver-streaked red hair, loosening the braid that blended with and altered the pattern of the red plaid she wore. It did not have to keep away the chill, for it was summer and the night, for once, was warm; she wore it because the plaid was old, comfortable and poignantly familiar.

Ailsa raised her head, chestnut hair falling down her back to pool on the rock behind her, and stared up at the interlocking pattern of leaves. "Sometimes I wonder if my father dreamed it all, conjured up this night, the magic lantern that makes only this place real in all the world, and all of us here, together." She nodded toward Genevra and Lian, her newly discovered half-sisters, in amazement and affection.

Lian was twenty-five, tall and lithe, with the thick black hair and bronze skin of the Chinese, while Genevra was eighteen, small and slender, with translucent skin and fine blond hair that refused to stay bound. At thirty-eight, Ailsa had the sturdy wholesome beauty of a woman of the glen, with her sun-browned skin and scattered freckles, her strong legs and callused feet, which had carried her over this very burn many times when she was younger.

The single feature the half-sisters shared was the reflection of their father's light blue English eyes. Ailsa's were blue-violet, Lian's sky blue, Genevra's blue flecked with gray.

"I do not think Charles Kittridge has that kind of power," Lian offered, legs pulled close to her body. "To create this place and us as well." She kept her voice neutral, stifling a flash of the rage at her father that had shaped her childhood. He was a British diplomat who had traveled the Empire, leaving behind Ailsa in Scotland, Lian in China, Genevra in India. He had abandoned his daughters and their mothers, though it had not been his choice. Nevertheless, the result had been the same. He had left them helpless and far apart, from him and from each other, except for the invisible strands that bound them through their dreams. They might never have met, but he had called his three daughters to his bedside here in the Scottish Highlands, where it had all begun, where—in the end—he had chosen to die.

Charles Kittridge's widow, Mairi, and the half-sisters had passed through the fire of the first violent rush of grief over his death nearly two months ago. Tonight they'd become restless, in need of grace and stimulation, rather than sorrow. So here they sat in the glow of the lantern, losing themselves in the songs of the river.

Genevra, the youngest, looked up, eyes alight. "Of course our father has that kind of power." She had been drawing on her ever-present sketchpad, trying to capture, not the image, but the essence of her sisters in the mellow light of the glen. "We're here, aren't we? Still here, though he's gone, buried, no more than a ghost." She looked about, shivering. "Yet I feel he's hovering about us, watching. I know he is." Her tone held more longing than certainty. "Because we need him."

Roused from her thoughts, Mairi raised her head warily. She'd seen the copper gleam of the eyes of a wildcat darting through the shadows, pausing soundlessly to watch from the safety of tangled ferns and reeds. She was undisturbed.

She'd been aware of golden eyes upon her many times in her life and had felt an inexplicable reassurance. There were things in this glen of the Celtic gods that she could not explain, and did not try.

The moon had begun to rise from behind the mountains, outlining the jagged tips with silver, muting the light that permeated the water, made it incandescent. Ailsa felt comforted; in the midst of a storm of anger and sorrow, forgiveness and loss, she had found a moment of stillness, of peace.

"I believe ye can keep the spirits of those ye love by ye if ye choose," Mairi offered. " 'Tis no' a matter of how far they are from ye or if they can come back again, but only how much ye believe. There're spirits everywhere. In the water, in the sky, in the earth and the ever-changin' moonlight." She smiled knowingly. "These things are older than we, older than memory, older than man. They remember what we never knew—every soul that's lingered here, leavin' his image in the water or his voice in the wind or his imprint in the soil. Here, earth, sky and water are close enough to touch, to recognize."

Lian felt dazed, as if the moonlight had enfolded her in an enchanted cloak, blocking out the past. "How do *we* leave our mark upon this place?" She wanted very much to do that single, simple thing.

Glancing upward, Mairi gazed at the point where the burn disappeared over the hill into the secret green woods. The water poured over an ancient stone that protruded above the *linne* in which she dangled her feet. "Ye leave your mark, ye make the land remember, by takin' a risk that proves your sincerity and commitment."

Craning her neck, Lian saw the rock, the clear curtain of water falling from it in small steps, bit by bit, over the wide boulders and through the slender rushing channels of the burn.

"When the moon's full, ye stand there and dive into this *linne*, which is deeper than ye imagine."

Lian drew in her breath and glanced at Ailsa.

"I've heard it whispered the rock is sacred, that the water remembers such risks, such courage." Ailsa pondered. "But do ye think 'tis wise for us?"

Genevra leaned forward eagerly. "It doesn't matter. What matters is adventure, magic, all the things you've taught me to believe in, though they be wise or practical, foolish or brave. Don't you see? Only we three will have dared."

Ailsa looked from Lian's unreadable face to Genevra's and back again. She turned to her mother. "Should we take the chance?"

Mairi considered solemnly, fearful for these women who had learned so much and lost so much in the last several months. Perhaps she should have kept silent. But then, she could not hold them safe beside her forever. " 'Tis your decision to make, no' mine. But I think 'twould be a fine thing to know you've conquered your fears and doubts." And, she thought, mayhap the invisible hand that holds ye fast inside your anger and grief for your father.

Lian was beside Ailsa in an instant. "If Ailsa is willing, so am I."

Despite her eagerness, Genevra was slow to rise, but as her older sisters approached, she closed her sketchbook firmly and stood, back straight and chin up. "Let's go up together," she said.

"Without our shifts," Ailsa insisted. "They're more likely to trip us up or catch on a branch and pull us down than to protect us." She drew the flimsy garment off, dropping it at her feet. "There'll be nothin' between us and the water, nothin' to hold us back but ourselves."

Genevra hesitated, then stripped off her chemise and drawers, but Lian looked uncomfortable.

"You've done it before," Ailsa urged softly. " 'Tis only us. Do ye no' trust us?"

It was odd, but she did. A few months ago she had neither met nor conceived of these two women, but since her arrival, the distance and resentments that might have become barriers among them had collapsed under the weight of their shared grief. They had held tight to one another, combined their strength to keep from falling deep into their sorrow. "You must know that I do, but it is not proper—"

" 'Tis no' a question of proper," Mairi interjected. " 'Tis a question of faith, of the comfort ye feel with your sisters. No' one of us is here to judge ye or stare at ye. 'Tis a little thing, Lian, and of no import when ye think of what you've already shared."

Lian gazed into Mairi's eyes, amazed that this woman, who might well have resented her and Genevra, sent them away or treated them with disdain, had instead taken them in like birds with broken wings. Slowly, she'd begun to try to heal those wings. "It is as you say. We do not hide from one another. To try to do so would be pointless. We dream each others' dreams. No woman can know another better than that."

Besides, this night, this sense of contentment was a gift, a blessing Lian could not refuse. Carefully, she removed her cotton shift and folded it neatly beside her sisters'.

Because she knew the glen better than the others, Ailsa lead the way. The three made a wavering line of pale flesh against dark earth and stone. When they reached the crest of the hill, they stood on the boulder, their feet barely covered by the water that flowed over it, and stared at the moonlit scene below. The river became an unruly ribbon of silver threaded through green moss and yellow lichens, thick ferns and striped boulders. It tumbled and raced, slowed and meandered, whispered and sang in a voice deeper and more enduring than the wind.

Without speaking, they agreed Ailsa would go first. They could feel her excitement in her vibrating body, see her Highland pride in the way she stood a step away from the edge of the slippery rock, solid and unwavering.

What Lian and Genevra could not see was Ailsa's reluctance to take the last step. Ye fool, she thought. Have ye gone daft? She was thirty-eight years old, no longer young, no longer the nimble, fearless girl who'd leapt into the air and flown across a Beltaine fire, arms wide, plaid streaming behind her like fiery wings. She'd been away too long to leap from this high place as easily as she'd risen above the flames.

Uncomfortably aware of her half-sisters watching, waiting for her to plunge over the edge of the deceptively smooth surface, Ailsa realized she was unnerved by the steep drop, afraid and ashamed of her fear. If she did not dare, would Lian and Genevra? She felt their trepidation, their exhilaration laced with doubt, their anticipation as her own.

She heard rustling in the bushes and caught a glimpse of amber eyes. A wildcat crouched nearby. Quickly, she looked away and saw her mother staring up at her, saw the compassion and confidence on Mairi Rose's face. "No' for them," Ailsa whispered, straightening her shoulders, "but for myself, for my father, who never had the chance to take this risk or claim this victory."

Exhaling, she spread her arms wide, beginning at her sides and bringing them up slowly, hands open, fingers spread, as if to embrace the air, the breath of the wind, the voice of the water singing at her feet.

She tipped her head back and let the wind blow through it, staring at the stars through a canopy of leaves. "For this moment alone I would've come home long ago, if I'd known." She paused. "But 'tis no' a night for regrets."

Ailsa murmured a prayer to Neithe, God of Waters, and dove. As she descended, she felt the wind on her falling body, knew that wind's caress as a promise. She closed her eyes, did not know when she would hit the water until it enveloped her—cool and familiar. She curved her arms up toward the surface, then burst back into the night, shaking her wild, wet hair from her eyes, inhaling great bursts of sweet Highland air.

"Why did ye close your eyes?" Mairi asked.

"I'd no need of them. I came by touch and smell, and was a little afraid, but when the fear left—I can no' describe the feelin' of bein' free, untouchable."

"Look!"

Mairi pointed to where Lian stood resolutely at the edge. It was difficult to see her expression. The moon was suspended behind her tall, slender body, and her black hair glowed like onyx against her bronze skin. She raised her arms above her head, palm to palm, and froze, edged in moonlight. She was willowy and graceful—magnificent, unfaltering. In that moment, her grief fell away, revealing pride and a spirit so strong it transformed her into the image of an ancient Celtic goddess, or her own Kwan Yin, Goddess of Mercy.

Lian did not really see what lay below. There is nothing to fear now, she thought. Not when everyone she loved had been taken from her. She alone had survived. Except she was not alone. Not now that she'd come to know Ailsa and Genevra, who had always been part of her, and Mairi, who seemed to have been waiting, ready to open her home and her arms.

It was easier to jump than to think ahead, to wonder. Easier to plunge off this rock than to look inside her heart. She had lived with eyes downcast all her life. Now they were wide open.

Lian bent at the knees and launched herself into the air. As she descended, tears fell of their own accord, pushed by the rushing air over her temples and into her hair, leaving her shaken, yet relieved. She was free.

Mairi and Ailsa, who could not see her tears, watched in admiration as Lian's body curved sinuously into a perfect dive. Her hair streamed behind her like a banner of victory, and then, too soon, she hit the water, slicing it into waves that rose to the edge of the *linne*.

She had not closed her eyes, even at the last moment. Now she gazed in wonder at a new world. The water was deliciously cool on her skin; she let it flow over her, along her back and down her legs. She turned to feel it rush over her breasts and belly and thighs. She curled her toes in the soft silt at the bottom, letting her feet sink deep, while her hair floated around her. Finally, reluctantly, she rose toward the light, taking in one deep, long breath, making her way to the rock where Mairi and Ailsa waited, dripping.

"Most remarkable. Breathtaking. I do not know if I have

made my mark on the river, but it has made its mark on me." She would not soon forget her exultation as the water had flowed sensuously around her.

Together, the three looked up to where Genevra stood alone, shivering. They could see the water rolling over her feet, her fine hair, loosened from its pins, falling in soft curls around her neck, the apprehension on her shadowed face. She, too, was silhouetted by moonlight, caught in the glow like a reluctant Madonna.

Holding her breath, Genevra wondered what had possessed her to pursue this ridiculous quest. It would not change her. Tomorrow she would be the same as she was tonight. She gazed down and grew dizzy, swaying from side to side.

With an effort, she forced her eyes open, shivered once, then was still. She did not want to back down. Not when the others had already succeeded. Genevra wanted more than anything to be like them, but, though Mairi told her she was wrong, she was not certain she had the strength.

Frightened, she started back from the edge, then heard a noise and glanced over to find the wildcat perched on a boulder, staring. More afraid of those amber eyes than the sharp drop, she stumbled forward and jumped. She tried to steady herself, straightening her body as she fell, feet first. She crossed her arms over her chest, gripping her elbows, holding tight to protect her body with nothing but her two small hands. She kept her eyes open, fixed on Lian and Ailsa. The connection among them, and that alone, would bring her safely down. Her hair blew about wildly while the water misted on her skin. Anxiety retreated beneath an unexpected rush of determination. The cat had taken the choice from her, but as she felt the air rush past her naked body, her skin tingled and a shout rose within her, a burst of courage.

Genevra was overwhelmed. She had done this unthinkable thing, and just before she struck the water, she'd felt as if a pair of hands reached up to catch her—her father's? Her fiancé, Alex Kendall's? Her own from her reflected image? She'd plunged in knowing she was safe. Now she wanted to explore by moonlight what she'd seen only in the sun.

She trailed her hands through the water grasses that undulated like the pale green hair of mermaids, brushed up against the sides, striated with so many shades of gold, brown and rust that they bled one into the other. She touched the round, smooth stones, feeling the shape of them, the size, absorbing the colors as she did all color, until it blended with the palette in her mind. She would paint this scene someday.

At last she ran out of breath and reached the surface just in time, coughing and gasping for air. Ailsa and Lian were poised on the bank, ready to pull her out, but Mairi whispered, "Don't ye dare. She'll never forgive ye. Ye two did it on your own. To offer help would diminish what she's done, make her less than ye."

By now Ailsa could see that Genevra was smiling as she coughed and stumbled toward a boulder, where she lay face down, quivering with exhaustion. After what seemed like an eternity, while her half-sisters stood by anxiously, she raised her head.

"I was terrified," she admitted blithely. "But I did it just the same. And once I was under water, I saw so much. It was amazing." She ran out of breath and lay inert. She did not tell them about the reassurance of invisible, anonymous reaching hands. That moment was hers alone.

"I wasn't graceful like you," she said at last. "I just jumped, and I'm glad I lived to say so." She closed her eyes as the flush of triumph faded from her cheeks.

When Mairi took Genevra's head into her lap to smooth the snarls from her fine, wet hair, the others realized how tired they were. Lian and Ailsa collapsed, leaning on either side of Mairi, absorbing her warmth. It was finally sinking in—what they had done, how dangerous it had been, how easily they might have been hurt. Yet they hadn't.

" 'Tis because ye were already known somewhere in the deep ancient heart of this earth, but now ye'll no' be forgotten. Not ever."

The three looked at one another long and steadfastly, sky blue eyes meeting blue flecked with gray meeting blue-violet. Finally, Lian spoke the words that hovered among them, touched by moon and lantern light. "We will not be forgotten because we will not forget. If he gave us nothing else, our father gave us that."

With a burst of energy, they rose together, as if they shared the same body, and slipped back into the water of the silver golden pool.

The wildcat shook itself, languidly licked its paw, then turned to disappear into the shadows where the moonlight did not reach.

2

"WHAT AILS YE, GENNY?"

Genevra was startled by the unexpected appearance of Alanna Sinclair, Ailsa's twenty-year-old daughter. In the muted light of the croft, she looked as Mairi Rose must have looked at her age, with sun-kissed cheeks, violet eyes and Highland red hair. There was something mysterious in her gaze—something that intrigued, bemused and calmed.

Genevra had to make herself look away. Several days had passed since the revelations at the *linne*. Today, while the others went out to revel in the lovely summer air, she had stayed behind. She had had enough of heat and sun, and craved the cool dimness inside the small dirt-floored cottage where Mairi Rose had been born.

She found comfort in the smell of earth and peat and heather that lingered there. The walls were coated in soot over layers of patterned clay over stone, the thatched roof damp from a brief thunderstorm that morning. The kitchen, with its press full of dishes and herbs and a sturdy cloth for the scrubbed pine table, was fragrant with the nutmeg and cinnamon of fresh-baked black buns. The boxbed sat sturdy against the wall, its side panels open to reveal the window cut to match the one in the old stone. The heather and straw mattresses were piled on the floor, one atop the other to leave room to move about. The leather coverings were tied back from the windows, the weathered oak door left slightly ajar. The scent of rain, rich loam and summer flowers drifted through the croft.

This place made Genevra feel placid, safe. She needed to feel safe; she had just received several letters from her fiancé, Alex Kendall. Apparently they had gone astray in the wild Scottish countryside, and though written over several months, had arrived in a single bundle. She clutched them to her chest, troubled, trying to understand the erratic beat of her heart. Genevra realized Alanna was waiting patiently and looked up, blinking in confusion. Alanna had asked what was wrong. "I'm not sure, actually. I just don't feel quite . . . right. I'm nervous, really, distracted."

Genevra closed her eyes and conjured Alex behind her lids. Alex challenging her: *Say it, Genny. Say the words.* Alex holding her while she shook with despair. Alex, with his deep blue eyes, watching her leave him at the train station, his hand outstretched as if to catch her if she stumbled or changed her mind.

"Should ye no' be happy? Had ye no' begun to wonder if he'd write at all?"

Genevra blushed, embarrassed that the girl had guessed her secret fear. Alanna was her own age, yet she seemed so much older somehow, so certain and secure. "I *am* happy.

It's just . . . I miss him so much. Miss him and need him. And now that I hear his voice again, it frightens me."

" 'Tis no' so strange," Mairi Rose said, joining the two girls unexpectedly. "Much has happened to ye of late. You're no' the same woman who left him in India." She was glad the girl was talking; she'd worried about Genevra from the beginning. She was so very young and insecure. "Mayhap you're wonderin' if he's changed too."

"Perhaps." Stomach fluttering with nerves, Genevra placed her elbows on her knees and her chin in her hands. "I remember the first time I saw Alex, I thought he was my father's ghost. I need someone like Charles Kittridge to keep me strong. Someone wise, who's lived enough to understand what I can't."

Mairi grew very still, but the girl did not notice.

"Alex will give me a family of my own, children who'll love me absolutely, without question or doubt, as he will."

The older woman shook her head. "He can no' *give* ye a family or bairns who adore ye. Ye must make a family together."

"We *will* be together, just us; we'll care for one another. Alex will protect me and keep me safe. He'll make me happy." She said it emphatically, covering her doubt.

"And what of ye? Will ye make him happy?" Mairi sat next to Genevra, shoulder to shoulder, reassuringly. " 'Tis something to think about. 'Tis also dangerous to depend on one person too much, to place the weight of your happiness and survival on his shoulders. 'Tis a heavy weight to carry.

"From what you've told us, Alex Kendall has faith in ye and loves ye," she added. " 'Tis a great deal to depend on, Genevra. And ye must know, too, that I'll always be here for ye, and your sisters as well. But ye mustn't make the mistake of seekin' a father in your Alex. Don't do him the unkindness of marryin' him because ye need someone to fill the hole my Charlie left inside ye. I'd guess 'tis a partner your fiancé wants, a true friend of the spirit, a wife. You've strength of your own; ye don't *need* his to survive. Ye have to believe that."

Genevra blinked as the color drained from her cheeks and her hands began to flutter liked trapped butterflies in her lap. "Sometimes I do, but sometimes I can't think straight, or my thoughts get tangled with my feelings, and I can't sort them out."

Mairi cupped the butterflies in gentle hands. "Mayhap then ye should write your feelin's down, when you're confused and distraught. It might help clear the cobwebs away. Write for yourself alone. Things ye might no' want to say, even to Alex."

Shuddering, the girl leaned heavily against the kindhearted, generous woman who, from the first, had treated her as a daughter and not a burden to be borne. "Emily Townsend kept a diary. I don't want to be like my mother. Not ever."

"You're no' like her at all," Mairi whispered. "I know because Charlie told me. You're young and hurt and vulnerable just now, is all. 'Tis normal to feel a little lost."

Genevra shook her head. "You never did. You always knew what you wanted."

"You're wrong about that, little bird."

Finally, Alanna spoke up. She had been hovering, unsure whether to stay or go, but now she could not keep silent. "I *thought* I knew, but till I saw the glen for the first time, but four months past, till I felt it in my blood, I knew nothing. When I opened my eyes at last, I was sure I'd come home. I've always belonged here, where my soul's at peace. Ye'll know you've made the right choice when ye have that same feelin'. All ye must do is listen to your heart."

Genevra could not imagine her soul at peace, and the voices in her heart were so many and so disconcerting, she did not know which ones to heed. She envied Alanna her conviction, the glow of happiness in her eyes.

"Aye," Mairi said, gazing at her granddaughter with

affection. "Always your heart and spirit will guide ye and no' lead ye astray. If ye let them. Ye can do it, our Genny. I know ye can."

3

"HOW WILL I LIVE WITHOUT YOU?" AILSA WHISPERED AS SHE slipped into the bed she shared with her daughter in the crowded croft. Long after the girl had fallen into peaceful sleep, Ailsa lay awake, trying to fill her head with the sound and rhythm of the water, unwilling to close her eyes and let her thoughts take over. Alanna had chosen to stay in the glen, but her mother had to leave soon and return to her family in London. It was the first time Ailsa would be parted from her eldest child—the closest to her heart. In spite of her heartache and apprehension, Ailsa finally drifted off.

For the third time in as many nights, she fell deep into a disquieting dream. She awoke shaking, not with fear or despair, but because she felt empty. Hollow. She knew she would not sleep again before dawn. Instead of lying restless and uneasy, she rose, slipped on leather sandals, took up a plaid and left the croft in silence.

As Ailsa made her way in the darkness, her own mother's voice echoed in her mind, and she remembered vividly the words they had spoken not long past, as the others lay sleeping.

" 'Twill be too painful," Ailsa whispered, "to leave Alanna behind."

"I once thought I could no' live without ye, when ye married William Sinclair and went away to London," Mairi reminded her, "but 'twas no' my choice, my heart, 'twas yours."

" 'Tis just—'Tis so hard."

Mairi's strong, weathered hands closed over her daughter's. " 'Tis a mother's obligation, her heartbreak and her joy to set her children free." She smiled her bittersweet smile. "First ye give her the gift of life and teach her how to use it, then ye give her the freedom to make of her life what she will. Ye know as well as I that ye can no' protect your bairns from growth and change and sorrow, nor shape them in your image, nor fashion the nature of their joy."

Ailsa felt a rush of gratitude, of deep affection, of guilt. "Did ye know all that when I left ye here alone?"

Mairi kissed her forehead. "No. But over the years, I learned, just as ye will."

"Mayhap she'll give ye back what I took from ye so long ago."

Eyes damp with tears, Mairi whispered, "Ye didn't take it; I gave it. The same benediction ye'll give your Alanna."

Will I? Am I as strong as Mam? Ailsa wondered as she stumbled across the clearing. Then she stopped still, overcome by the eerie feeling she had heard and said all this before, an absolute certainty that she would hear and say it all again. How was that possible?

Ian Fraser slept fitfully for the third night in a row, tumbling the covers about him as he turned and stretched and tried to get comfortable. He knew it was no use—his stubborn determination to ignore his troubled spirit, to shut out the voice that whispered in the back of his mind, refusing to release him or grant him a reprieve. This time, when he woke from the nightmare he could not remember, except for a feeling of emptiness, he bent over his wife, Jenny, watching her peaceful face, relaxed and young in sleep. "Ah, my Jenny, forgive me, but there's aught I must do," he whispered. He kissed her temple where the pulse throbbed gently, ran his fingers down her long braid and rose from their large heather bed in the loft he had built with his own two hands. He slipped away without waking the children; the sound of their deep, even breathing soothed him.

He knew where to go; there was only one place that called to him like this, one voice that he had thought long silenced.

Ian found her, as he'd known he would, in the copse beside the burn where they used to meet as children. The moon was still bright enough to glimmer on the peat-colored water, revealing the bright stones beneath.

Ailsa Rose sat on a stump in the middle of the copse ringed by ancient oaks with roots that had twisted upward from beneath the earth, by spruce and silver fir, whose needles made a carpet on the soft, damp ground. She wore only her nightrail and a plaid that had fallen off her shoulders and caught in the crooks of her elbows, where the aged wool lay in graceful folds, the long ends of the red Rose plaid across her empty lap. She had not yet braided her hair for the night; it fell down her back in chestnut waves, tinted golden by the moonlight. She was staring blankly into the shallow pond too far away for her to touch, her hands pale and motionless on the dark ringed stump.

Bowing his head, Ian knew he should not have come. He should have stayed, restive and uneasy, in his own bed. But he'd known Ailsa was in trouble, and he could not simply let her suffer. Still, it had been a shock to see her sitting so hushed and bereft in the copse of their childhood. The pain in his chest stunned him, it was so sharp and deep.

He had shut her out of his mind and his life twenty years ago, but that did not make him immune to the sight of her raw grief. He could tell himself, as he had for the past two nights, that her sorrow was no longer his to bear, but it would be a lie. For this was not Ailsa the lover he'd lost and mourned so long ago; this was his friend, who needed him.

As he stepped from under a ceiling of oak leaves, Ailsa looked up, startled by his presence. Perhaps she did not know he'd shared her restlessness these past few nights. That was the irony. She went pale at the sight of him, shaking her head from side to side. He realized she was not aware that she had called him here. She had finally accepted the withdrawal of his soul from within hers.

"Why've ye come?" she asked foolishly, for she knew, somehow, at the first glimpse of his face.

"Because you're lonely and afraid, and ye'd no' have the others guess. But even now, ye can no' fool me." He came forward slowly and sat cross-legged on the ground, careful not to brush the edge of her nightrail or her hand, still poised on blackened wood, looking fragile, breakable. Not like Ailsa at all.

She turned away from him to stare once more at the burn where Neithe, God of Waters, slept, though Ailsa herself could not. " 'Tis natural, this feelin'. My father's dead, my mother's husband gone forever. Too soon."

"Is't Charlie ye mourn? Are ye certain?" Ian murmured.

She tried to answer and found she could not lie. "No' tonight, nor last night nor the one before."

"Alanna." He did not have to guess; he could see it on her face and in her heart, which was open to him tonight, for this moment, as it might not ever be again.

Ailsa pulled her legs up close to her body, resting her head on her knees. It was no use pretending or denying what she'd known for some time. "Aye. She's with me yet, and will be, though I can't say for how long, but I've lost her just the same." She shivered at a chilly breeze. "I don't *want* to lose her. She's often been my refuge from the gray chill of London. She understands this place, which is buried in my soul." She could not quite yet accept the inevitable, though she knew it *was* inevitable.

"Then let that be enough. Ye don't want to hold her back, to keep her near when her happiness lies elsewhere. I know ye better than that, Ailsa Rose. Mayhap 'tis only that you've lost your father too, that ye know now he's naught but a man who can no' fight death or fate any more than can we."

"Mayhap." She did not raise her head; she could feel his eyes upon her, seeing the truth, forcing her to see it too.

" 'Tis because she's grown too fast and too far and she no longer needs me that my heart breaks."

"She needs ye more than ever. 'Tis as hard for her to let go of friend, mother, confidant as 'tis for ye."

"Aye, weel." Glancing around, absorbing the sights and sounds of the glen at night, Ailsa was not so sure. For Alanna would keep these things, these tiny nightly miracles, which Ailsa must leave behind.

"Even the greatest pain heals in time," Ian said, startling her with his perception. "I promise ye that. I know."

Ailsa fought back tears that came from nowhere. "Does it, Ian Fraser? Does it truly heal? Ever?"

He was silent for a long moment. "Aye, if ye allow it. If ye let go of the bitterness, the bewilderment, the sense of an emptiness never to be filled, if ye let those who love ye help turn a raw wound to a scar, then aye, the sorrow fades.

"But 'tis no' only your grief we're speakin' of. 'Tis your daughter. You're strong, Ailsa Rose. If ye love her, let her go, freely and without regret, findin' joy in her joy and compassion in her sorrow."

She knew he was right, in her heart and in her soul, but her spirit was bleeding; she feared she would drown. "Just now, I'm no' certain I can do it without bitterness."

Ian stared up at her until she turned to meet his gaze. "I'm certain, *mo-charaidh*. Besides, there're others who need ye more than she. Your husband is losin' his daughter, too. His first born. His secret pride and treasure."

Struggling, Ailsa fought for air. "How do ye know that?"

Waving his hand nonchalantly, Ian shrugged. "It doesn't matter. All that matters is that ye don't let him grieve alone. Only ye can console him, because she's a reflection of ye—only ye can give him what she's taken away." He stopped, pulling great tufts of grass from the damp ground, shifting his weight uneasily, observing his hands as if they'd moved beyond his power to control them. His voice was little more than a whisper. "Go ye to your William and console each other, Ailsa-*aghray*. Hold to each other and don't let go. Remember why ye love *him* as well as why ye love her. Remember how much he cares for ye, all that he gives ye, all that he is. If ye do that, then ye'll be all right."

Ailsa knew what those words had cost him, and an old weakness crept over her, stealing her will, her determination, her distance from the man who sat beside her, a thousand miles between them. "Will I?" She dared not move or turn her head or lift her hand.

Ian knew what that restraint cost *her*. "Aye," he whispered in the rhythm and the cadence of the river. "You've courage enough, and kindness enough, and faith enough. Ye must never doubt it, nor your strength nor your will nor the instincts of your heart. They'd no' lie to ye, ever, any more than I would." He rose to his feet abruptly, the image of her desolate eyes burned into his own. It was time and long past time to leave her. "Don't ever stop believin', Ailsa, *mo-chridhe*. I never did."

Before she could thank him or touch him, he was gone.

Within the deep, dark shelter of the trees, little Glenyss Fraser blinked and shook her head. She had been awakened the last few nights by her father tossing and turning and mumbling in his sleep. Usually, Ian Fraser slept soundly, for her mother had told her he worked hard in the fields and claimed his rest gladly. But with the intuition of a child, Glenyss knew something was bothering him, keeping him half-awake.

So when he'd risen earlier and crept from the croft, she'd been so worried that she'd followed without thought. Now, eyes wide with shock, she watched him head toward home. She was overwhelmed, knocked breathless by the feelings that had simmered in the air between her father and Ailsa Rose.

Though not once had Ian reached out or grazed her hand or her hair or the white drift of her nightrail, Glenyss felt he had touched this woman, held her, made the pain in her tear-filled eyes a little easier to bear.

She saw Ailsa standing stiffly, looking after Ian Fraser, lips parted in silence, hands outstretched with words unspoken lying on her open palms.

Seven-year-old Glenyss rocked from the heels to the balls of her bare feet, entranced and bewildered by what she had seen. She did not understand it, but she knew absolutely she would never forget it.

4

"WHAT WILL YE DO NOW?" MAIRI ASKED AS SHE AND LIAN sat on the low, crumbling dyke surrounding the garden beside the croft.

Charles Kittridge had died on Beltaine, the first of May, while throughout the glen bonfires burned in celebration of spring, but now it was summer and none of his daughters had left the croft, nor spoken of leaving.

Lian had no answer. Instead, she glanced at Mairi, red Rose plaid draped over her hair, violet eyes gray with melancholy. "You are *kuei-chieh*, a widow who refuses to remarry. In China women like you are looked upon with great respect. But you have been twice widowed by the same man. Not many would have survived that sorrow."

Mairi shook her head. "He gave me joy as well. Never forget that."

"Charles Kittridge must have been an extraordinary man to inspire such fidelity."

Staring off into the woods where the sound of water over stones was just audible above the breeze, Mairi mused, "He was ordinary in many ways, though he'd a great curiosity and need to see mysterious foreign places, did my Charlie.

But ye know all about that." She picked at her worn plaid, glancing down so Lian could not see her face. "Ye know too that he had a likin' for the lassies, and they for him."

"Yet you loved him. You love him still." The young woman was trying to understand, because she respected Mairi, not out of obligation, but out of affection.

"I can no' explain it. I know only that his heart touched mine and our lives became entangled so even the fairies who weave our fates from gossamer threads could no' separate us." She turned, catching Lian's earnest and baffled expression. Mairi squeezed her hand. "He was no' perfect, nor ever claimed to be. But then, neither am I. 'Twas easier to love him *because* of his weaknesses. With human flaws comes the need for forgiveness and understandin'. If ye can love someone when ye know all that's ill or wantin' in them, ye'll love them no matter what." She shook her head, as if shaking away her husband's ghostly image. "Besides, if it weren't for Charlie, ye'd no' be here now."

She smiled. "No' till he was dyin' did Charlie find what he most desired, and then only for a little. But he left it behind for us, for me, for ye, for Genevra, for my own daughter and granddaughter. A family. A future different from the lonely past. 'Tis so much, Lian. 'Tis more than enough. So I love him. 'Tis that simple."

Lian felt tears well in her eyes. She could not fathom simplicity; her life in China had been complex, structured, shaped by centuries of tradition and restraint. Mairi's artless declaration shook her so deeply chills rose on her arms.

It was true that Charles had brought them together, but Mairi had made them a family. Even Lian, who had lost everything—mother, lover, country, the comfort and beauty, rituals and history that had sustained her in a childhood filled with terror. To her own surprise, she had let herself be drawn into the warmth of Mairi's affection, and Ailsa's and Genevra's, even Alanna's. All four had touched her heart, and the unaccustomed intimacy made her uncomfortable. Wan Ke-ming had taught her that it was not safe to let others inside. *There is danger in intimacy*, her mother had said often. *He who knows you well can destroy you more easily*. But her father had made her break her own rule. And then he had died.

He was one too many to have lost. One too many to mourn.

Sensing Lian's withdrawal, Mairi took her hand. Though the girl's inbred instinct was to draw away—in China, physical shows of affection were not encouraged—she did not move. She liked the feeling of Mairi's warm fingers on her chilled ones.

"Remember, Lian, as I told my Charlie when he feared he'd lost hope, that our hearts are stronger than we believe." She paused for an instant, shifting to face Lian directly. "But we were talkin' of ye, no' me," Mairi reminded her gently. "You've spoken of goin' to America. Is't truly what ye want?"

Lian frowned, perplexed. The concept of her future was too huge, too all-encompassing to think about. "No one has ever asked me what I want." She realized the older woman would find that odd, perhaps incomprehensible. Because Mairi, Ailsa, her granddaughter Alanna, and in the end, even Charles, had chosen their own paths. Lian sat up, intrigued in spite of herself. She did not dare give voice to the new thought that had caught her off guard, inspired in her a flicker of longing.

"I only know it was what my mother wanted." She could still hear clearly Ke-ming's voice, rough with emotion on that last night in China. *I am a captive of my own history, but I have raised you to be free, to move toward the future—and the future is the West.*

"I was no' askin' what your parents wanted, but what ye want for yourself."

"It is not important. It is not a question I ask myself. In China *shun*, compliance, is the rule for women."

"You're no' in China now, Lian. You're free to do as ye

please." Mairi nodded toward the towering black and silver mountains in the distance. "There's a whole world out there, waitin'. Do ye really think your mother would've wanted ye to go to a strange country where ye had no friends, no relatives, no future, if ye wished otherwise?"

Lian looked away. "My mother chose that I come here."

" 'Twas only because ye'd no' have done so else. She wanted ye to know your father. 'Tis different, ye ken?"

Lian knew all too well. Had her father not sent for her, had she refused to answer the summons as she wished to do, she would have died, as her mother died, in flame and fear. But Charles Kittridge had called her away from the turmoil, the betrayals, the violence of a China trying to purge herself of enemies.

Her father had called her away from chaos and into the soothing comfort of Mairi Rose's croft, built into a Scottish hillside in an isolated glen.

You are my hope, Ke-ming had said. *Promise me you will survive.*

Mairi stood, raising Lian's chin with gentle, sun-browned fingers. "I guessed ye might be thinkin' of stayin' here, of burrowin' into the solace of Glen Affric." She glanced around at the vast, inviting cocoon of the glen. The smell of pine and silver fir drifted on the summer air, while dog roses, the last of the wild violets and blue speedwell littered the green sloping meadow. "This place never changes. Mayhap ye think 'tis what ye need just now. I tell ye from my heart that ye'll always have a home here; I think ye know it. But I doubt ye'd be happy here for long. Ye need to find a home of your own. There're so many other places, other choices to be made. And you've the strength to make them, of that I'm certain. 'Tis a beginnin'. A chance for ye to start again."

For the first time, Lian began to believe in the possibilities Mairi spoke of with such conviction. It struck her like a flash of brilliant fireworks on a dark, still night, that *she*, like the others, was completely free to choose her own path. But she could not conceive of freedom, what it meant or how it felt. "I do not know what I want," she said. "I am no longer the girl who cared for her mother in the beautiful Western Hills, who planted and cooked and sewed and cleaned and was content. Everything is different now." The lights and colors flickered and went out. "There is nothing to reach for, to turn to. Ailsa has her family in London, Genevra her fiancé in India, and Alanna has you." Lian held out her hands with their long, slender fingers and stared at them bleakly. "My own hands are empty."

5

MAIRI SAT WEAVING WHILE THE OTHERS SLEPT. AS THE shuttle flew back and forth among the threads, a sense of confusion kept intruding on the pattern, making her fingers clumsy, leaving a slit in the fabric. When the shuttle slipped from her hand for the third time, she sighed. She would have to unravel the cloth and start again.

She glanced at her daughters, dreaming around her. *There's a reason they've come to me like this. I feel it in my bones.* Frowning, she curled up alone on the heather mattress she'd so recently shared with her husband, her Charlie.

Mairi's dream was laced with melodies, compelling and seducing her into the woods where she had met her Charlie, and lost him, and found him again. But she had not wept for him.

She found herself at the crest of the hill, on the stone above the deep, clear pool. She was aware of the glittering stars, the dim light of the quarter moon, and the copper eyes of the wildcat, darting in the darkness.

For a long, breathless instant, the night grew still.

Then, from the bottom of the deepest pool, a tree rose where none could grow. Its trunk was spindly, but as the branches developed one by one, sprouting layer upon layer of new leaves, the trunk thickened, grew sturdy—indestructible. The leaves began to unfurl in such abundance that they made a solid pathway as the branches reached for Mairi and lifted her into their heart.

She was walking, floating, on a fabric of leaves woven of different colors—silver-green, gold and vibrant rust. From the original branches grew others, and the pattern became more intricate, more beautiful as burgundy and deep blue and rose entwined themselves into the weave, into a bright, ever-widening path.

The wind lifted the fabric, ruffling it like a length of ribbon. As she struggled to keep her footing, Mairi saw that Ailsa would bear a child, another who was yet to come. A girl, born of the earth and sky and river from which the tree had sprung.

Then the wind fell away and the cloth stretched out ahead until the pattern of leaves curved back, inevitably, toward the glen.

The future lay before her—a lacery of strands in living fabric, interwoven webs of color and tensile strength and fluid time.

Mairi saw it all, and was moved, afraid, enchanted.

It was promise enough to adorn her dreams in the years to come with bits of ribbon from the fabric she had walked that night. The Sight had come upon her and she had seen both sorrow and joy, for there was never one without the other. She had known that before she started.

Mairi watched as the pattern faded and the leaves curled up and the tree disappeared into the deep green pool from which it had sprung.

Then she noticed the wildcat crouched beside the burn. She saw its eyes blazing copper in the moonlight; then it stepped back, drew its body inward and launched itself in an arc across the stone on which she stood, across the river, across the path of time unwinding. It landed on the far bank, leaving footprints in the loam.

In the stillness left behind, Mairi realized her cheeks were wet with tears that flowed into the water at her feet. The cat had touched something within her, set her free. She wept, releasing a deluge of grief held tight and close to her heart for too long. "I'll miss, ye, my Charlie, always," she whispered. "But 'twill be a sweet sorrow, for my memories are bright and fierce within me."

Mairi raised her wet face to the waning moon before it sank behind the mountains, invisible in the sudden hush of the darkness.

"What is it, Mairi Rose? Are you in pain?"

Blinking hard, trying to focus through the curtain of her tears, Mairi felt Lian bent low beside her, Lian's arms tight around her. The young woman was trembling, her eyes reflecting Mairi's sorrow.

She reached up to brush Lian's cheek. "No, *mo-ghraidh*. 'Twas just a dream." Her smile through her tears was poignant and disarming.

Lian felt her own eyes grow damp and her chest tight. "Was it about my father?"

Reaching up, Mairi enfolded Lian in her arms and they held each other, rocking. "No, Lian. 'Twas time. I let my Charlie go."

Book Two

❧❧

Just one small step
yet light-years away;
Somewhere there lies the moon.

London, 1879

ALL HER LIFE, WAN LIAN HAD BEEN PLAGUED BY NIGHT-
mares so vivid, so full of menace, that she was often astonished to awake and find herself safe within the embroidered
silk butterfly curtains of her bed in China. Her sweeter
dreams had been equally as vivid, brilliant with color and
vitality, so that when she woke, she could not understand
the dim confines of that same bed.

But this particular morning on the London docks, enveloped by muffling wisps of fog, was neither nightmare nor
dream. It was strangely unreal—devoid of clarity or color.
The dock bustled with figures without substance; they were
neither men nor women but phantoms. Even the blasting of
ships' horns was muted, and the carts of luggage and cargo
that trundled past, clacking over rough, warped slats, seemed
like murmurs in the distant background. Lian moved slowly
through the drifting air of her dazed waking-dream. She was
a shadow puppet—walking, breathing, running against a
screen of light. But she did not know who held the strings, or
how the story ended.

Plans are made by man, the voice of her childhood
teacher whispered in her head, *but their accomplishment rests*

with Heaven. She tried to remember his face, to absorb the meaning of the ancient proverb, but both had been left behind. She could not reclaim them now.

The only thing that was real to her were her half-sisters clinging to her arms, grasping the heavy cloth of her dark wool gown. Even they were dimmed by the mist inside her and without. Ailsa Rose Sinclair's normally bright chestnut hair seemed dull brown, her pleasant features, bronzed by the sun, were blurred and indistinct, and Genevra Townsend shimmered and faded in her pale prettiness.

Lian had come to this noisy, bustling dock in the unseasonable chill of late July, to say good-bye. Again. She had grown weary of leaving those she loved. For the third time, she was abandoning everything she had known—forsaking her past, leaving London, leaving Genevra, leaving the lush Scottish Highlands where Mairi Rose remained, along with the first sense of home Lian had felt in a very long time. Leaving Ailsa. It was time to discover her own place.

'Tis a beginning. A chance for ye to start again, Mairi had told her.

Today she would step off English soil into a world she had never seen and could not imagine. Yes, it *was* a beginning, a new chance. Mairi Rose was very wise. At the remembered sound of that melodic voice, Lian half-smiled and felt a sense of excited expectation.

You're free to do as ye please. There's a whole world out there, waitin'.

"Are you certain this is the right thing to do?" Genevra asked anxiously. Her forehead was creased in a frown, and her features seemed more fragile than ever, as if a single touch might break her.

For the first time since they'd met, the three would be apart. Tears filled Genevra's eyes but she fought them back, knowing if she wept, all three would weep.

"I am certain of one thing." Lian said. "That this day is *pen-mo.* The beginning and the end of all I have known. If I look into your face," she turned to Ailsa, "and yours, my sister, I feel that T'ien-hsia, all under Heaven, are as bewildered as I."

Ailsa managed a faint smile. "I think you've chosen wisely. Do ye no' see ye must do as ye wish, Lian, no' as ye learned?" She wanted desperately to reach her sister. Lian had been withdrawing, a little at a time, since the day they'd come to the docks to purchase Genevra's passage to India. If the three had not stopped to catch their breath at one precise moment, on one precise spot, Lian would not have encountered that odd family. She thought it was Fate, the hand of the gods. Perhaps it was true. Ailsa did not argue with the power of things she could not see or touch. She shook her head, but she could still hear the sound of the greeting, could see and feel all that had followed as if it were happening again.

"Wan Li-an!" the excited voices of strangers had called between the blasts of a ship's horn. "Is it really you?"

Slowly, Lian had raised her head to find a man, a woman and two young girls gaping at her while trying to keep their eyes politely lowered. The man was dressed in a poorly tailored worsted suit with no waistcoat, the woman and girls in plain muslin gowns with long, tight sleeves trimmed with ribbon at the wrist. Nevertheless, their thick blueblack hair and bronze faces, turned slightly yellow by the London climate, were unmistakably Chinese, as were their slanted almond eyes.

Taken aback, Lian stared blankly until she recognized Chin Yun, Chin Shu and their daughters. She bit her lip and tried desperately to gather her thoughts into some kind of order. Why should it be these people of all those from her past who came back into her life, reminding her of what could have been? Chin Yun and Chin Shu were uncle and aunt to Lian's secret husband, Chao, a traitor to the Manchu government. She did not think the family knew of her tie to their nephew; the lovers had been careful.

Then she realized the adults had given up all pretense of good manners and were staring, stunned, at her clear blue eyes.

Instinctively, she lowered her lids. In the months since she left China, she had forgotten what it was to be blind. Mairi, Ailsa, Genevra and Charles had accepted her without question. In the sanctuary of their acceptance, she had nearly forgotten the need for intrigue, deception, forgotten the pantomime she had played out for the first eighteen years of her life, pretending to be what she was not. She stiffened, but in spite of her determination to remain impassive, her hands shook.

A chill passed through all three sisters, as if the other two felt her apprehension as keenly as she did. Ailsa and Genevra moved closer. "What is't?" Ailsa whispered.

For a long moment, the Chins and Lian stared at one another, frozen. It was as if the London dock had faded and memory transported them to the land they had left behind. To the smell of spring gardens, the low reverent voices of scholars, to the shouting and the clash of weapons and the smell of blood hanging heavy in the air.

When Madam Chin's gasp broke the strained silence, the sounds of the busy dock returned—the swish of lace petticoats and the murmur of distant voices, the looming bulk of huge ships, tall and imposing against the lapping sea. The sharp tang of the air that skimmed over the choppy water was bitter with soot and sweat, and the wind was chilly.

"It is the daughter of Wan Ke-ming," the stranger exclaimed. "I visited their house in Peking often enough to know." Both she and her husband had gone pale and rigid, while the girls stood, hands clasped before them, staring at the warped boards of the dock, as was appropriate.

"She is one of *Them*," Chin Yun hissed to his wife. He, too, used awkward English. Lian wondered why. He did not point to the undeniable evidence of her blue eyes; it would have been a breach of courtesy. They who had first called out her name with pleasure were regarding her with anger and disgust.

As he spat out the words, Ailsa and Genevra flanked Lian protectively. Oddly, Lian felt sympathy for Madam Chin, whose husband's stare was an accusation.

He spoke in a whisper the sisters heard clearly. "Why did you not tell me she was born of a foreign devil?"

Despite her doubts, their open animosity, their relationship to Chin Chao, whose name still hurt after all these years, Lian moved toward the Chinese family. Ailsa and Genevra tried to hold her back. They wanted to protect her. She was touched, and her throat ached at their instinct to shield her. She gave them a half-smile and took a step forward.

The Chin's moved back. "Why did you not tell me?" Chin repeated.

His wife bowed her head. "I did not know." Her voice shook, not with anger but with hurt at Lian's betrayal.

"I do not believe you visited Wan Ke-ming's house for so many years, and yet did not guess. Were you blind? Did you not see her eyes?"

His daughters, who appeared to be about ten and fourteen years old, shifted from one foot to the other in agitation, but did not speak or look up.

Madam Chin lifted her head in a small gesture of defiance. "You know how the women of the household behave. We remain inside the walls of the women's compounds; we are demure and quiet, as our mothers have trained us to be. We walk with eyes lowered politely, and may not look higher than a man's breast. Young unmarried women are even more modest and submissive, so they will make good wives." She drew a deep breath. "Wan Li-an was one of the most polite, the most modest. She rarely spoke a word and kept her eyes lowered always, fixed on the tea tray or her hands in her lap or her embroidery."

Pale with shock, Ailsa took a step, her mouth open in protest, but Genevra silenced her. Having been raised in

Anglo-India, the youngest sister understood confinement and restriction and the rules of politeness as Ailsa, born in the wild Highlands, never could.

Lian did not move. She dared not look away from Chin's accusing stare; she would appear weak and afraid. "I did not deceive you out of malice but out of fear." Why was she bothering to explain? "My honorable mother told me that I must pretend, to protect my life and hers."

Diffidently, Madam Chin nodded, but her husband was not impressed. The two girls seemed to be struggling to remain silent.

"You call me one of Them because of my blue eyes, a legacy from my father. I did not ask that he should be my father. Had I been given the choice, I would have chosen otherwise. It would have been much easier, safer, to be like everyone else. But we cannot change the fate the gods have chosen for us, no matter how hard we wish it."

The couple glanced at each other, then away. Their response had been involuntary, bred of a lifetime of hatred and fear of the foreigners who had brought destruction and humiliation to the Middle Kingdom. The Chinese could bear anything but loss of face—their sense of worth, their pride. "She is right."

The two girls risked a quick glance at Lian, a fleeting smile of conspiracy. During Chin Shu's visits to the house of Wan, her daughters, Lin-Mei and Yi-niang, had grown fond of Lian, who was usually bored by the gossip among the older women. She had slipped away with the children to write them poems and give them embroidered tokens, which she taught them how to make. She had even let them hold her calligraphy brush, dip it carefully in the ink and make a stroke on parchment.

The girls had learned Lian's secret as they sat on satin pillows on the floor. If she had not been so lonely, she would not have taken the risk. She must have been mad. They had promised not to tell, but they were children, and she had feared they would blurt it out unthinkingly. But apparently they had been loyal to their friend.

She could not return their quickly hidden smiles, but she moved her hands just slightly, gracefully, in the motion of butterfly wings she had taught them long ago. Lin-Mei and Yi-niang lowered their heads, but Lian knew they were grinning.

Mister Chin was thoughtful. After all, his family had been living among foreigners in France for months, had begun to grow accustomed to their strange ways. Perhaps he had been too harsh. "Please forgive our rudeness. You did not earn our cruel judgment, nor did we have the right to make it. It was the sight of those blue eyes in a Chinese face that shocked us into being unkind and unwise."

Inclining her head in acknowledgment, Lian said, "My gown and eyes are of the West, but I was born, and I remain Chinese in my spirit, which sings in the rhythm of flowing streams; in my soul, which yearns for hills of pine and gardens of beauty and order; in my mind, which treasures the words of the Wise Ones. Those things run in my blood as surely as my blood runs through my beating heart."

This time Genevra could not stop Ailsa from coming forward. "Ye need no' defend yourself to them."

"I have said what I feel, what is the truth. That is all. Mairi Rose taught me to do that. It was my choice."

Mister Chin was impressed at her unbending spirit. He looked at his wife, whose compassion for Lian shone in her eyes. "We are all exiles," he said, when he had collected the words carefully in his mind. "We are rootless, when once our roots went deep and spread wide—over ten thousand *li*, through ten thousand legends. In exile one must not cling to old superstitions and traditions." He paused, sighing. "China is crumbling, but I wish to remain standing with my family beside me. That is why I have chosen to forget the past, the old language, the old ways, and think only of the future. Perhaps it is the same for you."

Lin-Mei, the older girl, thought it safe now to tug on her father's sleeve. When he bent down, she whispered urgently in his ear. He regarded Lian with new interest. "We are looking for a governess, a teacher for our daughters and ourselves. First Daughter reminds me that it is said you have been educated in English, Latin and French, in philosophy, the Classics, history and astronomy. I heard rumors of the tutors Wan Ke-ming hired to teach you, though I did not believe them then." In China, no woman was taught much more than cooking and sewing and the graceful art of pleasing her husband. "First Daughter also tells me you were friends, that you cared for my children when others did not. I am grateful. But more than that, I would ask a great favor."

Lin-Mei and Yi-niang looked up boldly, nodding and smiling. Lian could not help but respond.

So it was that, in the end, the Chins had asked her to accompany them to France as companion and governess to the children and tutor to the whole family. Within the week, it was arranged. They had given her a place to go.

A luggage cart colliding with a pile of wooden cartons brought Ailsa back to the present with a jolt.

She and Genevra had come today, reluctantly, to say good-bye and see Lian safely onto the ship. Their sister stood staring at the choppy, cold gray sea.

"It is right, what I am doing," she murmured. She had agreed to go with the Chins because of her affection for the girls, because she would be useful and productive, and because, by staying with a family who shared her memories of a beautiful and violent civilization, she was, in some small way, clinging to her past.

"I'm not so certain," Genevra said. "You hardly know these people you're going away with. We only just met them a fortnight past."

Lian looked up, brow furrowed. "I have known the Chin's all my life."

Blushing, Genevra realized the girls had grown so close in the past months, that she'd begun to feel she knew everything the other two had ever done and everyone they'd ever known. But of course, that was impossible. Still, she was uneasy. Or was it bereft? "I just—do you *want* to go to France?"

There're so many other places, other choices to be made. And you've the strength to make them. Of that I'm certain. Lian nodded, suddenly optimistic. That would have pleased Mairi Rose. "The Chins are familiar. I am comfortable with them. I have always been fond of the girls. And they know this small town on the Seine; they will make a place for me."

"Ye'll be part of a family," Ailsa said in encouragement, though sorrow was a shadow across her lively face.

"There is no blood tie among us," Lian said, thinking of her lost lover, of the melancholy expression on her Scottish sister's face.

"If they care for ye, it makes no matter, Wan Lian, and well ye should know it. I thought my mother taught ye that, at least."

Lian smiled sadly, because she was leaving all that behind. "Of course she did. I will never forget what she taught me." *I tell ye from my heart that ye'll always have a home here. I think ye know it.*

Lian felt the grip of Ailsa and Genevra's hands holding her back, keeping her near them. She did not allow herself to return their grasp. To touch them now, though they be sisters, friends, the keepers of her dreams and nightmares, was against every rule of politeness and dignity. In China one did not touch in public, expose emotion or a tender caress to strangers. That is what she told herself, but she knew Mairi Rose would have brushed her excuses away in disbelief.

Lian's back was straight and her face impassive as she

glanced across crates and carts to see that the Chins had arrived. They stood back, their faces without expression. She knew they would not approach or interfere. It would not be polite.

They could not possibly understand the tumult of emotion inside her, how little and how very much she wanted to walk away from Ailsa and Genevra. They had become her family, an unfailing source of strength to replace what she had lost.

"Must you go?" Genevra asked again.

Lian answered slowly, speaking each word distinctly, with confidence. "Yes. *T'ien Hon*, Heaven's Ruler, will protect me as he does all travelers on the sea."

When the ship's horn blared, Lian saw the Chins glance anxiously toward the line of passengers. Her sisters were weeping. "If ye need us, we'll come for ye. Ye know that, don't ye?" Ailsa asked.

"I know," Lian replied, staring at the Chins. They represented all she had ever yearned for. They were a family, whole and unbattered, familiar in their foreignness. They had given her the chance to move away from the numbness and into the future.

A family. A future different from the lonely past. 'Tis so much, Lian. 'Tis more than enough.

Lian's hands began to ache and she realized that, unconsciously, she had linked her fingers with Ailsa's and Genevra's. Now it was *she* who was holding on to *them*. Until now, her sisters had bound her in this cocoon of unreality, where she was comfortable, safe. She had to let go of them to move forward, but her limbs were rigid and unresponsive. She was caught like the child she had been, frightened to leave the safety of her bed with its shield of butterfly curtains.

The two families approached one another warily as the ship's bell called and the biting sea air hit their faces. Lian had become rigid and Ailsa knew she had to help her sister go. For Lian's sake. Genevra had stopped trembling and forced herself to be still. It seemed she and Ailsa must be the strong ones now.

All at once, Lian surprised them by whispering softly:

> "As the fire died and the white round moon
> Disappeared behind the purple mountains,
> The image of your face grew indistinct;
> But not the touch of your hand or the sound
>   of your voice,
> Beloved and familiar in the darkness."

The pain in Ailsa's chest was suffocating, and Genevra was pale with grief at their sister's poem of farewell, an offering, a last fragment of Chinese beauty.

Unexpectedly, Mister Chin released his daughters, who had been calling out for the friend of their childhood. As the two girls met the women face to face, they reached out for Lian just as Ailsa and Genevra released her, pushing her slightly to force her into motion.

Lin-Mei and Yi-niang grasped Lian's hands. Only for a second were her fingers free of human touch in the cold, damp air. Lian turned to face her sisters. She would not insult them by turning her back as she walked away. Her throat constricted and her mouth grew dry. They had talked long and intimately into the night; just now they could not speak. They said farewell with their eyes as the Chins moved purposefully toward the ship. The impatient girls tugged Lian closer to the future. Slowly, with each step backward away from her sisters, she felt a tearing inside that left her weak.

At the base of the gangplank, she held Ailsa's and Genevra's gazes one last time, and knew she could not bear this parting. A thought vibrated in the air among the three, unspoken, heavy with sadness, yet also a sense of anticipation.

She smiled, eyes veiled in tears, and the thought faded

like music, like an unfinished song, settled like dust in an unused room. Lian closed the door to that room so firmly that not a grain of dust or a note of music could escape. She would no longer rub the dust between her fingers, hear the song within her head.

She turned resolutely up the long ramp to the ship, felt the weight of the two girls clinging to her tightly. Lian had dreaded this moment, dreaded it deep in a dark corner of her heart that she did not explore. But now that the moment of parting had come, as she moved toward the deck, as her sisters were enveloped and consumed by fog until she could no longer feel their presence, she realized, with a small leap of hope, that her hands were not, after all, empty and cold.

1

Two years later: Chervilles, France, 1881

INTENT ON DESCENDING THE STAIRS SOUNDLESSLY, WAN LIAN moved toward the street.

She had been awakened earlier than usual by the pigeons on the ledge outside her window and had dressed quickly in a satin tunic and overvest. While combing and braiding her hair, she had heard the high, clear song of the goat boy piping his herd along, the cacophony of small bells, the clatter of hooves and plaintive bleating magnified by the stillness of a sleeping town. She had picked up a cracked pitcher, a basket and a bag of coins and started out before the day had quite begun.

She went down the stairs as silently as smoke, as she had learned to do in China. She loved this time by herself, this lingering darkness, this cool gray expectation of the fast-approaching dawn.

Often, she tried to reach the sidewalk before the landlord, Cheng, the alchemist whose shop of healing herbs and teas and mysterious powders faced the oddly curved Rue Salubre. Not once had she succeeded. Cheng was always there when she arrived, seated in his favorite chair, hands folded, smiling enigmatically. His almond eyes, heavy-lidded and surrounded by fine wrinkles, gleamed with a trace of laughter, as if he knew she was trying, just once, to best him, though he would not admit it.

Shaking her head, she stepped onto the sidewalk and paused, captivated, as always, by the sight of the hushed streets.

Wreathes of mist curled through the maze of new leaves and graceful branches, hovered like gauze haloes around the gas lights that burned pale yellow in the soft gray air. Ivy climbed sinuously up the black poles, gilded by light from the globes above. The stables and blacksmith, catty-corner to Cheng's shop, were still dark, though the pungent odor of horses and damp straw revealed their presence.

A thread of musical notes caught Lian's attention; she turned as Jean-Paul, the goat boy, approached.

"*Bonjour*, Mademoiselle Lian," he called cheerfully. "I have Annabelle for you, as always." One of his small herd nudged him fretfully behind the knees and Jean-Paul nearly fell over. "Behave yourself, Gertrud," he said in an attempt to sound stern. "You will make me look the fool in front of Mademoiselle."

"*Non*, never," Lian assured him as she crossed the damp cobbles that gleamed like crushed and re-formed gems. Already the street cleaners had flooded the gutters to wash away leaves, dirt and debris from the day before, so the morning smelled of smoke and newly green acacias, of magnolia blossoms and wet stone.

Lian ducked under the branches of a chestnut tree to hand over her pitcher. In his plain, homespun shirt, rough-woven trousers and worn boots, Jean-Paul chattered about the arrival of spring as he milked Annabelle, who watched Lian with limpid eyes.

The goats became restless, butting heads and bleating, their tiny bells ringing in an erratic rhythm. The boy looked up as Cheng approached with a large bowl.

"Ah!" Jean-Paul said as he handed Lian the full pitcher

and accepted the *sous* she gave him, "Monsieur Cheng prefers Bridget." The boy reached for the second goat's collar; she came meekly, without a sound. "He says her milk is sweeter."

"Not sweeter," Cheng corrected him softly, "but purer, for Bridget is a goat at peace, so no bile spoils her milk."

Jean-Paul shrugged, rolling his eyes at the way Cheng viewed the world in general and goats in particular. When he had finished his task, he paused, listening.

"I must go now. There are many other bowls to fill. And if Bridget becomes bored, her milk will go sour along with her mood." He smiled impudently at Cheng, waved and flung *"Au revoir!"* over his shoulder as he turned the corner, lulling his restless goats with the notes of his flute.

Smiling to herself, Lian turned in the opposite direction, toward the open-air market on the Seine. She walked the entire length of Rue Salubre, all five buildings, before crossing to the four rows of stalls along the quay. Several people greeted her pleasantly as they passed. She had been surprised at first by how readily they accepted her Chinese features and oriental clothing, her unadorned black braid and sky blue eyes. But by now she had become accustomed to the tolerance and warmth of these people.

This, after all, was Chervilles, created thirty years ago by François Duchamps for his American wife, who had been harshly snubbed by aristocratic Parisian society. On land his family had owned for generations, he built an estate in the woods by the lake. Because of the prejudice they had suffered, Marie and François welcomed foreigners and French alike to the small town that sprang up around the estate—a German butcher, a green-grocer, a seamstress, Cheng the Chinese alchemist, an English tobacconist and many others. It quickly became more like an eccentric family than a group of tradespeople and their wealthier neighbors who depended upon one another for survival.

Lian paused as the rising sun edged the pine forest on

the far side of the river, spread slowly across the meadow until it met the silver-gray rippled water. The fragile light was colorless, so clear it shone like crystal. Gold rose from the luminous band, transforming itself into orange, then red, then violet. Color bled upward as light filtered down into the Seine, imbuing the pastoral tranquillity of meadow and woods with a soft luster. Slowly, the gaslights on their iron posts flickered out.

The market began to take on life and color and motion. As if voices had been stilled by the dimness before dawn, they erupted into a flurry of greetings and bartering and good-natured insults. The scents of fruit and vegetables, fish and brightly colored heaps of flowers blended with the distinct, quicksilver smell of the Seine. Lian had tried to describe that smell in poems, but always the words eluded her.

Moving briskly down the rows, she put fresh cherries, asparagus and cabbage in her basket, along with a posy of sweet william. From the fish seller, she bought a turbot; though the fresh carp looked tempting, it was too dear. Finally, she added a small wedge of brie and one of cheddar.

She thought of the year she had spent at the Chins', when the serving girl had been sent out every morning to do this task. Until six months ago, Lian had never guessed what she'd been missing, lying wide-eyed in her bed or crouched over her books. But Monsieur Chin had freed her from her ignorance when he hired a French governess for his daughters and told Lian it was time she find her own way. *It is too safe for you here*, he had said obscurely. She had been too stunned by his rejection to ask what he meant. Yet she spoke no word of argument. It was Chin Yun's choice. He had offered her refuge when she needed it, after all, just as François Duchamps had given it to the Chins.

Fortunately, she had met Cheng when she discovered his shop of familiar herbs and teas and ancient cures. He in his long silk gown and cloth-soled shoes, his hair in a neat queue down his back, and Lian in her plain Chinese gown and tunic, had understood one another at once. He had asked her to work in his shop and offered, in exchange, the flat on the top floor of the house on Rue Salubre.

She had not sought the change, but did not regret the result. Except for the girls. She tried not to allow herself to think of Lin-Mei and Yi-niang. Mairi Rose had once told her: *Our hearts are stronger than we believe*. Lian had begun to think it true.

Her basket nearly full, she turned toward home and the bakery next to Cheng's. Breathing in the smell of bread fresh from the oven, the tang of yeast and flour and warm butter, she slipped inside and was enveloped by a fragrant warmth that made her weak with hunger. She saw a Chinese boy engulfed in a huge white apron working busily at the back of the shop, though he paused long enough to notice and smile approvingly at her Chinese tunic and vest.

Henri Arnaud and his wife, Claire, both spoke at once. "We have grown too busy and had to find help. Yen Tai is a hard worker and makes it easier for us."

Lian wondered why Cheng had not told her about Yen Tai; he always knew such things before anyone else. She purchased a brioche and baguette, still speculating as she left.

Pensively, Lian crossed the alley between the bakery and the apothecary shop. Her landlord was seated in his chair out front, eyes closed and head back. Guiltily, she glanced over her shoulder to be certain no one was following. Though she had tried, she had never quite broken herself of the habit.

Despite Cheng's stillness, she knew he was watching. He was always watching and listening. Yet she started when he spoke. "Are you seeing Bannermen in the street today? Are the armies of T'zu Hsi on the march? Or is it only *kuei*, the ghosts from your past?" He smiled gently and peered up and down the street. "Rue Salubre is empty of your enemies. They exist only inside your head."

Lian stiffened, unable, as usual, to ignore his challenge. "Perhaps the *kuei* are in my head, but the Bannermen are real."

Cheng smoothed his wispy white hair. "Real, yes, but they are not here. It is too far for them to come and the journey is too difficult." He smiled. "Besides, you worry too much. If they did come, I would have heard them."

In spite of herself, Lian returned his smile. "Sometimes they walk on cloth-soled feet and are as quiet as the cats that creep along the roofs at night." The smell of turbot began to drift upward. "I must go or the fish will spoil."

As she turned away, Cheng stirred. "It is your choice, Lian," he murmured cryptically. "Remember, 'The green waters have really no sorrow; it is only the wind that wrinkles their face.' " He closed his eyes once more.

He had said all he was going to say, leaving her with another riddle to decipher. But before she could move, Cheng surprised her by rousing himself.

"I had nearly forgotten. I have letters for you again. They arrived in the late post." He drew them out of his wide sleeve and tapped them on his palm, gauging their weight. "Those sisters of yours must have a great deal to say. Perhaps the postman should begin to sleep in my shop, so he need not come so far so often."

"At least it is a pleasant journey, now that it is spring," Lian replied, unimpressed by Cheng's long-suffering sigh of pity for the postman. She smiled as she took the two heavily stamped envelopes. Holding them, however briefly, was like touching her sisters' hands for an instant, feeling their strength and affection flow through her like a tonic. She slipped the letters into her basket. "Now that I have relieved you of your heavy burden, you can rest your frail and weary bones, Old Master."

Cheng eyed her narrowly, muttered something and sank back into his chair, arms crossed, hands buried in his wide silk sleeves.

Lian left him looking inscrutable and made her way between the buildings to the rear door leading to the stairway to her flat. She noticed from the loud noises and raised voices that the butcher across the street had begun his business for the day.

She pushed open the bright blue door, its panels carved with garlands of leaves and flowers that bloomed around the heavy knocker—an intricate twisted braid of brass. Pausing cautiously at the foot of the stairs, she began to climb slowly, shivering at the cool dimness inside.

She stopped when she realized she was being enveloped by drifts of smoke tainted by the smell of burning that billowed from the butcher's open door and windows. Before she could pull back, the smoke crept over her, and with it, the odor of charred flesh and blazing wood. She backed away, but it was too late. Despite her desperate attempt at denial, the years disintegrated and she was a child again, quivering in terror before her mother's house.

The smoke lay over Canton like a harbinger of desolation, foul drifts of fog raining ashes from the sky. Everywhere she looked, the city burned; the smell of charred wood and flesh poisoned the air so she could not breathe.

"My Mother!" she shrieked, though her voice was lost amid the tumult of gunfire and explosions. "My Mother! Please!" the child shouted again. There was no answer.

Earlier, the Wans had gathered the few things they could carry and stuffed them into sacks to sling over their shoulders as they fled. Lian hovered at the door, frightened of going out and terrified of staying. In the streets, she would be attacked by the Westerners as a Chinese, but inside the house, even the few loyal servants who had kept the secret of her heritage, those who had always been her protectors, watched her in a way that made her want to hide.

Ke-ming knelt before her young daughter, whose hands trembled with fear. "I must go quickly to say good-bye to my lover."

Lian clung to her mother, nails digging into Ke-ming's flawless skin. "Do not leave me alone!" she plead. "The soldiers are coming."

"It is only for a moment, precious jade. You will be safe here with the servants until I return."

As soon as she was gone, the servants fled. Then the courtyards caught fire and the house began to blaze, its rice paper walls and wood frame feeding the flames. Alone and uncertain, Lian dragged the sacks of treasures and stumbled through the courtyards into the street, staying close to the front wall, which was made of clay and stone and had not yet been touched. "Come back to me, My Mother!" she cried, tears streaming down her cheeks, leaving snakelike trails through the soot and dirt.

She gasped at the bedlam in the streets: Everywhere, people were running. Foreign soldiers with rifles and bayonets, families dragging their possessions in rickshaws and carts and wheelbarrows, clasping their children close in a futile attempt to protect them. All were coated in ash and debris like sullied rain. The air shuddered with explosions and the ground beneath Lian's feet shifted dangerously.

She could not stay here. Dragging the heavy sacks on the ground, Lian moved slowly, stopping every few li to call out, "I am here, Wan Ke-ming. I need you!"

Then the child heard a familiar voice.

"Wan Li-an! What are you doing in the street alone? You must go and hide. Where is your mother?"

She glanced up warily to see the family from the next compound, the Lu's, huddled across the street from her. The Lu's were old friends. Surely they would help her. The leaden weight in her chest lightened a little.

"I cannot find my mother. She turned, only for an instant, but the crowd swept her away." She did not tell the truth because she was ashamed.

The ominous thunder of soldiers' feet came closer, and the heat of the flames changed the air into a blurred, undulating mass. The sacks were heavy, Lian's hands raw, her heart despairing. The

Lu's motioned frantically. "We cannot wait, but neither can you stand there. Come with us. We will try to find Wan Ke-ming."

The child hesitated, glancing over her shoulder. The fire raged high above the courtyard walls, but Ke-ming was not there. Turning back to the only shelter she could find, Lian took one step toward the family gathered across the street. In her fear, she forgot herself and her secret, and gazed at them directly.

She saw their eyes widen, but before they could speak, before she could move or explain or cry out, there was a strange whistling in the air and the ground exploded at their feet. Suddenly, where the Lu's had stood an instant before, there was no one.

Lian blinked in disbelief, screamed as the smoke engulfed her, but not before she saw that the cobbles in the street were wet and slick and stained.

Then, out of nowhere, Ke-ming appeared, sweeping her daughter into her arms, holding her so tightly that Lian gasped for breath. Her mother had meant to protect her child, both from those who would destroy her because of her foreign blood, and from the horror and ugliness that filled the swarming streets.

She was too late.

The Lu's had seen, been horrified by the sight of Lian's eyes, and though the Lu's were no more, Lian's face, her hands, her gown were covered with their blood.

"Save the blood for the sausage!" The butcher's voice reverberated across the street and through the open door in the alley.

"I know my own business, you big bloated ox. Go away and leave me to it!"

Lian blinked, startled back into the present by the shrill bickering. Profoundly shaken, she crept up the rest of the stairs in silence.

2

Chin Lin-Mei and Chin Yi-niang stood inside the apothecary shop, the echo of the hollow bell fading overhead. The two girls blinked rapidly, disconcerted by the contrast between the bright light of day they had left behind and the cool dimness that enfolded them now. The fragrance of incense and boiling herbs—musky, bitter, sickly sweet— curled through the gloom, an exotic but reassuring odor of things unknown. The girls clung together, staring at the brass Chinese character *fang hu* above the door, representing the square kettle—the symbol for immortality.

"So, my young friends have returned," Cheng observed, appearing silently from among the long rows of shelves that rose toward the ceiling, the aisles of Chinese medicine chests with their many small drawers for storing herbs and pills and other medications.

"We have." Yi-niang's voice was hushed; to speak loudly in this place would seem a desecration. "We wish to see Mademoiselle Lian. It is not the same since she left the house of our father." The younger girl could not hide the trembling of her hands, nor the nervousness in the furtive glances her older sister cast behind them.

Cheng spread his hands wide in welcome. "So you have said before." The alchemist was delighted to see Yi-niang and Lin-Mei; he knew Lian missed them greatly. She had told him Chin Yun had sent her away, laying no blame at the feet of her employer, but Cheng had heard what she did not say. He hoped this time the girls would not lose their nerve. "Yet not once have you climbed Wan Li-an's stairs or knocked upon her door. Is that because your honored parents have forbidden it?"

"Partly." Lin-Mei replied diffidently. "We have always

been obedient daughters." But *hsiao*—filial piety—could not stop her from thinking of her teacher and friend, from being drawn to this house often. Mei could still see Lian's face clearly, hear the sound of her musical voice. She glanced upward, heart racing.

"If you are hoping she will appear and solve your dilemma, you are wrong," the old man said solemnly. "She cannot come to you. You must go to her."

"But—" Yi-niang began obstinately.

"You may object as long and loudly as you like, but that will not change anything." Cheng regarded Mei and Yi intently. "You are a woman now, Lin-Mei, and must begin to think for yourself. Look into your heart to see if your intentions are right and proper and kind. Then decide."

Cheng felt compassion for the two girls who so clearly longed to obey their father and yet defy him. Judging by the number of times they had appeared in his shop, their affection and respect for Wan Lian was deep. But so was their doubt. "Once you have asked yourself these questions, you must find the strength to follow the voices which answer. Are you willing to do that? If you are, you know the way."

He gestured toward the back of the shop, past the carefully labeled vials and bins and drawers that contained his skill, his knowledge, his strength. His silk sleeve stood out in the dimness, pointing the way to the door that led to the upper floors.

All at once, Cheng tilted his head sharply, listening. "Someone is coming. I must leave you. Perhaps in the stillness you will think more clearly." He smiled benignly and was gone in a rustle of silk and the faintest whisper of his steps against the wooden floor.

Lin-Mei looked at her sister, almond eyes full of questions, though there were none left in her heart.

* * *

Lian closed the door to her flat, her pulse pounding in her ears. It had been a long time since the past had come to her so vividly, a long time since she had felt this piercing chill. But she had changed in those days and weeks and months of freedom from memory; she had learned the past could hurt her only if she allowed it to permeate her thoughts, to feed the apprehension she managed to suppress for prolonged, peaceful intervals of time. Now and then, she convinced herself she had forgotten altogether, but that was mere obstinance and yearning. Still, she had grown stronger with each day that passed.

Now, although it was not easy, she caught her breath and her heartbeat slowed. With determination, she forced the memory of Canton away. Eventually, the disturbing images faded into the dim stillness of her flat. The air was cool, laced with the evanescent presence of whispering ghosts that brushed her cheek, the muted quality of light and sound that soothed and reassured her.

Knowing it would help to keep herself busy, she put the food away in the compact kitchen and pantry, the milk and fish in her tiny icebox—the block of ice had been replaced the day before, and the chilly air caressed her face in a cloud of white mist when she opened the door. Those chores done, she flung open the tall red shutters in the parlor, inviting the early morning sun to illuminate the room.

It was then that she heard a hesitant tap on the front door.

For an instant, she froze. When she was very young, her mother had taught her to listen well, to hear approaching footsteps and never be taken by surprise. But there was a great deal on her mind. "I must take more care," she murmured as she drew the door inward far enough to see who stood outside.

"Lin-Mei, Yi-niang!" Stunned and gratified at the sight of their faces, which were nearly obscured by shadow as they hung back uncertainly, Lian opened the door wide. "I did not hear you coming."

"You didn't? But you always heard everything," Yi-niang said softly.

"Too much," her older sister replied, barely above a whisper. "We had no secrets from you. Until you went away." There was a trace of accusation, a trace of hurt in her voice and dark brown eyes, as well as a hint of uncertainty.

The girls remained in the hallway out of Lian's reach. She extended both hands in welcome, though her smile was bittersweet. "I did not mean to steal your secrets any more than I meant to leave the ones among us three behind. Whatever happened at your parents' house on Chemin de Marie, you need not hover in the chilly hall as if afraid to come in. You are welcome in my house, always. I have missed you greatly for these past six months."

"You see!" Yi cried in triumph. "I told you she would be glad to see us." Recovered from her shyness, she skipped forward, while Mei followed more slowly, hands clasped tightly before her. She regarded Lian closely, then lowered her lids as was proper. She looked as though she might say something, but Yi interrupted her.

Glancing around surreptitiously to make certain no one was watching, the twelve-year-old pointed to her Chinese shoes. "We wore our cloth-soled shoes and hid our high-button boots in the bushes by the gate. We hate them, don't we, Mei?"

Mei nodded, watching her tutor and friend steadily, trying to read the emotions Lian was so adept at disguising. Most of the time.

"Of course you do," Lian said, knowing Monsieur Chin would not approve of either the shoes or the deception. And probably not the visit itself. But she said nothing. It was no longer her job to see the Chin girls made their parents happy. Still, she felt a flicker of guilt; she had absorbed too well and too deeply the concept of *hsiao*. She could not simply dismiss it, no matter how she felt about the way the Chins were raising their daughters. "I am so glad you have come." Her face shone with delight, surprise, relief. "I had begun to wonder if I would see you again."

Shaking her head, Yi-niang exclaimed, "How could you not see us in such a small town? Everyone sees everyone, whether they want to or not."

"Why didn't you come to visit?" Mei asked coolly. Sixteen now, she was considered a woman and was intensely aware of the obligations that came with adulthood. Lian had taught her those obligations. Besides, her teacher's defection had hurt her deeply.

Yi's grin disappeared. The sight of her old friend's familiar face had made her forget her anger and hurt. "Yes, why didn't you?"

The girls stood with arms crossed, awaiting an answer. Lian would not have recognized the effort it took for them to remain aloof if she did not know them so well. If their lips had not trembled as they tried to frown fiercely.

"I did not think I would be welcome." Indeed, as she noticed how the two were dressed, she became certain. Yi's hair had been cut into thin bangs that someone had attempted to curl. It was drawn behind her ears and held by a band over which a ribbon had been tied in a bow. The hair in the band was braided, while the rest fell loose to just below her shoulders, where a wide, thick clasp tidily contained the blue-black mass. She wore a dress of violet grosgrain in the French style. The front was ruched and pleated and set off with a lacework collar and a large bow above the ruffles of the skirt. Several inches of beige wool stockings showed above the ridiculously incongruous cloth-soled shoes.

Mei's hair was drawn up in a more mature style, softly braided and curled, leaving her neck bare. She wore a cashmere gown, intricately draped, pleated and ruffled. Her skirt just reached her ankles, where the edge of an expensive lace petticoat showed. Clearly the Chins were trying to make their daughters look as French as possible, though their heavy blue-black hair proclaimed their heritage as distinctly as their dark almond eyes and their bronze skin, even beneath a layer of pale pink powder. Lian was perplexed and dismayed by the girls' unnatural appearance. She had feared this might happen, known it in her heart since the day Monsieur Chin sent her away.

"*You cling to China, and you teach this yearning to my daughters. I wish them to forget they have lived anywhere on earth but here.*"

Lian was appalled. "*How can they forget when for so many years you instilled in them Chinese values and customs? When they experienced a culture so different from this?*"

Chin went on as if she had not spoken. "*You insist on using their Chinese names, though we have asked you many times to call them May and Nan. I want my girls to fit into French society, but they are deeply attached to you. Because of this, they imitate you, worshipping at a shrine to their ancestors, feeding the Kitchen God honey at New Years, clinging to a past they should leave behind them. They will not let go and move forward, become truly French, until you set them free.*"

As if she had been holding them prisoner, forcing upon them some distasteful ideal, even the thought of which made their father look ill. Lian had stood perfectly still, wounded, uncomprehending.

He paused portentously. "*It is not that you have not done well, but that you have done too well. So well that we no longer need you. You have given us all you can.*"

It was not true, but she could find no words to fight him. He was obdurate, distant, unreachable.

When she did not blink or look away, he added quietly, "*It is too safe here, Li-an. There is no challenge for you anymore.*"

Why, after so many months, did the memory hurt so much?

Lian pressed her fingers to her temples; her braid was too tight. Impatiently, she unraveled the woven strands, spread her fingers wide and fanned them through her hair as she shook her head in relief.

The pain faded, but the unrelenting sound of Chin's voice did not. "I did not think I would be welcome," she repeated.

Mei was bewildered by the look on Lian's face. Forgetting her anger, her intention to remain aloof, she murmured, "We would have welcomed you." She covered her mouth with her hands, surprised by her own outburst.

Her sister continued to stare at the polished hardwood floor. "Perhaps not at first," she said without looking up. "We disliked you more than high-button boots when you left. My mother said we shouldn't, that you needed your own life and we were being selfish. I didn't care. We missed you and wanted you back." At last, she raised her eyes to meet Lian's troubled gaze. "You didn't even try to see us."

Lian looked away. It was no easier to face the girls now than it had been six months before.

"Don't leave us!" Mei and Yi cried, their faces stricken.

"I have given my word," Lian managed to reply.

"You gave your word to us," Mei said. "You promised never to go."

Her younger sister grasped Lian's tunic, leaving smudges on the pale lilac cloth. "You promised!"

"You are our only true friend," Mei said, "our teacher and protector. How can we bear to lose you? Do you not see how much we need you?"

Lian had seen, had felt their tears as if they were her own. In that moment, that single instant of suspended time, she'd had to choose. She could tell them the truth, that this was not her choice, that she ached at the thought of leaving, but then they would have blamed their father, the head of the family, who deserved their respect, obedience and devotion. She could leave them angry, confused and hurt by her, or by the man they trusted and adored. There was, after all, no choice to make.

"We shouldn't have stayed away so long." Mei spoke with more assurance, so her voice pierced the cool, dim stillness of the flat. She wondered how she could have doubted Wan Lian or thought she did not feel their grief. "We missed you." She tried to keep her emotion under control, as was proper, but she wanted to hug her friend, to weep with relief that there was one who understood. She leaned heavily against the narrow ebony cupboard in the entryway.

Lian was moved by Mei's confession, the need and affection in her liquid dark eyes. She touched the girl's hand, brushing her fingers over the smooth bronze skin, startled when Mei turned her hand palm up, linking her fingers tightly with Lian's, releasing them abruptly.

Lian wanted to weep at the hunger for tenderness in that single gesture. "How long can you stay?"

Mei hesitated; she could not yet think. She was rescued by her younger sister, who had overcome her reserve long enough to peek around the corner, while the others stood as if caught and held there by the past.

"Look, May, she has a Kitchen God of her own." Yi did not know what made her cry out, except the dampness of tears in the air. She could not bear it if anyone wept.

They turned gratefully toward the paper image of the brightly colored God on the wall beside the range with its tiny grate. His wide smile brought light to the dim nook, while his green and red robes brought color.

"I still make him offerings of food and candy twice monthly, and before the New Year, I gave him honey and sweets to seal his lips so he will not carry tales of my transgressions to Heaven."

The girls touched the colorful image reverently. "*Maman* took ours down the day you left," Yi murmured, "but I rescued him from the rubbish and hung him at the back of our closet."

Lian was touched, but also concerned. "Was that wise?"

Yi turned to face her defiantly. "No, but I couldn't let them toss him away."

"We keep a bag of sweets for him hidden in a tiny cupboard in the wall," Mei added. Even at sixteen, she was not too old to admit her fondness for a tradition her parents had explained was pointless and had sprung from ignorance. Like Lian, she enjoyed the ritual and did not wish to give it up. "They took away the altar to our ancestors as well. We had to keep *something* of the old traditions. We couldn't bear to lose them all."

Choking back anger she could not express, Lian guided Mei and Yi into the parlor where the light streamed through the open shutters at the front and back of the flat. For the first time, the girls noticed the decor. Not so much the handwoven rugs, bright embroidered pillows and twin rocking chairs, but the plaster itself.

A former tenant had painted a likeness of the Seine, which flowed from wall to wall under gracefully arched bridges and along grassy banks, through stands of pines and around docks, where boats moved with the current. A single child floated on a roughly built raft. The painting continued on the ceiling, where birds swooped, clouds drifted and two kites, one pink and one yellow, bobbed in the deep blue sky.

"Oh, it's lovely," Mei exclaimed with more animation than she'd shown since she arrived. "How lucky you are to have this always around you, even when it rains."

Yi simply whirled, gaping, eyes shining with admiration.

3

THE SOUND OF MUTED LAUGHTER ROSE FROM THE STREET below, followed by the chatter of voices. Lian turned toward the balcony beyond the open shutters. "Ah! Already Cheng has guests, and noisy ones at that." Tilting her head curiously, she pushed the French doors open and stepped into the morning air.

The girls pressed themselves against the wall on either side, peeking around the red shutters while trying to hide their presence.

"Nothing ever happens at home," Yi whispered. "Besides, you will want to show us your view." Her anticipation was tangible.

Mei ducked her head, hiding a smile.

Lian sighed with pleasure, breathing in the mingled fragrances of stables, bakery and river. From her snug perch, she could see the neighboring houses opposite, and the quay along the Seine. She often leaned here for an hour at a time, watching the breeze play in the ivy that climbed the stone walls of the houses, whisper through small beds of roses, iris and hollyhocks, tease the petals of geraniums, peonies and marguerites in the bright window boxes. Or she lost herself in the flow of the river, the passing of boats, the wind in the leaves of the plane trees.

Yi and Mei were not looking at the view. Bodies concealed, only their foreheads and eyes—apparently politely lowered—visible, they stared at the group near the apothecary shop. Lian smiled at their restraint in spite of their obvious eagerness.

"It is only Cheng and the baker, Henri, his wife, Claire, and a stranger in a dark felt hat." Lian knew quite well who stood beneath that familiar hat; Émile Drouard was unmistakable, with his broad shoulders and solid body, the negligent grace of his posture.

"That's not a stranger; it's Monsieur Drouard. He's famous all over Chervilles." Yi squinted at Lian, trying to read her expression.

Since Chervilles comprised precisely three streets of five buildings each, a dairy, a herd of goats and one of sheep, a church, which also served as schoolhouse and town hall, as well as the Duchamps estate and four smaller chateaux grouped in a half circle behind the town, Lian was not unduly impressed by the man's supposed fame. She was far more interested in how Yi and Mei had heard about him.

"Everyone knows he often comes all the way from Paris to work with Cheng," Yi whispered. "Though most believe that's not his only reason."

She spoke softly, but Lian heard. She also saw the girl's knowing wink. "It is not wise to speculate about the intentions and feelings of others."

At last Mei spoke up. "Then I suppose few people are wise. I've heard them say he comes to see you, My Teacher. Only this time he has brought a fish."

"What?" Lian looked down to see that indeed, Émile Drouard was holding a large carp in his arms. The very carp she had admired at the market earlier.

As if he sensed her presence, he looked up, hazel eyes full of amusement as he rolled them toward the chattering group caught up in intense discussion. He shrugged as if to say "What can one do?" and grinned.

He has a pleasant smile, Lian thought. His face, too, was pleasant, especially with the morning sun caught in his blond hair and his curly red beard. She returned his smile, as everyone did; they could not help themselves. Monsieur Drouard had a kind, inviting smile without guile or cynicism. Lian lifted her hands, palms up, and raised her eyebrows in dismay at the commotion below.

Émile froze where he stood. Wan Lian had unbraided her hair. He had never seen it loose before. Never realized it would fall, thick and blue-black, below her waist. It touched her face gently, softening her expression. Usually, her braid was pulled back and her features starkly revealed. They were striking; her high molded cheekbones and narrow chin, straight nose and well-shaped lips revealed the best of both her Chinese and her English heritage. But combined with her natural reserve, her face had seemed exotic and coldly lovely—unattainable. Now, curtained by hair shimmering in the morning sun, she looked warm, mysterious, accessible.

Émile looked away to hide his thoughts.

Mei shook her head regretfully. "He'll ruin his lovely greatcoat. It will smell of fish now, no matter what he does."

"Perhaps that is why he has come. Cheng is known throughout the city and countryside as a fine alchemist. He can diagnose an illness more quickly than most doctors, and treat it more successfully. Even the wealthy come to him in disguise, trusting him to keep their secrets. He is also clever with formulas and mysterious concoctions which accomplish all manner of things. He might even be able to remove the odor of fish from wool."

"Monsieur Drouard doesn't look ill," Mei mused, with her sister's suggestive smile. "He looks quite well. And I doubt he brought the fish from Paris. The other passengers would have thrown him from the train." She paused dramatically. "The townspeople think him quite romantic and mysterious."

Just then the Chinese boy appeared from inside the bakery to shake out a floury cloth and see what was happening next door. Mei grew still, regarding Yen Tai half in admiration, half in panic. "Oh!" she squeaked, then reached out as if to retrieve the sound before the others heard.

Lian was too quick for her, as was the young man, who glanced up, curious.

"I wish you good morning, Chin Yi and Chin Mei," he said with careful formality. His glance lingered on Mei, who blushed and restrained her hands behind her back.

"Good morning," she replied stiffly.

"You know him?" Lian asked in surprise.

"He is First Son of Yen Yung, who, like my father, was a banker in China. He moved to Chervilles years ago. It was he who suggested my family come here. He and my father take the train to the city every day. Yi and I know all the Yen children."

Yi remained silent, staring at the young man, brow furrowed. Lian felt a stirring of discomfort. Be careful, Lin-Mei, she wanted to whisper. You cannot even hide your wistful smile as you watch Yen Tai.

"Ah, Li-an is here," Cheng said, unaware of the little drama unfolding on the balcony. "She will solve our problem."

Émile shook his head. "She has guests to see to." He had noticed the girls peeking out shyly, seen how they looked at Lian with deep affection. Perhaps that was why she seemed different today, more at peace and more alluring both at once. Unlike Cheng, he had also noticed Yen Tai's arrival and silent departure, been intrigued by the interplay between Yen and Mei.

"You have finally found your courage," Cheng called to the girls. "I am glad to see it."

Yi and Mei slipped out of sight when everyone began to stare.

"Tell Yi-niang and Lin-Mei they need not hide from us. We are friendly and harmless," Cheng said. There was a twinkle in his eye that belied his soft tone.

"But I digress." As the girls took the risk of revealing themselves to the group below, the alchemist called up, "See here. Émile Drouard has brought me a beautiful carp of white stomach and slender shape, as the best fish are, so I might have carp in red pepper sauce." He peered at Lian, one hand shading his eyes. "To turn down his offering would be churlish. But I do not cook such dishes. I was quite nearly forced to turn him away, when I remembered, fortuitously, that you, Wan Li-an, are an excellent cook of Chinese delicacies. Would you be willing to prepare this carp for my supper and share it with me?" He paused for a fraction of a second. "Only so I do not offend."

Émile shook his head, grinning, balanced the fish on one arm, swept off his hat and made a graceful bow that emphasized his height and broad shoulders. *"Bonjour,*

Mademoiselle Lian," he said, greeting her officially for the first time.

"*Bonjour*, Émile." Lian was surprised at how easily she spoke his name. "I hope you are well."

"I am well, but burdened, as you see, by my own whim, which told me to bring Cheng this excellent fish. His expertise, it seems, does not extend to the kitchen."

Aware of the giggling girls behind her, Lian could not hold back her own smile. "A predicament indeed. I suppose I will rescue you this time, but cannot promise always to save you from your whims." She tapped her finger thoughtfully against her lips. "As it happens, I am particularly fond of carp in red pepper sauce."

He looked astonished at the coincidence, but Lian was suspicious. "The fish is large," she observed.

"Then we must invite our friend Monsieur Drouard to join us. The gods would surely frown if we wasted a single bite of tender flesh," Cheng said.

Lian bowed toward the alchemist. "You must do as you think best."

"I always do as I think best," the old man replied. "It is the only way to accomplish one's goals and desires." Smiling obscurely, he motioned Émile toward the shop, no doubt to put the fish on ice before it spoiled. "You will join us for dinner tonight, Monsieur?"

"You need not invite me," Émile pointed out. "I brought you a gift; I did not mean to force my presence upon you." Yet he could not stop staring at the luxuriant black hair that fell over the railing when Lian leaned forward. He wished, fleetingly, that he might run his fingers through it, and was surprised by the strong impulse.

"The fish is too large for two. Indeed, you must join us." She felt no urge to take back Cheng's invitation and was pleased he had thought of it. She wondered if she only wanted to show off her skill at cooking to the "famous" Monsieur Drouard.

"In that case, I'm delighted to accept," Émile said. "I shall see you tonight, then."

"Tonight," Lian replied.

As she turned to shepherd the girls inside, she remembered Mei's interest in the Yen boy. She felt a rush of affection for the girl, and though she knew Chin Yun would not approve, she wanted to see again and again Mei's shy smile of happiness.

4

"AH! SUCH A MAGNIFICENT MEAL!" CHENG HAD EXCLAIMED as he leaned back, replete, fingers intertwined and resting on his belly. "The fish sliced thin and white as snowflakes, the flavor delicate yet spicy."

"I've never tasted carp so fine," Émile had added, not to be outdone. "And the tang of the fish head soup lingers on my tongue along with the sweetness of the melon."

"I had forgotten how succulent a good carp can be, how subtle the interaction of the spices," Cheng countered, taking another sip of chrysanthemum wine, oblivious of Lian's acute embarrassment at the excessive flattery. "It tastes of home."

They had continued showering her with praise as if it were a game, and he who spoke most eloquently the winner. Their hostess had shaken her head and shooed them away so she could clean up in peace, so they would not see her smiling with pleasure at their outrageous compliments. So she would not reveal her pleasure and unease in the intense awareness with which Émile Drouard had watched her closely throughout the meal, absorbing her words and movements as certainly as his blood had absorbed the flowery wine Cheng had brought from China.

Now, order restored in her kitchen and parlor, she made a last stroke with her brush, dusted sand across the ink on the rice paper she had impulsively laid out on the empty table. When the ink was dry, she took the small scroll, rose and glided down the stairs outside her flat. She knew she would find Cheng and Émile sitting over coffee, or perhaps jasmine tea, at one of the tables on the sidewalk in front of the bakery.

As the cool night air touched her flushed cheeks, she heard laughter and saw the glowing lights at the other end of the alley. Rolling her scroll carefully, she followed those lights to the small group gathered, as they often did, to enjoy the mild evening. Besides Cheng and Émile, there was Henri and Claire Arnaud and the butcher and his wife, Claude and Pauline Gustafson. Yen Tai had no doubt returned long ago to the house of his father.

"You have a new suit, Monsieur Drouard," Pauline said. "It is very fine. And no doubt very dear."

"Yet you never seem to do anything," Claire put in, "except sketch and paint, and certainly that does not buy such clothes. It's curious, is it not?"

"Come, Émile," Claude wheedled. "Tell us where your wealth comes from. My wife says your clothes are always of the latest fashion. Your patron must be very rich."

They spoke lightly, teasingly, but beneath the laughter was a hint of more than simple curiosity. Cheng sat with elbows on the table and hands pressed together beneath his chin, frowning. Lian knew that frown well. But no one else seemed to notice; they were too caught up in their friendly interrogation.

"If you don't tell us who your patron is," Henri the baker said, "we'll begin to suspect you are a spy for the government or the morals police. I hear they pay handsomely to know what people say when, in the late hours of the night, drink has made us honest and unwise."

"What are we to think, when you remain so stubbornly silent?" Claire asked.

Émile Drouard shifted uneasily on his wrought iron chair, increasingly uncomfortable as the voices grew more demanding. The sight of his distress overwhelmed Lian with an unexpected sense of fierce protectiveness. Resolutely, she glided forward on cloth-soled feet. "Why should you think anything at all, when it is not your concern?" she said, as astonished as the others by her firm but soft-spoken outburst.

In Chervilles, Émile had always been generous, often purchasing more than he could possibly eat. Regularly, he brought small practical gifts, or vibrant sprays of roses, peonies and gladioli to the baker, the butcher, the goat boy's mother. Today it had been the carp Lian had thought too dear. But he never sought thanks for his gifts, only the pleasure of those who received them. She admired him for that.

Lian stood tall, unmoving, as she said quietly, "In China it is not polite to ask how a man acquires his wealth." She regarded her neighbors with compelling, almond-shaped blue eyes. "Is it so different here? There, when a man is your friend, you have faith in him, enjoy his company and do not doubt his character or his motives."

She did not raise her voice, yet the people of Chervilles heard every word, and were ashamed. They had always been intimidated by her presence, the melodic lilt of her voice, her tall, willowy body in its Oriental tunic, her extraordinary blue eyes. All had watched as she sat silent among them, intrigued by her solitude, her dignity and beauty. Never had they expected her to challenge them so boldly.

Lian looked from face to face, lit from below by wavering lamplight. "I have asked a question. Will no one answer?" She was aware of Cheng listening and waiting, but did not turn to him for reassurance.

"It is no different here," Henri Arnaud said at last. "My apologies, Émile."

Only then, as everyone spoke at once, attempting to make amends, did Lian begin to realize what she had done, how much attention she had drawn to herself. She was chagrined but unrepentant. She nodded at Émile, who was gazing at her in disbelief. There were other things in his eyes, things she could not decipher, and did not even try.

For a moment, they stared at one another openly. Before, she had been careful to avoid such encounters. But for that moment, she forgot, and Émile, looking as if someone had struck him, inclined his head in gratitude. She felt it like cool relief in her own body, saw it blaze like fleeting flame in his eyes.

When she turned away, Lian found Cheng watching with an odd expression—part pleasure, part foreboding. He tugged pensively on his long white beard, and Lian felt the weight of his gaze like a hand lying heavy on her shoulder. His secret smile was unsettling, as was the unfamiliar gleam in his eye as he glanced from her to Émile. But, as always, Cheng kept his own counsel.

"You will join us?" Rising, Émile held out a chair for the exotic woman who usually hovered behind a patterned veil that protected and disguised her. Tonight she had stepped out of the darkness into the golden light, blue eyes full of outrage, though her voice was deceptively soft. She had silenced them all, something Émile had failed to do. He, who was never at a loss for words, did not know what to say to her.

Lian thanked him politely, but sat beside Cheng, making the round pitted table a kind of barrier. She had stepped too close to Émile tonight and wanted only to change the subject. She was relieved when Claire presented her with green tea in a translucent cup and a pear tart baked in a delicately designed pastry shell prepared especially to complete their elaborate meal.

Émile began to sketch, remembering Lian's grace as she moved lithely from kitchen to table to kitchen in her satin tunic and silk gown of pale green. She had spilled not a drop, seemed to flow easily from room to room, her hair loosely woven in two braids that became one. The gaslight on her bronze skin had given her a golden cast, and the fragrances rising from her pots made him dizzy with hunger and curiosity.

Aware of Cheng's amusement but refusing to meet his twinkling onyx eyes, Lian contemplated Émile through the steam rising from her tea, perplexed by what she saw.

Head bent over his sketchpad as it often was, he leaned back in his wrought iron chair, making it seem fragile. The lamplight masked his face in dancing shadows and glimmered on his blond hair and curly red beard.

Lian was intrigued by his absolute concentration on charcoal and paper, by the tinted light moving across his aristocratic cheeks and nose and the more common breadth of his wide forehead and square chin. He was a strange contradiction, this man. His shoulders were broad, and though he was not tall, his solid frame spoke of strong peasant stock in the blood of his ancestors. Yet he carried himself with an ease, grace and assurance that had not come from toiling in the fields. Lian glanced at his hands— not artists' hands, not long-fingered, slender and graceful. He had taken off his coat, and his sleeves were pushed up to reveal strong, sun-browned forearms. His face glowed with health, with color, with the red cheeks of a man unafraid of the sunlight.

Just when she was about to ask what he was drawing so attentively, as if he sensed her intent and wanted to forestall it, Émile inclined his head at Cheng. "How is it that you come to be here in Chervilles, Monsieur Cheng? The town is so small, one could easily lose it. Why are you not in Paris, the center of the world, where the people would appreciate your talents?"

Lian was startled by the question. Had Émile Drouard never asked it before, in all the months he had been visiting the alchemist?

Cheng, however, did not look surprised. "I came because

my friends François and Marie Duchamps invited me. I was treating them when they abandoned Paris, or rather, after Paris abandoned them. I was as ready as they for the peace, the lack of smugness, the tranquillity and unaffectedness in this sylvan place. Here no one cares where you were born or how old your family is or what language you speak. They care only if you are kind and open and willing to share your skill with others."

"We, too, came at François's request," the German butcher said. "In the city we were strangers, renounced because we were foreign; here we are accepted, at home."

"It was the same for us," Claire Arnaud agreed. "We came from the south of France and Parisians thought us ignorant and unsophisticated. But we knew François and Marie would make us welcome."

"A toast to the Duchamps!" Claire cried. "I'm only sorry we must have cider instead of wine. The disease that's withered our grapes has left us with little choice. They say we will thirst for a long while yet."

"Still, we'll make do," Fraulien Gustafson said.

While everyone raised their glasses of cider to the founders of Chervilles, Lian noticed that Émile was pale and his eyes had lost their shine. He was once again ill at ease. She wondered why. Her hand shook, spilling a few drops from her glass. Carefully, she set it on the table. "I am weary after wrestling with the carp. I think I will retire."

The front legs of Émile's chair hit the ground and he closed his sketchpad with determination. "I hope you will allow me to walk you home. It's not always safe after dark for a woman alone, even in Chervilles. The least I can do is offer an escort, after all the trouble you've gone to. Besides, a brisk walk after such a fine meal would be healthy."

He stared at Lian as if he meant more than he said. She began to object, but Cheng spoke first. Leaning back, he glanced down the alley that led to the young woman's door. "I can see the streetlight from here," he murmured. "And I doubt very much that such a short distance will aid in your digestion."

Lian had intended to refuse, but was inexplicably angry that the old man should interfere. Even if he was right. "We could take the long way, in order to enjoy the mild evening."

"Ah! The long way. Well, that, of course, is an entirely different matter." Cheng suppressed a wicked grin. "The long way" meant simply crossing in front of the apothecary shop, following the building to the back and turning the short distance on Rue les Soutiers along the back until one reached the alley. "It is a pleasant night for walking, I suppose."

"A pleasant evening for friends, yes," Lian said quietly, aware that the Arnauds and Gustafsons were listening with great interest. She suspected Cheng had tricked her, but she could not back down now. Pride would not allow it. She refused to admit there might be any other reason for accepting Émile's invitation.

Cheng considered, his wispy beard trailing over his clasped, age-spotted hands. "Yes," he said at last, so softly that only she could hear. "Monsieur Drouard is your friend. One has few enough true friends." His gaze caught Lian and held her. "I will remember that, but you will forget. You are good at forgetting. I suppose that is why you have survived to be 'escorted' home by this good man on this fine night."

Lian stiffened as the two men regarded one another and she sensed an unspoken undercurrent in their silent exchange.

"I was just thinking of the old proverb: 'Man does not attain the one-winged birds of our childhood tale; they must rise together,' " Cheng murmured portentously, glancing from Émile to Lian and back again. "But go, my children. By all means, go. The danger increases by the moment, I suspect."

In your company it does, Lian wanted to snap, but she

knew her annoyance would only betray her. She rose with Émile, saying farewell to the others and nodding at Cheng, who smiled beatifically, unrepentantly.

When they had moved out of the lamplight, Lian murmured, "Cheng enjoys being inscrutable."

Émile drew her hand into the crook of his elbow, closing his own hand lightly over her cool, slender fingers. "What worries me is, I think I know what he means."

5

ONCE THEY HAD TURNED THE CORNER OF RUE SALUBRE and passed the cultivated plot of herbs beside Cheng's shop, Émile and Lian did not turn toward the back of the building. Instead, by unspoken mutual consent, they took the street leading to the meadow behind the tiny town, and eventually to the lake and the Duchamps' estate.

They could smell magnolia blossoms, still furled in the darkness, and the cool, damp scent of cobblestones and trees bursting into spring leaf. There were no clouds to dim the brilliance of the stars against the inky background of the sky, and the air was brisk, invigorating. The two walked slowly, taking it all in.

Lian was unusually aware of Émile's bare head, the curly hair made ruddy by the lamplight. Had he forgotten his hat? She did not remember if he had been wearing one. Then there was the scent that clung to his suit, subtle as sweet tobacco. Perhaps he had visited the Englishman's shop today. She had been busy, first with Yi and Mei, then with preparations for the dinner, and had not wondered until now how Émile had filled the time since she'd seen him this morning.

For a while, they were content with the comfortable

silence between them, content to let the other voices fade into the still night air. Then Émile could wait no longer. He stopped at the edge of the road, where the tall spring grass brushed his pant legs. Turning Lian to face him with the slightest touch on her shoulders, he asked, "Why did you defend me tonight?"

She attempted to avoid his searching gaze. "I do not know. The words came, that is all."

Shaking his head, he murmured, "I think maybe you do know."

She started to deny it, but of course he was right. She looked directly into his eyes, but hers were veiled, unreadable. "Perhaps I have become oversensitive to injustice."

He felt her slight retreat, the distance that had sprung up between them, thin as the veil on her eyes, but palpable just the same. He did not want to push her away, yet he could not let the question go. He wanted to know more about her, to find some key to dissolving her calm detachment as the unwelcome prying of her friends had done earlier. "Do you ever dream of your homeland? Is that where you learned to feel this way?"

Keeping her gaze steady with an effort, Lian shivered. He had not exactly read her mind; he could not possibly see the memories of China whose vivid colors dimmed and dwarfed all else. But Émile Drouard had sensed something. Again, her impulse was to turn away, but somehow, the pull of his gaze—gentle, not demanding, curious but kind— would not let her. "I never dream of China. I have left it behind and vowed to forget the chaos of the past. I promised Mairi Rose, a friend and more than a friend, that I would try to live in the present, to enjoy each moment as it comes."

"Promises are easier to make than to keep, though, aren't they, *mon ami?* Especially when you struggle to forget what is painful and vivid and wrenching. The past has a power and presence that doesn't fade easily, if at all." She was trembling ever so slightly. Émile wanted to pull her close, but he sensed it was too soon. Besides, merely by answering, she had given him a rare gift. He had known she had secrets the first time he'd seen her in Cheng's shop. She never spoke of her past, but once or twice, when she thought herself unobserved, she had looked haunted.

It was more than the shadows, banished quickly by the sheer force of her will, that intrigued him. She was lovely, elegant, contained, and though she tried to hide her intelligence, her quick wit often betrayed her. She was never rude, did not reject any friendship she was offered; she smiled frequently, even laughed aloud now and then. Yet she remained mysterious, separate. Her Chinese tunics and gowns only emphasized the distance she kept between herself and others; they swathed her in her own protective coloring.

"Of course I cannot forget what is seared into my memory," she whispered, interrupting his thoughts. "I can only use my strength and determination to put it behind me. I must not dwell on the past, but look only forward, seeking what might be. It is not easy, but I think I am succeeding, bit by bit and day by day."

Émile was so startled that, for a moment, he could not think what to say. "But what of your clothing?" he asked impulsively. "Your hair, the calligraphy on the scrolls that adorn your walls? What of your distinctive Chinese cooking and your poems in the rhythm of Li Po and Wang Wei? Are those things not from your past?"

Lian grew still, aware of Émile's hands open at his sides, trembling as if he wanted to reach out but dared not take the risk. His face seemed to soften and blur in the moonlight. "There were good things as well as bad, moments of beauty I hold close to my heart, where they are protected, cherished. I have sweet memories, Émile Drouard, that I would not lose or forget." She paused, brushing a blue-black strand from her cheek. A breeze had come up, ruffling the perfection of her hair, disarranging the graceful folds of her gown.

"But in China, every minute of every day there are rituals to be performed, traditions to be preserved." She looked away. "Even in the House of Wan." *You are very good at forgetting.* She had thought Cheng was right. Now she began to wonder.

Sensing her growing discomfort, but loathe to release her when she had begun to speak at last, Émile persisted. "Why do you say that?" Over and over in his mind he saw her fingers graze her cheek and tuck her hair behind her ear. He could imagine the texture of her skin, the softness of that strand. Again and again, he wished it were he who had stroked her hair, her flushed cheek. His fingers tingled with that single, mindless desire.

Lian took a step back, dismissing her unwise words like the dragonflies that flitted in the breeze. "It was a long time ago. The House of Wan is no more." She risked meeting his gaze again. "Why try to bring it back, even in my mind?" *Promise me you will survive!* Ke-ming had cried. *You are my hope.* Lian sighed. She did not understand what her mother wanted of her, seemed to need so desperately.

"Because it's where you came from, your heritage."

Ke-ming's voice faded at the sound of Émile's—real and palpable, not disturbing and out of reach. Lian sagged with gratitude.

"One can't let go of such things easily," he said fervently. Too fervently.

All at once, Lian was curious about the tautness of his expression, the vehemence in his voice. She was glad to turn the conversation toward him, away from images that burned in her lungs like cold winter air. "Have *you* let go of your heritage?" she asked. "It sounds as if you have tried to do so."

He stiffened, and before she could stop herself, she said, "Or do you fear you will lose the legacy of your blood and your own past?"

Émile was stunned by her perception, and disconcerted.

"Your voice, your face, your eyes gave you away." She was not certain why she felt the need to explain. "Please forgive me. I did not mean to distress you."

"Nor I you." He was as astonished at her apology as he had been at her probing questions. *He* had chosen to stop here. *He* had chosen to ask what he knew would not be welcome. She had answered anyway. He owed her the same courtesy, the same risk, the same gift. But not just yet. Not tonight, when the willows and chestnuts whispered around them, and the breeze turned the meadow into an undulating sea whose tiny white wildflowers were the reflection of the stars.

A sheep swam up through the ocean of grass. Lian knelt to scratch behind its ears, grateful for the distraction. She suspected Émile felt the same. "Have you lost your way, little one?" she murmured. "Or are you looking for adventure?" She glanced up. "They say Marie Duchamps often talks to the goats and sheep." It was not much of an explanation.

"Does she?" Émile looked more intrigued than surprised. "I wonder why."

Giving the ewe one last pat, Lian sent it back the way it had come. "Perhaps she thought they were lonely."

He frowned. "But they're part of a herd. How could they be lonely?"

Lian merely looked at him in silence.

"But of course," he whispered. "One can be lonely anywhere, whether alone or not. I had forgotten."

"Then you are lucky."

The words might have been the song of the breeze, so low and insubstantial were they. When Lian began to walk again, Émile followed, searching for a hint of unhappiness in her face or the lines of her body. He found none. "Perhaps it's my background that makes me so obtuse. It was you, after all, who learned the rules of polite behavior while I was tumbling in the vineyards and entangling myself in the vines. You can't expect a peasant to recognize such fine distinctions."

Lian looked sideways, considering him in the pale light of the setting moon. She discounted his hand-tailored clothing, gold embroidered waistcoat and watch, the cravat at his throat. A peasant could become wealthy, learn to dress with style, but could never imitate Émile's aristocratic features, the elegance of his stride, his self-assurance, the ironic quirk in his smile. "I can expect a great deal. Sometimes too much, as was expected of me. But I am not often mistaken about human nature." My mother taught me that, she added silently. "And you, Émile Drouard, are a liar."

Émile saw a low gate across the road ahead. With so many sheep and goats and cows about, the gates were a necessity in this small town. Because he was a gentleman, he lifted her across and set her down gently on the far side before jumping nimbly over the worn wooden railing. He was as comfortable climbing stiles as he was swinging his ebony cane with its gold lion's head. But he was no more comfortable with her accusation, though it had been spoken teasingly, than he had been with the taunts of Henri and Claire, Claude and Pauline. He *would* not discuss it, though by keeping silent, he was telling a kind of lie. "I suppose, then, that I am a lost man."

Wondering what had possessed her to challenge him, Lian tried to lighten the tension between them. "You are not lost at all. You see the lamppost just ahead? That is the junction of Rue Verchamps and Chemin de Marie, which ends at the Duchamps estate. It is impossible to get lost in Chervilles. The name of every street or road points the way to where it is going."

As they arrived in the glow of the street light, Émile recovered his sense of humor. "Your Monsieur Duchamps is a straightforward man, isn't he? I've not seen another town where everything is named for precisely what it is. It's no coincidence, I suppose, that the street which houses Cheng at one end and Dr. Ricard at the other is called 'The street of good health'?"

"No coincidence at all. And this, as you have no doubt gathered, is the end of 'The way to Marie.'"

They stepped onto the cobbled road and regarded in silence the impressive estate across the way, with its high walls, large rooftop distinguished by many twisting stone chimneys and fancifully shaped windows. There was an air of neglect about it. "Have they left? I'd begun to wonder why I've never met this paragon."

Lian sighed as she approached the front wall, covered with vines, creeping jasmine and honeysuckle. "They have gone to America for a year or so to visit Madame's family. I gather she was missing them sorely. Since he built this town because they were cruel to Marie in Paris, you can guess that Monsieur could not bear for his wife to be unhappy."

Émile was barely listening. He was enthralled with the expression of longing and regret on Lian's face, the way she glided toward the two high doors through which carriages would pass. Vacant or not, gaslights shone brightly above the double doors.

Gingerly, reverently, Lian touched the warm, rose-colored paint, caressed the brass knockers shaped like large chrysanthemums. Each side was decorated with intricately carved and painted roses intertwined with ivy that followed the inner, recessed panels. Lian brushed the large brass handles and sighed. "I have always wondered what lay behind these doors. I hear Marie has a beautiful garden that she cherishes like the children she could not have. Before I could see it, the Duchamps went away. Now that they've been gone for so long, the garden must have gone wild. I wonder . . ." She trailed off, staring at the heavy doors as if somehow she could see through them.

"Surely servants come and go to keep the house in good repair. The doors might not be locked. Why don't you turn the handles and see what's inside, rather than imagining? It can't hurt anyone, certainly not the Duchamps, who share everything so willingly. It's because they're not afraid, because they feel safe here that Chervilles even exists." He reached toward the handles, but Lian blocked his hands.

"I am certain they are locked."

Émile was shocked at her intensity, the determination with which she turned him away. "You won't even try to find out?"

Shaking her head, she stared fixedly ahead. "There are doors for a reason. They are meant to be closed, keeping what is inside safe, what is outside away."

"Perhaps that's so, if what's inside are horses and small children who might otherwise stray," he said. "But that's not what you meant. You seem to think doors are to keep people out. I say they're to let people in. Do you believe this entrance was so lovingly created so outsiders would pass it by?" He shook his head. "No, these beautiful doors are an invitation."

He was inordinately disappointed when she turned away.

"It is late. I did not intend to stay out so long." Sensing his mood, she hurried, unwilling to say more. She had already said too much.

Émile caught up with her, noticing that she glanced with a different kind of longing at the next, smaller chateau they passed. He wondered if this was where the two girls who had hovered behind Lian so trustingly this morning lived. She straightened, seemed to grow taller, to regain her dignity and her distance from those who might, or already had, hurt her. Only then did he recognize how many layers of her woven veil she had let fall tonight, how close she had let him to the heart of her. He wished they had not encountered the damned carriage doors, that they'd returned the way they had come, rather than stepping on to Chemin de Marie. That was when Lian had begun to retreat from him. "I'm sorry," he said, not certain what he was apologizing for.

Turning, she regarded him quizzically. "Why?"

Her eyes gave him the answer. He was sorry she had remembered the need for her elegant restraint. He wished fervently that they were back in the meadow, talking to the sheep. She had been smiling then, relaxed. "You seem sad. It's that, I suppose."

"But that is not your fault. Besides, if I am sad just now, it will not last." She glanced back at the silhouette of the Chins' chateau. "There I lost something I valued greatly. When I see the house and know it is closed to me, I cannot help a moment's regret." She looked away. "Perhaps several moments. But even several moments pass." She smiled a little stiffly.

Why, Émile wondered, did he want to weep with both regret and admiration?

In silence, he took her hand and wrapped it around his arm, lacing his fingers through hers. Lian did not object, but leaned against him as if she had used more of her strength than she realized. They did not speak again until they reached her door and stood in the circle of light beneath the street lamp.

Resting her weight against the carved blue door, Lian turned to bid Émile good night, but he did not release her. Instead, he moved closer, brushing his fingers across her cheek as he'd longed to do beneath the stars. She shivered, alarmed by the desire in his eyes, more alarmed by her response to the whisper of his fingertips on her skin—the erratic beat of her heart, the tingle of expectation and longing down the center of her body.

Warmth turned to heat; she shivered as though chilled. Émile wanted her, if only for now, and she did not wish to turn away. She wanted to feel that heat again, the rush of her pulse as he touched her gently, demanding nothing, but telling her he wanted everything. Just as Wan Ke-ming's lovers had wanted everything. Lian's mother had had many men. Ke-ming had given her body and affection willingly in exchange for shelter, protection and the fulfillment of her own sensual desires.

But I am not my mother, Lian thought. I have a home where I am not afraid. I am not ruled by the needs of my body. And this was Émile, who was not like other men. Émile who had eaten at her table, whom she had defended fiercely, to whom she had spoken of the past and her yearning for beauty and memories that had given her happiness. That made him dangerous. Because he was safe, their friendship easy, encouraging her to trust him. She twined her fingers together in a rigid pattern.

Émile was not surprised or dismayed by the ember that lingered long after his brief caress. He had known from the moment they'd stopped in the road, when she'd tucked that blue-black hair behind her ear and met his gaze instead of running from his questions. He had guessed this moment would come, but Lian had not.

Her blue eyes reflected the light above, shifting to silver, then gray before she lowered her lids. "I fear you think too much, *mon ami*. Do not wonder what will be or what it means or if you are in danger. Not from me. Never from me."

He reached into the large pocket of his greatcoat to remove his sketchpad. "I want you to have this." He tore off a page and handed it to her, grazing her fingertips, though he wanted to pull her close and hold her until her wariness disappeared. "I will see you perhaps another day in Cheng's shop, another night outside the bakery, now that spring is here."

"Yes." She did not recognize her own voice. She reached for the doorknob as he turned to go. He looked somehow diminished, his shoulders hunched as if he were cold. Cold and empty, as was she since he'd taken his hand away. Yet in the past hour, he had awakened her from a long sleep; she had begun to feel invigorated as she never had before. Until caution rose like a shadow tiger, warning her away.

"Thank you for the walk. And for this," she said inadequately.

"You are welcome," he said. "You know that. Good night, *chérie*. May your dreams bring you comfort." He disappeared around the corner and she was alone with the cold brass doorknob in her hand. She hurried up the stairs, fumbling with the key, pushing the door open with relief. She was glad she had left the gaslight burning in the hall. The yellow radiance was welcome.

Pausing to catch her breath, she stared at the paper she had crinkled in her hand.

The sketch was of her face in three-quarter profile. She was resting her cheek on her hand and she looked regal, distant, her pensive expression revealing nothing. But her eyes revealed too much—pain, fragility, sorrow, and beneath the sorrow, fear.

She was shaken by the knowledge that Émile had seen beneath her mask. He had recognized what she did not admit even to herself, what she thought she had conquered. Recognized it and put it down on paper with a blunted charcoal pencil.

Dazed, she dropped the creased paper and wrapped her arms protectively around herself. Émile, her friend, had seen her too clearly and knew her too well.

It was her own fault. Even if she wanted to, she could not deny that tonight she had revealed herself to him. In spite of that, in spite of the shadow tiger's warning, somewhere deep inside, she was not really sorry.

6

LIN-MEI FELT THE FEATHERY MIST TOUCH HER SKIN AND tilted her head back in pleasure, grateful the new governess had not done her hair that morning. Instead of the usual curls and upsweeps and intricate knots, with myriad pins to keep everything in place, her hair hung unbound down her back. The first soft drifts of rain settled on the thick, shining mass in hundreds of tiny drops, making a clear meshwork over the blue-black strands. She closed her eyes, enjoying the cool, fresh moisture and her freedom, both unexpected gifts. She held her palms out flat to capture the mist and her own elation.

Pausing in front of the apothecary shop, she recklessly pressed her wet palms against the window and smiled as a few drops trickled away. She knew she was misbehaving, but today, for once, she did not care.

Yen Tai saw the mist begin to float down in translucent curtains touched with rainbows where the last of the sunlight struck in thin rays. Courteously, he called over his shoulder, "I have put the baguettes in the oven, Monsieur Arnaud. If you do not mind, I will take a break now, since things are slow for the moment."

"Go!" Henri shouted above the pounding of dough.

Tai hurried out the door. It was too warm inside, where the huge ovens were always fired. The air was permeated with flour dust; he craved the relief of open air and the rain on his flushed face.

He stopped still when he saw Lin-Mei, took in her blissful expression and the long swaying fall of her hair. Infinitesimal drops, connected one to the other, glistened against the dark strands. She wore a simple blue gown with a long flowing skirt that swirled around her ankles, revealing plain black kid slippers. He had never seen her so unadorned— or so lovely.

She made an odd contrast to the exotic objects displayed in the alchemist's windows. Sharks' teeth strung together under a huge shark fin, the collar bone of an ox, the jaw of a tiger, turtle shells in a pyramid, small and large fossils, groups of leaves arranged in strange, mystical patterns, strings of garlic and dried flowers and roots. The townspeople often stopped to stare, mouths open, when Cheng changed the display. Yen Tai heard their whispered comments and knew the bizarre objects only added to his mystique, his reputation as a healer of extraordinary power.

Therefore, he should not be surprised that there, miraculously, stood Chin Lin-Mei, unescorted, smiling dreamily, obviously having escaped her mother's and governess's scrutiny. Inhaling deeply to make certain he could still breathe, the young man wiped the flour from his hands and joined her at the window.

Lin-Mei saw his reflection in the glass and leaned more heavily against her hands. She felt heat rising in her cheeks and hoped he would not notice through the rain.

"Good day to you, Chin Lin-Mei," Yen Tai said formally, as he always did. He did not meet her eyes, but spoke to her reflection in the window.

Mei tried to look calm and composed, so he would not realize her heart was beating far too quickly. "Good day, Yen Tai." She, too, could be polite and proper.

"Are you looking for Mademoiselle Lian? Or perhaps you've come in secret to obtain a potion that will strike your sister mute for a day or two?"

In spite of her resolve to remain aloof, she giggled, covering her mouth with her hands, as she'd been taught in China, missing the long full satin sleeves that would have hidden her expression completely. "As for Yi-niang, she is merely high spirited," she told the blurred image of his face in the glass.

"Spirits, especially high ones, can be dangerous," Tai countered. "Ask Monsieur Cheng."

Mei fought a widening grin and lost. "I do not need to ask." She paused. "Besides, you were right the first time. I am looking for my teacher. My family and governess have gone to Paris on the train, so I thought it safe to seek her out."

"Ah!" he said softly. "Now I understand." With her parents gone, Lin-Mei had felt free to leave her hair down and dress as she chose. "But I fear Wan Lian is not at home. On Tuesday she teaches the village children at the church in the meadow. Thursday and Saturday as well."

Deeply disappointed, Mei remembered the open books, stacks of papers and scrawled notes that had covered Lian's table. "I should have asked before I came. It is not easy for me to get away. I am sorry I was so thoughtless."

"I am not sorry." Tai turned to look at her, face to face. "I am glad."

Without thinking, Mei met his gaze and was astonished by its warmth. She had long admired Yen Tai because, unlike her, he was not meek or shy or uncertain. From the first time she met him, she had noticed his independence, his confidence. "Why are you glad?" She was not being coy; she simply did not understand.

Tai stared at his feet. "I know I should not speak of such things, but surely you know I am fond of you. You remind me of the Middle Kingdom in your modesty and shyness, yet I sense a spark in you that is also of this world, of France, of Chervilles." He cleared his dry throat. In China, they could never have spoken together unless they were married; nor would they have glimpsed each other's faces in passing, so carefully were the boys kept separate from the girls. Tai was painfully aware of all the strictures he was breaking. This is France, he reminded himself, and our fathers introduced us to one another.

He remembered well his first glimpse of Lin-Mei, eyes downcast, hands folded demurely in her lap. Then Chin Yun spoke her name and she looked up, barely smiling, her emotions clearly visible in her dark eyes—bashfulness, hope, the desire to please and eagerness. He had been charmed by her sincerity, her black winged eyebrows, her smooth bronze skin and parted lips. "Of course, your beauty has nothing to do with it."

"I am not beautiful." Her voice was heavy with disappointment, bitter with regret.

He glanced up in trepidation. "I have not said so to beguile you, but because it is the truth. If you do not believe me, you should look more closely in your moon mirror." When she did not answer, he closed his eyes in an agony of embarrassment. "Please forgive me if I have shocked or offended you. It is merely that I was so surprised to see you here like this." He indicated her long hair and sky blue gown. "Forget everything I have said."

He was staring over her shoulder, so he did not catch her fleeting smile, the tears that sprang to her eyes, the unnatural color in her cheeks. Mei was stunned into silence, partly because he had spoken so openly, when he'd always been perfectly correct, partly because his words and the cadence of his speech were like music to her—moving and indescribable. She was afraid to respond; she did not know about men and compliments and the longing she had never dared admit she felt, even to herself. "What if I do not wish to forget?"

She whispered, but Yen Tai heard. He looked into her glowing face; her onyx eyes said all he needed to know. Before he could think of a response, it began to rain in earnest.

" 'Only a fool drowns standing in the rain,' " a third voice intoned warningly. "Come inside, Lin-Mei, Yen Tai, before you fulfill the ancient proverb."

Startled by Cheng's sudden appearance, the two hesitated, but when they saw him glance warily up and down Rue Salubre, they realized he was worried about more than the rain.

"It is warm inside my shop, and dim," the alchemist murmured. "The small porch in the rear is screened; you can speak there in dryness and safety." He did not say that they would not be seen, that their conversation was less likely to be overheard and repeated in every house in

Chervilles. They did not object when he ushered them inside, pulling the door closed firmly.

They stepped into the gloom, spiced with the smell of burning incense and herbs, with a feeling of relief. The rows of medicine boxes were familiar, the bin of garlic bulbs pungent as they paused beside it while Cheng went in search of a blanket.

They could not help staring at the walls hung with a shark fin, the long, serrated snouts of swordfish, rocks full of minerals to be extracted, interspersed with the wisdom of centuries painted in Chinese characters on long rice paper scrolls. On the counter were bowls full of stones with healing properties, tiny vials and large ones, ointments and decoctions, folded rice paper and seaweed packets of herbs. Lin-Mei shrank away from the jars of crows' liver and bleached seaweed and the livers of fatty fish, along with other indistinguishable organs floating in cloudy liquid. Yen Tai stood close, so she could feel his presence and reassuring warmth, but he did not touch her.

"I have, perhaps, the means to cure your sickness," the old man said with a wink, draping the blanket about their shoulders, drawing them closer together, "but I suspect you are not yet in need of such treatment."

Yen Tai smiled. Lin-Mei blushed.

Shrugging, the alchemist pointed toward the porch, now hidden from view. "It shall be as you wish. The young are often stubborn in this regard and refuse to listen to the wisdom of we who have lived too long."

"We are grateful for your help, Monsieur Cheng, and would listen to your wisdom all day in return for your kindness, but I think, in the end, we would all be frustrated."

Sighing with exaggerated melancholy, Cheng shooed them away and turned back to the log that lay open on the desk.

Tai and Mei went gladly, locating the tiny porch and drawing two stools close together, so they could clasp the blanket tight. For a moment, they sat in shock, staring at the silver streams flooding the cobblestone street beyond the screen and wondering how they'd gone so quickly from a simple greeting to sitting so close their thighs touched. Both stiffened but did not move.

After a minute, the rhythm of the downpour soothed them and Tai reached out tentatively to take Mei's hand. She shivered at the warmth of his palm against hers, the sensation of their linked fingers, which made her quiver inside.

She knew she should pull away, but she could not do it. Instead she tried to make normal conversation until she could think properly. "Why are you working at the bakery, covered in dust and flour, sweating among the ovens, when you could be in the city with your father?"

Tai, who was nearly eighteen, and therefore much wiser, considered for a long moment. "I do not wish to be a banker; I enjoy cooking, especially making pastry. It is not simply putting together dough in different shapes. It takes concentration, patience, a delicate touch. It is an art. Working there makes me happy, that is all."

Mei was enchanted by the look on his face. His smile was guileless and open, his eyes bright, revealing his pure, uncomplicated joy in what he did. It had been so long since she'd seen that look. She smiled back at him, sharing his pleasure.

Tai swallowed and concentrated on brushing a strand of hair from his eyes. If he looked at her one second more, if her smile remained as innocent and honest, making her pretty face more lovely, he was afraid of what he might do. He was glad, after all, that Cheng was in the shop out front. Forcing himself to contemplate the sheets of rain that could not reach them, he sought a distraction. "Of course, my honored father does not understand, though I have tried to explain many times. He says I am demeaning myself. But I do not want to follow in his dedicated footsteps any more than you wish to be a young Frenchwoman. Especially when it means forgetting the old ways, the traditions, the rituals in which I find such comfort. I believe you are the same. It is one reason I noticed you. You never seemed quite happy in your fancy gowns and coiffed hair. Several times I observed you trying to bury your hands in your sleeves as you used to do in your Chinese gown and tunic."

Startled by how much he had guessed, Mei was reluctant to meet his gaze for fear of what he might read there. She did not want him to see the turbulent feelings churning inside her. She was not certain *she* wanted to feel such things. They confused and frightened her because she could not make them stop.

"Besides," Tai continued, "you seek out Wan Lian with a dedication I admire. You do not desert your friend, though your father sent her away and forbid her to visit you and Yiniang. Everyone knows it is because she clings to the old ways that he dismissed her."

Stiffening, Mei withdrew her hand and dropped her corner of the blanket. "I did not know it." Her mind was spinning with words and images and emotions—a kaleidoscope of too bright colors. "She told us it was her decision, that she wanted to go, even when we pleaded for her to stay." She stopped, dazed and appalled. "Yi and I accused her of breaking her sacred vow to us, of abandoning us, yet she did not defend herself." Tears stained her cheeks as she realized how much they must have hurt their friend and teacher.

Yen Tai's eyes widened in admiration for Lian. "She could not defend herself without hurting many others."

"No, I suppose she could not." All at once, Mei understood many things that had perplexed her. But understanding did not stop her tears. "We should not have doubted her."

This time Tai took her hand firmly. "You could not know,

Lin-Mei. Besides, it does not matter now. I saw you smiling on her balcony last week, did I not? Do not blame yourself. Too many already carry that weight."

She looked at him, eyes swimming with tears and gratitude. "You are kind, Yen Tai."

Embarrassed, he ducked his head. "It is not kindness, but selfishness. I cannot bear it when you are unhappy."

Mei was speechless. She stared at him, and he at her, for so long that the damp air seemed to penetrate their clothing, though the rain was far away.

At last Tai said hoarsely, "We are the same, you and I. Is it not so?"

She nodded, still mute.

"Then I would wish," he stumbled with his words, "I wonder if you would permit . . ."

"Do not wish and do not wonder, Yen Tai. You are only wasting time." She smiled tentatively and nodded.

Slowly, very slowly, Tai released her hand and placed his palms on either side of her face. He wiped away a lingering tear gently with his thumb, then leaned toward her, at the same time drawing Mei toward him. For a moment, they stopped; in the chilly air, their breath became mist touching their parted lips. They looked at one another for a moment more, then closed their eyes, inched closer and closer still until their lips met and they lost themselves completely, blissfully, irrevocably in their first kiss.

7

LIAN AWAKENED ABRUPTLY, DISORIENTED. SHE GAZED ABOUT as if she'd woken in an unfamiliar room. Then, slowly, she began to recognize her flat, the smell of flowers from the street, the oak table on which she leaned. She saw that besides the books she had been studying, beneath her hands lay an unfinished letter to Genevra. She ran her fingers over her sister's name; the letters felt like flame for an instant, before the sensation of cool ink returned.

She paused, one hand in the air. Something had awakened her, she realized. A sound, a memory, a voice from the past.

"Wan Lian! Are you there?"

Lin-Mei, calling from outside the door.

With relief, Lian rose and went to welcome her young friend and the real, palpable present—her cozy flat with the sun streaming through the open shutters and across the table, transforming the Kitchen God into a blaze of red and green.

Mei was smiling when Lian opened the door. Had she grown taller, or was she merely standing straighter? Though the girl wore a fashionable gown of Swiss muslin, her hair was woven into a fat braid and wound simply around her head.

"You are different today," Lian observed, closing the door and revolving slowly to contemplate her guest.

"I am two weeks older. That might explain it." Mei smiled brightly, and without giving Lian a chance to reply, she bent over the narrow ebony cabinet in the entryway. She ran her fingers over the ivory inlays delicately. "I didn't notice this before. It's beautiful."

"A gift from Cheng. He said I must have something to keep the letters from my sisters in." Kneeling down, Lian opened the intricately inlaid door and revealed stacks of smudged and well-read letters.

Mei was more interested in the framed watercolor and poem that hung side by side above the scalloped shelf on top. The painting was of a rushing moonlit river with low waterfalls and striped flat stones. A woman sat among moss and ferns, gazing up at a rock from which the water cascaded in a long clear curtain. Within that fall of water, the figures of three naked women hovered, almost as if they were one person, each the ghostlike echo of the one below her. The colors were muted, everything tinted golden, so that the image shimmered. "Oh! How lovely."

Having examined it while Lian stood mute, Mei turned to the poem—graceful Chinese characters side by side with the English translation.

Mei turned to find her teacher at her shoulder. "The poem is surely yours. The watercolor?"

"My half-sister, Genevra."

The girl knew all about Lian's half-sisters, and the woman, Mairi Rose, who had unofficially adopted Charles Kittridge's two illegitimate daughters. Lian used to sit between Yi's and Mei's beds at night and read to them from the letters, making them laugh and cry and ache with her and for her. "They're very beautiful."

Lian's answer was a reminiscent smile. "Come inside. While I make tea, you can tell me why you are here."

Leaving painting, poem and letters with regret, Mei entered the parlor and sat on the colorful cushions beside a low rosewood table. "Need I have a reason to visit?"

"No." Lian spoke from the kitchen where she arranged a tray with cups, her favorite dragon teapot, ginger cookies and sesame toffee. "But I see that though your lips are smiling and your attitude light, your eyes are troubled." She brought the tray, set it on the low table and sat on a cushion on the floor.

When Mei blushed as she used to do, Lian realized she had missed her pupil's shyness and restrained delight more than she knew. She closed her hand loosely and rubbed it over her heart as if to soothe it.

"It is just—" Mei broke off, then began again. "My honorable parents have begun to take Yi and me to church in the city, and sometimes to parties where they introduce us to 'suitable French children.' The church is huge and echoing, glittering with colored glass and high vaulted ceilings. Yi and I sit there in all that beauty and vastness and feel lost and miserable." She paused to take a sip of dragon well tea, to smile at the remembered flavor and savor it on her tongue. "More and more often my father and mother want us to accompany them on the train, but we don't like it in Paris. It is too loud and bright, like a circus. And behind my parents' backs, people are cruel to us. I try to forget when we're back in Chervilles, but it isn't easy."

Tears sprang to her eyes, but she blinked them away. She must behave with dignity, not like the child her sister still was.

Lian picked through her words with care before responding. "Your parents do not mean to be unkind. They only want you to be accepted, to become a success in your new home, to be like everyone else. They believe in this way they can ensure your happiness." Lian did not believe as they did, but refrained from saying so.

"But we're *not* like the others. We can never be like them. You know that, don't you?"

Of course she knew, but she must keep it to herself. She could try to comfort Lin-Mei, give her a refuge where she need not pretend, but she could not criticize the decisions the Chins made for their children.

Watching Lian's still face, sensing the struggle behind the stillness, Mei remembered what Yen Tai had told her about the way in which her teacher had left their home. She began to speak, to wave away the difficult question she had asked, the position in which she had placed Lian, but Mei decided to remain silent. She would not force her friend to make that painful choice again. Instead, she voiced the doubts and worries that had kept her awake the night before.

"I don't understand," Mei said quietly, calmly, "why my father is so determined to forget everything about China—his culture, his soul. He became rich there; he was respected and my mother revered. Why does he want to push those things away, to pretend they never happened?"

Lian stared down at her feet. "You and your mother and your little sister were very sheltered in the Middle Kingdom," she said thoughtfully. "You lived in beautiful courtyards surrounded by thick walls, so that no sound, no uninvited guest could impinge on the perfect harmony of your courtyards. You lived in the midst of beauty, of gardens planned to enhance serenity, to please the eye and the spirit, the manmade streams that flowed through your dreams in your embroidered curtained bed. The bridges you crossed were graceful and narrow and led only to greater tranquillity. Is that not so?"

"Yes, but—"

Lian rested her hand on Mei's, forming a link across the small table. "I have not finished. Your father lived in a different world. You cannot imagine the threats he withstood, the ugliness and corruption he tried to ignore, the horrors he witnessed. As I did. Perhaps your honored father *needs* to forget. As I did. To believe there is something better, more just, kinder in the hearts of men. As I must believe."

Mei was stunned. Lian had never mentioned these things before; her voice had never quavered, even briefly, when she spoke of the past. The girl was not quite ready to admit there might have been such cruelty and pain in Lian's life.

"But what about the beauty, the scholarship, the poetry, the feast days when lanterns glowed all over the city? What about the Kitchen God, and Kwan Yin, Goddess of Mercy?" She was desperate to repeat every bit of goodness her teacher had described. "What of all the things you taught us, showed us through your eyes?" She did not mean it to be an accusation, but the words came out that way.

For the first time in Mei's memory, Lian looked disconcerted, ashamed. "I taught you and Yi-niang only about the good things, the lovely things, the things to be proud of, and there are many. I felt you should know your heritage, carry it in your heart as you carry it, and always will, on your skin and in your features and your black hair." She toyed with her tea cup, spinning it in her hands. "There is another side to that heritage, a darker side, that I thought you did not need to know. No one should ever have to know how ugly, how unjust and cruel that side was. As I know. As your father does." She spoke softly, in a matter-of-fact tone without self-pity or even sorrow.

Mei made one last try. "But you do not reject the good because of the bad. You remember and rejoice in so many things that could only have come from China. Why must my father deny all that as well as the rest?"

Lian met her young friend's gaze and held it. "I have been able to put the ugliness behind me, to separate the two. Perhaps Chin Yun is not so lucky. You cannot blame him for that. You do not know what he feels in his heart." She leaned across the table to take Mei's face in her hands. "But this I do know: Your father loves you and your sister deeply and sincerely. He would give his life for you; he has already done so by coming here to give you a new chance. If the ugliness had ever touched you, it would have broken his heart. He did the single thing he could to protect his family, to preserve the ties that bind you all—he left the only life he had ever known."

Tasting salt on her tongue, Mei realized she was weeping. She covered Lian's hands with her own, pressing them hard into her cheeks, trying to understand through touch what she could not through words. "What does he want from me, Wan Lian? Even for him, I cannot be who and what I am not. How then can I make him happy?"

"By finding your own happiness." Lian answered automatically over the distant echo in her mind. *I have raised you to be free, to move toward the future*, Ke-ming had said firmly. *And the future is in the West.*

Was this what her mother had meant? This complete rejection of the old culture in order to embrace the new? Lian could not, would not believe it. She was shocked from her own thoughts when she heard at last what Chin Lin-Mei was saying.

"I've found my own happiness. His name is Yen Tai."

8

THOUGH MEI HAD LEFT LONG SINCE, LIAN COULD NOT FORget her sweet smile or the luminous light in her eyes when she spoke of her feelings for Yen Tai. Lian herself had been drawn into the girl's pure joy in her discovery of love.

In China, her father, Chin Yun, would have been pleased by such a bond with the Yens. He would have seen no impediment to a lasting relationship between Tai and Mei. But now, here, today, Lian guessed he would not approve of his daughter being involved with a Chinese boy. That was not what he wanted for his oldest child, not what he had planned.

Still, Lian had been unable—more than that—unwilling to shatter Lin-Mei's newfound delight. She had never seen the girl so animated, heard her speak with such enthusiasm and optimism. Mei had never suffered deeply, so her happiness was unspoiled, chaste.

"I've been a prisoner until now, and all at once, I'm free," the girl had exclaimed. "I do only what my heart tells me to; I feel like I'm flying. There are no longer any rules to bind me to the earth."

Watching the girl's radiant face, Lian had envied her uncomplicated happiness. She'd remembered when *she* fell in love, how full of intrigue and danger the world had been, how deeply that had shaped her emotions, her troubled relationship. But Mei had no reason to fear the world beyond her father's house. Her feelings were natural, naive, uncorrupted by the fear of loss.

"Tell me about it." Lian had wanted to soak up every moment of this girl's joy.

"We don't do much really, Tai and I, except talk and talk, take walks along the Seine when we can get away, share picnics in the meadow, sit on Cheng's back porch laughing. Yet every moment is magical. I wouldn't trade one day for a hundred festivals of lights."

I promised Mairi Rose I would try to live in the present, to enjoy each moment as it comes. Lian had told Émile she thought she was succeeding, bit by bit. But Lin-Mei was doing it wholeheartedly, without doubt or hesitation. "I would like to feel that way," Lian said wistfully.

"What's stopping you?" the girl asked guilelessly. After a moment, she added in a whisper, "I heard you went walking with Émile Drouard." She examined the sesame toffee to hide her secret smile.

"You hear, I think, more than you should." Lian tried but failed to sound stern. She was too full of an awareness that Chin Lin-Mei had found a reason to continue, something—someone—to fight for. Her shyness had evaporated, and her elation brought a sheen of tears to Lian's eyes.

After the girl left, skipping down the stairs, Lian had tried to return to her letter to Genevra, but it was not long before she found herself gazing out the open French doors, reaching instinctively for Émile's drawing. She glanced at it briefly, forced herself to look away into the cool, murmuring shadows at the corners of her flat. Her heart raced, slowed, raced again, as she remembered the night she had walked with him, the things she had said and the things he had seen.

She had not joined the group in front of the bakery since that night. Instead, she wrote letters and studied and made up lessons for the children of Chervilles. She realized she was tracing the lines of the sketch without looking, running her fingertips over and over the image of her face, but seeing instead Émile's gentle smile, feeling his hand brush her cheek, losing her inhibitions in the kindness of his hazel eyes. She wanted to see his face again, to hear the sound of his warm, deep voice, but she was not ready. Not quite.

Then she heard them—heavy footsteps at the bottom of the stairs. Despite her preoccupation with Émile and Mei, despite her attempt to ignore the slow, laborious sound, she could not help but stop and listen. There was no doubt; the footsteps were coming toward her.

Lifting her finger from the charcoal drawing, she moved toward the door. Though she tried to stay calm, her palms were clammy. "You are being foolish," she told herself. "You are no longer in China. There is no threat." She was ashamed of her reaction and forced a smile to her lips before she opened the door and glanced down.

The first thing she saw was the dark, bent head of Madame Chin. Below her, Chin Yun struggled with a burden that had made his face red and his breathing labored.

Lian held herself very still. She had not seen the couple since she left their house, and knowing what she did, she was wary of their unexpected visit. Had they discovered Yi and Mei were slipping out to see their teacher, though they had been forbidden? Or did the Chins know about Yen Tai? Either way, Lian was not certain what to say. She only knew she could not betray her young friends.

Madame Chin looked up as the door opened. She paused at the sight of Lian's face. Her own eyes were shuttered, her face oddly blank, as it had been that day they'd met on the dock nearly two years ago.

Lian felt a prickle of apprehension, and when she saw what Monsieur Chin carried, she wanted to close the door and lean against it, as if that would keep the inevitable away. But she had chosen to be ruled by fear no longer, so she waited.

No one spoke, not even when they reached the top of the stairs and stood panting outside Lian's door, Monsieur Chin struggling under the weight of an ebony Chinese chest. All three seemed frozen, unable to move forward, unable to retreat. After one glance, Lian did not look at the chest again.

She knew she should invite them in; she should speak or nod—anything but stand like a jade carving. Once before they had stood thus, staring at each other across a chasm too wide to cross, carved of thousands of years of history, of prejudices so deep they could not be eradicated by mere common sense.

Madame Chin finally broke the silence. "Please, may we come in? Perhaps we have no right to ask, but . . ." She trailed off, staring at her tightly clasped hands.

Lian shook herself awake. "Of course you have the right," she said. "It is just that you startled me. I have been unforgivably rude." She stood back so Chin and his wife could enter. Carefully, she closed the door without latching it. She felt better that way.

By the time she joined them in the parlor, the couple stood facing Lian, clearly uneasy, unwilling to meet her eyes.

"Shall we sit?" she said politely. "Would you like some tea?"

"We have come about the chest," Chin Yun said with unsettling abruptness. He pointed to the spot where he had placed it. "Please."

She was not certain what he was asking, except that he wanted her to look at something, remember something she had managed to forget. *Never let them see your fear*, Keming had warned more than once, *or they will know your weakness and use it against you*.

Moving with the natural grace she had learned at her mother's side, Lian crossed the room until the intricately carved chest stood between them—she on one side, Chin Yun and Chin Shu on the other. "What is it you want of me?" She had not meant to sound so fierce, but the sight of the chest was painful.

She had first set eyes on it a few months after the Chins settled in Chervilles. It had arrived from London, sent by Ailsa Rose Sinclair, who had received it from Mairi Rose, on whose threshold it had arrived months after Lian's departure. It had been protected by frayed cartons with address after address marked off and replaced with a new one. But the first address, written in careful script rather than Chinese characters, was the only one Lian had truly seen. It was her mother's handwriting. Apparently Ke-ming had sent it after her daughter; the chest had followed Lian nearly around the world, missing her time after time until finally it had arrived here.

At her request, the servants had carried it to the Chins' attic, then left her alone to cut away the rope and the disintegrating boxes. In the dim light of the dormer window, she had sat on the floor, oblivious of dust and dirt, and stared for a long time at the beautiful carvings of winged dragons, Chinese symbols and other fantastic creatures. She knew the chest at once. It was one of the few she and her mother had taken from Peking when they fled to the Western Hills. But she did not know what was inside, or why it was here in the dust-laden light of a strange house in Chervilles, reminding her with wrenching clarity of the family, the friends, the home she had lost.

At last, reluctantly, she had worked the intricate lock and lifted the lid with trepidation. On top was a folded parchment letter with her name in Chinese characters written by her mother's hand. Beneath the letter lay a purple gown embroidered with plum blossoms and a sleeveless silver tunic worked in a bamboo pattern. Lian did not open the letter or touch the gown. Instead, she had slammed the lid shut as memories washed over her like high ocean waves, filling her lungs until she thought she would drown. She could not bear those memories and the pain they carried with them. She had fought too hard to put them behind her.

She had pushed the chest into a corner and done her best to forget it. She did not want to see into the past. The present was challenge enough. *You are good at forgetting,* Cheng had said lightly. *I suppose that is why you have survived.*

She looked up, startled, when Monsieur Chin cleared his throat.

"We did not come to upset you," he said. Quietly, he and his wife seated themselves on the floor cross-legged. "We came to return what is yours."

"I am grateful," she replied tonelessly.

Sensing her unease, Chin Shu said, "Will you not sit with us? There are things that must be said."

She raised her hand. "This I know, but there is something I must do first. I must respect my honorable mother's wishes."

Finally, now, she had to take the risk and open the untouched letter inside this chest. No matter the pain it caused her, she could no longer ignore Ke-ming's voice speaking long after it had been silenced. She raised the lid slightly and removed the folded rice paper.

Lian, My Daughter,

> You left too suddenly, and with too little. As I sat
> here waiting for my destiny, I knew I must gath-
> er that which you cherished and send it after
> you. I told you, you see, to move toward the
> future, but you cannot do so without your past.
> This I have come to realize too late. Now I must
> return to you some of what you have lost, and
> speak to you once more, when I thought my last
> hope disappeared with the smoke of the dying
> fire and the rise of the mist on the morning that
> you went away.

I cannot leave your treasures for Barbarians to steal or trample like the ashes of a fire that once warmed them, but no longer serves a purpose. I send the most precious of the jewels to help you on your way. Sell them to keep yourself alive and healthy, so that my dreams for you will not have been in vain.

I want to know that you will look at these things and touch them, feel in them the luxury and warmth of the years you spent here. They are the last pieces of your life in the Middle Kingdom; let them help you remember that there was beauty as well as suffering, love and joy as well as loss, that there is hope. Always there is hope, so long as you survive.

I am happy, my daughter, please believe that, no matter what might come to pass. Know that I am not afraid, that I love you as I have loved no other in my lifetime, because you were mine alone to protect and care for and nurture, and because you believed in me always. These thoughts I will carry in my heart, and no blade or rope or heat of fire can take them from me.

Always Your Mother,
Wan Ke-ming

Lian's hands trembled. Not only did the words shred her carefully woven defenses, but so did the rice paper itself, covered with familiar Chinese characters, some smeared, the paper puckered as if marred by tears. Lian had never seen her mother weep, yet she had wept over this letter. Rocking silently, she fought for control.

"May we speak?" Chin Shu asked.

Though she wanted to refuse, Lian knew she could not;

they were only trying to do what was right. "As you wish."

Chin and his wife exchanged a glance. She nodded and spoke in a low, uncertain voice. "You must have forgotten this chest because it was left in the attic," she began. "May and Nan were playing there one rainy day and found it." She blushed so her bronze cheeks turned chestnut. "They thought it was ours and were so enchanted that they put on the clothing and jewelry, playing a game of ancient China. Of course we put it back exactly as it had arrived." She looked at Lian beseechingly. "We would not have allowed this violation of your privacy if we had known—"

She broke off when Lian held up her hand to stop the flow of remorse. She could not tell them she was more disturbed by the unnatural sound of the names May and Nan than the girls' supposed transgression.

Nodding, Chin Yun continued. "We did not know what they had done until we found them in their room with some of the things from your chest. Naturally, we replaced what they had taken and forbade them to open it again." He paused, glanced down at the ebony chest, then up at Lian. Both he and his wife stared at her resolutely. "We have come to return it to you, but because of our daughters, we saw things—" His eyes locked with Lian's and did not waver. "We would very much like to open it now."

Lian was perplexed by their vehemence. Against her will, against her better judgment, she allowed curiosity to draw her in. She nodded.

With deliberation, Chin Yun worked the Chinese lock, then lifted the heavy lid. The purple gown and silver tunic lay on top, unwrinkled, cool and smooth, as if the Chins had replaced them with reverent care. Lian felt a stab of dismay; at least that was what she called the pain that pierced her already battered heart.

When Chin Shu lifted the satin gown, a packet of letters bound in aged and dirty twine fell to the floor. Lian stared, remembering a pallid face and dim gray eyes. Her father, Charles Kittridge, as he lay dying. She had been drifting back toward China, toward the day when she wore the purple gown, but now she forced her thoughts to the letters on the floor and the memory of crouching beside a rough heather bed in a dim, chilly croft in the Scottish Highlands. Her father had held her, but his hands had been cold. Then, after he died, Mairi had given Lian these letters Charles had written but never sent, because he knew they would endanger Ke-ming and his daughter. Charles wanted Lian to have them now. She thought of her father's hands, writing year after year to the daughter he had known only as a very young child.

She had kept the letters, unread, in a corner of her room until the chest arrived from China. Without even trying to see what else lay inside, she had thrust those letters deep against the ebony dragon walls. As Mairi Rose said, Lian had known enough sorrow. It was time to forget.

But it seemed they would not let her.

Though she fought her own inclination, her gaze was drawn to the gown Madame Chin had lifted out so her husband could reach underneath and withdraw something large and bulky. Instinctively, defensively, Lian closed her eyes.

"Our daughters were acting empress, wearing this like a crown," Monsieur Chin explained shakily. "My wife and I recognized it at once. It has been in the Chin family for many generations." He noticed Lian's tight-closed eyes, but continued doggedly. It was the least he owed her. Yet he owed her so much more.

Chin Yun held up an old-style Chinese headdress—a peacock fashioned from mother-of-pearl. The only bright colors were the fine pieces of lapis lazuli that gleamed from the eye of each tail feather. The cleverly woven veil was stained and wrinkled, but it did not detract from the magnificence of the headdress, which glowed pink, ivory and beige with a hint of the palest blue.

The Chins waited for her to respond, but she knelt across from them, unmoving. Finally, Madame Chin nodded at her husband and he sank back, the headdress cradled in his lap. "Long before we left the Middle Kingdom, in the days after our nephew Chin Chao was arrested by the Imperial Guard," he began, his voice gruff with suppressed emotion, "many stories passed through Peking. Rumors and accusations and tales that seemed too fantastic to be true." He paused, waving his hand before his eyes, glancing unconsciously over his shoulder, forgetting, for an instant, that he was in France and could speak as he wished without fear of reprisal.

"One story in particular was told again and again, by servant and soldier, scholar and matriarch. They said that not long after the Bannermen took Chin Chao to prison in the Imperial City, a young woman went to the head guard at the Vermilion Gates and asked to see my nephew."

Lian raised a hand to try to stop him, but he would not be silenced.

"It was foolhardy for anyone to ask to see a prisoner being held for treason, but this woman did it nonetheless, risking her own safety by quoting Confucius on the quality of compassion, pointing out to the guard, quietly and with dignity, that he was not following the rules of the Master in keeping my nephew isolated in his fear." Chin Yun cleared his throat at the sight of Lian's face, drained of color until her skin looked sickly white.

"When still the guard refused her entry, she told him she would wait for him to come to his senses, crossed the street and stood beneath a willow tree. The guard did not relent, so she returned the next day, and the next and the next. Day after day she stood in the shade of that willow, within reach of the Imperial Guard, and simply waited, silent, determined, bereft." He coughed, his throat parched.

With a sigh, his wife murmured, "We all wondered how she had obtained Chao's mother's headdress to hide her face. A headdress no one could mistake, so rare was it, so unique. A peacock fashioned from mother-of-pearl and lapis with a veil of finely woven ivory chain so light it swayed like fabric."

She kept her gaze on Lian's pallid face and blind eyes. Blind by choice this time. "Some said she was his lover, some even thought his secret wife. We will never know, for she disappeared when Chin Chao died and was never seen again."

"Whoever she was," Chin Yun said, "she was extraordinarily brave, with the kind of courage we did not have. We hid, we ran, we remained silent in the hope that the furor would pass us by. But that mysterious woman was not intimidated. Her courage humbles us. Her determination makes us feel weak and inadequate."

Perhaps your honored father needs to forget, Lian had told Mei. *As I did. To believe there is something better, more just, kinder in the hearts of men. As I must believe.* Always, always, her words came back to haunt her.

"My wife and I have harbored for years the fruitless hope that someday we would have the chance to tell that remarkable woman what her sacrifice meant, to Chin Chao, to us, to others too afraid to speak for themselves. To explain how great was her long, fruitless vigil, how reverently remembered."

There is another side to that heritage, a darker side.

Silence eddied around them like the shades of ancestors long dead, like the voice of Kwan Yin, Goddess of Mercy, like the *kuei* of those who died in violence. Then, at last, Lian spoke. "I think, perhaps, that the woman was very much afraid. Perhaps she was not brave or strong, but only fulfilling a promise she had made in order to save face. Perhaps she was more of a fool and a coward than anyone could know. More simpleton than paragon."

No one should ever have to know how ugly, how unjust and cruel that side was. As I know. As your father does. Lian thanked the gods a thousand times for Lin-Mei's ignorance, her innocence.

Lian glanced at the radiant mother-of-pearl in Madame Chin's lap. She swayed forward, reached out, drew her hand back. She could not touch it, because touch would bring memory. Even the sight made her throat dry and her eyes ache with tears she dared not shed. She looked up to see the Chins too were misty eyed. But their eyes were full of shame.

I don't understand why my father is so determined to forget everything about China—his culture, his soul. Lian understood. How could she not?

"You should not regret your will to survive," she said, pronouncing each word with care. "Sometimes, when the mind is in turmoil, foolishness wins out over common sense. It is nothing to be proud of."

Before she could stop him, Chin Yun took her hand. "You are wrong."

He stared into Lian's eyes as he had the last time she sat in his library. He knew he had hurt her with his claim that she was holding his daughters back by keeping China alive for them. It was true he wanted May and Nan to become more French, less foreign and exotic. But that was not enough of a reason to break Lian's heart, when she had worked so hard to guide and teach and counsel them. She had been more than governess to his children. She had been part of the family. Her strength of will had held them together through the homesickness, the confusion of a language and culture to which they only slowly grew accustomed. She alone had made it possible for them to face the future.

"She gives the girls everything she has to give, and what is left, she gives to us," Chin Shu had pointed out. "She will not stop giving and learn to take if we do not release her. Her sense of *shun*, compliance, obedience, responsibility will not allow her to contemplate leaving. She would never desert us, so we must desert her."

Chin Yun had let Lian go, partly for his daughters' sakes, but mostly for her own. He'd told her she was no longer needed in order to force her to seek out her own happiness. As he watched her now, he realized he'd been arrogant to think Wan Lian needed *him* to set her free. She was so much stronger than he. She did not need his protection or his guidance.

Lian wanted violently to keep hold of Chin Yun's hand. She wanted him to take her other hand and close his fingers about it tightly, to keep her from falling—falling far and deep. But she could not ask that of him. He released her, his fingers uncurling and withdrawing until he was too far away for her to reach.

The Chins replaced the discarded letters and satin gown, closed the lid and laid the headdress on top. As one, they rose, bowed and started to leave. At the door, Chin Yun turned back. "I once thought no woman worthy of being my nephew's wife. But when I heard of the woman in the peacock headdress, when I saw what became of Chin Chao's burning need to make his world safe and just, I began to wonder if, despite his brilliance, his scholarship, his passion and his courage, he, after all, was not worthy of her." In less time than it takes to draw a breath, he and his wife were gone.

Vaguely, Lian heard the front door close. She sat unmoving, paralyzed by the past that swept about her like the hungry sea, eager to pull her into its cold blue heart.

She knelt for hours, motionless, hands clenched in her lap. She thought if she did not move, if she summoned all her strength and willpower, if she did not touch the shimmering mother-of-pearl, she could keep the past away. If she disturbed nothing, not even the air around her, she could survive and forget as she had once forgotten.

I have been able to put the ugliness behind me. She had believed that lie with all her heart. *Perhaps Chin Yun is not so lucky.* Chin Yun did not have to forget; he had been embarrassed and ashamed, but those wounds would heal eventually. What about Lian's?

She heard no noise from the street below, smelled no flowers or herbs or cooking meat. She was not aware the sun was sinking, that the room darkened and the shadows lengthened, whispering like *kuei* who could not rest. Around her there was darkness, utter stillness, while in her head images swirled in dizzying bursts of color.

Even without touch, memory came, and she had no defense against it.

9

ÉMILE DROUARD TAPPED IMPATIENTLY ON THE DOOR OF THE apothecary shop, listening for the sound of Cheng's muffled footsteps. Finally the old man peered out, brow furrowed until he saw who was waiting. He did not seem at all surprised, but it took a great deal to surprise him. "At last your interminable patience has run out," he said with exaggerated relief. "I had begun to wonder if it ever would."

Émile stared blankly. "I don't understand."

With a wry smile, Cheng explained. "You grew weary of waiting like a good and proper gentleman for Wan Lian to appear and decided to come demand to see her."

Émile should not have been alarmed. Cheng observed everything and missed nothing. He must have seen the young man watching Lian's balcony every morning. The shutters were usually open, but Émile had seen no glimpse of her in all this time. Frequently at night he gazed up at her lighted windows. He'd noticed the alchemist watching now and then. He might easily have guessed at Émile's tense anticipation and constant disappointment when not even her shadow darkened the glow from inside.

Cheng nodded wisely, as he was prone to do. "Frustration will erode even the best of manners and the finest intentions if left to simmer long enough." He sounded quite cheerful about the whole thing.

"You've been expecting me."

"Certainly. Have I not eyes in my face and a brain in my head? Only a blind fool could have missed the signs." There was more than a trace of irony in his tone.

Émile did not enjoy being so transparent, even to Cheng. "I am merely worried about Mademoiselle Lian. This continued absence is not like her."

Narrowing his eyes, the old man considered. "Since the night you shared a walk, she has worked with me in the shop every day, as usual. She has spoken as usual, behaved as usual. Only she has not said your name."

Émile's stomach felt hollow. "I see."

"No," Cheng intoned, "you most certainly do not. I thought you had come to know her well enough to realize that Wan Lian is most vigilantly silent about those things which disturb her most."

Feeling faintly ill, Émile replied, "I had no intention of distressing her. I only wanted to talk, to learn what she thinks about, what she's been through." I wanted to touch her, he added silently, to hold her and kiss her, to feel her cool defenses melt.

Cheng looked thoughtful, the early morning light making his face seem more wrinkled, his hands more frail. "Did she talk? And did you learn?"

Unsettled by the old man's piercing onyx eyes, Émile nodded.

"Ah! Now all is clear." He paused, rolling words in his head like marbles in his hand. "Émile, my friend, to Wan Li-an you have transformed yourself into the most dangerous of men, because you made her feel safe." He looked troubled. "If you are sincere in your desire, I hope you have great energy and persistence, for Wan Li-an is very good at building walls. You must take them down stone by stone, until the breach is too wide to be repaired; then you must keep her from escaping through it. Are you dedicated enough, obstinate enough for that kind of heavy labor?"

Émile, whose dreams Lian had invaded, whose mind churned with the mysteries still unspoken, squared his considerable shoulders. "I'm strong enough for your difficult task. I'm not a man to reject a challenge. Besides, it's the only way I will find peace."

Cheng smiled benignly, nodding in approval.

"Is she in? Shall I go up?" The young man was eager to begin.

"Go." The alchemist touched his arm in warning. "You should know that today the Chins came by with a large chest. They arrived looking determined and left with tears on their cheeks. I have heard no sound since from Lian's flat. So take care. Patience is your greatest weapon, the best gift you can give her."

"I'll remember." Émile left Cheng precipitously, without a single sign of patience, and disappeared down the alley.

The old man watched him go, shaking his head and muttering under his breath.

Émile knocked on the door several times, but Lian did not answer. Cheng had said she was in, so Émile persisted; he was not only patient, he was stubborn. Eventually the eerie silence after the fading echo of his fist on wood unnerved him. He turned the knob experimentally.

It moved. The door was unlocked. Quietly, so as not to startle her, Émile pushed the door open and glanced inside. He stopped, gripping the wood with rigid fingers, when he saw Lian in the middle of the room.

She was kneeling in front of a black chest, hands in her lap, her body unyielding as marble. The shadows had taken the room back from the day, except the last dim rays of light that fanned through the open shutters and fell across

Lian's motionless form. Even as he watched, the light was fading, leaving her face in shadow, but it was enough to show him her vacant expression, her fingers so tangled against her satin skirt that the skin was mottled red and white. Her shoulders were slumped forward, as if something lay heavily on her back.

Émile felt ill, as if someone had struck him hard in the stomach, and he understood at last the sense of urgency that had brought him here. From the moment he awakened, his mood had been darker than the storm clouds in the western sky.

But he had never expected to find her like this—deaf and blind and rigid. Her skin, when he touched her arm gently with a brush of the fingertips, was cold, her face a lifeless mask.

He realized her condition was dangerous, that the cold would seep into her body until it drowned her. At least there was one thing he could do for her. Moving silently, he found her bedroom with its low sleeping pallet, the duvet spread neatly, without a wrinkle. He gathered it up, twisting his fists in the thick, soft fabric.

Quickly, he returned to Lian's side and draped the duvet over her shoulders, folding it awkwardly about her ice-cold hands and tucking it under her knees and around her rigid legs. With great care, he made certain she was covered from just beneath her chin to the bottoms of her feet. Then he sat behind her, pressing his chest to her back, wrapping his arms and legs around her, attempting to infuse her with the heat from his own body.

For a long time he sat immobile, afraid to move or speak, to awaken her too abruptly from her stupor. *Take care. Patience is your greatest weapon, the best gift you can give her.* The words echoed in the uncanny stillness, and Émile knew, from the tightness in his chest and the rasp of his own breath, that he stood on the edge of a precipice. If Cheng had not told him he'd seen her this morning, Émile would have thought she'd been sitting for days, star-

ing blindly at the odd headpiece shaped like a white peacock that shone, even in the dimness, against the ebony
chest.

It was as though her spirit had left her, though her chest
rose and fell, telling him she was alive. Alive, but little
more. He could not imagine what had frightened her so
badly. If he called her name, if he woke her from this living
death, would she thank him? He did not know the answer,
and it was tearing him apart.

In the end, he had no choice. It seemed an eternity ago
that he had enfolded her with his warmth, trying to think
while his mind and his heart spun wildly with questions
and insecurity and fear. "Slowly," he murmured, "I must go
slowly. I want to help you, Lian, but my hands are blunt
and large and clumsy, except when I hold a piece of charcoal or a brush."

He realized he was talking to himself and forced some
air into his lungs. He felt helpless. He wanted his compassion, his affection, his tenderness to be enough to break
this spell, but he sensed his feelings were paltry in compari-
son with whatever force had taken her away. He had
guessed her will was strong. Was it stronger than his?

"No," he said, not caring that he spoke aloud. "I can do
this."

Lian did not move so much as an eyelash. She had not
heard.

Nevertheless, she seemed less chilled beneath the heavy
duvet. Émile rose, suddenly chilled himself, oppressed by
the lack of light. He turned up the gaslights on the walls,
dissolving the dimness that had settled around her.

Quietly, he resumed his place on the floor. Closing his
eyes in a brief fervent prayer, he began to move his hands
in slow, hypnotic circles that barely touched her rigid body.
He touched her, first with fingertips, then with palms, heart
racing, face damp with sweat. He pressed his ear against her
back to reassure himself her heart was beating, the blood

still flowing through her veins. He sighed with relief when he heard a faint irregular thump.

He was alarmed by the color of her skin, the shadows beneath her eyes. He knelt, trying to breathe his breath over her and into her, to bring her back by forcing heat and life into her body. He sensed it was dangerous, but he was growing frantic.

"Lian," he whispered, "it's all right. You're not alone. Come back, Lian, from wherever you've gone. Come back and let me make you warm."

He thought he saw a flicker in her eyes, but she did not respond. Taking one deep breath, he grasped her arms and the duvet slid to the floor. "Come back, Lian," he said more loudly. "It's all right. You're safe now."

Her eyes did not blink nor her expression change, but with a violent thrust, she pushed him away, striking the ebony chest with her closed fists. "It is *not* all right."

Émile's heart raced and he was sweating, despite the cool evening. He had known Lian was more than she seemed, but this was beyond his comprehension. "There's nothing to fear now. You're safe with me."

Lian turned, glared at him for an instant, in which his heart stopped beating, then flung her arms around his neck. "I'll never be safe again, do you not see that? Never!"

She clung so hard he had to struggle to breathe, but he barely noticed. He was appalled by the slightness of her body in his arms, which closed around her automatically. She was inflexible, her muscles twitching from long confinement. For a long time he cradled her, too stunned to gather his wits, too frightened by the reality of Lian, unconscious of the world around her, shivering in his arms like a child. She who had always been in control, always dignified and withdrawn, was completely vulnerable, broken, lost.

He guessed she would have sent him away if she'd had the power, but he would not go. Not only out of simple human kindness, but because the impulse that had sent him to find her would not allow him to abandon her now. Nothing mattered except her need.

Lifting her easily in his arms, Émile carried her to the kitchen and set a kettle boiling for tea. Then he drew a chair as close to the stove as possible and settled her in his lap. She was barely conscious, muttering incoherently in Chinese, French and English. Two words came through clearly, over and over. Chin Chao.

Émile stifled his curiosity as he fed her tea and a soft piece of bread, rubbing her feet and hands until some of the cold left her, but her eyes were still blank.

She continued to shiver violently, and he rose with his burden in his arms. "You're too cold. You need to be in bed." He headed toward her bedroom, stopping long enough to grasp the duvet and drag it behind them. She did not protest when he lowered her onto the sleeping pallet, removing her outer vest and tucking the bulky quilt around her. He hovered while she trembled. He leaned close, wondering what he would do when he *had* to leave. He decided he would go to Cheng. The old man would know what to do. He cared about Lian.

Slowly, reluctantly, Émile rose. He gasped when Lian grabbed his hand.

"I do not wish you to leave me." Her eyes were panicked, an odd contrast to her formal words. "It is so cold here," she whispered, "and I am so alone."

Émile was shocked by the desolation in her voice. Her eyes remained glazed, looking through him.

She clung to his hand, her grasp a silent plea. She needed him—someone, anyone would suffice, so long as they were calm and did not ask too many questions. She didn't recognize him. He knew it was childish, but the realization hurt. Yet he stayed. Carefully, he maneuvered past the foot of the pallet and stretched out, pressing his warm body against hers.

Just before she drifted off to sleep, still shuddering now and then, she whispered, "I am grateful, Émile."

He stiffened, ceased breathing for so long his chest began to ache. She *had* recognized him. When? How long ago? Certainly before she asked him to stay. For the second time in her presence, as he felt Lian go limp in his arms and begin to breathe regularly, he wanted to weep.

10

LIAN DREAMT A CRUEL AND VIVID DREAM. SHE AWAKENED soaked with sweat, head throbbing and eyes blind. She could not shake the terror, the sense of emptiness and loss. She stood in China, dust on her shoes, the Vermilion Gates looming above like a promise of things to come. "No!" she cried hoarsely. "No!"

Émile had not closed his eyes, had watched her fall asleep, begin to mutter, to toss and turn and finally cry out. When he took her in his arms, she wept dry tears, one arm around his neck, grasping his hand in a biting grip.

"I can never get away," she cried. "The Imperial Guard will come for me. I hear them coming."

In her mind, she was in China, caught so wholly in the past that her nightmare was more real than her pallet in France. "Lian," Émile said firmly. "Listen to me. You are safe. You were only dreaming. Open your eyes. Please."

His certainty broke the grip of the nightmare. She looked up at him until slowly, the red walls of the Forbidden City faded along with the choking dust and the fear.

"Tell me," Émile murmured as the film left her eyes. "Tell me your dream." He ignored the voice inside that said he did not want to know.

She collapsed against him, and, her face pressed to his chest, she told him in vivid detail of her terrifying, hopeless vigil across from the Imperial Palace. She told him of Chin

Chao—her secret husband—his editorial condemning the Son of Heaven, the charge of treason and his imprisonment, of her frantic need to let Chao know she had not abandoned him like the others.

Émile shrank a little within himself. This man, this martyr, had been her lover? She had suppressed her own terror to prove to him her constancy? How could he, Émile Drouard, hope to compete with such a memory? How could he hope to win the heart of such a woman? He rested his cheek on top of her head, arm wrapped tightly around her. He had no power, no strength to match hers and her lover's. He had no more than a compassionate heart and a little wit and some skill with a pen. He was empty; he was nothing.

"Weren't you angry with him, even for a moment?" he murmured.

Lian stiffened. "Angry?" The word seemed foreign to her, incomprehensible.

Émile frowned in dismay. "Because he chose to voice his opinion at the cost of his reputation, his family's welfare, even his life. And in making that choice, he left you alone and vulnerable to his enemies."

"No," she murmured, perplexed. Then she shivered, her eyes grew wide at an image he could not see, and she gripped his hand so hard he gasped. "I cannot go back. Not ever."

I never dream of China. I have left it behind and vowed to forget the chaos of the past, she'd told him in the starlight. *Promises are easier to make than to keep,* he'd replied. *The past has a power and presence that doesn't fade easily, if at all.* He had not known then how right he was.

He realized she had stopped shaking, that there was moisture on the hand she had been clutching. In the dim, colored light of the red paper lantern above her bed, he saw four moon-shaped wounds in her palm where her fingernails had pierced the skin. He took her other hand from around his neck and opened it to reveal four identical crescent wounds.

Whispering meaningless words of solace, he carried her to the kitchen and found her store of herbs and ointments. With one elbow, he cleared a space on the table, pushing books and papers away. He could not find a bandage, but discovered some soft cloths in the cupboard. He settled her into a chair at the parlor table and made certain she could sit upright. She leaned heavily against the scarred wood, watching him with dazed, reddened eyes, her hands lying in front of her, palms up.

Carefully, he cleaned away the blood, disinfected the eight wounds, spread ointment on each and wrapped the clean cloths around her palms, one at a time. He knew it must hurt, but she did not flinch.

She was the first to speak. "You do that with skill." Her voice was oddly flat.

"I learned while growing up in the wine fields, where injuries are common, and Cheng taught me about more effective herbs and ointments."

When the color began to return to her skin, he rose to search for wine but, finding none, he settled for making tea. While the water was heating, he made more space on the table, piled books on top of one another and left the papers in an untidy stack. He was about to turn away when an unfinished letter on top caught his attention. "My Dear Sister Genevra," it read. "I dreamed of you again today. Tell me where the danger lies. In *your* heart, or those of your enemies?"

Genevra, the half-sister who'd created the magical watercolor of the women in the rushing river. He'd seen it the night he came to dinner. Émile touched the fresh ink warily. More dreams of danger. More mysterious links with others that he could not understand. How, then, could he hope to understand Lian?

Émile turned his attention to the whistling kettle. He must focus on practical things, like urging her to eat. He put hot tea in front of her, along with bread and cheese and fruit. She was still trembling and tended to gaze vacantly at the steam rising from her tea cup rather than the food on her plate.

Émile wiped the perspiration from his forehead, but the rest of his body was damp with sweat. The last few hours had been more difficult than he realized and had exhausted him so he felt light-headed. He had known it would not be easy to break through Lian's carefully layered shell. But he had never imagined this. How in God's name could he deal with *this*?

Lian ate slowly, one bite at a time, sipping her jasmine tea and tasting nothing.

"Tell me the rest," he said. "Now, before you retreat behind your deftly woven Chinese veil."

"You do not really wish to know."

"You can't say what I do and do not want, Lian. I've seen you looking like a doll without breath or life or hope, and I need to know why." He paused when she grew rigid.

"I would rather be alone now," she said abruptly.

It took a moment for Émile to absorb the shock, to wonder, and finally, to speak. "I don't think it's wise when you're in this condition, but if that's what you want, I'll go. You should know I'll never force my company upon you, whatever your reasons or my doubts. You need only ask and I'll be gone. I swear to you, Lian." He paused. "But now, right now, is that really what you want?"

She bowed her head, so he could not see her expression. Then she reached out tentatively to touch his hand. "No. Please stay. It is just that I am afraid."

From far away came the memory of his voice. *Do not wonder what will be or what it means or if you are in danger. Not from me. Never from me.* Tonight she wanted to believe him. She was surprised to find she did.

"There is an old French proverb," Émile said quietly. " 'Nothing is so burdensome as a secret.' You have carried a heavy burden of secrets for a very long time. Didn't you ever think that sharing that burden might lighten the weight on your shoulders?"

Lian searched his kind hazel eyes, full of concern, compassion, tenderness. He was offering consolation. He understood that she needed someone to hold her while she spoke of the unspeakable and bore the unbearable. Slowly, inevitably, she began to talk.

She told him about the terror that had begun when she was four years old and Charles Kittridge left her, about Peking, her mother's lovers, the sound of soldiers marching in the street, about how they had fled, Ke-ming and her daughter, after Chin Chao's trial when the marching feet were turned toward the house of Wan at last. "At least the waiting was finally over," she murmured. "I had known all my life that they would come. I had dreamt of that day, of the blood and the fear, expecting it every moment, except sometimes when I was with Chao. But in the end, they did not catch us after all. In the end we were just ahead of them as they marched through the streets of Peking toward our compound." *Why did you defend me tonight?* he'd asked, perplexed. *Perhaps I have become oversensitive to injustice.* Now he understood.

She told him of the Western Hills, her journey to the Highlands, the loss and kinship she'd found there. It had begun, as it had ended, with Charles Kittridge.

Émile sat stunned, attempting to imagine her suffering. It was too far beyond anything he had ever known, too strange and violent and incomprehensible.

When she had finished, she rested her head wearily on her outstretched arm. "I am a fraud. I have lied to myself, believing I could forget."

One can't let go of such things easily, Émile had warned her. *Of course I cannot forget what is seared into my memory. I can only use my strength and determination to put it behind me.* Even then she had known.

Silence hovered, binding them yet holding them apart.

Resting his chin in his hands, Émile sliced through the invisible barrier. "Do you hate your father now?"

"It would be easier if I could. Then there would be someone to blame."

"Do you need that, some one to blame? Not a crumbling civilization or corrupt officials or a government so weak it tried to destroy all that was worthy?"

She shook her head. "There were others who lived with all those things and yet lost little."

"But your mother—" Émile began, changing direction when he saw Lian's face. "If you don't blame Charles Kittridge, why have you not read his letters?"

Had she told him that? Lian raised her head. "Because I do not wish to think of him with compassion."

"You don't love him either?"

"I did not know him long enough to love him."

You're wrong, Émile thought. He is with you as your mother is still with you, and much as you may wish it, you can't silence his voice. But he did not speak his thoughts out loud.

Lian looked dazed, as if she had lost the thread of the conversation. She was staring at the chest.

"Will you do me one more favor, Émile?" She was glad to change the subject.

The sound of his name on her lips made him ache. "I'll do what I can."

"Will you put the headdress back inside," she waved vaguely toward the carved ebony chest, "and put the chest . . ." She rubbed her temples in distraction. "Somewhere where I will not have to look at it?"

"You don't want to see what else is inside, ma petite?"

Lian did not seem to notice the endearment. She shuddered and shook her head. "Please, no."

Her resolve to ignore the chest and all it represented disturbed him, but he did as she asked, despite her soft voice whispering in his memory: There are good things as well as bad, moments of beauty I hold close to my heart. Might not this last gift from Wan Ke-ming hold such moments, such beauty? He thought of the doors to the Duchamps' courtyard, which Lian had refused to open, and knew she would not change her mind. After placing the headdress inside, he moved the chest to a far corner of the room, where he draped it with a large embroidered shawl. Then he dropped into the pine chair across from hers.

"Why?" he asked.

She knew he was not asking about the chest. Émile wanted to know why she had told him her story. "Because I trust you." *I am not often mistaken about human nature.* She toyed with the soft white bandages on her hands. "Now you know. Now you have seen . . . everything, too much."

Wistfully, she touched his face. He covered her hand with his, easily, naturally, as if their fingers were meant to be pressed to his bearded cheek, tangled together in the red hair. She could not bear the sweet ache that spread through her, the tingling sensation of their intertwined fingers.

Émile felt her tremble. "It doesn't matter what I've seen. Not if you trust me as you say. Just don't shut me out." He leaned so close she could not escape, holding her delicate wrists in his square hands. "I will not let your fear defeat me."

"Defeat you?"

He rose and began to pace, head bent. "We've both been wounded tonight, I think. We're both in pain, though I can never feel what you have suffered." He turned to face her. "Like it or not, we've shared something unthinkable. We had no choice. In China you weren't given a choice, nor in Scotland. Those things I cannot change."

Kneeling, he put his hands on her shoulders. "Tonight, Lian, we have a choice. We can part, aching, and try yet again to forget, or we can hold one another, console one another, remind one another that there are good things left to feel." He looked into her amazing blue eyes, unprotected, revealing her desire. She could no longer hide from him. It was too late for that.

Lian swallowed dryly, thinking of her mother. Ke-ming

had found what pleasure she could in the arms of her lovers. Perhaps Lian was more like her mother than she thought or cared to be. All she knew was that she could not face tonight alone. Still she hesitated.

Clenching his hands into fists, Émile garnered the last of his pride. Even if she rejected *him*, she deserved for someone to give her happiness. If she did not find her way out of the morass in which she was struggling, she might be caught forever. "Don't you understand yet? I'll never hurt you, no matter what I know."

After a moment, she said, "You see a great deal, and did, even before this night. That sketch—" She shivered. "It frightened me, how much you had discovered, how easily you caught me with your pencil. You see what others do not or cannot or will not; you see what is concealed behind shadows and walls of mist and smoke. Tonight you have seen all I am. And you are right. We know each other, Émile Drouard."

She brushed his temple with her fingertips, touched his cheek with her bound hand. "I do not know if there are good things left to feel. I do not quite believe you. I do know that I want you near." She cupped his face in both hands. "Let us see if there is something more, and if there is not, then at least, for a while, we can help each other forget."

11

ÉMILE AWOKE TO THE SOUND OF A FLUTE OUTSIDE THE SHUT-tered window. Lian lay beside him, the duvet thrust away in her sleep. Last night he had held her, warming her with his hands, touching with wonder her long, slim body and golden skin, surprised by the passion with which she responded. She touched him everywhere as if intent on devouring him. After both had found their pleasure, she had smiled without hesitation. Briefly, before she drifted into sleep, she had cupped Émile's face, the bandages on her palms brushing his cheeks; the blaze in her blue eyes had dimmed to a soft glow. Now she slept deeply. Even when he tucked the comforter around her, she did not stir. He suspected she would sleep for a long time.

Dressing quietly, he went to her small kitchen, surveyed the contents, then took her pitcher and basket and crept out of the flat. He hurried down the stairs, hair uncombed, beard tangled, one arm in the sleeve of his expensive overcoat, the other hanging loose, his shirt cuff barely held in place by a crooked stud. He was aware of none of these things, only of the need to catch Cheng before he went to buy his food for the day.

Émile was lucky. Cheng was just closing the inner door to his shop, empty milk bowl in hand, when the younger man caught up with him.

Cheng stared, startled out of his normal imperturbability. He looked Émile up and down, neither smiling nor frowning. He was surprised, but not distressed. "You are, perhaps, up earlier than you planned?"

Émile ran one hand through his disheveled hair, realizing how frazzled he must look. But that was not important now. "Lian is not well," he said, being deliberately vague. "I don't think she'll leave her flat or wish to have visitors today. She's obstinate enough to starve rather than appear in public, but I don't mean to let that happen." He proffered pitcher and basket before Cheng could voice the questions in his shrewd black eyes. "She'll need milk, some cheese and bread and fruit—bananas and apples. I have the sous here. Will you get these things for her? I can't do it myself; the entire street would see me, and I don't want them gossiping and asking questions." He mentioned a few other items he needed. "Will you do this for her?"

"My friend, you know I would do much more if she

asked. This is but a simple task which I will gladly undertake, and I am well aware of what she needs day by day." Cheng showed no surprise, and despite the concern in his almond eyes, he asked no questions. Weak with relief, Émile leaned against the nearest wall for support.

"Before you go," he said, "would you be kind enough to lend me paper, ink and a brush?"

Eyes half-closed to hide his trepidation, Cheng guided the young man inside, leaving him slumped on a stool with paper and ink before him. As soon as the alchemist had gone, Émile leaned on the counter, rubbing his temples, trying to think. By the time Cheng returned from the market on the quay, he had struggled with his brush strokes until he was satisfied. He took the half-full pitcher and bulging basket Cheng offered, grateful for his friend's discretion. "I can't thank you enough—"

"No, you cannot, because there is no need. She is my friend."

Émile smiled wryly, glancing at the paper in his hand. "Still, you have been very kind and discreet, and your silence is a gift beyond price."

"One that is yours whenever it is needed. Now go take these things to Li-an, for I am too old to climb so many stairs." He smiled at the obvious lie. "Afterward, I beg you to go and rest, for you too look ill."

Émile tried to dissipate the fog of weariness that had curled through his mind, obscuring thought and instinct. "I must take more care when I return."

Cheng rested his wrinkled hand on Émile's shoulder. "We always take care. We are too cautious, you and I. This, I think, we have in common with Li-an."

Sighing and nodding, Émile thanked the old man, folded three pieces of paper and slipped them into the basket. Laboriously, he climbed the stairs to Lian's door.

He touched the folded rice paper gingerly, wondering if she would understand.

Finally, he slid the smallest fragment under the door, leaving the basket and milk on the floor. He stood for a long moment, staring at the blank face of the door, wondering what would happen to Lian, to himself, to the two of them.

He had no illusions. It would not be easy to draw her away from the overwhelming power of the past, far enough that she could feel the allure of the present. As she had, for a while, last night. To her, such fulfillment was fleeting, ephemeral. He wanted her to understand that pleasure, kinship, warmth could last longer than a moment. Perhaps even a lifetime.

He did not know if he had the perseverance for such a task, but he had the desire, the determination. Especially now that he had held her in his arms and felt her passion through every inch of skin and blood and bone.

Émile leaned against the unyielding oak, feeling light-headed. He could not remember when he had last eaten, except that it had been yesterday—a very long time ago. But hunger was not the source of his discomfort, nor lack of sleep, though he had closed his eyes not two hours before the flute woke him. "I will be back. I'll not disappear docilely," he said, pressing his fist against the wood as if to reach through and seize her so she could not slip away.

12

LIAN LAY PERFECTLY STILL, EYES CLOSED. SHE ACHED ALL over from the hours she had sat unmoving, and her shoulders were hard knots of tension. But the outward pain was nothing compared to the inward.

She remembered everything from the moment she'd heard the Chins' footsteps on the stairs, and she wanted to draw her legs in close to her body and hide beneath the duvet. If she stayed wrapped in her cocoon of silence, she would not have to think of yesterday or wonder about tomorrow.

She remembered the feel of Émile's arms, remembered crying out as she lost herself in the seduction of his callused hands and hungry mouth. She remembered the power and urgency of her longing, the blaze of elation. Afterward, they lay tangled in her hair, holding each other so tight that their labored breath was an agony and a profound fulfillment.

She strove not to move or change the rhythm of her breathing. She knew she would open her eyes to find Émile beside her. He would observe her kindly, his gaze fond and tender.

She could not face him, knowing he had witnessed her weakness and fear. He had seen what no man should ever see—her naked beating heart, open and vulnerable.

Aware she could not hide forever, she steeled herself to confront Émile, to face him calmly. Opening her eyes, Lian gaped at emptiness. Émile was not beside her and his clothes were gone. She recalled vaguely that he'd fed her last night; perhaps he was preparing breakfast.

She rose stiffly, found her green silk butterfly robe and slipped it on. She tied the belt awkwardly and took a deep breath to make her heartbeat slow to normal. She felt confused and irrational, especially when she saw that he wasn't in the kitchen. She stood in the doorway, staring at the empty parlor, the table, uncluttered with plates or cups or rolls. Her gaze flicked toward the balcony, but the shutters were closed, allowing a few pale shafts of light to touch the floor.

Émile was gone.

Lian felt light-headed and bewildered. He had left her alone. Without a word, without a good-bye or a note propped on the table. Disbelief robbed her of breath and she blinked back tears. *I won't let your fear defeat me,* Émile had vowed. Had he lost the battle after all? She refused to believe it.

Lian crossed the parlor, arms wrapped around herself.

She shivered at the sight of the shawl-covered chest. For one brief moment, she hated the Chins for bringing it here.

Yet they had done the most difficult thing possible—admitted their own weakness. Their honesty had not come easily. To be honorable, she must deny her anger and admire their strength of will. She knelt, eyes closed.

It was difficult, because she was alone now, enveloped by memories as palpable as dust.

She could see Émile's face in the red-tinted darkness. Why had he come? Why hadn't he left her in peace? Why, *why* had he gone? She shook her head in denial, until, out of the corner of her eye, she saw a piece of folded paper under the front door. She bent to pick it up, holding it by the edge. It must be from him.

Warily, she opened it to find a poorly drawn Chinese character. *Fu*, the symbol for happiness. Anger flared at his insensitivity. Happiness, after all he'd seen and heard last night? The image seemed to burn through the paper, leaving a charcoal scar on her palm. Then, in a flash of enlightenment, she remembered the character for happiness was formed by symbols which, together, represented a full stomach.

She cracked open the door to find her pitcher filled with milk, her basket with food. There was nothing else. Just the sustenance she needed to keep herself alive.

She shivered, unnerved that he had chosen to remind her, neither of anguish or desire, but instead, of practicalities, the need to eat and drink. Yet he had done it with the symbol for happiness, and in Chinese. How could he have known what was just enough—not too little or too much? How could he have guessed it would be too difficult to face him today, to see the image of herself in his eyes?

Tonight you have seen all I am. You see what others do not or cannot or will not. Suddenly, she was not hungry.

Leaving pitcher and basket, she turned to the refuge where she found comfort at such times—the altar to her ancestors, where she worshipped every morning.

Raising the reed blind that screened the shrine between the end of her pallet and the wall, she ducked beneath. She knelt before the altar—a teakwood table with a marble top and an embroidered silk skirt that hid the stone soul tablets honoring her ancestors, her dead mother and father. She lit the incense in the jade holder until the smell of sandalwood drifted about her shoulders, fragrant and familiar. The wilting white jasmine that filled the small porcelain vase gave out a sweet scent that calmed her, urged her toward action, toward creation.

She took out her supplies and soon became engrossed in writing poetry. She spent hours bent over rice paper, with inkstone, brushes, sand and sticks of ink. She enjoyed the ancient, elegant, studied ritual of calligraphy, the brief vivid images in the style of the Chinese poets. These things brought her some measure of peace.

Eventually, she realized she was hungry after all. Brushing her butterfly sleeve across the rice paper, she rose to bring in the pitcher and basket Émile had left outside. This time she noticed a nosegay of peonies on top, which made her pause. With trepidation, she read the short note.

Lian,

Cheng suggested you might need to replenish the flowers at your family altar. I hope these are appropriate.

Émile

Relief washed over her at the simple, harmless gesture. She steeled herself against the gratitude she felt. That was what she called it—gratitude.

Hands shaking, she examined the rest of the contents of the basket. Besides vegetables, fruit, bread and cheese, she discovered a small box tied with several colors of ribbon in bows and curls—as necessary to a French gift as the object inside. Nervously, she pulled away the ribbons, opening the box to find two fragrant pear tarts. The note read: *Thought you ought to vary your diet. Good for the digestion.*

Pear tarts were her favorite. Somehow Émile had found out one more secret, made one more gesture of friendship, asking nothing in return.

Giving in at last to the urgings of her heart, Lian sat on the floor and wept.

13

THE NEXT MORNING, SHE WAS AWAKE WELL BEFORE DAWN. She sat at the table in the parlor, listening. When she heard soft footfalls coming up the stairs, she went to the door and opened it. "Do you think there is enough for two?" she asked.

"*Oui,*" Émile said, dazed, "there is plenty."

When he'd closed the door behind him, he stood just inside, waiting for Lian to speak, to move, to give him a sign. But she seemed to have been struck mute.

They stared at one another for a minute that had the shape and feeling of an hour. Then, without warning, she took the basket from his hand and set it on the table.

She moved with the grace of a willow branch. She had dressed carefully in a soft rose gown and burgundy tunic embroidered with peach blossoms falling like tears from a dew-touched leaf. Her blue-black hair hung down her back; she had brushed it long and thoroughly.

"I am cold," Lian said at last, breaking the tension on the thread pulled taut between them. She looked up and, for the first time, met Émile's eyes directly.

He could not fail to read the invitation in her sky blue

gaze. "Are you sure?" He had sworn not to push her and did not wish to break that vow.

Lian crossed the space between them and her body brushed his. "How can you doubt it?" she asked. Awkwardly, she reached up to trace the sun-bronzed line of his cheekbone.

Without conscious thought, he closed his arms around her protectively, but he wanted more than simply to warm her trembling body or to keep her safe.

Lian sensed his reluctance and pressed closer, closing her arms around his waist.

Émile released his breath in a long, ragged sigh. Resting his cheek on the crown of her head, he held her tenderly but tightly, in case she should escape, as a fragile butterfly escapes its captor's net.

But Lian did not wish to escape. She leaned into him, seeking his warmth and strength. He was solid and real; she could feel his desire in his rapid heartbeat. She did not want to let him go, but to hold him like this, and he her, until the past had retreated for good. It came to her that she was no longer alone with the past. She had not realized how lonely she was. She looked at Émile and realized she had chosen ghosts and shadows when she could have had much more.

Émile knew everything, so she need not hide from him or pretend she was invincible. She did not know how much effort it took to keep her protective wall in place until she let it crumble. It lay now at their feet, ignored and irrelevant once she lifted her face and her lips touched his.

Groaning, he buried his hands in her hair and kissed her deeply, fiercely, till the heat of his body burned into hers, melting the core of ice at her center.

Lian was both excited and afraid, enticed and surprised by the pressure of his arms, his body, his searching lips. She could not catch her breath, but it no longer mattered. She did not want to end the unexpected radiance, the kiss that bound them one to the other. She had waited too long, denied herself completely; the cold had crept into her soul. She could not, now, put out the blaze that aroused and warmed but, miraculously, did not burn.

Later, shutters pulled back and French doors open, they sat on satin pillows, gazing at the river, silvered by the cloudy light.

Lian had not yet spoken of the ebony chest, the nightmare and what had followed. Émile had not pushed her; instead they had laughed and talked of ordinary things. Safe things.

Now, leaning back against him, his arms clasped at her waist, Lian murmured, "I want to talk about the first morning."

Émile sighed with relief, glad she was finally ready to face it. But wisely, he remained silent.

"These wounds in my hands, even the presence of the past, hovering like a thunderstorm at my shoulder, did not frighten me." She picked up an embroidered pillow and held it close to her chest. "What frightened me was the anger. I was full of rage, shaking with it. There was room for nothing else. Why?"

Émile considered the ease of a lie, but she trusted him. He chose to tell the truth. "Perhaps anger is easier to feel than pain, despair, helplessness? Those things debilitate, while fury makes you feel strong, invincible."

"It's true that over the years my anger at my father became my backbone of steel," she mused. "But I was not just angry, Émile. I was enraged at the Chins who had merely fulfilled an obligation, and more enraged at you, who rescued me and tended me and held me." The words did not come easily. She wanted to lean back and see, in his eyes, what he was thinking. His arms tightened around her.

"Could it be," he said, "that you were angry at us so you

need not be angry at yourself?" He was taking a risk and hoped he had not judged her wrong.

"At myself?" She did not sound outraged, only perplexed.

"For allowing the Chins to bring your lover's ghost to sit on your shoulder? For letting the memories conquer you, for being weak enough to hurt again from pain you thought long buried? And most of all, for the loss of the peace you had created?"

Lian shook her head with wonder woven into ineffable sadness. This time she sat up and turned to look at him directly. "You are always honest, are you not? Even when the risk is great."

"*Oui*, unless it is pointlessly cruel to be so. But what I have told you is not cruel, Lian. If it is the truth, then so is this: You are not weak or foolish; you are stronger than I, or you would not be here now. A coward would never have asked for the truth, or hearing it, would have denied it. Yet you are willing to look into the darkest part of yourself to see the nature of your imperfections. What you can't see is the beauty, the understanding, the luminous compassion that is also you. I know, because I've seen it, touched it, felt it all around me like a benediction."

Lian shook her head, eyes filmed with moisture.

Émile was beginning to grasp how many tears were dammed up behind her wall of smoke. "You doubt me. But it does not matter. Even if you never recognize that incandescence, it will not dim or flicker or fade. You don't have to know you are beautiful for it to be true."

For a long moment, they stared at one another, motionless. "I do not believe you," Lian whispered, "but I thank you."

Chest aching with compassion for all she could not see, Émile leaned forward to kiss her tenderly. Lian sighed and let her lids drift closed, not to become blind, but to feel rather than see.

He reached for her, and she for him, hearts beating one

into the other, lips parted, seeking and finding heat and fire and absolution.

14

LIAN SAT AT THE BACK OF THE APOTHECARY SHOP AND watched a customer open the door with the odd, hollow bell and step inside. The woman paused, letting her eyes adjust to the gloom, her nose to the biting scent of incense and boiling herbs.

Cheng went to meet his customer, bowing graciously, speaking in his low-pitched courteous voice, asking not only about her physical condition, but also her life, her home, her frustrations, her joys. As she talked they shared a pot of jasmine tea.

To cure the patient, I must find the root of the illness, not merely the symptom, he told Lian often. *I must earn their trust, which is as important to healing as the herbs, ointments and decoctions I prescribe.*

Sitting on a high stool, cutting and sifting dandelion leaf and crushing the dried root to powder, Lian rested her head on her hand, glancing down the rows of Chinese medicine chests. Those chests reminded her of home, of the beautiful rosewood box on her mother's dressing table beside her moon mirror. Sometimes Lian ran her hands caressingly over the smooth dark wood, remembering through touch the pleasant mornings when she'd sit on Ke-ming's teak bench padded with down and covered in tapestry while her mother treated a cut or her daughter's sore throat or the cold in her chest. Ke-ming's hands, like Cheng's, had been gentle, her scent subtle but sweet. Lian thought she could smell it now.

She sat up with a start when Cheng appeared beside her. "Drifting in your memories?" he asked.

"How did you know?"

The alchemist did not answer, but pulled up a stool and sat beside her, hands resting on the edge of the drying table. "Émile Drouard was here while you were out with Mei and Yi. He seemed downcast that he had missed you, though he cannot complain that he has seen you too little these last two moons."

In spite of herself, Lian blushed. She was unsettled by how much she enjoyed seeing Émile, delighted in his company, his wit, his warm hands on her skin. The two had grown close in laughter and friendship, as slowly, tenderly, they came to know each other's bodies in the red-tinted light of the silk lantern above her bed.

"You are embarrassed by your friendship with such a man?" Cheng asked in surprise. "It is good, what you have with Émile, is it not?"

"It is. But it was born from something ugly and destructive."

"And because of that you fear it must end. You refuse to understand, Li-an. You have blessings, rare blessings, yet you spoil them with your doubt. Each time Émile holds you, do you not wonder if it will be the last?"

Mutely, she nodded.

" 'If you are lacking in faith,' " Cheng muttered, " 'others will fail you.' " He regarded her sadly. "Perhaps you believe Confucius decreed that each man is allowed just so many beautiful dawns, so many years or months or days of happiness."

Lian was disconcerted by the truth in what he said. She had not realized how she felt until he put it into words. Chills rose along the back of her neck. "It cannot continue. It is too good to go on forever."

"You are wrong, oh foolish one. There is nothing on this earth that is too good, only that which is unappreciated or taken too much for granted." He rose, pacing in a tiny circle that expressed his agitation.

Firmly, he took her shoulders in his clawlike hands. "Know this, Li-an. Hear me. Your future is in your hands and no one else's."

"I do not believe that."

"The exalted one says, 'Curses and blessings do not come through gates, but man himself invites their arrival.' I repeat, it is your choice."

"The exalted one also says: 'Pearls belong of right to her whose soul reflects the color of youth's purity.' I am not certain I ever knew the purity of youth. I expect no pearls; I must be content with colored stones."

"And Émile Drouard?" Cheng demanded. "Is he nothing but a colored stone? Do you think so little of him? Because he does not hide what he feels for you."

"I know that he feels friendship and desire." She faltered on the last word. She did not discuss such things, especially not with her friend and teacher.

The old man leaned on the cutting tray so Lian had no choice but to meet his gaze. "He feels much more than that."

She tensed. "Then he is hiding the truth from me."

"Perhaps you are not looking. Did you ever guess you might be hurting him, thinking always of the loss to come? That you are giving him less than he deserves?"

Head bowed, she murmured, "I hope not. We agreed. He knew—"

"An agreement is merely words; it cannot shape the emotions, or stop them from growing as they will. Émile is only human, after all." He paused, considering her intently. "You never realized you had the power to hurt him," he said in amazement. "And most certainly you will not give him the power to hurt you."

Unnerved by his appraising stare, Lian replied unwisely, "It will hurt to lose him."

"But you need not. I have tried to tell you so."

Unblinking, still as stone, Lian replied, "You have tried."

Cheng raised his hands, the palms impressed with the texture and fragrance of dandelion. " 'When a man has been burned once with hot soup, he forever after blows upon cold rice,' " he muttered in helpless anger—at the gods, his own ineptitude and Lian's obstinance. A sheen of tears blurred his rheumy black eyes.

"Besides, we are different, Émile and I. There is no place where our worlds meet. He does not take life seriously," Lian insisted. "He is too quick to make a joke, as if laughter can make problems disappear." Because she was afraid he would tire of her many sorrows, she spoke heedlessly, condemning what she valued most.

Cheng saw Lian grow pale, but wisely did not comment. "Perhaps laughter is his defense. He tries to smooth the harsh edges, so they cannot wound himself or others. You would be wise to follow his example. Do you not know that every Parisian is a child at heart? Many come from far away simply to discover their childhood."

Lian stood unmoving. "I do not know how to be a child," she said with a melancholy that wrung Cheng's heart. She regarded him wistfully, eyes full of longing. "I do not think I ever did."

15

"Shhhh!" Yi-niang hissed unnecessarily. "All in the house of Chin are asleep and you'll wake them if you're careless. You must make no sound." Peering dramatically, suspiciously from side to side, the girl tiptoed through the kitchen with elaborate caution.

"Since they're asleep, it's easy for them to be silent. Less easy for me; I am awake." Mei's voice quivered, and she glanced timidly over her shoulder, certain the two would be discovered.

Yi shook her head in disgust as she fiddled with the locks on the back kitchen door. Though Mei yearned and languished and pined for her young love, it had taken Yi weeks to convince her sister to meet him at night, when they would be unobserved and need not hide from curious neighbors. Then Yi had planned carefully to engineer the "escape," wishing all the while that it was she who was sneaking away.

She pulled the door open as soundlessly as possible, guiding Lin-Mei toward the narrow gap. "Don't forget to put your head down as you duck across the road in the glow of the gaslights. After that you should be safe. I'll make certain the locks are open when you return."

Mei turned on the top step. "But what if someone sees me?"

Rolling her eyes in exasperation, Yi whispered, "I've told you already. How can they know who you are, dressed like that? Now, go have your adventure or all my planning will be wasted." She sounded wistful. "Go!"

Mei went, stumbling in the loose dark cotton Chinese trousers and tunic Yi had discovered in the attic. Her sister had tied Mei's hair back with a blue silk scarf, then twisted it up under a shapeless gardener's hat. Yi was right, beneath a full moon, Lin-Mei was unrecognizable. Nevertheless, she kept to the shadows until she found the break in the tall, tangled barrier of box hedges, bushes and shrubs that edged the grounds of the chateau.

Mei paused beneath a poplar, gathering her courage before she crossed Chemin de Marie into a swaying wilderness of tall grass and daisies, then ducked under a chestnut tree. Light filtered through the leaves of the huge old tree, making black lace patterns on the ground. She ducked across Rue Verchamps, head down, caught in the light for a few moments before she reached the reeds and ferns clustered around the lake. Only then did she feel safe.

With each step, her heart beat more loudly in her ears,

and by the time she reached the far end of Lac de Bois, where François Duchamps had built a charming stone bridge nearly twenty years ago, her breath was coming in short gasps. As Mei tripped up the curved incline, Tai glided out of the shadows from the other side. He had come the same distance, but from the opposite direction.

Tai and Mei met in the middle of the bridge, leaned on the edge and stared down at the water, over which a light mist lay.

"You had no trouble?" he asked when her breathing had settled.

She looked up, beaming, her dark eyes luminous. "Nothing could have stopped me." Her sister would have been astounded to hear it.

Tai could not help it; he drew her close and kissed her again and again, as delighted by her refusal to be daunted as he was by the sweet, warm pressure of her lips. "You are wonderful," he murmured.

He had looked forward to meeting her, but not until he saw her welcoming smile and extraordinary eyes did he realize what a beautiful night it was. The moon was high and full, in the distance a nightingale sang, and nearby, the water lapped rhythmically on the shore, underscored by the cicadas.

When Mei laughed, the ducks floating on the surface rose with a muted flapping of wings and escaped in graceful formation across the broad face of the moon. "For our pleasure, I am certain," she said.

"You almost make me believe it." Taking her hand, Tai led her off the bridge to a small clearing. Behind it the woods grew thick and green, like a forest of soldiers protecting their backs.

From his pack he produced a blanket, baguettes, cheese and a bottle of chrysanthemum tea. But for the moment, they were hungry only for each other. They clung together, kissing and laughing. Tai knocked the hat from her head so her hair tumbled around her shoulders. He unfastened her scarf and used the long, fine length of silk to bind their wrists together loosely, as if he were performing a sacred ceremony. When he'd finished, they raised their hands, first palm to palm as if in prayer, then spreading their hands outward. Tilting their hands, they made enough space to lean close and kiss, with the scarf brushing their chins and their thumbs cupping their cheeks.

"I see why you can't be a banker, Yen Tai. You have too much imagination. You'd rather make beautiful things." She indicated the elegant weave of the silk around their wrists.

"Or look at them," he replied, watching her face in the moonlight.

Mei blushed. She was not accustomed to being complimented, had always believed she was plain, especially when she compared herself with Wan Lian, whose delicate features and exceptional blue eyes were so lovely. Monsieur and Madame Chin seemed to prefer European beauty, which Lin-Mei could never hope to attain. So she became uncomfortable when Tai called her beautiful.

He shook his head, lowering their intertwined wrists. "You've been listening to others again; I can tell," he admonished her. "About this, at least, you must hear only me, for I am the one in love with you."

"Are you? Truly?" Tai's eyes shone with admiration and affection, and he turned his hands within the scarf to lock his fingers with hers. Though she tried, Mei could not stop her wide, artless smile or the racing of her pulse.

"How can you doubt it?" he said quietly. "I spend every free moment with you, and when we're apart, I am always thinking of you, imagining your face, your smile, your skin, your lips." He gave her a wicked wink. "And I nibble at your glorious earlobe as often as I do at my pastry creations." Caught in her eyes, he asked, "Do you feel the same?"

"How can *you* doubt it, when I risk my father's wrath by seeing you at all?" She chewed her lower lip pensively.

"When I'd rather be with you than anyone, even if you're working on Monsieur Arnaud's account books. I like watching you do figures; you furrow your brow and look quite fierce about it."

They stared at each other in silence; neither was laughing. Tai undid the silken bond and pulled her close. He could feel her breasts against his chest, her rapid breathing, the thundering beat of her heart.

"It's warm tonight," he said suddenly. "And Lac de Bois beckons." Turning away from temptation, he removed his plain cotton Oriental gown, revealing common French woolen drawers.

Slightly dazed, Mei nevertheless nodded. She wanted to feel the water on her tingling skin and warm face. Without hesitation, she tossed away her loose tunic and trousers. She wore a soft muslin chemise underneath, edged with lace at neck, sleeves and hem, which came to just above her knees.

She did not protest when Tai grabbed her hand and ran toward the lake, though she waited demurely on the bank while he plunged head first beneath the surface. For a moment, the silvery liquid churned and bubbled, then his head appeared. He shook away the great drops that whirled about him in a wild, glittering ring.

"You seem to be in a great hurry. Surely the warmth of the night did not overwhelm you so suddenly," Mei observed, testing the water with one foot.

Tai was glad she could not see his expression. She might be innocent, but she was not foolish. "We don't have forever. I didn't want to waste any time," he lied.

Wading out till the water came to her thighs, Mei dove under. The water running along her body felt lovely as she made her way toward the center.

Tai's arms closed around her, and despite his resolve, he kissed her hungrily. She gave herself to that kiss as she would have given her spirit if she could.

"Let's swim," he suggested in a strangled voice.

When they grew tired, they flipped to their backs. They floated side by side, one arm stretched out over the water's surface, the other supporting one another's shoulders. The undulation of the water was a gentle caress up and down their backs. Lightning bugs darted and dragonflies hovered above the surface while a tall willow swayed on the bank, its graceful, feathery branches gilded from above.

Eventually, Mei and Tai climbed out, heavy and dripping beneath the willow, wringing as much moisture out of their underclothes as they could. They paused several times to kiss and cling to one another's hands, so their progress was slow. When they'd stamped away as much moisture as they could, Tai stood behind Mei, grasped her thick hair and smoothed the water out a little at a time.

She tilted her head, loving the motion of his hands as they brushed her shoulders and back. Finally, she straightened. "If you're thinking it will dry while you stand there, you're wrong. We would be here well past dawn. Come, I'm hungry."

"Yes." The single word was enigmatic as her hair slid from his hands.

They returned to the blanket, where he poured out tea and divided baguettes, concentrating on the task so he would not stare at her wet chemise clinging to her breasts, outlining her nipples, raised by the chill of the breeze. Finally, he produced fresh strawberries, watching in delight as she bit into them and let the juice run down her chin, catching it in her cupped palm.

"I didn't think I'd ever be hungry again after dinner. How did you know?" Mei was always astonished at how much Tai knew about many things—things she cared about or needed or desired.

"I know *myself*." His answer was abrupt. He had caught another glimpse of the thin white fabric clinging to her skin. His body was hungry as well, but he could not tell her that. He stretched out so he could not see her from the front.

"Something is wrong," Mei said. "I sense it. Please tell me."

She ran her fingers lightly over his dark hair, and that was his undoing.

"Lin-Mei," he managed, "when I see you like this, I wish to do things, to touch—"

"Then why don't you? I like it when you touch me."

Though it was long past time, no one had ever told her about the allure of her body, about what happens between men and women, about physical desire and yearning, about passion and danger, right and wrong.

Yen Tai knew this and refused to take advantage of her ignorance. "I care about you too much, Lin-Mei. There are things that can only happen between husband and wife. That, at least, is the same in Chervilles as it was in the Middle Kingdom. You must trust me, little flower."

Braiding her fingers together thoughtfully, Mei remembered things she had not understood, conversations cut off at her arrival, pictures she had seen in a secret book. Such moments had confused her, yet no one would explain. "You know I trust you. You know I'm only happy with you. At home they watch me and try to change me, make me into someone I do not know. I feel they're suspicious of me and Yi, as if we're trying to hurt them by refusing to enjoy what they think we should enjoy, learn what they think we should learn. And when we go to Paris, I'm unwanted, disliked."

She sighed and leaned on her elbows so her face was level with Tai's. "I wish I could be with you always."

"I would like nothing better. But we are too young, our families too close, this town too small. You're only sixteen. You might change your mind, find another—"

Mei put her hand over his mouth. "I will not change my mind. I will not find another. I love you, Yen Tai."

Oddly, he believed her. Chin Lin-Mei had never had

anything to fight for. Now that she did, her determination alarmed him. Because she was so chaste, so innocent, so vulnerable. "I think we'd better go." He had to struggle to get the words out.

She looked hurt, as if he doubted her. Yen Tai rose and took her in his arms. "I know you love me as I love you. But we must be patient, or we might ruin any chance of being together. Will you listen to me? Believe me? I don't want you for a few moments if it means losing you for a lifetime. That is one risk I will not take."

Mei smiled. He looked so strong, so wise, and yet so lost. "I will listen. I believe. I will even wait, though that will be most difficult of all."

Yen Tai did the only thing he could—he kissed her again.

With the blanket around her chilly body, Tai walked Mei home. Both had replaced their clothes, but their under things were not yet dry and the water seeped through the lightweight cotton. They crept around the side of the orchard, and with one last, heated kiss, he bid her good night, glad to know that at least she was safe.

When she'd heard his footsteps fade, Mei turned toward the back of the house, realizing too late there was a gaslight on to welcome her. She was staring at the ground, puzzling over the things Tai had said, when she stepped into the circle of light. She stopped short at the sight of her father's grim face.

Behind him, in the gray light of the kitchen, she caught a glimpse of Yi, pale and frightened, wringing her hands helplessly. Their father must have discovered Mei's absence and guessed she would have left by the back door. Mei inclined her head slightly. Yi hesitated, formed the silent words, "I'm sorry," and disappeared. The older girl took a deep, shuddering breath as her father's face filled her vision.

Chin Yun looked his eldest daughter over from head to toe, noticing the mud on her servant's slippers and the hem of her trousers, the damp stains down her front, the heavy swathe of her still-wet hair. Most damning of all were her lips, parted in a secret smile, and the dreamy distant look in her eyes.

Lin-Mei stood, frozen by her father's expression—grave and accusing. His eyes were hard and black, and for the first time all night she felt cold and began to shiver.

16

LIAN HAD LEFT THE BALCONY DOORS OPEN WIDE TO ALLOW the late spring air inside, along with the glow from the full moon, which bathed the room in a mellow light. The gas lamps flickered in the breeze, casting alluring shadows over the floor and along the walls. The fragrance of roses drifted through the flat, tantalizing in its subtle sweetness.

Lian and Émile had just returned from a walk that took them along the lake, rippled silver in the moonlight, and beyond, to the edge of the forest.

They sprawled, heads close together against the wall, in the center of a particularly rapid current of the Seine, a boat bobbing above them. Émile turned his head, smiled, and stopped admiring the painting of the river to admire the curve of Lian's neck. He nuzzled the exposed skin, and she reached up so her deep green sleeve flowed over his shoulder with the soft murmur of satin.

Lian smiled at the sight of Émile's legs stretched out before him, his wool socks rumpled. He had discarded his boots, which lay on their sides next to his gray fedora. His blond hair was tousled from the night breeze, his skin ruddy above his curly beard. His hazel eyes glistened, more green than brown in the warm light of moon and low-burning lamps. He looked completely comfortable and at home.

It is good what you have with Émile, is it not? Cheng had asked pointedly. It was good. Better than she could have imagined. She was amazed at how easy and natural she felt with him.

Lian pushed the thought aside, rose and held out her hand in silent invitation. Émile closed his fingers over hers and brushed the back of her palm with his lips. "You are cool tonight, *ma chérie.*"

She smiled enigmatically as he rose, sliding his arm around her waist. They crossed the parlor, pausing to bask in the feathery light of the moon that spilled over the floor. Leaning her head against Émile's shoulder, Lian noticed a letter from Ailsa lying on a chair where she had been reading it earlier. Her sister had written of the moonlight, hadn't she? What had she said? Ailsa's words hovered at the edge of her mind, then faded into the shadows as Émile lifted her in his arms and carried her toward the bedroom.

The red silk lantern cast a warm glow over Lian's skin as Émile removed her tunic, exposing smooth shoulders, the curve of her back, the delicate shape of her small breasts. When she stepped out and away, he draped the gown over a chair and began to unweave her braid. He caught his breath, aroused, as always, by this simple ritual. She sighed as he kissed her neck and then her shoulder, trembling as he drew her hair around him like a cloak. For a long time, they stood unmoving while she leaned into him and he breathed in her scent. She could feel his heart pounding against her naked back, and she melted in his arms, murmuring his name.

Émile removed his own clothes while she slipped into bed. She enjoyed the sight of his body, tall and imposing, his broad shoulders and long, strong legs making a shadow like a giant's on the wall. The silk-tinted light softened the curves and angles of his face.

Lian smiled and reached for him, unaware of how defenseless, how irresistible she looked with her arms outstretched and her breasts half-covered by the duvet. In a moment, Émile was beside her, holding her close, his hands moving up her back and down again. She kissed the golden hair on his chest, teasing one nipple and then the other. Then he leaned down to kiss her, nibbling at her lips until she put her arms around his neck and opened her mouth to him. As the heat rose within her, the conflagration he conjured with hands and mouth and body transformed her into pure, smoldering sensation. Fevered as she was, she trembled when chills rose on her skin and he warmed them away with his open palms. Leisurely, he stirred awake every nerve and tissue; there was no part of her he did not melt and then re-form with clever, gentle hands.

Finally, he groaned and covered her body with his as desire swept away control. They shuddered and held tight, gasping in exultation as they rocked and clung, cried out into each other's mouths at the ferocity of their need. He moaned her name, burrowing his face in her hair, and together they filled each other with flame and shimmering light and haunting colors.

Afterward, they lay side by side, filmed in sweat. They talked of Henri Arnaud's influenza, which Cheng had stopped from spreading through the neighborhood, of Mei and Tai's growing affection, the increasing difficulty of keeping their meetings secret, of Monsieur Chin's inflexible attitude about his daughters and their needs. They spoke of the aristocrat who had bought one of Émile's paintings. "My first," he said, unable to conceal his delight. "It won't ever feel the same as this again. Though he seemed interested in seeing my other work."

Lian smiled with him, feeling his pleasure as her own. "Did your patron introduce you? Is that not usually how it happens?" She asked partly out of curiosity and partly out of mischievousness. Émile often teased her, made her laugh at her own foibles, but there was little she could tease him about.

As she expected, he colored and cleared his throat uncomfortably. After a pause that lingered a little too long, he said, "I believe that is often the case."

She had thought he would avoid the significant part of her question; now she was amused and intrigued. "I begin to think," she said, "that either your patron is so ridiculous that you are embarrassed to acknowledge him"—Émile closed his eyes as if in pain. He should answer her; she deserved the truth. But he could not find the words—"Or, better still, he is a she—a woman of great wealth, also greatly unattractive, who wants you, not for your talent as a painter, but for . . ." she looked up and down his naked body, "other attributes."

Groaning, he tried to keep his face impassive, but his discomfort was obvious.

"Or perhaps you do not have a patron," Lian mused, lips pursed, brow furrowed in thought, as she tapped her chin with her forefinger. "You might work for the government after all, I suppose, but you would make a dreadful spy, so it cannot be that. Besides, I have never seen an official dressed as well as you, and since they have no taste, they would not have recognized your potential, nor taken you on in the first place. And from what I have seen, the morals police have altogether less taste and intelligence. They would have been terrified by your cutting wit, if they had the intellect to understand it, and intimidated by your air of elegance and refinement. No." She rolled over, staring up at the ceiling. "I cannot see it at all." She counted three revolutions of the lantern before he responded.

"At least you have enough sense to discount the ridiculous stories the others seem determined to repeat. Why do they believe there must always be a villain?" His tone was light, but she felt the tension in his body. "You're very curious tonight."

"I was teasing you, Émile. Only you forgot to laugh."

He brushed her cheek with the back of his fingers. "Forgive me, *mon amour*. When I cannot laugh at myself, I have become too serious indeed. It's my pride, you see. I forgot to warn you; pride is my particular sin. Ah, I have surprised you. You wouldn't have guessed it, would you? But it's true. Never forget that it is true."

They fell silent, fingers intertwined, each thinking their own thoughts. When the lantern swayed, infusing the moving shadows with color, Lian murmured to herself,

> "Today a plum leaf fell onto my shoulder.
> I could not feel its weight,
> though I knew it was there—
> tiny and lovely—resting easy,
> desiring no other place
> but the padded seam of my tunic,
> until a breeze came to lift it away.
> I watched it float and drift and turn
> as I smiled in contentment,
> the sun a caress upon my cheek;
> I remembered your touch
> in the moonlight."

"I haven't heard that one," Émile said.

"It has been drifting through my mind in fragments, but just now the words fell into place and became a poem."

He was touched and leaned over to grope for his trousers where they'd fallen on the floor. He riffled the pockets until he held up the stump of a pencil in triumph.

"What are you doing?" Lian asked, laughing.

"I shall write it on the wall so you'll never forget that you felt this way."

"I will not forget," she murmured.

Émile did not hear. Instead he asked her to repeat the poem line by line, so he could scribble it on the wall beside his pillow.

The sight of his naked back, of the words taking shape and meaning on the wall was lovely in a way that made her ache. The affinity, the intimacy between them was tangible; they had given their trust along with their bodies.

Émile finished his task, then twined his fingers with Lian's. She turned toward him deliberately, gratefully, so they lay face to face, lips nearly touching.

She felt safe and sated, glad that she was not alone. She thought of Ke-ming, of the men she had used and enjoyed. Except for Charles Kittridge. *He was the only man I ever knew who had no secrets in his eyes. He gave me everything and did not ask for more than I could give. There are few men who ask so little yet give so much.*

Like Charles, Émile gave everything and asked only for her company and affection.

Bracing himself on one arm, he gazed at her face, tinted by lantern light, her eyes open but guarded. Gently, he put his hand on her forehead, brushing the tendrils of hair away, resting his palm lightly on her skin.

Lian closed her eyes and leaned into his hand, craving his reassuring touch on her forehead. His palm was cool, the gesture sensual in a way she had not imagined possible, because it was so simple and so fleeting.

Émile felt her pleasure vibrate through his body. "I wish we could lie together continually, so we would always know this feeling."

"Yes," she said drowsily. "Always." Her pulse slowed when she saw the naked, tender look in Émile's eyes. *I know he feels friendship and desire*, she'd assured Cheng.

The old man had shaken his head. *He feels much more than that. Émile is only human, after all.*

As was she. She wanted him so much, needed his tenderness, his compassion. But—

Each time Émile holds you, do you not wonder if it will be the last?

He stared at her stricken face, puzzled. "What is it, *chérie*? Come, let me hold you."

Did you ever guess you might be hurting him, thinking always of the loss to come? That you are giving him less than he deserves?

Émile Drouard deserved a great deal. More, perhaps, than she could give. She went into his arms. "I do not know if I can do this."

I hope you have great energy and persistence, Cheng had warned Émile, *for Wan Li-an is very good at building walls.* "Tell me what you fear."

As always, he knew her too well. She rolled away. "While we lie here, alone, intimate, I can leave the past, forget, live only in my feelings for you, your companionship, your hands on my skin." She could not look at him, but stared fixedly at the silk lantern.

"I know it's easier to talk to the lamp because it doesn't glare or demand, but neither does it respond." He had heard the misery in her tone and was trying to make her smile, though he could guess what was coming. *Remember, patience is your greatest weapon, the best gift you can give her.* Cheng was no fool.

She turned to face him. "You are right. I am taking the coward's way."

"You're saying you're afraid of *me*?" Still, he spoke lightly, as if he were joking. *Émile, my friend, to Wan Li-an you have transformed yourself into the most dangerous of men, because you made her feel safe.*

"Not of you. Of myself." Sighing, she caressed his naked shoulder. "I am too comfortable with you. It is too easy to forget—"

"To be careful? To be vigilant?" His smile was rueful.

Lian tangled her fingers in the golden hair on his chest, feeling the steady beat of his heart. Tears stung her eyes. "Many have tried to make me believe I need not doubt everyone or question their motives—Mairi Rose, my sisters, Cheng and especially you." She kissed him, drawing away with reluctance. "You, above all others, make me believe in trust and loyalty and faith. Here." She pressed her open hand to her chest. "But I cannot be certain I will ever learn those lessons in my head, deep inside where my instincts lie." *If you are lacking in faith, others will fail you.*

"I know that. I understand." *You must take the walls down stone by stone, until the breach is too wide to be repaired; then you must keep her from escaping through it.*

"To understand is one thing, Émile. To live with it another."

I'm strong enough for your difficult task. I'm not a man to reject a challenge, Émile had declared. But what Lian said was true. He wanted to say it didn't matter whether she could overcome her doubts. But he knew it would not be easy to live each day, go to sleep each night wondering if he might wake to find her crying out, soaked in sweat with bloody palms. To wonder if he might walk in one day to find her sitting like a statue, lost in a past he could not imagine. Émile was not certain he could withstand that pain, that despair and helplessness again.

"I have come far," Lian whispered, "but I cannot make my past disappear. No matter how hard I fight." *Know this, Li-an. Hear me. Your future is in your hands and no one else's.* She examined the crescent scars across her palms.

Go, my children. By all means, go. The danger increases by the moment, I suspect. Cheng was wiser, perhaps, than even he knew.

When Émile said nothing, Lian thought she understood. *You never realized you had the power to hurt him.* She hadn't known, but she did now. "I see your easy laughter, your honesty, your unabashed pleasure in living. You deserve someone who can give you openhearted affection in return. You will never know what it is to wake from a nightmare, surprised to find you are alive. I pray to the gods it will always be so." *I do not know how to be a child.* "You deserve someone who is like you."

He took her hands between his. "I've found someone better."

She shivered at his touch. *It is too good to go on forever,* she had cried. "You are too good." Against her will, her fingers intertwined with his. *There is nothing on this earth that is too good, only that which is unappreciated or taken too much for granted.* "I know that happiness such as this does not come without obligations. There is always a toll."

"You have it wrong, *chérie.* There is no recompense to make."

Unable to withdraw from his caress, his stirring voice, Lian faced him squarely. "I want you too much, care for you too much, need you too much. That frightens me." *Most certainly, you will not give* him *the power to hurt* you.

Émile tensed when her words sank in and he realized he, too, was afraid. Never before had he become so entangled that he feared he could not break free. He knew Lian had seen it in his eyes and it had hurt her deeply.

With great care, with regret, in torment, he murmured, "I have business in Marseilles for the next fortnight. We've been together nearly every day. We've acted too quickly, instinctively, with no time for thought. Only passion. Perhaps . . ."

"Yes." Her voice was little more than a whisper, as insubstantial as the lantern flame. "It is wise to take time, to think, to consider . . ." Finding no more words, she trailed off as he had, forlornly, as if she were lost.

"I'll write," he promised. "It won't be long."

"No. A fortnight. Not long at all."

When she turned, eyes downcast, Émile caught her, pulling her close. Cheek to damp cheek, they collapsed among the pillows, holding each other so tightly that they ached, so tightly that, when they finally fell asleep, they lay tangled inextricably together.

17

"HURRY!" CHIN YI-NIANG HAD CRIED. "HE IS WAITING. BUT be back in twenty minutes. I don't know how long I can keep them away."

Her younger sister had disappeared, leaving Mei in an unaccustomed panic. She wasted precious moments looking frantically for her scarf, realized she didn't need it and made her way awkwardly to the narrow door she and Yi had discovered soon after they moved into the house. She knocked a rosewood shelf askew, righted it, then stumbled on a wrinkle in the Persian runner in the seemingly endless hall.

Barefoot, wearing a pale rose gown not fastened properly in back, she opened the door as she heard raised voices and scurrying steps upstairs. When the night air struck her, cool with the breeze off the river, she straightened her shoulders. "Think, Mei," she told herself sternly. "This might be your only chance."

Following Yi's instructions, she ran for the flowering rose tree well back from the house. She saw a figure in the darkness and hurled herself forward until she reached Yen Tai's arms.

He held her close, drawing her with him to the far side of the tree where the twisted branches and massive red blossoms hid them from the house. "How long?" he whispered against her lips.

"Fifteen minutes," she replied breathlessly. "Yi's creating a distraction. She wouldn't say more than that; I think she enjoys the mystery."

Her heart was beating so fast he was afraid she might faint. Then he realized it was his own. "She is astonishing, your little sister. It was clever, managing to slip a note beneath the linen in the basket Gabrielle brings for the baked goods every morning." He cupped Mei's face in his hands with great tenderness. "She says you're a prisoner, that your father found us out and won't allow you to leave the house."

"I may go into the courtyard and about the grounds, so long as Madame Garat, the new governess, is with me, watching." Mei hung her head, unable to meet his gaze. "It's all my fault. I should have been more clever. My father caught me in my wet clothes, sneaking into the house. He wouldn't leave me alone till I admitted I'd been seeing you."

Yen Tai hugged her so tight that she gasped for breath. "It's not your fault. It would have happened sooner or later. I'm only glad you're not ill. When you didn't come for so long, I thought . . ." He trailed off. He did not want to put into words the things he had imagined might have happened to her. He pulled her close again, his cheek on the crown of her head. "At least you're safe."

Mei tried to look up, to see his face, but he wouldn't release her. "What will we do?" she murmured against his shoulder. "I'll go mad with boredom, though my honorable mother noticed I'd grown pale. Now they're talking of sending me to a school in Paris—" She broke off. "I can't bear being without you. Not seeing you every day. There's a weight in my chest so dark and heavy that sometimes I can barely breathe."

When he remained silent, she wriggled out of his arms and grasped his shoulders. "They'll hate me in Paris. My mother doesn't want to believe it, but it's true. Even if they accepted me, how could I stay there without you?"

It was more than a question, and Yen Tai knew it. She was asking him to do something to make her parents free her from the lovely but constricting prison of the chateau. More than that, she was asking him to find a way to stop them from sending her away. And last, most crucial of all, she was asking him to find a way for them to be together openly.

His arms and legs felt like lead, and when he swallowed, the air burned his throat. "Surely Mademoiselle Lian can convince them the school is inappropriate." He felt her tense, and the air now seared the inside of his chest. He felt foolish, helpless, weak. Yet he knew in his heart there was nothing he could do. Not now. Not for a long time. "They can't keep you here forever. Eventually you'll be free to roam Chervilles again. Then we'll think of a way to meet now and then."

Mei took a full step back, away from him, from the despondent blur of his face to the defeated slump of his shoulders. " 'Now and then' isn't enough. It will never be enough. Help me, Tai. I'm so unhappy." She held out her hands, palms up. "Please."

" 'Great happiness often leads to greater unhappiness,' " he whispered so she could not hear. She was breaking his heart, tearing him in two with her pallid face, the dark bruises under her eyes, the plea in her voice, her reaching hands—empty hands that he had no power to fill. "I have thought and thought, but I don't see how, unless we change your parents' minds."

Swallowing her disappointment, which tasted bitter and made her feel ill, Mei shook her head. She did not withdraw her hands, which were trembling now. "They will not change. Though they would deny their heritage, one thing they brought with them from China, buried so deep inside that they don't know it's there—the belief in the absolute necessity of filial piety and obedience, and an unalterable stubbornness."

She reached up to touch Tai's cheek, cool and smooth beneath her fingers. "We are the only ones who can change our destiny. I pray secretly at the family altar every night for an answer, a release. I thought, perhaps if I saw you, if we talked . . ."

"There's nothing we can say that will change this dreadful circumstance. We can only be patient and wait and believe that our time will come." Yen Tai closed the space between them, wider by far than it had been a few minutes past, and kissed her gently, then demandingly.

She leaned against him in despair, opening her lips to him as she had once opened her heart. Too late now to close that door inside. Too late to alter her dreams of him each night. To late to forget the feel of his fingers on her skin. He could not help. She must accept that. Accept it and take as much pleasure as she could now, with his arms warm around her and his mouth against her mouth. Lin-Mei breathed in his breath, holding it for as long as she could, felt tears sting her eyes when he held her face in his hands and looked long and yearningly into her eyes.

It would have to be enough for both of them. For now.

When he'd gone and she'd crept back inside, closing the door behind her, she clenched her hands into fists. If Yen Tai could not help, then it was up to her.

Lian leaned against the bin of garlic bulbs in the apothecary shop, regarding the counter crowded with vials and ointments and seaweed packets. The scent of herbs and musk, the incense burning at the four corners of the room, the cool dimness and Cheng's presence combined to give her a sense of safety. Here was a refuge that could not be violated.

"I can see why your customers return so often, even when they are not ill." She concentrated on the dish of healing plaster that Cheng fashioned into the shapes of birds. The plasters themselves were black and unpleasant, but when put directly on an open wound, they rarely failed to draw out the poison.

Uncomfortably aware of the old man's searching gaze, she roused herself and went to the mysterious back room to gather supplies for the day. She had asked Cheng once what he did there when he was alone and the shop closed and silent.

I experiment. I mix and test, guided by intuition and my fancy as well as my knowledge of herbs. But until I have in my hands something correct in its balance and purpose, I will say no more. That, Li-an, is my little secret.

Today she barely noticed the room that usually fascinated her. Her thoughts were elsewhere. Having collected her supplies, she turned to go, then caught a glimpse of something glittering on the narrow counter at the far end of the sink. She felt compelled to follow that gleam—bright and unexpected in the gloom. When she reached it, she bit her lip and pressed her hand to her chest.

On the battered surface lay Émile's mahogany cane with a lion's head of gold. Beside it was his gray fedora, tossed casually, as if he had just stepped out for a moment. Hat and cane did not look out of place; they looked as if they belonged.

Choking on the pervasive fumes, she stumbled back into the shop, pulse pounding. "Émile Drouard has been here. You have seen him," she accused Cheng.

He tilted his head solemnly. "I meant to tell you he had returned this morning, but you did not ask. He wanted you to ask, I think."

Lian raised her chin and stood motionless—tall, slender, erect. "He once told me pride was his greatest weakness." She clasped her hands together tightly. "I, too, am proud. It is not easy for me to ask. Especially when I care so much about the answer." She flushed at the admission, at Cheng's startled expression. "Are you surprised it should be so?"

He was not surprised at her feelings, only that she had expressed them so openly. She had grown unusually quiet and self-contained in the weeks Émile had been away on business. Cheng had not ventured to ask her why. In his heart he already knew the answer. Her eyes had betrayed her—tinted gray with uncertainty one moment, bright blue with hope the next.

"I have wanted to ask numerous things," Lian admitted, glancing away so her old friend could not read her thoughts. "I blotted and crumpled countless sheets of rice paper in writing to Émile." She paused, looking inward. "But I have written him many poems. I even painted one on the wall beside my pallet."

She remembered holding the brush in her hand, stroking the ink over the plaster, wishing her fingers were curled in Émile's hair. She remembered all too well how it felt when he lay beside her, hand on her forehead, teasing her with affection. She remembered his smile and the sight of his legs stretched out, rumpled socks visible, boots forgotten. "How is he? He says he is well, but—?"

Cheng raised her chin with one gnarled finger and answered the question she had not asked aloud. "Émile has never hidden his devotion. What do *you* think, little jade?"

A flush of color reddened her cheeks. "I . . . think he is not a man of mercurial moods. He does not change easily. But to know that in my head does not soothe the uncertainties in my heart." She had not guessed she would miss Émile so very much.

"Sit down," her old friend said firmly. "I have something for you."

Dazed by the things she was revealing carelessly, Lian obeyed. Besides, she realized, her limbs were heavy with fatigue.

Cheng drew a scroll from his voluminous sleeve and dropped it in her lap.

Lian looked down warily, untied the ribbon, then stopped. "He gave this to *you?*"

"He was not certain you would welcome it."

There was an uncomfortable tightness in her chest as she unrolled the parchment to find a detailed drawing of Émile's hand, palm up. Every line and curve was familiar, each bent finger and rough callous. He had sent her his open hand. Just that. Then she saw the message scrawled across the bottom: "As the Empress Eugenie once wrote to her dying Napoleon, *'Je t'envoie mon coeur tout plein de toi.'* "

"I send you my heart, completely full of you," Lian whispered. She could not catch her breath. It was the first time he had spoken of love. Always, he had been careful not to cross that line. This, then, was his answer to the question that had echoed from the walls, yet remained unspoken, the last time they lay in each other's arms. All at once she felt giddy with relief and happiness.

Cheng should have been pleased, but instead was uneasy at the hectic color in her cheeks. "I told him, 'One must not expect a lace handkerchief to hold tears,' but he does not always listen."

Lian barely heard him. It was most peculiar, but she felt agitated and uncomfortable, as if her relief had stirred awake impulses in her body that she had been trying to ignore. All at once she bent forward, pressed her fingertips to her temples; her head ached and her stomach churned.

Alarmed at the sudden transformation, Cheng rested his hands on her shoulders. "Are you ill? Let me help you."

Lian tried to deny it, but no sound escaped her parted lips as he counted her pulse, brow furrowed. The touch of his cool fingers felt like heaven on her skin.

"Something is wrong," he declared. "I will make you a decoction, then get you up to bed."

Again she tried to protest, but could not find her voice. Perhaps she *was* ill. The thought surprised and distressed her.

Cheng scurried about collecting tiny bottles and pinches of herbs.

Lian could not watch as the movements blurred and wavered, making her dizzy. It was as if she had been holding herself upright by sheer force of will, and somehow Émile's message had undermined that will. The smell of the shop became unbearable. She slid from her stool and ran to the back room. She vomited, clutching the sides of the sink, until she sank to the refuge of the slatted floor.

From the corner of her eye, she saw Cheng's small room next door, its rice paper doors partially open. There was a simple pallet, and beside it, an oil lamp and ebony chair with a thick embroidered cushion. Slowly, holding her breath against the sickness that broke over her in waves, she made her way to the chair and curled up, her face making a stain of sweat on the ancient silk.

The alchemist found her there, shivering and clutching her stomach. He held a steaming mug in his hands, but he set it on a narrow teak table and knelt beside her. "This is not the first time."

It was not a question, and she realized he was right. She had been preoccupied with wondering about Émile and had dismissed the signs of illness. "It has happened before, though not so violently."

Cheng rubbed his bald head in distraction. "Are you carrying a child?"

Lian looked away in embarrassment. Or was it anger? Now that she stopped to consider, it was true she had missed her monthly flow. She had not wondered why because it had happened before. But she should have guessed that this time might be different. Why did I not think? she berated herself silently. The question, the answer frightened her.

She became aware of Cheng's gaze fixed upon her, unblinking. "It is possible. My body has felt strange of late. Not like my own, as if I wore someone else's skin."

Cheng touched her temple, felt the pulse there, lifted her wrist again and peered closely at her skin and eyes and hair. "You are with child."

Lian felt as if she had walked hard into a closed door. She could not begin to catch her breath.

"Did you not take herbs to prevent such a thing? I have

given you the packets when you asked." Cheng's voice was gentle but firm.

"I used the herbs as my honorable mother taught me, each time Émile and I were together."

Without a word, Cheng took her in his arms and held her while she shivered. "So how can this be?"

"To wonder is useless," he whispered. "It is time to act. You have fooled me, and yourself, it seems, with the appearance of your usual good health. But you are weak and ill; this is not auspicious. I must build up your body so you can withstand the new demands upon it. But there is more than your body to think of." He paused, blew his breath through parted lips and said, "When will you tell Émile?"

Lian lay back, momentarily stunned. "Émile." It was a vow, a breath cut off, a plea. *I do not know what I want,* she had told Mairi Rose in another world, another life. *It is not a question I ask myself.* The time had come to ask. "I think— I wish—"

"Wait," Cheng murmured. "You are distraught. This has come upon you too suddenly. How can you be expected to think sensibly? You must dream and rest, in order to consider your future with care and wisdom." He waited until she stopped shaking, then reluctantly drank the decoction he had made. He waited longer, until the herbs began their work and she grew quiet.

"Now, in this moment, I sense the child is not yet real to you." He paused again, considering, his rheumy eyes distant. "But in any case, you must know Émile deserves to share in this miracle. Remember what Confucius said:

" 'Is any blessing better than to give a man a
son, man's prime desire by which he and his
name shall live beyond himself; a foot for him
to stand on, a hand to stop his falling; so that
in his son's youth he will be young again, and
in his son's strength strong.' "

A tear slid down Lian's cheek. She wrapped her arms close to her body, cradling herself. Of course Émile deserved the truth. He always had, since honesty was the first gift he had given her. Honesty and a refusal to pass judgment. Her thoughts blurred and drifted.

Cheng shook his head in alarm. When her eyelids fluttered, he asked, "Have you eaten in the last day?"

Lian tried to think, but her gaze was vague, unfocused. "I cannot remember." She had not been eating much of late. She was not often hungry.

Now the alchemist was truly concerned.

"First," he said with grim determination, "we must make your body healthy. For you and for your baby. You must stay in bed, rest and re-invigorate your spirit. For now I ask only that you do not give in—not to fear or weakness or the pain of being human. You are stronger than that. You have told me so ten thousand times, and I have believed you.

"So, I will make tea for you, and broth and rice flour dumplings," he said as he lifted her in his arms, despite her protests and started toward the stairs. "Soon you will grow strong and fat and happy, you and your child." Only he heard his own hollow voice. Only he knew how anxious he sounded. And felt.

18

LIAN LAY RESTLESS ON HER PALLET, FROM WHICH CHENG had forbidden her to rise. *We must make your body healthy again. For you and for your baby.* The words echoed in her head, bringing with them jumbled questions. "How could this happen?" she asked. "What will I do, not knowing what Émile will think? How he will feel?" She exhausted herself with the need for answers that did not come. Her feelings were so confused she did not know if she was glad or desperate or if inside, hope was beginning to stir itself awake.

At Cheng's insistence, she nibbled on rice flour dumplings, sipped hearty broths and teas and herbal decoctions. "This is marjoram with chamomile and gentian to soothe your stomach and improve your appetite," he told her needlessly, for she knew as much about such cures as he. "I have violet tea and peppermint for your headaches, powdered crows' liver to build up your blood, and hawthorn leaf to give you strength."

I ask only that you do not give in, he had told her, *not to fear or weakness or the pain of being human. You are stronger than that.*

She knew he was wise to insist. She felt hollow, felt the need to fill that hole and nurture the scrap of life growing inside her. Often, she rested her hand protectively on her stomach, an instinctive and involuntary gesture. "What of Émile?" she asked. "I want to see him, to explain, but—"

The old man tugged at his wispy beard, deep in thought. "I believe it would be better if you do not face him just yet, at least not for a day or two. Wait until you are more yourself, in your heart and in your head. I know it is difficult," he added when he saw the glitter of defiance in her eyes, "but it is wiser and safer for both of you."

Propped on her elbow, she regarded him steadily. "What is truly difficult is lying here, useless and helpless." One or two days seemed like an eternity, yet also a respite. She half sat up and realized ruefully *why* she was confined to her bed. She had worn herself out in missing Émile, used herself up in ignoring the clamoring discomfort of her body. The knowledge only frustrated her more.

"You will never be helpless, Li-an, of that I am certain." Cheng was pleased by her outburst. "But you must give yourself time to adjust to your condition."

"Yes," she said, smiling wistfully. "Time will make all things right."

* * *

The next morning the door opened softly, the rhythm of quiet footsteps moved toward the bedroom.

"Lian?" a timid voice whispered. "Are you—?" Chin Lin-Mei stopped in the doorway, rigid with shock.

Though it was not proper or polite, though it went against all she had been taught, the girl stared at Wan Lian sleeping on her pallet. Her skin was paler than usual, perhaps from being so long inside, and she was sleeping deeply. She did not stir at the sound of the girl's voice. She must be very weary to be so oblivious, Mei thought. It wasn't like Lian. She was always alert, conscious of every sound; she sensed when someone entered the room long before she could see them. She did not look ill, but certainly she was not herself. She seemed fragile somehow, vulnerable.

Mei was speechless and bit back tears. Her teacher, her friend had always been strong, healthy, wise. Lin-Mei had thought her invincible. She was ashamed of a momentary impulse to turn away.

"Mei," Lian said, awakened by the pull of staring eyes. "You are here."

The girl started at the sound of the familiar voice and wondered if Lian could read her thoughts in her expression. "Monsieur Cheng told me to go because you were ill. But he was so mysterious, it frightened me. I had to come."

The girl had been weeping all night, thinking of Tai, had known there was only one place to go for solace—to Lian. Desperate to talk, Mei had tried to sneak up the stairs, but Cheng had caught her and sent her away. She had felt rejected, abandoned. As soon as he disappeared, she had returned.

Now she realized she'd been thinking only of herself, had refused to believe in the seriousness of Lian's affliction because she did not *want* to believe it.

"I am glad you did," Lian said. "I have missed you."

The girl was doubly ashamed because she had come for

help and advice, had disregarded Cheng's warning because she needed her friend so much. Now Mei realized she would have to forget about Yen Tai and her own loneliness. Those things seemed far away, like a bad dream.

Because, for the first time, Mei saw that Lian needed *her*. This woman had never failed the two sisters, and Mei could not fail her now. But she did not know how to care for others, only how to be cared for. "I'm very spoiled, aren't I?"

"Of course you are not. It is only that you have seen little of the world. Your parents have protected you from ugliness and pain."

"Perhaps," Mei whispered, leaning close to Lian's warm cheek, laying her head on the pillow. "But now that I've opened my eyes, I will take care of you, Mademoiselle Lian. Yi and I and Cheng together. You've always healed our pain and dried our tears. Forgive me for not noticing you had pain and tears of your own."

"Your parents," Lian repeated, dismayed. "You are not allowed . . ."

"Don't worry. They knew I was coming. They no longer forbid me."

Lian nodded, relieved that Mei was free to visit her again. The girl hesitated as tears filled her eyes. She blinked them back. "I don't know what to do for you. I don't know how to give back what you've given me." Lian's face was blurred by a film of moisture. "But I'll learn. I promise."

She rose abruptly and found the kitchen, groping desperately for something to do. Lian always made tea when things went wrong. Mei could do that at least.

But she found broth on the stove and some boiled chicken and leeks. Apparently Cheng had been preparing a meal when he was called away. With determination, she assembled a tray. She took it to the bedroom, drew a small table near and watched Lian eat, though she took tiny bites and swallowed little.

"I am not hungry," she explained. "Besides, I would rather talk."

With an effort, Mei hid her concern, removed the tray and came back to kneel beside the pallet. "Is there anything—what can I do—"

"Please, just sit. I like you near." The girl's presence was distracting, and the sight of her beloved face soothing.

Mei sat with Lian's hand in her lap, talking quietly in a cadence that seemed to comfort her friend. At last Lian relaxed and drifted back to sleep.

Mei watched her for a moment, then slipped under the reed blind into the nook where the altar to Lian's ancestors stood. Kneeling, the girl began to tremble. Mei let her tears flow, rocking back and forth before the low ebony table. "I love her," she told the gods in a whisper, not quite certain why she was so upset, "and Yi loves her, and I think even my parents, though they don't say so. We need her strength and compassion and goodness. Don't take that from us, please."

She thought of Yen Tai and their separation and the school in Paris. "No," she said sharply. "Those things will wait. I'll have to be patient, as Yen Tai said. Not for our sakes now, but for Lian's."

When she slipped out from under the blind, she met Cheng in the doorway. She started to explain, but he put his finger to his lips and led her to the kitchen.

"I know you told me to leave her be, but I couldn't bear your worried face."

Cheng shook his head, indicating the tray, which she had tidied as best she could, and the food, carefully saved. "You have done well, Lin-Mei. You cared for her and helped her sleep; resting is most difficult."

Mei was ashamed by the praise, because she had been selfish for so long, because she had never before considered Lian's needs or desires, because it took the fear of losing her friend to make her open her eyes.

Putting a reassuring hand on her shoulder, Cheng gave her a small smile. "I know you have your own sorrows and fears, and that you had to push them aside for her. It is not easy, is it, to put someone else's suffering before your own? Yet Wan Li-an has done that all her life. I think, in realizing that, you have suffered more deeply than you thought possible. Yet you did not run. You stayed and tried to give back what she has given you. I am proud of you, Chin Lin-Mei."

Cheeks wet with tears, Mei whispered, "It takes more than one afternoon to repay a lifetime of devotion. My debt is large and weighs heavily upon me."

Taking her other shoulder, Cheng forced the girl to look at him. "Li-an would not want you to suffer such regret. She gave because she wanted to, because it made her happy. Her reward was the friendships with those she loved. I think she would hope only that you find the same pleasure in giving. She would want you to realize how precious is any affection, how necessary, so long as it flows, unlike the river, both ways, from one to the other. Do not grieve for what you have not done, little jade. Only vow to do what you can. That is all Li-an would ask. Your affection, your occasional presence, the sound of your voice to help ease her into her dreams. These small things will give her joy and peace."

19

LIAN WATCHED AS SUNLIGHT AND SHADOW MADE PATTERNS on the floor and tried to find answers there. The silence only increased her deepening determination to recover her health, to face the future squarely. For herself, for the child, for Émile.

Mei and Yi's visits were a welcome distraction. The two

girls helped prepare her food—arguing all the while about the proper amount of this spice or that vegetable—and fed her. She could have done this on her own, but she saw how much it meant to them to feel they were helping, so she allowed them to spoil her. Between meals, they told her stories of their adventures, which she suspected Yi had concocted for the occasion, and when letters from Mairi, Genevra and Ailsa arrived, Mei sat in the rocking chair and read them.

"You're not the only one with eyes in your head, Mei," Yi complained good-naturedly. "You save the best task for yourself because you're older and more selfish."

Lian smiled inwardly, grateful for the sound of young, energetic voices. Then she turned her head and found herself staring at her poem scribbled on the wall in Émile's handwriting. She stared, mesmerized and aching.

> I smiled in contentment,
>   the sun a caress upon my cheek;
> I remembered your touch
>   in the moonlight.

"It's time to get up and let us put clean linen on your bed," Yi announced loudly, breaking the spell.

Lian protested when the two girls put her arms across their shoulders and helped her to the rocking chair. "I am not weak or helpless." Nonetheless, she let them settle her in the chair, smiling fondly while they smoothed new sheets onto her pallet, fluffed the pillows and replaced the duvet.

Her gaze returned to the poem. She was drowning in memories of Émile—his writing on her wall, his arms reaching for her, his heart, which he had given her in a drawing of his open hand, and which he did not know beat literally inside her now.

Listening to Lin-Mei reading from the *Tao Teh Ching*, trying desperately to concentrate, Lian sensed an unusual tautness in the girl's face. "Is something troubling you, Mei?"

The girl fell silent and hung her head. "I can't burden you with my tiny problems when you are unwell."

"I am better every day. Have you not noticed? My thoughts give me no peace, and I would be glad of someone else's problem to consider. Besides, you are very unhappy. I see it, though you hide your face from me."

Ashamed of her intense relief, Mei told her everything.

"But I've thought of a solution," she added. "Yen Tai and I could run away and be married. He is too good to suggest such a thing, so I've been planning."

Reaching out to touch the girl's warm hand, Lian said simply, "No. That is not the answer. You must stay here."

Certain Lian would be her ally, as she had been in the past, Mei was deeply disappointed. "How can I stay when I'm so unhappy?"

"You will learn that such sorrow fades in time. To run would be neither responsible or wise. You are too young to make a wife yet, Lin-Mei, and Yen Tai too young for a husband. Especially if your families cast you out. The pure sweetness between you now would soon turn sour. That would be wrong and would hurt many."

Her eyes were drawn, inevitably, to that poem on the wall.

Upset and unthinking, Mei lashed out. "This child you carry, though you have no husband. Is that not wrong? Its birth will not hurt many?"

Lian was struck silent by the truth, spoken so baldly by such a young girl. Mei was more perceptive than Lian had realized if she'd so easily guessed the secret.

For a long time, she struggled with the emotions that churned within her—apprehension, uncertainty, remorse and, buried deep among them, hope. "The child cannot be wrong," she whispered. "It did not choose to be. But I have been careless and unwise. I should not have let this happen." Before Mei could reply, she added, "Just as you would be careless and unwise to toss aside the gift you have been given. You must stay and try to work things through with your father. I have told you before, he only wants what is best for you."

"You also told me that to fulfill his hopes for me, I should find my own happiness." The girl leaned over to clasp Lian's hand. "I told you I had found it, and every day, it becomes more true. I can only be happy if I'm with Yen Tai. He gave me so much that I'd never imagined. Without him, I have nothing except misery." As if the weight of her sorrow were too great for her slender shoulders, she lay her head on the pallet, weeping and heartbroken.

She spoke with all the passion and certainty of a sixteen-year-old girl in love for the first time. Lian freed her hand to rest it on Mei's blue-black hair. Gently, with regret for a child's dream lost, she ran her fingers through the soft, dark strands. "I felt that once, a very long time ago," she mused. "I felt . . . no I was sure . . . I could not survive without my lover, who was taken from me by cruel injustice. When I knew I would never see his face again, I did not want to go on alone. When the Imperial Guards took him away, they took with him my love, my hope, my joy. I gave him my whole heart, and in giving it, lost it forever. Or so I believed.

"I was older than you, and I knew more, too much, about cruelty and fear and bitterness. I thought I was alone, completely and forever. But I was wrong, Lin-Mei, about so many things. My life did not end with his loss, and I have loved many since, including you. And there are yet many years to come."

There're so many other places, other choices to be made, Mairi had said as they sat in the womb of the Highland glen. *And you've the strength to make them.*

"Mei, my precious one, always remember how lucky you have been, carefree and full of elation, unafraid of your emotions—to feel them, share them, show them. So few ever have that freedom, or realize they have lost it."

Mei stopped weeping and lay still. She wanted to cover her ears to shut out Lian's voice, not because she didn't believe, but because she knew it was the truth.

Aware of the girl's resistance, of the effort it took to listen to what she least wanted to hear, Lian whispered, "You were blessed, for a time, with a pure, untainted joy. You should treasure it always." It was difficult to keep her voice steady. "Only the very young receive that gift. But it cannot last forever. If it did it would lose its shine, its splendor, become ordinary. That would be tragic. It is the fleeting nature of your happiness that makes it so remarkable."

She paused, stroking the girl's hair wistfully. "The innocence of youth fades, but in its place comes a depth of feeling you cannot imagine, a passion so compelling and fulfilling it overshadows all that came before. You cannot always have what you want, little flower, but if you are patient you will have so much more."

Motionless, Lin-Mei stared at the wrinkles in the duvet, letting the words sink in as moisture might sink into the valleys and rivulets of the thick cover.

"Talk to your father. Do not shut him out or think of him as your enemy. He has not a woman's heart, but he is not heartless either."

"I will try," Mei promised. In spite of her heartache, she was curious about Lian's references to her own youth, the cruelty and injustice. She had never spoken of that part of her life, had carefully avoided doing so. "What of *your* father? Did you ease his heart and he yours? Did he want you to be happy?"

Lian stared up at the red silk lantern. "I do not know what my father wanted. I was a very small part of Charles Kittridge's life."

"But he wrote you all those letters. Cheng says you won't even read them. How can you know what he thought or felt or wanted if you're afraid even to look?"

Mei's intensity surprised her, and her perceptions, which

pricked Lian like needle points. The girl was right; she was afraid to know what Charles Kittridge felt. She had tried to forget his letters to an absent child. Before she could change her mind, she called out to Yi, who had been ostentatiously tidying the kitchen while her sister bared her soul. "There is an old packet tied with string in the chest. Could you bring it to me, please?"

Thrilled at the chance to open the ebony chest again, Yi found it quickly. Gingerly Lian took the letters, weighing them in her hand. Slowly, while Yi and Mei watched, openmouthed, she untied the string and spread them on the duvet.

Seeing Lian's expression, Mei nudged Yi. "I think we should leave her alone."

Lian did not notice as they slipped away. Gingerly holding the worn pages, some so yellowed and faded she could hardly make them out, she began to read.

Charles Kittridge's letters were full of his adventures, his exhilaration, his loneliness. In each he spoke of his love for Lian—"my daughter," he called her often. His regrets, guilt, yearning, told her all he'd never had a chance to say out loud.

She ached with pity for the man she had once blamed for her misfortune, a man who had spent many hours sharing his heart and dreams with a daughter he knew would probably never read his words.

Sadness crept up on her like a shadow—for her father, for herself, for the years when she hadn't known he cared. She remembered Mei's soft hair beneath her fingers, the girl's faith in Lian's wisdom, and the memory tore at her heart. Charles Kittridge with three daughters he had never truly known. Lian with a pupil who had become more like a daughter. Within her now, another life beginning.

Lian caught her breath. Touching her stomach with her free hand, she was seized by an invisible burst of illumination. She was carrying a child. A baby of her body and her blood, a life, a miracle. She was struck with wonder and amazement. The shimmering illumination lingered, and for an instant, she felt warm and whole.

20

"I MUST SEE HER!" ÉMILE DROUARD'S VOICE ECHOED FROM the back of the shop. "I need to know she's all right."

Lian sat up abruptly, listening, but the voices had grown dangerously quiet.

The words were indistinct, but Lian knew Émile's tone. He would not wait any longer. She was surprised he had waited three days. At least she was healthier now. But as she rose from the tousled bed, she realized she had not had enough time to untangle her turbulent feelings. Not nearly enough.

When, having made his extraordinary revelation, Cheng disappeared inside the shop, Émile paled, gaping in disbelief. A child? A *child?* Now he understood the old man's wariness, the glitter in his eyes this past fortnight.

Émile ran his fingers through his hair, trying to stop the world from rocking at his feet. "Lian is with child." If he said it aloud, perhaps he could shake himself out of the trance he had fallen into. He did not know how he felt. It was too much to take in, to comprehend.

He stood stiffly, unable to take a step. Here he was, caught in a carefree life of pleasure, of friends and art and laughter, without ties or obligations. That was why, in the beginning, he had been drawn to Lian in her dignified isolation. But that had changed the night he found her kneeling beside the Chinese chest. Changed irrevocably. But a child . . . What should he do now? He was numb; he was amazed; he was mystified.

* * *

Lian dressed blindly, overwhelmed by guilt and expectation.

She knew now that her feelings for Émile Drouard were both devastating and irresistible, but how was she to embrace him with so much unsaid between them? "What am I to do?" she cried to the empty room.

She reminded herself the child was not hers alone; it was also his. *Charles left behind a family. A future different from the lonely past. 'Tis so much, Lian. 'Tis more than enough.* Mairi Rose believed it with all her generous heart and spirit. Could Lian believe it too?

She heard the door slam closed at the bottom of the stairs. Heard Émile's familiar footsteps approach. He opened the door quietly and saw her waiting, watching. She had never been more aware of his physical presence, the width of his strong shoulders and long, muscled legs, the elegance of his movements in contradiction to the solid toughness of his body. His fine-honed cheekbones and aristocratic nose, broad forehead and square chin were softened, the distinction blurred by his wavy blond hair. He was not handsome so much as compelling, and when he smiled and his hazel eyes grew tender, she could not look away.

She stared at his fists, tensed against his sides, and remembered in every detail his square hands, scarred by calluses, his blunt fingers that had touched her with the skill and sensitivity of an artist.

He stopped a few feet away and she wanted nothing more than to grasp his hands and cup them around her face, to lean into him and let his steady heartbeat calm her, as it had done so often.

"Lian."

His voice was rough with a concern that shook her deeply.

But not as deeply as her appearance shook Émile. She

was still slender as a reed. He had expected her to look different, but the change in her was not physical. "I didn't intend to come today, *chérie*, but Cheng told me—"

"Yes," she whispered. She had thought she would be angry, but instead, she was relieved that Cheng had taken the burden from her shoulders.

Émile could not stop staring. Lian's cheeks were flushed with an emotion he could not identify, and she seemed stronger than before, as if forged of steel toughened by fire. "You look well, carrying our child."

The tenderness and wonder in his voice undid Lian. She could not bear his kindness. She took refuge in panic, turning away abruptly.

"I want to marry you." It cost Émile a great deal to keep his tone matter-of-fact. Until this moment, he had not guessed how *much* he wanted this woman and the child she carried.

She glanced down at her stomach, looked up, eyes closed. "Because I am pregnant? To marry for that reason would not be wise, I fear."

"Perhaps, but it's not only because of the child. I've cared for you for a long time, waited patiently, not pressing you for what you felt you could not give. But now things are different."

"Yes. You think they are easier, clearer, but they are only more difficult." She clasped her hands together to hold herself steady. "When we were last together, we were afraid of our feelings for each other. But a child? Is that not more frightening still?"

"It's terrifying. But I've told you before, I won't let your fear defeat me. Nor my own. We are strong enough and wise enough to make this decision together." He sounded less certain than he would have wished.

Lian leaned against the Seine flowing behind her on the painted wall. "I do not think it is kind or fair to bring a child into this world. There is so much suffering and struggle." She held her hands out in a plea. "Do you not see that?"

"What I see," Émile said quietly, "is that *this* world is not the world you were born into." He paced, hands clasped behind his back. "It's true that in China the struggle was hard, the sorrow deep, the decay pervasive. You couldn't escape the poison that tainted mind and heart. You couldn't come away from such horror without dread so deep that it colored everything you did or felt."

He stopped, facing her. "But look around you, Lian. This is a different time, a different life. This world is not perfect, but it does have one thing you never had in China, not even in your mountain retreat with your mother."

"What?" she asked, unnaturally still.

"This world has hope. Enough to build on. Enough to give a child. Hope."

Her eyes were so dry she knew she would weep.

"Think, *mon amour*. Did you ever *really* know hope? I don't believe you did."

Lian wanted to look away, but could not. "You are wrong. I lived on it, breathed it like air, like salvation, until the day I lost Chin Chao. That day I lost everything, except rage and caution and the ability to numb myself. Those were my shields, layer upon layer woven of smoke that kept me safe. There are not many layers left, Émile. You have torn them from me one by one, until the smoke is thin and no longer blurs my sight. If you blow the last of the smoke away, you leave me naked and defenseless."

Émile was shaken, as he always was at the sight of her vulnerability. But he had not been born to surrender quietly. He noticed her hands were cupped over her middle. "Yet you're cradling your belly gently, as if to protect something fragile and precious. You *want* to protect it, give it your strength, no matter the risk or the cost. Part of you wants that."

"You are right. Too often right, I fear."

His heart thudded loudly. "Lian, it's a miracle. Have you never wanted a child?"

Lian gasped as if he'd struck her with the sleek, sharp blade of a Chinese soldier's sword. With difficulty, she caught her breath, staring at the light dancing on the painted surface of the flat silver Seine. "I carried a child once before." She paused, seeking words she had never meant to speak. "She is gone now. I lost her before she was ever born." Stumbling, she turned toward the refuge of the shadows. She remembered how she had sensed from the beginning that it was a girl child, tiny and helpless within her. "I cannot hold this baby in my arms, come to care for it, then lose it. I cannot bear such loss again."

Émile was stunned. "Why are you so certain you will lose it?"

"I was not strong enough to keep my daughter before. My body and spirit and will were not strong enough. And I was still young, resilient." She had silenced him at last. "The other was taken from me. All the others. My mother, my lover, my child, my friend, my father. I could not protect them." Tears streamed down her cheeks but she did not care.

"What makes you think you were *supposed* to protect them?"

Lian could not see through the clear salty rush of her tears. "It is what you do for family, for those you love. Keep them safe."

Émile trembled at the exertion of speaking calmly. "You try, yes, but you can't always succeed." He cleared his throat to give himself time. "There are some things you can't shield another from, no matter how strong you are or how hard you try. Pain, loss, loneliness."

Lian winced.

With a deep breath, he said succinctly, "No matter how much you wish it were different, they make their choices; you make yours. That's as it should be. You *have* choices, Lian, even you."

"Yes. I made a choice once. I chose to keep my child, knowing I would be shunned, that I would be watched and judged and lose the respect of the people. Not only would I be an outcast, but everyone around me as well. I knew it would not be easy, but I was young and passionate and stubborn. Because of me, Chin Chao lost everything except his virtue and his honor."

"We are back to Chao and his legendary honor."

Lian was shocked by the disdain in his voice.

"You say he was virtuous and you weren't. But you told me what happened, how he chose to become a martyr." Émile knew he was treading on dangerous ground, but he was desperate, for Lian as well as himself. "You told me once you needed someone to blame. Yet you say you never, for an instant, blamed Chao."

"I was to blame. I kept the child inside me, though I knew full well the danger. I made the easy choice, he the difficult one."

Émile turned his back so she would not see his fury. "Chin Chao's choice was difficult; he suffered terribly. But nonetheless, it was a smaller risk." He ignored Lian's cry of disbelief. "He knew exactly what would happen when the government turned against him. But with you, his lover, with people, you can't predict the outcome—whether your feelings will strengthen or fade with time, how close you may grow to one another, how dependent. How much they will see of your inner self, how much you'll come to need that insight and intimacy. It's a greater risk, Lian, because it's unpredictable, and therefore frightening."

"He was not afraid!" she cried too loudly. "He was a hero."

"Yes, he *was* a hero, a man with more status than one who stays with his family, has children and raises them to be good people, who loves his wife and learns from her as much as she from him. Contentment is not a sin." Émile placed his hands on the oak table, leaned heavily on the wood until he felt the pits and scratches with his fingertips. "Yet Chin Chao chose China over you, even knowing he would lose."

"He had to. For honor, for pride. To stay with me might have made him happy for a while. But that would have been too easy. To make a family instead of a stand, that would have been weak, cowardly."

Émile leaned harder into the table. "Just because something is easy doesn't make it less valuable or worthy. Just because a man is brave in one way, doesn't mean he's not afraid of his own heart."

"He suffered to show his dedication to the Middle Kingdom." Why did her voice sound so hollow, her protestation so empty?

"And because he suffered, because you suffered for and with him, you became terrified, living in a prison you created out of sorrow and fear, pride and despair. A prisoner, Lian. You don't *have* to suffer to survive. You're allowed a little happiness. Besides, your prison is woven of shadows too fragile to withstand attack; as you say, it will soon disintegrate and you'll yearn for the contentment you turn from now."

She did not reply, her face white and set against the onslaught of his words. They had the far and distant ring of truth. A truth that belied all she had clung to, refusing to set herself free. Her head was whirling and her vision blurred. He had knocked her off-balance and she could not seem to recover her equilibrium.

Unaware of her thoughts, Émile sighed and forced himself to go on. "Yet you're still the strongest of them all. The others stayed behind, remained tied to a land, a civilization that could only destroy them. How much harder, *ma petite*, to free yourself from that land, that civilization, that affection for what had long disappeared, to go forward toward something new. Only you did that. Only you were that brave."

Strange, is it not, Wu Shen, her friend and teacher had once said, *to live in a world where she who is most afraid is braver than all the rest of us together?* And their last night together, Chao had told her: *You are a tiger indeed, my pale jade, and every one of us a coward.* Then there was Ke-ming: *I am a captive of my own history, but I have raised you to be free, to move toward the future. Here we have only shadows of the past and I was meant to die among them. I could not bear to see you destroyed with all the rest. You are my hope. Promise me you will survive.*

Suddenly, Lian threw herself at Émile. "I am alive!" she shouted. "I did not die with them. Why, then, can I not free myself of their shadows?" She beat her curled fists against his chest in futile protest. Her skin felt cold, then hot, then numb again.

Very gently, Émile took her hands and held them. "You can, but you choose not to. You choose to cling to a tragic hero who selfishly left you alone and defenseless, rather than a man who would never value anything or anyone above his family."

The accusation, the promise shattered her—one a slap, the other a caress.

Émile did not notice; he had retreated into outrage, a temporary madness. "Don't think that because I've been content, because I laugh often, because I'm kind to those in pain, that I am also weak. We French have a proverb you'd be wise to remember, since remembering is what you do best. 'Dread the anger of the dove.' I am that dove, Lian, and I have never been so full of anger." Please! he wanted to cry. Don't deny our child a chance.

He glanced at her stomach, then looked away, his face twisted in pain. "Inexplicably, you believe your survival and escape are a curse, not a gift." He faced her rigidly. "You are wrong, *chérie.* Someday you must accept that."

Lian could not speak; she was still reeling.

"You see, Lian, it is a gift, an incomparable gift that few

are given. A second chance to find the happiness your family could not." His face was luminous in the slatted light. He held her with his gaze, trying to make her believe by the sheer force of his will. "Treasure the gift. Don't toss it away. Take the risk of being happy."

"I do not know how!"

Émile recoiled, appalled by the passion of her response. "You are bright and you are human." He made one last attempt to reach her. "You can learn."

For a moment, she felt a spark of something bright and warm begin to smolder. "Can I? Do you really believe that?"

Considering her closely, he saw what he should have seen long ago. "It doesn't matter what I believe. *You* must believe it. And you don't." He did not know whom he pitied more: himself, because he could not be happy without Lian; Lian because she did not know how to be happy at all; or the child, who might never know the safety of its father's arms, the depth of his love.

He wanted to break something, to destroy and, through destruction, release some of the rage at everyone who had brought Lian to this moment. It should not happen this way. He should be holding her close, her skin smooth and warm beneath his fingertips, their souls full of wonder and their minds full of plans. He remembered too well how it felt to hold her, to feel her give herself into his hands, trustingly, as she let him inside. He remembered how her hair slid through his fingers, fell around them as they made love, binding them in strands of blue-black silk. He remembered the scent of honeysuckle on her skin and the slow, satisfied smile that transformed her when they lay side by side, speaking intimately, without reserve.

He was suffocating and Émile knew he had to go. He could not give up hope. "I can't stay any longer among your ghosts and shadows," he said grimly. "I am going. For now." He hesitated briefly, shoulders taut and body rigid, then turned and left her.

Lian stared after him, swaying unsteadily, trying to speak, but unable to find her voice. She feared she had just lost the most precious thing she had ever known.

21

FIRECRACKERS EXPLODED OVERHEAD, FILLING THE NIGHT SKY with shimmering stars of red, green, blue and luminous white, which hovered, suspended for an instant, smoldering, before they fell back to earth and fizzled into ash. With each new explosion of light and color, the people of Chervilles roared their approval and delight. They had gathered in the courtyard of the Chateau Duchamps, for though the couple were away, it was a tradition that on Bastille Day they opened their house to the entire town to give them music and firecrackers, dancing and jubilation. The people celebrated as if the prison, the ancient symbol of repression, poverty and suffering, had been stormed and the prisoners set free just hours past, instead of a century ago.

Lian stood just inside her open balcony doors and watched, remembering other celebrations that had filled her senses and made her pulse race, fragile silk and horn and shell-covered lanterns that had turned the dark Peking River into a radiant ribbon of light. People shouted as they passed, demanding she come down and join the party, but she kept back from the seductive incandescence outside her window, fingers laced beneath her slightly rounded belly. She was moved by the people's joy in their freedom, caught up in the exhilaration as if this were *her* country.

"Why do you not go out and join them?" Cheng murmured, gliding up behind her.

She looked at him in surprise. "Would they not be distressed by my condition?"

Cheng shook his head. "You know the people of Chervilles; they would make it part of their celebration—a new life, a child. There is nothing the French like better than a child."

"Are you certain? Even when the mother has no husband?"

Cheng stared at her in frank astonishment. "You are worried about the rules of social propriety? You who broke every rule in China, and proudly, as did your mother before you?" He had heard, as had everyone who passed through Peking, of the Wan women's fearless disregard for the dictates of society. Ke-ming and Lian had followed their own hearts, their own rules, and for that they had been much envied, and much hated.

Lian stared wistfully at the sky, fragmented into showers of white and gold. "When I broke the rules before, I paid a high price." She brushed at the words like hovering gnats. "Besides, if my friends turned away now, it would break my heart."

In spite of himself, Cheng was touched. "You deserve a night of happiness as much as they. Perhaps more. Do not hesitate to take it."

She knew he was referring to more than the Bastille Day celebration. She saw in his wise black eyes, almost hidden by wrinkles and folded lids, sympathy and a flicker of something very close to anger. He who was always so calm and dignified.

She vacillated, and the spark became a flame. He pulled his hands from his wide silk sleeves, dropping something that he ignored as he grasped her shoulders. "Why are you so obstinate? So determined to remain up here alone, cloaked only in your dignity?"

He stared into her eyes piercingly; she could not hide her doubt. "I told you long ago it is your choice. It has always been your choice, even in China when the fates took your happiness and crushed it in their hands. Now they are tired of you, daughter of my heart, for you are no longer sport to them. Even when you were, you did not let them rule you. You forged your own path and it carried you to freedom. Freedom, Li-an. Of the body, of the spirit, of the mind. Yet you insist you are still bound. Perhaps that belief is your refuge from men like Émile Drouard, who have the power to touch your heart."

Lian turned as if mesmerized by the many-hued radiance outside her window. "I am afraid that he despises me now." She was shaken by the aching regret that filled her chest and the watery hollow where her baby lay.

"If he did, would it be simpler?" Cheng asked quietly, bending down to pick up the object that had fallen from his sleeve. He waved it through the air in dismissal. "It does not matter anyway. He would marry you tomorrow if you wanted him. He has loved you long and cautiously, respecting your reticence and your need to be alone, delighting in giving you what pleasure he could, drawing you out, bringing you laughter. He might have run far and forever after the night your ebony chest came home, but instead he courted you, befriended you and gave you a child.

"You may think he is weak because he did not force you to accept his proposal, but he is wise. Patience is a great strength in a man like Émile." He paused. "Still, even Émile has not patience enough to wait for the end of the world, even for one as remarkable as you. I warned you, pale jade. Do not break a good man's heart because you are afraid. Look at him. *Look!*" Abruptly, he handed her the rolled white page and left her. He could no longer bear the unshed tears that glistened in her eyes, revealing her heart as words never would.

Slowly, Lian unrolled the rag paper. She knew who it was from, and now Cheng had raised Émile's virtues and Lian's guilt like palpable things that lingered in the ghost-littered air long after he had gone.

Monsieur Drouard is your friend, he had told her once.

One has few enough true friends. I will remember that, but you will forget as it suits you. You are good at forgetting. "But I am not!" she cried to the walls covered with the work of a painter whose whimsy had no doubt already been forgotten, while outside, the world was jubilant, splendid, full of light.

With shaky hands, she unrolled Émile's offering and stared, stricken.

At the top of the watercolor, he had written "Bastille Day" in large clear letters. Beneath those stark words was a portrait that drained the blood from Lian's face.

She stood at her favorite rose-colored doors at the Duchamps, where she and Émile often paused while she imagined the garden inside the massive walls.

In the sketch, Lian had opened the doors to reveal a lush garden full of roses and lilacs, peonies and lilies, thick climbing ivy and banks of marguerites. The colors were bright and alluring, begging her to come inside the wildly disordered, lovely tangle of flowers and vines and color and scent.

Though she had turned the giant double knobs and pushed the doors open, Lian was looking over her shoulder, back into the empty street, strewn with the ashes of bonfires, with burnt out firecracker casings, limp, faded streamers and confetti crushed and dirtied by many feet. The remnants of a celebration that had blazed until it burnt itself to cinders. Lian did not see the garden or feel its enticing invitation. And though the doors, the flowers, the vines and the walls had all been washed with brilliant color, Lian alone was sketched in black and white. So close to a paradise she refused to see and could not enter because her own vitality had been drained away like the power and exuberance of the party in the street.

Why don't you turn the handles and see what's inside, rather than imagining? he had asked.

There are doors for a reason, she had replied. *They are*

meant to be closed, keeping what is inside safe, what is outside away.

Do you believe this entrance was so lovingly created so outsiders would pass it by? No, those beautiful doors are an invitation.

She had turned away without even seeing if the doors were locked.

Lian tried to swallow and found she could not. Gradually, the meaning, the devastating judgment filtered through her tangled thoughts and she forgot to breathe.

It was much later when she heard Cheng's footsteps once more. "I would not disturb you again, but you have visitors. You have mentioned you wanted to speak to them, and they most assuredly want to speak to you."

Lian heard the slightest warning in his tone, but she would not turn away again. Not anymore. Not from beauty or joy and not from this. "The Chins? Please send them up."

"But tonight? Are you certain?"

She smiled sadly, affectionately at the old man who had become her friend and champion. "It is kind of you to try to protect me, but tonight is as good as any other. If we must speak, and if our words should turn to anger, then at least we have the appropriate background for it." She gestured toward the bursts of blinding light, the sparks, the fire in the sky outside.

Cheng had not the heart to argue, but he could not help admiring her spirit, her attempt to lighten the tension that vibrated in the air like a thunderstorm about to break. "As you wish."

When Monsieur and Madame Chin stepped through the open door, Lian was seated in the rocking chair, the silken folds of her gown falling around her, her hair clipped back with a jade clasp. She sat upright, hands resting gracefully on the arms of the chair, her long sleeves rippling softly toward the floor.

The couple paused, taken aback by the resemblance to her regal mother.

Lian did not wait for them to begin. "You have come to speak of Lin-Mei. I, too, have things to say."

Forgetting their awed hesitation, they approached, eyes blazing.

"You knew our daughter was seeing a Chinese boy, yet you allowed her to be corrupted."

"You sneer when you say the word 'Chinese.' Do you not find that hypocritical? All that you are, all that you have, you owe to what you learned in China." Before Chin Yun could release his pent-up rage, Lian continued. "Forgive me. That was unkind. I knew of Mei and Yen Tai, it is true, but what they shared was pure and chaste. They were happy together. Lin-Mei was not corrupted by Yen Tai, but allowed to be free, unfettered. She told me she felt she was flying without chains to bind her to the earth. I envied her that freedom."

"You encouraged her to creep around behind our backs, to discard her *hsiao*, her training, her virtue, and all for personal pleasure?" Chin Yun spat the words at her, as if they were poison on his tongue.

You were blessed, for a time, with a pure, untainted joy. But it cannot last forever.

"I did not discourage her from seeing Yen Tai, whose name you refuse even to speak. Nor did I encourage her. You yourself had declared her a woman. It was her choice to make. Yen Tai is a fine young man, virtuous, hard-working, kind, and always aware of the need to protect your daughter, to preserve her filial piety and her virtue, whatever the cost to himself. You are lucky it is he she loves, and not some French boy who does not understand the sanctity of family, purity, tradition."

"How dare you defend him when he's ruined Lin-Mei? How dare you defend yourself?" Chin Shu, in her stylish French gown, her hair curled and pinned and netted, spoke quietly, fiercely.

Lian's gaze remained steady. "He has not ruined her; he has only made her happy. I tell you he has protected her, that he would never knowingly harm her, because it is true. Perhaps you would prefer to believe ill of your eldest daughter, whose love and respect for you are great, though she does not understand why you try to change her and Yi-niang. As for me—I do not defend myself."

They were nonplussed by her determination, her refusal to shrink before their wrath. Madame Chin began to wonder if they might have been wrong after all. Then she remembered. "You cannot deny you put the idea in her head of running away with that boy when she heard we meant to send her to a school in Paris. You must have told her escape was the only alternative."

Leaning forward, blue eyes flashing, Lian said evenly, "The idea was hers—that of a desperate young girl who has lost her joy and foresees only sorrow and rejection. I understood those things; I have felt them. Nevertheless, I told Lin-Mei she must not go. I told her it would cause more sorrow in the end than she bears now. I told her it would break your hearts, that instead she should try to tell you how she feels. I did not say, though I know it is true, that it would have broken her heart as well, for Yen Tai would have refused. He understands their youth, their innocence, their need for knowledge, experience, guidance. All Mei understands is that she is in pain, that you want to make her French, when her heart, body and spirit are Chinese. She does not understand why you send her to Paris, where she is disliked and made fun of."

"Naturally, you encouraged her in this thinking as well," Monsieur Chin said caustically. "It is, after all, your dearest wish that she remain tied to what we left behind. You must have made her hate us for trying to change her."

Lian looked at him with pity, seeing for the first time the sag of his shoulders, the despair in his almond eyes. "I told her you loved her deeply. I said you would give your lives for her, that you had done just that by coming here to build your daughters a chance at something other than cruelty and corruption and injustice."

What does he want from me, Wan Lian?

"She said she did not know how to please you. I could see it was tearing her in two."

Even for him, I cannot be who and what I am not. How then can I make him happy?

"I told her you only wanted her safety and her happiness. She could not see it then, but she is young. She will understand someday how much you have given up for her. How hard you try to make her life better than your own. Please do not blame her for being a child. She is lucky to have had that chance, that ignorance and innocence. She will learn about the world and its harshness as well as its beauty. I beg you, do not make her learn too soon. Though I have no right to ask this."

For the second time, the Chins were ashamed of their doubts, their unjust treatment of their friend and teacher. For she was as much to them as to their daughters. "You have the right." Chin Yun and Chin Shu spoke in unison, softening the sharp edges of their anger.

Lian rose, half-smiling. "Then may I ask one more thing? Do not send your daughter away. She will be an outcast in Paris, as I was once an outcast in my homeland. You cannot imagine the anguish of a young girl, alone and despised, too far from everyone she cares for. Let her stay here, where she is loved, respected, known. Let her see Yen Tai if she wishes. He may not always give her joy, but for now, he makes her feel cherished. She is a good and honest girl and will not risk her virtue or your pride or your fine name. She did not realize before how much she put in jeopardy. But I think you will find she has grown up, your little Lin-Mei."

She saw they were not listening, but staring at her belly. "She'll preserve our good name as you've preserved yours?

She'll value her virtue, her honor? Why should she, when you, her idol, do not?"

The bitterness and condemnation in Monsieur Chin's tone hit her like a gale of wind, knocking her back into the chair. Painfully, she rose again. "First you despised me because I would not let go of the traditions of the Middle Kingdom; now it seems you judge me more harshly because I carry a child, with no husband, no family to claim it. In France, such things are common."

The Chins turned their backs, but she stopped them with her unwavering strength of will. "No! You will listen to me as I once listened to you, though I did not wish to hear, though your story wrapped itself around my heart and squeezed until I had no pulse, no breath, no shield against the pain. But I listened. So will you."

Against their will, their inclination, they turned as one to face her as they had faced her once before.

"She whom you so admired, whose grief and agony you could not imagine if you tried, she who waited outside the Imperial Gates of the Forbidden City to see your nephew one last time, or if not that, to let him know she had not fled in fear—she, too, carried a child in her womb. Chin Chao's child. She was proud to have been his lover. She, who loved Chin Chao, his honesty, integrity, sensitivity, humor, who loved him with all the stifled love of nineteen years alone, was not afraid of the miracle they had made together. She feared death, loss, violence, the marching feet of the Bannermen, but she did not fear discovery. There were more important things at stake."

She caught the arm of the chair as she grew light-headed and nearly fell, but she righted herself without touching Chin Yun's outstretched hand. "Is she—am I—to be unhappy for the rest of my life because I loved a man who valued honor and pride above family, above happiness, above life, above the forming body of his own child? Because he chose to die rather than give me his name, his family, his protection? I lost that child when I lost him. Part of my heart, my soul, my spirit have been missing ever since. Perhaps I have at last found a way to replace what I lost so long ago.

"I have told Mei, who guessed my condition, that I was unwise, wrong." *The child cannot be wrong. It did not choose to be.* "I have told her of the danger of having faith in one whose heart may be false, though I know Yen Tai's is true. I have told her if he is true, he will wait.

"Wan Ke-ming left me with no such need to protect my reputation. I was born illegitimate, and worse, tainted by English blood. In my mother's eyes, in her heart, which only she could know, what she had done was not a sin, but a miracle. I was conceived in love and raised to follow my heart as she did, but I was afraid. Not of what people would say, but of being lost, hurt, abandoned yet another time. There have been too many.

"And now, because I have been taught to mistrust joy and kinship and my own right to be content, am I to suffer because, for a moment, a week, a month or two, I took what was offered with open hands and open heart? Am I to regret that a good man, a faithful man, a patient and kind man, cared enough to give me love—more love than he ever took. Am I to be forbidden happiness because the finest man I've ever known is fool enough to love me? I would be lucky now if he would have me, for I have caused him more grief than joy."

She stared Chin Yun and Chin Shu in the eyes and murmured softly, "You once wondered aloud if Chin Chao was worthy of his faithful lover. Émile Drouard is worthy and more than worthy. He gives me joy untainted by laws and traditions and cruel strictures that keep the heart in check. I do not regret my past, no matter how painful, because it has taught me much and brought me here. It is time now to go forward."

The Chins had no answer, no defense, no explanation. It did not matter. Lian would not have heard them.

"As for Mei—she is sensitive, intuitive and strong beyond her knowledge or yours. Have a little faith in her and she will make you proud if you allow her to do so, if you do not turn her away because you are afraid that she loves a boy from China."

She crossed the room and took their hands—they gave them up limply, without a struggle—just as the thunder and lightning of fireworks exploded outside her window, illuminating her in surrealistic radiance.

"You see, my countrymen, my second family, my friends, in the end, neither you nor I can escape completely the legacy of the Chinese gods, the rituals and ways of thought that shaped us. China is bred deep into our blood and bones. We cannot simply close it out, ignore it, pretend it never was. No one who was part of it can. You know that in your heart though you pretend you do not feel it. You know it in your mind, though you pretend you cannot see. Open your eyes, your beating hearts, and you will know what you must do, what you must acknowledge, what you must give your daughters Lin-Mei and Yi-niang. The freedom to choose. There is nothing more I can tell you, except that anger, your resentment of me, will one day turn to bitterness that will poison your blood and your contentment. I do not ask you to like me. Only to forgive me and to let me be."

22

WHEN THEY HAD GONE, LIAN LAY ON HER PALLET, BATHED in soft red light, certain she would not sleep. The revelers were dancing and singing with unflagging energy. Now and then her tiny bedroom was lit by the blaze of a firecracker. She could not escape the celebration even if she wanted to, and she knew now she did not want to. The sound of laughter and exuberant voices, of music filling the cobbled streets, the glow of brilliant explosions against the dark night sky were oddly soothing.

So far, she had managed not to examine the significance of what she'd said to the Chins and what it meant to her, to Émile, to their tiny, half-formed child.

Defending Mei and herself had drained her, using up a source of strength, a string of thoughts she had not guessed existed. Now she was so weary that her eyelids fluttered closed of their own accord and in spite of the noise outside, she lay back, drifting into sleep.

Ailsa Rose Sinclair stood with her family at the edge of her husband's grave. A breeze rippled the sunlight, lifting her mourning veil. Though the air was heavy and warm, she felt a deep chill and clenched her teeth. With that breeze, that chill, came memory.

Just so had she stood three years ago by a gaping hole in the valley where Charles Kittridge had chosen to be buried. "Let me rest, Ailsa-aghray," he had said two days before. "I'm so tired. And I have so much." Her father had touched her cheek with affection and looked at his other two daughters and his wife with satisfaction. "I am content."

At the foot of his grave, with nothing but the lid of a plain pine coffin to stare at, Ailsa had wanted to shout, "But I have nothing!" She'd looked at her pale, stricken sisters and added fiercely, in silence, "We have nothing!" Ailsa, Genevra and Lian had come here at the summons of their father, who had bidden them know him, forgive him, and watch him die.

The landscape only deepened her depression. The fierce mountains, beautiful and frightening in their distant splendor, the valley with its melancholy voices and shadows, the cold, savage wind in this wild, abandoned place.

She wanted to fall to her knees and plead for her father to come back and give her some of the peace he'd found. She and her sisters were teetering on the edge of that grave, stricken and helpless. They were bound by an invisible thread that held them together in grief and desperation. Ailsa knew that if she stumbled, if she broke the thread, they would collapse, one after the other. She saw in their faces that they too felt the unraveling thread. The only thing that kept them upright was the knowledge of each other's weakness. If one fell, they would all fall, endlessly, into the gaping black hole of Charles Kittridge's grave.

Now she stared at the polished mahogany of William Sinclair's casket while the breeze threatened to lift her veil, exposing her. As suddenly as it had come, the wind faded into the May sunlight, over the manicured English lawn scattered with expensive marble stones and monuments.

Like those monuments, Ailsa was cold and rigid. Three years ago, her anguish had consumed her; today she stood far away from all that was happening around her. Her beloved husband was dead, but she could not grieve. She viewed the burial through a distant haze, as if she had no part in the ceremony of farewell. Just now, she was closer to the past than the present.

Lian sat straight up, body rigid, eyes scratchy and dry. Her heart thundered in her chest as if the god of storms were using it for his drum. She could not breathe, and struggled to draw air into her lungs. William was not dead, she told herself firmly. She had just had a letter from Ailsa saying everyone was well. Even on paper the half-sisters could not lie to one another. They always sensed the truth. But dreams of her sisters were never idle or unimportant. She had hovered inside Genevra's body as the color of her life seeped out of her, stood beside Ailsa at their father's grave, and felt the helplessness, the darkness, the loss of hope.

William was not dead, but Charles Kittridge was. The pain had been so real, she had felt the chilly keening of the wind and smelled the freshly turned earth from the long gash in the ground where his coffin rested. She, like Ailsa, had stood once more in the past. The present had disappeared in the desperate fear of falling, all three sisters falling endlessly into the open grave.

Though William Sinclair was alive now—she felt certain he was; her heart had stopped pounding quite so fiercely and there was a vibration of calm in the air that came from Ailsa, wherever she was, whatever she was feeling—but someday he would die. The scene in the dream was true, or would be in the future. She was also certain of that. When William was gone, at least Ailsa would have her family, her mother, her children and grandchildren for solace. She would bear the loss, no matter how difficult, because her family would give her a reason to go on.

"Is that what you are trying to tell me, my sister? Is that why you walked through my dreams tonight?"

Her hands were cold, her skin translucent in the tinted light. Her eyes burned with unshed tears. Was Lian afraid to take one more chance?

It was very cold in her room, very empty. The stillness was stifling, especially after last night's clamor. Then, without warning, she cried out at a sharp jab inside her belly. She felt a shifting, a slight stirring of limbs. She stared at the rise under her ivory gown in astonishment. The baby had moved. She had felt it as surely as she felt her own intake of breath, the dull thump of her heart. She cupped the mound lightly, fingers spread, a warm shock rushing through her body, making her dizzy in the still July heat. The child inside her had cried out its first silent cry. She was trembling, her face filmed in sweat.

She was carrying a child, a life, a new beginning. It struck her with the force of last night's explosions that she had not really believed in the baby until this moment. Not truly, with all her heart, with her clear, sharp mind. The baby was real, a person, not nightmare, dream or spirit. A child. Her child. Hers and Émile's.

She smiled slowly as waves of realization struck her. With them came the comfort that had long hovered within her grasp, ignored. She trembled with it, rose and whirled beside her pallet, laughed, and all the while kept her hands on either side of her expanding stomach. She was light-headed and brought up short when she crashed into the wall, but she only laughed again. "A baby!" she whispered in awe and amazement, stunned by the depth of her exultation. She looked toward the ceiling, but saw only the sky. "You have given me two lives—this baby's and my own."

She felt things stirring that she'd never felt before. A fierce, palpable joy, an equally fierce desire to protect and nurture, anticipation, exhilaration. She did not know she was weeping until she saw the tear stains on her pale silk gown.

Another child. Another chance. Another place. Cher-villes.

As she swept through the flat, unable to stay still, she saw Charles Kittridge's letters lying on the table. She touched them sadly, remembering her dream of Ailsa and their father's grave. It was all right now to break the thread that had held them all upright. She could stand alone, without her sisters to keep her steady. She could have what her father had desired above all things. *No' till he was dyin' did Charlie find what he wanted most, and then only for a little.*

He had loved her. He had tried in the only way he could to reach a daughter beyond his reach, knowing he would fail, knowing his task was fruitless. But perhaps it gave him hope, or the sense that he was not alone after all.

Lian wept for Charles Kittridge, at the futility of his self-imposed task. She wept with terrible sadness that he had been compelled to reach out blindly, week after week, year after year, for someone he could never touch. Except that he *had* touched her, even if it was too late. She knew, though he never would, that after all, his effort had not been wasted. She would never have known him as she knew him now, through his own words, through the many years and many changes scrawled across these pages. She would never have known how much he cared. She would do better for her child than Charles had done. He had never had a chance to be a parent, but *she* did. She would not let it slip away. "I promise you, My Father, to give all that you would have given me."

You will not speak your father's name, Ke-ming had told her daughter in a voice of steel, *until you speak it with love.* "Charles Kittridge." The sound of the words, ringing in the morning stillness, surprised her. She had spoken them without thought and without rancor. She curled her fingers around his last letter, weeping freely. Now she could grieve for the man her father had really been. And in mourning without questions and uncertainty, without constraint, she could finally let Charles Kittridge go. She had feared the darkness of his open grave because, in her heart, it had never been closed. But today she would bury him, and with him, Ke-ming, whose grave she had never seen. She could bury them both at last, because from the moment her baby moved inside her, she had known she had a future, not merely a past, a fleeting present. Émile had been right. *This world has hope. And that is enough to build on. Enough to give a child. Hope.*

A hope that she could share, believe in, *feel.* Now, for the first time, she understood the meaning of Ke-ming's final letter. *They are the last pieces of your life in the Middle Kingdom; let them help you remember that there was beauty as well as suffering, love and joy as well as loss, that there is hope. Always there is hope, so long as you survive.*

The parchment felt fragile between her fingers, the words faded to pale memories. She sat on an embroidered cushion, chin in her hands, lost in thought. *We are back to Chao and his legendary honor.* She had known, as Ke-ming had known, as Chin Chao himself had known, that their love was doomed from the moment it was born. They had loved each other deeply, but carefully, aware always of the inevitability of violence and loss.

Chin Chao chose China over you, even knowing he would lose?

Lian glanced up, the trails of tears barely dry on her face, when she heard the soft tread of a cloth-soled shoe. A moment later, Cheng peered inside. "I heard only silence for so long that I became concerned. I have become an old grandmother worrying over her young. Forgive me." He noticed her eyes, red from weeping, the letters strewn across the table, the stains on the breast of her ivory gown. "I will go."

Lian shook her head and held out her hand. "You are always welcome, my friend. You should know that." She drew him toward the rocking chair he'd given her.

Cheng was uncomfortably aware of the luminous glow of Lian's eyes, despite her skin, blotched and swollen from weeping. Her shining hair flowed unrestrained around her shoulders. He swallowed dryly, his heart beating slowly, rhythmically. "I did not sleep well, wondering if the Chins had hurt you. I could feel their anger like pulsating heat in the air around them."

"Their rage ignited my own and gave me a resolve I did not know I had. I do not think their words ever touched me. I pitied them in their blindness, which opened wide my eyes." *Always remember how lucky you have been, carefree and full of elation,* she had told Mei. *Unafraid of your emotions—to feel them, share them, show them. So few ever have that freedom, or realize they have lost it.* Last night Lian had realized. She did not regret her tirade; it had been the truth. *You deserve a night of happiness as much as they. Do not hesitate to take it.* She did not have to earn that right, to make herself worthy, to atone for what was past. It had never occurred to her that Mei had to earn her joy; it was a gift, and to refuse it would be unthinkable. Why should it be different for Lian?

"Remarkable," Cheng said. "What is it you saw?"

"The value of your wisdom, your insistence on my happiness. That Émile's laughter is precious beyond words, as is the offer of his heart." She touched her stomach with a new tenderness and acceptance.

Raising her head, she regarded Cheng. "But I need your help, if you are willing." At his silent look of inquiry, she said, "When you came in, I was thinking of my feelings for Chin Chao and Émile. How difficult was one, how easy the other." *Just because something is easy doesn't make it less valuable or worthy. Just because a man is brave in one way, doesn't mean he is not afraid of his own heart.*

It took a moment for Cheng to accept that he had heard correctly. She had spoken of Émile softly, pensively, sounding honestly perplexed.

She looked him in the eye and said, "I cannot make sense of my feelings. But I must. It is imperative. Can you help?"

He had been trying to do just that. Tears came to his rheumy old eyes because, at last, she had asked for what he had to give. "I will tell you what I have heard and what I think. That is all I can do."

"That is enough." Her face was calm, expectant, her eyes full of trust.

Cheng cleared his throat. The question should have been difficult, except he had been thinking of little else when he lay alone at night. "Your relationship with Chao was built of desperation and need, of daring and courage beyond imagining. Chin Chao was brilliant and obstinate, powerful and faithful to those things which he believed, but I suspect he never knew you as Émile Drouard knows you."

Lian leaned forward, brow furrowed. "You believe that?"

Smiling, Cheng nodded sagely. "Émile has been your friend, your companion, your lover, your challenge. These things you know, and have always known, even before he touched your face with tenderness and you opened your tight-closed eyes. I do not know what was last said between you, but this I do know. He cares for you as a man rarely cares for a woman, especially one who fights him every moment."

The innocence of youth fades, but in its place comes a depth of feeling you cannot imagine, a passion so compelling that it overshadows all that came before.

Remembering Émile across the parlor, Lian bowed her head. She started to speak, but Cheng stopped her with a light touch on her arm. "It is not easy to change when your character was shaped by violent, angry forces. But you have begun. Émile knows that. He knows you from the inside out; he has seen beneath your skin to your true heart. He has seen your weakness, your fears and desires. Your friendship with him is more risky to you than the danger you experienced with Chao. Fear, peril, intrigue—these things you were born to. The ease, the honestly, the openness you have with Émile is far more terrifying than the glint of any sword."

'Twas easier to love him because of his weaknesses. For with human flaws comes the need for forgiveness and understandin'.

Cheng perceived her agitation. "To let someone inside who actually knows you, day by day, hour by hour, in boredom and happiness, ordinary times and celebrations, is most difficult. With Émile there is no bravado, no dramatic and devastating proof of loyalty and courage. Just your heart and soul laid bare because you allowed him behind your protective walls. You think what you share with him is less intense and dramatic, but, ah, my jade flower, my Lian, it is far more dangerous."

It is a bigger risk, Lian, because it is unpredictable, and therefore frightening.

"But I am not a coward," Lian murmured to herself after much thought. "I thank you, Cheng, for telling me the truth, as you have always done. Now I must go, if you know where Émile lives and will tell me how to find him."

He smiled tremulously; he had begun to doubt this moment would ever come. "I will write it for you while you put on another gown. A pretty one that will make your eyes bright." He drew forward a brush, her inkstone and a piece of rice paper.

Lian slipped into her room to change into a pale blue gown and dark blue tunic. She returned to pick up the drawing Émile had called "Bastille Day," and roll it in her palm. She took the address from Cheng, touched his cheek briefly and started away.

She stopped, cheeks flushed and hands shaking. "What if I pushed him too hard and too far? What if he doesn't want me—us—anymore?"

Cheng was astounded by her honesty, by the anguish she did not try to hide. "Take the chance, Li-an. Ask him. You will only learn the answer if you find the strength to ask the question."

You cannot always have what you want, little flower, but if you are patient, you will have so much more.

23

SHE KNEW THAT SOMETIMES ÉMILE ARRIVED IN CHERVILLES via the train from Paris, but just as often, he came by boat. The distance from the town to the city up the winding Seine was much longer than the more direct train route, but the trip infinitely more scenic. That was partly why Lian chose to take a boat half-full of other passengers. Besides it would give her time to think.

She soon saw that the artist who had painted the Seine on her parlor walls had known his subject well. There were forests and meadows in vibrant shades of green and yellow, rickety docks and large well-built ones, occasional small towns whose life spilled onto the river in more than its reflection dancing on the water. Colorfully dressed people had picnics on the shore, fished from the bridges and the quay, ate and sketched and laughed and swam. Though the sun was not bright, the moving clouds changed the Seine from blue to green to gray to silver, while the dappled shadows of the leaves made shifting patterns on the rippled surface.

As the water lapped against the side of the boat, Lian wondered what Émile did in Paris. He had mentioned frequenting the cafés in Montmartre, where he'd become close friends with artists, writers and poets. But she'd gotten the impression that was not where he lived, that his heart was divided between Montmartre and Chervilles, while he stayed somewhere else all together. As often as he was in Chervilles, he must spend little time at home.

When she reached the busy, crowded dock in Paris, she quickly found a hansom cab and gave the driver Émile's address. She settled back on the worn seat and wondered how he would greet her. The image of his face as she had last seen it, unrelenting, sharp as stone, was burned into her mind. Beneath that stone his rage and hurt had rushed like an underground stream. *I am going*, he had said grimly. *For now.* His tone had been so cold. *We French have a proverb you'd be wise to remember, since remembering is what you do best. "Dread the anger of the Dove." I am that dove, Lian, and I have never been so full of anger.*

Looking out the window to distract herself, she had a vague impression of ancient stone, a hundred shades of gray, of wide boulevards bustling with people and omnibuses and wagons. Everywhere there were trees—plane and horse chestnuts and magnolias and acacias—and green parks. The streets were full of motion and tension, color and noise. As they entered the residential section, she noticed children rolling hoops or playing stickball or skipping rope in the street. She smiled.

The cab stopped, and her heart began to thrum with apprehension. She could not remember all they'd last said to one another, but she knew it had been explosive, unkind, uncontrolled. Still, whatever he felt for her, he would see her because of the baby, his child. She paid the driver with shaking hands and turned, surprised by the obvious wealth of the neighborhood.

Émile's house was made of huge old stones, mellowed by time to a soft, indiscriminate color between gray and gold. His door, up two steps from the street, was painted green, and the knocker was a lion's head of bronze. She realized she was crushing the rolled up watercolor she had brought so carefully from Chervilles. Loosening her grip, she raised and lowered the lion's head with her other hand. The sound reverberated through her body.

The door was opened by a tidy little man who regarded her curiously. "*Oui*, Mademoiselle? May I help you?"

"Is Monsieur Émile at home?"

The man frowned, face wrinkled in thought, then his eyes lit up. He stepped back, opening the door wide. "But of course. You are Mademoiselle Wan. I should have known at once." He bowed formally and made a sweeping gesture, inviting her inside. "I am Pierre, Monsieur Émile's valet. If you'll make yourself comfortable in the sitting room, I'll fetch him at once." He bowed again as he disappeared.

Lian was too anxious to notice the rich Persian rug on which she stood or the fine brocade draperies over Belgian lace. She did not notice that she stood beside a tapestry love seat with warm rosewood trim. She heard distant voices, then footsteps, and she stiffened, not knowing what to expect.

Émile entered the room in a rush. "You're here." He noticed she was flushed, her hair loosely braided, as if she had hurried. Her eyes were clear and sparkling. That made it harder. He had spent the last days nurturing his anger in order to ease his pain, while he tried to decide what to do about Lian. Finally, after pacing a ragged pattern into his bedroom rug, he'd concluded he could do little if she was not willing to let go of the past. The one thing she would not, could not do.

Lian looked into his shuttered eyes and felt his fury cut a swathe through the room like an icy wind.

Her hands shook and Émile saw in astonishment that she was nervous, afraid of his reaction, that she held no shield of pride and dignity between them. Dare he hope—? "I didn't expect you to come," he said. The wind of his anger lost some of its chill. His curiosity and expectation were demolishing his common sense. "Please sit. You shouldn't stand for so long."

At the hint of concern in his tone, Lian sank onto the settee. She felt as if someone had knocked the breath from her body and her pulse rushed in her ears. She had forgotten, in the turmoil since she'd last seen him, how compelling he was, his blond hair disheveled, his beard still glistening with water, as if he had just bathed his face. Affection overpowered her. She did not know until that moment how deeply she had missed him—his tenderness, his humor, his irony and optimism.

Before she lost her courage, Lian rose until they stood very close. Gingerly, she held out the sketch, "Bastille Day." "I want you to paint me."

Émile, who had not yet recovered from her appearance and what it implied, stared blankly, afraid to believe what he was seeing. He glanced at the sketch, which she had unrolled. "Why?" It was the only word he could manage. He who was known for his unfailing wit.

With an unsteady finger, Lian pointed to her penciled figure outside the glorious color of the garden. "Because gray and white are the color of ashes, and ashes are the color and substance of mourning, and I do not wish to mourn any more." She met his gaze steadily. "I want to see the beauty of the garden, not the abandoned street, the future and not the cold, dead past."

He felt a rush of pure joy and reached for her, but paused, his hand near her shoulder. "Are you sure?" he asked. "Or will you allow your ghosts to haunt us?"

I have come far, but I can never get far enough from my past to make it disappear.

He was asking for a promise he knew she could not give. All at once, Lian was desperately afraid, not of the violence that had been, but the emptiness that might be. *I want you too much, care for you too much, need you too much. That frightens me.* "Do not leave me," she said, tears in her eyes. "Do not give up on me, I beg you."

Your future is in your hands and no one else's. She prayed Cheng was right as she took a step closer, her face naked of pretense or protection.

His fingers closed tightly on her shoulder and he felt her shaking. "I thought *you* had left *me*. I thought *you* had given up." He pulled her close, crumpling the sketch between them. His arms closed around her and finally she felt safe; she had found where she belonged.

He held her gently, his touch as light as when he held brush or charcoal in his hand. Her expanding stomach pressed against him and he massaged her back in slow, mesmeric circles. "The child is well?"

Lian rested her head against his shoulder and let the fear flow out of her. "Our baby thrives. This morning I felt it move. But, Émile, the things I said—"

"You said what you believed. It didn't leave me unscathed, because I care too much, but it was the truth through your eyes. I can't blame you for that." Resentment flickered and was gone.

Lian did not move, did not wish to move ever again. Her body, which had been cold for so long, grew warm as she listened to the beat of his heart. "You could, if you were not the man you are." An extraordinary man, Cheng had said. A rare man.

She slipped her arms around him and held on, letting him hold her upright, allowing him to give her his strength, admitting she did not have enough of her own. "Are you certain, *mon amour*? Because I won't be told to go again."

I forgot to warn you; pride is my particular sin.

"I will not want you to go. I want us to be together, a family." She looked up, remembering why she had come. "Our child will know both parents. It would be wrong to take that chance from him. I know what it is to grow up with a shadow for a father." *You cannot escape your destiny,* Ke-ming had told her, *to be Charles Kittridge's daughter. His blood, his history, his energy have made you strong.* What then, might his presence in her life have done? She saw the question in his eyes and understood. "I do not merely want a father for my child; I want you. I want your kindness, your affection, your faith in me, which you never tried to hide, though I gave you little in return. I want *you*, Émile Drouard, and no other."

If ye can love someone when ye know all that's wantin' in them, ye'll love them no matter what, Mairi Rose had said as they sat on the stone wall. Surely by now Émile knew all that was wanting in Lian, yet he seemed to love her anyway. Mairi Rose was as wise as Cheng.

She spoke so impetuously that Émile could not take it in. She was like a different woman—the one he'd been waiting for, who'd hid, until now, behind her smoky veils.

"This morning I was reading the letters my father wrote to me, and I saw his pain and loss clearly for the first time."

"You read them?" She had vowed never to open that packet, never to look inside and see the kind of man her father was. Émile was astonished and delighted.

"Yes, Lin-Mei thought I should, and perhaps because I was carrying a child, I began to wonder what it was to be a parent, and more than that, I wanted to know the person Charles Kittridge was."

He was no' perfect, nor ever claimed to be. But then, neither am I. Lian smiled at the sound of Mairi's matter-of-fact voice. Then she turned back to the letters.

"I never imagined the loneliness, the rage and frustration Charles Kittridge felt, knowing he had a child he would never see again." Her eyes were suspiciously damp. "I knew I could not take your child and cause you that loneliness, that rage, that pain. Having felt my father's sorrow, I could not leave you that legacy."

Émile held her at arms' length, moved by the remorse in her voice. "You will marry me, then?"

She stared at him, afraid her voice would fail her. "Yes. Because you are foolish enough to want me, even knowing me as you do. My child will have a father, and I a husband. I will not be alone as my mother was. And our child will know happiness."

Émile heard every word as if she carved them on the wall, because he had imagined them for so long, yet been certain he would never hear them. "What about *our* happiness?"

Lian backed away and he let his hands fall, setting her free. "I will give all I have to make you happy, but for myself . . ." She trailed off.

Take the risk of being happy, he had implored her. *I do not know how!* she had cried in despair.

There was a long, taut silence. When she could bear it no more, she said, "I cannot forget my last night in the Western Hills when my mother told me she wanted something for me. She had planned my whole life, and hers, so I could escape China and achieve this thing, this elusive victory for which she sacrificed all she had."

Émile tried to control his resurfacing anger at her past, her mother, her own stubborn blindness, but he too had suffered in the last few weeks. He too had come to doubt things he had once held sacred. "The trouble with sacrifice is that it leaves a heavy burden on the one sacrificed for. Often that burden is impossible to carry." He paused, waiting, but she remained silent. "What did she say? Tell me her words, exactly."

The words were burned into Lian's memory like the ashes in which her mother had died. "She said, 'You must be more, my pale jade. I raised you to be more.' She said, 'Promise me you will survive. You are my hope.' But I do not know what she meant, what she wanted, why she spent so much time and money educating me, so much care to make me stronger than the others, so I could accomplish what she could not. I have failed her, for I do not understand."

Always, my Charlie strove to meet the expectations of others, but rarely were they satisfied. So he was lonely and vulnerable. Lian actually glanced around to see if Mairi Rose was in the room. But it was only her wistful memory of her husband.

Émile paced up and down, thinking, groping for an invisible thread. Gradually, comprehension dawned as he put together the pieces of the puzzle of Ke-ming that Lian had reluctantly revealed. "What do you think your mother wanted in her own life, for herself? What do you think she regretted most?"

Tugging on her braid until her scalp began to ache, Lian considered. "She yearned for safety, freedom from fear, comfort, love."

"What about happiness?"

It is sad to remember being happy again. "Yes," she said. "I think she yearned for that most of all."

Émile contemplated Lian closely. "If you are her hope, wouldn't she want you to have the things she dreamed of but never found? Wouldn't she want more than anything for you to be safe, loved, happy? Did she ever once tell you that to seek happiness and fulfillment was evil, weak, selfish?"

Lian pondered until words from years before came back in a hollow echo. *It is not wrong to find pleasure where you can. To enjoy the few moments in your life when beauty is greater than sorrow or fear. Such moments are as rare as perfect pearls and must be treasured accordingly.*

One at a time, the words sank in until she understood them with more than her mind. It was so obvious that she'd never thought of it. That Ke-ming wanted her daughter to have what her mother could not—a normal life. Her confusion evaporated and she ached for Wan Ke-ming, who deserved so much more than she had found.

Lian stared at Émile unblinking as a wash of memories nearly swept her off her feet. Ke-ming weeping at an altar to a stranger because she dared not reveal her ancestors. Ke-ming trying to warn her away from the danger her daughter would face with Chin Chao. *Do not make the same mistake that I did, I beg you.* Ke-ming defending Charles Kittridge for his honor and affection in a court full of deceivers. Ke-ming sending her daughter away to the father she had never known, so that she might survive. *You are my hope.*

Slowly, incredulously, Lian looked up. For so long she had misunderstood. "She wanted more for me than a chance to raise my child in safety. She wanted me to find a man I could trust, as she trusted no one, that I could care for without doubt or fear or blame. What she might have found with my father in some other time and place." She touched Émile's face tenderly, in amazement, as if seeing it for the first time. "She wanted to give me the chance to choose freely, out of desire and affection, not necessity or the need for protection or simply to keep loneliness at bay." She raised her other hand and cupped his bearded cheeks, while tears ran unabated down her own.

"She wanted me to live a life not bound by walls stained with centuries of Chinese blood. She wanted *me* to have hope. It is so simple. She wanted me to know that there is such a thing as happiness, and that it can endure."

So I love him. 'Tis that simple.

She rested her forehead on his chest. "She needed to believe those things were possible even more than I. But I swallowed all her anger, mistrust and pain and so could not hear how clear her wish was." *Do not let your grief turn to bitterness that poisons the blood,* her teacher, Wu Shen, had warned her, *for that would break your spirit mother's heart.*

She smiled sadly through her tears. "She did not hope for much. Only that I let go of my sense of obligation. To take the world off my shoulders is more difficult than to become a famous poet or philosopher. Easier for me to change the lives of all the poor and hungry in the world than to change my own."

You're saying you're afraid of me? he had asked. *Not of you. Of myself. I am too comfortable with you. It is too easy to forget.*

"I'll help you." Émile lifted her chin and looked into her eyes. "I want to be happy, and I want our child contented. But if you are forlorn or merely free of sadness, what will it mean, in the end? Let me try to show you how."

She could not seem to stop the tears. "I will. I believe you might even succeed." She, more than anyone, knew the depth of his patience and commitment. He alone had freed her passion, held carefully in check, denied and ignored for so long that even she had not recognized its power until the first time he touched her.

We've acted too quickly, instinctively, with no time for thought, only passion.

In the end, that was Émile's most precious legacy to her. The longing, the hunger, the desire he had awakened that had turned her from cool flesh to a warm, passionate woman. It was her salvation.

You see, Lian, it is a gift, an incomparable gift that few are given.

She raised her lips to kiss him long and tenderly, holding tight as their mouths opened to let each other in. This time the fire, the pleasure, the sweet fulfillment was not a sin for which she would have to pay. He was right. It was a gift. And the gift was freedom.

24

A WEEK LATER, ÉMILE AND LIAN STOOD ON HER BALCONY, hand in hand, watching the preparations in the street below. They had decided to be married on Rue Salubre, in front of the apothecary shop, since Lian was neither Catholic nor Protestant and could not imagine being married in a church. Nor could either fulfill the ritual demands of a traditional Chinese wedding.

"Once I attended a French wedding. It was for the seamstress's daughter in an ancient church in a town farther north. I stayed back in the shadows of the huge gilded church, out of the colored streams of light through intricate stained glass windows," she told Émile. "I stared in horror at the crucifix before which the bride and groom took solemn vows in Latin, made binding by a priest who claimed he was speaking for God. I was shocked that any mere man should do that."

She waited for her fiancé to reply, but he'd been caught off guard and could think of no argument or explanation that would satisfy her. "And the bride wore white—the color of mourning in China. I simply did not understand, that or the reverence the people had for the huge, violent symbol of a man twisted in agony on a cross. Where is the need for all this ritual? A wedding is a simple enough thing."

Normally Émile would have smiled at the irony of her protestation. She had described to him in detail the sending of the matchmaker, the formal acceptance of the groom's family by the mother of the bride, the courtship, beginning with the ritual declaration of names and details of birth, the exchange of gifts. Finally, when every minute rite of preparation had been fulfilled, there was the ceremony of dressing the bride in the red bridal gown, the tiny red slippers, the red headdress and veil to hide the face of the virgin bride from all but her husband. The procession itself, formed and carried out in each detail as it had been for thousands of years, wound its way through the streets like a huge serpent pinned by hundreds of darts with red flags flapping from its top and sides. Tradition and her father's men carried the bride away from her home, held high in an ornate red sedan chair, and when the procession arrived at the groom's family compound, more rites and traditions were fulfilled before the bride was released and taken to the great hall, where she must be greeted in just the right way with just the right words, introduced to the relatives in the correct order, according to their rank and importance in the household. Then the new wife must cook her husband's supper—a certain kind of fish or fowl, prepared in a certain way, with spices that insured the favor of the gods and many children. And that was that.

Émile shook his head. He was painfully aware that this wedding would not fulfill a single familiar tradition for Lian, and though she said she did not mind, he wondered.

"Do not worry so much," she had admonished him. "Those rituals have no meaning for me. They are very cold, very rigid, born from superstition. The bride and groom are not seen as people with feelings and desires, only puppets who fulfill expectations and traditions from a thousand years before. I hope I can be more spontaneous than that." She'd slipped her arms around his waist and showed him that she could be.

Though he could not help but smile at the memory, Émile was uncomfortably aware that on the day he would become one with Lian, who had unveiled all her mysteries and laid bare her soul to him, she did not yet know him as fully, because he had not been completely honest. He had not told her all his secrets; he had not lied, but when she did not ask, he did not answer. He shivered, feeling unclean.

Lian felt the shudder as she felt every shift in his body, every change in his mood. They stood shoulder to shoulder, and her skin tingled at the contact of their arms, but she must not think of that. Émile was troubled. She put her hand over his. "If you wish to have a church, if that is part of your ritual, I will understand."

Émile had looked away, embarrassed because now it was she who was being gentle, thoughtful of his feelings, and he who kept his reasons and his doubts locked inside. He reached out to run his finger down a long, loose strand of her hair. "I do not need a church."

She turned to him earnestly, eyes as blue as the cloudless sky, lit from within by the summer sun. Unconsciously, easily, she took his hands, still startled and delighted by her body's response to his touch. "Then what troubles you? Your eyes are dark; I cannot read them."

He raised her hand to his lips, kissing the soft skin, saying a silent prayer of thanks that she had unwoven the threads of her cocoon and stepped into the light of day. "I'm nervous. It's expected of the groom, you know. We're already breaking enough rules and expectations today."

She smiled and kissed him, and in the rush of warmth as their lips met, he remembered that while she had said she cared for him and trusted him, she had never said she loved him. Then every other coherent thought left him.

The activity in the street had grown energetic. The flower vendors had obstructed the block at one end with their cart and risers; now the couple was arranging tumbled rows of vivid blooms. The children of Chervilles, whose teacher Lian had been, were helping with the preparations, crushing the petals that littered the street. The youngest threw the petals in the air, and the discarded flowers at one another, while girls sat weaving crowns and garlands from the blossoms. Herr Gustafson, the butcher, was laying out a large table with meats, while Claire and Henri Arnaud, with Yen Tai's help, set up a cake and rows of pastry and several kinds of bread. The dairy had sent brie and cheddar and Swiss to go with the hard rolls and baguettes.

People laughed and shouted to one another across the glistening cobbles, cleaned three times for the occasion, though they had been sparkling before the cleaning began. The neighbors were fond of Lian and Émile—the charmingly generous, funny and mysterious *bon vivant*—but mostly, they were pleased at the prospect of another celebration so soon after Bastille Day.

Lian shook her head in amazement, leaning close to Émile. "It is a good thing they know how to enjoy themselves, or this would be a very dull wedding indeed."

"I don't think there's any chance of that, *ma chere*." He closed his arms around her and enjoyed the weight of her head against his shoulder.

She turned to look up at him, suddenly uncertain. "There is one thing I would ask of you."

"What is it?"

"I would have you kneel with me before my family altar. To ask the spirits' blessing and tell my ancestors of our happiness." She blushed till her bronze skin glowed. "You must think me a fool, but it is one ritual I value, one superstition I cling to. Will you come?"

"Of course I will. I don't think your ritual foolish. Don't forget, I'm Catholic. We're not without our own superstitions and altars and saints that we pray to. And as for rituals—well, there are more than I can keep track of." He held her cool, elegant hand between his square callused ones. "Everyone needs comfort sometimes that people cannot give them. To kneel before the memory of your loved ones is, I think, a wise and very human means of praying."

Lian was amazed again and again at how much he understood. In silence, her fingers laced with his, she took him to her room and rolled up the reed blind so that he saw the altar to her ancestors for the first time. He thought it simple and very lovely and was touched that she wanted to share it with him. Together they knelt and Lian lowered the blind so they were closed inside the tiny sacred corner where she had so often wept and prayed and asked for inspiration.

As she lit the candles and incense, rearranged the white roses in the graceful porcelain bowl, Émile watched the flames reflected in the polished marble. Lian pulled out the soul tablets from beneath the embroidered curtain and pressed his fingers into the Chinese characters carved there, covering his hand with hers.

"This is my family, my past. I wanted you to feel it, not through me, but through their spirits, which linger here in stone and golden flame and curling incense."

Hand running over the smooth soul tablets with their deeply carved characters, eyes on the flames, Émile was intensely aware of the incense that swirled around them, binding them to each other and apart from the world beyond the blind. He was surprised to be caught up in Lian's reverence for the past, for her ancestors, for the spirits she kept bound to the earth by the fine, thin thread of her devotion.

When Lian drew out the intertwined white and yellow gold bracelet that had once belonged to her mother, the letter from her father asking her to come to the glen, and gave them to Émile, he held them as if they were infinitely precious, trying, as Lian did, to feel in these mementos the spirits of those who had touched them in life.

His head felt light and his vision blurred. For the first time, he felt the ghosts of Lian's past, not through her terror or nightmares, but through her veneration. He felt their power and their substance, and he understood, at last, why she found such comfort here, where she need never be alone.

Lian stared into the wavering candlelight, into the orange heart of the flame, and said a silent prayer, as she had done before, asking for a sign that the gods and the spirits of her ancestors approved of her marriage and her choice. She had received many such signs in her lifetime, before other altars—the guttering, then wild flare up of the candles when there was no breeze; the petals of peach blossoms falling from a branch into her hands spread open in entreaty; an indistinct voice inside a wind that rose and circled where no wind could be.

"Please," she whispered, gazing intensely, hopefully at the altar, "bless me and show me. Just once more."

Émile did not hear what she said, but he saw the vulnerability and entreaty in her face and his chest ached for her. Instinctively, wanting to comfort her, he reached out and took her hand, braiding his fingers tightly with hers.

The candles did not gutter nor the wind rise nor the rose petals tremble, and yet she knew she had her answer. It was very real and very human, and she realized that the physical sensation of Émile's hand was enough to tell her she had made the right choice.

If the gods were speaking to her now, they were speaking through human touch, as they never had before. Lian tilted her head. Or perhaps they had spoken, but she had not listened. Since meeting Émile, she had learned to hear with new ears, to see with new eyes, and to trust that the will of the gods was not jealous or destructive, would not let her go astray, unless she stopped listening to her own heart and spirit and the urgings of her soul.

She turned to Émile, her smile so radiant that it stopped his breath. "In China," she said, "it is shameful to show you care more for your sweetheart than for all your family, living and dead. But I think it must not necessarily be one or the other. To care for you, to free the feelings I have so long denied, frees me also to care for my ancestors, my mother, my father without anger or regret. My love for them is purer because of what you have taught me. Because I am not afraid." Her eyes were wide with wonder, like the eyes of a child who discovers his first miracle.

Without breaking the thread of their gaze, she put her free hand over their linked ones, tenderly, protectively, gratefully.

25

LIAN STOOD INSIDE THE APOTHECARY SHOP WITH CHENG when they heard a great commotion at the back and turned to find Lin-Mei stumbling toward them.

"I wanted to be with you on this day," she gasped, attempting to catch her breath. "And here I am."

Cheng offered the girl a seat and a cup of water. "Take a moment to rest and catch your breath," he suggested kindly.

"I thank you—" She broke off, staring, when Lian stepped into the light.

The bride was dressed in a purple satin gown embroidered with plum blossoms and a sleeveless silver tunic worked in a bamboo pattern. In her flat, she had braided her hair tightly, then, with a secret smile, shaken it free. Now it was held back loosely on one side with a clip of sapphires and silver filigree. Her skin was flushed with excitement, and her eyes were a clear, calm blue.

"You're so beautiful," Mei whispered reverently. "Like Maku, the kind fairy."

Lian smiled, touching the girl's shoulder briefly. "I bless you for coming, Lin-Mei. But how did you manage it?"

When Mei stood, Lian saw she was wearing a sky blue gown embroidered with butterflies, and a blue silk tunic with the suggestion of lotus leaves in the carefully dyed fabric. Her hair was braided simply, looped up and held with a silver butterfly clasp, as it would have been for any Chinese celebration.

"How?" she repeated, touched and mystified and anxious. If Mei had defied her parents yet again—

"I didn't run away." Lin-Mei stood tall and straight. "I told my parents that I would feel dishonorable if I abandoned you today, as we've all done too often. I told them it was your special celebration, and this the only gift that I could give you. I told them decency demanded that I come, that *you* wouldn't fail *me* on such a day, or Yi or any of us. You've always been there when we needed you. Yi told them I was right, that you'd never failed us." Mei shrugged, though the gesture was not natural to her. "How could they forbid me after that? What could they say?"

Lian's eyes were full of pride and gratitude, but she could not speak.

"Well, you look very lovely, very dignified, more mature," Cheng observed. "You carry yourself like a woman, a reed, slender and graceful, that bends with the storm but does not break."

Mei blushed like a young girl at the compliment. She knew Cheng did not toss them about indiscriminately. But she also seemed uncomfortable with her newfound independence. "I told them I wouldn't speak to Yen Tai. I didn't want them to think—"

Cheng put his finger to his lips. "Ah! That was wise, though I see it was difficult for you. But keep in mind that a woman knows in her heart that patience will be rewarded. In time I think you will find what you seek, though it may surprise you, this discovery."

She glanced at Lian.

"He enjoys being inscrutable. Do not try to understand. Only remember the words, because someday they will make sense." She smiled and took Mei's hand. "I am so glad you are here. You cannot know what it means to me." Lian thought of her half-sisters, worlds away from here, whose presence she also wished for. She would have to be content with the telegrams of congratulations and exuberance from Ailsa, Genevra and Mairi Rose. She had slipped them into her sleeve, so their words would be near her skin, reminding her that their thoughts were with her. It was easier to accept their absence now that Mei was here.

Impulsively, Lian drew her toward the front of the shop and indicated the street beyond the huge windows. "Have you seen Rue Salubre?"

There was color everywhere, the noise was loud and cheerful, the bustle vigorous, and everyone watched the door of the shop between sips of beer and bites of cheese. "Out there is the future, but now there is just us—my two dear friends and me."

Émile had disappeared into the crowd to make certain all was ready, and Lian stood waiting, clasping Mei's hand on one side and Cheng's on the other.

"The bride!" the people in the street were calling. "Where is the bride?" Across the way a single flute began to play, and the fine, clear notes drifted over the heads of the people of Chervilles, teasing Lian, beguiling her.

"The *bride!* The *bride!*" the word filled the air, pushing away the drifts of clouds like a mighty wind.

"We had better go out before they shatter my windows with their clamor," Cheng said. But he was smiling. He flung open the door and a cheer went up as he moved forward, followed by Mei and Lian.

The other two had already passed when the bride stepped onto the cobbled street and nearly tripped over a goat.

"Forgive me, Mademoiselle," Jean-Paul said, shamefaced. "I told them they must stay at home today, but Gertrud would give me no peace till I promised to bring her. She had her heart set on attending your wedding." He shrugged with the flair only young Frenchmen had ever mastered. "What could I do? Break her heart?" He leaned close to whisper, "When she sulks she does not give me her milk, and I could not risk that. *Quelle horreur!* You must see that I had no choice."

"Of course you did not." Lian smiled, choking back a laugh. A wedding should be a solemn thing, after all. Besides, she was afraid if she opened her mouth, it would be filled with flower petals, which people were tossing into the air with enthusiasm.

Through the velvet, soft colored, scented rain, Lian turned toward the small platform hastily erected, where Émile and the others were waiting.

Mei and Cheng preceded her along the path that had suddenly cleared. When she reached the platform, Lian saw that a stranger in a brown robe stood beside Cheng. Henri Arnaud had brought a priest to make the wedding legal according to French law, while Cheng would bestow upon it a Chinese blessing. Lian's eyes met Émile's and she shivered as if he had caressed her. Her silver satin slippers barely touching the cobbles, she crossed to the platform, carried on the lilting, silver notes of the flute and the expression in her bridegroom's eyes.

When she reached the step, Émile reached down to lift her up beside him. His eyes widened when he saw, not only how moved she was, and yet how close to laughter, but that she wore a gown that was familiar. Where had he seen it before?

The flute trilled out a few last trembling notes while Lian stood beside her groom. He looked quite sophisticated in his top hat and morning coat with tails, his snowy white shirt and elegant cravat.

Émile drew Lian forward as the priest stood before them with a bemused expression on his face. The tiny man, narrow as a reed, seemed to wield more power than anyone present. When he raised his hand, the crowd fell silent. Lian exchanged a surprised look with Mei.

The priest made the sign of the cross and spoke in Latin, first to Émile and then to Lian. They answered, clinging to one another's hands, echoing the words they were told to repeat, all the while aware of the people jostling for a better view. The priest spoke quickly, afraid that at any moment this boisterous French crowd would become over-enthusiastic. He did not wish to risk his life today, amusing as the scene was, and as often as he would describe it in the years to come. Bride and groom knelt to receive the complicated Latin blessing. The priest made the sign of the cross over their bent heads and pronounced them husband and wife, while the flute echoed hauntingly around and among them.

They rose, and Émile kissed Lian lightly, but she pulled him closer, until they blocked the tiny priest from view. The people called out their approval while the priest, wisely, skittered away. When bride and groom parted, Émile smiled broadly and touched Lian's loose hair. "My wife," he whispered, glancing again at her lovely gown and tunic. Then, with a shock, he remembered where he had seen it before. In the ebony Chinese chest. He had nestled the fragile mother-of-pearl headdress in these purple and silver folds the night Lian had asked him to put the chest away forever. She had opened it today. He lifted her off her feet in pleasure and relief.

Sliding his hand up inside the wide quilted sleeve of her gown, he said, "You aren't afraid anymore of the memories?"

"Not anymore," she answered breathlessly, because he was holding her so tight. Realizing how closely they were being watched, and that the others on the platform were waiting, she nudged him and they turned back to face Cheng.

He stepped forward, putting one hand on each of their outside shoulders. "Remember to seek always contentment, to find joy in the small things—the shape of a leaf of thyme, the fragrance of cinnamon, the last of the winter flowers and the first of the pale green spring leaves, in the laughter of your children and the lightest touch of one another's hand. You have begun your journey at last, though, Lian, you may think that today you have reached the end. Remember what Confucius said. 'Birth is not a beginning, nor death an ending.' You are always becoming what you will someday be. And remember these words from the *Tao Teh Cheng*: 'To be Great is to go forward, To go forward is to travel far, To travel far is to return.' Remember, wherever you are, if your heart and spirit are pure, you can always return to those places and people you love. And remember as I told you once before: 'Man does not attain the one-winged birds of our childhood tale; they must rise together.' "

He paused, hands clasped beneath his wisp of white beard. "Rise together, Émile and Lian, and know that the sky is endless in its boundaries and its beauty; it will never disappoint, nor will it constrain you. Rise."

Cheng pressed their shoulders and the couple turned to face the people of Chervilles. For a full minute, congratulations echoed off the ivy-covered stone houses, floating out over the Seine, rippled by a light breeze.

Lian and Émile stared in amazement at what they had not noticed before. The houses were draped with garlands of fresh flowers, the cobbles were not visible through the petals that had showered down from generous hands. The food tables were piled with pastries and breads, meats and cheese and fruit. There was also beer and cider, lemonade and jasmine tea from the creamerie.

A magician and a group of singers performed, while Claude the butcher juggled. Lian could not help but remember how secret her last wedding had been, how dark, the words spoken in whispers so no one would overhear. Today, all of Chervilles would hear; the street was a blur of color and music and laughter.

Just as they stepped down from the platform, Lian noticed three people standing formally erect, hands folded before them, apparently oblivious to the tumult. The Chins. She had sent word, but had not thought they would come, particularly not like this. All three were dressed in Chinese gowns, the women in satin slippers, Chin Yun in cloth-soled shoes. They wore embroidered silk and satin, jade and gold ornaments and pearls. Even Yi, who grinned at her impudently behind a lace fan.

Chin Yun and Chin Shu had chosen the only way they could show their affection and respect and yet retain their dignity. They had worn formal dress clothing brought from China and hidden away in cedar chests since their arrival in France.

Lian's eyes were once again full. Placing her hands palm to palm, she bowed. "I am happy to see you. It would not have been the same without my second family here." She had one arm around Mei and one around Yi-niang, who clung as if she did not intend to let go.

Returning her formal bow, Chin Shu murmured, "We give you our best wishes for happiness in your marriage. You *do* deserve it."

So the Chins had heard and understood her after all. Lian smiled.

In that instant, she became aware of Yi tugging on her sleeve. When she bent down, the girl whispered, "I promised to give them no peace till they agreed to come. I *wanted* to do it—for you *and* for us, Mei and me."

"I am grateful that you are so fearless and obstinate. But I would not wish to be your parents in the next few years. I do not think they realize the challenge they face."

Yi smiled sweetly, eyes discreetly lowered. "As you say, My Teacher."

Out of the corner of her eye, Lian noticed Yen Tai and his family hovering some distance away, watching. Lian called them over. "I thank you all for coming today."

Yen Tai replied politely, but his attention was on Mei, at whom he was trying to stare without appearing to do so. His gaze was worried and wistful and full of longing. She saw that the Chins and the Yens had seen it too. The two fathers looked hard and long at each other, nodded firmly.

"Perhaps the young ones are thirsty after so much excitement," Chin Yun said. "Yen Tai, will you escort my daughters, make certain they are safe?" He was asking much more, and Yen Tai knew it. He nodded, bowed, then led Yi and Mei away.

Lian saw the strain in Chin Yun's face and took his hands. "I know that was not easy for you, that you are not happy about it, but it was most generous and kind. Look." She pointed toward the three young people. Yen Tai was walking behind them, arms spread wide to keep away any danger that might approach. He was taking Chin Yun quite seriously. "He will not let your daughters come to harm. Either of them. I thank you, Chin Yun. From my heart."

"You care for Mei that much?" Monsieur Chin could not hide his surprise.

"For all of you. I think I understand what is in your heart. However your actions or your anger sometimes appear, I know that your heart, your intention is good."

The Chins could see she was telling the truth, and it shamed them. Despite their training, each put a hand on her shoulder and squeezed. Contrary to all tradition and rules of polite behavior, Lian leaned forward to kiss them on both cheeks.

"Now come meet my husband." She started at the sound of the word on her lips, then smiled.

They nodded to one another, knowing she was at peace with them.

As Lian turned away, people began to hug her and Émile, to kiss them on both cheeks and cry out congratulations, many with tears in their eyes. Lian recognized the butcher and his wife; Gabrielle; the flower vendor; the seamstress Nicole and her husband, the costermonger; Docteur Ricard; Henri and Claire Arnaud; as well as the children from her class at the small makeshift school in this tiny town.

All afternoon and evening, the couple ate and accepted gifts and danced on the cobbled street. They drank a second bottle of chrysanthemum wine Cheng had hidden away years ago, toasting each other silently. Always Émile was beside Lian, his hand on her arm or around her waist or, now and then when they caught a moment alone, cupping her growing belly tenderly.

Lian did not notice the exact moment when she forgot her dignity. She laughed aloud, kissed Émile openly and swung from one set of arms to another, so that her feet rarely touched the ground. She was enjoying herself without inhibition. Émile was her husband and she carried his child. The couple were embraced by a whole town of friends as exuberant as they. She had never in her life been this awake and alive and free.

"My Mother," she whispered, "I have fulfilled my promise. I have more than survived. I have found joy. I thank you for believing this foolish one would someday open her eyes and see how vivid was the world around her, when before it had been dull and gray. I thank you for this chance, this gift. Nothing could have been more precious."

Always there is hope, so long as you survive.

26

ÉMILE AND LIAN SETTLED INTO THE BOAT THAT WOULD take them to Paris, huddled back to front, their feet up on the seat. It was very quiet on the Seine, and they could hear quite clearly the water lapping against the hull. The intermittent moonlight sparkled on the silver waves of the river, and they listened to one another's breathing, taking comfort in the rhythm and the sound.

They were met at the dock in Paris by a plush hansom cab. By then, they were too relaxed and tired to speak, but the silence between them was comfortable, even soothing. When the cab rolled to a stop in front of Émile's house, the horse snorting and shaking its head, Émile helped Lian step down and paid the driver. They stood for a moment, leaning on each other, watching the cab drive away. Lian's eyes widened when she saw that the small oval window was wreathed in a garland of flowers, the wheels were twined with flowers and ivy, and several long ropes of roses hung from the back. She had not noticed the decorations before; she had been nearly blind with exhaustion when she climbed into the cab and sat down, sinking back on the red leather seat with a sigh of gratitude. Now she smiled wistfully.

Émile put his arm around her waist. "What are you thinking?"

Because she was too tired to consider, she answered honestly. "I was thinking of my last wedding, of how very different it was from this one."

"Different in what way?"

Lian heard the tension in his voice, but did not recognize what it meant. She leaned back against him, head on his shoulder. "It was forbidden, secret, traditional and rigid, only half a marriage, empty because we could let no one know, not even our families." She paused, her mind drifting back to that distant past. "It was very beautiful and very sad, and I knew even then that it would bring more sorrow than joy. I simply did not know how much, or how far and how long that sorrow would follow me—even to this moment."

"Even now you think of him?"

Lian turned to consider her new husband closely, so that, in the golden light of the street lamp, she saw his vulnerability. She was shocked that he did not bother to hide these things, as she would have done instinctively, defensively. Émile was not afraid to let her see through the layers of his skin and bone and blood to his heart. She felt a wave of gratitude and envy as she put her hand on his chest. "Today, for me, our wedding was full of affection and jubilation and sweetness: I taste it on my tongue in the gifts of food and candy, hear it in my ears in the laughter and generosity of the people, smell it in the thousands of flowers and the scent of your cologne. I feel the pleasure in my heart, the delight your touch gives me, the lightness and the freedom I thought never to know. I feel all that and more in the movement of our child inside me." She cradled her belly with her free hand.

Émile responded to the musical flow of her pleasure, but he was still wary. "The foreboding you felt then, the sorrow you foresaw?"

Lian put her other hand on his chest, one on top of the other, covering his slow-beating heart. "Today I feel no shadows upon me. You have destroyed them one by one, so that now there is only happiness, and gratitude, and hope."

Finally, Émile smiled and bent to touch her lips with his.

After they had eaten artichokes, *foie-gras* stuffed quail, and pear slices in brandy, after they had drunk a little champagne in a toast to their marriage and their already growing family, Émile took Lian to his bedroom. She stopped inside the door to stare in dismay at a huge four poster bed with a brocade canopy and intricately carved rosewood posts that nearly reached the moulded ceiling. There was a huge marble fireplace, two wing-backed chairs and a settee upholstered in velvet, and a Persian rug so beautiful it took her breath away. The mahogany night tables were large, trimmed in the same design that adorned the bedposts, and draped with Belgian lace as delicate as spider floss. She froze, mouth open, not quite sure how to respond.

"I know," Émile said behind her. "It's ridiculous, isn't it? But it came with the house, and I could hardly remove it all by brute force, although sometimes when I waken in the morning to see that canopy hanging over me like the shadow of doom, I'm sorely tempted."

He folded her into his arms and held her for a long moment, resting his cheek on her sleek black hair, until a discreet knock on the door surprised them into pulling away.

"*Oui?*" Émile said. "*Entrez.*"

Pierre stuck his head around the door carefully, averting his eyes and managing to look dignified, nonetheless. "*Pardon*, but will there be anything else, Sir? Madame?"

"*Rien de tout*, Pierre." Nothing at all. "Please go and get some rest."

"*Oui*, Monsieur, and may I say congratulations to you both."

Émile smiled broadly, grasping Lian's hand and drawing her close. "You may say it as often as you like."

"And so I shall," Pierre said, returning his master's smile. "But for now I will wish you *bonne nuit.*"

He was gone before they could respond.

Lian stared at the ornate gold paneled door through which the valet had disappeared. "This house," she said, "how did you find such a place?"

Émile became uneasy, his jaw tensed and his smile faded. "In just a moment, *mon amour*. But first I wish to give you a wedding gift." He went to the opposite wall and turned up the gas jet.

Lian watched curiously. He was behaving oddly, as if he were ashamed—or apprehensive. It was very unlike his usual confident manner. Her heart began to beat rapidly. Émile removed a piece of fine cloth draped over a frame on the wall that she had not noticed before. "Come," he held out his hand to her. As she went around the foot of the bed, she saw that her carved ebony chest had been placed there, but the sight of it inspired no terror; her thoughts, her affections, her questions were focused on Émile. She was watching his face, not the frame on the wall, so for a long moment she did not see the painting he had uncovered.

Her new husband clasped her fingers and drew her into the circle of bright light. She leaned against his side, turning slowly toward the wall. Spellbound, she moved closer, staring in wonder at the oil painting depicting the scene he had done in watercolor and titled "Bastille Day," only this time Lian wore a teal blue gown and emerald tunic, her hair was loose, caught up by the wind, held only by a small jade hair pin. She was smiling, holding open the double doors that had ignited her curiosity for so long, and gazing with wide eyes into the wild, chaotic, colorful garden. She was clearly entranced by the untamed beauty of pink, red and yellow roses climbing up walls thick with ivy, so that thorny branch and supple vine were intertwined. The banks of small white marguerites had nearly been obscured by golden peonies and lilacs and red geraniums run wild. Only the calla lilies seemed to stand alone. Behind Lian, even the remnants of last night's celebration—multicolored confetti and streamers and the shiny red, blue and white tubes of burnt out firecrackers—were vivid reminders of an extravagant, unruly holiday, proof of the excitement and light and exuberance that had filled the streets hours before. A small engraved gold plaque at the bottom of the frame bore the inscription: *Le Jardin*, and beneath that in much smaller letters, Bastille Day, 1881. The last line read simply: For Lian.

She felt tears rising and fought them back, not because she did not want Émile to see her weep, but because she was happy, astonished by his gift. He had understood that she had not thrown the sketch at him without thought and asked him to paint her; she truly wished she could turn her face toward the garden, open the doors unafraid, become part of the picture, part of the life and blood and energy that flowed through those vibrant colors.

She turned and wrapped her arms around his waist, speaking so quietly he had to bend down to hear her. "It is beautiful, my husband. More than I ever expected."

"You have never expected enough, *ma petite,* not *for* yourself, only *of* yourself. You deserve a great deal more than this. But that we will discover together." He paused for a moment, then murmured, "*Je t'aime,* Lian. So much."

She held him closer, the feel of his sturdy body against hers both comforting and alluring. She could not speak, so she raised her head to kiss him. For a long time, they held each other, feeling the heat of each other's breath, of their bodies pressed so close together, of their mouths, moving eagerly, hungrily, their lips moist and sweet.

All at once Émile pulled away and held her at arms' length. "Before we go on, I must tell you the truth about myself. You deserve that. I can't hold you this way, feel your yielding body leaning trustingly against mine, when you don't know."

She stared at him, mouth dry with misgiving. A moment ago she had felt so safe, so aroused, so right. Now she did not know what to feel. He had taught her to trust him, a little at a time, and now, suddenly, he had a secret that disturbed him deeply. His eyes were dark, even in the bright light of the gas lamp.

"Come," he said, "sit with me and I will tell you. I would have done it long ago, but for my uncertainty and my damned pride." They sat side by side on the high, ornate bed, the canopy casting a shadow over their faces. He stared straight ahead, not meeting her eyes, his face rigid, his lips unsmiling. "You asked where I found this house. I didn't find it; it was here, waiting for me, or any one of my family who cared to visit Paris, though they haven't done so for many years. It belongs to us. This, and the chateau in Burgundy, and thousands of acres of vineyards." His face flushed with embarrassment, he took a deep breath, as if he were starved for air. "I am one of two sons of a wealthy landowner and vintner. I have two sisters as well."

When he fell silent, Lian took his hand. "Go on."

Émile closed his eyes with a heartfelt sigh. He put his hands on his knees, gathering his thoughts, and continued woodenly, "Our vineyards made the family rich more than two hundred years ago, so my grandmother felt secure enough, or stubborn enough, to ignore the family's admonitions and marry a peasant with whom she happened to be in love. It turned out he had a good head for business, and though the family was appalled and predicted disaster, together my grandparents increased our fortune considerably." He smiled at the irony; he could not help himself.

Lian was more and more perplexed. "But what—"

He touched her lips with his finger. "It was difficult enough for me to begin. Please let me finish."

Lian sat back and waited.

"After many years, just when the family had begun to accept this peasant, my grandmother, who had grown old and less tolerant, announced that her joints ached with arthritis and she was tired of the strain of living with such a large family. 'I love you all dearly,' she said, 'but I can't bear to live among you anymore. You will surely kill me with your care and attention, which comforts you and drives me mad. So, my Jacques and I,' even after so long, her voice softened when she said his name, 'will go back to his family cottage where we'll grow old and senile in peace.'

"There was quite an uproar, which in my view only proved her point. But then, they said I always took her side. They say I am most like her. They thought it an insult, but I was pleased, because even when I was a child, I sensed a core of goodness in her, kindness and a well of strength that never ran dry. It was that which compelled her to flaunt the family traditions, to jeopardize their social standing. Though it could never be diminished, no matter what she did; we were too rich. She married a good man who loved her and stayed by her her whole life. I always hoped my family was right, that I have just a little of her strength of character."

He paused, a tender smile on his lips, apparently having forgotten this was a confession. "I was the only one who ever visited her in that cottage. I spent more time there than in the chateau. It felt safe in her warm kitchen, comfortable. No one pretended to be what they were not." He sat upright at those words, remembering why he was telling this story. He flushed again and would not look at his new wife.

She was confused and faintly relieved; her stomach fluttered with a feeling she could not identify. "So this thing which you have kept from me, this thing which I deserve to know—what, exactly, are you telling me?"

He turned slightly toward her and bowed his head. "I'm afraid I'm an aristocrat, that my money, which people wonder about so openly and often, comes from a fortune more than two centuries old."

He made it sound like a sentence of death. Lian wanted to laugh in relief and building hysteria, but Émile looked so dejected and ashamed that she could not do it. "An aristocrat," she repeated. She knew what that meant to the people of Paris, particularly in Montmartre, where so many of the rebellions against the old, wealthy, arrogant and oppressive establishment had begun. Where Émile had told her he had many friends. To Lian it meant nothing. She, of all people, understood what it was to be unable to choose your birthright, to wish every day that it had been different. Why, then, was her husband so distressed by the admission? And why, if she did not care, was her stomach churning and her head spinning? She knew she must say something; he was waiting for her reaction. "Why are you here, and not at home in the vineyard, and why did you lie for so long through your silence?" Her voice shook, but it was not from fear of his answers or shock at what he had revealed. It was something else, something . . . dangerous.

Émile finally faced her. "You have heard of phylloxera, which wiped out the wine crops in France a decade ago? Ours were not exempt. There's nothing to do now that the vineyards are row after row of dead, twisted vines. It's depressing, and we're absolutely helpless. My parents' only comfort is that the fortune is large enough to carry us through many more years, mostly because of my grandmother and her clever peasant. I was going mad with the futility of it, infuriated and frustrated by my own impotence. I used to walk the dead land and want to weep at what had once been lush and green, red and full of beauty with the wine to come. I tried to paint, as I've always wanted to. My family deplored it, of course, compared me to 'those useless Bohemians in Paris.' Only my grandmother encouraged me. She said I should leave my frustration, stop carrying the weight of responsibility for something I could not change, and at least enjoy what was left of my youth.

"Still, I hesitated to leave my family, until one day I heard of a brilliant alchemist named Cheng, who lived in a small town outside Paris and was famous for diagnosing and curing what other doctors could not. He was also a scientist, experimenting with concoctions he'd made to help the earth as well as the people who lived on it. I heard he was working on a formula to kill the poison in the ground, to keep it from coming back.

" 'Now you will go,' my grandmother told me, shaking her head in disgust, 'because you carry responsibility with you, and do not simply seek your own pleasure or pursue the dream of your heart—to paint. Promise me you'll absorb every last morsel of pleasure and freedom and knowledge of your craft as well as working with this Cheng.' She would not let me go until I promised. So, now, here I am."

He rose to pace restlessly. "As for why I didn't tell anyone, aside from the virulent hatred of the aristocracy that flows through France—as wine once flowed down their throats—" he paused and swung to face her. "I was ashamed of the wealth I had done nothing to earn. All my friends are poor, struggling artists who have given up everything to come here and pursue their dream. The true artists and intellectuals scoff at money, especially old money." He shook his head, smiling slightly. "Yet those very purists are often shameless in the pursuit of what they claim to disdain. But that doesn't matter." He cleared his throat. "I was embarrassed, Lian, by how much I had when they had so little. And as for the chemical experiments, I did not speak of them in case they failed. Pride, you see, always pride, foolish as it may have been. I told you once, but you probably didn't believe me, or even remember."

Lian remembered. *Pride is my particular sin. You would not have guessed it, would you? But it's true. Never forget that it's true.* And Cheng. The ease and familiarity between the two men, Émile's regular visits to Rue Salubre, the stick in the back room that she'd found on the day she discovered she was carrying a child. Suddenly it all made sense.

Noticing how pale her skin was, how cool ice blue her eyes, Émile knelt at her feet. "I didn't ever wish to lie to you, deceive you. But especially after I learned what you'd suffered, my idiotic pride wouldn't let me admit that my life had been easy, at least until the plague hit our land. But even then, all I felt was helplessness." He took her cold, unmoving hands in his. "Can you understand that? Can you forgive me?"

She nodded, but her face was blank. Without a word, she rose, stunned, and stood at the window with her back to him. She stared blindly at the leafy green trees below, the glowing gas lamps, the hansom cabs coming and going, yet she saw nothing. Her silence was so long that Émile feared she was retreating as she had that day when she knelt beside the chest and faced her past in the shape of a peacock headdress. "I did not ask. I married you, but I did not ask who you really were or what you did besides paint, or about your family. I did not even pause to wonder," she said at last. Her voice was toneless, unrecognizable.

Her husband was frightened by her stiffness. It was true that such behavior—marrying a man about whom she knew no particulars—was not like her. "Why not?" He wondered if he wanted to know the answer.

Lian turned jerkily, like a puppet whose strings are tangled, inhibiting its movement. She looked directly into Émile's eyes and said slowly and clearly, "I did not ask because it did not occur to me. I did not think of the rumors, the speculations, the ugly insinuations about your wealth. I did not think of the secret alliance with Cheng which he would not explain. I remembered none of these things. They did not matter."

"I don't understand. You're so careful about everyone and everything."

Lian smiled tremulously, shaken by the realization that had struck her like a hot spark. "I used to be. Always. It was what my mother taught me, what kept me alive more than once. But that was before I met you." She paused, gathering strength. "I did not take time to think this through, to analyze, to wonder who you are, where you came from, why you are so secretive about the past." She ran her hands through her hair, astonishment lighting her bronze face. "I simply—acted."

A physical shock propelled her forward. "It did not matter—your past and your secrets. *Nothing* mattered but what I felt here." She rested her hand over her heart. "I trust you. I—" She stopped.

Émile had begun to understand. "You trusted your instincts instead of your mind with its stringent rules and restraints."

Lian nodded. "Yes. Never before have I acted so blindly, yet if I stopped to think now, to examine and question, I would not change what we have done." *The choice is yours, and always has been.*

"I knew I was safe, that what we had was right, because I listened to my heart. I knew, I've always known, because I love you."

The words, so long unuttered, hovered on the air in a whisper, clear and real. Lian could not hold back her tears, and Émile held her, amazed at the enormity of her admission. She had finally, finally, let go of her caution, and therefore, her fear.

27

THEY TURNED THE SETTEE TOWARD THE WINDOW AND SAT IN silence, holding each other's hands loosely, leaning shoulder to shoulder, absorbing each other's heat and contentment. There was more to discuss, but for now, they wanted peace in which to consider this new and astounding discovery. Lian put her head on Émile's shoulder as they looked out at the night full of vague but comforting shapes and sounds.

Her entire body had been drained of fear, of memory of conflict and doubt. She felt boneless and drowsy and light-headed, without the burden she had carried on her shoulders all her life, in one form or another. She was weightless, free, ecstatic. "You have done this for me, my husband, though I fought you every moment, through each step forward and each stumble backward. You have waited and believed and clung to hope when I thought there was no hope to feel. I thank you."

Émile put his hand under her chin and looked into her eyes. "It's not your gratitude I want, Lian."

She reached up to kiss him, her lips warm and pliant, one hand caught in his curly hair, the other on his shoulder, both tense with passion and need. He leaned into her and put his arms around her, drawing her close, so he could smell the honeysuckle in her hair. They held each other, taking with hands and mouths all they could, until the scent and pulse and heartbeat of one fused into that of the other, and they shuddered with desire.

Lian drew away, gasping for breath. "Does that feel like gratitude to you?"

Touched by her open display of affection, aroused by the kiss that had ended too soon, he reached for her again. But she was looking over his shoulder, brow furrowed. He turned, annoyed, until he saw what had caught her attention. The Chinese chest at the foot of the bed. He started to speak, then thought better of it. This was her private struggle; he could not make it right for her.

She turned, eyes veiled by a sheen of tears. "Finally, tonight, with you beside me, I would like to look deeper into the chest I have opened twice before, but blindly and in fear. At last I *want* to know what my mother thought precious enough to send so far over so many seas. And I want you beside me."

Before he could misinterpret her meaning, she smiled and touched his cheek. "Because you are my husband, my friend, and I want you to see that there was also beauty in my past. Only you. I want to take you on a treasure hunt as you took me on a hunt through the dark clinging web of my memories. And Émile," she met his gaze steadily, "I am no longer afraid of what that chest holds, what memories it might bring. I have faced the worst and left them behind me." She stood up, suddenly eager, her face lit to a golden glow in the lamplight. "Come. Come with me."

So they sat and rediscovered her past, as she took out item after item and told him its history, its purpose, its meaning to her. The simple cotton trousers and wide-sleeved top she had worn in her mountain retreat, where she had dressed and worked like a peasant and been content. The poem she had written the night before she left her mother for the last time. Lian put it aside for Émile to read. She was too emotional just now. Ke-ming had included a dried peony and a lotus leaf, a handful of willow bark tea, which she'd used to ease her daughter's blinding headaches, some jade hairpins and Lian's favorite moon mirror of ebony inlaid with mother-of-pearl.

Such an odd assortment. It told Lian as much about Ke-ming as it told Émile about his wife. Surprisingly, gently folded and preserved with camphor, was one of the gauze curtains decorated with satin butterflies that had hung from Lian's bed in Peking. There was a simple blue tunic with Ke-ming's scent, which Lian held to her face for a long time. No one had ever imitated the fragrance that was her mother; it was uniquely Ke-ming, and one of the things that had intrigued and comforted Lian in her youth. There was a carefully folded silk lantern in the shape of twin nightingales, *The Analects of Confucius*, which her teacher, Wu Shen, had inscribed to her when she was seven. Some smooth colored stones taken from the pond at their compound in Peking, to remind her of the beauty of the gardens and their healing power. At the very bottom was Ke-ming's jewel chest, filled with sapphires and pearls, white and green jade, gold bracelets and ruby earrings, a brooch of pearls shaped like a butterfly and much more. Lian looked up at Émile, smiling. "You see, I, too, was rich all along. Only I did not know it. That is what my mother meant when she mentioned the jewels that would keep me safe."

Émile regarded her solemnly. "What of the gown folded so carefully on top?"

She stared down at her hands. "I wore it the first day I went to stand at the Vermilion Gates."

Émile was appalled. "Yet you wore it at our wedding?"

She took his hand and squeezed it hard. "I wanted to eliminate the sense of tragedy and replace it with my serenity. Now, when I look at this gown and tunic, I will think of this amazing day, of the street transformed for our wedding, of the vows we made and the advice Cheng gave us as I turned from China and toward you. Now when I stain it with my tears, they will be tears of joy."

Because he could find no words, Émile kissed her.

They emptied the chest and refilled it until nothing was left but the peacock headpiece. Lian smiled sadly, but her hands were steady when she laid it in a bed of cloth and slowly closed the lid. She was weeping, but it was with happiness and relief that she could touch her past again without pain or regret, feel the beauty and pleasure, the memories of all she had once treasured.

Émile leaned against the ornate headboard of his monstrous bed while Lian slid down so her head rested at the crook of his bent leg. There had been long minutes of silence between them, but it was an easy, comfortable silence, and when they spoke, their quiet voices threaded through the air and intertwined.

Staring out at the ornate room, Émile felt again the elation he had experienced when Lian shared her past with him. First she had shown him the horror, now the beauty. Until tonight, he had begun to believe there had been only ugliness, and he was moved at the moments she had described, the beauty of the objects she drew from the large chest. He had been amazed and humbled as she showed him her treasures. He thought of the altar to her ancestors, her family to whom and for whom she prayed every day, as if their spirits hovered just above her shoulder.

Gently, he put his cool palm on her forehead—a simple gesture, but intimate and soothing. She sighed with pleasure. "Never take it away," she murmured.

"No," he said, surprised by the shock of heat that ran through his body, at the sensation of his callused palm on her smooth, bronze forehead. "But we must talk about the future."

She did not shift or pull away, but lay contentedly beneath his hand. "Yes."

"I've been thinking that perhaps it's time to go back to Burgundy, back home. I've done what I can with Cheng; I have some formulas to try on the barren vineyards. He'll continue to work here, but he doesn't need me. And I miss my family, my eccentric grandmother. Would you be willing to go soon?"

Lian sat up so quickly that Émile had to brace himself against the bed. "Of course you must go home." She looked down, flushing. Home. She did not know what that word meant anymore, yet suddenly she recognized that she *had* a home. She touched the baby moving inside her. "We must go. They are your family and they need you, just as you need them. I think you have missed them more than you know."

Émile was disconcerted. "What makes you think they need me?"

Kneeling, Lian placed her hands on his knees. "I have come to know you well in these past months. I know that their loss of your patience and thoughtfulness and humor would leave a void no one could fill. And you have missed *them*, not only because you love them, but because you feel you abandoned them."

Now that her eyes were open, she saw too much. Émile looked away. "I thought, when I came here, that I wanted to leave my family behind. I found friends in Montmartre, others in Chervilles, and then I found you." He gazed into the distance. "But you're right, I do miss my bickering sisters and brother and my parents and Grandmere, who always knew me so well. I miss them especially deeply having seen your loneliness at losing a family to whom you can never return."

Lian's eyes were dry, but she felt bereft. She had never really had a family, except for a few months in a Scottish glen. She would never lose the intimacy, the bonds that tied her to Ailsa, Genevra and Mairi Rose. *I tell ye from the heart that ye'll always have a home here. I think ye know it.* Lian did know it, and thanked the gods every day for that blessing. Those three women were her family as surely as Ke-ming had given birth to her. But Ailsa, Genevra, and Mairi were not physically with her day by day. She had a kind of family, but not a real home. She wanted one more than she had wanted anything in her lifetime.

Émile read her thoughts easily. "I want to give you my family, even as we make our own."

She looked him in the eye and asked quietly, "Will they want me?"

"Yes," he said, "because I love you. Because you're my wife, they'll try to love you too, and it won't be difficult." He rested his forehead on hers. "I want to thank you."

"Thank me? But it is you who have awakened me from my long nightmare."

Émile shook his head. "I'm grateful to you for making me see what my family means to me. I hoped all along that I was helping you to heal. I didn't realize that at the same time, you were healing me."

Lian looked up at him, holding back tears. "Is that true, Émile Drouard?"

He pulled her against him and murmured, "It's true."

With her arms locked tightly around him and his warm breath in her hair, Lian wept with relief, with happiness, without sorrow or regret.

Epilogue

Fourteen years later: Burgundy, France, 1895

"YOU SEEM TO HAVE LEFT ME, *MON AMOUR*. WHERE ARE YOU now, this moment?"

"In the glen with my sisters," Lian responded without thinking. "I had a disturbing dream last night, and it clings to me still." As she spoke, she kept a close eye on her two youngest boys, Vincent, nine, and Marc, seven, wrangling across the room. Their trousers and loose blouses were already smudged with dust and what looked to be soot from the empty fireplace. She did not ask how it had gotten all over their faces and hands. Probably they had decided to excavate the chimney, having nothing more exciting to do. At least they were tussling on the wood floor and not the nearby Persian carpet. Her mind was half on her children, half on the images that lingered from her dream.

"Another one?" Émile asked in concern. "That's the third this week." Over the many years he and Lian had been married, he had come to recognize and respect the strange bond among the three half-sisters and their dreams. If his wife had dreamt of Ailsa three times, uneasy dreams from which Lian woke distracted and apprehensive, then something was wrong. "Tell me."

Lian and Émile sat in the parlor, savoring the taste of the Drouards' second good year of wine since phylloxera had struck in the 1870s. Émile had worked hard with the help of his family and the local people to revitalize the poisoned earth with the mixtures Cheng gave him. They struggled to make the soil rich again and fertile, to plant and nurture grapes with extra care, until finally a full, sweet crop had been brought in and transformed into the wine that had made the Drouards rich nearly two hundred years ago. He tipped his glass toward his wife's and they touched rims, always grateful for the rebirth of the wine, never taking for granted the miracle of full oak vats and the musky red liquid in their glasses.

Lian rolled the wine around on her tongue, turned to glance at the noisy boys, who were shouting at each other over a game of checkers they had laid out on the floor. She turned back to Émile. "I cannot remember much of it clearly; it was blurred and out of focus. But I remember as if she were beside me now, the heat of Genevra's body next to mine, the dismay and dread that consumed us as we watched Ailsa on the far side of the glen. We were calling out to her, but she did not hear. The furor in the glen held her attention."

"What furor?" Émile prodded.

Lian sighed. "That's the part I could not see, except that I knew, as Genevra knew, that there was trouble and confusion and pain so palpable it pulsed in the air. Ena was there, and Mairi Rose, holding onto each other as if they could not stand alone. We were frightened for them, Genevra and I."

Her husband saw her hand was shaking, took her glass and called out to his sons, "A little quiet, *s'il vous plaît*. Maman is distressed."

Immediately, both boys rose and started toward Lian, oblivious of their disheveled state and filthy clothing. "What is it, Maman? Are you ill?" Marc demanded, throwing himself at his mother.

Not to be outdone or forgotten, Vincent also curled against her, dusting her silk gown with soot. "We'll take care of you."

Smiling and shaking her head, Lian ignored the smudges that were transferred from her sons' clothes to hers and put her arms around them. "You must not worry. I am not ill. But your grandmother will certainly be so if she sees what you have done to the settee."

They looked in horror at the gray smears on the pale cream tapestry and began to brush at them frantically. Lian helped, while Émile pulled out his handkerchief, dipped it in a pitcher of water and brushed gently until all signs of the soot were gone. Then Lian surprised the boys, who looked like twins with their curly blond hair and brown eyes, and the knobby, awkward bodies of growing children, by pulling them close and holding them tight, despite the damage to her gown. She buried her nose in their tousled curls, dimmed by dust and soot, kissing one and then the other on the top of the head. When she looked up, her nose was dusted gray, but she did not care. With the nightmare lingering in her mind, she felt an almost savage need to feel her own sons' wriggling bodies, to hear their affectionate, high-pitched voices.

Vincent and Marc broke free when their older brother, Sebastian, entered, holding a disordered pile of envelopes and folded stamped parchments in his hand.

"*Bonjour* Maman, Papa," he said, shaking leaves and seeds out of his shoulder-length black hair. "It seems we're very popular today. We have letters from all over the world—" He broke off when he saw his mother's expression. He had a tendency to exaggerate. Lian had spoken to him about it often, but he couldn't seem to stop. He loved to make each drama a little more dramatic. He attempted to look repentant, but his blue eyes sparkled with mischief.

Lian was not frowning at Sebastian's exaggeration. She

was staring at the pile of letters in his hand. She rose while the two younger boys fell over each other in an effort to grab the mail their brother held just out of reach, but Émile was faster than all of them. Sebastian looked surprised by all the interest, then apprehensive. "Is something wrong?"

"*Non*, my son, *non*. Don't worry yourself. It's just that your mother had a dream last night, and now you say there are letters. . . ."

Sebastian understood at once, handing the mail over to his father while Lian stood anxiously waiting. "Two from the glen—one from our cousin Ena, one from Mairi Rose—one from Aunt Genevra in Kent and one from Cheng in Chervilles."

"All in one day?" the younger boys asked together.

Émile nodded as he handed the four envelopes to his wife, who sank down on the settee, the image of the dream more vivid than ever. Something was certainly amiss. It was not odd that Ena, Ailsa's youngest daughter, had written to her aunt. She did so often, pouring out whatever thoughts and feelings flitted through her fey, imaginative mind. She liked to see her own words on paper, as if she were shouting them aloud to the wide blue Scottish sky. Mairi wrote once every month, as did Genevra, to keep in touch, to remind each other that they were an unusual but unshakable family, bound by threads invisible to most eyes. But Genevra had written only two weeks past, and Mairi had been silent for three months. It was most strange that all three should arrive together, along with a message from Cheng—on the day after Lian's third warning dream.

Lian read the letters quickly, squinting at Ena's free flowing scrawl to make out the words, noting Mairi's handwriting was not as steady as usual, and while Genevra's flowing hand was as elegant as always, it was what she said that disturbed Lian.

She passed each letter to Émile when she was done, while the boys circled their parents impatiently, full of questions at the darkening expressions on their faces.

Lian had them sit at her feet, except for Sebastian, who was thirteen and far too old for such indignity. He drew a chair near as Lian sighed.

"My half-sister is worried about what she hears from the glen. Apparently, Ailsa's eldest daughter, Alanna, is uneasy, though Genevra cannot understand precisely why. So she lies awake, anxious and restless, and dreams of the glen every night. She feels compelled to go back, and wants me to come also."

"I see," Émile mused. "It's all very confusing and unsettling."

"And then there's Cheng's obscure warning. 'He who builds his house at the foot of a mountain of stone must move quickly at the sound of falling pebbles.'" They felt his deep concern, though they couldn't understand the words of his message.

The boys watched, mouths open, as their parents looked at one another, gazes locked, as if they need not speak their thoughts, but read them in each other's eyes.

"You must go."

"I must go."

They spoke at the same time, almost with the same breath. Émile regarded his wife closely. "But you're dreading it."

Lian twined her fingers together and stared at the braided shadow on her blue silk skirt. "I want to see them, be with them, feel the strength we share, but this time they are not strong. Do you realize only Ailsa is silent? Ailsa, the strongest of us all. If she is lost, what am I to do? I, who am helpless, who have always leaned on her?"

"That's not true!" Marc said, rising abruptly. "You're not helpless. Why do you say that?"

"He's right," Sebastian added seriously. "Remember the

time I lay on the ground, unable to move because I'd broken my leg trying that new bicycle? The rest of the family fluttered, wept and moaned while you fashioned a makeshift splint and sat by me and fed me something that eased the pain while Papa went to get the doctor."

"And when we had the influenza," Vincent cried, "and you had to take care of us all at the same time. You did it, and we all got well."

"Or the time when the family was brawling over the next step to take with the grape vines, and everyone became hysterical and lost the ability to think straight?" Émile said. "You remained calm and spoke quietly until we stopped to listen to what the other was saying. Then again, you've borne three children, a task I contemplate with horror. You don't go about waving a sword, *ma chérie*, but you're powerful nonetheless. I have long known the strength of your soul. I told you once long ago, that will never weaken or dim, whether or not you believe it's there."

The children watched expectantly, startled when tears filled Lian's eyes and she leaned down to kiss each boy on the forehead. Even Sebastian, who, for once, did not pull away in embarrassment. Émile sat beside her so his shoulder touched hers and she felt his breath on her cheek. "Almost you make me believe, the four of you." She smiled and her family collapsed in relief.

"So will you go to Scotland?"

"When will you leave?"

"Is Papa going too?"

Lian waved away the swarm of questions as Émile caught her hand. "I think I must go alone. This is among us, Ailsa, Genevra, Mairi and me. That much I know." She glanced at her husband apologetically. "Can you understand?"

He smiled, stroking her long, elegant fingers. "I can, though you speak of Glen Affric so warmly and wistfully that I've often longed to see it for myself. Perhaps another time, when it's peaceful there again."

Blinking eyes suddenly dry and burning, Lian clasped her husband's hand tightly. "Thank you."

The boys were less accepting. "Why can't we go with you?"

"Must we stay here and wonder what's happening to you every minute?"

"We won't sleep at all, we'll be so worried."

Though their concern was real, there was a hint of mischief in their eyes.

"We've never been anywhere, but Sebastian went to London with you. It's not fair." Marc and Vincent stood sullenly, arms crossed.

Émile spread his hands in a gesture of helplessness, leaving the boys to Lian. He could not hide his own disappointment.

"It is not fair," Lian agreed with her sons. "You are right, but nevertheless, it must be this way. Some things I know deep inside."

Sebastian was not convinced. "All right. But you're depriving your poor children of an educational, edifying experience."

As he had intended, Lian laughed aloud. "Edifying indeed. I see you have your father's sense of humor. And irony," she muttered under her breath.

She looked from Émile to Marc to Vincent to Sebastian with deep affection. She was happy now and rarely afraid. These blessings had once seemed beyond her reach, until Émile had shown her how long her reach was, how tight the grasp of her fingers. She glanced at him tenderly and kissed the hand that still held hers. "I know you are not happy. That you want to go with me and see us all together in one place— my sisters, Mairi Rose, little Ena. I appreciate your generosity in not arguing, in letting me do what I must. The boys are right; waiting at home is not easy. I know that only too well."

Émile held her tight, amazed at how much he still desired her. "I'll miss you, that's all," he lied.

Tangling her fingers in his hair, Lian smiled wistfully. "And I you. All of you."

She did not realize for several hours that in the excited discussion of her trip, the planning and repeated requests and arguments of her persistent family, she had not once thought of the glen, of Genevra's worries and Mairi's frailty, or of Ailsa, far away and unreachable in her dream.

Book Three

❧❦

Fly your Santa Maria
through the dark of the night,
crossing shadows
in the blink of an eye.
And in between the valleys
and the highest constellations,
Somewhere there lies the moon.

1

Glen Affric, Scottish Highlands, Spring 1895

THE AIR WAS STILL AS ENA ROSE CREPT ALONG THE BRAE, grateful for the soft turf that muffled the sound of her movement, grateful that the wind had not risen, so it could not carry her scent to the animal crouched in a nearby thicket, wary, in pain and dripping blood into the moss.

Ena could just see the wildcat's head from where she paused, holding her breath, silent as the unborn wind. It was a week after the first spring thaw; the air was bitingly cold, the ground slippery with thick mud and dotted with patches of snow in small shadowed hollows where the sunlight could not reach. It had not been easy, even for her, to follow the wounded animal's erratic path. It would have been more difficult yet if not for the trail of blood left behind. She was fiercely determined to get this cat, no matter that the chase had been long and grueling, no matter that her body was soaked in sweat turned to ice by the cold, no matter that her muscles ached, her face was flushed, her breath raw and ragged.

"All we've to do is see which path she takes," the girl murmured to Connor Fraser, who crouched nearby, trying to muffle the sound of his harsh breathing. "She'll no' make it to her den; 'tis too hard a climb over rocks and hills. No, she'll find a place to burrow in, and then we can catch her."

Connor nodded vaguely, thinking of how they had come to this moment.

They crouched in the greenery, watching a hunter doing his best to stalk the wildcat, though the season had not yet begun.

"He's no' even huntin' for food, but only because he's bored. Ye can tell from the look on his face. Bored," Ena said fiercely. " 'Tis why my father didn't want strangers usin' the glen for their pleasure. 'Tis cruel, that kind of pleasure, so unkind it near breaks my heart.

"Now the snow's melted, the guests are returnin' to the Hill of the Hounds. Why can they no' just stay away?" she cried like the defenseless child she was. The Hill was a mansion built by an English family who had long ago returned to London. The house itself, splendid and elegant, had never belonged in this wild place. The formal gardens the owners tried to shape of the untamed Highland landscape had been enveloped and reclaimed by the potent forces of nature that ruled here.

"At least the Sassenach come less often," Connor said reassuringly. "Mayhap the animals have grown too wise for the hunters at last."

Well-hidden by shadows and bushes, they fell silent when the stranger raised his gun. The children hissed at the frightened wildcat, propelling it into flight as the hunter aimed his rifle. He fired a single shot, shouting with pleasure when he saw the cat freeze and shudder in mid-air, then tumble to the ground. The man sauntered expectantly after it, smirking.

Ena was glad the wildcat sprang into the cover of the forest. It was momentarily stunned, in shock, so she and Connor rustled the bushes, changing places so the wind would carry their scent to the wounded animal, warning it of danger. As she'd hoped, it had shaken itself out of its trance and run deep into the wood where the hunter could not follow.

The children watched, breathless, as the hunter reached the spot where the animal should have been, where its blood should have stained the earth. He found only a muddle of footprints in the soft, damp loam.

Ena did not wait to see more. As she sprinted among the leafless oak and larch, the deep green pine and silver fir, the sound of her passage was muffled by soft earth covered by a layer of fallen needles.

"What're ye doin'?" Connor'd called quietly.

"Goin' to find the cat to see if I can save it." Her reply floated back to him in the hushed, cool air.

Connor did the only thing he could; he joined her. "Someone has to watch over her," he muttered to himself. After all, he was a man . . . well, at thirteen, very nearly, and two full months older than she. Besides, his heart was pounding with anticipation. A day with Ena Rose was never dull. He caught up with her where several paths crossed and a ray of light penetrated the thick forest around them.

Kneeling, Ena put her hand on the ground, feeling the texture of the loam, listening in absolute concentration. She had spent many hours reading books and teaching herself about the rhythms of the earth, the patterns of the water, the vagaries of the wind and the ways of the animals—their footprints, their smell, their instincts, their limits. Thus she had learned to follow where they led.

And Connor had decided to follow Ena. It was much more than a habit, accompanying his friend. Though they weren't sister and brother, they'd grown up side by side, both with auburn hair that changed color in the sunlight, gray eyes flecked with green, lithe young bodies, browned from long exposure to the sun. Because they looked so much alike, were so close in age, and were nearly always together, the Highlanders thought of them as twins, two halves of a whole.

The two of them followed the wounded cat for what seemed like hours, through knots of trees, over steep hills and braes, across rocks and down streambeds. Connor was weary and *acutely aware of the way Ena's body vibrated with tension.* "Why can't ye let the cat go? Ye don't even know if ye can help it, and since the snow damaged the pens where ye keep your sick creatures, you've no' even a place to take it."

Ena was silent, taut with concentration.

Connor's legs, coated with mud, ached from running and climbing, but he refused to give up. "Ye always told me we can no' save every animal in pain." He shifted on his elbows to get a better look at her face. "You've always known when to give up before. Why not now?"

"I can't." Her response was low, unyielding, and she met his gaze with a kind of desperation. "Mayhap you're right and 'tis already too late. But the wound can no' be too bad or the cat would've collapsed long since. If we turn back now, 'tis sure that animal'll die slowly, in torment, alone in the cold. 'Twill bleed to death, after runnin' so far and so hard, or infection'll set in, and that'll be slower yet." She stared down at her filthy hands to hide the threat of tears. "I can't walk away, knowin' how it'll suffer. At least I can make it easier, quicker, painless." She gestured toward the bulging rectangular pockets on her skirt, which held her traveling medical supplies.

For a long time she was silent. Finally, she looked up again. " 'Tis because I chased her off that she's out there hurtin' and afraid. I've got to make it right. Ye need no' come along. I ken how tired ye are; I feel the same. I also know no other who would've stayed by me till now." She put her hand on his arm. "Can ye understand?" She knew his answer before he spoke the words. He wished he could end her torment, but only one thing would do that.

He was brought back to the present by the sound of his friend's ragged breathing. He waited a moment then asked, "Have ye a plan? What's to do next?"

Ena hugged him so tight that he felt her exhaustion. "Bless ye. You're a rare, true friend, Connor Fraser, and I'll no' be forgettin' it." She paused. "I didn't want to do it alone." Quickly, to mask tears of gratitude, she explained. "If we let her corner herself, which's bound to be soon, she's so tired and hurtin', we can catch her easily. But we'll need a basket and old blanket." She was thinking out loud, but Connor snatched at the excuse to return to paths he knew and purposes less arduous. Ena had a natural "feel" for the chase that her friend did not share.

"Are ye certain 'tis safe?" he asked again.

"Aye, so long as ye know how, and ye never look her in the eye. She'd think that a challenge and fight ye, even if she was too weak to win."

"Then I'll go for the basket and blanket. I know where ye keep your winter supplies. How'll I find ye again?"

"Follow the trail of blood, or mine. Ye can see how the grass clings to the mud in our footprints." She clasped his hand as he turned away. "Thank ye, Connor."

"Ye'd do it for me, would ye no'? Weel then." He started back the way they'd come. Or so he thought. He turned several times, trying to determine where they were, then thought he recognized the sound of the river and the leafless larches that crowded its banks. He began to run, knowing he must hurry or Ena might try it alone.

She'd not been long out of sight when he saw fresh blood on the cotton grass and stopped short, holding his breath. He knew the wildcat was near. This time, like Ena, he could smell it, hear its low growl, its ragged breath. Then he saw the cat crouched in a clearing, its sides heaving, its eyes dull with pain. It could not run this time, weak and ill as it seemed. It had worn itself out.

So long as ye never look it in the eye . . . Connor's mind was racing. He had the cat in view and Ena was nowhere near. He could do this. He could immobilize the cat and solve at least half her problem. He'd felt how weary she was, how ready to founder. 'Tis for her sake, he told himself, to make it easier on Ena. He took a few steps into the clearing. Of course, it'd be excitin, bein' the one who was no' afraid to take such an animal. But 'tis mostly for Ena.

His heart thundered in his ears as he began to move

through the cotton grass, staying to the side of the wounded wildcat, taking care to avoid its gaze. He took off his overcoat, intending to use it as a blanket, but the animal saw the movement. It stiffened, hissing, and Connor felt a jab of apprehension. The animal must have smelled his fear. Lungs aching with the cold air, he pounced, attempting to wrap his coat around the squirming cat. Without thinking, he looked down, saw the copper gleam of its gaze just before it swiped at his arm and blood welled from four parallel scratches ripped in his shirt. Stunned by the shooting pain, the boy loosened his grip. The cat twisted in his arms, scratching Connor's neck and trying for his throat.

He dropped it, clutching his empty coat, watching, dazed, as the cat burst from the clearing to a thicket of ferns and bracken, sending greenery flying. Even dragging its back leg, it was faster than Connor, who would not have followed anyway.

Shivering and humiliated, grateful Ena had not been there to see, the boy wrapped his coat tight around him, concealing the marks of the wildcat, the leather thick enough, lined as it was with thick wool, to absorb the blood. He could hear Ena coming, tracing the trail of blood. He ducked into the trees and slowly, painfully, went in search of basket and blanket.

Hair stuffed beneath the cap she was rarely without, skirt split down the middle and restitched into full trousers that did not restrict her movement, Ena crawled on hands and knees to the dark hollow where the wildcat had found refuge. It was half hidden in a burnt-out oak surrounded by gorse and broom, heather and bracken, where the shadows were long and the animal felt safe. She could feel in her own body the heat and coiled strength, the hot, dry breath, exhaustion and pain that seared the wildcat's side. Her own fear and the warning beat of her heart she refused to recognize. She did not know if it was too late.

Staying well out of the animal's sight, she approached from the side, half singing, half talking in a slow, soft cadence that would calm the injured cat.

Often, that cadence cast a spell upon the wounded, weak and exhausted, lulled into acquiescence by the soothing clarity of the song, by an intuitive understanding that the girl wanted to help.

Ena was waiting for Connor. It seemed he had been gone a long time, but she could not really judge, so intent had she been on following the cat. Then, at last, she heard, then saw him at the top of the hill, standing stiffly, heavy basket in one hand, staring at the trail of blood until he saw the small, dark place where the cat lay.

Connor felt sick, but he kept his face blank when he spotted Ena's cap in the bushes nearby. He could hear her chanting, murmuring as she often did to animals; he could see the cat was not frightened, that its breathing had eased, and he felt twice the fool.

Ena stood carefully, indicating he should circle around the other side, getting as near as he dared and passing her basket and blanket high above the cat's head. She knelt to arrange the blanket so a long corner hung over the edge, then motioned to Connor. "So long as we come from behind and above, she won't fight us. She's too weak and in pain for one thing, and so long as we don't come head on, she'll no' see us as a threat."

Connor looked skeptical, pulling his coat tighter about him.

"Cats are very intuitive, ye ken. She'll soon see we want to help. I've the basket ready. Can ye help me lift her in?"

For a terrible moment, he thought he couldn't do it, but he didn't want Ena to know. Reaching out inch by inch from either side, they scooped up the cat and laid it in the basket as Ena whispered and murmured, murmured and sang.

She was so busy trying not to hurt the cat further that she didn't see Connor wince in agony, or how quickly he drew back his arms, though the animal offered no resistance. She covered the basket loosely to keep out the cold, crooning and chanting all the while in the Gaelic. Only then did she reach from the side, letting in just enough light for her to see. The cat's heart was beating strong, and its breathing, though labored, was only a little shallow. She slid her hands out, letting the blanket fall back into place.

Looking up, she grinned at Connor. "Mayhap we're in time. I'm willin' to take the chance." She regarded him steadily. "I know I've asked a lot of ye today, but I can no' manage this alone. Can ye take one side of the handle and I the other?"

He nodded, but when she began to pick up the right side, he slid in before her. He could not carry anything with his wounded left arm, but he would not tell her that.

Ena shrugged and took the left side and they began to walk home slowly, the basket swaying slightly, in a soothing motion, while Ena talked and talked to the now invisible cat.

There was no sound from inside except, now and then, an odd purring that shocked Connor. The sound was neither threatening nor harsh.

He raised his head, blinking back tears at the searing pain in his arm and neck, fascinated in spite of himself. Ena always walked as if on air and not earth, so easily did she move through the glen. But now she seemed to float— an odd contrast to the careful, strong rhythm of her footsteps, meant to soothe the cat. She grinned, unable to hide her elation at their success, her optimism and confidence that she could save the wildcat.

She glanced sideways, offering a triumphant smile. "We did it, just ye and me."

Connor smiling thinly. "Aye. But then why're your hands shakin'?"

"Weel, I hope I no' fool enough to forget the hazards of such a thing. I'd read about it, aye, and I know a bit about animals. But in the end, ye can never be sure what might happen. I'm tremblin' with relief, is all."

Connor gaped. "Ye crouched beside a wounded wildcat, put your hands under it, and did not know if 'twould sleep or turn its claws on ye?" Shaken, he let his coat fall open.

Stopping short, Ena stared in horror at the inflamed scratches on his neck. She went so pale her skin was translucent. She set the basket down, and he had no choice but to do the same. "Oh, Connor! How did ye—when— why did ye no' say—"

Before he could stop her, she was drawing him among a group of pines where the snow had not yet melted. "Take off your coat. I must tend to those at once."

"What about the cat?"

She was already pulling things out of her pockets, but she stopped to stare at him, appalled. "The cat's only a cat. 'Tis in no danger. You're Connor, my friend, and you're bleedin'. Come." Her hands trembled so badly she wasn't certain she could do what she must.

When she saw his arm, the blood streaked down to his wrist by the sleeve of the coat, tears burned her eyes. "I'm sorry," she said over and over. "I'm sorry." She found she could not look at him. "I never meant ye to be hurt."

" 'Tis nothing to fret over, Ena. Only a few scratches." Trying to comfort her, Connor shrugged in unconcern, but his wince of pain gave him away.

"Only a boy'd say something so daft. Don't ye know what muck is on a wildcat's claws? 'Tis serious, this. The wounds could get infected and leave awful scars."

Connor quirked an eyebrow, a gesture he'd perfected just the day before. "Girls like scars. They like the feel and love the excitin' stories that go along with them."

Lips pinched together, Ena packed snow on the wounds to cool them and clean away what dirt she could. He'd frightened her so much she wanted to shout at him. It was hard to keep him from sensing her fear. She picked out bits of wool that had stuck in the deep scratches, and though her hands had been steady and her voice firm as they lifted a wounded wildcat into a basket, now her fingers were clumsy and she could not speak at all.

Removing the vial of tincture of iodine from the collection of herbs and paraphernalia she carried in her pockets in case she came upon a wounded animal, she held Connor immobile. Fortunately, many herbs worked on man and animal alike. " 'Twill hurt like the very devil, but ye hold my ankles and squeeze when ye must."

Carefully Ena spread the iodine along each scratch, and with each movement, felt Connor stiffen another muscle. But he did not squeeze her ankles.

" 'Tis all right, I'll no' shatter, ye ken? Hold them as hard as ye can."

The pressure did not increase. Ena sighed. "You're a man and can no' admit weakness; is that it?" She daubed iodine on a new gouge. He clenched his teeth but made no sound. "At least the animals let ye know when they hurt," she muttered. "Unlike people, who're too stubborn and proud." She paused, feeling woozy. "Why did ye no' tell me ye were hurt?" Her stomach was knotted with unfamiliar nerves.

"Because ye would've ended the chase."

"Of course I would've, Connor Fraser. Do ye think me daft or heartless?"

"Neither."

She chewed dried kelp to moisten it and packed it on the wounds, then ripped strips from her shift to use as bandages. She was face to face with him now and could see the pain in Connor's eyes. "Then why?"

"Ye told me why 'twas so important. Ye would've mourned and blamed yourself forever if ye'd given up. I could no' do that to ye. I had to let ye try."

2

ENA'S GRANDMOTHER, MAIRI ROSE, USUALLY KEPT HER CROFT alive with animated voices when the light shifted to deep lilac in the gloaming. But it was quiet that night when Ena stumbled in with the wildcat in its makeshift litter. The croft was heated by a large peat fire, the chill stone walls obscured by shadows and smoke, thick handwoven blankets draped over the rocking chairs waiting to enfold her, the kettle bubbling on the single gas burner, and her mother and grandmother waiting fondly for her return. Now, for the first time all day, though the air had been crisp and she'd forgotten her jacket, Ena Rose began to shiver with cold.

Startled by the girl's abrupt appearance, Mairi and her daughter Ailsa leapt from their comfortable chairs, staring in horror at Ena and the large basket she held in arms too small to balance it. Her hair straggled from under her filthy cap, tangled and stiff with dried mud. Her arms were scratched and grimy, streaked with layers of dirt and sweat and fresh bruises, her face and torn gown soiled and smeared with blood. She'd lost one brogue and her ankle was swollen, but she didn't seem to notice.

"Are ye hurt?" Ailsa cried. "I've had a feelin' for two hours past that something was amiss, and 'twas growin' stronger. What's happened?"

Mairi hovered while both women tried to peer into the basket. "Connor and I rescued a wounded wildcat." Ena turned to her mother, whose blue-violet eyes had a cast of gray upon them. " 'Tis no' me who's hurt, but Connor. I wanted to bring the cat here, where 'tis warm, then go back to him."

Ailsa and her mother exchanged a look over the girl's head. Ena often brought home injured animals—squirrels, birds, a fawn, wood mice and, once, a fox. But never before a wildcat. Ailsa knelt, taking the covered basket. "The cat needs your particular kind of healin'; no one else can do it. Don't be arguin' with me; ye know 'tis true. *I'll* go to Connor." Tenderly, Ailsa brushed the hair back from her daughter's face, where it had caught in the mud and blood. "Ye clean yourself up and see to the cat. Mairi'll help ye. Let *me* go." Now she understood the unease that had haunted her all day, the restlessness, the apprehension. Connor and Ena had been in danger.

Throwing her arms around her mother's neck, the girl cried, "Thank ye, Mam. 'Tis all my fault, and I know ye can help him." Her mother and grandmother had always been healers as was Ailsa's eldest daughter, Alanna—Connor's mother.

"I'll do what I can." As Ailsa went in search of her basket of healing potions, herbs, leaves and roots, she asked, "How is't that 'tis all your fault? I've not known anyone who could force Connor Fraser against his will." She swept up the basket and reached into the press for the disinfectant she sent for regularly from London.

Ena caught her mother's arm and looked up, gray eyes full of doubt. "I wanted ye to know I wasn't heartless, nor afraid for myself when another creature was in trouble. I could no' leave that cat in the hills to die in pain. No' if I could help it. Ye always told me—" She broke off, staring at her muddy feet. "I only wanted to do what was right." Her gaze, the grasp of her fingers were imploring, asking for approval.

"And so ye did. Ye followed your kind heart and your instincts, as I taught ye, for naught else is so trustworthy a guide. I can see from your face that ye made the only choice ye could." Ailsa met her daughter's gaze. "I'm proud of ye, and angry and terrified at once." Though she would turn fifty-four in two months, Ailsa still worried about this child as she had her first, born when she was only eighteen.

Gently removing the girl's hand from her arm, she took

her red plaid from its hook and threw it around her shoulders. " 'Tis a fact that I begin to fear you're as brave and foolish as your father." The tenderness in her voice was unmistakable.

For an instant, the girl was diverted. "Do ye really think so?" she asked eagerly.

Mairi answered before Ailsa could take a breath. "Och, aye, you're more like Ian Fraser every day. Just don't be feelin' the need to prove yourself like he did. The glen survived long before the Frasers came to save it from the modern world. I've a feelin' it always will. 'Tis timeless, ye ken, its splendor and serenity, its mountains and stones and rivers and lochs. It'll go on, this place, this beauty, however many feet traverse its paths, however many years pass over its mountains."

Ena heard the warning implicit in Mairi's soft-spoken words. Ena's father, Ian Fraser, married to another woman, had once tried to stop industrialization from coming to Glen Affric, and in doing so, had rediscovered his childhood sweetheart Ailsa Rose, given her a child—Ena—and lost his life. Unnervingly, she thought of Connor and his angry red wounds.

Ailsa seemed to be thinking the same. "Now, ye see to finishin' what ye started, and I'll go to Connor and give him all that's in me." She held the basket with both hands to keep them steady.

"I told him why I couldn't leave the cat to the cold and the wolves, or he would've come home safe." The girl could not seem to let it go.

Mairi Rose shook her head in resignation. "Ena, *mochridhe*, ye'll never stop surprisin' me, were I to live a hundred years. Leave a wounded, half-mad wildcat out there tonight? Of course ye couldn't."

Ena's eyes filled with tears. "I've got to save it now, for his sake. Else 'twas all for naught." She blinked rapidly. "I cleaned Connor's wounds with snow and doused them with tincture of iodine, then bandaged them with kelp. 'Twas all I could do." Just now she felt as helpless as the red-gold flame that flared then faded to a curl of smoke.

"Just remember," Mairi said firmly, "nothing is for naught when ye've fought hard to win it. But sometimes, mo-run, 'tis no' for the reason ye thought."

Ailsa Rose, her crown of chestnut braids half covered by her plaid, had one hand on the latch. When she thought of her grandson, she felt a foreboding that urged her to be gone. "Listen, our Ena. Ye cleaned and treated Connor's scratches early. Mayhap early enough to stop infection altogether. Be grateful for that. And for the rest, as I've told ye before, listen to your heart. 'Twill no' misguide ye."

Glancing from her grandmother to her mother, Ena half-smiled. "Thank ye," was all she said.

David and Alanna Fraser sat in their padded rocking chairs, reading in the stillness of gloaming, by the fire roaring in the hearth. They were content in one another's company, content in the hush that had fallen upon their cottage, content in the knowledge that they were warm and comfortable and safe.

Safe. The word echoed in Alanna's head. She looked up without marking her place, her eyes unfocussed, her skin chilled. She tensed, hands locked on the arms of her chair. "Somethin's amiss."

Her husband closed his book at her tone, which sent a chill down his spine. She had done this before.

"Connor's late." Her voice was toneless, yet full of implications, full of fear.

"He's often late," David said, trying to ignore the light in his wife's violet eyes, now veiled in gray. It frightened him, that look, as much as what she said. And David Fraser feared little.

Suddenly Alanna reached over to clutch at her husband's hands. "Our son's in danger. I know it."

David gave in to a kind of dread he could not conquer. He clasped her hands tightly and they stared at each other, unable to move or think or speak. There was nothing to say. All they could do was wait.

Connor pushed open the heavy oak door and stood holding on with one hand, keeping the other cupped over the wound on his neck. He felt strangely disoriented, and his vision blurred, became clear, blurred again. His arm and neck throbbed, so he leaned against the door, out of breath and vaguely uneasy. With the gloaming at his back, he was as aware of the swirling lilac mist as he was of the warm yellow light within the roomy cottage. He looked about, comforted by the bright light of oil lamps, by the clean kitchen with its fine oak table—one of the few in the glen that was not scrubbed pine. His father had painted one wall of the small room with primroses and wood anemones, as a wedding gift for his mother, he'd been told. The soft, muted colors were a pleasant sight after the day he had spent.

All was warm and cozy, but oddly different. The walls shifted slightly with the throb of pain in his neck and arm. He thought he could feel them swelling, pressing against the loose bandages, could hear the loud pulse of his own blood.

A fire burned low in the potbellied stove, and the smell of scotch broth wafted toward him. He swayed, realizing he was weak with hunger. He had not eaten for many hours, so caught up had he been in the chase and his concern for Ena. But he knew that before he tasted that fragrant broth, he would have to face his parents and tell them what had happened. He stiffened his shoulders, wincing at the pain.

Alanna and David Fraser sat at the far end of the croft, near the fireplace built into the wall, a luxury compared to the circle of stones on the floor in other cottages. The fire burned high and warm, adding its golden light to the oil lamps with crystal globes that sat on matching rosewood

tables beside his parents' rocking chairs. They faced each
other, knees nearly touching, gazes locked, holding hands,
absorbed completely in one another. They often read by
the hearth in the evening, chairs on the thick woven carpet David had brought from Glasgow, enjoying each other's
company as well as the light and warmth of lamp and fire.
They looked so peaceful, heads bent close, Alanna's Highland red hair loose around her shoulders, now that evening
had come and visitors were unlikely. The light glinted off
the bright tendrils in orange sparks, while David's dark
hair, curling to his shoulders, seemed to absorb the light
rather than reflect it. He could not quite make out their
expressions, though something disturbed him about the
tension in their bodies.

Their son stood across the cottage, feeling a thousand
miles away. His parents' relationship was so close, so intimate, that he sometimes felt excluded, like an intruder on
their harmony and happiness. They didn't seem to need
him—only each other. Besides, he often brought them
trouble, such as now, when he feared he might fall forward.

The boy shivered with the cold at his back, uneasy
about entering the welcoming warmth of his home, which
embraced his parents naturally. He knew they would be
angry he had spent the day with Ena, "chasing her phantoms," as David often said.

He stood quietly, watching his parents in their compan-
ionable silence, and hesitated to shatter that peace
irreparably, as he knew he would the instant they saw him.

Just then Alanna and David looked up and his flash of
panic passed, forgotten. He was so glad to see them. To be so
close to safety and comfort. Their expressions were so concerned, their exclamations of relief so real that he was
drawn into their little circle. As he always was. They never
left him alone and apart. How could he have forgotten that?

"Connor, my love, 'tis good beyond words to see ye
again. Where have ye been? Are ye safe?" At first Alanna

saw only the shape, the height, the strong, wide shoulders of her son, and not his condition. Then, at David's sharp intake of breath, she noticed the boy was covered from head to toe with mud, his clothes were wet and dirty and torn. His hair was tangled and oddly stiff, and he was very pale. He swayed, one hand clamped tightly to the side of his neck, the other hidden behind him. It struck her like a physical blow when she saw that all the stains on his shirt were not dried mud. "Connor!" Fear took all other words away.

David rose abruptly, sliding his arm around his wife's waist. She felt him stiffen as Connor stepped into the circle of lamplight and both saw how their son swayed, how pallid was his skin, how huge his eyes in his face. He was trembling, yet trying with all the strength that had deserted him to force his body to be still.

"You're hurt," his father said, his tone edged with apprehension. He glanced at Alanna uneasily. She had known. She had sensed Connor's peril but been helpless against it. Now their son was hurt; they could not even guess how badly.

The boy heard the tenderness in his mother's tone, saw the concern on his father's face, but still he was wary. They did not wholly approve of the way he wandered the glen with Ena day after day, especially now that he was old enough to help at home.

"Dear God!" David whispered when Connor's arm fell away from his neck, revealing the blood-soaked kelp and, underneath, the long, bloody claw marks on his skin. Already the wounds were red and swollen, caked with blood.

" 'Tis no' so bad," the boy said. "It hardly hurts at all."

His pallid face belied his brave words. When Alanna reached for him, she took the arm he had been holding behind his back and he tried but failed to choke back a cry of anguish. For an instant, Alanna and David were frozen in shock, staring at the two deep wounds from the claws of a wild animal. Connor's arm, neck and chest were covered with blood that blended with the drying mud that had begun to flake onto the wooden floor.

"Was it—" Alanna murmured.

"A wildcat, shot by an early hunter. But ye've no need to worry. Ena cleaned them with snow and put iodine on." His strength was fading alarmingly.

"Don't . . ." Connor coughed and tried to hide a grimace, "blame . . . Ena. My fault." He closed his bloodshot eyes, licked his lips and added, "Wanted . . . to be . . . stronger. Show . . . I'm . . . no' . . . afraid. Had . . . to . . . save . . . the cat. And we did." He paused again, then opened his eyes wide. "My . . . fault. My . . . pride. Daft." He stared. "Please."

He slumped, unconscious, into his father's arms.

David lifted him easily. He knew where Connor had gotten that damnable destructive pride, and it wasn't from Alanna. He was appalled by where that pride had led. But underneath the guilt smoldered anger.

Finally, David met his wife's violet eyes, dark with worry. "Even now he defends her," she said, "trying to take the blame on himself." She paused, surprised by what she said next. "He must care for her very much."

Her husband stared at her, stunned. "Does that matter now, with him injured, in danger?"

Alanna took Connor's legs and they placed him on the bed. They could hear the heavy rasp of his breath. "It always matters, David-my-heart. In the end, 'tis all we have, that carin'. Good and bad, angry or grievin', full of joy or lost in sorrow, we love and are loyal to each other. We've no choice, nor would we want one." She touched her son's cold grayish cheek. "It doesn't mean I'm no' afraid and angry and terrified. But all we can do is take care of him and love him, just as he does Ena, and she him."

3

WHEN AILSA HAD GONE, ENA CONCENTRATED ON THE CAT lying in the covered basket. It was the only way to keep herself busy enough that thoughts of Connor were no more than bright hot sparks that singed, then faded.

"How did ye manage to catch him without gettin' hurt?" Mairi asked, while she rummaged in the press and came out with disinfectant, linens and the box of medicinal herbs they always kept at home.

"Thank ye, Gran," Ena said. To her grandmother's astonishment, she took the clean linen folded on her unmade bed, found two large baskets, and arranged a snug bed in one of them. "Francis McPhee once told me how a friend caught a wounded cat near his huntin' lodge, and glad I am that he did." She described the chase, thinking with gratitude about the roving veterinarian she'd first met when she was eight. Francis McPhee traveled about the Highlands attending the herds of cattle and sheep. Ena had been fascinated by the tall, wiry man and his knowledge of animals, more so because she'd always had special feelings for the wildlife in the glen.

Once, he'd come upon a wounded fawn, and with the gentlest touch she'd ever seen, he'd worked on its injury. His face, usually rugged from exposure to the sun, had softened, and he'd cradled it tenderly. " 'Tis from the herds I make my livin'," he'd told her, "but 'tis the wild ones I love. Someone has to take care of the little ones."

She had decided then that her ambition was to be that someone. Mr. McPhee had told her many stories while he worked, and when he left that first year, he'd given her the gift of a book on treating wild animals he'd had since veterinary college in Edinburgh. He'd smiled at her and cocked his brow, interested to see if she pursued what was apparently becoming her passion.

"He's so docile," Mairi observed of the inert animal.

When she'd arranged the sheeting and a bit of warm rug to her satisfaction, Ena put the baskets side by side near the fire, half in the shadows, and, with Mairi's help, they came low on either side and scooped the animal into her new bed. Then the girl covered the basket with another, making a kind of litter for the cat, leaving a place where the animal could see what was going on around it. "I think, I hope, she knows I've no wish to hurt her. Francis says cats are very wise. They sense if you've good intentions just as they'd know if ye were afraid."

"And you've no fear at all?" Mairi had treated many people with many illnesses in her life, but never one that was likely to bite her or tear deep gouges in her skin.

"She's in too much pain to hurt me now. She's very weak and lost a lot of blood, besides the damage of the wound. Even if we left her lyin' free on the rug, she'd be no threat." Francis had told her his friend had kept the injured wildcat in his dark, warm study on a pile of linen.

Mairi was silent for a long while, watching in surprised admiration. Ena seemed to know just what to do. Her grandmother settled into her rocking chair, arranged the blanket around her shoulders and over her legs and observed the girl. "If ye need be usin' your own sheetin', why could ye no' use your gown?"

Intent now on what she was doing, Ena did not raise her head to answer. "My gown and shift smell like other animals. That'd upset her." Her body glided and her fingers flew as she found some chicken broth, heated it slightly, put it in a shallow dish and left it in the wildcat's reach. To Mairi's surprise, the animal lapped at it, though weakly. Next Ena got out her blackwillow and hops for sedation, wrapped the herbs in a piece of garlic, and again, coming from the side and slightly above, slipped it into the cat's open mouth and gently crooned and rubbed it under the chin until it swallowed without realizing. Her body might have been a wisp of smoke, so swiftly and lithely did she move, her hands light and sure, and all the while, she kept up a low chant, a murmur, almost a purr that echoed the cat's.

Caught up in the soothing rhythm of her song, the cat grew drowsy, then slept, both from exhaustion and the effect of the herbs.

Ena knelt to draw the top basket away. Then, bringing a lamp as near as she dared, very gently, very slowly she used a soft cloth to clean away the dirty, clotted blood, then examined the wound delicately. "Seems the bullet passed through the thigh and came out the other side, breakin' no bones and tearin' no important muscles. 'Tis a lucky cat, this." Ena's earlier elation returned. She might have a chance after all.

"Aye, lucky indeed. To have ye to care for it."

The girl pretended not to hear, but secretly, she was pleased by the compliment. Mairi was not one to pass praise out lightly. By now Ena had emptied her voluminous pockets of herbs, stones, pieces of bark, a half-carved squirrel and small whittling knife, and various other things. She put her treatment journal on the floor, resting her palm on it for an instant; it held a great deal more than simply her methods of dealing with different animals and their injuries. Inside were her thoughts, imaginings and dreams. She brought one hand out full of thin broken glass stained ugly yellow. "I've broken my vial of tincture of iodine again. Thank the gods 'twas no' before I used it on Connor." She sighed, picking at shards of glass that left a permanent stain on the fabric. "But the gown was ruined anyway." She stared at the mess of blood and dirt and stains of moss and lichen and grass, and shrugged, unconcerned. It was by no means the first gown she'd ruined.

"Surely she'll no' stay here while she's healin'?"

Ena shook her head. "Ill as she is, she'll feel protected in the warmth and darkness and comfort of the baskets. On her own she would've sought somewhere shadowed and protected, like her own cave. She'll no' be wantin' to move about."

Mairi could see how much Ena enjoyed tending her patient, warmed by the fire, safe in the familiar croft. The shadows of flames danced on layered mud walls, creating intriguing, exotic patterns. Her expression was intent, yet animated as one gesture flowed into another and she disinfected the bullet hole on both sides, filled it with herbs to help it heal, and stitched it up with catgut. Then, in a hypnotic motion, Ena bound the wounds with a soft bandage. Gingerly, she replaced the basket on top, still and always murmuring, singing, chanting. It was the first thing she'd learned from her friend the veterinarian—to establish a connection with the animal, to both calm it and tell it, in the only way people could, that she meant it no harm.

At last she leaned against the settle, looking peaceful, contented for the first time since she'd walked in the door. "If ye learn to listen well," Ena replied, smiling in exhaustion and contentment, "animals'll speak to ye in their own way."

The girl knew a great deal on the subject. The second year he'd come, Francis McPhee had seen her dedication and determination and told her the names of the books she should study. Since they could not be found in the glen, Ailsa had tucked the list into letters to her sisters. Lian and Genevra had begun to send them to Ena, one by one, as gifts.

McPhee had talked by the hour, teaching her as much as he could each time he returned. But Mairi knew all that information was useless without instinct, a natural affinity, the ability to listen to a patient and sense what was wrong. How much harder with an animal, whose language, if it could be called that, was subtle and difficult to understand, than with a person who could tell you exactly where it hurt. It was the same with the whole of the glen—trees, moors, rivers, braes—the child seemed to understand them intuitively, their cycles and their beauties and imperatives. "Ena, you're remarkable, ye ken."

The smile disappeared. "No I'm not, or Connor'd no' have gotten hurt. I can help some animals, aye, but no' people. And 'tis people I need, Gran."

"Particular people or people in general?" Mairi asked shrewdly.

Caught off guard, Ena stared down at her broken, ragged fingernails to hide her flushed cheeks. "Och, I don't—" She made some noises like garbled words. " 'Tis no' so much . . . I really can no' . . ." She threw her hands in the air in defeat. "I might be thinkin' of someone or other, but there're many I couldn't do without. My aunts, my mother, my cousins," she added hastily, "ye, Connor, Mam . . . and mayhap a father, for but a day or two, to know what 'tis like. But mayhap he'd no care for me anyway. I'd not know how to charm him, or anyone, as ye and Mam do."

She sounded so forlorn that Mairi wanted to sweep her granddaughter into her lap as she used to, singing and rocking her till she was calm or asleep. "Mayhap you're bein' too hard on yourself, as usual."

Standing abruptly, Ena began to pace. "No. I used to sense things and feel they were true. But now, I'm naught but confused. I don't know how to *be* anymore."

Mairi leaned forward, hands outstretched. "Ye be as ye are, birdeen. 'Tis as simple as that."

The girl leaned toward those gnarled, comforting hands. " 'Tis only, I've been feelin' . . . funny and sad, like things're wrong, but I don't know why or what or how to fix 'em." She stepped in and out of the firelight, unable to stay still. " 'Tis like I'm fightin' something, fightin' it with all my might, but I don't know what it is. I sound daft, I know."

"Ye sound to me like a girl who's nearly thirteen. Old as

I am, I remember what that felt like. I was too old and yet too young, and I'd not have known which way I was goin' if Mena stepped down from the moon and pointed the way."

Ena gaped at her. "Really?"

"Have I lied to ye yet, *mo-run*? 'Twill pass, these feelin's that seem no' your own. Ye must be patient, lass. I know 'tis hard, but 'tis your only choice."

At a sound outside, both looked up expectantly, but the door remained closed.

"Where can she be? Is Connor so very ill? Why does she no' come home?"

Her hair had straggled loose when she took off her cap, the strands full of leaves and twigs like awkward ornaments in the thick auburn hair that fell to her waist. She tugged on it until it seemed it would come out in her hands. Mairi's heart went out to her, but she could not help Ena. Not now. Not just yet. "Listen, wee one," she reverted to the old name unconsciously, "ye'd best get comfortable on this rug with this blanket about ye, for if you're goin' to wait for Ailsa Rose, 'twill be a long while." Sighing enigmatically, she leaned back into the cushions Ena had made for her seventy-second birthday.

The girl followed her grandmother's suggestion and sat on the thick warm rug that had been her half-sister, Alanna's, gift to Mairi. Feeling the cold now that she'd finished her task, Ena pulled a wool plaid blanket around her, but she crossed and uncrossed her ankles, leaned one way and then another, unable to calm herself enough to get comfortable.

Finally, she made some chamomile tea, and they sat listening to the cat's uneven breathing, the sounds of the nightbirds and the wind in the trees as they sipped the steaming liquid. The firelight gilded them, turning sun-browned skin golden and hair to shades of glowing fire. Mairi's violet eyes and Ena's gray eyes flecked with green stared into the flames, each seeing thoughts and memories created, melted, created again. The mist curled about the cottage, sneaking around the edges of the leather window coverings, swirling into the smoke to create a soft, tinted haze.

The cat's breathing changed, and Ena was beside it in an instant, trying to determine its condition without disturbing it. The animal settled again, but the sound, the heat, the smell conjured the image of Connor's face, the two sets of parallel scratches, the jokes he'd tried to make to hide his pain.

Ena had been growing sleepy, but she sat upright, fully awake at a wave of heat followed by a deep chill. She knew instinctively that she was feeling the fever in Connor's body as if it were her own.

Ailsa found her daughter kneeling beside Connor's bed, torn between watching her son and glancing at the front door, waiting for it to open. Alanna had felt her mother coming, just as Ailsa had felt her daughter's apprehension, when the two were still far distant from one another.

Rising stiffly, Alanna met Ailsa in the kitchen, where the two clasped hands tightly. Ailsa offered strength and consolation without words, with the force of her blue-violet eyes.

"How's the lad?" she whispered as she knelt beside the small boxbed.

"We hoped ye could tell us."

She was startled by the sound of David Fraser's deep voice. He rose from his seat by the fire, skin pale, face lined with panic. "We only know he's very ill." He paused to touch his wife's shoulder. "Alanna's wild with worry, and she'll no' sit; she'll no' leave her son. Now that you're here, please, try to make her rest."

" 'Tis near impossible for a mother to do when her child's ill. Besides, I can see he's a fever, which means some infection. 'Tis best if two work together."

David's face was gray, his words clipped and abrupt. His body vibrated with coiled anger and frustration at his impotence. He could not cure his son, nor could he force his wife to give up her vigil. Unconsciously, he clenched his hands into fists.

Ailsa was overcome with compassion. "Alanna'd no rest even if ye forced her into bed. She needs to be useful as much as Connor needs her care. I know ye understand that; I can see it in ye."

Reluctantly, David nodded. Ailsa often saw too much, and it unnerved him. But his mother-in-law was right. Why should Alanna suffer this exhausting sense of inadequacy when she had the skill of a healer?

Ailsa saw how her daughter's hands trembled, and she cupped Alanna's face in her hands. Her touch was light, her gaze commanding. Alanna had pulled her hair into an awkward braid from which long tendrils straggled over her flushed face. The Highland red seemed faded, though her violet eyes glittered as if she also suffered from a fever. "I'm here, *mo-graidh*. We'll do this together. But I can see you're ready to drop where ye stand. Mayhap ye *should* relax for the while, take some tea and eat some broth and a bannock to restore your strength."

"I knew ye'd come," Alanna said, leaning her head against her mother's shoulder as if she were a young girl and not a woman of thirty-six. "I saw Ena used iodine and kelp on the scratches. Do ye think 'twas soon enough?"

Ailsa hugged her daughter, surprised by Alanna's helplessness. She was usually strong and self-confident—a survivor.

Alanna was the first child of Ailsa and her husband, William Sinclair, a British barrister with whom she had lived in London until his death fourteen years past. Once the girl discovered Glen Affric, she had never returned to London and never regretted her choice. She belonged here, where Ailsa had been born, and Mairi before her and many before *her*.

Ailsa knew her daughter had never understood why her

mother had left this paradise to live in London, a world in which she never truly belonged. Long ago, Ailsa's obsession with her absent father's mysterious world had led her to give up what she treasured most—the glen and the friend of her spirit, Ian Fraser. Much as she'd loved William Sinclair, she'd never forgotten Ian, who knew her thoughts before she spoke them and her pain before she felt it.

Ailsa had been delighted when Alanna married Ian's nephew David. She had returned to the glen after William's death to attend the wedding, and against her will and her vow, become entangled with Ian once more. The result had been the conception, in one decisive night, of Ailsa's last child—Ena.

The birth created chaos in the lives of those in the glen, giving Mairi a new grandchild, Alanna a half-sister, David a cousin, and Connor—Ailsa stopped the useless muddle of her thoughts. No one had been able to figure out exactly what Connor's relationship to Ena was. It was difficult to define.

But that was not why she was here. Ailsa wondered what had brought her history back so vividly, now of all times. "Of course I came," she told Alanna. "Just as ye would've come to me if my child were in pain." She knelt beside Connor, who thrashed about in twisted sheets and blankets. His face was flushed, then pallid, his body hot, then clammy cool. His eyes were glassy and did not seem to recognize his mother or grandmother.

"As for your worryin' about the danger; Connor's no' likely to . . . succumb." She changed the word at the last instant. "Though he's no doubt very ill. Ye must treat his symptoms as they come, and no' fill your head with doubts and fear. Believe, Alanna-my-heart. I thought I'd taught ye that. 'Twill help your son as much as ye."

Alanna did not seem convinced. Ailsa clasped her daughter's hands till they ached. "Listen to me. Give me your faith and your trust. And have some faith in Connor as well. He knows how to fight, mayhap better than I know how to heal. He's David Fraser's son, isn't he?"

Her daughter half-smiled. "Aye, that he is." The smile disappeared and she swayed a little. "Mayhap I'll take just a moment . . ." Alanna stumbled but David caught her, guiding her toward the kitchen, where he set tea and broth and bannocks before her. At least there was *something* he could do.

Ailsa was glad for a moment alone with the boy. He was so small and fragile now, had been so large and robust yesterday. She breathed deeply, her eyes damp. Ailsa understood too well what it was to see someone you loved so ill, to be unable to stop the sickness or ease the pain. She had watched her beloved husband, William, fade day by day, until she couldn't reach him anymore. 'Tis different now, she told herself sternly. Connor Fraser's young and strong enough to fight off this fever. She had not lied to Alanna. The danger of death was very slight. Then be at it, ye daft old bessom. There's work to do and no time for wanderin'.

While Ailsa unpacked her basket, Alanna sipped and nibbled, wanting nothing, but knowing her mother was right; she'd need all her strength. David paced, holding in anger and panic, clutching them so close and tight they burned.

With care, Ailsa removed the soiled dressing from Connor's neck, revealing the angry red swelling, the viscous liquid oozing from four raw wounds. She tried to keep her face expressionless. She spoke softly to her grandson as she worked, first giving him a decoction of yew for the pain, then cleaning the wounds and preparing poultices. "Ye'll have to help me, Connor Fraser, with all the energy ye have." She could feel the boy's pain shoot through her hands each time she touched him.

"Besides, though ye think ye know the heart and spirit of the glen, there's so much more to learn, and ye can't do it lyin' in bed. Ye'd be leavin' Ena to discover the rest alone. And she'll no' want to do it without ye."

"Ena," the boy rasped. It was the first coherent word he had spoken.

Ailsa winced as if her own daughter had called out a fevered name that was not her mother's. At least Alanna had not heard. Fiercely, she wrung the moisture from her cool, soft cloth and pressed it against Connor's forehead.

After that, Alanna and Ailsa worked side by side making skunk cabbage and kelp poultices to draw the toxins from the wounds. They did not speak, but sensed one another's needs and responded instinctively. Together, they fought to get a decoction of pennyroyal and yarrowroot down Connor's throat to make him sweat and break the fever. Constantly, one or the other wiped down his burning body with a cool cloth.

Without realizing it, they sang very softly, old Celtic chants and prayers, creating natural harmonies with soft, slow rhythms and indistinguishable words. The sound seemed to calm them, and sometimes their patient.

David was half wild with his churning emotions; he could not bear to be powerless when his son was in such danger. He wanted to hunt down the cat that had done this, to stalk it and watch it flee, to release some of the tension.

"David Fraser."

He found Ailsa watching knowingly.

"I'm thinkin' you're not enjoyin' our singin'. More like, 'tis drivin' ye daft. But 'tis therapeutic for us and for Connor. Mayhap ye should go out for a bit. There's naught else for ye to do here, and I fear ye'll catch the rug on fire with your pacin' and the burnin' in your eyes. Go, before ye lose control. See to the sheep lost in the night, who need your care after this harsh winter, or the cattle that've fallen ill. Go ye and heal what ye can heal, and take your rage with ye, for 'tis no' healthy for your son to feel it in the air. Even I feel its heat against my cheek. Ye need to be movin', to be useful. 'Twill ease ye, I promise."

"Mayhap." Disturbed by her knowledge of his emotions, he sounded doubtful, wary. He glanced at Alanna, who nodded, her eyes full of compassion and her own helplessness. "Aye then. Send someone if ye need me." Abruptly, he turned and left them alone.

Finally, when they'd done what they could, they gave Connor a sedative of blackwillow and hops to help him rest, though that seemed unlikely. Weary as he must be from the battle his body was fighting, he could not stay still. He tossed and turned, tangling himself in the covers, kicking them away, reaching out blindly.

Alanna knelt beside her son and rested her hand on his hot, damp forehead. His eyes were glassy and did not change at the sight of his mother, but she tried to reach him through her familiar touch that might awaken a deeper memory—one the fever had not eradicated. Connor stirred, muttering under his breath, then shifted from one side to the other and back again.

Rising, his mother leaned heavily against Ailsa. "This is hardest to watch, because I can do naught to help him. If only I could give him a bit of peace. That would be enough—for now."

"Aye. 'Tis wearin' when so little means so much. But don't worry yourself. We'll no' give in. Not to this." Purposefully, she drew two rocking chairs near, so they could watch the boy while they sank into the comfortable cushions. Both were aching and weary and needed rest themselves.

Mother and daughter rocked, soothed by the motion. Suddenly, the creaking of Ailsa's chair stopped and Alanna looked up to find her staring at Connor, but her eyes were unfocused; she was seeing something far beyond the boy's boxbed.

Alanna touched her mother's hand. "What?"

Ailsa came back to herself and stared down at her hands. "I was thinkin' of Ena. She's crazed with fear for Connor and blames herself." She glanced up. "But I hope ye understand she'd never knowin'ly cause him pain."

"Connor was afraid we'd condemn her. 'Tis easier when

there's someone to blame, but how can we put the responsibility on her? As my son said, 'twas his choice to go, his choice to try for the cat. I know Ena's sufferin' too." Her throat was tight and dry, but she managed to get the words out.

Recognizing it had not been easy for her, Ailsa murmured, "I'm glad ye understand. Ena's naught but a child, though sometimes we forget. She needs our comfort now nearly as much as Connor does, though her wounds are on the inside."

As mine are, Alanna thought. I need your consolation too, Mam. She regarded her mother intently, wretchedness in her violet eyes, but Ailsa said no more. Finally, Alanna grasped the hand lying on her mother's knee in an unmistakable plea.

"Och, Alannean," Ailsa cried, and took her daughter in her arms, holding her, rocking her, smoothing back her tangled hair. "Why did ye no' say something?"

After a time, Alanna said with her lips, "Because I'm a woman grown, a wife and mother, actin' like a helpless bairn, needin' ye to hold me." But with her heart, she cried, "Because before I'd no' have had to tell ye. Ye would've sensed it without words or a look or a touch of my hand, with the same certainty ye sensed Connor was in danger or that Ena's mad with grief. Ye simply would've known."

"Don't be daft." Tenderly, Ailsa rubbed slow circles between her taut shoulder blades. Her eyes grew misty with memory. "On my first visit to the glen after leavin' it a half-formed girl, comin' back to a stranger who called himself my father and a life I'd missed every minute I was in London, do ye no' think I needed Mairi Rose? I was older then than ye are now, but often and often she comforted me, held me, and I her. 'Tis a bond between mothers and daughters so powerful that it never tears or fades or weakens, no matter how old and wise ye become. 'Twould honestly break my heart if ye needed me no more."

"I know," Alanna whispered. But the knowledge, certain and immutable as it was, could not ease the ache of regret for something lost.

4

AILSA ROSE AND IAN FRASER MET IN THE SHADOWS OF THE chilly cave and knelt to build a fire. The sparks came from their fingertips, setting a small hoard of peats aflame. In the hallowed secret cave, they kissed, creating an auburn-haired girl-child of mist and smoke and the love they bore for one another.

But when the sun rose, they disappeared into the shadows, leaving their daughter alone and afraid. She felt insubstantial, less than flesh and blood and bone. Made only of vapor and the exhalation of her parents' hope, she began to unravel. Mist and smoke and dreams dissolved until nothing remained but a tendril of hair, curled like the edge of the last flame, flickering golden-red.

Then the flame went out.

Ena sat up, wide awake, arms locked around her knees until her trembling ceased. She listened to the sigh of the wind through the trees, saw the mist creep under the leather window coverings, heard the distant rush of the river, and below those seductive voices, the rhythm of Mairi's deep breathing. But not Ailsa's. She had not yet returned. The girl longed for the beat of her mother's heart against her ear, the heat of Ailsa's body, the sound of her voice, soothing and calm—all centered on Connor now, because he needed her more than Ena did.

She could barely breathe. It was too still inside the croft. All at once, Ena felt she would suffocate.

She left her bed, gliding across the room in her nightrail, pausing soundlessly beside the cat's baskets. She forced herself to concentrate, to repress what she could not deny—Connor's suffering. Because of her.

She brought a lamp near, then gently removed the upper basket and stroked the sleeping animal, it felt warm to the touch and lay stretched out as far as it could. Trying to spread the heat inside, to find some relief from what must be a fever. She was certain when it opened one eye halfway and she saw the normally copper iris had turned orange tinged with red. Francis McPhee had taught her to watch for that.

She made a tiny ball of dried hops and blackwillow wrapped in garlic and slowly, carefully, imitating as best she could the animal's purr and a low, rhythmic chant, she drew back so the cat could not see her eyes and worked the herbs into its mouth, stroking its throat to make it swallow. Then she gathered clean linens and bandages and warm water with disinfectant. When the animal's breathing was slow and regular, she replaced the soiled linens. Ena undid the bandage, cleaned the wound as gently as possible and replaced the bandage, noiselessly. She had learned long ago to move in silence. Last, she put some drops of water down the wildcat's throat with a dropper.

Ena sat back on her heels, heart racing. There was really nothing more she could do. Reluctantly, she replaced the basket that half-covered the lower one. "I've done what I can, Connor," she whispered. "I only hope 'tis enough." She knew Ailsa and Alanna would do their best for the boy. Rising like a wraith, she glided out the door, choking on the smell of blood and infection in the dirty linens and bandages she set to soak in an old barrel beside the croft.

Wrapping her plaid around her shoulders and pulling her cap onto her head with her hair tucked underneath, she slipped into the night.

Soon the first hardy cotton grass of spring brushed the hem of her gown with dew, and she paused, head back, taking in the vastness of the sky glittering with stars. She glanced around as she always did, at the clearing, the woods, the river, the distant hills, barely visible in the darkness draped in mist. This was her true home, her enchanted world of wind and woods, the sharp smell of pine and fir, the promise of water rushing over singing stones. This was her peace and her joy.

She had never feared the glen at night. Even as a small child, she'd sensed she was safe here, protected by the ancient gods and the animals of the darkness, whom she had made her friends. Often, she went out while others slept and only earth, water and moon were awake.

Out here, she was able to capture the pure, untainted happiness of her childhood. But tonight there was a shadow on her pleasure.

Connor.

Every instinct told her to go to him, but she knew that would be unwise. She stared at the sky in frustration. Then turned toward the woods. She knew she would not sleep again that night.

In his dream, Connor was enveloped first by heat, then chilling fog. His vision blurred as he blinked furiously, seeking the wildcat, chasing it, then running away. "Connor!" Ena's voice rose from the earth, desperate, urging him, pleading.

Strange, haunting music ran like a thread through his body. The river had always been their music, rushing and tumbling over stones and boulders, creating the murmur of waterfalls. Suddenly he was running, racing with Ena through the woods. The song of her flute called him in the middle of night. "To swim!" she exclaimed, elated. He wanted to feel icy water on his heated skin, wanted to be cool, to calm his tortured body. He reached the linne and was about to slide into its chilling comfort.

Then the music of flute and river and shifting leaves fell silent, and he was in bed, tangled in damp sheets. Trapped. He floated above his body, escaping, for an instant, the pain, heat and delirium that made him turn and groan and stifle his cries. Beyond was a blur of worried voices and the blaze of a fire and a thick fog that filled the room, choking off everything that tried to penetrate its cold, thick haze. Blinding him, leaving him paralyzed.

He drifted, was wrenched back into his body, held there by throbbing wounds and the burning that would not go. If only he could break the heat that made him struggle against himself. But he could not do it. No one could.

The cat was above him, staring with its hot amber eyes. Connor tried to scream, but his mouth would not open. Then the wildcat's piercing eyes became Ena's, calling out in silence, reaching for him, trying to swallow him in their gray-green depths. She appeared out of the fog, unhindered by clinging white.

He tried to think of water to cool himself, to control the quaking of his body, the wrenching and twisting that would not end. He tried to tell her to go, to shout that he could do this alone. But no sound came.

He could not deny that the sight of her face, the rhythm of her breath, the touch of her hand took away the fear. Sighing, he stopped fighting, gave in to Ena, as he always did. With her hand on his forehead he fell, far and gently; the amber gaze of the wildcat faded, and then the fog consumed him.

5

JENNY FRASER WAS DREAMING, AS SHE OFTEN DID, OF HER dead husband. She had tried, at first, to keep him from disturbing the only rest she'd found since his death many years before. But she had known when they were children he was stronger than she, so Ian Fraser crept through the darkness—the temporary reprieve of the solitude and stillness of night—and into her dreams.

He held her lightly, swaying in the firelight, so the shadows from the flames transformed his face. She ran her fingers through his dark curly hair, gazed into his green eyes and fell deep and far, as she had before and would, no doubt, again. His sun-browned skin was golden in the flickering light, his arm strong against her back as he whirled with her, dancing to the music of the river outside the open door.

They were young again, and fair, and happy in one another.

Jenny woke with a start, staring into the darkness for the slightest flicker of time, reaching for that dream, for the blissful feeling of hope and youth and joy it had brought back to her. The night snatched it from her grasp, though oddly, this time she did not feel Ian creep away as he had before.

Was it he who drew her out of bed, shivering as her bare feet hit the rag rug on the packed dirt floor, who drew her away from the smoldering peat fire, toward her plaid, which she wrapped about her, trying to dissipate the chill that would not go? Did the young Ian of her dream guide her to the window, or the older Ian who had left her alone, afraid and heartbroken? Or was it just her fancy, pulling her toward the moonlight that transformed the glen?

She leaned on the wide windowframe, staring into the gilded darkness, curious and oddly uneasy.

Then she saw the girl standing motionless beside the river, caught in veils of mist that swirled around her, holding her captive, for the rest of the night was clear.

Jenny stiffened. Ena Rose. Daughter of Jenny's husband and Ailsa Rose Sinclair.

Except when she saw Ena and was reminded of her husband's betrayal, Jenny had taught herself to forget, to occupy herself with her children and grandchildren and their ordinary lives. The success of her children, their survival, their love and the laughter of *their* children were enough to make Jenny content.

Still, she did not withdraw from the window, but continued to stare at Ena Rose.

Letting her breath out in a sigh, Jenny felt the distant figure staring at the Fraser croft. Staring and staring as if to will herself inside it. Sadness touched Jenny's heart, as it often did when she saw the girl who stood outside, alone and enwrapped in cool, damp mist. And her loneliness broke Jenny's heart.

Jenny had sensed that loneliness the first time Ena Rose knocked diffidently at the cottage door when she was barely six.

Ena's arms were wrapped around a bundle of fabric, her feet bare and her gown gathered into a knot that left her calves exposed. Her legs were covered with dirt, and judging from what Jenny could see of her skirts, tying them up had not kept them from gathering grass and turf and loam; there were brown and green stains all over the fabric.

But it was Ena's expression, and her youth, as well as courtesy and decency, which kept Jenny from closing the door in the child's face. Ena's gray eyes were wide with hope and apprehension mingled, and she stood back from the threshold as if moving any closer would be presumptuous, or threatening. She'd held her bottom lip with her teeth and had difficulty meeting the older woman's eyes.

In spite of herself, in spite of years of being haunted by hurt and helplessness and envy because this child had ever been born, Jenny found she was curious. She had heard only stories and whispers, caught fleeting glimpses of the girl before. They had never once stood face to face. Jenny was struck hard by the recognition of the courage it had taken for the child to come here.

"I know we've no' spoken before, but we're no' really strangers either," Ena declared in a single breath. "Ye'd no' be wantin' to help me, but I'm askin' just the same."

Jenny stiffened, incredulous. "Ye need my help?"

Forcing herself to stand up straight in an attempt to disguise her trepidation, Ena nodded toward the bundle in her arms. "Aye. I've heard ye sew a lot, and I pick up too many things in

*the woods and hills. I can no' hold 'em all. Connor Fraser said I
need pockets, big ones, on every gown. So I came to ye."*

Jenny remained silent and Ena gnawed on her lip. *"I'll go if
ye like."* She could not hide her disappointment.

Jenny was overwhelmed by Ena's vulnerability and honesty.
Most children hadn't the first idea when they were not wanted.
But Ena more than half-expected to be turned away. Still,
Jenny was not quite ready to relent. *"Why come to me? Why
not go to your mother? Ailsa Rose is quite good with her hands."*
Jenny had not spoken that name aloud for many years. As
always, the thought of Ian followed.

Ena ducked her head, clearly uncomfortable. *"I don't
know."*

Jenny was intrigued. Besides, this girl was neither Ian nor
Ailsa. She was a child clutching her bundled fabric tightly, her
knuckles white with uncertainty. *"Come in,"* Jenny said impulsively.

After that, Ena had come to the Fraser croft to learn to
sew and spin and card and weave, though she was hopelessly
clumsy at these small tasks. She could not seem to make her
fingers do as she wished. She learned to cook broths, but her
bannocks and biscuits and cakes always burnt, and her buns
never rose; her thoughts tended to wander, and she came
back to herself too late. Giving up on cooking, Jenny
devised a way to split Ena's skirt into trousers so full they
looked like a proper skirt unless she was climbing or running
or crawling through the grass. The child could not hide her
pleasure in the constant noise and motion, laughter and
shouting that made the croft more welcoming.

After each lesson, Jenny found a small gift left behind—
a wood carving or pressed leaves or a small bouquet of flowers or a smooth sparkling stone.

Jenny had become very fond of Ena Rose.

A tear fell on her hand, and she gazed at it in wonder.
She enjoyed Ena's company, but had not realized until that
moment that she cared enough to weep for her.

* * *

Ena stood for a long time beside the river, watching the moon's silver light dance on the water and shimmer in the treetops. Often, when she wandered at night, Connor sensed her restlessness and came in search of her. But tonight he could not. She felt cold inside, and afraid and lonely. The mist held her prisoner in the iced silver moonlight.

Just before dawn, Ailsa returned, tugged off her clothes, slid her nightrail over her head and fell into bed, too exhausted to fold her gown and shift and drape them over the back of a chair as she usually did. She intended to think over Connor's condition and what else might be done for him, but she was asleep and dreaming of heather as soon as she sank into the mattress, drawing the blanket around her.

She was walking barefoot in the darkness, through the woods and distant foothills. Her feet ached, and her arms, from the low branches of trees and bushes as she hurried heedlessly past. She felt exhilarated, free, as she ran, the smell of the woods, the caress of the mist, the feel of the wind in her hair, coming free from its braid to rise and fall with her shallow breath and the motion of her agile body.

Ian was waiting. She knew it and hurried faster, pulse pounding.

He was singing for her, calling her to him, murmuring her name in the notes of an ancient Celtic chanson.

She could feel his joy, his relief, his elation as deeply as she felt her own, and then, suddenly, he was there and she was in his arms and he was whispering in her ear, telling her all that she wanted and needed and yearned to know.

Then he held her face, stared into it, delving into the thoughts in her eyes and leaned down to kiss her, brushing his lips over hers and telling her something she could not quite hear.

He vanished into the air, into the stone, into the wind.

She waited, knowing he would not be back. Yet she could not leave.

Then there was darkness and she awoke with a start, half in, half out of bed. She remembered nothing but the faint cadence of a song that faded as she sat up.

Ailsa shook her head to clear it, but it felt heavy this morning; her thoughts were mere smudges and blurs. Her eyes burned as if she'd not slept for days. Then she felt her nightrail clinging to her ankles and looked down in alarm at the wet stained fabric. Stained with dew and mist and loam and grass and blood. She gaped as, through the haze, she looked at her bare feet and saw they were scratched and scraped and bleeding. There were scratches on her bare arms, too.

She stood abruptly, ignoring the pain, and whirled toward Mairi. Her mother had been lying awake when Ailsa stumbled in, barefoot, wearing her nightrail and no plaid. Mairi had expected Ailsa to stay all night at Alanna's and breakfast with her daughter before she came home. The old woman was surprised to see her at all. But her condition was more than surprising; it was shocking. She stared, openmouthed.

Ailsa looked at her pleadingly. "Where did I go last night?" She was perplexed and anxious and dazed. So weary that, though it was a blur of fog, she could not seem to pull herself out of her dream. Faintly, she recalled sounds—the wind in the trees, the splash of falling water, the skittering of small animals, and perhaps, far away, a voice. She remembered smells—loam still damp from melting snow, heather and grass heavy with dew, celandine and primroses and daffodils, and an acrid odor that made her shudder. Why should those memories be so vivid, yet the dream itself faint as a watercolor left in the sun too long?

Mairi worried the cloth of her skirt into pleats, trying to take it all in. "You've done it before, mayhap three times in as many years. You're gone mayhap an hour, and when ye return ye throw yourself into your bed and sleep at once, without speakin'." She paused, frowning. "I thought ye were awake and knew where ye were goin'. Usually ye stopped to put on your brogues and carefully wrap your plaid about ye. When ye made no mention of it, I thought 'twas a private thing, so I didn't press ye. But now—" She broke off and spread her hands wide. "I don't know, my child."

Blinking helplessly, Ailsa realized her skin was clammy. She paced, trying to think, but instead nearly tripped over the wildcat's temporary home. Could it have to do with the wounded cat? With her concern for Connor and Ena? But no, Mairi said she had done it before. All she remembered from arriving home from Alanna's was sliding between the sheets and into the comfort of her dreams. "I can't believe I'd no' awaken. I can't believe I'd no' recall."

Mairi took her daughter's hands, as much to steady her own as Ailsa's. "Weel, ye'd best believe. Look at ye, scratched and bruised and your feet bloodied. All I know is, 'tis dangerous, this dream of yours."

Ailsa felt light-headed, confused, a little desperate. She could not deny the evidence of wandering in her sleep. Neither could she explain or understand it. "Aye, I see the danger," she replied in whisper. "Only I don't know how to stop it."

6

ENA PULLED HER LEGS IN TIGHT AGAINST HER BODY AND leaned toward the tiny fire she had laid. She was not seeking warmth so much as a moment's stillness in her unquiet thoughts. She had been here, in her secret place, since the darkest early morning hours, when exhaustion had overtaken her. She'd pushed open the hidden door and slipped inside the hollow trunk to huddle, like the wildcat in its basket, in dark and warmth and safe familiarity.

Connor had discovered this little hideaway. He'd found the huge, bent old tree, hollowed by age and disease and fire until there was an oblong space inside high enough to crouch in. Immediately, the children had claimed it as their own.

It had been Connor who found that where the tree split, there was a knothole curled into the aged wood directly above the hollow. He had struggled and sweated, dragging his small saw through the thick bark, until the knot came away, leaving an opening for the smoke to rise from the small fires they built when the wind was cold and the cavern of their own making warm and cozy. They had kept the knot and wedged it back into the trunk to keep out rain and snow and intruders who might discover their haven.

Connor had hauled clay in a bucket and spread it with care inside the curved trunk to keep out the cold. Ena had followed behind, making swirls in the drying mud, so the hollow tree began to look like a miniature croft.

Everywhere she looked, she saw her friend. "Be well, Connor, *mo-ghraidh*. Please be well."

Mairi Rose raised her head as the song of the wren, the herald of spring, drifted to her from a copse of birches. The full skirt of her linsey-woolsey gown, fraying at the neckline and uneven at the hem, undulated in the breeze, as did her long silver hair, which she had left unbound. She stood barefoot in the soft, fertile loam of the cottage garden, enjoying a moment of solitude. She held a packet of letters in one hand—stained with age, nearly torn through at the folds, the edges bent from the touch of her fingers. Mairi smoothed the borders patiently, smiling.

Putting aside her own bewilderment for Connor's sake, Ailsa had returned to Alanna, her basket under her arm. Ena, who had left sometime during the night, had not yet reappeared. Realizing she was alone, Mairi had not bothered to braid her hair and wrap it into a crown around her head, nor to put on her brogues to protect her from the damp earth of early spring. Feeling unusually lighthearted and undisciplined, she wandered out to the garden, where new spring sunlight beckoned.

She walked among the rows of cabbages, beans, carrots, peas and leeks; she had forgotten how good soft loam felt on bare feet, how sweet and pungent the garden smelled, though the plants had barely begun to come up through the soil, after the long, snow-laden winter. The sun was warm on her head, though it had not yet summoned the strength to heat the earth. Mairi raised her face to the light, letting it soak into her pores, taking it in like water to cool a long, dry thirst.

She paused when she reached the far end of the garden, where Ailsa and Ena grew their herbs. She used to love the mist more than the sunlight. It roiled and billowed with mystery, with possibilities. But now she was seventy-two years old, and the mist that had been her comfort and inspiration had become her enemy. The chill dampness made her joints stiff and uncooperative. In the last few years, she had turned to the sunlight, which warmed her bones and muscles, eased her little aches and pains. Yet the light often burned too bright, revealed too much.

She shook her head, distracted by the sharp scent of rosemary that had spread along the ground at the bottom of the low, rough stone wall that surrounded the garden. The long spiky branches grew thick and green up the crevices between stones and over the flat top of the wall. She could smell thyme and peppermint and the newly blooming honeysuckle that climbed the outside of the wall, as well as the plethora of medicinal herbs that Ena cherished and cultivated like children, culling the weeds and breaking off the flowers with tender hands.

There was a small stone bench in the center of the fragrant herb plot, and Mairi lowered herself onto it gingerly. Then, ensconced in her small silent kingdom, she looked around, surveying with pleasure the croft where she had been born. Her small stone cottage with its roof newly thatched by the young men in the glen, the low warped door hanging open in welcome, as it had always done, except in the worst storms. Her home, familiar and dear to her beyond words, because it had once been her mother's home, and was also her daughter's home, and her youngest granddaughter's.

On the back of the breeze, it came to her softly, almost imperceptibly that those she loved would be all right, would prosper, each in their own way. She need not worry for them. When had her concern ever changed the course the gods had chosen? She chuckled, because that lesson was the easiest to understand, the most difficult to learn.

Letting her thoughts wander, she gazed at the clearing, sprinkled yellow and white with wild daffodils among the new grown grass. In the near distance were the woods where she, and then Ailsa, then Alanna and now Ena had run free, discovering the magic of earth and the voices of history in wind and trees, river and loch. She could see clearly the pines and Douglas firs, the larches with newly sprouting green leaves, the grand oaks and ash that would soon make an impenetrable canopy of green over the river. In the far distance rose the dark purple mountains, brooding and magnificent.

Everything was clear, vibrant, familiar. Mairi smiled to herself. She could see the beauty around her so clearly she felt she could touch it and feel its texture on her callused palm. She took out the letters from her husband and opened the one on top. It was easier to read in the sunlight, and there'd been little enough of that lately. Wistfully, Mairi read and re-read Charles Kittridge's long ago messages to her, finding comfort in the familiar words and well-used paper. She missed him a great deal just now, missed his support and his unwavering faith in her. She was surprised at the feeling, though he had been on her mind often in the past months.

She decided to stay where she was for awhile, absorbing

sun and sky, color and sound, her senses intensely awake and keenly perceptive. Looking up every now and then to renew her sense of delight in her surroundings, she slowly and fondly read the words her husband had written years and worlds away from here.

Ena sat in the semidarkness, raising her head when the notes of a wren singing its dawn song aroused her.

Pale light filtered through the knothole as the smoke curled upward, mingling with and staining the new light of the sun. She sat on a soft bed of pine needles, heather and moss she had replaced at the end of winter. Ena glanced around the small, circular room, staring at each object in turn. The misshapen pinecone she had rescued, the wild daffodils she had brought yesterday, only slightly wilted, the squirrels and small birds and the tiny red deer she had carved and placed in natural indentations in the trunk. A pile of smooth colored stones.

There were dried flowers scattered about, and a shallow set of wooden cubicles for her herbs and roots and dried flowers and leaves. She had found a tiny stump nearby, and Connor had uprooted it, cutting off the bottom in a straight edge, then carefully sanding the top until it was smooth. She used it for her table, pretending it had been here all along, one tiny tree trying to grow inside the hollow shell of another.

Tacked to the walls were drawings and notes from her cousins Sebastian, Vincent and Marc, Lian Drouard's sons, as well as Genevra's children. She wrote to them frequently, and also to her uncles and aunts, and they to her. She felt she knew them almost as well as the people in the glen; it was much easier to put on paper secrets and doubts and dreams and expectations than it was to speak them aloud. She discovered, through them, another world beyond her own, so different, so fascinating, so huge and full of things she'd never seen, ideas she'd never heard. They asked her to visit in nearly every letter, to come to Burgundy, France or Kent in England.

You have to come, Sebastian had written. He was not alone. *When are you coming to visit?* Elizabeth Kendall wrote. *If it isn't soon, we'll all be old and married and shriveled, and that won't be any fun. Come now, while the damask roses are in bloom, and the garden a tapestry of color and scent.*

Ena closed her eyes to picture that garden and felt a nagging guilt because she yearned so much to see that other world. She should be content to stay here, she told herself firmly, in the place her father and mother had loved above all others. But, oh, the lure of those voices, those promises, the deep affection she felt for all her cousins. Except for Connor, they were her best friends. Her favorites of their letters were tacked to the walls and spread on the stump of the table, so she felt they were nearby when she was in her secret place.

My Esteemed and Beloved Niece, Lian said in her boxlike hand, because she'd learned to write in English from Chinese ideograms, *Despite your stories of running deer and pools of clear crystal water that reflect the moon, you are missed here, where we speak of you daily. We have never seen or touched you, nor you us. Strange, is it not, the affection we share? When will you make what is now invisible, real?*

Ena ran her fingertips over the words longingly. How much she missed them all just now, how much she wished they were friends in the flesh as well as in the mind. She realized with a start that for the first time in her life, she was lonely. She shuffled through the vellum until she found her Aunt Genevra's last letter.

Ena, my child, she had written in the elegant, flowing script of an artist, *I see your face shimmering in the foam-edged ocean waves. I think of you often of late, perhaps because you are the future, yet never once set foot on this soft, crystalline sand or saw this azure ocean, so full of secrets and shells and beauty I've not yet discovered.*

Ena read it twice, then folded the page carefully, thinking fondly of the family, who made her feel she was one of them. She was not sure why it was so important to her, that family, except that her aunts and cousins were not at all like the people she knew in the glen. They were intriguing, exceptional, and they tantalized her with their other world. Over the years, she'd come to love them.

In the past few months, the yearning to meet them had been growing stronger. She wanted to go away to a magical place she'd never been, to make a trip, perhaps to Kent *and* Burgundy. She thought about it often, a strange, tight feeling in her chest that only made the longing more intense. She knew her aunts asked Ailsa if her daughter could come to them, but her mother had delayed, saying the girl was too young. Ena had wanted to argue, but had kept silent. Recently, feeling as strange as she did, Ena'd almost mentioned it again, but her mother had been so funny and affectionate that night, had so obviously wanted her daughter near, that the girl had kept silent. But that did not stop the desire.

The girl dropped Genevra's letter from tingling fingers, staring and listening and hearing only the thrum of her own heartbeat. Something was amiss. She raised her head sharply, smelling the fragrance of new morning air, hearing the sounds of the animals stirring, seeing the clear quality of a light that was usually dimmed by mist at this hour.

There was a discordant note in the light spring breeze, but she could not decide where it had come from. Her stomach growled, reminding her how long it had been since she'd eaten. Perhaps she'd return to the croft, where nourishment and Mairi waited. Without a thought she abandoned her letters and her treasures, knocking a jar of ink among the moss and heather.

As she hurried toward the croft built into the hillside, her footsteps quickened, and her heartbeat, and her trepidation. Something was wrong; someone was calling. She closed her eyes in a fervent prayer to the gods of the glen and began to run.

7

MAIRI ROSE SAT ON THE LOW STONE BENCH IN THE GARDEN, head bowed in concentration. Her arms were tense, stretched to their limit as she tried to lift herself from the bench, her hands curled like claws at her sides. The veins throbbed, dark and swollen beneath skin worn thin by work and sun and time. Her body was unnaturally rigid, straining for an effort unaccomplished, a goal unreached. Mairi's face was pallid in the sunlight, her lips a taut line, her eyes closed tight against the glare, hiding the frustration, the supplication. Her husband's letters had fallen among the herbs like white flags of surrender, fluttering in the breeze.

"Aye, 'tis very strange." Kneeling at her mother's battered feet, Alanna removed the basin of warm water and blackberry leaf powder in which they had been soaking and dried the soles gingerly with a soft cloth. "Wanderin' in your sleep? Yet ye always seem to know where you're goin'."

Ailsa smiled and shook her head. "Or I'm wantin' to make ye think I do. Mind ye, now and again I've found the right path." Her smile was fleeting, and she leaned back into the deep cushions pensively.

Emptying the bowl and collecting the things she'd need to attend her mother's injuries, Alanna remembered with dismay how Ailsa had appeared at the door earlier. She'd worn an old dress of moss green, somewhat wrinkled and disheveled. Ailsa's hair had been braided quickly, but already the strands were coming loose. Her scratched arms and legs looked as though they'd been washed too quickly; a thin layer of dirt and spots of blood still stained her skin.

"But," she'd said bluntly, "we must see to Connor first."

With difficulty, Alanna withheld her questions, wincing at how cautiously Ailsa moved about on her sore feet. Together, they replaced Connor's bandages, discovering that while his wounds were no better, they were also no worse. His fever seemed a little lower, partly from the pennyroyal that had made him sweat out the unnatural heat and partly from the constant bathing of his body in cool water. David had taken over when Alanna fell exhausted into her chair by the fire and slept. He'd worked assiduously, grateful for something to occupy his hands.

After mother and daughter cleaned and rebound the wounds, they left David to his task and retreated to the kitchen, drawing chairs close to the coal-burning stove.

Ailsa told Alanna about the dream she could not fully remember, the evidence of her struggle, and her bewildered realization that she must have gone outside in her sleep.

Leaning forward, elbow on the chair arm and chin in her hand, Alanna listened, perplexed and intrigued. But when Ailsa's shawl fell over her arm and she winced, her daughter leapt up, determined to ease her mother's physical pain, if not her emotional distress. She'd used white willow bark, witch hazel and comfrey on the abrasions, then tenderly washed Ailsa's soiled arms and feet.

"Looks as though you stumbled through the woods without botherin' to find a path, Mam." Alanna pushed herbs, cloths and dirty water aside, considering. "Ye must've been goin' somewhere. I mean, I can't believe ye were wanderin' aimlessly."

"I don't know what to believe. But it's set my head fairly spinnin', I tell ye."

"Aye, I suppose 'twould." Alanna was touched that her mother had confided in her. " 'Tis a delicate thing, this. A disturbin' thing." Yet Ailsa had not hesitated.

"How can I explain when I can no' understand?" her mother said, idly fingering the scratches on her arm.

Automatically, Alanna brushed her hand away. "Ye don't want to inflame them."

Ailsa didn't notice. "What shall I do?" She looked suddenly defenseless and bereft.

Alanna's chest ached, and she rose, eyes damp with tears. "First ye'll let me tidy your hair. Ye look like a barbarian, ready to shout the English to death if need be."

Nodding, slipping back into her reverie, Ailsa closed her eyes with pleasure as Alanna slowly unwound her braid, then used the silver comb David had given her to smooth out the tangles, the bits of leaves and tiny twigs still clinging in the untidy mass. Gracefully, she drew the comb through the thick chestnut hair, noticing how many more gray strands there were than her daughter remembered. Alanna spread the waves across her palm, picking at a tangle strand by strand until it was gone, then combed out the thick mass over her arm. " 'Tis aye bonny, your hair," she murmured.

While water heated for tea, she made a thick new braid and tied it with a green ribbon she found in the drawer of the press. Then, with a cup in each hand, she sat across from Ailsa once more.

After half a cup of tea and a black bun—her favorite since she'd been a child—Ailsa was more relaxed and her violet eyes were clear and alert.

"Bless ye, child," she said. "I'm better now in every way." She leaned forward intently, though there'd been no change in Alanna's expression. "What is it?"

" 'Tis just . . . do ye remember anything that moves ye when ye think of it? Anything from the dream, I mean."

Ailsa closed her eyes and concentrated until suddenly, beneath her hand, she felt slightly rough, cool stone, remembered a fragment of a song and an ache so deep it stopped her breath. She described the feeling to Alanna.

"I've naught but instinct to guide me, Mam, but I wonder if you're followin' a path you've followed before, so often that ye know it even in your sleep? I wonder if you're lookin' for something ye can no' find at home."

Ailsa considered. "What could it be? I've all I need and more. Why risk my life for this mysterious and unlikely thing in the dark and unconscious mist of sleep?"

"Because it means that much to ye. Because some part of ye needs it enough . . ." She trailed off.

"You're thinkin' of Ian Fraser, are ye no'?"

"Mayhap. What else could it be?"

Ailsa shook her head firmly. "I'm no' yet clingin' to him or his memory. 'Twas a long, long time ago, Alanna, and too painful to go back to."

"Not so very long when ye think of the age of the ground ye walk and the mountains and forests ye see every day."

Ailsa felt uneasy, as she had when she awakened, and she did not like it. But what if Alanna—serene, practical Alanna—was right?

Briskly, her daughter took her hands and held on tight. "Whatever 'tis, it makes no matter. We'll find out in time. Don't fret."

Ailsa's throat felt tight. Despite everything Alanna was suffering, despite her son, lying fevered and ill at the far end of the room, she could feel her mother's distress, share and try to lighten it. " 'Tis grateful I am to have ye for a daughter," she said. "Always here, always ready to listen, no matter your own troubles."

Alanna met her mother's gaze, feeling infinitely old and wise and foolish all at once. " 'Tis glad I am *ye* need *me* now and then. 'Tis a satisfyin' thing, to be needed. And much more than that as well. But ye know. You've always know that, Mam."

Ena was possessed by a sense of urgency. As she reached the garden, she glanced toward the plot of herbs that had sprung up rapidly since the snow and mud had gone. The girl stopped still when she saw Mairi, but was wise enough to hide her dismay. "I'm back, Gran. My mouth is waterin' at the thought of your barley-corn bannocks and milk, I'm that hungry."

Mairi relaxed slightly, feeling her granddaughter's young, vibrant presence, hearing her everyday voice and knowing it meant freedom from this painful captivity. She sighed—a single, fragile breath released.

After gathering the scattered letters, Ena helped her grandmother to her feet. The two walked slowly through the garden, hand in hand. In mutual accord, they paused at the gate to catch their breath.

Ena had long been aware of Mairi aging, becoming less active, less agile, but the sight of her on the bench, struggling as if against a rough Highland wind, had struck the girl like the icy water of the loch in winter.

Mairi had been momentarily shocked by her helplessness, but the feeling passed as the two of them leaned on the weather-worn gate, which held them upright as it had for generations. "I'd no' go inside yet," she said. "If ye can tame your hunger for a wee bit. The sun feels good on my face. Tranquil." She felt her granddaughter's hand in hers, and the child's fingers seemed nimble and small. Once Ailsa's hands had been like that.

" 'Tis past now, birdeen," she murmured. " 'Twas only a moment, and that created by my own foolishness. I'd forgotten how low that bench was. But don't ye see, 'twas worth it, that hour of sunlight and memory."

"Aye?" Ena was skeptical. "You've no pain?"

Mairi actually laughed. "Of course I've a little pain now and then and my body's more frail than before." She squeezed her granddaughter's shoulder in reassurance. "I'm growin' older, or hadn't ye noticed? If I had no aches and swollen joints and as much strength as when I was younger, 'twould be unnatural."

"I suppose." The girl sounded dispirited.

Turning toward her, Mairi commanded, "Ena-my-heart, look at me. 'Tis normal, what's happenin' to me, and no' necessarily a bad thing. There're inconveniences I could do without, but on the whole, I'm content. I've a vivid memory, even if my hands are no' so skillful as they once were. I carry every person, every moment of my life inside as surely as I carry Charlie's letters in my pocket. 'Tis a cycle of nature, is all. Ye, above all, should understand that."

"I understand that you're wonderful. I know ye say this partly to calm me, but when I look in your eyes, I think mayhap ye really believe it."

"I believe, my granddaughter. I've always believed. In the Celtic gods, in the sacred glen, in each of my family, that we've all of us a privilege and obligation to be happy, and that it comes right in the end, though sometimes ye can no' see it. More than ought else I might yearn for, I hope ye learn to believe as deeply. Many and many's the time that faith'll bring ye comfort."

Ena smiled; her grandmother surprised her again and again with her strength and her conviction. "I'm learnin' a little at a time, and so I'll go on." She considered Mairi unobtrusively. "But I'd have ye know that we're grateful you've always cared for us, Gran. You've cared for everyone but yourself. I just . . . I want to say, don't ye worry, because I'll take care of ye when ye need me. Always." It was more than a promise; it was a sacred vow.

"Aye, weel, that's as may be. And I thank ye from the heart, child. But just the same, I'd ask ye no' to mention this to anyone."

Ena drew herself up straight. "Ye need no' ask. 'Tis between us, what happened here today. It always was, Gran."

Mairi smiled with affection. "Of course it was. Forgive me."

Together they ducked under the lintel, Ena to plunder the bannocks and porridge, and when she'd eaten her fill, to check on the sedated wildcat sleeping by the fire. She'd not have to sedate her today, she noticed. The cat was so ill with fever and pain, so weak from loss of blood, that it lay inert, the only motion the rise and fall of its chest as it breathed. Ena could only give it some drops of chicken broth infused with yarrowroot, hawthorn leaf and nettle, for fever, heart and blood. The normally copper eyes were still orange, but the tint of red had faded.

Mairi collapsed into her rocking chair, closed her eyes and rested her head against the soft cushion, enjoying the sounds of her granddaughter moving about, murmuring to herself as she saw to the cat's wound.

All at once, the old woman looked up, listening. "Ailsa's comin' home. 'Tis time for ye to be off to see Connor."

Ena stiffened at a wave of nausea.

"Don't fash yourself, my girl," her grandmother said kindly. "Think of the many animals you've treated for many unpleasant things. You've seen them bleed and even die. Connor's past that danger, I think, if he was ever near it at all."

"But he's my dearest friend. I've never tried my 'touch' on someone as ill as he."

"That's no' what's eatin' at ye, is it?"

Sometimes Ena wished her grandmother were not so perceptive. "I've never seen grief and anguish so close, felt it so near my own heart. And his parents—"

"Don't be worryin' for David and Alanna; 'tis Connor needs your help. Go ye now, *caraid.* 'Tis time and past time. You're strong enough and skilled enough, and have compassion enough to carry ye through. I'd remind ye of your promise to believe. 'Tis a good time to start. Don't let fear or sorrow into your mind as ye work, for they'll take the power from your hands and the wisdom from your memory more quickly than lightning takes a whole forest. Don't be doubtin' yourself, not even for a moment."

For a little longer, Ena gazed at Mairi, unmoving. Then her grandmother's affection and faith broke through the haze of doubt. She nodded. "I'll be goin' now, but I'll no' forget the lightning, nor the vow I made ye." She turned and was gone, swift and sure as the red deer she loved.

8

ALANNA AND DAVID STOOD SIMULTANEOUSLY AT THE SLIGHT knock, hoping for something to save their son.

"As if such would come knockin' at the door," David muttered wryly.

"Mayhap it would. 'Tis not unheard of in this place." Alanna's whisper was barely audible, as surprising as her undiminished faith.

David looked at his wife askance, more longing than skepticism in his eyes. He opened the door to the sight of Ena Rose hovering uncertainly on the threshold.

The girl looked from one to the other, troubled and agitated. She did not know what to expect. "I know Connor's very ill," she said quietly. "I know ye blame me, as ye should. But mayhap I could help him now. I'll no' ask ye to forgive me, not until we're certain he's safe." She straightened her shoulders without much affect. "But then I *will* ask. I can only hope ye answer." She waited, heart pounding, wanting desperately to go to Connor. She could feel his heavy, slow breathing, the rushed beat of his heart.

David took his wife's hand. He was a vigorous man of unusual strength, shaken and angry because, looking into Ena's face, he saw his own impotence reflected in her eyes. He wanted to rage at the girl, but he was mute. He would have liked to blame her, but he knew Connor had made his own choice.

Alanna and David exchanged a long look, while Ena waited on the doorstep of a house that had been as much her home as Mairi Rose's. She clasped her hands to hide their trembling, her growing desperation at each wasted moment. Connor! she called in her mind. There was no answer. Only a cold all-enveloping fog. She could not bear it, that his affliction had taken him away from her, from everything but itself.

She frowned at the Frasers' hesitation, which fed her new-found insecurity and uncertainty. Ena had been raised among the memories, emotions and events of the past, but no one had told her about the future. About doubt and panic and mistrust. About rejection, which she had never known.

She felt the foundation of her world shift and tilt and knew no way to hold it steady, keep it safe and unchanged. Ena's stomach churned.

She fought back tears because these people were uncertain, angry, afraid. Of her. She who loved Connor more than any other on this earth, except for Ailsa and Mairi. "I only want to help," she said. "And if I've no' the power to do that, I promise I'll never hurt him. Mayhap at least I can see him rest more easily."

"Nothing makes him rest easy," Alanna said. "How can he heal when he can no' sleep for the pain and fever?"

Ena's mouth went dry. "I can try." It was a plea from her heart.

The Frasers could not ignore or deny it. Together they opened the door wide, allowing Ena to step from the sun on the clearing to the cool, dark croft, which smelled of peat and mutton stew and home.

Ena went directly to Connor's bed, stopping, skin pallid, when she saw him. His upper body was splotched with red from the fever. The tangled sheets were soaked in sweat and smelled of sickness. He thrashed about wildly, disturbing the bandages, through which blood and pus oozed. The infection had gone deep and she struggled not to look away. She was not squeamish, only afraid of failure.

"I want to clean the wounds again. I've a new brew of

herbs, a powerful disinfectant." She glanced up, hollow-eyed. "He must be made to sleep. Will ye let me try?"

"He'll no' stop ravin' and thrashin'. I've tried everything, but naught works. Oh, aye, ye can try. I'd be grateful." Alanna's voice was weak with dwindling hope.

Ena removed her leather bag of herbs and decoctions from her gaping pocket, while Alanna went to get bowl, cloths, warm water. As she laid out her tools and medicines on the floor, the girl began to speak softly, reminding her friend of midnight swims in the chilly burn, of the song of the wind and the sway of the trees, of the voice of the water—cool, soothing, beautiful. Quietly, she began to sing a healing charm upon him, comforting herself as much as her patient. She sang, and her song was an invocation to the gods to take the poison from his body.

> "May it go with the beasts of the heights,
> May it go with the wild ones running,
> May it go with the streams of the glens,
> May it go with the winged ones flying."

Holding her breath, she put her hand on Connor's fore-head as he tried to twist away. Almost at once, he grew still and his arms fell to his sides. He lay immobile, his breathing audible in the sudden hush.

Alanna folded inward, hands across her middle. Tears filmed her eyes and she turned away. She could not comfort her own son, but Ena could, with a single touch and the sound of her voice.

For a long time, the girl kept watch, cleansing the wounds and rebinding them, feeding him herb teas, cooling his body with a wet cloth, and, eventually sitting beside his bed and playing her flute, hoping to reach him, as she often had, through music.

Ena started when Connor half-rose, eyes wide and shiny

as silver, croaked out incomprehensible words, then fell back against the pillows. Her heart paused, pounded too hard, paused again. His body was covered in perspiration, but his skin was no longer burning. His forehead felt warm and clammy, but beneath her hand, his eyes closed naturally and he slipped easily, soundlessly, into sleep.

"The fever's broken," she said, unable to suppress her relief and elation. "He's no' yet completely out of danger, but with your care, I think he'll be all right. I hope it, aye, but I believe it too. If 'tis all right, I'd like to come back tomorrow."

Alanna smiled with tears in her eyes—half relief, half heartache. "Of course ye'll come. He'll be askin' for ye as soon as he can speak, and 'twill be like before."

Ena knew somewhere deep within that it would not be like before. Connor would carry with him always two sets of long jagged scars, and because of that, no one would forget. So much had happened, yet so little, that things had shifted oddly, and the world she knew would never be the same again.

9

ONE WEEK AFTER THE ATTACK ON CONNOR, ALANNA AND David welcomed their neighbors back into their cottage. The men transacted their business at the kitchen table, while the women brought homemade gifts for Connor— which were mostly for his poor, beleaguered mother, fighting an infection from the claws of a wildcat.

Alanna smiled and shook her head as she sniffed the mutton stew Catriona Grant had brought, the woven scarf—"blessed by sacred water, ye ken, to save ye from future mishaps,"—from Flora Munro, the rich sweet cakes from Kirstie Maclennan.

"Was't truly a ninety pound cat mad with pain and eight feet long?"

"Did Connor grab it by the paws and hold it till Ena Rose could subdue it?"

"And did they chase it forty miles into the mountains with the spring snow meltin' around their ankles and the hidden rocks makin' 'em slide down the scree?"

Even David, engrossed in the exchange of seed for coin and coin for new implements, of cattle and sheep for both, heard that last and actually smiled for the first time since Connor had come home.

Turning away so she'd not disgrace herself by laughing, Alanna faced her visitors solemnly. "No. Here's how it happened, ye see. Ena and Connor were out enjoyin' the first true day of spring, when a Sassenach hunter came out of nowhere—"

David had to force her voice into the background and deal with the men around the long oak table. His kinsmen and partners as well as his friends. Malcolm Drummond, Ewen Grant, Alistair Munro and Archibald Maclennan had come that morning. There would be more in the next fortnight; just prior to the wildcat's attack, David had been to Inverness to collect the last payment for the crops from last fall, to sell off the weakened cattle and sheep and buy heartier, healthier specimens, along with chickens aplenty, new plows and scythes and shovels to begin the spring planting.

"I'll tell ye this, Fraser," Ewen Grant said, taking a swig of the customary whisky—*uisge beatha*, the water of life—that sealed all Highland bargains, " 'tis damned grateful I am, and many a man more than me, that you're willin' to take on the collectin' and sellin' and tradin' for Glen Affric. With your other life in Glasgow, ye learned more than all of us put together about strikin' a bargain and makin' a profit."

"A profit in particular," Alistair Munro added. "For I've ne'er seen so many good years runnin' but since ye took over sellin' the crops and meat and kine."

"A fair genius, ye are!" Archibald Maclennan cried, "And no' a man in the glen hasn't learned it to his benefit."

David kept his head buried studiously in the books he'd opened for their perusal, though only a few could read. They knew he'd come here a rich man, but no one knew how rich, since he didn't swagger or brag or toss gold coins about after a few too many whiskies. They only knew that when he sold the combined crops of oats and barley and wheat, which before each man had traded on his own, he got a better price because of the men he knew, his bargaining skill and the tricks he was wary of.

They never guessed when, say, Maclennan's crop wasn't as good as Munro's. All profited equally and lived in fair comfort, which was what they cared about most. That was one reason he'd wanted to combine the products from the glen. They also didn't know, nor would they, that he bought more expensive plows, finer seed, healthier animals, and made up the difference with his own money. He charged the men half what he paid and wished he needn't charge them at all. But Highland pride was a formidable thing, as he'd learned to his grief more than once. So he made his transactions far away in a big city where quality merchandise was to be found and no one from home would come upon him using his money to supplement their own.

No one would argue the glen wasn't prospering.

David looked around their comfortable croft with its wooden floors, the glass at the windows and the stove Alanna valued so much. Then there was the down bed in the loft, softer and more welcoming than the beds of heather and straw the others slept in. He could not regret those improvements to their lives, but it was easier to bear knowing the others benefited as well. He felt the money he'd earned in Glasgow was unclean; that was why he'd left father, brother, sister and shipbuilding/importing business behind to return to his family in the glen.

"How's the Widow Fraser gettin' on now?" asked Malcolm Drummond, who'd recently lost his wife, and once, long ago, had had an eye for young Jenny Mackensie before she married Ian.

"Tolerable well," David replied, catching his wife's warning glance. "She's well enough. No' wantin' for anything, last I heard."

" 'Tis amazin' how that woman does it, and her so long without a man." Malcolm sounded just a bit wistful.

"Aye, weel, she's a smart lass, is Jenny Fraser. And careful. Very careful."

Alanna would have glared at her husband, except the others would've noticed. It had been difficult enough for David to distribute the money his father had left for Jenny Fraser and her family; guilt money for bringing the Strangers who'd killed her husband. She would have flung Duncan Fraser's offerings in his son's face, had she known, so great was her grief and her pride. He'd helped her in small ways, as he'd promised his father, giving her a little more than her share of everything he could.

Now that her son and his family had moved south, and she had no men in her house, David watched over her with special care, coming up with creative ways to give her his father's money. She could have been rich, but wouldn't have wanted that. As long as she was comfortable, had food on the table and was never in want, David was content, because Jenny herself was content. Only Alanna and Ailsa and Mairi knew the truth, and not for the world would they whisper a word that might damage her pride— one of her last and most precious possessions.

"To the Widow Fraser!" Malcolm Drummond cried, and every man drank an enthusiastic toast. But they would have toasted a dry roof or a new hoe by then. No doubt by the time the third bottle was empty, they'd done just that, and worse.

When the day ended at last, and the happily burdened

and swaying men were accompanied home by their sober and disapproving wives, David and Alanna settled outside, watching the gloaming descend on the mountains like a shawl fashioned of lilac mist draping itself over looming dark shoulders, bathing them in violet light to soften their forbidding aspect. David had brought a lantern and the books to work on, while Alanna spun wool into thread. They were grateful for the hush that lay over woods and river and moor, especially after their boisterous guests.

"Do ye know what Connor wanted to do today?" Alanna asked after a long, tranquil hour. "Go see the new brood of sheepdogs born last week, clear down the moor and across the loch. Said he could walk, thank ye kindly. I'm no' certain 'twasn't better when he was too weak to talk."

"Weel, if ye must be makin' him stronger, ye have to expect the worst." Her husband sounded unsympathetic, but he was being driven as wild by his young son as Alanna. Connor's fever was completely gone and his wounds had begun to heal. He was well enough to want to be up and away, chasing another wild animal no doubt, though every time he moved, he winced with pain. He refused to recognize how weak he was and was eager to be out exaggerating his adventure.

While Connor was ill, David and Alanna had clung to each other, growing closer, more intimate, more affectionate. Nearly losing their son had reminded them how much they meant to one another. When he was not needed to help treat Connor, David worked the muddy land, cared for the injured animals, rounded up the sheep that had wandered. "I have to slay my own demons," he'd told his wife. "I'm mad with frustration and my anger burnin', because there's naught I can do to help my lad. So I tramp the fields, doin' as much heavy work as I can, hopin' the anger'll seep through my pores and dry with my sweat." Somehow, husband and wife had survived.

They fell silent, watching the moon drift among dark clouds that moved above the lilac-tinted earth, pushed by the wind into a slow gliding dance. Alanna would not have been surprised if Mena, the Moon Goddess, had stepped lightly down to earth.

"Things'll have to be different from now on," David said, breaking the fragile mood reluctantly. It was time to talk about the future.

"Aye, so they will. I'm afraid Connor's gotten too comfortable in his childhood and his freedom." Alanna looked down sadly. " 'Twouldn't matter so much, mayhap, if he had brothers and sisters we could tend to."

Grasping her hand, David showed his understanding. He, too, had been disappointed that they'd had only the one son, pray though they might for more children. In a way, that made Connor more precious to them both. He cleared his throat roughly. " 'Tis no' that he doesn't help out with the crops and the animals when I ask, but by now, with his size and strength and age, it should be natural for him to go to the fields most days. But he still gets away whenever he can."

"I wonder if he knows he's well on to becomin' a man," Alanna murmured. "And she a woman." She stared at the round pitted face of the moon, gauging the shadows and the secrets. She thought she heard Mena's voice in the distant murmur of the burn. "I think mayhap he does. He just doesn't know what it means."

David ruminated, lighting a rosewood pipe and puffing out his thoughts. "We can no' tell him when to see her. He's my son, in the end, stubborn as the birch is tall. He'll sneak away often, just to prove he can." He paused, coughed on an artistic puff of smoke that backfired, then added surprisingly, "And, to tell ye the truth, I'd no' want to interfere."

Alanna regarded her husband in surprise.

"Och, Alannean, we've talked and talked and can no' decide what to do with young Connor. Mayhap we should ask Ena Rose."

Alanna was silent.

Her husband noticed the shuttered expression in her eyes. "What is't about Ena you're no' sayin'?"

"There's nothing to say, after all. I'd like to resent her, blame her for everything, but I can't. 'Tis no' her fault." At least, that's what she told herself. She sat very straight, her shoulders back. " 'Tis merely who she is that seduces Connor." She stared at her hands in her lap for a long, tense moment, then cried, "She only had to touch his forehead and speak and he grew calm." She covered her face with her hands, slumping forward. The words had been torn from her without her intention.

For the first time, David realized how much Ena's magic touch had hurt his wife. He should have known. Why hadn't he seen it before?

Alanna was truly torn. The girl had broken her heart by saving Connor further pain. How could she hate her, or even dislike her, when she gave all she could, patiently, modestly, unobtrusively?

David read her feelings in her eyes, and he ached for his wife. He stood beside her chair and put his arm around her, brushing her cheek tenderly. "I'm sorry, Alannean. I wish there was a simple answer."

"Connor's all we have," she murmured. "And Ena's all he loves. That's the only answer he'll understand." She twined her fingers with David's, kissing his raw knuckles lovingly. "He thinks 'tis his choice, the path he takes. He knows so little, our son, and believes he knows so much."

10

WITH AN UNOPENED LETTER FROM HER AUNT LIAN IN HER pocket, Ena skimmed along the path to the river, etched so deeply into her mind that her feet carried her through the woods toward the copse without thought. Everywhere she looked, she saw new life. Wild daffodils clustered among the celandine—the yellow seven-petaled stars that, along with white and lilac wood anemones, carpeted the ground among the trees. There were violets hidden in niches where the wind did not reach, creeping wood sorrel, with its white petals, spread open to the sun. Ena seemed to move just above the undulating design of whites, yellows, violets, blues and greens.

The rowans were marked by silky, silver-green furled spears; the larches had sprouted light green tufts and the holly bushes sported their last red berries. The beeches with their criss-crossed branches were still tall and leafless, and the birches had begun to reveal dark green fans ready to open. The giant old oaks had a few pale yellow leaves, but the ivy climbing up their gnarled trunks was vivid green.

As the sound of the river rose with a murmur and a rush and a roar through the new spring trees, the pines and spruce and fir undulated regally at the playful breeze winding its way among them.

Ena tilted her head back, listening, relishing the kiss of the breeze, moist with water from the river, the blue sky painted with soft drifts of cloud, the verdant hush that fell upon her as she entered the woods. This was where she belonged, where her spirit took flight and her soul was at ease.

And now, well over a week after stalking the wildcat, she felt lighthearted, bursting with joy as if returning to a beloved home. "Connor's better every day," she told a passing red squirrel. "He'll have scars, aye, but no doubt he'll like showin' 'em to the ladies who'll gather round to hear his story." She frowned briefly, then smiled at a nudge against her hand. A red doe stood there with its irresistible liquid brown eyes, a distinct scar down one side of its back. "I wondered if ye'd be back, but then, ye know I'll feed ye and scratch your hide as well as the bark you're leery of.

But ye'll no' be eatin' so much as last time. There's plenty to be found on your own." She indicated the moss and low grass, wood sorrel and ferns that edged the river. "I'll no' be spoilin' ye this time, so don't think it."

The doe merely nudged her free hand again, rubbing her head against Ena's arm. The girl sighed and gave up. "Follow me, then." She had sewn up and treated a ragged tear on the deer's side from a sharp branch on the tree she'd been scratching her hide against last summer.

"There's no' a hint of infection in the wounds," Ena continued. "Connor's wounds, ye ken. If I'm to care for ye, ye have to listen to me blather. 'Tis only fair. So if he keeps still till they heal, he should be fine." The squirrel had gotten bored long since and disappeared into the dark green shadows, so she turned her attention to the doe. Hearing the words aloud made her feel more confident.

When she reached the clearing where she kept her injured animals, the small reed pens and roomy cages and larger enclosures, most with sheltered areas covered with thatch and straw, the doe stopped abruptly, scenting a natural foe.

"Ah, so you've smelled the wildcat. Weel, no need to fret; she can no' get to ye, and well as she's doin', ye can still run a mite faster." The deer hung back, so Ena set down the bucket she carried and went to find her stockpile of grass and seeds and acorns. She filled her skirt, holding it out like a dancer ready to take a bow, and took it to the deer. The animal began to munch contentedly.

"Connor'd no' believe it if he saw it with his own eyes," Ena muttered. "Told me it couldn't be done with wild deer or squirrels or even wood mice, no matter what Francis McPhee said. Scoffed at me, he did. Yet here ye are, and 'twas ye found me, no' the other way round." She scratched the red hair in ever-widening circles. "Ye know I'll no' hurt ye, is why. Ye know the sound of my voice and the approach of my feet mean food and care. But be off with ye, now.

You've your own life to lead." She waved the deer off and it turned and disappeared into the trees without a backward glance.

Ena shook her head and returned to her wounded menagerie. It was small, since she'd spent the last week repairing the damage done by winter wind and snow—drying out the ground with straw, rebuilding the pens that had fallen under the weight of the snow, or the branches soaked through that had snapped. Surprisingly, most of the shelters were in good condition, though she still spent a lot of time collecting wood and reeds and thatch and straw to make each area as secure as possible. Fortunately, the food she'd collected, the blankets and bandages and needles and scissors and catgut had been carefully stored deep in a partially hollow tree and protected by several layers of straw and thatch and woven reeds, so her supplies were intact.

Her heart began to beat expectantly as she approached the pens, washed in sunlight and warmth. She noticed a sheltered nook of primroses on the bank of the burn and stooped to admire it, to run her fingers through the icy water till she touched smooth stone. Soon she would see the wildcat again and judge its progress. She grinned and rose, letting the water drip from her fingertips in a wavy pattern of sparkling drops on the moss.

Intent on her mission, she checked the young bird whose wing she had splinted when it collided with the blowing branch of a larch. There was also a red squirrel that had torn its paw on a jagged bit of broken rock. She had disinfected the wound, soothed it with blackberry leaf, then sewn it shut. The bird attempted to flap its wings, and chirped at her when she fed it the grub worms she'd collected. The squirrel chittered away as it always did; squirrels were perhaps *too* easy to tame. It hobbled about on three legs, trying its best to escape her when she reached in to change the bandage on the swollen paw.

"Now," the girl said, smiling broadly. "Now." Without

appearing to touch the ground, she made her way to the pen where she'd confined the wildcat. This was the most suspenseful moment of the day, when she uncovered the cave-like structure inside a larger pen and checked on the cat's progress. Somehow she was always afraid it would be gone.

Ena had taken her from the croft after several days, when the fever faded and she became alert. The girl put her on a soft bed of grass and heather in a shadowed cage that made the cat feel secure. The sun had been warm for so early in spring, and once the animal was awake and eating solid food, she thought it would be happier outside, so long as it had a place to retreat to. The wound was better every day, the pus gone, and the redness and swelling. Yesterday the girl had seen the cat hobble about the pen, trying out her injured leg, dragging it behind her, but walking just the same. Ena, down wind and out of sight, had watched in amazement. In her heart, if she told the truth, she'd not really thought she could heal that wounded, worn out, weakened cat.

Now she only sedated the animal by mixing hops with its food when she needed to examine the wound, making the cat drowsy and slow, so she could approach without the danger of meeting it eye to eye. She still included herbs in its food to make certain the infection was gone, to strengthen its blood and renew its strength. At first, the cat nibbled at the chopped up chicken she'd included in its broth in small and then larger portions. But it devoured the fish Ena had caught and cut up for her and finally had eaten whole a recently dead bird the girl had found, then an entire cooked chicken, tearing the legs away with an appetite and energy that made Ena smile with relief and pleasure.

Just then the wildcat went to the bowl of water outside the shelter and drank deeply. "Wobbling about with an injured thigh must be thirsty work," Ena murmured, crawling up to the cage from the side. The animal was still wary of her, but had realized she brought food and not harm, so it allowed her near. Just not too near.

Ena admired it from where she lay, elbows bent and chin on her crossed hands. She guessed it was about five feet long, though she could not tell its weight; it had lost so much while ill, but now was beginning to gain it back a little at a time. Its reddish brown coat, fading to beige underneath, which had been matted and dull when she brought it home, had begun to take on a new sheen. Ena longed to brush it, or just run her fingers along its back, but she didn't want to take any chances. "You're so bonny," she murmured. "And soon you'll be strong as well." She noted the way it held up its finely shaped head, how symmetrical were its silken ears, tufted with soft beige hair. She was mesmerized by its copper eyes that flashed gold in the sunlight.

She noticed it was a bit more steady on its legs today, though it seemed to take an effort to move without dragging the injured leg. "Aye, and you're stubborn, too. Same as Connor Fraser."

The cat knew she was there; its ears were pricked up, and it was alert, sensing no danger, but like her, not wanting to take a chance. "I've brought a letter from my Aunt Lian today," she announced. "She's Chinese, ye ken, and married to a Frenchman. Mam says she still wears Oriental clothes."

The animal still responded to the cadence of her chants, so she read to it every day in a stilted, rhythmic tone. Sometimes books of Celtic myths and legends, sometimes letters Ena herself was writing, sometimes correspondence she'd received.

Stretched out on the grass, she smoothed the rice paper her aunt had folded in the shape of a bird. As always, there were Chinese characters brushed on the outside: Ena could not read them, but they made Lian's letters more beautiful and mysterious. "My Most Beloved Niece," it began, as always.

There was the usual news about the family, this year's

crop of grapes, Lian's amusing anecdotes and fascinating observations. Then the tone changed.

I have had your face in my mind these last weeks, have been wishing you were not so far away. You sound weary in your letters, but I think, not from physical exertion. There comes a time for every girl when keeping your balance and your faith in ordinary things becomes so difficult that it wears you out. Oh, little flower, how I would love to sit beside you and listen to the silence filled with invisible webs of things beyond our understanding which mystify and disorient us. One of these, I believe, is the absence of our fathers, more painful somehow, as we become women. Do you miss Ian Fraser? Do you love him? I wish you were here, gazing out over the acres of grapevines that make one seem small, as does the glen, because it is so old, so powerful, so full of other lives and cultures past. I made my mark upon it once, and Mairi Rose said the earth would remember me. I wonder, is it so? For surely it remembers you.

Your Loving Aunt Lian

Ena sat up, trying to avoid the shadows nudging at her. It was a bonny day, she reminded herself. Both Connor and the wildcat would recover; the sun was warm, the sky blue, the burn whispering behind her. She took off her cap, allowing her auburn hair to tumble over her shoulders, and leaned back till her hair brushed the ground. But the rice paper with its elegant folds was still in her hand.

Ena stuffed the letter back in her pocket. She knew her aunt only meant to reassure her, but Lian had brought back vividly what she'd said to Mairi the night she brought the wildcat home. *I used to sense things and feel they were true. Now, I'm naught but confused. I don't know how to be anymore.*

She'd hoped the confusion had disappeared in the last week, but it had only been hidden by her fear for Connor and her guilt and the many things that had kept hand and head busy. *'Tis like I'm fightin' something, fightin' against it with all my might, but I don't know what it is.*

Strange that Lian had mentioned Ian Fraser. Ena had visited his grave early that morning. Often she went to the kirkyard looking for her father, though Ailsa claimed his spirit was not there, but racing, drifting, singing on the wind. "I'll never know that part of him," Ena'd said. "His headstone is solid and worn and real. I can feel the nicks and indentations, lean against it, knowin' it'll hold me up." The stone kept her from falling, but it told her nothing. Never, in the shade of the rowan with the moss to cushion her, did she hear Ian's voice or feel his presence. To Ena, her father was real only through Ailsa's memories. Sometimes that was not enough.

She bent forward, hands across her middle, and leaned heavily against the post of the wildcat's cage. She felt light-headed and wondered, for a moment, if her aunt's spirit had indeed reached out to her. Then she looked down and gasped, pulling her legs in tight and close. She wanted to hide what she'd seen, to deny it and defy it. But as she sat there rocking, knees pressing into her chest, the queasiness turned to nausea and a kind of throbbing pain.

"No!" she cried, loudly enough to shake the naked branches of the rowan overhead. "Please, no." It was barely a whisper. She could feel the uncomfortable moisture between her legs, and her head ached with the rhythm of her pulse. No matter how tenaciously she held her body folded in upon itself, no matter how tightly she squeezed her eyelids closed, she couldn't ignore that single, telling glimpse of blood that stained the skirt of her dirty beige gown.

11

"DO YE FEEL IT?" AILSA WHISPERED TO HER MOTHER. THEY'D left Alanna's not five minutes past, attempting to keep a restless Connor entertained so his mother did not go in search of a high cliff top, as she'd threatened to do. Everyone had been in good spirits, if a little frustrated now and then. No sooner had they stepped onto the familiar path toward home than Mairi'd closed her eyes and raised her face to the sun, smiling the kind of smile that intrigued her daughter no end.

Mairi had already paused, alert and unsettled. "I feel something."

They had stopped under a willow tree, overcome by a sudden chill. "Mam."

Mairi faced her daughter, placed her hands gently on her shoulders. "I know."

"Something's amiss with Ena. Her name makes me ache and shiver both."

"Aye, so it does."

Ailsa shook her head to clear it. "She's no' at risk, but there's a shadow hoverin' above her." She paused, glanced about, rubbed her clammy palms together. "I think 'tis so. I can no' say for sure. All I know is we must hurry home. Whatever this shadow is, she's searchin' for help, and I can no' bear the thought of her pain. She hardly knows about sufferin', she's had so little in her life. I must hurry."

"Aye, go on ahead. I'll come along as I can." For a moment longer Mairi held her daughter. "Remember Ailsa, she loves ye more than she knows, that child. More than she should."

The words followed Ailsa on the breeze, and she frowned but did not pause. She wanted to get home; she must get home. What if she was too late and her youngest daughter, Ian's final gift, found naught but emptiness?

Jenny Fraser knelt in the vegetable garden beside the croft, gown wrinkled and stained from pulling weeds, her hands heavy with dark soil. Her straight hair, pulled back and twisted into what had begun as a tidy bun, was now more gray than brown. Loose tendrils strayed into her eyes and mouth, and she brushed them away, leaving plant dust and smudged soil behind. She was fifty-three, but it was more than age that had leached the color from her hair and the sparkle from her hazel eyes.

She worked here often. The sun on her back comforted her, as did the unchanging fertility of the Highland earth. With her hands buried in the soil and a ratty apron over her gown, she forgot for hours at a time her grief and the rage that had dimmed with the passage of years. She felt at home again, and blessed.

"Jenny!"

She raised her head, squinting into the sunlight. Most people called her Ian's widow. Only two called her Jenny: Alanna Fraser and Ena Rose.

"Jenny!" Without warning, Ena Rose appeared out of the woods, holding her skirts bunched up around her hips, exposing her bare legs to the world.

Jenny looked about anxiously, distressed by Ena's disregard for modesty and decorum. She could hear her grandchildren tumbling about and screeching with laughter nearby and did not want them to see the girl. "I know ye can't run with your skirts about your ankles, but just the same, ye should no' reveal your legs like that."

Ena stopped on the far side of the garden wall. "Why not?" Her brow was furrowed; she seemed genuinely perplexed.

Jenny cleared her throat, stared at the weed in her hand and said awkwardly, "Because people . . . the lads . . . can see too much of your strong brown legs."

Frowning, Ena brushed the dirt from one bare foot with the other. "Do ye mean they might see how fast I can run?"

Exasperated, Jenny threw up her hands, sending loam and weeds flying. Was the girl really so innocent? She was, after all, more than twelve. But Ena's sincere, distressed expression told its own story. Jenny was shocked at her lack of awareness. In the last several months, her body had begun to change, and the legs that used to resemble the fleet legs of a running deer had grown more shapely, while Ena's waist had begun to narrow. "Has your mother no' told ye about . . . men and women?"

"Och, aye, but what's that to do with runnin'?"

Jenny sighed and gave up.

Ena glanced about, wary and anxious and unaware of Jenny's expression. She shifted her weight from foot to foot and twisted her hands in the wrinkled, earth-stained folds of her skirt. Her uneasiness communicated itself to Jenny, who was suddenly alert.

"Is there something ye wanted to say?"

Ena started at the sound of her voice, her face pale in spite of the sun-washed day. "I—wondered if I could talk to ye." She spoke just above a whisper.

"Of course ye can. Ye know that. Come sit here." She patted the earth at the end of a row of leeks and beans.

Gnawing her lower lip, Ena glanced from side to side through narrowed eyes. "I wanted—I hoped—I thought we could talk inside?" Her gray eyes were imploring.

Jenny was dumbfounded. Ena had often come to ask advice, but usually she preferred sitting in the garden or on the low stone dyke. She did not like being penned up inside if the day was fine. Something was amiss; Jenny felt it in the fine hairs that rose on the back of her neck. She stood, brushing the soil from her apron and hands. "If ye wish. Come ye with me."

She stopped at the bucket of clear water by the door to rinse her hands, and though Ena usually did the same, this time she clung tenaciously to her dress.

When they ducked inside, Ena saw the children playing in the loft and watched them nervously.

"Robbie, Fiona, Simon, go join your cousins by the burn. But mind ye watch where you're goin' and try no' to fall in the bog."

The children laughed. She always said that, though not a single one of her grandchildren had ever set foot or hand in a bog. "How can we when we can no' find one to fall into?" Fiona asked pertly. Not bothering to wait for an answer, the three trailed out, laughing and shouting suggestions for a new game.

Ena stared after them in silence, then closed the door tight.

Jenny reached out to brush her cheek, but instead rested her hand on Ena's shoulder. All at once she could see Ian in his daughter's face. She ached at the memory of that face, of the man who had given so much to this child, though he died before she was born. She was surprised that the hurt went so deep after so long. She felt a flash of rage, quickly extinguished. It was not the girl's fault that she carried her father's image in her eyes—full of curiosity and secret knowledge and an innate kindness—that her mouth curved with the sensitivity, determination and humor of a man long dead and buried. The closer she looked, the more she saw—Ailsa Rose in the shape of Ena's eyes and nose and chin, and in her prettiness, which had not yet turned to beauty. Suddenly Jenny felt old. "Ye need no' hold your skirts high in here. There's no bracken or hawthorn to catch your gown on, no roots to trip over."

Ena swallowed, searching for her voice. " 'Tis no'—I don't—I can't—"

Usually words poured from her like water from a spring. Watching her stutter, tongue-tied, Jenny finally recognized how deeply upset she was. She took Ena's other shoulder and held her securely. She could feel her trembling, and that too was unnatural. It was a well-known fact that Ena

Rose feared nothing and no one. "What is it?" Jenny asked gently. "Tell me, *mo-run*."

Pacing the tiny kitchen while Mairi used the loom for the first time in a long while, Ailsa waited, trying not to imagine the cause of Ena's distress. Again and again the image returned of her daughter standing in the doorway, her gown covered with stains and blood, her hair half-braided, full of grass and leaves and matted with mud, her face barely recognizable beneath a mask of dirt and blood. For an instant, for the briefest span of time, Ailsa hadn't noticed the covered basket in Ena's hand, had believed the blood was her daughter's. Her fear had been so instantaneous, so deep, she thought she'd crumple where she stood. Her heart had stopped; she'd felt it cease to beat until Ena spoke, and the haze forming in Ailsa's mind dissipated. The girl was safe, uninjured. A rush of relief had left her dizzy, aching to hold her child tight and close, to feel her healthy heartbeat.

In all that followed, Ailsa had forgotten that moment of fear, her life suspended in anticipation of disaster. Now she could not escape the memory, as the minutes passed and there was no sign of her daughter. Twice Ailsa went out, following the path across the clearing toward the woods. Twice she'd paused halfway across, watching, waiting, listening. Something held her back, would not allow her to go farther, and she returned home, shaking her head at Mairi's unspoken question.

Frustrated and apprehensive, Ailsa began to assemble black buns, Ena's favorite as well as her own. It was a long time before she realized Mairi had not once spoken. She concentrated on weaving, guiding the shuttle through warp and weft, making a pattern that was known, predictable.

Ailsa willed her daughter to appear, concentrated her considerable intuition and imagination and understanding on the image of Ena's face.

The girl did not come.

"I don't understand. I can no' think where she might be."

"Can't ye now, *mo-ghraid?*"

Ailsa whirled as her mother's voice shattered the stillness like a stone a pane of brittle glass. "Ye don't mean, ye *can't* mean she's gone to Jenny Fraser? What I felt was so strong, like a wind with Ena strugglin' at the vortex. Surely she'd come to me if 'twas so urgent. Surely."

Mairi turned back to the loom, compassion in her violet eyes. They had known since the child was six that she was seeking particular kinds of help or advice elsewhere. Not once had she asked Mairi, the most skilled weaver in the glen, for instruction at the loom, yet Ena could weave, albeit poorly. She could sew, and neither Ailsa nor Mairi had once picked up needle and thread to show her how. There had been many hours unaccounted for, many tasks, usually the ones at which the girl was less than skilled, learned suddenly, after an afternoon lost.

At first they'd thought it was her half-sister, Alanna, and Ailsa had hoped the two would form a bond, despite the gap in their ages. Then one day, while she was wading knee deep in the burn, Ailsa'd seen Ena running in an odd direction, had called out, but the girl hadn't heard. There was only one croft along that path. They knew then who Ena had chosen for her teacher. Jenny Fraser. Ian Fraser's widow, to whom neither had spoken, whose face neither had seen since Ian's death.

"No," Ailsa had cried. "Not Jenny." She sat on the floor and drew her legs in close to her body, clasping them painfully with white-knuckled hands. "Why does she no' come to *me?*" She'd risen abruptly, besieged by so many feelings that she swayed with the impact. "I'll go and get her. I'll bring her home."

Sadly, Mairi'd shaken her head. "Ailsa-my-heart, she must come to ye of her own accord. She's no' a heedless bairn. She must have a reason. Mayhap she goes to comfort

Jenny; mayhap Jenny comforts her. Hard as it is, I think ye should let her go where she will. 'Tis the only way to keep her."

Jenny Fraser's kindness broke the thin membrane between Ena and her misery. Despondently, she let go of her skirts so they fell heavily from her hands. She stood still as marble, and as pale, unable, unwilling to look down.

Jenny could not help but see the blood that stained the fabric. Her first blood, the first sign of her womanhood. For a moment, Jenny was carried back to the day she had discovered her own first flow—her curiosity and anxiety, the physical pain and inexplicable excitement, the fear she could not name. It was as if she had become that young girl again, for what she felt was not memory, but the full, powerful, disturbing sensations she'd known those many years ago.

Ena's eyes had sent her back, gray eyes flecked with green, flashing in the dim, shadowed light of the croft. Eyes full of apprehension and doubt.

When Jenny did not speak, the girl said quietly, "I'd not be knowin' what to do. Will ye help me? Please." She faltered, afraid Jenny might refuse and send her home. She did not want to go there now. She couldn't bear for her mother to see her like this.

The uncertainty that was close to despair brought Jenny back. She was oddly pleased the child had come to her, and not entirely surprised. Before she could reply, Ena grasped her hand tightly.

"Please."

As if I might actually turn her away, Jenny thought. She should know better, after so long, after the hours we've spent learnin' to know one another.

"I'll always be helpin' ye, birdeen. Ye should know that by now. Come, take off your gown and put on one of these,"—she waved toward the chest that held her daughters' discarded dresses—"while I show ye how to care for yourself."

She took the soiled gown briskly, with no sign of distaste, and set it to soak in a cool mixture of liquid and herbs. Then she poured water into a small bucket from the kettle hanging above the smoldering embers of the fire. She gave Ena a soft towel to clean herself while Jenny gathered the thick, multi-layered cloths women used at such a time. Standing awkwardly in a stranger's dress, the girl watched as Jenny showed her how to use the cloths and clean them later.

By now Ena's head ached and Jenny guided her to a chair close to the heat of the dying fire. Unconsciously, Ena clasped her arms across her middle at the unfamiliar discomfort there.

"What you're needin' is some chamomile tea and ladyfern to soothe your head and help the crampin'." As she passed the girl, hunched miserably in her chair, embarrassed and ashamed, Jenny rested her hand on her tangled auburn hair in a light, reassuring caress. She was not aware she had done so. But Ena was.

Ailsa turned to Mairi, face streaked with tears. "Ye honestly think Ena finds consolation with that woman she can no' find here?"

"If she does, would ye take that solace from her? Would ye take it from Jenny, if she's able to find peace in that child's company? That child of all children?"

Ailsa shook her head. "No, I'd take nothing more from Jenny than I already have. She's suffered enough because of me." All these years, they'd kept their polite and silent distance from one another. That was why Ailsa could not interfere. "And as for Ena, if it makes her happy, I can't destroy that happiness. I made a promise, to myself and to Ian, that she would be free. How then, can I make her a prisoner?"

She left the croft, tears streaming into her hair as she

ran—away from the rejection of her daughter; away from the rage she had no right to; away from the failure, the inadequacy, for she must have done something to make Ena go; away from her reawakened guilt; away from the sense that she owed Jenny something as precious as she'd taken from her.

Ailsa ached in every part of her body, but she never let anyone see that pain.

She knew Ena's defection hurt Mairi as well, but wise Mairi, kind Mairi, compassionate Mairi said nothing. She had always hoped, secretly, fervently, that the silence between Ailsa and Jenny would one day be broken, the animosity resolved. She knew now that her wish would never be granted. Ena was one more barrier between the two women who were not really enemies, but only governed by unkind, inexorable Fate, as were they all.

Only once, in all those years, had she spoken as Ailsa paced the dirt-floored croft in Ena's absence. *At least ye can be grateful she chose no one dangerous or foolish. At least Jenny Fraser is sensible, kind, intelligent. She'd never use Ena against ye, use her to salve her old wounds by openin' yours. 'Tis a blessin', Ailsa, whether ye choose to see it or no'.*

Ailsa knew she was right, and that only made her envy, her anger more of a burden. She was certain Jenny would never knowingly hurt her, no matter what had come between them. Never knowingly hurt Ena, never take out on a child her own bitterness and grief. She was too good. And that, above all, was too difficult to bear.

Jenny and Ena held horn cups of steaming tea, sitting in silence, staring into the glowing peats, seeing many things and nothing. When the color began to return to Ena's face and she sat up, a little more relaxed, she noticed Jenny's eyes were clouded and her brow furrowed.

"I hope I've no' upset ye. 'Tis only that I could no' think where else to go."

Jenny raised her head sharply, though her tone was mild. "That's what upsets me. Did ye no' think to go to your mother? Did she no' show ye how to do these things, prepare ye for the changes in your body? Explain what they meant?"

Ena looked away. "She tried to, but I wouldn't listen." She stared hard at the floor, her eyes moist, her mouth grimly determined.

Kneeling beside Ena's chair, Jenny folded the girl into her arms, the shimmer of tears in her eyes. The same tears she had shed when her own daughters reached this moment, this fear and this uncertainty. " 'Tis natural, though no' pleasant, this change. 'Tis nothing to fash yourself about." She spoke gently, her voice soothing. " 'Tis part of growin' up, of becomin' a woman."

Ena buried her head on Jenny's shoulder. "I don't *want* to grow up. I don't *want* to become a woman!"

Jenny was shocked. Ena sounded so vehement, so frightened. The woman thought back to idyllic days when she and Ailsa and Ian had played together, when no shadow had fallen between them. She had treasured that time, but innocent as she'd been, she had always known there was something better, something she wanted even more. "When I was a girl, I longed to become a woman, to be free of the restrictions of childhood, to learn the things only women know, feel the things only they can feel."

Ena fought to control her turbulent emotions, her confusion, her doubt. "Growin' up hurts too much. 'Tis too hard and too sad. I've seen it. I know."

With an effort, Jenny found her voice. "*How* do ye know?"

"From my mother's journal. About her childhood in the glen. About ye and she and William and . . ." Ena decided to change directions. "Mam taught me to read by usin' it as a guide, word by word, and she read aloud from it every night."

I want ye to know everything about your father, Ailsa had explained, *so ye'll no' worry and mourn and wonder as I did about mine. Unanswered questions are unsettlin' and can lead ye so easily and so far astray.* The words, written from Ailsa's heart, and the power of the stories and the cadence of her voice had transfixed Ena on many a damp, inhospitable evening. Within those words, Ena could feel her father, see his tall, strong body and dark, curly hair, imagine he was real.

But he wasn't real. Not to her. She'd never seen her father's face or touched his hand or heard his voice, and she felt his absence deeply, because hers was a house of women. As much as she'd learned of Ian Fraser through the journal, as well as she knew the man he'd been, in the end, to Ena he was a stranger.

Twice today she'd thought of him. Twice felt bereft. Why now? Why?

"I want everything to stay as it is," she declared without warning. She crossed her arms and stood, feet planted firmly, ready to withstand a siege.

Gathering her thoughts into coherence, Jenny said, "Ye may want as much as ye like, but ye can no' stop it. 'Tis the way of time, to move forward no matter how many try to hold it back." She thought regretfully of Ian and his hopes for the glen he had loved. *That* heartache she kept to herself.

Arms akimbo, Ena faced her obstinately, refusing to bend. "So ye think ye can stop time, your own growth and everyone else's, stop this day from becomin' tomorrow, simply by ignorin' it? By refusin' to recognize that 'tis inevitable?" Her mouth was dry, but she added, "Have they made ye believe ye have that power?"

Ena's arms fell to her sides and she crossed them over her belly, swaying uncomfortably. "I'm no' powerful, Jenny Fraser. Just afraid."

They faced each other, Mairi and Ailsa Rose, on the lovely spring day that had promised so much, both feeling the shadow over Ena's head, but helpless to remove it or call it by name.

"Ena has needs and desires of her own," Ailsa said softly, unable, this time, to disguise the hurt. "Mayhap I don't understand them. And I'd no' stop her from fulfillin' them, even if I could. I'm no longer even certain of that." She grasped the rocker, pushing it resolutely forward and back. "Ye know how restless she's been these past months, how often she can't sleep and wanders the night instead. She used to go only when the moon was bright or the glen too alluring to resist. Now she's tryin' to hide there. I sense it."

"Aye," Mairi whispered. "She told me the night she brought that wildcat home that she was confused and strugglin' and didn't know where to turn. I told her 'twas her age and she had only to be patient. But now, but now—"

"Now I know Ena needs help. I feel it so strongly the need seems like my own. I should protect her; I want to wrap her in my arms and keep her safe and warm and fearless. But I can't." *Remember, Ailsa, she loves ye more than she knows, that child. More than she should.* Ailsa released the rocker, whirled away from her mother, then back again. "Just tell me I've no' lost my daughter. Tell me even if it is a lie."

She had realized at last what she'd long suspected in her heart. She needed her daughter as much as she hoped her daughter needed her. Perhaps even more.

Heedlessly, seeking warmth and sympathy and consolation, Ena Rose threw herself into Jenny's arms, shaking violently. "Have ye told your mother how frightened ye are? She's better than I at explainin' such things, and surely at easin' your fears."

Ena drew away abruptly to sit on a three-legged stool by the fire. She would not look Jenny in the eye. "If I told her, Mam would know I'm afraid." She twisted her long auburn braid tight around her hand, gradually cutting off the flow

of blood. "I don't want her to see that I'm weak and foolish. . . ." She trailed off.

Jenny was so disconcerted that her skin paled, as if the
sun had never touched it. With difficulty, she managed,
"Ailsa Rose Sinclair's a strong woman, Ena. She can bear
many things, has borne them time and time again."

By all that's holy, and sensible as I am, I should hate that
woman, Jenny thought. Ailsa Rose, linked forever with the
heroic Ian who had saved the glen, while Jenny was left with
the real Ian Fraser. Uninspiring, ordinary, like their marriage.
The Ian she knew had been kind, sensitive, generous, a good
husband and father. The only exceptional thing about our
lives is that Ian loved me at all, Jenny thought.

He'd broken her heart, but she had done worse; she had
broken his spirit, his faith in himself. Ailsa had healed him.
Jenny had not known how.

Usually she managed to force such thoughts away.
There were moments of rage and grief, quickly extin-
guished by Fiona's smile or Robbie's gift of wilted flowers.
She'd avoided Ailsa, not out of hatred, but because Jenny
Fraser was done with conflict. She lived each day forget-
ting, and in forgetting, found her life again.

But this was unforgivable, the obligation Ailsa had
unconsciously placed on the slender, fragile shoulders of a
child. Perhaps she did not realize. . . . Jenny's hands curled
into fists. She *should* have realized, *should* have understood.

Instead of turning to her mother, insecure, uncertain of
her knowledge, her skill, Ena had brought her problems to
Jenny, to a stranger.

Jenny raised her head, thinking, Is this what God
intended all along? Am I to heal Ian's daughter as Ailsa
once healed Ian? Is that my punishment for my lack of
faith?

Yet she did not resent Ena, but loved her. Perhaps, after
all, this was a gift—a chance to save Ian's daughter, though
she'd not been able to save him.

The girl stared, hypnotized, into the glowing embers of the fire. "After Gran, my mother's always been the strong one. Now, if I'm a woman, 'tis my turn." She was far too serious about what she thought her new responsibility. This was Ena, who found pure joy in the first spring flower, who heard a symphony in the music of the river.

At last Jenny realized that this young girl, who had today begun the journey to womanhood, needed more than lessons in household tasks. She needed an ally, a confidant, a mother who would not judge or expect more than a girl could give.

Jenny could still feel the clamminess of Ena Rose's hand on hers. Her hazel eyes were dark, her mouth determined. "You've never been weak or foolish. Remember that, *morun*. Child or woman, you're just what ye should be. Yourself. Listen to me, and believe. Ye know there are no lies between us."

Once the girl had gone, Jenny would turn the rage taking root inside toward those who had earned it. It was time, at last, to face the truth, and that meant facing the past, once and for all.

12

FOR THE FIRST TIME IN HER LIFE, ENA DID NOT LIKE THE HISS of the wind through firs and new leaves and long spring grass, the thrum of the burn that echoed through the trees, the hushed, clinging sigh of the darkening mist at gloaming. She was uncomfortable when she thought of what had passed between her and Jenny Fraser, as if, somehow, she had betrayed her mother, when she meant only to expose herself.

Shoving the door open with her shoulder, she stumbled

into the cottage, welcoming the scene that greeted her. The loom stood in its accustomed corner, the Celtic harp in its place atop the kist—the wedding chest beside Ailsa's low heather bed. The fire burned brightly in the center of the croft, the smoke curling lazily upward toward the hole in the thatched roof, leaving its gray mark on the layered and textured clay walls. The smell of peat and bubbling brose filled the air, one pungent and earthy, the other rich and spicy. The leather coverings had not yet been drawn down over the windows, so the gloaming crept in—a faint gauze of colored moisture—to Mairi Rose's croft.

Ena wondered if it would always be called that, long after Mairi left it behind. After all, each stone in the aged cottage held her image in its gray, cracked surface, while the crevices and fissures called her name in a winter wind. She had made it hers as thoroughly as she had made Charles Kittridge her husband, so that he had returned to her, after forty years' absence, because, in his heart, this place, this tiny, crumbling cottage was home. She had made it so to many more than her own child, Ailsa—not just Alanna and David and Connor and Ena, but Wan Lian and Genevra Townsend and Jenny Mackensie and Ian Fraser. She had gathered them together and bound them one to another with her generous heart, her strength and gentleness and perception.

Now Mairi was curled comfortably in one of the rocking chairs beside the fire, a skein of yarn wrapped about her hands and through her fingers in some ancient design. She was smiling into the golden flames until she looked up and saw Ena. Ailsa too looked up. She was laying the scrubbed pine table for supper with large carved bowls and horn spoons and cups filled with sweet milk. She'd taken one of the china plates she'd brought back from London from the back of the tall press and put out fresh oatcakes and mashed turnips and boiled potatoes. A single paraffin lamp burned in the center of the table.

Behind her, deep in the settling shadows, was the painting Charles Kittridge had done of his daughters before he died. Ena blinked at the indistinct image, unable to believe in the familiar reality of the croft that closed around her like a warm, welcoming hand. Nothing had changed; no one was ill or moody or withdrawn, and the light from fire and lamp was cheerful.

"Weel, close the door, birdeen, before the mist creeps in behind ye. 'Tis just in time, ye are," Ailsa added. "As ye can see, supper's waitin'."

She sounded both wistful and determined, and her eyes were piercing, probing.

Mairi looked at her granddaughter through the molten heat of the flames. She raised her hands, bound by twine, to get the girl's attention. "What is't, Ena? You've the look of a bairn chased home by a specter."

Ailsa put the bread down and swung around the table. "Are ye well, *mo-run?*" Her blue-violet eyes were dark and intense, making the question more momentous than it should be. For a moment, Ena was afraid her mother could see through her damp, wrinkled gown, through her skin and bones to the truth beneath. She thought Ailsa could feel her pain. Or was it she who was feeling her mother's?

Ena closed the door and sagged against it for support. Now that she was back where she belonged, where it was warm and safe and the two people she loved most were waiting, she thought she might collapse. Her legs felt weak and her skin chilled and damp. "I'm fine," she lied. "Just weary and a bit cold."

Ailsa smoothed her daughter's disheveled hair away from her face. "Aye, so ye are. But you're sure you're no' ill?" She pressed her warm hand to Ena's cheek and the girl leaned into it, closing her eyes with a sigh of pleasure. So they stood for a long, long time.

Leaving unspoken her questions, her concern, her anger and relief, was the most difficult thing Ailsa'd ever done.

But she'd not lost her daughter; that was clear from the weight of Ena's flushed cheek in her hand. She'd wait till the girl was ready to tell them what had happened. She rested her cheek on the crown of Ena's head.

All at once, Ena flung her arms around her mother's waist and clung, afraid if she didn't she would whirl away into the darkness that was the future and adulthood and responsibility.

Closing her eyes, Ailsa rubbed Ena's back until it was warm, and even then, was loathe to release her. "I knew ye'd come home tonight, whole and unhurt." She had prayed for hours to the Celtic gods for that favor, that reprieve. "We must eat." There was nothing else she dared to say.

Ena nodded as Mairi rose, unwinding herself from the twine and the blanket over her legs, and the three sat down, talking of inconsequential things.

Frowning, Ailsa whispered, "You're fidgetin' on that chair like ye can no' rest easy, Ena. Are ye certain you're well?"

There were shadows beneath Ena's eyes and her skin was filmed with perspiration. Her face, usually sun-browned and glowing, was pale. "A little tired only. I've no' slept much since . . . well, since Connor was hurt."

There's more, Ailsa thought. But she'd known that this afternoon, sensed that her daughter was losing her way, though she had not turned toward home for solace. Now Ailsa could not shake the feeling that Ena was ill at ease, perhaps even in pain. But her daughter remained silent.

Breathing slowly, the girl concentrated on her brose. It was true she could not get comfortable in the ladder-back chair. She was not used to the bulky cloths that made her shift from side to side. She felt cramping in her belly, but she'd have chamomile and peppermint tea after supper, and no one would wonder.

Jenny had told her she'd have to watch and change the cloths when necessary. She'd also have to prepare a bucket to soak them in. Those things she would do later, outside, where the moon would guide her and the mist and darkness hide her from curious eyes.

"I've no' eaten for a very long time. Mayhap my body is scoldin' me for my neglect," she muttered into her bowl.

"Mayhap." Ailsa did not believe her. She'd seen the condition of Ena's skirts, damp and wrinkled and slightly discolored. Besides, the girl's demeanor was different; she moved heavily, awkwardly. Usually, she flitted about the glen, wraithlike, though her strength and stamina belied her airy manner. The girl's unspoken misery reached out to her mother until she could not breathe for the weight of it. But still, she would not press her. She had promised. But it wrung her heart to see Ena like this.

Though aware of the undercurrents at the table, Mairi kept silent. This was between Ena and Ailsa. As she watched them, she felt that somehow time was slipping past, spinning away so quickly she could not grasp—and hold—a moment. But that was the way of things, and however wistful for the past, Mairi could not be sorry. She smiled and touched the letters in her pocket.

Only when they stood and Ena swayed at the sudden motion, when Ailsa caught her arm to steady her, did the girl realize she *wanted* to tell her mother. She did not want to be alone with her changing body and what it meant. But more than anything, she did not wish to feel isolated in the dark croft tonight.

She was searching for the right words when she felt something warm between her legs and gasped. "I must be away for a bit, but I'll be nearby." She slipped out swiftly, as she used to do. Chimerical, intangible, leaving Ailsa with an empty hand and more questions than before.

The girl thanked the gods and Jenny Fraser for giving her several sets of cloths to use and the voluminous pockets to hide them in.

When she returned, the scene was as idyllic as when she'd first come in, only Ailsa had cleared away the dishes and was sitting in her favorite chair, toying with a letter on the low rosewood table beside it. She reached for Ena. "Your stomach mustn't be easy after all. But 'twill settle when ye lie down and rest. Are ye all right, then, birdeen?" She spoke lightly, but the questions lay heavy on her heart.

"Aye, Mam." Ena leaned against Ailsa's side, absorbing her warmth. "*Now* I'm better." She thought of telling them the truth, settling their minds, except Ailsa reached out just then to draw her fingers through her daughter's loosened hair, pulling her down to the handwoven rug on the floor beside her, so Ena's head rested against her thigh.

Her mother was warm and Ena cold; the fire sputtered and flared, throwing heat and shadows and light around the room in friendly patterns that slowly, along with the languid, tender motion of Ailsa's fingers in her hair, made Ena drowsy and her eyelids heavy. She'd traveled far today and learned too much. It was good to sink into nights like those in her childhood, when she'd sat just so at her mother's knee and known that she was safe and blessed, that nothing could ever harm her.

13

"WHAT'S WRONG, GRANDY?"

Jenny Fraser jumped at the sound of her granddaughter's voice, turning away from the window in the loft where she'd sat all night, staring into the darkness. "Fiona! Ye startled me, appearin' that way at the top of the ladder. What makes ye think something's wrong?"

The child pursed her lips and shook her head. "Do ye think us all blind and daft besides? You've braided and unbraided your hair a hundred times since ye came up, and not once laid your head on the pillow."

Forcing her nervous fingers away from her hair guiltily, Jenny folded her hands in her lap. "I've been thinkin', is all."

Fiona regarded her thoughtfully. "About Ena Rose?"

Jenny's eyes widened in dismay. She should have known Fiona would notice something was amiss the day that Ena had stood silent, her skirts gathered at her waist. Jenny kept forgetting the child was ten and wise beyond her years. "Aye, among other things." All night her mind had spun with images, doubts and certainties, and the persistent, painful memory of Ena's stricken face.

I'd not be knowin' what to do. Will ye help me? Please.

Unsatisfied, Fiona sat cross-legged at the foot of the bed. "What other things? They must've been aye upsettin' if they kept ye awake till dawn." The girl seemed to be waiting, gazing at her grandmother steadily, expectantly.

"I've been wonderin' if I should visit Ena's mother to have a chat with her."

"With Ailsa Rose! But everyone knows she's your enemy." Fiona's face was flushed with outrage.

"Is that what they think? Everyone?" She had also forgotten how much children heard and understood when adults forgot they were about. She had known her grandchildren would eventually hear how Ailsa and Ian had betrayed her.

A wave of long-repressed jealousy, rage and loss swept over her, leaving her pale and shaking. She tried to speak, but couldn't.

When her granddaughter saw her distress, she crawled over to lean against Jenny, head on her trembling shoulder. "Weep if ye want to, Grandy. I don't mind. And I'll no' be tellin' the others."

Jenny rested her head on Fiona's uncombed hair, touched by the child's offer of comfort. With an effort, she pushed the sickening wave back into the dark ocean of feelings she'd learned to ignore and deny. "I haven't time to weep just now, but I thank ye, birdeen. From my heart, I thank ye."

Fiona nestled closer, into the comfort of her grandmother's kindness and unswerving affection. "If speakin' of her makes ye feel this way, if ye hate her so much, why would ye do it?"

"I don't hate her, *mo-run*. 'Tis only that Ailsa's always been my greatest test," she mused, more to herself than Fiona. "My first and dearest friend, my rival. But I'm thinkin' she's no' my enemy." She'd not spoken to Ailsa since Ian died, and only once, a long time ago, had they tried to discuss their unusual friendship. Perhaps it was time someone broke the silence. "Besides, there's Ena."

Sitting up sharply, Fiona crossed her arms over her chest. "Ye told Mam 'twas never wise to interfere. I heard ye. Ye said ye'd learned the hard way; once ye'd tried to change what ye didn't understand and caused a tragedy."

Jenny gaped at her granddaughter. It was time to start paying attention to this girl. She knew far more than was good for her. "When was it ye took to listenin' at doors? It can be dangerous, ye ken. Ye might hear things ye'd rather not."

Facing her grandmother obstinately, Fiona refused to back down. "But ye said it. Ye told Mam ye'd sworn never to do it again, that it cost ye too much."

Jenny remembered that vow made to her daughter Brenna. She remembered everything. But even her granddaughter's accusing eyes could not erase the image of Ena Rose in her bloodstained gown.

I'm no' powerful, Jenny Fraser. Just afraid.

"Aye, but things're different now. Sometimes ye make a vow and the years change its importance. As I told ye, I've been thinkin' for days. I can only hope I'm wiser now than I was those many years ago, that I know what I'm doin' this time. It'd help if ye wished me well instead of glowerin' like the sky before a storm."

The girl tried to look more fierce and disapproving, but

when her grandmother held out her arms, Fiona flung herself into them. "Ye know I do, Grandy. 'Tis only . . . we need ye more than she does. And I can't bear it if they hurt ye. When I see ye unhappy, when I see ye wantin' to weep, it scares me so much I feel sick inside." Her skin was pale, her eyes wide and imploring.

Jenny cupped the child's face in her hands. "There's naught to be frightened of, little one. That I promise ye. They'll no hurt me again. Not unless I let them, and 'tis something I've no intention of doin'."

For the seventh day in a row, the sun rose warm and unclouded in a blue sky. Encouraged by the lovely weather, Jenny dressed, fed her grandchildren porridge with milk and nutmeg, made certain Fiona and Robbie would watch over the others, and left the croft. She headed resolutely toward a path she'd not taken in many years, her plaid close around her, not for warmth, but for reassurance. The woods enfolded her and the burn filled dappled shadows with a music she had not heard, had not listened for, since her husband's death.

When she reached the edge of the clearing, sprinkled with bluebells and starflowers, she almost stopped and turned back. She could see Mairi Rose's croft from within the sheltering shadows of the wood, see the long, ancient dyke covered with honeysuckle around the garden, the misshapen cottage disguised by ivy and wood sorrel, the battered door, warped and bleached by sun and wind and rain. Jenny's breath caught in her throat and she fought for air. It had been so long since she felt this sloping path beneath her feet, crossed this flowery meadow where the cotton grass brushed her hem, headed toward the cottage built into the rocky hill, turned emerald green by moss in the undiminished sunlight.

She felt the blood drain from her face, the clamminess of her skin, the ache of her hands pressed knuckle to knuckle with her plaid gathered between. *You're strong, my Jenny*, Ian had told her once. *Stronger than ye think. Don't be lettin' the fear defeat ye when ye have the power to defy it.* He must have been right or she'd not be standing at the edge of her childhood, contemplating facing Ailsa Rose Sinclair. She'd not be standing here at all, for the guilt and sorrow and bitterness of the past thirteen years would have broken her long ago.

Letting her plaid slide into the crooks of her elbows, she stepped into the clearing, avoiding the dips and stumps by instinct. She had not forgotten. Finally, she reached the croft, enveloped by the sweet scent of honeysuckle and the warm sun.

She paused at the door, but not because she was afraid. She had made her decision; nothing would make her turn back. She cared too much for the auburn-haired child that should, by all that was holy and true, have been her own. She paused because as she stood in the hollowed-out place where many hundreds had stood before her, facing the door with its cracks and rivulets and scars, memories assaulted her. A few moments ago she'd stood at the edge of her childhood. Now that childhood came rushing back.

For, much to her parents' annoyance, she had been more often at Ailsa's cottage than her own, until the day her dearest friend left the glen as the wife of an Englishman. The Mackensie family had been devout Church of Scotland. *Ye know, our Jenny, that Mairi Rose and her young daughter are pagan to their souls. They'll corrupt ye, those two, make ye forget the laws of the Lord.* That's exactly what had drawn Jenny to Ailsa—her complete disregard for rules. She lived by instinct and the bidding of her heart. From the day Jenny met her, she'd been smiling, confident and alarmingly sensitive. Always ready for fun and excitement, to swim naked in the *linne* before dawn if the desire struck her, or to leap the Beltaine fires, not simply without fear, but with exultation. *'Tis happy I am this night, and happy I shall be forever.*

The youngest child and only girl, raised by her strict parents, Jenny had been timid, always looking over her shoulder, always worried and afraid. Ailsa had taught her to laugh and take a chance. *There's naught to fear if ye listen to your heart and no' the voices that tell ye 'tis wrong. 'Tis all there is, the truth in your heart, and all that matters.* It was Ailsa who'd introduced Jenny Mackensie to Ian Fraser.

Come Jenny or ye'll miss the fun. Come. 'Twill no' be the same without ye.

She'd been their friend, joined in their play and loved them both. But from the age of thirteen, she'd known her love for Ian was different, precious, sacred. He could never be hers; Ian and Ailsa had been born for one another. Jenny could not resent an affection so fundamental, an understanding so complete. When they brushed hands, however briefly, she felt a woman's longing, when they grew older and clung more closely, she experienced a woman's need. As well as a woman's loss.

Jenny had forgotten how much Ailsa had taught her, how generous and giving she'd been, and how honest. In her pain and anger, she'd forgotten so much that was good. No matter what happened now, she was glad she'd come to this familiar door today. She'd been given back the gift of her childhood, her uncomplicated happiness, the memory of a friendship long lost in the void that was grief and loneliness.

Placing her palms against the rough wood, Jenny rested her forehead between them, trying to regain her composure. Drawing a deep breath, she released it slowly, stood and raised her hand to knock. Before she could do so, the door swung open. For the first time in over thirteen years, Ailsa Rose and Jenny Fraser stood face to face, close enough to touch.

"Och! Jenny!" Ailsa cried, unaware that she'd done so. Seeing the Widow Fraser without warning, after so long, standing on her doorstep, shook her profoundly. What was she to do, when the sight of her old friend's face faded beneath the image of Ena. Her daughter still had not spoken of the day she'd disappeared. "Ye came back." Ailsa spoke stiffly, uncomfortably, half smiling through a sheen of tears. She wanted to welcome her friend, to pull Jenny close, to forget the time and torment that had passed between them. She must not think about Ena. That was not fair.

Resolutely, she rested her hands on Jenny's shoulders. "Ye chose to come back." She could not quite take it in, could not quite hide her disbelief and hurt.

Jenny's eyes were damp, so she did not recognize Ailsa's pale shock. "Aye," she said simply. "And was a fool to wait so long."

With an effort, with dawning realization, Ailsa drew her friend inside. If her hands trembled a little, no one seemed to notice. Or so she thought. "No, Jenny Fraser. Ye were never a fool. I envy ye that, and always did."

Jenny stood as if mesmerized, helpless against her emotions, so different from what she'd imagined. Helpless against the knowledge that she might have repaired a long broken friendship last week, last month, last year, but she'd been too proud. And now, for Ena's sake, she would probably end it again. It hurt deep, that loss. But she'd made her choice.

Mairi smiled tenderly, her once violet eyes warm with welcome. "It's been too long, Jenny, and we've been the less without ye." She sat forward in her rocking chair, hands folded, watching Ailsa, who had been struck mute.

"I'll leave ye then, the two of ye. Be kind to each other. There's as much good as bad. Ye just need to look hard enough and long enough and deep enough." She'd been expecting this for a long time, had been both apprehensive and hopeful. But the two women must settle it themselves. Quietly, in spite of the warmth, she drew her plaid around her shoulders and murmured something about enjoying the sunshine while it lasted.

Ailsa and Jenny watched her go, wishing she would stay, knowing she could not. It was not her conflict or her sorrow.

Jenny sat in one of the rocking chairs beside the fire while Ailsa tried to calm herself by gathering tea and gingerbread, cups and teapot and sugar, finally placing a tray on the settle. She stood, bemused, regarding Jenny expectantly. "Much as I'd like to believe it, I'm no' thinkin' ye woke up this mornin' and said, ' 'Tis time to see Ailsa and Mairi again.' Ye look, rather, like a woman with a purpose."

Which was what alarmed Ailsa, made her stomach clench. Since her visit to Jenny, Ena had been pallid and withdrawn. Now and then Ailsa found the girl watching as if about to say something important. Each time Ena caught her mother's eye, she curled back inside herself and silence engulfed her. The pain of that constant retreat, the apparent rejection of her mother's care and compassion, broke Ailsa's heart.

She sat on a straight-back chair and leaned forward, hands between her knees, cushioned by the heavy skirts of her violet wool gown, her silvered copper braid brushing the floor. "Why *have* ye come?"

She was partially concealed by the shadows—a comforting, cool dimness Jenny remembered with affection. She had moved her own chair into the streams of sunlight pouring through the windows. The warmth was exceptional for this time of year, and she wanted to feel the light on her face, to feel both the coolness inside the small cottage and the heat outside. Ailsa made no move toward the sun, but settled into shadow and waited.

"Pride, mingled with grief—for ye and for me—kept me away for a long time," she said at last. "Held me close to home like a strong thread from my spinning wheel."

Ailsa nodded, still partially stunned, letting her friend find her own words, her own way.

"And then there's—" Jenny broke off, cleared her throat.

She still did not know exactly what she should do or say, only that she must do something. She could not and would not ignore Ena's distress. Though it was not her right to tell Ailsa what her daughter had chosen not to, she'd made no vow, so it was not really a betrayal. Yet she felt she was betraying both mother and child.

"Ena." It was more difficult than she imagined for Ailsa to speak her daughter's name to this woman, whom the girl had chosen as her confidant. Her heart raced in dismay that was too close to fear. "Why now? Why today?" After all those years of silence, she thought. All those years of my daughter's childhood lost.

Jenny stared at the pale gray liquid in her cup, watched the tiny leaves swirl and scatter and settle. "Because a few days past, everything changed." She glanced up.

Ailsa now stood half in shadow, half in light, moving from one to the other restlessly, her feet making no sound on the packed dirt floor. But the sounds of her distress, her uneven breathing were unmistakable. "What do ye mean, 'everything changed'?"

Jenny set down her cup, studying with apparent fascination the ancient *clarsach* that hung on the wall. Ailsa's precious hand harp, which she played so sweetly that the wind wept, as well as the listeners. She looked away. She must stop letting memory intrude. Leaning forward, she willed Ailsa to listen and to hear. "Ena . . . sometimes came to me when she needed help . . . with little things, practical things, like how to make the pockets she'd devised for her skirt. How to spin and weave and cook. She said she didn't want to bother ye with such unimportant things."

Ailsa struggled for control. Little things, unimportant things—the kinds of things girls came to their mothers for every day. Except that Ena had not done so. She had not wanted to bother Ailsa with questions she would have delighted in answering, just as Mairi had once delighted in answering them for her. She felt like a child fighting back tears. "I know . . . I always knew she . . . went to ye, but I didn't know why."

"Ye knew? But Ena thought—" Jenny was stunned. All these years, Ailsa had known her daughter was seeking out someone else, no, worse, choosing Jenny Fraser over her mother. How must that have felt? A pain so sharp it took her breath told her. If she'd ever learned one of her girls had turned to Ailsa Rose . . . For a long moment, she did not think she could continue. Not when she could feel Ailsa's pain so easily and deeply. "Why did ye no' stop her, then?"

"Because she's my daughter, no' my prisoner. Because she's wise enough to choose her own friends. And because I could no' force her to choose me, even if I kept her ever by my side." Ailsa dared not risk the light; her face was veiled in gray.

Jenny shifted nervously, smoothing her skirt over her knees. Mayhap, she thought, ye gave your daughter too much freedom. Mayhap ye should've let her know ye wanted her to come to ye, of her own accord or no'. Still, this was not what Jenny had expected, not the mother she had conjured from the child's distress. "I first thought she was bein' kind. She has a good heart, your Ena, and room enough in it even for me."

"Aye. Heart and spirit and loyalty and a rare kinship with livin' things." Ailsa was reminding herself as well as Jenny that, wherever Ena had turned in need or sorrow or friendship, even if it was away, her mother did not blame her. Ailsa's tears fell inside, where Ena would not see their salt tracks on her mother's cheeks.

"What do ye mean, 'everything changed'?" Ailsa repeated grimly. She could no longer bear the suspense. "Is't no' what ye came to tell me?"

Swallowing dryly, Jenny wished herself away from memory, from friendship, from the task she'd undertaken. "A few days past, Ena came because she'd begun her monthly flow, and was so distraught by it, I began to wonder why. Ena didn't want to distress ye, so she kept her own counsel."

In agitation, Ailsa ran her fingers up and down her braid, feeling the texture, which was real and familiar. Jenny's features blurred; the outline of her figure softened like a phantom speaking a language Ailsa could not comprehend. This could not be true. It was not happening. Then why did she ache so? Why was drawing breath so hard?

She stared, stricken. "Ye must be wrong. She would've told me. I would've seen. I would've known." But Jenny Fraser never lied.

Unflinching, Jenny faced her, and though she did not move or speak, her eyes asked, *Would* ye have known?

There was no air in the croft, only murky, leaden shadows too dank to breathe. If there had been air, Ailsa could not have taken it into her lungs. She could feel nothing except the bruise where Jenny's words had struck her like a fist. But she saw the truth in the woman's averted head, which could not quite conceal her pity. Ena had become a woman, and Ailsa did not know it. Jenny Fraser had to tell her. Jenny, to whom Ena had run, bewildered, humiliated, in despair. "Why?"

"She thinks the moment she's a woman, she'll lose all that she cherishes—her freedom, her joy, her independence. She believes 'tis time to let ye rest, that since you've always been strong, she must take that responsibility on herself. That's what growin' up means to her, along with love and heartbreak and loss and sorrow. 'Tis a heavy burden to put on a child, Ailsa Rose, whether ye knew ye were doin' it or no'."

Ailsa wanted to strike out at Jenny in anger and bitterness, but she'd always known this day would come, this confrontation she had not asked for. Jenny obviously cared about Ena or she'd never have taken this risk. And apparently Ena needed them both. She could almost accept that, but she had not known this moment would hurt so much. And little as she wanted to admit it, she felt that Jenny needed comfort too.

Ailsa was standing at the edge of a cliff; the burn below was full of pointed rocks and hissing water, the sky above dark with storm clouds full of violence yet restrained, the land covered in brambles and mud and gorse and beautifully dangerous bogs. There was nowhere for her to escape the oppression, the threat, the aching grief. Afraid she would shatter, weep, reveal her impotence and anguish to this woman of all women, she took a step over the edge, caught and righted herself, then slowly, thoughtfully, looked Jenny in the eye.

A strange calm settled over her as she met her old friend's gaze. "This isn't just about Ena, is it? Returnin' after fourteen years, when you've so carefully and quietly stayed away, just as I've stayed from ye. 'Tis all so civilized, the silence and politeness between us. No' likely to stir up trouble. But trouble came and went years ago, Jenny.

"We're pretendin', by no' speakin' *of* Ian nor *to* one another, that nothing's amiss. That everything's all right. But 'tisn't, Jenny. 'Twill never be again; we both know that. We pretend there's no ill feelin' between us, no anger or resentment or blame. But we're only human. 'Tis there, roilin' beneath our well-bred masks, the rage we never examine, no' to mention speak of to each other. It has to be, or we'd be nothing but women carved from wood with no spirit, no feelin's, no heart." Wearily, Ailsa stepped from the shadows where the light struck her like a beacon and a curse.

"We're no' made of wood, nor are we saints. This pretendin', this denial of our feelin's, this calm silence is unnatural. Ye came today for Ena's sake, but 'twas no' the only reason. Admit it. Say what you've been feelin' all these years, stop holdin' it back like a dangerous animal that, once released, might turn and destroy the hand that held it. Tell me what you're feelin'!"

It was against everything she believed, a threat to every bit of armor she'd welded over the years. It was unwise, unkind and, yes, dangerous. But somehow, in that moment, with Ailsa facing her in the wash of sunlight, Jenny could not resist.

"Ye took Ian from me," she said softly, each word growing louder and less timid. "Ye discarded him and broke him and when he let me piece him slowly back together, ye came and took him again. He loved ye, damn ye, Ailsa Rose. Always and always in his soul he loved ye, no' me. Oh, he cared for me, aye, but his passion, his spirit were yours, and ye fool, ye gave it away. How could ye be so daft, so heartless?" She honestly could not understand, so she waited for an answer that could never be.

"Whether I gave ye my blessin' or no' that last night, whether my own guilt made me see that your loyalty was greater than mine—greater, though I'd lived with him, loved him, borne his bairns and raised them, cooked his food and fed that small part of his heart which was mine—in spite of all that, I bade ye go, run, hide, protect each other." Jenny paused, eyes as dry as if every tear had been sucked from them.

"And instead of tellin' me no, that whatever I lacked, I loved him with all 'twas in me, that I didn't deserve to lose him just because I doubted and was afraid, ye did as I bid ye. Ye took him back inside in every way ye knew how, and each was a betrayal of me, of my family, of Ian's honor." The accusation startled her as much as Ailsa.

"I know 'twas his choice as well. I know if ye could've ye would've stopped him from tauntin' those angry men to shoot him. I know ye would've stood in front of him and let the bullets pierce your heart instead. That's why I can't forgive ye, Ailsa Rose. Because ye would've died for him, and I had no' the courage." Had all this been inside her from the beginning? Had she always felt she was not good enough for Ian Fraser, yet better than he? Jenny swayed at the dangerous glitter in Ailsa's eyes.

"Ye deserved that night together, the child he gave ye in farewell, but only in violence, in rage, in struggle did ye earn it. For every day of every month of every year for over twenty, there was no violence, no need to sacrifice myself for him, nor he for me. All we needed was to love each other, care for each other, give each other peace and calm and happiness. And so we did, through ordinary work and harder times, through poverty and peace. I loved him every day of my life, and ye took him because ye had to be better, stronger, braver, more loyal. Ye may've been all those things, Ailsa Rose, but *I* was his wife, not ye. Never ye."

Though she had asked for, demanded the truth, Ailsa was stunned by the bitterness and envy, and in the midst of it, the understanding, pouring out of Jenny like a new spring after a boulder's rolled away. As her rage and long-repressed sorrow grew, as her face turned red and her knuckles white, Ailsa's anger came spilling out.

"No, I never was his wife, because I was too young, too foolish to see what I was doin'. Make no mistake, I loved William Sinclair as much as ye loved Ian. But he couldn't *be* Ian; he couldn't know the things Ian knew. We were reflections of one another, and I know, 'twas my fault, I chose to break the glass. But that didn't make the bleedin' less painful. When he married ye, he closed his mind against me, cut the cord that'd always bound us. Shut me out like an unwanted cat. When I came back to the glen, I never meant to piece the mirror back together or reweave that broken thread. Ye did that for us, ye and the strangers." Ailsa moved closer, then away, afraid of her own feelings.

"I was whole again, for one night and one day. 'Twas Ian chose to die; he chose to leave me and ye and your children, chose to blaze from this glen like a shootin' star so bright 'twas never forgotten. Do ye think it didn't hurt me, knowin' he'd chosen ye and loved ye, that ye bore his children and shared his life? I had one night. One day, and that runnin' from men who would destroy us. But I know, I knew then, I'll always know, that day and night should have been yours. I made myself hate ye for losin' faith in the one man worth believin' in with all your heart and soul. I had to blame ye, or I'd blame myself and my child. I could no' ask your forgiveness, nor did I think ye could give it. I took too much, and ye held too much, and so here we've lived for fourteen years, the two of us, angry, enraged, unforgivin', no' of each other, but of Ian's foolish courage, which took him from us.

" 'Tis strange that Ena, his daughter, was the only thing that kept the thread from snappin' wholly and forever. The thing that brought ye here today. Ian's shapin' our lives even now, can ye no' see that? Holdin' us apart, makin' us courteous enemies, strangers who know each other too well. And we let him. That's why we're both fools, Jenny Fraser. We let him do it then and we're lettin' him do it now."

They stood, cheeks flushed, a line of white around their lips. Having said too much, they could only face each other warily, suspiciously. Yet somehow the anger was trickling away, the resentment dissolving in the bright heat of the sun. The sound of their ragged breath filled the croft, and they stared as if an apparition had appeared between them, or more likely, disappeared for once and all. They saw, perhaps for the first time, their honest feelings. One of them was regret over the loss of something they had never grieved for. They saw fury, grief, mercy, compassion over so much shared—the good and the bad. And affection turned against itself. They saw the truth.

For a moment longer they stood as opponents, keeping a studied distance between them, unwilling to move, uncertain where to go. When the tension in the air was so heavy it lay upon them like a shroud, Ailsa could not bear it anymore. She took a step forward. Jenny hesitated, took a step of her own.

And then, as they should have long ago, they touched each other's hands, clasped tightly, released their grip, stepped closer, and finally fell into each other's arms. They held one another and swayed and wept. Shyly at first, and then without restraint, brown hair tangled in chestnut, tears mingling, running freely down their faces. For the first time, they came together and mourned, not a man, but years of friendship lost.

And now found again.

14

THE WIND WAS COLD AS IT SWEPT OFF ENA'S CAP, DEPOSITING it on a tree branch just out of reach. It crept beneath her plaid, leaving her chilled, but she did not mind. Every day the rowans and larches, birches and alders revealed a bit more green, in shades from forest to emerald to lime. Every day the woods became more a refuge of verdant muted light that closed around her in welcome, cloaking her in tinted stillness. The forest floor was a riot of flowers and vines and fallen needles from silver fir and spruce and Scots pine. Ena's footsteps made no sound on the springy, living carpet of scent and color.

She gazed up through the still-naked branches of the oaks and smiled at the clouds scuttling past, their fleeting shadows skimming the ground. "Today Connor's comin' back," the girl informed a group of sparrows. "I know he is, though he's no' said so. But he'll be goin' daft, pent up like that, and if I know my friend, they'll set him free." She whirled, arms high, sending pine and fir needles spinning around her.

She was not yet at ease with the changes in her body, but acutely aware of every ache, every swelling, every minute change. But the voices of the glen made her forget.

As she approached the animal pens, she fell silent, moving soundlessly to where the wildcat lay in the patterned sun and shadow as the clouds fled by. She sat beside it, scratching lightly behind its tawny ears. The last time she'd come, it had not objected, and she had been delighted.

Ena had wondered at its docility. But it had had over a fortnight to realize that she brought food and took away the pain. The wound was healing well; she'd removed the stitches the day before and the swelling was gone, along with the redness. Not once had the cat flinched or tried to move out of her reach.

It lay staring up at her with cloudy amber eyes, lethargic and disinterested. When Ena gently probed its hind quarters and belly, the animal mewled, as if in pain, but did not move. Almost as if it were not able.

"I thought ye were gettin' better," she murmured. "But I see the pain in your eyes." She wondered if the wound had healed while the infection grew inside its body.

The cat made a sound low in its throat, not threatening, but unsettling, when she probed more carefully, and she became aware of an unpleasant, bitter odor. It tried to rise, but seemed too weak, and without once ceasing the unfamiliar purring, it let its head fall on its outstretched paws and did not try again.

Wincing, Ena closed her eyes, listening for guidance, waiting for an inspiration. Francis McPhee had shown her how, sometimes, with her hand on the animal, if she closed her eyes and listened closely, she could filter its pain, and having felt it, know how to ease it. Nothing came to her except the feeling that she had failed this wildcat after all. Her heart heavy, she placed it gently in its comfortable bed of grass and straw, and it curled in upon itself at once.

She sat watching for a long time among the low-slung branches and twisted roots of an oak, the green in her eyes eclipsed by the gray. Her sadness was a palpable thing that clung about her like shimmering heat. While the wind wailed and whispered above her, the animal's pallor increased, along with its malaise. The painful sound, part purr, part growl, grew high-pitched and continuous. Connor was better, his wounds half-healed. But the cat was not so lucky. Glancing over her shoulder at the fast-flowing river, she murmured a prayer to Neithe, God of Waters.

Finally, she lifted it out of its pen. The wildcat that had once been strong and tough, felt like bones held together by skin and tissue as fragile as parchment. She settled with it by the tree, spoke to it, sang little tunes and blessings, took the carved wooden flute from her pocket and played softly, hoping to soothe and comfort. She did not know how long she sat stroking the cat's head, remembering the hissing, angry animal she and Connor had first seen in the woods.

"Och, I wish ye could speak to me, *mo-run*," she crooned, "and tell me what would ease ye."

At last the cat raised its head, responding to the tenderness in Ena's voice. It looked up at her, resting its chin on her crossed ankles. Gazing down into its once glowing amber eyes, Ena saw the blank, cold gleam of stone. There was no rage, no pain, no will—only a kind of naked plea, which Ena recognized at once. She had seen it before.

One of the first things Francis McPhee had taught Ena was that she could not always cure the animals she treated. Sometimes the struggle to remain alive became more difficult than the surrender to death, to peace, an end to pain. Over the years, with Francis's help, she'd prepared various strengths of herbs for such situations.

Now, as she looked into the wildcat's eyes, she felt its pain and hopelessness as if it were her own. She had done her best for this beautiful, feral cat that had once leapt gracefully from boulder to boulder, hilltop to hilltop. She had tried everything she knew, everything she'd read, followed every instinct, but it hadn't been enough. *They'll always tell ye when 'tis time to free 'em from their sufferin'*, Francis had told her. *Believe me, you'll know, if you're lis-*

tenin' weel, to their need and no' your own. The cat lay with its head on her bare ankles, a leaden weight, without courage or the spark that made it fight. "If you're certain 'tis what ye want, wee one," she murmured, as if it could understand. "I'll go and get the herbs."

Sitting with ankles crossed, so her legs brushed the matted, lusterless fur, she lifted its head and stared into its eyes, her heart pounding in a rhythm that made her body ache with grief. She opened the cat's mouth and slid the tiny balls of herbs inside, then held its jaws closed until it swallowed, slowly, painfully. She felt each ripple of its throat muscles in her own neck, the dryness of its mouth in hers.

She leaned as close as she could get, so the cat would feel her presence, her warmth, her spirit. Softly, soothingly, she sang a blessing for its soul.

Ena's eyes grew moist when the wildcat lifted head and paws and laid them in her lap, seeking the warm cradle there. She bit her lip and fought back tears. Gently, tenderly, she stroked its head between the ears and held its dry swollen paws. It looked up at her for a long time as the herbs moved through its blood and its eyelids drooped, slid open, drooped again. It moved a paw, touching her palm, and she swallowed a cry of despair. Never once did its eyes leave her face, not until they closed for the last time, then opened, blind and blank and gray as stone.

"Farewell, ye wild one. May your rest be sweeter than your struggle and your pain." She had to choke out the last words as she lifted the cat into her lap, its body curled against her belly, head on her knee, paws on her ankles. For an eternity, she sat and rocked and held the once proud wildcat like a helpless child, unable to release its body, though she had freed its spirit long before.

Connor, fully dressed for the first time in over a fortnight, was just slipping his brogues onto his feet when he heard the sound of Ena calling. There was such sadness in her voice, such desperate melancholy that his chest ached for her. Rising, he reached for his jacket on its hook by the fire, finding comfort in the warmth of the thick woven fabric.

"Where do ye think ye're goin'?" David Fraser asked his son.

"I'll soon be ravin' if I don't breathe some fresh air," the boy replied. "I'm fair bored out of my mind. The sun's shinin', and the view out the window too bonny to ignore. And I need to be with Ena," he mumbled.

Running his fingers through his dark, curly hair, David Fraser groaned in frustration. He and Alanna knew how hard it had been for their son to stay trapped in his bed, to remain unmoving so as not to open his healing wounds, yet he'd rarely complained. And the day *was* welcoming and warm. "Aye, weel, mayhap ye deserve a little freedom." With an effort, David kept his voice low and even.

Connor straightened, though the motion tugged on the scabs and sent sharp pains through his shoulder. "Aye." He paused. " 'Tis important. Ena needs me. *She* came when I needed *her*."

David wanted to mention the wildcat's attack, but that wasn't fair.

Reading his father's thoughts in his eyes, the boy stood as tall as he could. " 'Twas my choice to go with Ena and to try for the cat. Mine and no one else's." In the days of his recovery, he'd worked at obliterating his humiliation, because he had given his best effort, after all, *and* survived. Ena'd told him long ago that a patient, human or animal, had to *want* to live when wounded dangerously. Had to be strong enough to fight whatever infection or poison or heat was in his blood. Apparently, Connor had been strong enough after all. "So if you're after blamin' Ena, don't. 'Tis no' right or fair."

He tilted his head. He could hear her voice, this minute, calling in a sad, melodic keening that raised chills on his arms.

David put his hand on Connor's shoulder. "One way or another, we came too close to losin' ye. I don't think ye realize how frightened we were. 'Tis no' the first time ye followed your Ena into danger. And somehow, the cost's always higher to ye."

The boy could not deny it. But then, Ena seemed to scent adventure, excitement in the air, and Connor had never been bored at her side. From her he had learned fearlessness, absorbed it through his skin, like the mist at gloaming. He gazed over his father's shoulder, seeing memories in the shadowed corners of the croft. " 'Twas always worth the cost," he murmured. "Even this time."

The image came to him, vivid and wrenching, of Ena perched on the riverbank, a sick animal in her arms. He had dreamed it last night, and it came back to him in the cadence of her mourning song without words. He wondered his father couldn't hear it, so audible had it become. "I've got to go. She's callin'. She needs me."

David cocked his head, listening intently, but he heard only the wind. His neck prickled with discomfort. "How do ye know? You've no' spoken to her today." He should not have asked, he realized, if he did not want to know the answer.

Connor was aware of his father's skepticism, of how uneasy such things made him, but he'd never lied to his parents. "I just . . . know. The way Mam knows things sometimes. In here." He pointed to his head and heart. "It's happened before between her and me. I can no' ignore it. *She* never has. If she needs me, I've to go."

Turning away to hide his distress, David paced distractedly. He had never gotten used to Alanna's ability to see and feel things that weren't in front of her. He had wondered if Connor had that kind of bond with Ena, but had never admitted it to himself. Now he could no longer deny it. Perhaps, after all, that was why he so feared the girl's influence on his son. The two children were bound by a force beyond logic or alteration. David Fraser's stable, comfortable world had begun to spin, and he could not stop it. He could not control it or shape it to his will.

"I admire your loyalty to your friend," he said carefully. "And your honesty as well. But Ena'll have to wait a little longer. There're things to be said." Slowly, he turned to face his son. "You're near a man now, Connor. Men have obligations, and you're old enough and strong enough to be doin' your share of the work. Your mother and I've let ye put your enjoyment ahead of responsibility till now, but no more."

He sighed, forehead furrowed. "I need your help, son. I can no' do it alone anymore."

The look of weariness on his father's face made Ena slip from the boy's thoughts. "You're no' so old," he declared, as if saying it loudly and firmly enough would make it true and banish the niggling distress he felt at the thought of David Fraser aging. "You're one of the strongest men in the glen." When David did not respond at once, his son cried, "Besides, everyone knows we've enough to live on. You've no need to work so hard. I've never understood why ye do."

"Because I like the air on my face, the breeze in my hair, the sweat on my skin, the pure, powerful feelin' of achin' muscles and limbs. I live in my body, and use it, creatin' growin' things, nurturin' the sheep and cattle, feelin' the earth always beneath my feet. Solid, unchangin', rich and fertile and bonny. I do it for love."

He paused, eyes piercing. Connor had succeeded at distracting him from the subject at hand. "The point is that we need ye here, Alanna and I, no' out in the hills and braes wastin' time."

Connor shifted his weight uneasily. His father was right; the boy had known that long ago. But more and more, Connor felt the need, the imperative of spending as much time with Ena as he could. For months now, he'd been plagued by a sense of foreboding, that he didn't have much time, that something was looming, threatening to crumple their friendship like a dry autumn leaf before lifting it up and away on a chill, damp wind. He felt hollow and empty at the prospect.

And now she was calling him, and she sounded vulnerable, weak. He did not like the feeling. "Ena's my responsibility, just as I'm hers. I know she's in trouble, but no' if I can help her. I only know I have to try."

When he saw the bemused expression on Connor's face, David was afraid for his son. "Why ye?" he asked.

Connor retreated, taking a single step backward, away from a confrontation he did not wish to have. David knew the boy's retreat was more than physical; he was also shutting away his thoughts, his heart, his mind. David recognized that kind of withdrawal, because, as a boy, and more frequently as a young man, he had closed himself away inside a thick, impenetrable shell where his own father could not reach or hurt him. Eventually, the retreat had become permanent, and Duncan Fraser had lost his son entirely.

David could not let that happen here. He'd changed his life by following his heart and his instincts. Perhaps it was time to let Connor do the same. To have faith in the boy's basic goodness and capability.

"All right then," David Fraser said softly, "make me understand why 'tis so important that ye go to Ena now."

Connor released a great gusting sigh of relief. He did not like arguing with his father, whom he loved and respected. He leaned against the carved overhead panel of the boxbed and tried to think how to explain what he only sensed.

Alanna had slipped inside during the conversation, remaining silent in the kitchen, listening. She smiled fondly when David paused, thinking, then made his son an offering of peace.

Unaware of his mother's presence, Connor worked thoughtfully at the leather thongs on his coat while he searched for words. " 'Tis just that I'm thinkin' she needs me more than before." Her voice in his head, her heartbreakingly lovely and lonely voice told him that. "She's aye confused and very sad."

David Fraser was amazed. "Ena Rose, sad? The only time I've seen her when she was no' either laughin' or smilin' was when ye were ill."

Shaking his head as he tried to sort it through, Connor said, "Today's mayhap different." The image from his dream came again, more vivid this time, and beneath it the sound of her voice. Full of tears? He did not believe it.

Alanna heard the note of protectiveness in her son's voice, and stirred uneasily, not certain why the thought disturbed her.

"I need to go now," the boy repeated. "She can no' wait anymore." He turned and fled.

Alanna watched him disappear, frowning. He was so passionately determined to respond, now that he sensed Ena's need. Was it necessary for Connor to prove he was strong enough? Or that he was not the only one who had been injured.

15

MAIRI WAS WAITING ON THE LOW STONE WALL COVERED with ivy and honey suckle that surrounded her garden. Jenny had been inside for a long time, and her face and swollen eyes showed traces of recent tears. The younger woman—Mairi smiled ironically; Jenny Fraser was a mere fifty-two years old—looked bemused, yet her step was lighter than when she had arrived.

Mairi took her hands. " 'Tis glad I am ye finally came, no matter the reason or the outcome."

Jenny nodded, clutching Mairi's gnarled, arthritic fingers. "Aye, 'twas the right thing after all." She tilted her head diffidently. "Or so I'm thinkin'."

She needed reassurance, and that Mairi could offer. "I see your hands are strong and comfortin', and your smile the one I remember. You've no' lost your courage or strength of spirit. Or your selflessness. 'Tis those things that brought ye here today. 'Tis those things that count."

Jenny might have said the same to Mairi Rose, whose generosity of spirit was written on her weathered face, palpable in the firm, warm clasp of her hands. The younger woman could find no words to express what she felt at Mairi's touch, the sweetness of her smile, the ease with which she welcomed an old friend.

In the end, Mairi broke the awkward silence. "It's been many years without ye, and each a little emptier for your absence. I hope you'll come back, whether you've made your peace or no'. For Ena's sake, and Ailsa's and mine."

She did not expect an answer. They only held one another tighter, eyes dry, but full of years of feelings unrevealed and words unspoken.

Connor found Ena sitting by the hollow tree, face streaked with tears, the stiffening body of the cat in her lap, speechless as she stared into the sky—blind and grieving. Knowing her as he did, he guessed at once what had happened.

He sank down beside her till they sat shoulder to shoulder. "'Tis sorry I am, Ena Rose. I know what she meant to ye."

Ena blinked at him in astonishment. "Ye can say that, when ye were so ill because of her?"

"I can say it because I'm here and alive, and in spite of the pain, I'll never forget the thrill of the chase. It costs me nothing to sorrow for the death of a bonny, powerful animal, its darin' and beauty gone forever."

Ena leaned into him, her tears drying as the chill left her body, her warmth restored by Connor's. "I'm lucky to call ye friend, Connor Fraser, and glad ye came today, for I was feelin' aye alone."

"Weel, you're alone no more."

Looking up at him gratefully, she wondered when he had grown taller than she, his shoulders broader, the set of his jaw more pronounced.

She was still wondering when he insisted on accompanying her to the small, sheltered clearing where rows of mounds revealed the final resting place of other animals she had lost. Holding his injured arm rigid, he helped bury the wildcat, covering the fresh turned loam with a pile of stones when it was done. The two friends crouched at the foot of the new grave, regretting the loss of the graceful menace of the wildcat, the determination and intuition they would never know.

Then they wandered, hand in hand, trying to distract themselves with the multihued burgeoning life of spring. Finally, when Ena noticed Connor's labored breathing and heavy tread, she locked her arm in his and they settled in the copse by the river.

From the moment he arrived, Connor'd watched closely, hearing her unspoken distress, seeing how she dragged her feet, which once had glided along this same path. He'd thought her sorrow and guilt over the wildcat had brought him here, but now he wondered. "There's something different about ye today," he said.

With her back to him, Ena flung herself down, staring at the blades of grass, the dew, the tiny insects crawling along the earth. "I don't know what ye mean, except that I'm grievin'." Her face, like her tone, was expressionless.

Connor was startled and upset. He knew intuitively she was lying, and she'd never lied to him before. There was no point; they knew each other too well. He stretched out gingerly on the grass facing her, propping his chin up with one hand so they lay nose to nose. He suspected she wanted to look away but didn't dare. Her reluctance to meet his gaze would reveal too much. In the past he would not have challenged her, but he felt a compulsion to learn the truth.

"I think ye *do* know. We're both different than we were that mornin' in the woods. 'Tis daft to think otherwise. How could we be the same, especially when we feel each other's pain?" His voice rose commandingly on the last word, for he sensed she was trying to withdraw, to hide, which both hurt and frightened him.

Ena shivered. Connor's face was every bit as obstinate as his father's, and his eyes held hers steadily. For a moment she panicked. She could not tell him she'd begun her monthly flow. It was not something you spoke of to a boy. She could not explain that, along with his virulent fever and her failure with the wildcat, this step toward womanhood had turned her world upside down. "You're right," she said carefully. "I knew it the day your fever broke. Nothing'll ever be the same again. No' ye or me or our friendship. 'Tis all changin' now, and it scares me."

Astonished that she'd simply blurted out her apprehension, Connor frowned. As he stared into her gray eyes flecked with green, he saw what he'd heard in the melancholy song that had drawn him to her side. She was bewildered and despondent, as he'd never known her to be, and she *did* need him. But he did not know how to help her, because he could not understand.

Sitting up, Ena pulled her legs to her chest and rested her forehead on her knees. "I don't like bein' scared. I want to go back." She turned to him in supplication. "Make it so, Connor. Say a spell and make it yesterday."

Now it was he who was bewildered. "And why would I do that? I've no wish to go back, only forward. I'm weary of bein' a child. I can no' believe ye want any different." He swallowed his distress. "Besides, you're the one who knows the spells. I never have, and ye could no' teach me."

She did not raise her head, and her words were muffled

by the bunched fabric of her skirt. "Ye didn't really want to know. And whatever ye believe, you're wrong."

Astonished by her fierceness, Connor stared as if he did not know her. Perhaps, after all, he did not.

Ena felt his shock and uncertainty, saw the questions in his eyes, the doubt. Always before he had understood, and rarely disagreed. Clasping his hands, she felt, all at once, as if he were slipping away from her. "I'm no' wantin' to disappear," she cried, holding Connor tighter, as if to anchor herself to him.

"Growin' up doesn't mean ye disappear. Right now I feel ye and see ye and hear ye as clearly as before," he said. Though I don't understand ye, he added silently. He did not mind the painful grasp of her fingers around his. He was as reluctant as she to let go.

For a long time, they stared at each other, afraid to risk saying the wrong words. Afraid of expressing what both felt keenly.

It was Ena who broke the spell. "When ye become a man, ye'll no' feel the same. Ye'll leave me behind. Ye'll have no choice."

Connor was deeply shaken, because he suspected she was right. Desperately, he wanted to deny it, but he couldn't. Not honestly. He stared miserably at the ground.

She saw the flicker in his eyes, the knowledge and regret, and went cold. Somewhere, somehow, she'd always known that she and Connor could not share this carefree life forever. Now she'd put it into words, and the words became a tension in her chest like a weight of stones.

Groping for reassurance, he said, "There'll always be change. New places and new wonders. Surely ye'll no' stay here all your life."

"Why not?" Her tone was flat, emphatic.

"Ye'll want to leave someday, mayhap to go to veterinary school like your friend Francis McPhee. There's naught here you've no' already learned thrice over."

"Everything I need to know is here." Thinking of her cousins in Burgundy and Kent, of Genevra and Lian and their constant invitations to experience new worlds, she knew she'd lied. She was intrigued, seduced by her family and the wonders they offered, generously, enthusiastically. She wished she could ignore that tug of curiosity, that betrayal of all her mother loved and valued, but she couldn't.

Connor scowled. That complacency did not sound like Ena. "Have ye no wish to be more?" He could not hide his own longing, the questions that fascinated him.

"I'm happy here. 'Tis my home." She had not answered his question.

"Mayhap 'tis the world ye were born for, but that doesn't mean 'tis your prison."

With a sigh, she looked into Connor's achingly familiar face. He lived with his feet planted firmly on the ground, while she glided, buoyant, woven into the web of the glen, her feet caught in the delicate meshwork. Sometimes she envied Connor the solid earth beneath him, the solid prospect of his future, real as the land itself.

Cloud and earth could never be part of one another, but only fleeting shadows, one upon the other. That was why Connor would move slowly, inevitably away from her, day by day and month by month. She wanted to cry out in denial, to weep.

Connor touched her cheek, cool and smooth beneath his fingertips. He looked into her, the confusion cleared and he saw what she feared, what they shared, what would one day cease to be. "Ena." Her name, the only word he could find, hung in the pine scented air between them until it was obscured by the unending song of the river, swept away on the breath of a momentary breeze. "You're the dearest friend I'll ever know," he murmured, and wondered why he ached where the wildcat had left no marks, no painful wounds.

16

THE FLAMES CAST FRIENDLY SHADOWS ON THE PATTERNED
clay walls while Ailsa worked in the kitchen, still shaken
by her encounter with Jenny, though more at peace than
she'd been in a long while. She'd not realized until she
spoke the words aloud how much she'd missed her friend
and resented all that had kept them apart.

But Jenny was gone, and along with her the rush of con-
flicting emotions that had overwhelmed Ailsa earlier. Now
she could think only of Ena, who, for reasons she could not
understand, had kept from her mother the most momentous change in her young life. That, and so much more.

"Why?" she asked Mairi for the third time. "I don't think
I'll ever understand."

"Weeel," her mother said pensively, as her thoughts ran
like drops of dew down a silken string, "ye'll have to be
askin' Ena. She's the only one can tell ye what no one else
can know."

As always, Mairi Rose was right. " 'Tis late," Ailsa said,
glancing out the window at the dark, heavy clouds that had
brought nightfall early. "Ena should be home by now. 'Tis
no' hospitable out there, especially for a child who's lost."
She put out her hand and felt the rain on her palm, closed
her fingers tight and knew, with a sudden, startling intensity, that her youngest daughter was indeed lost, adrift, in
need. The sensation slowed Ailsa's heart and sucked away
her breath.

"This time I'll no' wait till she comes to me. I'm goin'
after her." She turned to her mother and said fiercely, "I'll
find her and heal her and bring her home."

Mairi nodded. " 'Tis time ye find what's troublin' our
Ena and make her whole again."

Without a word, Ailsa plucked her plaid from its hook and was gone, leaving only the sound of the hushed rain on the woven thatch.

Ena felt extraordinarily fragile and alone, though she knew she was not. But too much was happening too suddenly. Anxiously, she wandered the bank of the burn, tried to read or write inside the hollow tree, worked desultorily among the animal pens, shoring them up and cleaning out the one the wildcat had inhabited. But she could not concentrate. She was too uncertain and melancholy.

The clouds that crowded the sky as daylight faded into night brought with them a light misting rain, and she raised her face so the moisture settled on her skin. She draped her plaid over her cap and wrapped it tight around her. The sun had crept away and the spring chill returned.

On impulse, the girl climbed the oak at the edge of the copse where she'd bid Connor good day, as stiff and unnatural as he, troubled by the wary distance between them. Locating a thick round branch that reached across the burn, dipping close to the water before rising and disappearing into the woods on the other side, Ena settled in the natural seat formed by the depression, arms linked around the ancient limb.

"My heart aches," she whispered, knowing she sounded childish. "And I'd no' be knowin' how to stop it." She pressed her cheek against the rough bark, but the ache did not go. She wanted Ailsa, now, with such ferocity that she nearly fell. She needed the warmth and comfort of her mother's arms, her wisdom and her strength.

Thinking of the fire burning at home, Ena pictured the dancing golden-orange blaze and felt she was one tiny flame fluttering at the edge, that she had no more substance than smoke.

Suspended above the murmuring water, supported by the solid, unchanging oak, she was overcome by the feeling that there was no future. There was only here, now, the voice of the burn, the sigh of the wind, the darkening sky filled with rain that made sharper the rugged outline of the mountains. The beautiful seductive glen had taken her reason, leaving her weightless, aimless, straying toward the angry sky.

Once Ailsa had gone, Mairi Rose released the skein of yarn from her hands and reached into her pocket, taking out a packet of letters from her husband. They rested in her lap and she touched them fondly, blindly, running her fingers over the faded ink, the tattered creases and folds. "Where's it leadin', my Charlie? For I feel a tug at my heart, and voices whisperin' secrets I can no' understand. So much mended today; so much left to mend." The sound of her voice and the motion of her fingers over the worn, familiar letters mesmerized her and she leaned her head against the back of her chair, her lids irresistibly heavy. Her violet eyes had a cast of gray upon them, and though she stared into the heart of the fire, she did not see the flames. She was drifting, floating, falling away from the tangled yarn in her lap, from the thick soft cushions of her rocking chair, from the cozy lamplight in the croft to the gauzy veiled glow of a beckoning torch.

They were walking arm in arm beneath the silver-misted moon, she and her Charlie, among the spreading branches of an oak. New growth unfurled beneath their feet, making a pathway of multicolored leaves, a fabric of intricate, intertwined threads. They saw a break in the design where the wind whistled through the unraveled threads, glimmering and enticing, lovely as the ribbon she'd worn in her hair on their wedding day. She glanced up at him, and he drew her closer while the living fabric stretched out beneath them, curving back to where it had begun.

Mairi opened her eyes languidly, smiling at the remembered warmth of Charles Kittridge's touch.

"Soon," she told the swirling flames that kept away the

chilly night. "The oaks are beginnin' to feel the spring, and the leaves comin' out of hidin' at last. Soon now the cloth'll unwind and we'll see its colors, feel its weight, recognize its design."

17

ENSCONCED IN HER CHAIR OF LIVING OAK, ENA CURLED HER legs beneath her and fought the exhaustion that was drawing her toward sleep. It was too cold, her body damp from the light rain, and she sensed tonight the dream would come.

Then she heard it: the voice from her nightmare, lilting and oddly familiar, yet strange and unknown. "Ena-*mo-run,* ye need no' be alone like this. I'm with ye. I'm always with ye."

The woman appeared like a wraith, came closer, flowing through the mist in a long pale gown. "Will ye no' answer me?" she murmured.

Ena held her breath. She was dreaming while she was awake. Dreaming and bewildered, yet drawn to the woman's lovely, smiling face. With every step she took, she seemed more substantial.

Then the mist around her fell away, and Ailsa Rose stepped into the copse.

The child's breath escaped in a sigh of relief. Her mother had come to her at last.

Determined to reach Ena quickly, to hold her and hear her and lift the mask of misery from her face, Ailsa began to climb the tree, despite her fifty-three years. Before she had risen much above the ground, Ena scrambled up and slid along the branch, then swung from limb to limb until she reached her mother.

"I was comin' to ye; ye need no' have left your perch," Ailsa said.

Together they climbed down into the clearing, where Ena turned. " 'Twas too cold and too high. I wanted to feel the earth again."

"Aye? Did ye then?" Putting her arm securely around the girl, Ailsa sank with her onto the mossy bank, the ferns brushing her hem. She examined Ena's face, damp and cool from sitting above the burn. "What've ye been doin', little one? You've twigs in your hair and your face is black with soil." She bent down, dipping the hem of her muslin gown in the clear rushing water. Tenderly, she cleaned Ena's smudged face, then her palms, leaving the marks of her daughter's day upon her skirt.

"Come, Ena, come to me," she whispered.

The girl turned so she sat with her back to Ailsa's front and leaned her head on her mother's breast. Trustingly, without hesitation. It seemed this kind of intimacy came easily to the child, but there were other things she did not share. "What is't, birdeen? I know you're hurtin'."

"The wildcat's gone," the girl whispered. "I could no' save her." She paused, fighting for composure. "And Connor . . . If I've no' lost him today, I will soon. Things're changin' and 'tis like I'm fallin' after 'em, tumblin' into a place I don't know."

Her grief was very real; Ailsa's chest ached with it. "Ah, my child, I'm sorry about the cat. I know how much it meant to ye. But ye did all ye could and more, lass. Don't be blamin' yourself. And as for Connor, I can no' imagine ye losin' him, ever. Mayhap your friendship is maturin'. 'Tis true, 'tis no' the same as 'twas in childhood, carefree and easy, but that doesn't make it less, only different. 'Tis hard to accept what's new and unfamiliar, but ye'll learn in time. Mayhap ye'll even be grateful."

And what of yourself, Ailsa Rose, she thought. Can ye accept what ye'd no wish to hear? 'Twas Jenny brought ye to this place, after all. Can ye disregard your own hurt to help your child?

Ena . . . sometimes came to me when she needed help. She didn't want to bother ye with such unimportant things. "Jenny Fraser visited today," Ailsa said cautiously. "She's worried about ye."

Ena stiffened, tried to pull away, but Ailsa drew her closer. "I've long known ye went to her, though I didn't understand why. Only ye can tell me." She paused, fearing the answer, and dried her damp palms on her plaid. "Why did ye no' feel ye could come to me?"

For a long moment the humming of insects and the murmur of the river were the only reply. At last, Ena sighed and gave up the struggle. "I thought Jenny was sad, and 'twas a little because of me, because I'd been born, ye ken." She shook her head when her mother tried to deny it. "It makes no matter now. 'Twas only one reason." She plucked at the low-growing ferns that carpeted the ground. "I didn't want ye to see me the way I was when I visited Jenny."

Ailsa was bewildered. "I can no' imagine a time when I'd no' want to see ye."

Ena turned her head to glance up uncomfortably. "Can ye no'? 'Twas whenever I was weak or clumsy or confused." She was caught in her own tangled web, listening to the blood pulsing in her ears.

Stunned, it took Ailsa a moment to find her balance, to suppress the jolt of pain at Ena's revelation. "But that's when ye *should* come to me. I'm your mother and I love ye. I want to take care of ye. 'Tis one of the joys of my life."

Ena turned away, her clenched fist full of broken pieces of fern. "But no' when I'm bad at something, like sewin' or weavin' or cookin'. No' when I'm failin' at the simplest things. I wanted ye to think I was good and strong, that I was enough. But I'm thinkin' I can no' be enough."

Ailsa's heart began to beat erratically. "Enough?"

"To be yours and Ian Fraser's child. I knew I could bring

ye my hurt and fear, because ye two shared those things. But ye and he were clever at everything, and I thought if ye saw how awkward I was, 'twould make ye realize I'd never be good enough to fill the hole my father left when he died. I wanted to stop your grief and rid ye of your pain, but I can't. So I thought ye'd no' love me, that ye'd be disappointed. . . ." She trailed off, throat tight and full of unshed tears.

Ailsa was appalled. "Whatever made ye think I was judgin' ye every minute? That I expected ye to take your father's place?" She tried to make her daughter turn, but the girl stared stubbornly at the ground, so Ailsa circled on her knees, lifted Ena's chin and forced her to meet her mother's gaze. For an instant, she reeled at the resignation and sadness in her daughter's eyes. "Why?"

Once, twice, the girl opened her mouth, but no sound came. Then she whispered, "In your journal ye always said how exactly right my father was, how talented and wise. How much he loved ye and advised ye and kept ye whole."

Ailsa sank back onto her heels in the damp moss. Only then, when it was too late, did it strike her that the constant reading of the journal—which she'd written intending to show Ena the truth so she wouldn't have to wonder and blunder as Ailsa herself had—had instead made the child believe she had an obligation to continue the story, a responsibility to give her mother back part of what she'd lost. She'd never criticized the girl or held her up to a measuring stick of accomplishment that Ena failed to match. Nevertheless, somehow she'd made her daughter think she must be exceptional in order to be loved. Ailsa winced.

She rubbed her eyes with two fingers while she tried to think. "You're only a child. 'Tis no' your place to care for me. You've neither the experience nor the power to ease my pain. No one does. Nor should they. 'Tis my sorrow, my burden, no' yours. Besides, 'tis no' so heavy anymore, as the years pass and I watch ye grow. Don't ye know how much joy you've given me? How often you've made me forget completely? Have I been so cold and distant that ye don't know how I love ye, how you've filled and transformed my life?"

Brow furrowed, the girl looked into her mother's eyes. "I thought I should be more. I wanted ye to be proud of me, is all." She sounded lost and forlorn.

In the child's gaze Ailsa saw what she did not wish to see. She should have guessed. *I wanted ye to know I wasn't heartless, nor afraid for myself when another creature was in trouble. Ye always told me—I only wanted to do what was right.* Ena had been so desperate for Ailsa's approval the night she brought the wildcat home. When her mother said, *I begin to fear you're as brave and foolish as your father,* the girl had looked up at her with shining eyes full of pride and hope. *Do ye really think so?*

Remembering the tenderness she'd felt for her daughter when she'd spoken those words, she saw that now and then she'd had a wistful longing for Ena to be a living, breathing piece of the magic her parents had created. A physical reflection of what Ian and Ailsa had been to one another. It was not right or fair, and she'd dismissed those fleeting longings. But children did not always understand; they did not analyze or reason out impulses of their hearts. No matter what she'd intended, Ena's fierce belief in the necessity of her own perfection had been the result. *'Tis a heavy burden to place on a child, whether ye knew ye were doin' it or no'.*

Ailsa cupped her daughter's face in her hands. "Listen, Ena, and listen well. Ye don't have to be anyone or anything but who ye are—in your heart, in your spirit, in your soul. 'Tis enough and more than enough. Ye need never hide your fear or what ye call your weakness; I want only to help. Ye can be a child with me, and I'll never ask ye to grow wiser or better or older."

Uncertain and confused, Ena heard the echo of Jenny's voice. *'Tis natural, this change. 'Tis part of growin' older, of becomin' a woman*. She looked at Ailsa. "Do ye want me to grow older? You've told me often and often to treasure my childhood, to hold on to it as long as I can. What if I can no' hold on anymore? What if 'tis too late?"

So. The girl had found the words at last. Ailsa could still hear Jenny's voice. *A few days past, Ena began her monthly flow and was distraught. She didn't want to distress ye, so she kept her own counsel.* Ailsa had replied, *Ye must be wrong. She would've told me. I would've seen. I would've known.*

Now she wondered as a voice whispered, *Ye did see. Ye did know.*

She remembered vividly the moment Ena had returned that day. The girl had been wearing a damp rumpled dress, which was not unusual. She came home more often in a filthy, torn gown than a fresh one. But wrinkled and disheveled as she'd been, her dress had been clean. That was most strange. At dinner, Ena'd fidgeted, looking ill and wan and uncomfortable. Afterward she'd rushed suddenly from the cottage and reappeared with her arms crossed over her stomach and a headache.

Those symptoms in a girl nearly thirteen very likely meant only one thing. Ailsa would have had to be blind and deaf not to have guessed. She *had* guessed, but had ignored what she saw and heard and felt. She'd not pressed her daughter, had asked no questions. Instead, she'd taken them back to when Ena'd been a child and had sat at her mother's feet, head resting on her knee while Ailsa ran her fingers through the girl's thick auburn hair.

Ena had not fought it; she, too, had wanted to go back, to forget new feelings and discomforts she could not understand, to retreat to the safe, the warm, the familiar. Ailsa'd seen and recognized the signs, but she didn't want to know her child had become a woman, so she'd denied the truth and offered comfort and forgetfulness instead. She and Ena had joined in a conspiracy. Ailsa should have forced the issue, should have given her daughter every chance to unburden herself, to confess her confusion and doubt and pain. Instead, they'd both been children, clinging to something that had vanished.

"Mayhap you're right. Mayhap a selfish part of me wanted ye to remain a child, bringin' warmth and a sense of safety with your innocent smile. But I was wrong. Ye can hold on through memory, through a touch or a look now and then, but with your heart and your body ye must let go, grow up, live your own life, no' in the shadow of mine. If ye don't do that, you'll miss so much."

Unable to stop the words that tumbled out, Ena told her mother what she'd already told Jenny. "I don't want to become a woman. It hurts too much, 'tis too hard and too sad."

"What makes ye think that?"

"Ye told me. In your journal."

Ailsa wanted to collapse inward, to avoid the knowledge of how much she'd shaped her daughter's insecurities and fears when she'd wanted only to save the girl from them. "Och, Ena, mo-run, I also told ye of the joy, the tenderness, the fulfillment of lovin' a man, of bein' a wife, a mother, a friend. Did ye no' hear those things as well?"

The girl braided her fingers together and stared down at the shadow of a pattern in the darkness. "Mayhap 'tis harder to have faith in those things. They're bonny, aye, but fly away as quick as butterflies."

"Ye must have faith, my heart. Ye need no' see a thing for it to be true. Ye need no' touch it or hold it in your hands to feel 'tis near."

The girl shook her head. "Sometimes I need to hold things in my hands. 'Tis the only way I know for certain that they're real." She took a deep breath and plunged ahead. "Now that it's happened, does it mean I must be as strong as ye and Gran, that I should no' need ye anymore?"

Ailsa wanted more than anything to make up for her mistakes, to heal the wounds and tears her daughter had concealed. "Och, Ena!" Taking the girl in her arms, she murmured, "They say your bleedin' makes ye a woman, but 'tis no' to say you're all at once fully grown, feelin' and understandin' all a woman feels and understands. 'Tis only the first step on a long journey that takes years to travel."

She held tightly, cupping the girl's head against her breast. "I told Alanna when Connor was ill that it doesn't matter how old ye are, or how strong or how wise. There's a bond between mothers and daughters that lasts forever. I tell ye as I told her, 'twould break my heart if ye needed me no more. We grow up together, all of us, every day to the end of our lives, dependin' on one another, linked to one another, carin' for one another. 'Tis the woven tissue of our blood, our heritage and our promise. Invisible it may be, but 'tis stronger than time or age or distance. If ye believe in nothing else, believe in this. This and the love I bear ye, always."

Ena felt her mother's heartbeat, strong and steady in the dark. She wanted to have faith, to abandon doubt and lose herself in the honesty and passion of Ailsa's declaration. Her mother did not lie; she could feel the truth in the hypnotic rhythm of their pulses, indistinguishable one from the other.

Suddenly she was so drained and weary that her limbs were leaden and she could not lift them. All she could do was hold on and accept. "I believe," she whispered, cheeks wet with tears.

When Ena fell limp and exhausted against her, Ailsa made a great effort and lifted the girl in her arms. She carried her cautiously back to the croft where the fire burned low and Mairi slept, smiling benignly.

Ailsa helped her daughter out of her gown and shift and into her nightrail, drew back the covers and slid her into bed. Then, sensing Ena's reluctance to be left alone, she sat on the boxbed with the girl's head in her lap and began to sing quietly.

> "Deep peace, a soft white dove to ye;
> Deep peace a quiet rain to ye;
> Deep peace, light of the moon to ye.
> Deep peace I breathe into ye,
>   to bring ye rest."

When Ena began to breathe deeply, regularly, Ailsa knelt to brush the hair out of her face, drawing her fingers across the girl's forehead in a soft caress. "Believe, my beloved. Believe in me and the goodness of the gods who cradle your head. Goodnight, my child, my Ena."

The clouds outside the croft shifted and the cool white goddess appeared above the glen, lighting it with a silver radiance. Ena felt the glow on her face, her eyelids as surely as she felt disquiet approaching silently, like a weightless falling shadow.

Despite her mother's blessing, as the moon sank behind a wall of trees and clouds covered the cool white light, Ena fell slowly into the darkness of a peculiar dream.

Epilogue

Glasgow, Scotland, 1997

NOT FOR THE FIRST TIME, RORY DEY WAS AWAKENED BY THE emptiness of the bed beside him. While his eyes became accustomed to the darkness, he peered at the rocking chair across the room, where he usually found Eva when she could not rest. It had happened for the last three nights, but that did not make it any easier.

His lover was seated, legs curled beneath her, wearing a wrinkled white nightgown, a shawl draped about her shoulders, her chestnut hair falling unkempt around her shoulders. The pale oval of her face was dominated by gray eyes fixed in an unwavering stare that watched but did not see him.

Rory wanted to shout with frustration and dread. Eva shivered and he drew the duvet tight around his shoulders, as if by warming himself he could warm her.

"It's the nightmare again, isn't it?"

Her reply was a barely perceptible nod. "But just now, I was thinking of the sea."

He restrained the urge to go to her, to lift her in his arms and hold her close enough to feel her breath on his cheek. He wanted to see for himself that she was the woman he loved, not an apparition. But he'd tried it before and knew she would go rigid, like a stranger. "The sea around the island where you grew up?"

That was odd. But when she woke like this in the middle of the night, nothing was as it should be. It had first happened the night he'd asked her to marry him, when he'd awakened to find her side of the bed empty and Eva staring through him, her face frozen and blank. Later, she had told him a little about the nightmare, just enough to stop his questions. But he understood only that she was unhappy, restless, searching for a part of herself she could not find.

"Aye, the sea. My refuge," Eva said. "I was thinking of the cliffs of tortured stone, of the puffins and kittiwakes and the waves that were so beautiful and compelling, so violent." She spoke softly, remembering. "But sometimes it was calm, the sea around Eilean Eadar. Sometimes the waves did not batter the cliffs and the ocean lost its power and beauty."

As you do when you dream, Rory thought. He could not bear to see her like this. She could not concentrate, and he ached at the distant look in her eyes. She had left him again to follow her ancestors through the trials and tribulations of their past. Why? What was she looking for? He was overwhelmed by a sense of defeat, afraid he was going to lose her somehow.

On nights like these, she held Ailsa Rose's journal, clutching an aged cashmere shawl around her, finding comfort in its delicate webbed pattern and gossamer weight. "Why don't ye put the book down, leave the shawl and come back to bed?" he asked for perhaps the fifth time, hoping if she simply turned away, she might free herself from the dream that took her back in time, instead of forward. He knew that even before the nightmares, she'd been melancholy and uncertain what she wanted or who she was, but now she seemed lost.

"I can't!" Eva cried, holding tighter the worn book and

shawl that had come from the ebony Chinese chest. "Not till I understand what it means—the dreams and the sorrow."

He'd known what she'd say, but he had to try, just as he'd tried at first to tease her out of her moodiness, to coax her to smile again, perhaps even to laugh. Nothing worked. She'd gripped the papers close and stared at him in fear, as if he were trying to peel away her skin.

Still, now and then he wanted to force her awake, to rip the journal from her hands and the dreams from her mind, until there was only the present, where he, Rory Dey, was waiting. She was stubborn, his Eva, and she insisted on digging into those long-forgotten lives, which had begun to overshadow her own.

"I've told ye and told ye, I have no choice, Rory. I have to do this."

"Why?" Another question he'd asked more than once.

"I don't know. I just know I have to go on." Her eyes were wet with tears. "I know it isn't easy for ye to sit by and watch, but there's nothing ye can do. Honestly."

"If ye won't marry me, move in with me," he said, surprising himself as well as Eva. He had vowed not to press her, not to ask again until she was ready. "I need ye."

Eva shook her head. "It's no' that at all, Rory Dey. Ye think I need ye. Ye think ye can take care of me and hold me and make the nightmares go." She paused, swallowed dryly. "But ye can't. I only wish ye could." She wanted more than anything to say yes, to accept the comfort and refuge he offered, but it would not be fair. She would be coming to him out of desperation, not out of love. "I have to work this through on my own. I don't know how; I just know I have to do it." She leaned forward.

"But ye have to know that nothing—not a dream or a chest full of papers or a puzzle I can't solve—can change the fact that I love ye. With all my heart I love ye. I want ye and only ye. Always."

She did not tell him that tonight the dream had drained

her as it never had before. There had been a little girl with auburn hair and silver-green eyes who stood in a copse. Her feet had begun to sink into the mossy earth, deeper and deeper, like the roots of a tree. She could not move; the weight of the soil was too heavy, and ferns and moss crept up her legs to her hips and chest. The river left its banks and moved up her arms and across her shoulders like a shawl of liquid bronze light that took up her hair in its rhythmic flow, until the strands became one with the reeds and long waving grasses.

Eva had awakened feeling that if it could, the earth would claim her, like a lover who had pined for her breath and her touch.

Once that girl had been drawn beneath the wild green earth, had floated within the golden water, she would never return. Eva didn't understand why, but the knowledge chilled her. Her grandmother, her great-grandmother had been wise, had chosen their own paths, shaped their own legacies. But Eva didn't think she had their strength or determination. She didn't know what she wanted or where to turn.

"Then marry me," Rory insisted, jolting her back to the present.

Her smile was fleeting. "I want to. I *will*. Just not now, not yet." She yearned for the constant, unchanging warmth and tenderness of his arms more than he could possibly guess. But she needed to go there unburdened by insecurity or doubt.

Rory could not understand, yet he kept trying. Trying so hard and patiently to get through, to draw her back into his world—*their* world, full of light and music. Tears clung to her lashes but did not fall. She tried but could not touch him, could not reach him, nor he her. "I love ye," she said. "So much."

Rory buried his face in his hands to hide his anger and disappointment. "Then be with me."

Eva glanced at the aged book in her lap; she knew she would return to it once Rory fell asleep. She could not stop herself. She kept going back to the chest, submerging herself in faded feelings and words, looking for an answer of her own. "Who am I?" she asked those women, long dead. "When will I find peace? And how?" The answers eluded her. She'd not yet come close to the confidence she sought.

"Come back to me. Come now," Rory demanded.

Eva wanted to throw herself into his arms and forget everything but him. But no matter how hard she tried, she could not break free of the threads that tied her to the past. She cried out to him, but ghostlike, the words made no sound in the midnight air. She was bound up in silence. Bound as the girl in the dream had been bound, and afraid of going under. She did not know how to cut the fine, sturdy strands that both frightened and enthralled her. She only knew it was too soon.

but glanced at the aged book in her lap, she knew she would return to it once Rory fell asleep. She could not stop herself. She kept going back to the chest, submerging herself in faded feelings and words, looking for an answer of her own. "Who am I?" she asked those women, long dead. "When will I find peace? And how?" The answers eluded her. She'd not yet come close to the confidence she sought.

"Come back to me, Cora, now," Rory demanded.

Eva wanted to throw herself into his arms and forget everything but him, but no matter how hard she tried, she could not break free of the thread that tied her to the past. She cried out to him, but ghostlike, the words made no sound in the midnight air. She was bound up in silence, bound as the girl in the dream had been bound, and afraid of going under. She did not know how to cut the fine sturdy strands that both frightened and enthralled her. She only knew it was too soon.

Book Four

❦

Just traveling through
on a flying machine.
There's a million stars
in this kaleidoscopic dream.
Chasing moons and losing all direction,
Somewhere there lies the moon.

Delhi, India, 1881

AN OMINOUS SILENCE LAY UPON THE NIGHT LIKE A MOON-
lit shroud swallowing the darkness. The air was unusually
hushed and still—no rain, no wind, no swirling clouds
of sand and rocks that came so frequently in India.
Genevra Kendall had thought the absence of sound and
motion would soothe her, but the intense silence, heavy
with heat, was too deep. Every little noise was amplified,
startling. She froze when she heard a muffled human voice
and saw a dark figure crossing her porch, his stretched and
eerie shadow thrown onto the lowered blinds. For an
instant he stood perfectly still—just . . . waiting. His feet
scuffed the wood in a ragged pattern that matched her
breathing.

She'd thought, foolishly, that she was safe inside her
new home. Her husband had been gone only a few hours;
surely no one would dare disturb her. But someone had—
that shadow figure moving furtively outside. She shivered,
hands fisted on the arms of her chair. She hadn't guessed
she'd feel so exposed and helpless without Alex Kendall to
protect her.

It didn't help that she hadn't slept all night. Any sound

or smell roused her—the scent of climbing jasmine crept beneath the blinds, sweet and heavy, making her sneeze. The occasional whisper of plane leaves rubbing against one another made her burrow further into her rocking chair. She'd eaten a single mango, then bathed to remove the sticky juice, hoping the warm water would relax her. But still her thoughts were half-formed and hazy. It was easier that way.

Yet she remembered with complete clarity kissing her husband good-bye and watching him go, followed by the staccato sound of marching feet. He'd led his regiment away, riding in front, helmet in hand, moonlight gilding his golden hair. He was heading somewhere into the crackling heart of the land of Hind. The army did not allow him to tell her where; she had long since stopped asking. All she knew was that he'd be gone for several months.

Afterward, his twenty-one-year-old wife had perched uncomfortably in the old rocker in the parlor, wearing a white gauzy nightgown, pale blond hair unbound, and tried to fight off the taut stillness that was her only companion.

Abruptly, the figure crouched. Genevra watched, holding her breath, mesmerized by the sound of her beating heart. She would not have been so frightened if she hadn't been so alone. Her husband had paid a native girl, Pahari, to become his wife's servant and companion, but she had run away at the distant sound of *tabla* drums in the dark. Genevra had neither watched her go nor regretted her absence. The girl was a stranger, and silent at that.

Slowly, Genevra rose, back straight, hands clasped to conceal their trembling. She could not hide in this room forever. She had to know. Throwing a thin wrapper over her gown, she crept to the door and whisked it open before the figure could flee. "What do you want?" she said in English, spreading her arms wide. She was slender and looked fragile, but even in fear her voice was steady. When she saw the pajamalike whiteness of the man's shirt and pants, the shape of his small round hat, she repeated herself in Hindi.

The man rose, waving his arms to keep her away as she descended upon him. "The *bhootams* are here. The evil spirits will consume me!" His black hair stood up as if he had pulled it by the ends, and his white teeth gleamed in his nut brown face.

Freezing in astonishment, Genevra peered through the gloom. "Hazari? Why are you here, wearing a path in my fine new porch and frightening me speechless?"

"*Me*? Frighten *you*? I am certain my heart stopped at the sight of your pale hair and skin and muslin wings reaching for me." He looked away. "Or perhaps it had already stopped and you have frightened it into beating again."

Genevra sighed in relief as her fear dissipated. When she was a child, Hazari had worked for her family as a *mali*—a handyman and gardener—and they had become friends, to the absolute horror of the British. Later, the *mali* had become the right-hand man of Genevra's friend and surrogate mother, Phoebe Quartermaine. He did not wish to leave her employ, nor did she wish him to go. They suited one another.

"Do not listen to my foolishness," Hazari blurted out, bringing her sharply back to the present. "Forgive me if I distressed you, Genniji. But I heard you were alone, and that is not proper or safe, so I came to protect you. To make you easy in your mind."

Genevra was still surprised, after twenty-one years in India, at how news seemed to spread through the air, fly on the wind among the natives. But more than that, she was grateful for Hazari's concern. She did need him, especially tonight. Then she noticed the *mali*'s expression, how gray his skin was in the unforgiving light. "You don't look very easy in your own," she murmured. The round red hat in his hands trembled and he had unraveled a piece of his matching sash. "Besides, you shouldn't be here when Phoebe's waiting for you."

Hazari looked up mournfully, no hint of laughter in his black eyes. "The *memsahib* is not waiting. I made the mistake of speaking from my soul and for too long." He was crestfallen. "You know I always talk too much. It was written on my forehead at birth, and I cannot change it."

He sighed deeply with a melodramatic wave of his hands. "And now, because of my mistake, she has chosen. So here I am. I could not think where else to go." He glanced at the small front garden, barely cleared of weeds, with small jasmine vines and poppy stems beginning to appear, along with hints of iris and narcissus and the bare stalks of bougainvillea. He waved his hand to indicate the pitiful garden, the house, which badly needed a coat of paint and several boards nailed back where they belonged. "Do I not have eyes in my head? I see how much you need me."

She clasped her hands to keep from hugging him, certain that he needed her this time. He looked so young and helpless, like a child. Besides, when he'd spoken of Phoebe, he'd used the formal *memsahib*. Normally, he called her *Tamarsha Begum*, or when he felt particularly bold, *Tama*.

Genevra felt a chill of apprehension. Hazari of the Burning Heart she used to call him, because he was so passionate in all he said and did. Gently, she put her hand on the *mali's* arm. "If she's not waiting, and that I don't believe for a moment, she'll nevertheless be worried. You should go back."

He straightened his back and stood as tall as he could. "I could not leave you alone, even if she called and called for me. She would not blame me for that. She would have sent me on her own if she'd known Pahari fled."

No matter what had compelled him to come here, he meant what he said. He had known Genevra since she was a young girl living with her aunt and uncle in the nearby British cantonment. His loyalty and affection had always belonged to Genevra; she was curious about the land of Hind, not just marking time, like her countrymen. She wanted to know all she could about India, its customs and rituals, foods and fabrics and architecture. She was also kind and affectionate; most of the *feringhi* were not. She refused to think herself better than the natives, only different. The English were appalled by her friends and her interests, the subjects she chose to sketch, using her intuitive skill with charcoal and paintbrush. Because they were afraid, because she was stronger than they, even in her fragility, all who had loved her had eventually left her. Each time it had broken her heart.

As his was broken now. He pinched the rim of his round hat so she could not see his face. "If you will let me, I have come to stay the night. I will cause you no trouble. I will sleep in the back garden beneath the cypress trees."

Shocked by the bleakness in his eyes, she knew she could not deny him. That would be cruel. "Certainly you may stay. I'd feel safer knowing you're here."

Before she could say more, he ducked his head in acknowledgment and slipped past her to the path that curved around the house to the back, where the stone walls, enclosing several rooms, also surrounded the neglected garden of living waters—the reason she'd fallen in love with this house. But she feared Hazari would not be impressed.

He had been muttering to himself in Hindi as they turned the corner, but when he entered the desolate garden, he stopped, speechless. The gates hung open; dust lay in drifts about the courtyard and the marble walls echoed with an eerie, empty sound. The lizards and scorpions, centipedes and cockroaches had become brave. They were everywhere—on the ground, the stone, the tile, the walls. Snakes slithered in the shadows, escaping the rain and heat. In the moonlight, he could see the sun had burned the fallen leaves and juice of the rotted fruit into the pavement. The only places there were growing things were where they did not belong; creepers and weeds without scent or color climbed up dead fountains, filled the empty basin with leaves that had long ago clogged the drains and stopped the life-giving water from breaking through.

The trees had lost much of their plumage, which had fallen into the once clear pools, obscuring—along with sand and dirt and broken twigs—the vibrant turquoise of the long-dry tiles. The *baradari* was dull gray, the furniture topsy-turvy, the bright cushions lying on the filthy ground.

Genevra and Hazari stood side by side, contemplating the past glory and fresh possibilities of the garden around them. This time, each knew what the other was thinking. She pointed out the room along the side wall where he could sleep, and quietly turned, leaving him silent and appalled. In his mind, he was already planning how to make this forsaken paradise new again. He frowned deeply, concentration absolute.

Genevra was silent, avoiding rocks and stumps, so she'd not awake him from his trance. Better he should mourn for a garden that could be renewed, than a relationship she feared was crumbling before his eyes. She would have to talk to Phoebe, perhaps at first light, though she dreaded what she might hear.

The night shadows flitted about, settled on her shoulders, becoming premonitions of disturbances to come.

Hazari and Genevra stood rigid when they heard the sound of a coach approaching the house. They recognized the sound. In an instant, the *mali* faded into the shadows, Genevra closed her eyes and whispered a Hindu prayer, then turned toward the house to greet her guest.

Phoebe Quartermaine swept into the house like a flurry of warm wind. "He came here, didn't he? He told you!" Her voice was panicked, not angry.

"He told me he'd said too much and you wanted him to go. He did not choose to tell me what he'd said that's obviously upset you both so much." Genevra closed the door quietly. Her fear had disappeared in concern for her friends.

She thought she could guess what had happened, and she didn't want to know. Her gown whispering about her, she turned, face blank, to look at Phoebe.

The woman had made India her home for thirty years, following native customs more often than she did British. That was one of the reasons she loved it here. That, as well as the brilliant, abundant flowers and the turbulence of the seasons. As usual, her abundant red hair streaked with gray fell in wild curls down her back, and she wore a bright gold silk sari over a light muslin skirt. She wore jeweled leather slippers on her feet.

Genevra found she could not catch her breath when Phoebe glanced wildly about as if Hazari would spring at her from the darkness. The girl often saw people as vivid colors; Phoebe had always been bright and tranquil—blues and soft greens and a splash of red passion. Today she was deep purple like the clouds gathering for the monsoon. So deep it was like mourning.

Phoebe had always looked much younger than she was. Genevra had actually forgotten her true age until this moment. Tonight she looked all of her fifty years, perhaps more. "Oh, Genny!" she cried, shattering the tense silence as she buried her face in her hands. "It's so desperately tragic. Hazari has—" She broke off, tried to pull herself together.

"He told me his heart burns only for me, and I believed him." She looked up bleakly, her grief palpable. "I know now I have no choice but to leave India."

Genevra gaped at her, stunned. "But why? Hazari has felt this way for years, nor did he hide his feelings from you. Why, now, must you leave?"

"It's too dangerous to stay. They aren't tolerant of that which is out of the ordinary, forbidden. A young native *mali* linked with a titled Englishwoman? Neither side could ignore that relationship or condone it. But either Hazari can't see all that—"

"Or he knows and doesn't care," Genevra interrupted.

Her pulse had begun to race, partly in sympathy for the abandoned Hazari and partly for herself. What would she do if Phoebe left her?

"It doesn't matter. You know I'm right. You of all people. They're cruel and want to destroy anything that threatens them, especially if it's delicate and beautiful." Years ago, they had tried to destroy Genevra, and in doing so, had cruelly used a native girl like a pawn. Narain, once Genevra's closest friend.

Genevra cleared her throat, swallowing the bitterness of the memory. "That was very different." She was determined Phoebe should answer the significant question she'd been avoiding. "Because Hazari loves you, you must leave your home?"

Phoebe leaned into the shadows, blurring her expression. "No, my Genny." Green eyes full of sorrow, her body shaking with it, she said softly, "I must go because I love Hazari. Too much." She spoke with more passion than she intended, revealing a depth of feeling that surprised Genevra.

Haltingly, Phoebe continued. "He makes me young again. It's like paradise in my garden of waters, alone with Hazari's magic hands and burning heart. I don't give a fig for ugly words and cruel names, but all of them—British, Hindu, Muslim, Sikh, Brahmin, merchant, warrior and laborer would disapprove. If we gave in to our feelings, we'd find ourselves outcasts. They'd make us suffer for our selfish choice. I'm right, you know, though you don't want to admit it. Far better Hazari and I preserve our passion pure in our memories than let the others soil it with their fear."

The determination in her friend's voice was all too convincing. The vision of life without Phoebe struck her hard, and she could not speak.

Phoebe rose, unable to stay still, and began to wander about. "I told you a long time ago that, much as I regret it, underneath it all, I'm English to the bone. So I'll not be back." She stopped and turned.

"Forgive me for leaving you, like so many others. But you see, unlike them I know what I'm losing. I take nothing with me from this place but my memories of you and the monkey Hazari gave me. His first gift, which I can't leave behind."

She dug through the large bag over her shoulder, bringing out a mass of finespun threads. "I want to give you my cream cashmere shawl. You've often admired it, and I'd like to know you carry my memory with you whenever you wear it. I don't like to be forgotten."

"You know I won't forget. You've been so much to me— friend, confidante, advisor." She looked away. "It hurts too much."

Kneeling beside her, Phoebe clasped Genevra's hands tightly. "Just remember *asparaji*, little fairy, that forgiveness is a lovely gift to give and to accept, a great weight off your own shoulders, a greater off your heart."

The girl's eyes were filmed in tears. She blinked them back. "I'm losing you forever, then."

Phoebe recoiled at the raw grief in the simple statement. "Perhaps not forever." Her gaze wandered, and Genevra realized it had done so more than once—hungry and a little desperate. Perhaps, though she'd claimed she did not wish to see Hazari, she had, after all, hoped to catch a last glimpse of him. Unaware of her own actions, Phoebe held out her hands toward the garden, helpless with longing, overwhelmed by the pain of sending him away.

"When will you go?"

"In a few days, perhaps weeks. But I'm very bad at farewells. Please don't come to the station. It would be too hard to bear."

Before Genevra could open her mouth, Phoebe Quartermaine swept through the house, her scent lingering on the still air behind her, and disappeared.

Rushing to the door to watch the carriage rumble away, Genevra realized Hazari had crept up behind her to grip the doorsill with strained white knuckles.

"Will you forgive her for abandoning you? Do you have the kindness and courage to do such a thing?"

Genevra whirled toward him. "Will you?"

He shook his head firmly. "She is behaving like a coward, which she is not, toward you and toward me. She is hurting you when you need healing. Running from bhootams. She is turning away from the sunlight. I cannot forgive her for so much."

"She's doing it for you, Hazari, leaving what she most loves in order to protect you."

"I did not ask for her protection. I am strong enough to defend myself. She speaks of me like a naive child. I am a man, Genniji. A proud man."

Genevra felt his sorrow more deeply than she'd ever felt his laughter. "I know." Phoebe had doubted his strength and resolve and left him behind. Now he had no one but himself to believe in. She understood the feeling far too well.

The mali pointed to the moon hanging low in the predawn sky. "As the Wise Ones say, 'There is a black spot even in the moon.' How then can an ordinary man remain enlightened, when the shadow might fall on him at any time?"

"I can only answer as the Wise Ones would have. 'The sun denies his light to none.' Not to you and not to me. We must try to remember that, always."

1

HIDDEN IN THE FOLDS OF HER BLUE SARI, PULSE QUICKENING with exhilaration, Genevra Kendall hurried through the hushed Indian dawn. Today she need not hide her yearning for the cool, tranquilizing relief of the river Jumna; it showed on her freckled, sunburnt face and in her sparkling blue eyes flecked with gray.

Surya, the Sun God, had barely risen, the morning barely left the night behind, yet already there was no hidden corner he did not seek out, revealing the secrets within through his unforgiving light. The landscape was engulfed by his far-reaching power—the trees and bushes crowding the sacred river, the vast, sandy plains, the goats and pariah dogs searching for shade, and her own slight figure. The image was frozen, for an instant, by the quick, impatient heat of the sun.

Genevra glanced about warily to make certain she was alone. She knew if her husband were at home, she would not be running through the dawn at all. Some corporal or foot soldier, or one of his countrymen working for The Company, might catch a glimpse of her and make certain Alex Kendall knew how his young wife was behaving. She did not want to embarrass him. "The English are sleeping," she told herself firmly, shaking her head at her own foolishness. "And even if they're awake, they'll be safe inside the compound, protected by high clay walls and the presence of the army." Certainly none would be headed for the river where the Hindus flocked each morning.

Genevra shivered at an unexpected chill. She was being watched, she was certain. She'd known the feeling for too many years to mistake it. Ducking her head into the hood of her sari, she tried to shrink and disappear.

The ache of Alex's and Phoebe's absence had diminished a little in the last few weeks as she spent her energy working on the house. She felt surprisingly light today, as if a burden had been taken from her shoulders. She raised her head toward the glare of the sun, smiling. She was alone in her new home, beyond the view of the cantonment, alone and free to do as she liked, not as she should. She'd brought along her sketchpad and charcoal, though she hadn't painted in a long time. "You never know when inspiration might strike. Better to be prepared," she murmured.

When she reached the Jumna, she crept around a cluster of *aswatta* trees, beneath the twisted branches of tamarind into a depression in the earth that had made a wide pool in the river. She glanced around once more, but there was no one. Only the chattering mynahs and crows and the hushed flow of the water. The Hindus did not come to this particular pool, though they went up and down the river every morning to bathe and purify themselves among the Brahmin—the highest caste, the Twiceborn. This spot was too near the hated *feringhi*.

Without hesitation Genevra removed her sari, lay it on a flat rock and waded into the water. Though it was not quite cool, it nevertheless sent ripples of pleasure through her as it washed over her shoulders, made ever-widening circles at her waist, caught hold of her pale blond hair. The loosely woven braid floated sensuously; she moved her head from side to side, releasing the strands until they spread around her like a shawl. Genevra swayed, took her tiny container of soap and began to cleanse herself. When her skin tingled from the sand she'd used to clear the soap away, she looked up at the patterns of shadow and light. Raising her arms, caught up in the cadence of the water, she began to spin, almost, but not quite, dancing.

"Are you dancing to your freedom or your loss?" A voice spoke softly from the bank, unexpectedly splintering the fragile stillness. "Perhaps you are pretending you are not bereft, but it is only a game."

The girl was startled, but not for long. She heard the voice often when she came to the river. Pausing in her rhythmic movements, she glanced toward the hollow at the base of an ancient plane tree. As she'd guessed, her friend Munia crouched among the gnarled roots, her image blurred by the blue whorls of mist above the water. As always, she'd seemed to materialize from air and sand and shadow.

The aging wise woman in her simple burlap gown had befriended Genevra soon after she and Alex moved into the isolated house nearby. She simply appeared one day on the banks of the Jumna. Noticing Genevra's nervousness in being there, she had said, "Do not worry, *aspara*, the Hindus do not like this place, and the English are afraid they might. So both stay away."

Genevra had laughed with relief and appreciation. The friendship had grown only here, beside the water, for Munia did not walk the dusty roads and alleyways or the path to the house Alex had bought for his wife four months ago.

"To raise our children in," he had said with undisguised anticipation. He'd not seen Genevra wince and look away. More than anything, she wanted to have a family with her husband, but in the two years they'd been married, she'd not yet conceived. She'd begun to wonder if she were barren. She could not guess what Alex thought; he preferred not to speak of it, but instead, to depend on optimism and faith. But how could his faith give her a child when he was hidden somewhere in the boundless desert?

She pushed the thought away as she met Munia's dark eyes. Genevra was always grateful for her company and her wisdom. The old woman must have sensed it; inevitably, she was there when the girl was restless or troubled. It was uncanny.

"I asked if you were dancing to your freedom or the loss of your husband and friend?"

A light chill touched the back of Genevra's neck. Munia often spoke as if she could look into the girl's mind. She recognized, in that instant, that she'd forced herself into numbness to survive the past weeks, but the wise woman had known at once.

Munia shook her head. "You are not alone, Genniji. You never have been."

The girl blinked in surprise. Perhaps the old woman did carry magic in her worn leather bag. "What do you mean?"

Smiling her mysterious, thin-lipped smile, the old woman put her arms around her knees and lifted her face to the sky. "Have you not learned yet that I know you well? Your body speaks to me of a sleepless night, your face, under the relief the water has given you, speaks of an ache deep within. All I need do is look carefully, and ponder the reason for what I see. As the Wise Ones say; 'One can only dance when the drum beats.' What drumbeat entices you today?"

Genevra was perplexed.

"You need not answer. I can guess. And I must tell you not to despair, larla. Though you fear you are alone, it will not be for long. Many will come."

The girl ducked under the water, then sputtered, "I don't mind being alone. It's just that, sometimes it reminds me of . . ." She trailed off.

"Your parents," Munia finished her sentence. "It's true that because you were illegitimate, Emily Townsend thought it better to give you a new chance with her sister. As for Charles Kittridge, he did not know he was your father then. They abandoned you, yes. But that was many years ago."

Genevra remembered every minute of those long years. Her mother had died in a madhouse and she'd not heard from Charles Kittridge until he lay dying in the Scottish Highlands and had begged her to come to him. She'd almost refused.

Shuddering at what might have happened if she'd decided to stay in India, Genevra remembered the shock of first meeting her two half-sisters and Charles's wife, Mairi. Before long, the shock wore off, the three sisters became inseparable, and Mairi Rose gently and willingly became the only true mother Genevra had ever had. Lian—Charles's Chinese daughter—Ailsa, the Scottish daughter, Mairi and Genevra wrote to one another often, could not have stopped if they wished to. They were bound through their dreams and the grief they'd shared over Charles Kittridge's death. She thought of the others' strength, of all they had survived, and felt small in her disappointment and loneliness. But what had Mairi told her? *You've strength of your own, our Genny. Ye have to believe that.* She shook her head firmly.

"Ah, I see you doubt me, or perhaps yourself?" Munia interrupted her thoughts. "You are brave, Genniji, unfaltering and determined. Remember that. It is more than important; it is the path to your happiness." She smoothed her only adornment, the silver scarf that covered her hair. It contrasted sharply with her frayed gown.

"I've begun to think contentment is enough," Genevra said.

"Enough for *you*. At least today. But you have wounds not yet healed and demons not yet faced. To be truly happy, you must trust your instincts absolutely, instead of the counsel of others. Then you will discover—" Munia broke off, sniffing the rising wind.

Genevra sat up abruptly, splashing water everywhere. "What is it?"

Munia crooned a few words under her breath. "I think the world is burning. Go."

Genevra was disturbed by the unusual distress in the woman's face, much wrinkled, like the pattern of rare dew on grass that resembled a spider's web. Then she smelled the acrid odor. She glanced down at her simple chemise and drawers, made specially to wear under her sari. "How? I'm soaked to the skin."

"You are better off that way, safer. Listen."

"Fire!"

The hoarse cry came from the far side of the trees. Genevra leapt to her feet, groping for her wrinkled silk sari. She could see a thin black line of smoke billowing into the sky. There were some adobe buildings in that direction, some fields of weeds and little else. Except for her house.

She wrapped her sari carelessly, then turned to bid Munia good-bye. But the old woman was gone.

"Go." Her voice echoed among the leaves of the plane trees. "Do not wait a moment more. Run."

Genevra left her sketchpad and splashed across the pond, prodded, not only by Munia's insistence, but also by the desperation in the second cry of "Fire!"

2

GENEVRA HURRIED TOWARD THE BITTER SMELL OF SMOKE, and discovered that a few English had left the cantonment to walk the wooden sidewalk, the men with their bowlers, the women with their frilly parasols and tiny, useless hats.

As one, the group in front of her paused when she reached them.

"Been bathing in the river?" Martha Worthy, the major general's wife, asked superciliously. "You do realize the natives go there daily to defile it." She looked down her nose at the young girl with wild, damp hair, uncombed and unbraided. "And what, may I ask, are you wearing?" The garments clung damply to Genevra's slender body, betraying her.

The woman looked triumphant, just as other British had looked at her with disdain, because she was illegitimate, and her mother had died in a madhouse. There were worse things, much more recent, but Genevra refused to think of them now. She knew these imperious men and women wanted to spark her anger, making her speak unwisely, but today she would not give them that pleasure. "It's a sari," she replied simply. "You might have noticed the servants wear them."

"My dear Martha," one woman whispered to another, "look at her clothes. Disgraceful. How she can even *think* of stepping into that filthy water is beyond me." The whisper was just loud enough for everyone to hear.

"Actually," Genevra said, tossing her unkempt hair over her shoulder to emphasize its just-washed dampness, "it's quite refreshing. Much nicer than a hip bath." She heard more shouts behind her, saw billowing smoke creep toward her. "Forgive me," she said with a stiff little curtsey. "I should love to stay and chat, but I believe my house might be on fire. I'm sure you understand." Then she was gone, like a shadow melding into the smoke.

The group stared after her, forgetting themselves enough to actually gape. They shifted uneasily. They could not help feeling that somehow she had bested them, which made them angrier than before. One thing they could not, would not bear, was having their dignity assaulted. "I wonder what Lieutenant Colonel Kendall would think if he knew what his wife was up to?" Martha mused aloud. "He'd be quite shocked, I shouldn't be surprised."

* * *

Genevra had already forgotten the group as she fought her way through the thickening smoke. A huge gust of wind cleared her vision for an instant. It was indeed her house that was burning, or rather, the field of weeds in the empty lot beside it.

Hazari stood at the edge of the flames, buckets in either hand, calling for help, for thick rugs and water, looking puzzled and distressed.

Genevra covered her face with a corner of silk, to hide the fear in her eyes and keep the smoke out of her mouth. This was her fault. She'd wanted to live away from the cantonment, away from British eyes and ears. But she did not wish to live among the natives either, and it wouldn't have been proper for Alex, an officer in Her Majesty's Royal Army.

Together they'd discovered this wonderful house with a front that resembled the simple bungalows of the cantonment, except for the marble pillars that held up the porch roof. It had been built by a man who had been as disenchanted with The Company as she, as eager to stay in India, and wise enough to know he could not blend in in Shajehanabad, which the British had renamed Delhi.

Inside, the rooms were bright, reminiscent of the Mogul palaces that had once made Shajehanabad a paradise of color and stone and marble and water. At the back, he'd built a garden of living waters, digging trenches to the underground wells nearby. Neither Alex nor Hazari had been able to find those wells, which were badly needed to bring the garden back to life.

She shook the last of the sand from her ears and forced herself to move. That garden—what was left of it—might well burn to the ground if the wind shifted, carrying the flames from the field to the house. Her heart raced and she tried to catch her breath. She loved this house. It was the first she'd ever owned. She could not bear to lose it so soon.

Natives had begun to appear from all directions, some

passing buckets of water hand to hand from the small well beside the house until they reached the line of flame. Some threw down rugs and blankets and stomped on them rigorously, moving them as each new spurt of fire was extinguished. Nevertheless, more of the field was now blazing, and Genevra did not see how they could stop the fire in time.

3

THE SAME GROUP THAT HAD ACCOSTED GENEVRA HAD gathered on the sidewalk, watching in fascination. No one stepped forward to offer assistance, though in the nearby cantonment there was a new fire truck, four new horses to haul it and a thick rubber hose to pump a stream of water. Genevra thought of that fire truck, as she knew they were doing, despite their blank expressions.

Then sibilant whispers began to slither from one to the other. Genevra caught a few words here and there as she made her way through the crowd.

". . . said she was seen here last night, watching . . ."

"Says she's a healer. More like a disgrace . . ."

". . . furtive, like a wild animal."

". . . several reports of her loitering near this house . . ."

"She must be afraid to get too close."

The gossip made Genevra uneasy; she glanced nervously around, but saw no one who should not be there. She turned her attention back to the fire. She wanted to run into the field to help, but she held her worn leather sandals in her hand, stood barefoot on the front walk in a sari coated in ash that flew alarmingly about her like wayward wings. More and more natives arrived to help Hazari form an efficient line of workers from the house to the far end of the field.

The English stood watching, silent and censorious. Certainly they would not work side by side with Hindus, even had they been inclined to help, which most weren't. Genevra could not help herself. She stared at them beseechingly; she knew they saw her, yet closed their eyes to her plea. She should have known they would.

Staring down at her flimsy garments, she clenched her fists in determination and ran toward the front walkway. A native stopped her, shaking his head violently. "No! No! Memsahib must not go inside." He pointed upward to the churning wind and billowing smoke. "If the wind changes only a little, the fire will take the house. You must not be caught inside."

Genevra looked into the flames leaping across the field and her heart sank. "You're right. Of course you are."

As she turned away despondently, a burning leaf landed on her sleeve, setting it ablaze. Before she could call out, Hazari was there with a thick rug. He wrapped her in it, smothering the flames before they could spread, then set her down promptly. She began to thank him, but he had disappeared.

Finally, when a corner of the field nearest the house flared up, Major General Worthy, whose wife, Martha, had been so malicious a few minutes past—reluctantly removed his coat, draped it on a frangipani bush and plunged into the fray. At the gasp of horror from his friends, he called, "She didn't start it, and no matter what she's done, she does not deserve to watch her home burned to ashes before her eyes." His conscience would not let him linger on the sidelines any longer. As a major general, he should take control. Especially because he knew that if Lieutenant Colonel Kendall were here, most of the men who stood idle would have long since begun to save that field.

His friends stared after him, speechless, but he didn't care. There was too much to do. Too many places to be at once. He lifted buckets of water and helped dig a trench until he thought he would drop. It was in the corner of the field that he stumbled on the wet, blackened earth, and his legs disappeared while he tried frantically to hold on. Three natives appeared from nowhere to pull him out, and while they determined he'd not been hurt, Hazari stared down into the hole. He leaned close and sniffed as far down as he dared. Then he leapt up and shouted, "Memsahib! Memsahib!"

He spoke formally because the British were present, though most had left when the smoke began to make them cough, and worse, to soil their clothes. Nevertheless, Genevra came running at the excitement in his voice.

"I have found it. One here and another there."

He pointed, but she couldn't see where. What she could see was the dark narrow tunnel of a deep underground well. Like him, she could smell the water, hear it running far beneath her feet.

It was a good thing the fire had been contained; the natives were also fascinated with the wells. "Your garden will live again!" Hazari called, as if that were more important than saving the house from burning to the ground. "The water is here and we can follow it to the other wells." The few natives that remained walked the field with him, listening and calculating where the streams had become blocked.

She could not take it all in. Too much to think about. Too difficult to hide the stark fear that overtook her. Choking, covered with ashes from head to toe, Genevra stumbled inside. She found she was trembling because the house had been saved. Only in that moment did she realize how much she loved it here, how comfortable she felt, as if she'd found her home at last. All it needed was children.

4

IT WAS SEVERAL MINUTES BEFORE SHE SAW THE MARKS SHE'D left on the arms of the chair she was sitting in, and realized it hadn't been there that morning. At the same time, a voice that had been calling her name attached itself to a face.

"I would not disturb Memsahib, but you are very tired? And perhaps hungry? And a little bit—gray?" She indicated Genevra's appearance. "It is my job to help you with these things."

Leaning so far forward she nearly fell, Genevra felt Ameera's arms reach out to steady her. "You work for Phoebe, not me. And where have all these things come from?" She'd finally noticed the furniture stacked everywhere. She sat up stiffly.

"Miss Phoebe left yesterday. She said you had not much to fill your rooms and that she could not take all this to England when she wishes to wander there. She also said Master Alex would want a girl here to serve you, and that the one he chose had run away." Perplexed by the changing expressions crossing Genevra's gray-streaked face, Ameera took a step back. "You do not wish to have me here? I will go at once. Only, Miss Phoebe said I was to insist."

Her face fell, and the disappointment in her eyes broke through Genevra's dubiousness. Phoebe had gone, so she'd left her things and her servant to replace her. The girl wanted to shout at the unfairness, but Ameera made her realize that would be extremely ungracious.

"Of course I want you here. Phoebe's right; I need help, but I haven't had time to look. It was generous of her to send me so much."

Ameera smiled, her white teeth glowing in her chestnut face. "You see, already I have tried to help."

She had begun to unpack the boxes piled against the wall, using the pump in the sink and fine-grained sand to wash the dishes, then placing them on the tables, low walls, ledges in the garden. "I thought the men might like tea and melon after their labors, but they have gone home. Still, I have food for you, Memsahib, and for Hazari."

Genevra blinked at the slender Hindu girl in astonishment. She had accomplished more in a single morning than Genevra had in three months—or was it afternoon now? Evening? She had no sense of how many hours she'd watched the men work, her heart pounding with dread. "I hope you have something for yourself? We have plenty of rice and chupattis and fruit."

Ameera nodded, then faded into a dim corner of the kitchen and waited. Many natives behaved so with foreigners. They stayed in the shadows and said little, only watched and listened, absorbing the nature of the white men while they waited to be called.

That's what broke Genevra's heart. Ameera and Phoebe had been together for years, and the Hindu had always been at ease in the monstrous Mogul palace. She'd treated Genevra the same as her mistress, but would not be foolish enough to presume her life would be the same here. "You may stay only if you are as you were before. We aren't strangers, you and I. I thought we were friends. I won't have you pretending things have changed between us. It would hurt my feelings deeply."

The servant came slowly into the light, and before either knew it was going to happen, they were holding each other and weeping over their lost friend.

Genevra was too weary and sad to wonder why the fire had started, or where.

That night, while she tried to sleep, she heard voices outside her window and went to investigate. Hazari and Ameera were crouched at the corner of the house nearest the field, and Hazari held a torch as close to the ground as he dared.

"It was set here," the *mali* whispered. "See the end of a charred rag?"

Ameera's eyes widened. "Do you mean—"

"It was no accident. They wanted to burn the house. But for once, Indra was our friend and the wind lifted the flames to the tall weeds instead." He paused. "It was just after dawn. They would have thought she was still in bed." He scratched his head, frowning. "We are lucky that whoever did this was not good at such things. I would not be surprised if they had never set a fire before, even in the fireplace. If the flame had not caught on the weeds, the fire would have gone out completely."

Genevra felt ill and bewildered. Did anyone dislike her so much? Though she wasn't sure why, she covered her mouth to suppress a small gasp, then slid away from the window when Hazari glanced up, his face oddly pale in the torchlight. She sensed they didn't want her to know this. Perhaps they were right. Now all she could do was wonder who and why, and if it were true that someone might be wishing her dead.

She heard shuffling; when she looked again, they'd gone. Head reeling, she found her bed and lay, eyes open, seeing nothing. She did not even pretend to sleep. The only brief respite came when she decided to confront Hazari in the morning. If he didn't want her to know, it was all the more critical that she find out, and soon.

5

As she usually did, Genevra headed toward the verandah to watch the vivid colors of the rising sun burn away. She was pleased by the sound of Ameera working in the kitchen; the house had been too quiet for too long. But when she opened the front door, she froze, her head fuzzy from lack of sleep, to stare at the tall thin native girl who was vigorously sweeping the front porch, trying to clear away some of the soot that lay like dark, thick snow beneath her bare feet.

"Ameera," her mistress called over her shoulder, "did Phoebe send anyone else yesterday?"

"No, Miss Genny. Only me."

The servant started forward, but Hazari arrived from the back of the house first, as if he had been listening close by. He saw the girl, her hem stained with soot, drop her head, but not soon enough. "Go inside, Genniji. I will see to this."

He who once had loved to laugh, had never sounded quite so angry, but that only sparked her curiosity. She'd not have slunk inside to hide in any event. That was not her way. She stepped out into a pile of ashes and regarded the stranger intently. Reluctantly, the girl raised her head. It was a moment before Genevra recognized her; her face was so gaunt, her hair tangled and filthy. "You aren't . . . it isn't . . . Narain?"

Hazari leapt up onto the porch, arms crossed. "Of course it is. She had nowhere else to go. She knew you were too soft-hearted to turn her away. Just remember how she betrayed you. Remember, 'He who affects to be our friend should, if he attempts to hurt us, be regarded as our enemy.'"

"Do you honestly think I'll ever forget? But that was before. I want to know why she's here today. Why are you so irate, Hazari? What do you know?"

With a great effort, Narain straightened and faced Genevra fully. "I do not think it right that he should answer for me. Whatever he knows, he cannot know all."

It was true, Genevra thought, Hazari had many secrets of late. Still, she trusted him and had no idea what to think of the girl who had once been like a sister to her. Letting go of the door frame, she stood without support and spoke to Narain for the first time in three years. "Tell me then."

Just now, Narain retained little of her regal bearing and none of her pride. "Thank you. I was afraid you would not listen. But in my heart, I hoped you would. I am not as I once was." Her hand trembled as she pointed to her torn, soiled gown, her filthy hair, her sunken cheeks. "I have come to you because I, too, have been betrayed. Only now that I have been humiliated as I once humiliated you, now that my heart has been broken, and my hope, do I truly understand how you felt three years ago." She paused to clear her throat and winced as if it hurt. Her lips were cracked and raw and her feet covered with sores.

"I ran away from—the one who hurt me—and she said the only thing was to come to you and try to convince you to forgive me."

Genevra could not help but be moved by Narain's appearance and her pain. She did not want to believe in her, but a part of her sensed she was, at least partially, telling the truth. Neither belief lessened the ache in her body, the confusion and uncertainty in her mind. She must be very careful. "A woman hurt you like this?"

"No!" Narain was confused. "It was not . . . there was another who advised me."

"Why are you sweeping my porch?"

Narain swallowed awkwardly. "I thought I could show you I can help you. I do not mind how small the task. Or how demeaning. In that way I can show you my sincerity. I want to take care of you, to make up for my neglect."

She dropped the broom and it clattered to the porch, barely making a sound. "It is also true that part of my reason for coming was to seek a quiet place where you might give me a chance to recover." She whirled on Hazari before he could comment. "I have lived alone before. I can do it again. But I did not realize how badly I had neglected my body. It would be difficult . . ."

"When did you last eat?" Ameera interrupted. "And water? Your lips are very dry and your voice hoarse." She didn't know what Narain had done; she only knew she needed help. She turned to Genevra. "Memsahib, I believe she is near to starving and her body is deprived of water. She is very weak."

"Not so weak that I cannot—" She took two steps forward, began to sway. Her face was tinged yellow, and her legs wobbled. She tripped

The three others ran to catch her, but Genevra got there first. Narain was too heavy to hold upright, so the two of them sank into the ashes. For an instant no one moved, and the mistress of the house did not touch Narain, who lay unconscious, her head in Genevra's lap.

Then, very quietly, she leaned down to whisper, "You broke my heart last time I let you near, made me an outcast, left me alone. You lied to hurt me, abandoned me. Yet here you are, worn and broken on my porch. And fool that I am, I caught you when you fell." Her eyes swam with tears, but she did not weep. "What am I to do with you?

"You can't speak but it doesn't matter. You're ill. No matter how I feel, I can't turn you away. You must have known that. Either I have no choice or I have no heart." She could not leave the girl here or put her out on the sidewalk to take her chances. That would have been a worse sin than Narain's.

Quietly, Genevra called out, "Hazari, Ameera, I need you."

6

IN SPITE OF HIS OBJECTIONS, HAZARI DID NOT HESITATE. If Genevra needed him, he would help, no matter how unwise he thought she was. Ameera was there instantly.

The three lifted Narain and took her inside, winding

their way awkwardly through the stacked furniture. They were silent when Genevra headed toward her bedroom, silent while they held the girl and Genevra removed pillows and sheets and coverlets from her bed to spread them on the floor, making a comfortable place for the patient to lie.

As soon as Narain was placed on the makeshift mattress, Hazari faded away, shaking his head in disapproval. He did not object again; he knew that note of determination in his mistress's voice.

The two women did not see him go; they were examining Narain. Gingerly, they removed her filthy gown, which was little more than fragments barely holding together. They had not realized how badly crusted the bottoms of her feet were. Her hands were cracked and dry, bleeding across the palms. Under the ash that stained her feet and legs and face, her skin was badly sun- and windburned. *What has she done to herself?* Genevra murmured under her breath. *Did she choose to run herself almost to death? Or is she protecting whoever did this to her?*

While Ameera collected a basin of warm water and some soft rags, Genevra went through the lotions on her vanity, gathering what she needed. Then the two knelt on either side of Narain and gently, carefully cleaned her feet and legs, trying not to recoil from the smell. They replaced the soiled water with fresh more than once, and sponge-bathed her gingerly, unwilling to add to her discomfort.

"It is good she is not awake," Ameera whispered. "This would be very painful."

Concentrating on applying antiseptic ointment to the sores on Narain's feet, Genevra did not answer. She used her best lotion of pounded orange peel and fresh cream on the injured hands, then spread ointment on the wounds. Together, they worked for what seemed like hours, spreading the lotion over her body, applying balm to her split lips. Using her fingertips, Genevra put orange-scented cream on Narain's scorched face.

When they had nearly finished, Narain awoke briefly and began to thrash as if to get away. Disoriented and unused to the cool feeling of her skin, she finally focused on Genevra's face. "Ah," she murmured hoarsely, "I am with you. Safe." Then she drifted back to sleep. To hide her flush, Genevra went to find clean sheets to replace the ones that held the remnants of Narain's escape. From what? Genevra stopped herself. Later she could ask questions.

With the utmost care, they rolled Narain onto her side, drew the soiled sheets from beneath her, replaced them with fresh ones and rolled her back.

"She needs liquid immediately," Genevra said, oddly torn by Narain's faith in her and that one word, "safe." But she didn't have time to explore her chaotic emotions. There was too much to be done. "Perhaps if we soaked one of my handkerchiefs in mango juice—"

Before she could finish, Ameera was on her way to the kitchen. Genevra opened her small linens drawer and pulled out the first several handkerchiefs she found. The women took turns dipping the small white squares into the juice, then squeezing just enough to let some trickle into Narain's mouth, a little at a time. Genevra knew they had to go slowly; when a person was this dehydrated, one could not simply pour liquid into her.

"Later we'll give her some broth, the same way, with the handkerchiefs, but I think nothing else today."

"How do you know all this?"

Genevra smiled ironically. "Narain taught me. She's a healer, you see."

When they took a rest, Ameera shifted about uncomfortably, glancing at her mistress, then lowering her eyes.

"What is it?" Genevra asked.

"It is just—I do not know what happened between you to make Hazari so bitter."

Twisting her finger in a damp handkerchief, Genevra delayed answering. "Do you think I'm not bitter as well?"

Ameera watched her, brow furrowed. "Perhaps. But then why, without planning, did you bring her to your room and give her your linens and use your best French handkerchiefs to feed her? Why were your hands so gentle when you treated her with your finest lotions and expensive balms?"

Sitting back, Genevra frowned. "I did the best I could for her. As for using my bed, it's the only one set up. I had no choice."

The servant regarded her through narrowed eyes. "You could have taken her to the rooms beside the garden, out of your house, so she would not disturb your privacy." She played with the end of her long black braid. "No, I think you would have brought her here anyway. I think your heart spoke louder than your memories."

Genevra looked up. "She broke my heart, you know."

"I remember there was a scandal back then, but what it was about—" She spread her hands and shrugged.

Her mistress was amazed. She'd honestly thought no one would ever let that memory lapse. That Ameera apparently had forgotten lifted her spirits. "I'll remind you, then. From the time I came to Delhi, my ayah was Radha, and Narain her daughter. They took me in willingly, so I was much more part of their family than my own. As children, Narain and I slept in the same room, she in a *charpoy* beside my bed. We told each other all our secrets—at least I told her mine. We were like sisters, she and I. And I trusted her beyond all others. Then her mother was suspected of a conspiracy with the British to steal Indian antiquities, and I was the first to discover what Radha was doing."

Ameera tried to interrupt, but Genevra continued doggedly. She had to get this out. It was too painful to speak about. Even now. "To discredit me, to make certain no one believed my accusations, Narain announced that we were lovers. The English and my family were so appalled that it ruined any chance for me to be accepted, ever. Not that I wanted to be one of them. But it was Narain's lie, her betrayal that hurt so much. There were many things she could have said or done that would not have been so cruel." She coughed from lack of air and nodded at Ameera. "Now do you remember?"

"I understand, but I do not remember. Yet if this is true, I am more confused that you have taken such care and given your best things to treat her."

Genevra herself was puzzled. "Because I made a promise and now I must keep it?"

"Why are you *asking* me instead of telling?"

As Ameera left the room, her mistress sat very still, wondering.

By the time she took a break from her self-imposed task, changed her ruined gown and put on a muslin shift, Genevra was irritated. When she found Hazari moving the new furniture about the room so it looked less like an obstacle course, she stopped directly in front of him, head tilted back, nose practically touching his chin. "Why aren't you in the garden?" Her tone was brusque, almost an accusation.

Hazari stood up equally straight, equally stubborn. "I do not wish to leave you alone with her. My job is to keep you safe."

She had been volatile enough when she left Narain's side; now she lost the last of her restraint. "Do you think I'm so weak and vulnerable?" As the words left her mouth the scene from the night before formed in her mind. "It seems you don't trust me either. I heard you last night, saw you pointing out to Ameera where the fire had started. Why didn't you tell me? It's something I should know, don't you think?"

The *mali* shook his head, crossed his arms, and without moving, seemed to fade into the shadows at the edge of the room. That was how servants behaved when they did not like or trust their masters. He had never been like this before, and she didn't believe dislike or mistrust were his motives. He was still protecting her.

"Have you no faith in me, after knowing me so long? Do you think me a fool?"

He couldn't keep silent at the hurt in her voice. "I have never thought you a fool." He glanced toward the back of the house, where Ameera was speaking quietly to Narain. "But I told you not to let her in."

Genevra stared at him, aghast. "You think Narain set the fire? Why, when she needs a place to recover? That makes no sense. Whatever else she may be, Narain is not senseless." She heard a voice whispering slyly in her memory, *said she was seen here last night, watching. . . .* Then, *furtive, like a wild animal . . .* and, *They found her watching this house.* What did it mean? They could easily have been speaking of Narain.

"I hope not."

Startled by Hazari's deep voice, she jumped. Apparently she'd been speaking her thoughts out loud.

At her shocked expression, the *mali* looked contrite. He didn't want to upset her; he'd spoken without thinking. He moved forward and put his hand on her shoulder. "Please listen, Genniji. If I did not believe in you, if I had not seen your courage time and again, if I did not know the inner core of your heart and a strength that will not break, I would not be here. I am in this house for and because of you. We will find out who set the fire, and I will tell you everything. You are right. For a time, I had forgotten who you are. It will not happen again."

7

UPSET BY TOO MANY EVENTS IN A SHORT TIME, MOST OF ALL by her enigmatic response to Narain, Genevra went to *her* refuge—the river. Though her head was spinning, had begun to ache dully, she decided to bring lunch for two. She hoped Munia would come today.

She was lucky; the old woman was settled between the roots of a plane tree, enjoying the cool shadows of the leaves on her face after a brief storm. "So," she said without opening her eyes, "you have come again so soon. What is bothering you to make your skin so pale and your eyes gray?"

"I wanted to talk to someone uninvolved in this turmoil. Besides, you always make me stop and think, and that's what I need to do right now."

Munia took the curry, *chupattis*, papaya and bananas the girl offered, but the food seemed a distraction to her as she took a bite now and then. "Is it about Alex you have come?"

Surprised that Munia should ask when she always seemed to guess why Genevra was there, the girl was quite disconcerted to realize she'd not thought of her husband since yesterday. Was he part of these feelings? "I sense danger on all sides, and I know I'm not overly suspicious; it's happened before, and I was right. The fire, the burnt rag by the house, Hazari's misgivings. I don't know what to do."

"You know inside, I think. But until you recognize what you know, I will try to comfort you. Your house did *not* burn, and I feel strongly that whoever set the fire was not trying to kill you or even hurt you. It would have been a foolish way to try. I suspect they knew you would be gone so early; almost every day you walk before sunrise."

"Then why—"

Munia ignored her. "They are trying to frighten you perhaps, but that is all." She popped a piece of banana in her mouth, regarding the girl closely. For the first time since Genevra had known her, she seemed tense and expectant. "You have not told me all that is bothering you." There was no hint of a question in her voice or her piercing dark eyes.

Genevra didn't notice. "My old enemy arrived today, ill and weak, and I let her in. There was a horrible scandal about her and me. Her name is Narain. Her mother was Radha."

"*Aahhhh*! I remember that scandal." Munia even knew the names. She sat silent, concentrating on her food while she thought. "This girl, Narain, she hurt you a long time ago. I see you have not let yourself forget."

Genevra dragged her feet through the water, enjoying the relief from the heat and recent memory of Narain's battered soles. "I loved her once, and trusted her with my secret dreams and fears. I can't forget when the pain is still inside." She stared at Munia, unblinking. "She never paid for her sin, never apologized."

"What you have described, her injuries and thirst and hunger, these things make me believe she's paying now. She sounds contrite; you admit that yourself. You must realize, Genevra, that life has not been easy for her since her mother was arrested."

"How do you know?" She stiffened, digging her fingers into the wet sand.

"Narain is much talked of in Shajehanabad; all Hindus and Muslims and many of the British know her name. Most everyone dislikes her, or convince themselves they do. The Hindus think Narain unclean for many reasons: Her mother's perfidy, her years of living with the *feringhi*, where she could hardly avoid being defiled, her lies about her forbidden relationship with you. Yet she is so skilled a healer that the people call her to them in secret, pay her in secret, bless her in secret. Yet they spit and turn away when they pass her on the Chadni Chowk. You know what it's like to be despised like that. You cannot pretend otherwise. You are alike in that way, you two. For your own sake, think about forgiveness. She has paid for her sins many times over."

Genevra had heard some of the stories but she had worked hard to forget. She didn't want to feel sympathy for her one-time friend, but how could she help it when the girl lay in her room, nearer death than Genevra liked to think about. She put her hands over her ears to stop her thoughts from whirling.

The old woman had never ceased watching. Now she touched Genevra's arm. "Listen to me, please. It is important."

The girl nodded reluctantly.

"In our society, an unmarried Hindu girl is nothing. She has no place, especially when she is wise and unbroken by her outcast state. Especially when she supports herself on her skills alone. She is not defined by our customs, so she is no one. She's done the unforgivable," Munia chuckled. "She's learned to support, educate and entertain herself.

> "In childhood must a father guard his daughter;
> In youth the husband shields his wife; in age
> A mother is protected by her sons—
>
> Ne'er should a woman lean upon herself."

The old woman got up and turned in two slow circles, stopping eye to eye with Genevra. "*You* should understand that; you've done it yourself by choosing to stay alone, by refusing to let the *feringhi* break you. Most of all by convincing your Alex to buy you a house neither Theirs nor Ours, outside the lines of distinction. You've made clear your scorn."

"Just because we're alike doesn't mean I know her anymore, or ever did."

"Then trust your instincts. They are potent and true within you."

Genevra looked doubtful. "I'll try." She felt a tiny flutter of hope. Could she do such a thing? Mairi Rose, her father's wife, had thought so. *Always your heart and spirit will guide ye and no' lead ye astray. If ye let them. Ye can do it, our Genny. I know ye can.* Was she really that strong?

Munia nodded sagely. "If you wish to be."

IN THE NEXT COUPLE OF WEEKS, GENEVRA CONTINUED TO treat and feed Narain, who had been moved into the bed. She did not speak often, though Genevra asked many questions. Narain preferred to listen to the workers below, even smiled now and then.

Meanwhile, Hazari was full of restless energy. Every morning, his native friends came to offer help. Some spent hours giving height and strength to the stone walls or scraping pools and fountains free of the build-up of long years of neglect. Others worked on the tunnels—marking them on the ground overhead, then going down in a bucket to walk the waterways until they'd discovered what obstructed the running water. Another group would go down together to disperse the blockage and lift out the debris, which they used to sweeten the earth for planting time. The women and Genevra discussed the choice and placement of plants and trees to be purchased at just the right time of year for them to flourish as soon as they touched the earth. Ameera found her way to the garden as often as she could.

Everyone was anxious to see the garden live again. They had already cleaned out the layers of dust and leaves and gravel, cleared the spouts of the fountains and restored what paint they could. Hazari asked Genevra if she would paint new tiles for the fountain and the pool, but she hesitated. She would have to consider.

Hazari and a handpicked few of his friends went into Delhi one morning to get Narain's things from a small room off the Chadni Chowk. The *mali* had not changed his mind about their guest, but this was necessary. He didn't want Narain wearing the mistress' clothes; she wasn't comfortable in them anyway. So he went to retrieve everything she owned, oblivious to the fights he engaged in to get it. He just wanted to return home to his garden.

Ameera and her friends worked on repainting the walls inside the house, demanding that the mistress add small touches of color and life with oil paint, while the workers dug through the unpacked boxes for intricate silk runners for the chests, which they filled with linens and crystal and china. Genevra's earthen dishes were stacked in the kitchen, where she used them every day. Ameera unearthed a large case of Genevra's paintings and lay her discovery in her mistress's lap. Genevra touched them gently, her face radiant. She had forgotten what they looked like. Forgotten the colors and shapes. Reluctantly, but secretly delighted, she allowed Ameera to hang one in the parlor and one in her bedroom.

In the garden, she sat back, watching with a smile. Everyone had stopped to eat cold curry with *chupattis* and musk-melon, pears, apples and almonds. Many were talking at once, and Genevra enjoyed the soft cadence of low voices. There was much motion and sound and energy, and wonderful varied colors. It struck Genevra suddenly what Munia had told her the day of the fire. *Even if you are lonely now, it will not be for long. Many will come.* That day she'd returned to discover Ameera, the next Narain, and now many Hindus worked on her garden as if it belonged to all of them.

At one time she'd wondered if the Hindus who lived near the old house had been angry that she was so presumptuous as to call it hers, if perhaps it was they who set the fire, hoping to frighten her away. But looking around, morning and afternoon, she dismissed the idea. These were her friends. They welcomed her.

A week later, Narain explained to Ameera a pressing need to speak to Genevra alone. The servant led her to a sit-

ting room dug into the ground to keep it cool with all the
tiny streams and rivers flowing through the earth beyond
the hard packed walls.

Narain forgot herself and actually smiled at the decorations. This might as well have been a *baradari* with its bright
colors and sense of life. There were Indian silk scarves
and gauze gathered into a single knot placed high on the
wall, the fabric spreading down like giant fans. There were
carvings and bowls, drums and bells and beads—local treasures Genevra had collected. There were painted earthen
pots on the shelves, and brightest of all, silks intricately
embroidered with designs of peacocks, flowers and the
twisted pattern of tamarind trees. None had been simply
hung or draped. Each was done a little differently—the
flowers gathered into a glowing circle, the peacocks marching down the wall as if seeking this very refuge, and the pattern of tamarind branches covering the long narrow window at the top of one wall. It should have been the darkest
room in the house. Instead it was the most welcoming.
There was a hand-painted pitcher on a wildly clashing tray,
and two mismatched clay vessels that smelled strongly of
lemon.

Narain stood just inside the doorway, watching Genevra
as she relaxed among the plump cushions at the foot of the
sofa. She'd not yet seen such peace on her friend's face, and
now she must destroy it. She almost turned away, but she
couldn't. Not anymore.

Genevra heard the door and glanced up to find Narain
standing just inside. Her hair was neatly combed but carelessly coiled and unscented, and her sari was clean but subdued. "I have promised myself that from this moment I will
tell you only the truth, that there will be no lies between
us, even if they are unspoken."

Taken aback, Genevra blurted out the first question that
occurred to her. "Have you come here for forgiveness, or is
it for refuge?"

"A little of both?" They sat facing one another on the floor, legs crossed.

At Genevra's expression, Narain bowed her head. "I will tell you what happened, though I think you know I would rather not. But you were once my sister, in feeling if not in blood, and you deserve to know. Because this will not be easy for either of us."

"How can it be difficult for *me?*"

Narain shook her head. "We will get to that soon enough. Let me start at the beginning. Nearly a year and a half ago, I fell in love for the first time."

Genevra raised her eyebrows in surprise. "I didn't think it could happen. You were always so careful."

"I lost my common sense, my natural restraint, my wisdom with this man. I gave it all up—for a British soldier."

As if she'd been struck in the stomach, Genevra curled in upon herself. When she looked up she was pale and her hands trembled. "You and a foreigner? I can't imagine such a thing. You are so very much a part of India. And a soldier? They aren't all like my Alex, you know. They can be dangerously reckless and wild, especially when they're young. But you know that. You know, and yet—"

"Yet I tumbled from the healer's lonely sacred perch, tumbled into the dirt and opened myself to him with love."

There was a long, tense silence; they could feel it hanging over them.

Narain spoke first, unafraid of silence at least. "Besides, I knew of one British officer very different from the rest. Tender, understanding, willing to do anything to keep you by him. If one, then why not two?"

The torch on the wall sputtered out, but the one outside the window flickered over their faces, creating elongated shadows and light. "You let yourself fall because of Alex?" She hesitated, then asked diffidently, "Would he really do anything to keep me by him?"

"You doubt him?"

"Of course not. He's my husband. But he is away a great deal, and sometimes I wonder—"

"Then you're the fool here, not me. Alex is as faithful to you as my soldier was false to me."

Genevra was torn between anger at Narain, astonishment at what she'd done, fear at how the tale would end and guilt for any small doubt she'd ever had about her husband.

Looking uneasy, Narain began to talk more quickly. She wanted to be done with this. Forever. But that wasn't possible now. "He bought a cottage outside the cantonment, far enough away so it would not be discovered. He was very afraid of being caught with me, so he risked a lot to come every night, and sometimes in the sun at noon. I do not doubt that he loved me deeply. I often felt I might break him, the way he clung to me so passionately, so desperately. And I did break him. The irony was that the Army never caught him. It was I who caught him unaware." She took a deep breath.

Now Genevra lay back on the floor, staring up at the ceiling, attempting to hear each word, to believe it at the same time. It was difficult.

"That was the night I told him I carried his child. It destroyed him, drove him mad. He called me whore, said I made love with so many, I could not know it was his. I know now that he did not mean those things. He was frightened and he did not think before he spoke."

Genevra sat bolt upright, staring at Narain's belly, which looked as usual. "Pregnant?" she repeated in a whisper. "What did you think he would do? What did you want him to do?" Her questions were intended kindly. Now she was truly afraid for Narain.

"I wanted him to declare his love, his devotion for his unborn child. I knew we must part, that he could not bring us secretly from post to post. That would destroy his career." Narain's eyes glistened with tears. "I only wanted him to tell me that he loved me one last time, perhaps beg me not to go, understanding, as he surely must, that of all people, I had the wit to know that I had no choice. Just the words and the look in his eye I knew so well. That was all I hoped for. But for him it was impossible. He thought if he loved me he must marry me, that a good man would act from the heart rather than practicality. So he had to convince himself I had betrayed him; he had to learn to hate me in a single hour, or else he would be lost. But he is not lost, nor was he ever betrayed. And I—" she spread her hands wide, "I am both."

Without anger or bitterness, Genevra reached for Narain while she fought back tears. "I do not want to weep for him. I want to hate him; I am better at it every day." She grasped the front of Genevra's nightgown. "It is *because* he loved me, you see. If he had tired of me, or simply used my body, I would not have bothered to tell him. But I went to him that night, so certain, so naive. He threw me out, you know. Burned our cottage to the ground. I ran and ran and never stopped until I found your porch covered in ash. How ironic that is. How utterly right. I let myself believe and now he has left me with half a heart, perhaps none at all. I will never forgive him. I can't."

"Two hearts," Genevra said softly. "He left you two hearts. Yours, which I know is stronger than you say, and the heart of your child."

Narain retreated as far as she could. "Do you think I want this child? A memory of him to become forever my shadow?"

Genevra thought it sounded like bliss, but wisely did not say so. She glanced under her lids at Narain, trying to guess how far along she was. What if she had lost the baby in her frantic escape?

"I carry it still. I hoped it would not survive, but I am disappointed."

Genevra thought her heart would break. A tiny helpless child, unwanted, despised, when Genevra would pay many *rupees* to carry a life within her. It was almost as if Narain had struck a final blow. But she could not have known how much Genevra yearned for a family, could not have guessed that Genevra thought herself barren.

"She is mine more than his," Narain continued in shame, "but I cannot make myself love her. There are no words to put back together the pieces of my shattered heart. But I have left that place forever. The only reminder is this helpless baby. And I want so much to forget." She licked her lips, which had gone dry. "Besides, what will there be for her except prejudice, hatred, perhaps slavery. They hate half-breeds more than they hate us." She bent her head, hands cupping her stomach. "If she has a strong spirit, even if I give her some of mine, they would nevertheless break her in an instant."

"What is his name?" Genevra was desperate to change the subject.

Narain tilted her head like a cat, curiously. "I have told you it is a she-child, and she has no name, nor do I plan to give her one. That would make her real and break my heart again."

"No, I mean the man who brought you to this. What is his name?"

Sighing so deeply she swayed, Narain murmured, "I told you I would give you the truth, that there would be no lies between us. But I cannot give you this."

9

HAZARI HEARD A SOFT SOUND FROM A DARK, FAR CORNER OF the garden. He'd been thinking of all the animals he'd left at Phoebe's and wondering who was taking care of them. He knew Phoebe well enough to guess there would be someone. The sound came again and this time he raised his head warily. It didn't belong in his garden, that poignant muffled noise. He followed it silently, his round hat in his hands so it wouldn't fall off and betray him. Finally he stopped. The sound was coming from behind the newly planted fruit trees. He crouched and glanced furtively between the trunks, then fell backward, barely catching himself in time.

Narain was curled up in the angle made by two walls, face in her hands, weeping. Hazari had carried a hard heart against her for years, but tonight she looked so vulnerable, curled into as tight a ball as she could force herself, hiding far from the house, and obviously in pain. She did not expect anyone to find her; she wanted to grieve in private. She had always been very proud.

Except for this one girl, Hazari could not bear a woman's tears, and always wanted to stop them from falling. He didn't trust Narain. But the image of her limp figure, the sound of her wrenching sobs was already burned into his mind. He did not doubt her pain was real.

Guiltily, he recalled the conversation he'd had with Genevra this afternoon. "Narain the mighty healer followed a British soldier, loved him, and in so doing lost her power. It was a betrayal to the Hindus." Genevra had peered at him so closely that his palms began to itch. "But didn't you feel about Phoebe as Narain felt about her soldier? Were they not both *feringhi*? You even lived in Phoebe's house, where Hindu and Muslim, Sikh and British saw you, spoke with you, became your friends. You can't judge Narain unless you're ready to judge yourself. And I don't want that, Hazari. Because you did nothing wrong, and neither has she." He'd had no answer to that and had conveniently found something urgent to do.

That night, he waited a long time for the tears to subside, then a while longer, to give her time. Then he rose and walked about enough to warn her of his approach.

When he finally came upon her, he stared in astonishment. "Are you yet in pain?"

Narain looked up, ready to flee, but something in his eyes stopped her. She was not used to talking to men, except the one who had betrayed her, and years ago, Hazari. She sat up warily. "My feet and hands have healed, but it will not cease aching here." She put her hand over her heart.

Tentatively, the *mali* sat beside her on the cool, dry stone. "Is something wrong with the baby?"

Narain stared, the question in her head branded on her face.

"Did you think I did not know? There are few, but I am not the only one."

Narain bowed her head, but her eyes were blazing. She'd thought she could keep it a secret. All of it. But she knew the truth blew in the wind, carried by Indra across barren plains and lakes and rivers and into the cities, where words became gossip, and soon afterward, lies. Must she now learn every lesson she had taught Genevra in her thoughtless youth? Now she, too, was ruined. Without warning, Genevra's face formed in her mind. The bones were so fragile, the cheeks high and generally flushed with color, the eyes mysterious. Narain feared the girl was too fragile after all, and sorrow choked her. "No," she answered Hazari, "it is not the baby."

"The kind of sorrow and emptiness you feel, I feel too."

Narain nodded. "I heard Phoebe had gone away."

He did not acknowledge her comment. "This kind of suffering can last a long time, but it can be easier with friends around you and ways to occupy your hands."

"I thought you were my enemy."

Hazari tugged on his thick black hair. "I thought so too. Perhaps I was wrong about your motives. But you are afraid of what they are, are you not?"

A straightforward question deserved a simple answer. "I

cannot say for certain. I am not used to looking deep into my heart, or understanding what I find there. So, for Genevra's sake, I must be careful. No lies anymore. I made her a promise."

Ameera had come looking for Hazari, but when she saw the two figures outlined against the stone wall, heads close, talking quietly, she turned without a word and crept away.

That night, Genevra had restless dreams that kept her awake most of the time. She didn't know what the danger was; she only knew it was real. She woke and slept, woke and slept, disturbed and disoriented. She felt a figure leaning over her.

Narain stood next to the bed, head bowed, a supplicant, asking forgiveness with the graceful gestures of her hands, the submissive angle of her proud head. Or was Genevra still dreaming? Narain's face was blurred, and she thought there were tears on her cheeks. She took Genevra's hand and pressed a single kiss into the palm.

Genevra did not pull away. All she could think was that once this woman had been her dearest friend, keeper of her secrets and dreams. She'd slept near Genevra's rosewood bed, warming her when she was cold, cooling her when she was hot, holding her while she wept. Then they were both falling across a desert without water, a sea that had no end.

Narain floated beside Genevra in a green sari, brown skin glistening, black hair sleek, dark eyes liquid and warm. She wore a mysterious amulet around her neck on a woven leather thong. An oval set in gold with the Hindu gods etched in the soft metal, a perfect ruby at its heart. It was hypnotic, that stone.

But Genevra forced herself to break the spell with her rage and disappointment at what this smooth dark girl had done to her. Her body began to burn and the water became flame, then, at a motion from Narain, the fire went out and the river ran clear and cool again.

"In all my life," she murmured, "I have had no other friend

like you, nor would I need another, had I recognized what was written on my forehead. Now Fate has given me the chance to atone for my betrayal, to prove my sincerity."

Why didn't Genevra close her eyes and ears, refuse to listen? Why was the healer not ugly to her, as cruelty is ugly? Why couldn't she see the poison inside? She knew it was there. Or had been three years ago.

Just then, a crocodile rose from the water, slithering steadily toward them. Genevra's mind was empty of all but terror. Together, grasping each other's arms, Narain and she tried to reach the shore. Genevra fell back, and Narain caught her, letting go of her foothold on a rock to reach her friend. Then they were surrounded by crocodiles, their mouths gaping open, showing glimpses of yellowed, sharp teeth before they snapped closed.

Now it was Narain who fell, and Genevra who caught her, and they stumbled through the water, making a great splash and thunder as they went, and though the bank was slick, Munia, the ephemeral wise woman, stood waiting to pull them out. They huddled on either side of her, shivering against her warmth, and still the crocs moved forward, unstoppable in a pyramid of scaly death.

All at once, the heat of Genevra's fury leapt up, bringing the flames back to the river. The crocodiles thrashed in the shallow water, which carried them back to the deep, silty center, where they disappeared. She remembered a story Narain's mother had told her, of the Brahmin who rescued a crocodile that then began to eat him. When the Brahmin cried out that he had done the reptile a good turn, the crocodile paused long enough to say, "The only honesty of our days is to ruin those who cherish us."

The three women let out their breath as one, locked arms about each other's waists and watched the river burn.

Genevra sat up, wide-eyed. What did it mean? It was too vivid and arduous to mean nothing. Was her bitterness diminishing or growing deeper? She could not tell. In utter frustration, she pulled her legs in close and laid her cheek on her knee.

10

SEVERAL DAYS PASSED WHILE THE MOISTURE ROSE, INTENSI-fying the discomfort before the monsoon. It was too hot, too uncomfortable to sleep, so Genevra lay in her thin nightrail on damp sheets. The night was still and the air heavy. She was glad when she heard the door open and Narain appeared. "I could not sleep. Do you mind if I sit in here for a while?" She wore bracelets of glass and lapis beads, of gold and silver and copper that reached to her elbow on one side, well past her wrist on the other, jingling and clinking as she walked. Her anklets chimed with each step, so there was always music in her wake.

Genevra could not quite trust her. Not since she'd spoken so harshly of the helpless child she carried. Surreptitiously, Genevra reached over to touch the letters she'd been reading from her two half-sisters. That touch reminded her how naturally Lian, Ailsa and she had become a family, and Mairi Rose, who chose to be their mother. While she watched Narain, the recollection of warmth and family disturbed her. She could no longer deny that Narain was behaving unnaturally.

Tonight they decided to declare a truce. Genevra was immensely relieved. They had, after all, known each other a long time and were soon talking easily. Eventually, Narain climbed onto the mattress and perched at one corner of the bed, Genevra at the other. Her fluid voice reached her friend like a drink of cool water when her mouth was dry and parched. Leaning against the bedpost, bare feet hidden by the linen sheets, Narain regarded her friend through fathomless dark eyes.

Because the moonlight was so rare and radiant, Genevra drew back the reed blinds to let it in, to invite its white incandescence to fall across the bed, illuminating all but the corners where they sat.

Observing Genevra closely, Narain discerned how she held herself a little apart—not too far, just far enough. Against her better judgment, she spoke. "Sometimes I think you carry the past with you as if you must repeat it, as if it is forever your fate, your devastation.

"But nothing is forever." She was determined, regretful, tender. "Remember that, believe it, and someday it will give you peace. Just as I will find peace when I atone for betraying you, and begin to mend my karma." She saw Genevra's question and replied, "All acts have consequences; all consequences are the fault of she who acted. I will pay, in this life or another, for my ignorance and cruelty. That is as it should be."

Narain leaned back against the tall bedpost. "As a Hindu, I see all life, the ones I have lived before and the ones that will come after, as an endless flowing river carrying me along. Now and then, when the wind shifts and the breeze whispers that it is time, I step from one boat to another, each boat a new life, and my journey continues. There is no pause, no break, no painful leap from one boat to the other. I, we, all of us, step smoothly, effortlessly between conveyances. It is why we do not fear death, for we do not believe in it."

"Perhaps it's easier to say that if one has children to leave behind to fulfill what we've left undone." Genevra flushed and covered her mouth when she realized what she'd said. Narain's pregnancy was advancing rapidly; though still slender and lithe, she could no longer hide the changes in her body

"This child is different. It was never meant to be. Every day I hope to wake, free of this nightmare, this responsibility for another life." She broke off when she realized how she sounded, how bitter and cold-hearted. But she could find no other way.

Wincing, Genevra tried to think of something else, but

instead was seduced by the swaying pendant Narain had worn since she'd first awakened and asked for the tiny pouch they had found around her neck when they treated her. In the bright moonlight, it sparkled from within, mesmerized Genevra, easing her worries. The gold surrounding the perfect ruby glowed and she thought she could see the figures of the gods etched there dancing, though that was not possible.

"Anything is possible," Narain murmured, closing Genevra's hands around the pendant. It was cool and warm, soothing and exhilarating all at once.

She did not understand why, just then, her father's image slipped into her mind. Charles Kittridge had found her, too late, and called her to his family in the Scottish Highlands. Somehow it had never been enough. In spite of everything, she did not think of him affectionately. Half the time there was only anger. Once again, Narain seemed to hear her thoughts.

"Your father is gone, Genniji. He has stepped onto another boat and disappeared."

She leaned forward so the moonlight edged her face in bronze light.

In the luminous glow, Genevra saw, belatedly, her rage at Charles for luring her from the heart of India only to watch the Golden Man of her mother's dreams and nightmares turn first to silver and then fade, become transparent. It was too cruel. Worse, somehow her feelings for Alex had been mixed in with the yearning and the fury. Sometimes she felt abandoned all over again, and blamed her husband. It wasn't fair to Alex. She would have realized that, had she been thinking clearly. But she'd no idea those feelings existed.

Now she knew she was plagued by Charles's ghost, by the sense of things unfinished, families incomplete, opportunities lost.

She cried out for Charles Kittridge, who created her,

abandoned her, sought her futilely for years. He had shaped her life, even in his absence, but that had been easier to bear than his regret, his desire to make amends. Easier by far to endure neglect than love, trust, forgiveness—all cut short by death. And he had known it. All along he had known. She wept for him for years that night, in one long, wrenching hour.

And then she wept for the unborn child.

When Genevra ran out of tears, Narain suggested they might go to the garden which was nearly complete. Genevra agreed eagerly. She wanted to leave this stuffy room and escape its ghosts. She was afraid she would say too much. Tonight it was too easy to talk to Narain.

They slipped into the garden, enwrapped by moonlit stillness, walking narrow coral paths among beds of flowers—tube roses and narcissus, sweet jasmine and iris. Hazari had built a white fretwork overhead to defuse the unrelenting sunlight. Fruit trees in budding leaf would shade the paths in daylight, and the *baradari*, the summerhouse, with its carved pillars and gracefully curved roof, sat on its platform, scattered with chairs, vivid cushions and chaises.

Narain tilted her head, listening to the music of the fountains. She was enticed by the smell of jasmine, the bougainvillea that covered the bottom half of the walls and would soon consume the rest, the blankets of fuschia that sighed and rippled like water in the wind. "Hazari's a genius, isn't he?" Genevra whispered.

"Indeed. I think he is very sad and very wise."

Intrigued, Genevra was disappointed when she realized Narain had turned her head at an angle that said, Do not ask me more.

The women moved between rows of tamarind and date palms, listening for the rush of the underground wells. They had come for the magic of the water that fell in angles, splintering into waves and rippled designs from stone chutes in the walls. The *chadars*—white shawls of water.

They stood beneath a falls, Genevra in her nightrail, Narain in a scarf wrapped like a sari and the gold and ruby pendant she never removed. They lifted their faces to feel the rush of cool wetness on their skin. Without speaking, they plunged into the large tiled pool, gravitating toward the waterfalls streaming over graduated stones until they reached the surface and crashed into turquoise serenity.

The water was golden in the light of the full moon, and Genevra spread her arms, washing away the shadows, absorbing the life-giving water that sank beneath her skin, purifying her body while the moon goddess blessed it.

They swam, submerged themselves and exploded upward, sending water splashing over the sides. They raced along the painted tiles at the bottom, holding their breath, reaching the waterfall that was their goal at the same instant. Laughing, flinging their wet tangled hair over their shoulders, they clung to the mottled rock and swayed there, one arm stretched out, letting the water move them as it would.

The light glimmered on the ruffled waves, looking one moment like iced silver snow, another like a low-burning ember that lit the water from below.

They faced each other, smiling slightly, stunned by the beauty, luminescence and solace of the night.

When they'd stretched out long enough for their bodies to dry, they went back to Genevra's room.

Narain lit candles, setting them in a circle on the floor, and when she'd discarded her nightrail, beckoned Genevra into the center. Narain sat behind her while she gathered matted hair in her hands, began to work at it with her best silver comb. It reached the floor between them, making a spot on the rug beneath. Her hands were slow and gentle as she draped the fine blonde hair over her dark-skinned hand

and combed it, tangle by tangle, strand by strand. Genevra closed her eyes, mesmerized by the wavering light of the candles, brighter than she had expected, and by Narain's fingers sliding through her hair as each long tendril was freed and smoothed, drying as she worked, curling up around her fingers, around Genevra's face, on the rug where they sat cross-legged in the candlelight.

Genevra did not notice she was naked, as was Narain, for her body was cool, saturated with water and moonlight. To cover it now would be a desecration. Narain had always been as comfortable out of her clothes as in them. She hummed softly, rocking with the motion of the comb, spreading Genevra's hair over her legs and knees and crossed feet.

Genevra rocked with her, eyes closed, drawn by the flicker of candlelight against her lids, the scent of sandalwood as Narain warmed the oil in her hands and combed it leisurely through the gleaming strands. When she finished, she buried her face in the fine, curling mass, then let it fall. Genevra shivered but was not cold.

They turned, and Genevra took up Narain's thick black hair. She worked at knots within knots, smoothing a little at a time, draping it over her hand and arm. Like Genevra's, it had begun to dry, though the heavy dark strands did not curl, but lay blue-black and shining where they fell.

It was then that Genevra found the words she had been seeking. "I fear my heart is not pure."

Narain raised her head regally, like a queen in shimmering black. "You have the purest heart I have ever known. And I have known some very black ones, *larla*."

With the scented oil on her hands, Genevra touched her shoulders briefly. She thought of karma, of what sin she might have committed in another life. "Then why am I barren, do you think?"

"Barren? What makes you think that? You and Alex have been married barely two years."

"But I should have conceived by now, found peace and satisfaction in my child."

Narain lifted her hands in a helpless gesture. "It may be the memories in the land of Hind, it may be that the sun and dust and violent rains do not encourage growth in your womb." She looked up.

"But you are dreaming. A child cannot fulfill you. You must do that for yourself."

Strangely, Mairi Rose had agreed. *Alex can no' give ye a family of bairns who adore ye. Ye must make a family together.*

"I know I'm impatient."

"No matter how hard you wish it, you cannot change what is immutable. Do you not think that I, too, wish to relive my life, to avoid the mistakes?"

"The soldier too? You would choose to miss the love and joy to avoid the pain?" Genevra asked in disbelief.

"I told you once that dishonor is worse than death, and it proved to be true. But we are not talking of me. You, Genniji, have a chance to step from the boat of your childhood to the boat of your future, a chance to find your way into the light."

It seemed to Genevra, in thoughts that floated down from the heavens and up from the earth and intertwined themselves with the wash of moonlight and the circle of candles, that she was already sitting in the light.

Narain drew her toward the mirror. Candle in hand, she urged Genevra close, until her face came into focus in the oval frame. "Look," Narain said.

Genevra stared as at a stranger, golden hair curling around her naked shoulders, cheeks flushed with color from the exhilaration of the water, luminous blue eyes flecked with gray. She stood frozen, amazed and frightened by the change.

"Look closer, Genniji, and I will give you a small gift."

"I don't think—"

Narain shifted so both faces were reflected in the mirror. "To reject my offering would be unkind."

She turned back to the mirror. "Look, Genniji. The gift is there in the clear, guileless glass. Genevra Kendall, pure of heart, generous of spirit and beautiful."

She held her friend loosely, an arm about her shoulder. "I know you do not believe me. I tried to show you once before, but I was young and foolish and cared more for my own beauty than yours, so I gave in too soon. Tonight I will not give in until you take the gift of my loving eyes and *see* yourself through them."

Genevra stared, appraised, moved closer, then away, still clutching her uncertainty like protective armor. Narain smiled and brought a second candle, and for the merest splinter of time, for an instant, a flicker of candlelight, Genevra saw, and she believed.

But when she tried to return the gift, Narain was suddenly shy of the mirror. She cupped her hands across her belly and turned away. Genevra realized she didn't want to see herself. She was ashamed of her condition. After all they'd said tonight, Genevra thought she knew why. Narain's pregnancy was a physical sign of her weakness. And no matter what she tried to make others believe, she hated to appear weak, but she did not hate the child.

Narain said over and over that the baby was not meant to be, because she was terrified she would lose it. She could not begin to acknowledge the pain of that fear, and the emptiness beyond it.

11

AFTER THEIR NIGHT OF CONFESSIONS AND LOOKING INTO mirrors, Genevra found she was uneasy around Narain. Not only did she wonder if she'd said too much, she worried more and more as the baby grew. She had a secret envy and fear for the child. But mostly, Genevra was disturbed by something that had changed in her that night. She could not say exactly what it was, but she felt the difference daily. She wrote many letters to Alex in that time of waiting. She also began to sketch and paint with fervor; she could not seem to stop the vivid fragmentary images from coming. The energy those sketches and watercolors took from her was wearing her out.

One morning, in a blue broadcloth gown with no bustle or corset, Genevra loitered by the river, sketching the trees and calling silently for Munia.

Soon enough, the old woman appeared—though Genevra could not tell from which direction—and nodded, prepared to hear her young friend's question. She tightened the scarf around her silver hair and concentrated on the girl.

"It's about—Narain. Rarely do I find anger against her in my heart, yet neither do I find forgiveness." She hesitated. "But whatever my feelings, she's doing all she can to help me. And since I can't quite give her her desire, I thought—I want to relieve her as she's trying to relieve me. It's the least I can do for all her efforts. I wish I could just say it's over, forget it ever happened between us, but I can't. Not yet, at least."

Munia peered at her and through her, past her bones to her heart. "Remember, *aspara*, 'The prudent one will never divulge her thoughts to another before she knows that other's thoughts.' Narain knows your thoughts does she not? And do you know hers? She is very good at hiding."

Genevra went rigid. "How—?" She fell silent when she saw Munia had gone into a kind of trance; her eyes were half-closed as she swayed and chanted quietly. But her attempt came to nothing. For the first time, she could find no solution. "I have no answer for you, child. What she has, she does not want, and what she had does not want her. I am sorry I could not do better for you."

Genevra leapt up. "But you have done." As she listened to Munia's apology, an idea began to take shape in her head. Once there, it would not go, but grew into a firm resolve.

Narain remained stubbornly silent about the baby, except to repeat that her child was not meant to be, it had no chance, she would not give it a world full of suffering. Now and then, when she thought she was alone, she whispered to the growing life in her belly, murmuring reassurances, chanting the old blessings, speaking to the child as if it understood her.

Genevra noticed she escaped regularly to the garden, now in wild, fragrant bloom, where she went in search of Hazari. They never seemed to run out of subjects to discuss as they worked side by side. It was not long before Narain had regained her natural color, and her talks with the *mali* seemed to restore a bit of her spirit, but none of her energy.

That's why, one night when Narain fell asleep early, Genevra went on her own search for Hazari. "Please," she murmured, "do you know how we can help her? I feel she's giving up, letting go of a life she could shape into anything she wanted. How can we make her open her eyes?"

Hazari crouched beside her on his haunches, rocking slightly as he smoked his pipe. He'd seen the desperation in his mistress's eyes, but he could not understand it. "It is possible, is it not," he began slowly, "that she does not want the same things as you? That she has made her choices, even if they cause her, or you, pain?"

Genevra grew rigid beside him. "She's told you her plans, then?" It took a great effort, but she kept the emphasis off the "you." "Is there some way we can help, or must she do this all alone?"

Hazari puffed in silence, watching the thin curl of smoke rise from his pipe as if it held the answer to his dilemma. He was torn. He'd sworn not to betray Narain, but in the end, the mistress was right. "I fear what she is doing will damage her *and* the child."

Ameera found them near the back of the garden. She too was worried. "I remembered something I must tell you. It might cause trouble, I do not know. But I had to come. On the first night when I was watching Narain, she called a man's name, first with passion, then with fury. Andrew Taylor."

That night, at that moment in the damp darkness, Genevra discovered a shape and direction for her resolve. She hugged Ameera and, without thinking, Hazari too.

He suppressed a smile. When the mistress was excited about something, the feeling was catching. But he wondered if this time she had dedicated herself to a cause that would end in disappointment. He knew before he spoke what she would say to that.

"I'm going away for a few days. That's all I'll need, a few days." She was trying to convince herself.

When Hazari and Ameera began to object, Genevra stopped them. "I know what you would say. But it wouldn't stop me, and it might cause us to bicker. I've lived here all my life and traveled many miles. I know how to get by. I know when it's safe and when there's danger."

"Let me go with you," Hazari pleaded.

"No, you must stay with Ameera and Narain, to protect them. Can you have some faith in me and let me go without argument? Can you believe in me?"

He nodded reluctantly. He had no other choice.

When Genevra had extracted solemn vows from both that they would not give her away, she went to pack a small bag for over her shoulder, some preserved fruits and a canteen from the larder to carry around her neck. She meant to be waiting at the crossroads well before dawn, when the first carts and *dak-gharies* appeared.

She could not sleep and stopped by Narain's room to find her sleeping heavily. Genevra smiled at the familiar face, kissed the round, swollen belly and whispered, "I go for you. I hope you believe that." She slipped silently away.

It was not difficult to walk the two miles to the main road. She was early and had to wait. She knew even then that the waiting had just begun.

12

GENEVRA WAS EXHAUSTED. SHE'D SPENT ALL DAY GOING through the cantonment and nearby camps, using her husband's name and rank in an effort to convince someone to tell her what she needed to know. She was perfectly aware that everyone here or in Delhi proper, and possibly in half of India, had heard the gossip about Andrew Taylor and the native girl who'd "ruined him." No doubt most of them also knew where he'd been sent, but they remained stubbornly silent. The man must have been stationed here or in town, or he wouldn't have crossed Narain's path enough to make her notice.

Genevra had always known she was different from the other British, not really one of them. She preferred most of the religions and customs of India. Her countrymen sensed that and shied away from her. Besides, they knew her reputation as an outcast. A great deal of the time, they treated her primly and properly, but very few were friendly. The kindly couples she remembered had moved on long ago. She had hoped beyond hope that one of them would ask her in for a glass of lemonade or a chance to wash up. Before she was halfway done, perspiration was rolling down her face, and her clothes were damp. For once, making an effort not to offend them, she had worn her most proper British traveling suit of gray wool, kid gloves and a jaunty hat that accomplished precisely nothing. She feared the suit was ruined and her quest hopeless.

She'd tried every house but one—Major General Worthy's. When she saw him whistling in the little yard, water can in his hand, nurturing the roses, she decided it couldn't hurt to try. She could not say she'd made every effort if she left without asking, though she knew before she opened her mouth what the answer would be.

Certainly, if anyone devoured gossip like opium, it was Martha Worthy. Her life seemed to be dedicated to a relentless search for more. She wanted to know every rumor first, to be the one to spread it, especially if it were bad. Unfortunately, her frail niece Nellie suffered for her aunt's "habit." Nellie had no friends.

Tapping her finger on her canteen, Genevra realized Martha would be enraged when she learned that everyone knew of Genevra's errand but herself. It was only polite to inform her. Brushing off her jacket, straightening her hat, she scooped up just enough water from the fountain to clean the rivulets of dust from her face before approaching the major general in his garden.

"I didn't mean to disturb you, sir, but I wanted to thank you for helping." He stared at her blankly. "With the fire in the weeds next to the Kendall house—my house. Alex's heart would've been broken if he'd come home to find it no longer standing."

"Of course, the fire." She could have sworn he flushed uncomfortably and glanced toward the house. He puttered about for a moment, then abruptly dropped bucket and shears on the lawn. He took a deep breath and looked down at Genevra. "Your house, is it? And what's a young lady like you doing out in the sun at this hour?"

He was acting very peculiar. "I'm looking for some information, sir. I thought—" She stopped and began again. "Your wife might know what I need to find out."

The General really looked at her then, his face thunderous. "Well, come inside. We'll see what Martha knows, shan't we?"

Intrigued, Genevra found herself standing in a parlor done in velvets and brocade. The room was stifling.

"I've promised young Mrs. Kendall tea, some of those sandwiches I like so much, and a pitcher and bowl for later. Drat it! We'll fill her canteen as well and see if we have any provisions to add to her pack."

When she saw their visitor's face, Martha went ashen and called for her niece to come prop her up. Poor Nellie hurried in, brow furrowed with anxiety, and stopped when she saw Genevra. "You've come," she said. "Good."

Martha glared at her niece while the major general glared at Martha. "Says she's come for some information, and very polite about it too. So I brought her in. The more the merrier, don't you agree, Mrs. Kendall?"

"I might if I understood what's going on." She turned to Martha, who shrank back, clinging to Nellie's arm.

"Not being much of a hostess," he continued. "Rather rude to leave her standing like that when her boots obviously pinch. And she must be desperately thirsty."

Nellie came to help Genevra off with her boots while Martha disappeared, growling, into the kitchen. But she didn't object too loudly.

With no effort at graciousness, she produced tea and sandwiches and nodded once at Genevra to come and get them if she wanted.

Gracefully, Genevra took a chair and consumed two cups of tea and two sandwiches. "Forgive me," she murmured, "I've been up all night or I wouldn't have been so greedy." Gaze on Martha, she added, "I didn't expect quite so warm a reception."

"Warm, the young woman says. I find it diverting, don't you m'dear? Warm reception."

The truth was, the general was impressed at the courage it took for Genevra to walk through the door at all, then to manage to remain polite when she was offered tea ungraciously from his tight-lipped wife. She was persistent too. She had no idea what was happening, but she kept her expression blank and waited for the outcome. He found her glancing at him more than once. She'd probably guessed he was up to something and would let him do it in his own way.

"Information about your house? The one that nearly burned, is it? That the sort of thing you're looking for?"

Martha collapsed into the many cushions of her French settee and Nellie glanced at Genevra oddly, her expression revealing fear and admiration mixed.

Why should the mention of the fire disturb these ladies so much? The major general met her eye and waited until a flame of recognition struck her. *It was set here*, Hazari'd told Ameera that night. *We are lucky that whoever did this was not good at such things. I would not be surprised if they had never set a fire before, even in a fireplace. If the weed had not caught, the fire would have died out completely.*

Genevra was looking at two such people now. But Martha Worthy and Nellie? She was surprised, but mostly because, if she were right, they'd chosen a method that could soil their gowns *and* their gloves. What's more, they'd had to rise and dress before dawn, creep away from the cantonment without being seen. And, they had to return before their absence was missed. It could well have happened that way. Hazari had told Genevra the fire had smoldered for a long time before the wind gave it life.

By the time she caught her breath, Martha and Nellie sat primly, hands folded. There was no other word to describe their expressions but "guilty." What should she do? She remembered Munia's admonition, *I do not think they wanted to kill you, or even to harm you. Only to frighten you.*

"Now then, if we have your information, then you shall hear it. Won't she, m'dear?"

A barter of sorts, never spoken out loud or shaken on, but a barter just the same. She did not hesitate. She'd forgotten the danger of the fire in all that had happened since. She nodded to the major general ever so slightly, mentioned Andrew Taylor and gathered every piece of information on him that was likely to be found.

He'd been transferred to Calcutta, they said. It was a huge city, housing several regiments of the Royal Army. Though she was clean and replete and her supplies overflowing, she felt dejected. She knew almost everything, but it wasn't enough. How would she find him now?

"Pardon, Mrs. Kendall," Nellie whispered at the door. She'd been sent to see their visitor out. "He's in the regiment at the end of the bay. And thank you." The door closed without a sound and Genevra turned away grinning. She'd been born in Calcutta, several days away if she joined a boat on its way up the Ganges. She knew exactly where to look.

13

SEVERAL DAYS LATER, SHE STEPPED FROM THE CARRIAGE INTO a sky turned red by the last light of the sun, deepening to purple as the wind rose off the bay. She was certain she would find the soldier here. Every instinct told her so.

Corporal Andrew Taylor stood with his back to the room. His body, outlined by the blazing light, was muscular, his uniform ironed immaculately, his shoes a black mirror.

"How did you find me?" he asked, attempting to sound brusque and distant. But he couldn't disguise the deep musical cadence of his voice. Another reason Narain would have been drawn to him. Music was her soul, her greatest pleasure.

Genevra smiled and shook her head. "It wasn't easy. You've a lot of loyal friends out there but I know this city too well. I was born here. In fact, I used to love to escape and seek out secret places to make mine. This was one of them."

A shack out over the part of the lake that was always at low tide. It was just as rickety as she remembered; it hadn't changed at all. Nor had the secret path of solid sand that twisted among the reeds, turned back upon itself twice before one could reach the final curve to the stairs of the shack.

Taylor probably felt safe here, so her entrance must have shocked him. He knew she was looking for him, but she'd missed him—and been misled by his friends in the regiment—so many times that he might have believed he'd escaped her. If that's what he thought, he did not know her. Yet.

"Why've you gone to such trouble? I can't go back to Delhi; you do know that?"

"I did it for Narain."

Though the shadows were deep, she saw him wince and hunch his shoulders.

"I don't want to hear that name again," he said stiffly.

"I know you believe that, but I think you do want to hear it. If for nothing else than to berate yourself with it." She found an old crate and perched on it, watching the sun play across his features as he turned from the window to face her. He clutched the rotted sill with one hand.

"It could have ruined my career; it's come close already."

Genevra examined her dirty fingernails. "Such things have ruined other men. But you won through. Do you know why?" She didn't wait for an answer. "Because the other men trust you; their loyalty isn't fleeting as loyalty often is. You're a good man, loved by many. Not the kind of man to turn his back and walk away without a glance. Narain told me a little of this, but the rest I've discovered here."

With each word of praise, he drooped farther, until his head was in his hands.

"All that may be true, but the one thing I'll never have again is their respect."

He acted like a man who was embarrassed, ashamed. He wanted her to think it was because he'd lost his honor with the regiment, but she sensed it was something else. Because he'd left Narain, cursed her, called her a whore. The man her friend had described up to that moment had been tender and caring. Genevra did not believe a person changed so quickly, or so cruelly. "If you've lost their respect forever, which I doubt, don't you want to keep Narain's all the more?"

He met her eyes and his face was so open and guileless, so vulnerable, so full of desire and pleading in every line, that she wanted to weep for him *and* her friend. He was tearing himself in two. "Don't you think you should see her once more to say good-bye? You never really did you know. It will haunt you both if you don't."

Silence hovered in the air, rising from the corners, blackening the shadows in the hut.

"Narain," he said, the word wrenched from inside. "Is she—how is she?"

That single question told her everything. He could not hide the emotion in his voice. He did care for her, deeply. The bitter sadness on his face told her losing Narain had left a scar that would not easily heal. "She's well. She and the baby. She has what she needs. Only one thing is missing."

Taylor turned away, gripping the sill with both hands, probably full of splinters from the force of his grasp. "I told you, I can't go back there. My position is probationary. You know how they watch and wait and judge a man before they know the facts. I can't risk losing my job. It's all I have left, now that I've lost Narain."

He did love her. Genevra had suspected as much, and the tone in Andrew's voice only confirmed it. He'd revealed more than he realized.

"Yet you see no reason to come back to Delhi?"

He got control of himself with difficulty. "Perhaps to see Lieutenant Colonel Kendall once more. I'd hate to think he thought ill of me. He was always just and kind as well as courageous. Not like the commanders here. They don't wait for explanations."

Genevra thought long and hard before she spoke again. Was he trying to distract her? Disarm her? He couldn't know, surely. And if he did, he was not the kind of man to use the knowledge as a weapon. She thought of Narain, wet in the moonlight, of a ring of candles, of Alex and his dedication to his friends. She paused. "Won't you come to Delhi, for a single day, just one short day, if for nothing more than to wish her luck? Surely you owe her that much." He stared at her like a drowning man pulled from the sea. If she hadn't seen his face, naked of pretense or pride, if she hadn't heard the love in his voice, she would not have done it.

But she had seen and heard those things. She could not erase them now. "Lieutenant Colonel Kendall is my husband and Narain our oldest friend. What do you think *he* would want you to do?"

14

AMEERA, HAZARI AND NARAIN SPRAWLED LANGUIDLY IN THE garden, despondent and bored. They hadn't heard from Genevra; while Ameera and Hazari had long since begun to regret their promise, Narain feared she knew without asking where her friend had gone, and why.

At the moment when the three decided to rouse themselves and cool their overheated bodies in the fountains, Genevra stepped onto the back porch. The other three froze, waiting.

"Narain, my friend, you have done many things for me, but I would ask you for one last favor."

Their eyes met and held steady for a long moment, then Narain nodded. How could she refuse when Genevra had literally saved her life? "What would you have me do?"

"You'll find someone inside who wishes to talk to you."

Narain could barely move, her body had become so heavy. She could feel every heartbeat of the baby she carried, every movement, every kick. Nevertheless, she acknowledged as she made her way toward the house, Genevra was right. It had never been finished between Andrew and her. That last night hardly counted as a farewell. Glancing back at her friend for confidence, she stepped inside the house.

Narain met Andrew in the colorful, welcoming, underground room; it was cool, and she felt suddenly too warm. The light was dim; she didn't want him to see how shaken she was.

When he came in, she was lying on her side on the comfortable sofa among bright patterned cushions. Her face was exactly as he remembered it, though her pregnancy had changed her. Still, the sight of her transfixed him. Why and how, he asked himself silently, had he been foolish enough to let her go?

"I've come back," he said, "to make things right between us."

She stared at his tall, muscled body, his dark hair, which usually looked uncombed—but that was part of his charm. Mostly, she focused on his face—handsome, achingly familiar and so sensitive that it struck her powerfully how vulnerable he was, how much he had opened himself to her. She knew there were few men like him, and her body throbbed with grief and sadness. Whatever he had come for, whatever Genevra had said to bring him here, Narain was acutely conscious that he would not be here long. She couldn't let him get close again.

Andrew sat on an ottoman as near to her as he could get. He could see now she was swollen and uncomfortable, her lovely dark skin no longer glowed, and he guessed she'd not been sleeping. He reached for her hand, but she drew it away gently. "Why did you run so far?" he asked, his brown eyes full of torment.

She looked at him unwaveringly. "You do not know? You do not remember the things you said to me that last night?"

He flinched, because he remembered far too well. "Yes, but you must have known I was mad, that it wasn't me talking."

"Your lips spoke the words."

He rested his head in his hands. "But why did you keep running? Why did you hide yourself from me? I looked for you for days, but there was no sign."

"I might have known you were looking, but I did not wish to be found. Running was the only way I could survive those first few days, wearing myself down until I could not think or feel."

Glancing up, recognizing the mix of compassion and hurt on her face, Andrew drew a deep breath. "Please forgive me for driving you to that. When you told me about the child, I lost control; I couldn't think, only feel. As the days passed and I calmed myself, I also knew how cruel and unfair I'd been. And I miss you."

She brushed his fine dark hair with her fingertips, tenderly and with regret. "But you were right. We could not make a life together that would satisfy either one of us. And it would not be fair to the child." She cleared her throat and added hoarsely, "I have missed you too. You are a miracle I would not have missed, even with all that's come after."

His heart slowed and his head ached. "You're talking as though it's over."

"It's what you came to hear, is it not? You did not really think we could be together and happy? The prejudice of others, your frustration over your thwarted career, which I know you love, would poison our feelings in time. I believe you know that."

"I suppose . . . but I thought I should come anyway."

"To say good-bye?" she offered. Her eyes burned and her heart felt chilled.

"Well, that night, the last time I saw you, was hardly a farewell. I've felt unfinished, incomplete since then. But more important, I ask you again to forgive me."

Narain blinked back tears she would not allow herself to cry. "I forgive you. You had the courage to come ask me yourself; you understood, as I have all along, that we needed to change our ending, to make it kinder, so we can remember it without sorrow in the years after the pain has gone. I know it was not easy for you to face me, nor is it easy to look into your eyes and know I once fell into them so deeply that I was blind."

Andrew shifted uncomfortably, for he had actually thought, during the several days it took to get to Delhi, that she might come back. But she was wise, as always. In the end, no one would be happy, and the bitterness would have increased tenfold.

"I have loved you long, and now that you are here, I am not sorry that I did. But I think you must go. We cannot let ourselves fall under the spell again. You only live a miracle once. Let us not sit and watch it disintegrate into our grief."

"I will help take care of the child, of course," he said despondently.

For the first time, Narain's eyes flashed. "No. That would bind us further. I can care for her myself." She did not tell him what she thought about the fragility of the child, her poor chance of survival. Oddly, it would have broken his heart more completely, though it was the child who had parted them.

He shook his head back and forth. "You're very obstinate."

"Yes, and just as I forgave you, I hope you will forgive me for my faults and my mistakes." She put her fingers on his lips to keep him from objecting. "We were both there; we both knew the truth. We are both responsible. Do not carry that burden alone. It is not fair to you *or* me." Her eyes stung so much that she knew she could last no longer. "Please, go now, Andrew. Remember that I loved you and you me, for that is worth saving. Forget the rest; it will only cause unnecessary pain."

He could find no answer, as wave after wave of dejection washed over him. He loved her—only now did he realize how much—and he knew they could never be together. He knelt beside her, smoothed back her hair and murmured. "Don't forget the good; it was perhaps the best part of my life."

Narain knew she was going to lose control at any moment. "You are young," she said, nestling a little closer so his hand cupped her cheek. "You have barely begun to live your life. How can you think this was the best?"

"I don't just think it," he whispered, kissing her palm lightly. "I know it."

"Please," she said.

He felt the plea all through his body, and he understood. "I'll go. You're not well. I realize now I *had* to come, to see you once more, and to say, finally, farewell, my beloved. I will not forget."

She closed her eyes as he rose and left the room, closing the door behind him. The sound of his boots on the tile gradually faded. Only then did she begin to weep.

Everyone was sitting in the garden when Genevra heard a door close, then another. Automatically, she rose to go to Narain. She had to search the house until she found her in the last place Genevra thought she'd be—the underground room. Narain was still weeping, so her friend occupied herself rearranging cushions and painted pottery. Narain looked pale and drained and a tiny bit relieved.

"Thank you," she said as she wiped away the last tear with her handkerchief.

Genevra knew she meant for not speaking. She sat on the floor, holding Narain's hand. She did not ask questions, but simply waited.

"I sent Andrew away," Narain announced. "When I saw him today, how torn he was, how broken, I had no other choice. I did not want him to stay." She put her hand on Genevra's arm. "But I forgave him."

"Why?" She was truly curious.

"Because today you called me 'my friend.' Because if you tracked him down and brought him here, *you* must have forgiven *me*, at least a little. If you can do that, how can I withhold forgiveness from a man who loved me—I know that now—but had to follow his own nature. He cannot help being British, being afraid of what others think. Sometimes we don't understand that. Especially you, who have never been truly afraid."

Genevra breathed shallowly, a lump in her throat. She was very moved, very sad for her friend, and very proud of her. "I just wanted you to have the choice. Not him, but you."

Late that night, Narain escaped to the garden of flowing waters and began, slowly, to sing. Her dulcet voice rose and fell, cascading over the waterfalls, settling into the still pool at the heart of this magic place. She felt light, free. A heavy burden had been lifted from her shoulders. Though it hurt her to remember, she was glad she'd sent Andrew away. A life with him would have been hard, perhaps impossible. It was inevitable. But what was she going to do now?

As she rose, her lower back throbbed dully and a sharp pain nearly knocked the breath from her. She knew she should tell Genevra and Ameera immediately, but she was too uncertain. She wanted to *know*. She was weary of being in ignorance about her own body, her own child.

Silently, she went into her room, took a vial of herbs to relax, and fell into a deep sleep.

Genevra should have been exhausted. Instead, she was restless. Hazari and Ameera plied her with questions about the search, but she could not yet answer. She opened Narain's door to check on her and found her sleeping peacefully. She had not done that in a long time. Genevra was glad for her.

At dawn, unable to stay cooped up in the house any longer, she took her sketch pad and settled at a place along the river Jumna that Munia did not share. Genevra was drawing a heron, though she hadn't looked at the sketch since she began. She was trying to clear her head, to think, to plan, but she was accomplishing nothing. As usual, without warning, the wise woman stepped from out of the mist, frowning and stumbling. She appeared to be in great distress.

"What are you doing here?" she demanded. "You are needed at home. I see much pain, much confusion, much sorrow."

"Ameera is more skilled at helping with births. She's done it most of her life."

"But Ameera does not know your friend Narain as you do. No one does. With knowledge comes responsibility. You've always understood you had no choice in this, and if you did, you would not leave your friend's side anyway. That's who you are. Go now. Go!"

Numbly, the girl rose, but was struck by an impulse to look at her sketch of the heron. Now. This minute. Instead of a graceful heron in the reeds, she'd drawn Alex on a horse surrounded by clouds of dust. Often her fingers did not know what would show up on the page, but the picture was always true. She'd not drawn Alex in a long time. Clouds of dust. Hmm. She closed the pad. Was Alex coming home?

The house was very still, ominously so, when Genevra returned. She soon found Ameera in the sunken room with the tile floor. She'd removed everything from around the sofa and low tables, and for the second time, fashioned a bed for Narain to lie on. It was made of old clean linens, and there were more spread around her like a pale, wrinkled corona. All the cushions had been pushed to the sides of the room where they would be protected.

Ameera looked up in relief at Genevra's approach. "When she awoke this morning, the pains had started. Everything is ready. Please call when I am needed."

"Everything is *not* ready. I am not ready." As a pain contorted her body, Narain grabbed Genevra's arm; she had stretched out beside her friend on the floor. "I told you, this child was not meant to be. I told you what she would suffer. But whatever happens to her, I will not make it through the night." She squeezed Genevra's hand. "You had better accept that. Do you think you can?"

For an instant, Genevra's eyes filled with tears, then she brushed them angrily away with the back of her hand. "No, I can't. Because you have decided not to live. You have many choices, but you can't choose to die." Narain lay unblinking, and Genevra remembered the strength of her will. If she wished to die with all her heart, she could make it happen. If she gave up the spirit so vital in her, she would, especially in the blood and pain of a child's birth, flicker out like a candle. "Don't," she whispered. "Please don't."

Narain regarded her sadly. "I fear we will both step onto another boat tonight, myself and my daughter. She will be born into a different life and perhaps it will be kinder. Surely they would not blame her for my sins."

Rising, breathing in, then breathing out, over and over

in her own necessary ritual, Genevra thought, It will be a long day. Perhaps the longest of my life. But she did not intend to let her friend win. Narain had taught her too much. Soon they would see who was stronger, more determined, who would win a battle of their spirits and souls.

15

THE HOURS PASSED, ONE STRETCHING INTO ANOTHER, WHILE narain lay on her makeshift bed. By evening, sweat covered her body, beading on her forehead, rolling down her back. She was faintly aware of the rhythmic whine of the punkah stirring the hot, heavy air. Sometimes she was floating and sometimes she fell, but always she could hear the water below and beside her, running deep, carrying thousands of years of secrets and mysteries.

She heard fragmented voices. ". . . too weak. The loss of blood."

"No," Genevra insisted, as she had been doing for hours.

Narain concentrated on the pain that ripped through her; she wanted to scream, but instead bit down fiercely on the rag soaked in sweet herbs Genevra had put in her mouth. More hours passed before she heard sudden movement, felt Genevra touch her gently. Narain winced at the pressure and pain as something was pressed against her. She could not bear it. "Let her go. I am willing to do so. You have not spoken of blood, but I know there is too much. Let us go, I beg you."

"I can't," Genevra replied. "It's not the kind of person I am. You knew that when you first came here."

A knock drew everyone's attention, and Hazari poked his head around the door. When the Hindu women who had come to help saw him, they gasped. "He must not come in. It is unclean to have a man in the room at a birth."

"I don't take your taboo's lightly, but I must do what's best for Narain. Perhaps he can convince her to try. Please, Hazari, come."

The women were uneasy, but they remained silent.

Hazari knelt next to the pale figure, appalled by the amount of blood. But he gave no sign of his reaction on his face or in his eyes. Gingerly, he took Narain's hand and held it tight. "I am here, *larla*, and here I will stay. Genniji is right. You will survive—you and the child. You are very wise, but tonight you cannot see your own face in the mirror."

She smiled at him, surprised by the comfort of his cracked, callused fingers around hers. "What would I do with a child who is neither this nor that? Who has no chance in the world? Where would I go?"

"There are places in the lush green hills where we could live quietly, you cultivating your herbs and I my garden. And when you are better, and easy with the child, you can begin healing again."

Narain stared at him in disbelief, and this time, when her body filled with pain, she wept.

Kneeling beside Hazari, his mistress took Narain's free hand. "I won't lose her," she said doggedly, biting her lip until it bled. Narain's eyes were half-closed and strangely colored, and she coughed raggedly. She looked at Genevra in supplication.

Hazari and his mistress called her name softly, holding both her hands, and she knew they wanted to infuse her with their heat and energy. And hope. She did not want their hope; it was too bright, and the losing of it hurt too much. She mumbled words that made no sense—part Hindi and part English—her eyes bewildered.

But Genevra stood resolutely, pressing against the pain, trying to stop the bleeding.

All at once, Narain screamed. Thank the gods, Genevra

thought, for I was certain she'd not allow herself this relief because it might appear weak.

Dawn was creeping close when a flurry of movement began. Hazari was sent from the room and, with the help of four hands, Narain's child—a girl, as she'd predicted—was born and washed and wrapped tightly in swaddling clothes.

For the first time, Narain raised her head. "Is she—does she look—is she alive?" Her voice trembled in a way Genevra had never heard. She reached out to grasp both her friend's hands.

"She is alive, and Ameera, who knows these things, says she is a beautiful child."

Narain lay back, smiling. Then she sighed deeply. "Now I am free. Now I can go."

Genevra sent everyone away to give her a moment alone with the new mother. She kept hold of Narain's hands, and though her own were shaking with fury, she hung on. Then, turning on her friend, she said fiercely, commandingly, "You will not die, not today. Not in surrender."

"I surrender only my body, a shell, nothing more." She could barely speak. Genevra put her ear to her friend's lips to hear. "I am not leaving you. I will return in another guise, a better one, perhaps. Because of you, Genniji." She stared up at the earthen ceiling, drifting.

Not for a moment did Genevra release her grip on those two hands. "I don't understand."

"Neither did I until the day you brought my soldier home. I knew then there had been a sadness and a silence between us for too long. You took away my transgressions and sorrows; now I am ready to shed my skin and walk new and clean and lightly into the rest of my life. Please." She was finding it difficult to breathe and her chest rattled alarmingly. "Take this amulet from around my neck. It is yours."

Genevra did as she asked, but her expression was grim. With difficulty, as Narain had once taught her when she was ill, she cleared her friend's air passages and the wheezing stopped. The blood had stopped long since.

Genevra let the amulet hang from her wrist. "I can't take it."

"But you must. Only you may have it, because only you have shared my secrets and my weakness and my reborn strength. You must take it, and in doing so, admit that you have given me a gift of new life, because you have forgiven me, and loved me. I want you to understand that I choose to leave the earth."

"The earth," Genevra whispered, "and two friends who need you, and your own newborn child. That's what you're leaving behind."

"It was not meant to be."

Genevra had all the while been washing her, removing the soiled sheets. She put a cloth on her forehead, but realized it was not needed. Narain's fever had broken and her skin was warm, yet no perspiration lingered. She did not mention these things. "I don't understand how it was not meant to be. The gods gave you that child, and with her, the responsibility of raising her and loving her. For you to go now doesn't make sense."

"Not all things do." Narain's voice was becoming stronger, but she did not notice. "Please take the amulet *asparaji*. Hold it and feel the potency within and listen." She paused to catch her breath; she was determined to finish what she had to say.

"For time past time remembering," Narain continued, "the women in my family have been healers, and since the great-grandmother of my great-grandmother, this amulet has been our strength, our single treasure. The first who wore it gave it to her daughter, and each daughter to her own, until my grandmother became ill and thought she might die. She called me to her and said my mother's soul was bitter with hatred that would smother the kind spirits within the stone. She wanted me to have it instead. I almost lost my soul as well, but then I set out to find you because I cared for you, because I'd wronged you and wanted to atone, because I wanted to be worthy of the amulet I valued above all things.

"Now I give it to you, and with it, my spirit, which I have sealed within, as all the women of my family have done. This is my gift to you. Your gift to me is that you have forgiven me and loved me, and so changed my karma, for you are the only one I truly betrayed, the only one I truly loved. Please accept my spirit as my soul is born again. Please be happy for me, as I am for you."

Genevra's expression softened, but her voice was resolute. "I'm as happy for you as I am determined to see you joyful again."

Narain chose not to listen.

Genevra met Hazari at the door and saw that outside the light was gray and growing lighter. The *mali* did not have to ask his burning question about Narian; his mistress answered at once. "She'll live, if we can convince her that's what she wants. Tonight you and I must be stronger than she."

He released his breath in profound relief.

Worried that he was assuming too much, Genevra pressed her hand against his chest in warning. "Hazari, in the end it's her decision. She must make the final choice, no matter how much we want to guide her. Tell her the truth, then we must leave her alone. Can you do that? Can you leave the room and let the Fates turn as they will?"

He hesitated, chewing on the stem of his pipe. "I can try. It is worth the risk."

He went at once to Narain. His heart froze in his chest. "You look as if you've given up." He sounded hurt and angry.

"I am not giving up," she whispered. "I am following Brahma's will."

"Is it Brahma's will that you slip away and leave your child alone?" Hazari asked angrily. "Is it his will that you should leave me, now that you have shown me how to love you? I do not believe in such a will. I think you are frightened of the world after all. Afraid people will not revere you, will not look at you, even in secret."

Narain pressed his hand to her cheek, but he looked away. "You are afraid of being ordinary like me." He glanced at Genevra warily.

"You're right; she's afraid. But you don't die from fear. You simply learn to put it behind you."

Hazari looked at the faces of the two women he loved. At the strength and certainty in Genevra's, the softening in Narain's. She was listening, at least. She was giving them a chance.

Realizing Hazari had touched a chord Narain could not ignore, Genevra rose and slipped away. In the hall, she quickly found Ameera and took the baby from her.

She was stunned when the two walked into the hall before she had taken a step, Hazari holding Narain up, his arm around her shoulders. She turned to Genevra.

"I think Hazari is right. I am afraid to simply live again."

For a moment, Genevra was speechless. "You shouldn't be up yet," she said reflexively. That Narain stood here, upright, could only mean one thing. Genevra was delighted for her friend, glad she had not given in, and most of all, elated for the baby.

"Ah, but I should. If I continue to lie helpless on the floor, how will I hold and nurture and care for my daughter, Simla? I did not really look when you held her up before. I am eager to find her, to gaze at her tiny features and flailing hands and learn the face which you say is beautiful."

Genevra put the child, sleeping with her hands beneath swaddling blanket, into her mother's arms. To her surprise, she felt no envy, only relief and joy at her friend's decision. Perhaps Narain was right; perhaps she'd been too impatient. She would wait and pray for her own children, and someday, perhaps, they would come.

"The first thing I will tell you, little Simla," Narain murmured to her newborn baby, "is that your mother has grown up tonight. Perhaps, someday, I will be as serene and contented as you are, my daughter, simply lying in my arms." She turned to her friend. "I must also tell you, Genniji, that I was wrong when I said a child could not fulfill you. You and I, we have done that for ourselves through all the years we have fought the people, the Fates, the cruelty of our world. Fought them, and, finally left them behind. I should have believed you. You are wiser than I." She buried her face in her baby's powdered blankets, laying her cheek against Simla's so tenderly that there were no doubts or questions left.

16

GENEVRA LEFT THE HOUSE IMMEDIATELY, WITHOUT TAKING time to change her blood-stained clothes. She was not aware of the state she was in, and did not care. She had expected to feel mourning and trepidation because Hazari and Narain were leaving as soon as the baby was strong enough to travel. But the long, emotional night had turned to dawn and dawn to a morning unexpectedly cool and cloudy. She was grateful for the relief and smiled to herself. After all, alone she had tracked down Narain's soldier, convinced him to come back so they could put their love to rest. She had helped rebuild her crumbling house into the inviting, pleasant home she'd always wanted. Now she had delivered a baby, plead for her life, then, difficult as it had been, left the choice to Narain.

Genevra did not feel sad or regretful; she felt triumphant, invincible. She had learned of a strength of will she did not guess she had; she thought she would not often be afraid anymore. She danced along the paths, singing Hindu prayers. She was hardly aware of where she was going; her feet barely touched the ground.

Then, in an instant, Munia was there blocking her way, staring at the ruby pendant around her throat. She had forgotten it was there. She had offered it to Narain for Simla when she grew up, but her friend had insisted they were starting a new life. The amulet was beautiful, it was powerful, but it was from before. "Keep it," she'd said. "I meant what I said. I want you to have it."

Munia was transfixed by the amulet, caught in its ruby depths for a long while. Then she looked up, her wrinkled face softened by tears. "I see that you have forgiven my granddaughter in the end."

"Your granddaughter? A child of your blood?" Genevra found she was not so much surprised as angry. Another betrayal. She had opened her heart to the wise woman, told her all about Narain, and never once had she hinted the girl was her granddaughter. "You knew. From the first time I mentioned her name, you knew."

Nodding pensively, Munia agreed. "It was I who sent her to you. This time, only you could save her. For years, she's carried you on her shoulders like heavy stone, and now you have removed the weight and she will be herself again."

"Not precisely herself. I think you'll find she's changed a great deal." Suddenly, Genevra stepped back. "But how did you know all this? Did she come to see you?"

"Not since the day she arrived."

Caught off guard, the girl retreated a step, looking into the woman's glowing dark eyes, her piercing gaze, remembering how often she had come from nowhere just when she was needed. Perhaps it was not coincidence, but something more powerful. She fondled the amulet uneasily, then gripped it tight.

Munia shook her grizzled head. Today she was not wearing her silver scarf or sacred thread. "No, I had no grand vision. The look on your face told me all I needed to know. And, of course, the amulet." She reached out to brush her finger across it reverently, as Narain had done many times.

"Then you do not know that she has a healthy daughter named Simla, and Hazari the *mali* wants to take her into the cool green hills and make her his wife."

The wise woman considered. "That is good. She has waited a long time for a man like him, who will take her with him into *his* world." She picked up her burlap gown, which was drooping in the mud. "But will you not be lonely when they go? Afraid to live alone?" There was a sparkle in her eye that could have been a challenge.

Laughing jubilantly, Genevra shook her head. She was alive; she was safe, wherever she might be, alone or not. She knew now she had friends who loved and helped her, believed in her and turned to her for guidance.

She had done a great deal by herself in the last months, without Alex, filling her house with people and color and life. Now he, too, would have a real home to return to. She discovered the amulet with the deep red ruby in her hand again and felt its warmth and vitality. "I am satisfied. I am at peace."

Munia's eyes grew damp and she lay her hand on the girl's cheek. "I am proud of you, Genevra Kendall. You are free." She motioned toward the water, her smile poignant.

Genevra ran forward, stripped off her blood-stained shift and chemise, and dove naked into the water. It closed over her head, accepting her and blessing her.

She smiled as she cleansed the blood and sweat and turmoil from her pale white body in the very heart of the sacred river Jumna.

Epilogue

Fourteen years later: Kent, England, 1896

IN THE DREAM, SHE WAS RUNNING THROUGH THE GLEN, *stumbling on fallen trees and hillocks and at the edges of bogs. Then she saw Ailsa ahead, moving blindly, and knew she must catch her, stop her before she lost her way. Genevra called and shouted, but Ailsa did not hear, did not look where she was going. Her sister realized someone else was near, that Ailsa's attention was focused on that figure. Genevra had to catch them both, to make them recognize her warning or all three would be lost in the tangled night forest of naked trees. The distance between them widened, and her skin grew clammy with fear, but she could not make them see her. She might as well have been a shadow. Then she heard thunder and a great grinding of stones, and knew it was too late.*

The amulet slipped from her hand, the soft sound as it hit the carpet waking her from the nightmare. For a moment, she was not certain if she were in India or Scotland, then high-pitched voices brought her home. She'd fallen asleep in her favorite chair facing the bay windows and a pair of French doors. Soft sunlight drifted through the glass, lighting the room with an unusual glow.

"Give it to me, Lizzie. You always grab it first when Mummy

brings it out of its fancy box," four-year-old Anne moaned, her blonde sausage curls having already begun to unwind.

Elizabeth Kendall, the oldest at twelve, cried out when her brother John took the pendant while she tried to disengage herself from Anne, who was clinging to her peppermint-striped skirt with grubby fingers.

Motioning to his brother Jeremy, John crept behind the lilac velvet settee, where the boys, aged nine and six, bent to examine their treasure.

"Mummy! They've done it again," Lizzie said as calmly as possible. She was practically grown up now, and she must behave with decorum, she told herself. She liked that word, decorum. The governess had taught it to her yesterday. Besides, she did not want her mother to think she considered the pendant a toy as the other three did. Genevra Kendall thought it very important indeed. She got it out rarely, and when she did, she sometimes fell asleep and had strange, upsetting dreams; sometimes she sat staring, head tilted, as if listening for something. Did the ruby talk as well? Lizzie wondered, but did not have the courage to ask.

"Something wrong?" Alex asked his wife, sliding into the wing-back chair she occupied and settling her on his lap. "You're pale this morning. And from the look in your eyes, I'm not entirely certain you can see me." He worried about Genevra, who looked delicate at thirty-five, with her fair skin and pale blonde hair, which was, as usual, coming loose from its carefully crafted chignon. But she was no more delicate than she'd been at eighteen and burned brown by the Indian sun.

Genevra smiled softly, aware of her husband's distress. Caressing his cheek, catching her fingers in his thick blond hair, she murmured, "It's just the dream again."

"Of Ailsa and the glen?" His arms tightened around her. These dreams made him uneasy.

She nodded, staring at the portrait of her husband above the fireplace—the last she'd painted of Alex in

India. They'd stayed one year after Narain's daughter was born, then received word that Alex's older brother no longer wanted to care for Ladybrooke, the family estate. He'd begged Alex to take his place.

By then, India had begun to wear on Genevra and her husband, so they'd come home to England. Once again, Narain had been right. The climate in India had not been completely healthy for Genevra; the children were proof.

She caught the dream in her wandering thoughts. "I know there's regret and sorrow lurking in the shadows, but Ailsa's turned her back and I can't reach her." She shivered, chilled despite the roaring fire in the morning room. She could not explain the feeling of helplessness that enveloped her when her sister did not look back or respond to the sound of her voice. Once, in the dream, Lian had been with her, equally fearful, equally impotent. She knew Alex did not understand the depth of the connection among the half-sisters, could not comprehend what it meant when one of them turned away from the others.

But the nightmare had come three days in succession, filling her with apprehension. In truth, she'd been uneasy since Ailsa had stopped writing, and Mairi wrote less often, with a strained tone in her usually flowing words. Only Genevra's niece, Ena, continued to send her whimsical letters as always.

"Mummy! Mummy! the boys took your pretty and they're going to hide it from Lizzie and me." Anne stood, arms akimbo, feet apart, ready to do battle.

Only when she met her youngest daughter's accusing gaze did Genevra remember she'd gotten out the amulet this morning. She'd been holding it loosely in her hand. One of the children must have crept up and snatched it away. "John, Jeremy! Where are you? What have you been doing?"

Anne stamped her foot, but spoiled the effect by smiling and revealing her dimple. "I've been telling you and telling you, but you just keep looking at Daddy."

With a great deal of aplomb for her age, Elizabeth drew her sister into the circle of her arm to explain solemnly, "Mummy gets upset when she dreams about unpleasant things, and she wants to fix them, but she can't. So she turns to Daddy. Sometimes he makes her smile and forget, sometimes he only listens and she feels better for having told him."

Alex and Genevra were astonished at how much their daughter perceived. They'd not realized she'd been watching quite so closely. How could they have missed this change in her? They spent as much time as possible with all four children, at the beach when it was warm enough, playing word games and singing their favorite songs in six off-key voices. They read to each child alone every night, so none would feel favored and none neglected. Alex took the boys out to the stables and let them watch the horse trainers, and Genevra taught Elizabeth how to draw and embroider, though the girl often slipped away to read a book in a private corner she'd discovered. Genevra and Anne had created a virtual kingdom of dolls in the parlor, where guests were either delighted and charmed or quietly, politely appalled that the lady of Ladybrooke allowed herself to engage in such ridiculous behavior.

That made Genevra smile and think of Phoebe, whose outrageous behavior was legendary. She still remembered vividly the day Phoebe had appeared at their door, her hair as wild as ever, though more gray than red, her gown apparently constructed of a proliferation of large, bright, cleverly draped scarves. "I've been waiting an eternity for you to get here," she'd exclaimed. "Always thought I was rather good company, but I recently began to bore myself. Mali is delightful, of course, but his conversation's somewhat limited." She indicated the monkey on her shoulder; he looked up at the sound of his name, then went back to pulling the few remaining pins from her hair.

After an emotional reunion, in which she described her

travels through the Lake Country, where she'd walked the grief and regret out of her system, Phoebe had asked to see the children and demanded to know which was her god-child, as she intended to spoil him or her outrageously. There'd only been Elizabeth and John at the time, and both had volunteered with gratifying determination.

Not wanting to cause discord, and discovering the chil-dren already had godparents—"But they're quite dull, not nearly as fun as you," Elizabeth offered—Phoebe had declared she would be their honorary grandmother instead. Since neither Alex nor Genevra's parents were alive, this met with everyone's approval. Now she came several times a year, staying for a week or a month, depending on her current whim.

The children adored her generosity, creativity, humor and absolute fearlessness in the face of the proper matrons who deplored her outlandish behavior. They called her "Gran" and were delighted at the matrons' distress. She had become a fixture in the Kendall family's lives, and Genevra was delighted.

Genevra shook herself and tried to concentrate. She simply could not keep her thoughts still today.

"It's all right, Mummy," Elizabeth said reassuringly. "We don't mind when your eyes go gray and you leave us for a lit-tle in your head. But you'd tell us if anything was wrong, wouldn't you? You'd not leave us out as if we can't under-stand. We can, you know. Quite a bit in fact. And one thing I know is that after you come back from wherever you've been, you always paint a lovely picture, though I can't always guess what it means. Only Gran seems to know at once."

Genevra's eyes widened. Now it seemed her daughter was reading her thoughts. Alex tightened his arm around his wife's waist, cleared his throat uncomfortably. "We often find you missing in the afternoon. Where is it that you go?" It was the only response he could think of to her intense perceptions, which were making him uneasy.

Elizabeth let go of her younger sister in order to stand perfectly straight. "I've planted a little herb garden and I'm learning which ones help the ache in your shoulder, Daddy, and Johnny's ear infections. I even know what to do the next time Jeremy falls on a splintered fence post."

Genevra leaned forward, suddenly intent. "Do you now? You never seemed interested in that sort of thing before." Was there a hint of hope in her voice, of restrained anticipation?

"Well, a person changes, Mummy. You should know that. I shan't be a child forever, and I want to know things and be wise and have people respect me. Though what I should like best is to be just like Gran and shock them all as often as possible."

Alex groaned while Genevra hid her bemusement by calling her sons over and retrieving the amulet. She rubbed the ruby stone, then the carved gold setting with her thumb. She did that sometimes when she had a difficult problem to solve. She had meant to think about the dreams and the disturbing news from the glen, but was momentarily distracted. "You may do anything you like, become anyone you want to be, if you have strength enough, and courage."

Elizabeth smiled, grateful that her mother was listening, not dismissing her daughter's desires as ridiculous or unimportant.

The girl was unquestionably lovely when she smiled.

"Beth, darling, you reminded me of someone just then, only I can't think who," Alex mused.

Smiling widely, his daughter waved her hand in the air in an undulating curve. "It doesn't matter, Daddy. It's only me."

Perplexed by Genevra's stillness and Elizabeth's odd remarks, Alex became aware that his four children stood clustered about the chair, staring, mouths agape, as if waiting for some momentous event.

Quickly, before she could change her mind, Genevra slipped the amulet into her oldest daughter's hand.

"Oh! It's so warm," Elizabeth cried. "The light's caught inside the ruby."

"Of course it is, silly. I just lit it behind the settee. Secret place for the match, but I shan't tell you where. Gran showed it to me." John tried to remain solemn, but by the time he was finished, he was snickering. Jeremy laughed loudly, poking his sister, since he couldn't catch his breath to make fun of her.

"But it is!" Elizabeth insisted. "Isn't it, Mummy?"

Genevra considered carefully. With all the children so near, her eldest daughter stood out. The other three had the same untamable glossy blond hair, the same clear, creamy complexions, the same clear blue eyes. It was not that Elizabeth looked as if she didn't belong in the family. She had Alex's obstinate jawline, for one thing, and Genevra's hands and skill with a sketchpad and brush. But she was different. More pensive, less boisterous, and she mothered the others, keeping track of them when they went to the beach or on a picnic, making certain everyone got enough to eat without giving them anything that would upset their sensitive tummies.

Genevra stared at the stone glowing in her daughter's hand. Lizzie'd always liked to hold it, and her mother had trusted her to do so when she was very young. Genevra'd been more careful with the others. They were children with children's boundless energy and disregard for furniture or vases or knickknacks that might get in their way. But not Elizabeth.

Meeting her daughter's steady gaze, Genevra allowed herself to wonder for an instant. Was it possible? Could an amulet hold that much power? It had, after all, been Narain's sacred pendant. Afraid the girl would guess her thoughts, Genevra shook her head emphatically. No. There were other things to think about just now.

She had already written to Lian suggesting they return to Glen Affric. She could not escape the feeling that it was vital, not just to Ailsa and Mairi, but also to Lian and Genevra. She could not think why, but the idea would not leave her in peace.

"Alex," she said, tearing her gaze from her daughter's, "I'm sure I won't rest till we know what's happening in the Highlands. I think I should go, and soon, even if Lian decides—"

"Of course you must, if you're dreaming those dreams. I'm certain Aunt Lian will go as well. She's just as worried about Aunt Ailsa." Elizabeth spoke with quiet certainty. When she saw how the rest of her family stared at her, aghast, she added quickly, "I mean, knowing Aunt Lian. She wouldn't let you go alone, would she?"

"No," Genevra said slowly, "she wouldn't."

"You needn't worry about us. Gran mentioned in her last letter that she'd probably be here soon. She'll take care of us," Elizabeth said.

"Oh, I'm sure she will," Alex said with more than a trace of irony.

His daughter ignored him. "And they need you in the glen, Mummy. I feel it inside. If you follow the path in your dream, then perhaps you'll sleep soundly and not wake trembling."

"Well, then you shall go," Alex said before he heard more. He had never felt comfortable with the half-sisters' shared dreams, though he neither doubted nor feared Genevra's ability to draw what she had never seen. In spite of his wariness, he could not deny his own feeling that Genevra must go. His wife had never been able to ignore a call from the depths of her dreams. And he would never try to change her.

She had already written to Liam suggesting they return to Glen Athie. She could not escape the feeling that it was vital, not just to Aissa and Mairi, but also to Liam and Geneva. She could not think why, but the idea would not leave her in peace.

"Alex," she said, tearing her gaze from her daughter's. "I'm sure I won't rest till we know what's happening in the Hebrides. I think I should go, and soon, even if Liam decides—"

"Of course you must, if you're dreaming those dreams. I'm certain Aunt Liam will go as well. She's just as worried about Aunt Ailsa." Elizabeth spoke with quiet certainty. When she saw how the rest of her family gazed at her, aghast, she added quickly, "I mean, knowing Aunt Liam, she wouldn't let you go alone, would she?"

"No," Geneva said slowly, "she wouldn't."

"You needn't worry about us, Gran mentioned in her last letter that she'd probably be here soon. She'll take care of us," Elizabeth said.

"Oh, I'm sure she will," Alex said with more than a trace of irony.

His daughter ignored him. "And they need you in the glen, Mammy. I feel it inside. If you follow the path in your dream, then perhaps you'll sleep soundly and not wake trembling."

"Well, then you shall go," Alex said before he heard more. He had never felt comfortable with the half-sisters' shared dreams, though he neither doubted nor feared Geneva's ability to draw what she had never seen. In spite of his wariness, he could not deny his own feeling that Geneva must go. His wife had never been able to ignore a call from the depths of her dreams. And he would never try to change her.

Book Five

✣

And on the dark side of this journey,
we all need a little love to get us home.
We touch the sky and then we fall down
to the ground;
we dust the dirt from our sleeve;
we stumble free,
And there lies the moon.

Prologue

Glen Affric, Scotland, Autumn 1895

FOR THE FIFTH NIGHT IN A ROW, AILSA DREAMED SHE FROZE *at the foot of her father's grave. She was acutely aware of Genevra standing on one side and Lian on the other. Sometimes she had felt warmth and pleasant expectation, but tonight she was plagued by a sense of foreboding. There was no mist to obscure the crisp darkness, to weave a veil between the full moon and the three women, linked hand to hand.*

Ailsa did not feel their warmth in the cool autumn night, though the fingers curled around her half-sisters' ached and throbbed. There was no wind, and the Valley of the Dead was eerily silent in the cool gleam of the moonlight. She was afraid to look down at the gaping hole of her father's fresh-dug grave, afraid to relinquish her hold on Lian and Genevra.

She glanced toward the lid of the plain pine coffin, but found instead a grave long filled, scattered with the last of the summer wildflowers and mounded with years of multicolored stones. There was no raw soil visible, no wound in the earth, and Lian and Genevra were not shaking or afraid.

Turning warily, Ailsa regarded her sisters. Both were immeasurably older than they should have been—not the girls who had once stood here, afraid to release one another for fear of falling forward into the open grave. There was sorrow and wisdom in their eyes, perhaps even compassion. But no fear.

It was impossible that the ~~three~~ women should be standing together again in the spot where they had once abandoned hope, yet the scene was very real. Ailsa could smell the moist night air, the sweet scent of wildflowers, feel the cold silver moonlight on her face. The grip of her sisters' hands was tight and painful, their palms moist against one another. It was not as it had been before, just after Charles Kittridge's death. Everything around her had aged and changed. The thought made Ailsa uneasy.

Suddenly Ailsa found herself standing in the door of the croft where everyone huddled around Charles Kittridge's bed, where he lay dying. But again, it was not the same. The faces were older, and the grief, while just as wild within, was more muted on the faces of the mourners. Other things had changed as well; those she felt but could not see. She only knew they should not have stood at the foot of his grave covered with stones before they knelt beside her father's deathbed. Chills ran up her arms and she shuddered. Something was very wrong. So wrong that it propelled her upward, forcing her awake.

Ailsa sat up in her heather bed, rubbing her arms to warm herself. She was deeply disturbed by the dream and could not shake the feeling, make it slide away into the early-morning mist. Slowly she became aware of another presence and turned to find Mairi Rose sitting up in bed with the same cold fear on her face, rubbing her arms in the same helpless way.

Mother and daughter stared at one another, speechless, for a long, tense moment, knowledge and sorrow heavy in the air between them. Ailsa opened her mouth, but no words came, just a deep chill that left her shaking. All she could see was Mairi's eyes, wide with foreboding, reflecting the look on her daughter's face.

Her mother had been dreaming Ailsa's dream, and was afraid.

1

AILSA HAD BEEN WALKING ALL AFTERNOON, TRYING TO alleviate her inexplicable agitation by losing herself in the summer woods, following the rush and flow of the burn. She had braided her hair, but had not bothered to put it up, so eager had she been to get away, to be moving. She had calmed a little as the hours passed, but was full of expectation, which only increased, until it drove her back toward home.

She paused at the sight of thick smoke curling into the sky above the croft; the fire must be larger than usual. Then she noticed dark shapes against the garden wall that looked like travelers' trunks. She began to hurry, holding her breath. Yes, she discovered as she approached the cottage, they were indeed trunks. And the fragrance of some unfamiliar food wafted toward her through the window.

Ailsa's heart skipped like a young girl's, and she didn't bother to tuck her disheveled hair behind her ears or smooth her gown before she ducked under the door to find Mairi seated in her usual chair, her hands idle for once. Ena sat near her on the settle, and both gazed, mesmerized at the two women who sat across the blazing peat fire. Ailsa saw only the back of their heads—the ebony hair caught up in a butterfly clip, the blond tendrils that drifted free of the chignon—but she had no doubt who the visitors were. Her pulse raced as she paused noiselessly on the threshold.

They could not have heard her, but they turned, aware of her presence without the need for sight or sound. Slowly, Lian and Genevra rose, and for a moment the three half-sisters stood unmoving, taking in the sight of one another, looking for changes, not in looks, but in feeling.

"Why did I no' guess ye were comin'? Why didn't ye say?" Ailsa murmured, dissolving the stillness among them. Then she thought of the last several nights, of the images that had followed her through the days. She'd barely slept the night before, had been excited and expectant all day. "But of course I sensed it. I just didn't quite believe. No' after so long. I should've known better."

"Aye, so ye should've." Mairi beamed at them all, luminous in the firelight and the force of her joy.

Ena was speechless, watching, absorbing the actual presence of the aunts she knew only through their letters. She had never heard their voices or felt their embrace until today.

She had been thrilled to find them waiting when she came back an hour since, had been unable to take her eyes from these two women who had befriended her from afar. She'd listened, breathless, as they talked with Mairi of a time long before she existed, answered eagerly when they asked about her animals and Connor and the changes in the glen. She'd gone willingly into their arms when Mairi introduced them, feeling as if she'd always been there, leaning against their experience and strength. She'd waited, barely able to contain her curiosity, for her mother's return.

Now, she and her grandmother watched while, as if propelled forward, Ailsa, Lian and Genevra met in the center of the packed dirt floor.

They had not yet touched, but Ena could feel the connection among them. The meshwork of blood and dreams and history that bound them was palpable, and as they stepped closer and slid their arms about each others' waists, it became, for an instant, visible.

2

THE THREE SISTERS STEPPED INTO THE PREDAWN MIST, AILSA wrapped warmly in her plaid, Lian in her padded jacket and Genevra in her wool pelisse. They walked quietly; everything around them slumbered, and they enjoyed the hush, the stillness. Without discussion, they knew where they were going; besides Mairi's croft, only two places lured them with a force they could not ignore. And of the two, one voice was louder, more compelling than the other.

They linked arms, partly for warmth, partly so Ailsa could guide them easily over the paths she knew so well, partly for reassurance. When the woods had closed around them, the mist clinging in the treetops and drifting downward as gray light began to rim the horizon, Genevra whispered, "I'm not sure I'm quite ready. Can we walk round a bit first, till the sun's up and this place feels real again?"

Ailsa glanced at Lian, who nodded. "I, too, would rather arrive after the sun has risen. I have had enough of shadows. I want to remember the feel of the loam beneath my feet, the scent of pine and the taste of sweet, misted air. I wish to go softly, comfortably to a place I remember as harsh and unwelcoming."

"Aye, then," Ailsa agreed. She, too, was nervous about returning to the place where their grief and anger had last mingled. She'd been there many times alone, but not once with her sisters beside her. She could only imagine what emotions their presence would resurrect. "We'll wander till 'tis right, 'tis time."

"How will we know?" Genevra murmured.

Ailsa looked from one to the other. "We'll know. Just as ye knew to come back."

Mairi drew her red plaid close about her to keep away the chill that hovered in the air. Head bent, she wound her way toward the valley where Charles lay. She did not have to watch her feet for fear of stumbling, though night had draped the woods and braes in purple-gray shadows that had not quite been lifted by the sun. Mairi could walk this path blind, as one day she suspected she would have to, with nothing to guide her but her longing and her willing spirit.

When she reached the Valley of the Dead, she slipped through the narrow opening in the tall stones and stumbled toward her goal, her joints stiff from sleep and cold. She scrutinized the rock-strewn ground, found one flawed but beautiful silver stone, and knelt beside her husband's cairn.

Gently, tenderly, she kissed the stone, tasting the salt on its surface, catching her tongue on the single rough edge. She warmed it in her cupped palms for a moment, then placed it with care above Charles Kittridge's head. For a long time, she did not remove her hand, but pressed it, fingers spread, palm down, onto the uneven mound of stones.

Closing her eyes, she tilted her head back, allowing her plaid to fall to her shoulders so she felt the first warm rays of the sun find their way across the majestic and dangerous mountains. Mairi remained unmoving, listening to the voices in the wind that spoke only to her. She let the chilly morning wind enwrap her, the tears of the dead surround her, the sound of one voice soothe her.

"I remember it, my Charlie," she said at last. "I remember it all. Every moment of solitude, each eternity of joy. You're with me, my husband. I feel your cold lips on my withered cheek. Not soft and smooth, as when ye last touched it. But mine just the same, and so, I hope, dear to ye."

Completely alone with her past, she lingered, unwilling to return to the hard earth of the valley, to the cold wind and the silence within it that sometimes stole her breath and left her gasping.

At last, because she had no choice, she opened her eyes and stared down at the barrier of stones between her and the long, sweet stillness of rest. So easily she could brush the stones away until she reached the barren earth above her husband's grave, so easily expose raw loam, that, having been disturbed once, would not mind another violation. "Not now, Mairi Rose, ye weak daft fool," she murmured aloud. "There's too much to be done."

She fixed her gaze intently on the grave and began to speak, as if to a nearby companion. "They're home, Charlie-*mo-chridhe*. Every one of them back home. I knew they'd come. They found their way to me as once they found their way to ye, when ye cried out from your heart, and despite their doubts, they came." She was surprised, touched; her voice shook as if she had not truly expected Lian and Genevra to return now, when it mattered most. She had not expected the sweet recognition in their eyes when they first held her. She felt again their warm breath on her cheek and knew they were skin and blood and bone, not ghost or phantom.

She ran her gnarled fingers above the grave. "I need them now, ye ken. And it makes me afraid, yet content, knowin' they're here."

For the first time, she let fall the mask she wore when she did not wish her thoughts to be known. She had not the power to maintain the pretense. Her face, no longer deeply browned by the sun, was pale and weathered and marked by wrinkles and curves and narrow lines that could tell many stories to one with the Sight. Her eyes were full of sorrow and elation, yearning and trepidation. "I never thought to hear myself say it, but without them, I'm thinkin' I could no' go on much longer. I need your daughters, my daughters by me. I need their vigor and dignity; I want to see through their eyes. Young eyes, new eyes." She lay her hands on the many-colored stones and her cheek upon her hands. "I need, them, my Charlie, my lad. We all do."

She was silent for a long time with her cheek pressed painfully against her hands and the pressure of the smooth round stones. Closing her eyes, she whispered, so the words were caught and captured by the wind, "Ye see, for the first time in my life, I can no' say how 'twill end. Only that the time is comin'. Where my secret knowledge used to glow and taunt and promise me, there's only darkness now. I can no' even guess."

Another long silence. Then, "Mayhap, after, they'll let me rest wi' ye at last. Mayhap we're closer than ye ken, ye and me."

Jenny Fraser had thought she'd be alone when she reached Mairi Rose's croft. She'd wanted to come last night, when she first heard of the arrival of the visitors, but had restrained herself. They would be weary, in need of peace and rest. And Jenny had become very good at seeing to the needs of others, very adept at restraint. But she suspected the Roses and their visitors would not be thinking of practicalities today, so she had come, partly to make certain all were fed, and partly because she could not bear to stay at home and miss all the activity.

"Jenny! What're ye doin' out and about so early?"

She started at the sound of Alanna Fraser's voice coming out of the mist just before the woman herself appeared. Jenny was surprised at how relieved she was to see a friendly face. Ever since she'd heard about the guests, she'd felt restless, had wandered through the croft and garden listlessly, unable to concentrate. It seemed to her she was waiting, but she did not know for what.

She pointed to the huge iron pot she carried, full to the brim with potatoes and carrots and cabbage and mutton. "I knew Mairi Rose would need extra food, with all the goin's on tonight. No doubt they'll be comin' from far and near to see for themselves the legendary sisters of Ailsa Rose Sinclair in flesh and blood. Who could resist such a temptation?"

"Aye," Alanna agreed, glancing about regretfully. She'd known they would all be off on their own, but that didn't make her curiosity any less relentless. Now that she looked closely, she saw her feelings reflected in Jenny's hazel eyes. "There'll be a *ceilidh* tonight in this house, and naught but a snowstorm in summer could prevent it." She too had baskets of food over each arm—freshly baked oatcakes, black currant buns and crowdie and cold boiled eggs wrapped in mince. She also had apples and fresh onions and gingerbread.

She and Jenny stopped at the door, ducked down to peek inside and saw that no one was home.

Jenny shook her head in dismay. "What are they thinkin' of, runnin' off without leavin' even a broth to simmer for their supper?"

"Mayhap," Alanna mused, "they're no' thinkin' at all."

Jenny's gaze locked with Alanna's in silent understanding. "I've no doubt you're right. 'Tis feelin' they are, and rememberin'." She spoke wistfully, because she'd been excluded from this reunion. She and Alanna both. She paused on the threshold. "Why do ye think they've come? Why now?"

Tilting her head, considering, Alanna murmured, "I'll wager 'tis more than a whim that brought them suddenly, without warnin'. They're so like Mam that something must've compelled 'em to come. I wonder what it means."

Seeing how serious she was, Jenny tried to imagine a force beyond her control or understanding leading her where it would. She could not quite do it. "Ye really believe it means something more than that Lian and Genevra missed their sister and wanted to see her because it'd been too long?"

"Och, aye. Mam sent Ena to fetch me last night to greet my aunts after so many years. They were content in bein' together again, but there's something more, something unspoken. I'm no' sure even they know what, but they're lookin' for something or waitin' for something. I can feel it." She'd been glad to join the visitors, for thus they'd drawn her into the circle of their presence and their purpose, and she'd felt a faint tension in the air, anticipation. "We talked long into the night," she said, "and I saw how they watched Ena and Gran when we sat huddled around the fire. There's a reason they've come and no mistake."

Jenny sighed and rolled her shoulders back and forth, feeling inexplicably as if a weight had been lifted from them. "Aye, weel, we'll have to wait and see."

Mairi sensed that she was not alone and raised her head, the marks of the stones pressed into her cheeks, her face wet with tears. Ailsa, Lian and Genevra hovered nearby, hesitating. Quiet contentment flowed through her at the sight. She lifted her arms, stiff from the chilly air, in invitation. "Ye need no' be goin'. I've spent my time alone here, rememberin'. Come."

Lian was the first to notice Mairi had not risen because her limbs were weak from kneeling on the cold hard ground and her curved walking stick was beyond her reach. Nimbly, she crossed the uneven ground, idly picked up the larch branch, smoothed by the constant touch of Mairi's hand, and dropped the walking stick at her side.

Mairi paused as she struggled to get her feet beneath her. Swiftly, Lian and Ailsa flanked her, appearing to stare at the cairn, leaning so close that their legs touched Mairi's shoulders. They did not move away until she had used the weight of their bodies to brace herself as she rose, clutching her walking stick with both hands.

Smiling her wise, sweet smile, Mairi turned her head, listening to the cry of the wind as if trying to discern its message. She stared at the leveled tops of the standing stones, where mist had begun to creep among the tall, unchanging sentinels of rock. "I've had my time with my Charlie. Ye stay and have yours. I'll start back, and mayhap you'll catch me on the way." She glanced down at her walking stick. "I'm no' as quick on my feet as I used to be." She said it matter-of-factly, without self-pity. Smiling, she reached out, and the sisters did the same. She covered their hands, one atop the other, with hers, and they stood for a moment, suspended in time. Mairi felt a sense of peace that warmed her aching bones, looked from Genevra to Lian to Ailsa in gratitude, then released them and headed unerringly through the billowing mist toward the hidden entrance to the valley.

3

LIAN, AILSA AND GENEVRA STOOD IN THE VALLEY OF THE Dead, wrapped in the chilly wind's embrace, staring at Charles Kittridge's grave. They had come as if drawn by a magnet that pulled them in its wake regardless of their will, though by taking a circuitous route, they'd prolonged the inevitable. Despite their apprehension, this was very different from the last time they had come. Sixteen years ago, united by their overwhelming grief, they had been unable to accept the loss of their father, the abrupt end to a relationship newly formed and, therefore, doubly precious. His loss had left them drained, angry, bereft.

Now, as then, the voices of ghosts cried out, caught inside the wind that whirled through the valley and upward toward the huge, tilted circle of standing stones.

Violent tinted light infused the air, coiling into the heavy mist that rose from among the tall patterned boulders of this ancient, sacred place, as the sun rose behind the stark mountains in the distance, shattering the darkness and announcing the arrival of another day.

The sisters stared in silence at the long, narrow mound formed from thousands of colored stones—a palpable reminder of their father and their loss.

All at once the wind stopped, filling the expectant stillness by its absence as wholly as it had by its presence. The sisters glanced at one another, and without the need for words, bent to search the ground for a special stone to add to the mound. Lian found a long oval of polished rust shot through with a thread of silver. She held it, waiting, as Ailsa discovered a deep violet and Genevra a soft, earth-colored stone. Then, as one, they knelt to arrange the stones over the place where Charles Kittridge's heart would have been.

Genevra's hand shook a little as she placed her stone, but she steadied it and gazed down, eyes filmed with tears. "We shouldn't cover his heart, for that is Mairi's," she murmured, trying to sort out the sadness and gratitude she felt.

Without looking up, Ailsa replied, "No. Our father's spirit belongs to my mother and his soul and his true nature, which she cradles inside like a secret treasure." She noticed the glimmer on Lian's wrist as she rose, and the shining braided chain around Genevra's throat. The bracelet Charles had given Ke-ming, the necklace Emily Townsend had cherished, each made of intertwined white and yellow gold. Each a unique gift to the women who had borne his daughters. Mairi Rose still wore Charles's gift; her wedding band, dulled and battered by years of soil and sun. The ring did not gleam in fire or sunlight, but the intricate weave of the strands of gold was still beautiful, made more precious because in the years of her joy and the years of her sorrow, when Charles and Ailsa had been lost to her, she had never once taken it off. It was her promise to the man she loved, a vow as sacred as the words she had spoken to become his wife.

Lian and Genevra caught Ailsa's hand on either side. The wind, usually full of fury, seemed to hold its breath as the sisters stood motionless, pulse beating into pulse, thought blending into thought, grief echoing grief, until the force of their silence drowned out all other sound.

They were frozen in time, circled by stone, awed by the current coursing through them. They shivered as the cool wind wound around and among them, creeping under their skirts, lifting the fabric in shallow ripples to forge a chain that secured their ankles one to the other. The morning breeze, the wind that circled in this place of stones, crept up their legs and their linked arms, through the pattern of interlocked elbows—a thick, invisible cord of wind and memory, past and present, what had been and what might be.

When it seemed the silence would go on forever, until it became a barrier rather than a link, Genevra took up the heavy bag that held her drawing supplies. Her husband, Alex, had had it made specially, of heavy hemp with long straps she could toss over her shoulders. She was rarely without it. Now she opened the knotted closures and withdrew a piece of her special paper, smudged and bent at the edges because it had been handled often. "I drew this over a month ago," she said, holding it up so the others could see.

It was a sketch of the three of them standing beside their father's open grave, staring into the gaping hole in the earth. The high flat stones rose in the background, casting long shadows across the scene. The wind circled the valley in slashing sweeps of charcoal carrying leaves and dust from the freshly disturbed ground.

Lian and Ailsa contemplated the sketch uneasily.

"When I drew it, I thought it was a memory of our father's death, but now I'm not so certain. Now I feel it was a vision of the future."

"So do I," Ailsa breathed, grasping the sketch in shaking hands. "I saw it in my dream." Fingers numb, she dropped the paper and it settled on the grave. The sense of foreboding she had shared with her mother night after night came back to her, but she tried to push the image away.

"Yes," the other two said at once.

She saw the recognition in their eyes, felt her apprehension in their slow beating hearts.

"We have been worried," Lian explained, "because of Mairi's infrequent letters and your silence. Then the nightmares came and we knew we could not stay away. We had to see you, speak to you, touch you, in order to understand."

"And do ye?"

"Not yet," Genevra mused. "But the moment we saw Mairi, how much she'd changed, we guessed it was partly for her we'd come."

Ailsa stiffened. "There's nothing wrong with Mam. She's older, aye, but we all grow old." She spoke with a fierce determination that betrayed her unacknowledged fear.

Lian met Genevra's gaze over their sister's head. "Are you certain it is no more than that?" she asked gently.

"As sure as I can be." This time her voice faltered.

Lian decided to leave it for now. Ailsa was not yet ready. "It is not only Mairi we are thinking of. Ena's letters have been as always, yet we watched her last night, and I think something is disturbing her as well." She did not want to push Ailsa away—as far away as she had been in their dreams—but she could not bear these unspoken doubts among them.

Sighing with relief, Ailsa's face relaxed. "She's havin' a hard time growin' up, leavin' her childhood and becomin' a woman. She's at that age, ye ken, when 'tis hardest for girls to understand what's happenin' to their changin' bodies and feelin's. She's come to me, and I've tried to ease her fears. I'd suffer these years for her if I could, but 'tis something she has to do herself."

Genevra nodded, willing, eager to accept the explanation. But Lian looked thoughtful. Brief as it had been, in that moment the night before when Ena had turned inward, her aunt had sensed something deeper than the difficulty of adolescence. But she could not give it a name, so she did not press the issue. Not yet.

At that instant, the wind came up, snaking under Ailsa's skirt, whipping the folds around her, tugging her hair loose from its crown of braids. The force was so powerful, she lost her footing and began to fall.

Lian and Genevra caught her, grasping her upper arms firmly. They would always catch her. She knew that. Why, now, did it make her want to weep?

"We must go," Ena said, eyes glittering like polished silver. She peered intently through the graceful branches of silver fir, alert and utterly still.

Connor watched the change in her with misgivings; a moment ago she had been relaxed, sitting with her back against the gnarled root of a larch tree in the cool, shaded woods. Now she was a wild thing, a spirit aware of every noise, smell and motion. Now she was the Ena he could never truly know, because he could not crawl inside her skin the way she seemed to crawl inside her wounded animals, seeking out their pain so she could stop it.

He'd seen this transformation many times, but it never ceased to make him anxious. "Go?" he repeated blankly. "I thought today we were settin' the deer free, to send it home where it belongs."

Without taking a breath, she replied obscurely, " 'Tis a bad day for freedom, I'm thinkin'."

More and more perplexed, Connor knew something was happening, but he didn't know what. He hated not knowing, being excluded from the premonitions that sometimes took hold of Ena.

"They need us." She turned to look at him directly, her

gaze unwavering, as if she'd read his thoughts and wanted to include him in the urgency she felt.

Connor wanted to look away, but could not. "Aye, weel, if there's need, 'tis for ye, no' me."

With a gossamer brush of her fingers along his cheekbone, she communicated her understanding of his frustration. " 'Tis both of us they'll be wantin'."

He shook his head, certain she was trying to appease him.

"I'd no' lie to ye, Connor. Ye know that." Taking his hand, she drew him up beside her, aware of the strength and size of his maturing body. Unlike her, with her inexplicable impulses, Connor was steady and practical. Leaning close, Ena touched his arm to reassure herself. Instantly he felt her distress and covered her hand with his.

She leaned against him briefly, closed her eyes and sighed. One more moment of peace before the furor. "Come," she said. "The danger's aye approachin'. Come."

4

JENNY AND ALANNA HAD BUILT UP THE PEAT FIRE, FILLING the sink with water, separating out the vegetables and meat from the baked goods. Both women worked by instinct, their thoughts far from the tiny rooms dark with soot and the smell of fresh peats in the settle.

They sat for a moment, staring out the door at the late summer clearing. "My husband was fond of this time of year," Jenny murmured. "And I know he would've loved the excitement brewin' in the glen today. . . ." She trailed off, wondering where the thought had come from and why she'd spoken it aloud. "My Ian was that proud of this place and its wonders, even if he alone could see them."

Silence lay suddenly and heavily upon them, and though neither looked at the other, both were thinking the same thing. Of the time when the glen had been threatened and Ian Fraser had given his life to save it. Jenny had not been beside her husband that day, and she often wondered if she would ever forgive herself—or him.

"We're a proud lot, are we Highlanders. Fiercely proud." Alanna stared at Jenny's bent head, at her wrinkled neck burned red by the sun, her once brown hair wound into a tight silver crown on her head. "Look at me, daft and imaginative bairn that I was. I used to envy the tone in Mam's voice when she spoke of Ian Fraser."

Jenny dropped her knife with a clatter that made her shiver. She was jumpy today, yet she'd thought herself calm. But then, Alanna had truly shocked her. She turned, hands out to offer comfort for the pain she'd felt as a child. She clasped her fingers together when she realized she was shaking. "She *told* ye? When ye were but a bairn? She told ye about the two of 'em?" She whispered the last words, found she could not utter her husband's name. Though not long ago, Ailsa and she had voiced many truths, begun to forgive many wrongs, the healing was slower than she'd imagined. Just because they now understood how Ian's memory had held them apart, shaped each of their lives, they could not simply banish him and his power over them with words of reconciliation and abundant tears.

Shaking her head emphatically, Alanna bent to pick up the fallen knife and place it gently on the scrubbed oak counter top. It gave her a moment to think. "No. She never said a word, except that he'd been her childhood friend, as ye had." She stopped at Jenny's skeptical expression. " 'Tis true, ye ken. Do ye think I'd lie to ye? I'd not be so cruel. Believe me."

Alanna touched Jenny Fraser's shoulders until she looked up. " 'Twas only that, when Mam spoke of him,"— she also could not use his name—"her face changed and her voice softened. I'm thinkin' she was no' aware of how much those things told even a bairn." She released Jenny and paced around the kitchen table. "Of course, Cynthia and Colin didn't notice. They heard different voices, from a world I could no' be part of. But Mam . . . I was too much like her, ye ken. I knew her too well, before I was ready. So I wanted to turn away every time she said his name, because I had no place in that world either, with that stranger."

"Aye," Jenny whispered, "I know. I used to watch them together, see how they moved and acted and thought as one. And I knew I was no' like them. I didn't believe in the spirits or the Celtic gods, but Ailsa and Ian inhaled them, as if they were sunshine and air that kept them warm and breathin'. I sensed even then they could see inside each other. That frightened me. I was afraid of many things as a bairn. I saw nothing where they saw so much, and I knew, though I was their friend, I'd never truly be part of their magical world."

She peered out at the gathering fog, closing them off from the rest of the glen. "I've forgotten that feelin' many times over the years. Ian made it go, and just lately, Ailsa. And for ye?"

Marveling at Jenny's strength, her ability to see the truth clearly, yet bear no ill will, Alanna felt small. "The day I first came here and saw the mountains towerin' over paradise, I forgot my envy. I understood how, once she'd known a place like this, Mam could no' speak of it without the wonder of it showin' on her face. Ian was only part of that wonder. I loved the glen, the feel and touch and taste of it. I knew I'd found my home at last." She bent over the counter to separate the carrots Jenny had sliced neatly. Just when the silence grew uncomfortable, she raised her head. "Something's happenin' here, changin'. I suspected it before, but now that my aunts've come, I'm sure, and it frightens me." She was ashamed by her admission.

Jenny took Alanna in her arms, and they rocked, each giving and receiving comfort, both sensing a deep, abiding affection and compassion for the other. "There're many kinds of pride," Jenny said at last, "and none better or truer than another. We each chose our own paths, and some take all our courage and strength just to keep us upright. We're strong as well as proud, Alanna. Ye and me and Mairi and your mother. And, though mayhap she doesn't know it yet, Ena."

Alanna smiled. "Mayhap none of us know till we need to."

Connor trailed reluctantly behind as Ena slipped through bushes, ducked lithely beneath low branches, and adroitly avoided twisted roots. Red squirrels darted among the foliage, sometimes pausing to chatter. Or so it appeared to Connor. Finches twittered what sounded like a welcome, and the silvery trill of the robins seemed to speed her on her way. Sparrowhawks fluttered above and around her, as if to protect her. From what? Connor wondered. Or was it from whom?

She'd always had a unique affinity with the animals, but never had it been so obvious to her friend as it was today. She was only a few yards ahead, but his path was undisturbed by squirrels or the welcome, warning songs of birds. They were speaking to her alone. Which was only fair, since her impulse had brought them here. He had felt nothing, had seen no approaching shadows, though often in the past he'd shared her premonitions.

Sighing, he called to her, but she did not pause. "Ena, wait. I'm needin' to talk to ye."

She did not hear him. He knew she did not because she was engaged in kicking away loam and pine needles to uncover something in her path. She knelt to pick up the long, thin branch of a rowan that had broken off in the wind. "Ah," she murmured, as she always did at the discovery of something that might prove useful in the future. "Look!" she cried waving the branch toward Connor. " 'Tis narrow but strong, not yet dried or brittle. Mayhap I'll use it for the new pen we've been after makin' so the bigger animals have more room."

Connor nodded, but Ena did not see as she forged ahead, brushing the earth from the branch, running her callused fingers over the wood in a careless caress. "Only ye'd be delighted by an ordinary stick of wood, Ena Rose. Others would see it as a piece of kindlin' for their fires."

"Then they'd be foolish. 'Tis aye useful, a long, nearly straight branch like this. For splints for the animals, enclosures for their pens." She leaned on the slightly curved end heavily. "Even as a walkin' stick, though 'tis a bit thin for that, I admit." She smiled over her shoulder until a thin veil obscured her friend's face, reminding her of her duty. She did not try to guess what she would find at the end of this brief journey. Ena Rose never asked the voices that called her *why* they called; she simply followed their urging. To pick up this fine rowan branch for example. She did not know why she had. It had looked tempting, so she'd rescued it from the damp and the dark. She waved it toward Connor, motioning them onward.

She was off again, knowing he would follow, that he would never be far from her, despite the mist that drifted down from the treetops, draping the forest in shimmering white.

Connor kept close, unsettled by the way Ena kept her gaze ahead, on whatever invisible lure had drawn her through the woods, its colors now dimmed by gauzy moisture.

He saw her run her hand idly down the branch, circling a raised knot with her fingertip, frowning slightly as she reached into her pocket for her carving knife and worked at the knot, sliver by sliver, until the stick was nearly flat. She dropped the knife back into her gaping pocket without looking; her gaze was fixed straight ahead.

Connor was fascinated and troubled by her skill and carelessness, by the suppressed energy like the spring of a tightly strung hand harp, vibrating with each breath of wind.

Without pausing to measure the branch, or even look at it, she broke it neatly into smaller pieces with brisk efficiency and dropped them into her pocket after her knife. He doubted if she was aware she had done so. Another ripple of apprehension ran up his spine. She was behaving very mysteriously, and there was about her a sense of determination he had never seen before. She paused once at a distant cry of a bird, but she stood for a long moment, head tilted, eyes narrowed, concentrating long after the sound had died away.

The mist had turned to a fog that Ena tasted on her tongue and in her throat, filling her as it did the forest, falling through the trees and hiding them from sight. A bird's shriek had stopped her, but now she could not hear it. She could hear nothing, not even Connor's muffled steps.

Her heart began to pound. "Connor!" she cried, inexplicably afraid. "Have ye gone from me?" An instant of silence and she repeated, "Connor! Where are ye?"

Connor paused at the sound of her panic. He rarely heard her cry out like that, rarely felt her fear in chills up and down his neck. She drifted in and out of sight as he hurried forward, calling her name. Her eyes remained blank, her face desperate, until he grasped her hand and held it to his racing heart. "I'm here, Ena. Of course I'm here. I'll never go from ye. Ye know that."

Swallowing convulsively, Ena's soul returned to her eyes and she touched her friend's cheek with affection. "I do know."

She seemed as perplexed as he by the sadness in her voice.

Only then did Connor remember what had brought them here. *We must go,* she'd said, her fingers clutching his until he ached. *The danger's aye approachin'.* Ena was never wrong. Suddenly the mist seemed thick, a series of white veils he must push aside in order to reach her. "To protect her," he murmured, his voice muffled by the clinging fog. But that was ridiculous. *He,* protect *her?* She was the strong one, after all. He almost stumbled on the red squirrel standing on its hind paws in the middle of the path, exhorting him, he thought, but that might have been the nebulous descending mist, which blurred and altered everything.

Surely he was lost, confused, mistaken. Then, in a voice that seemed to come from outside himself, he repeated, "I must protect her."

Just beyond the entrance to the valley, Lian, Genevra and Ailsa found Mairi sitting on a hummock, her back against the wall of stone.

Before they could speak, she gave them a dazzling smile. "I decided to wait for ye after all, so we could walk together. Every minute of the time we share is precious."

The sisters agreed, though all three felt something in her tone rang false. Yet they could not guess what it was.

With Ailsa in the lead, they started along the familiar path toward home.

"So," Mairi said when the path widened and they could walk abreast, "Ye left before dawn, but the sun was well up when ye reached the valley. Where else have ye been?" She gazed at them innocently, full of curiosity.

Ailsa regarded her mother in suspicion. "We wandered a bit. Lian and Genevra wanted to recapture the feelin' of the glen and watch the dawn from a hilltop."

"And which hill would that be?" The twinkle in Mairi's eye that told them she already knew.

"We went to the Hill of the Hounds." Genevra was unaware of Mairi's teasing, had forgotten Ailsa's aversion to the house built by the English that had caused more than one problem among the Highlanders.

"What an extraordinary place it was to find here, in the midst of all this." Lian gestured around her, but only shapes and shadows were visible through the mist. "We only peeked inside a few windows, but we saw enough." She caught Mairi's repressed smile, stopping as she was struck with an idea. "Émile and I live on the Drouard estate with his family, and we have been talking of finding a second home, for the boys and ourselves, where we could go for holidays. We want them to experience more of the world, to educate them by perhaps giving them adventures to discover as well as new places and people to come to know." She thought, fleetingly, of Ena, who had lived her entire life in this isolated Eden, who knew so much and yet so little beyond her limited experience. But that was a subject for later, when Lian was alone with Ailsa.

Her expression was pensive, and the other three waited eagerly for her to continue. "The Hill is lovely, from what we saw. It might just be perfect. It is a shame to leave a house like that empty for so long."

Abruptly, she turned to her sister. "Genevra, would you and Alex not bring your children here? There is plenty of room for both families, and in that particular house, the children would be comfortable, yet able to step outside and be in the wilderness."

"Och, aye," Mairi said, barely able to hold in her excitement. "And ye'd no' be strangers here. Ye'd have a family just waitin' to welcome ye home."

Whirling in her wide, belled skirt, Genevra turned to face the others. "It's a lovely idea, Lian. I'm sure Alex and the children would adore it. But would there be any trouble about our buying it together?"

"No' now," Ailsa said, "after bein' empty for near a year." She too turned, eyes glowing with pleasure. "Och, and 'twould make it ours at last, no longer a lingerin' memory of the *Sassenach* who've left it time and again. Ye two and your families could rid us of the ghosts who haunt it now, no' in the house itself, but in our hearts."

Smiling affectionately, Mairi added, " 'Tis always good to make something full of unpleasant shadows into something bonny and welcomin'." Both hands firmly on her walking stick, she moved through the mist, unintimidated or confused by the heavy drifts that had turned the air white and wet and sweet.

"But could we afford it?" Genevra asked anxiously. Now that the thought had been put in her head, she could not wait to get back to the croft to write Alex about the house.

Lian smiled mysteriously. "I think it can be done. We will have to plan carefully, that is all. It needs a great deal of paint and carpentry and new drapes and carpets, but the house itself seems sound. I would delight in having a tie to this place that has meant so much to us, somewhere of our own in this magical glen I have dreamed of for so long."

Mairi stopped abruptly and would not meet their eyes. She drew her plaid close to her face and tightened it around her shoulders, either to keep out a sudden chill or to hide her thoughts from them.

Disturbed by her silence, her stillness, Genevra rushed to fill it. "Perhaps we're going too quickly, bringing upheaval into your peaceful lives?"

In spite of herself, in spite of the sudden sadness that filled her bones, Mairi smiled. "Peaceful, is it? You've no' learned much after all, have ye?"

Lian, too, felt Mairi's distress. "Perhaps we should have let you know we were coming—"

Mairi reached out with one gnarled hand on the head of her stick, and took Lian's and Genevra's proffered hands. "I can never regret your desire to come so far, or your presence. Have ye no' learned yet that 'tis a sin in the Highlands no' to honor your guests and be grateful for the chance to serve them?" Her once vivid violet eyes were dim with age, but her wisdom shone as bright as ever. " 'Be no' forgetful to entertain strangers, for thereby some have entertained angels unawares.' "

For a moment, Genevra was at a loss.

"Be ye angels? Ye and your husbands and children?" she asked, eyebrows raised in polite inquiry.

"I doubt it very much," Lian said, half-seriously. "Though

if it would please you, I should endeavor to become one. But that is not the point." She clasped Mairi's hand carefully, tenderly. "Can't you imagine our children on the brae, in the woods, at the edge of the loch, again and again as they grow older and see these things each time through different eyes? It really could be a second home for them. And for us." She caught the older woman's gaze and held it. "Because we will come back. It is what we want above all things. For Émile and Alex and the children to know you as we do."

Mairi's eyes clouded over and her hand grew cold. She stared fixedly at the edge of the loch that shimmered in the distance. She could see it even through the mist. It had become part of her thoughts and visions, just as she had become part of the wind and the water and the soft scent of heather on summer hills. "Aye, indeed ye will come back." She spoke, not to them, but to the air, to the swirling mist. "Again and again will ye come, and your bairns with ye and after ye. And when they've grown, they'll bring their own bairns and those who follow. Each generation, till—" In the leaves and threads entwined behind her lids she saw the face of a young woman with short chestnut hair, wearing an odd shirt with no sleeves with trousers and shoes with no backs. And her face! So full of confusion and pain. Mairi did not understand what the image meant, but she knew it was important. What was it Ena had said about her nightmare? Mairi could not remember. That happened more and more often of late.

Her body trembled as the shadow lifted from her eyes. Her gaze was wistful and touched with longing.

"Would you not like to see it happen?"

Mairi summoned all her strength to fight off the vision and bring herself back to the moment, the place she had not forgotten. Could never forget. "Och, aye, more than ye'll ever know." She breathed once, deeply, and her bones ached with it. "But come, we're wastin' time, the four of us. They'll be thinkin' we've lost our way like wee bairns who know no better. 'Twouldn't do, ye ken. I must keep my dignity for their sakes. So enough of this bletherin'."

She took her hand from Lian's—determined and unstoppable—stepped forward and a little sideways, still caught in the web of a waking dream.

They had stopped at the top of a brae that sloped downward, slickened by moisture on the long clover grass dotted with bell heather. Ailsa leapt forward and tried to catch her mother before she stepped blindly off the path and her walking stick slipped from her grasp. Lian and Genevra lunged at her, but their hands met empty air.

They heard Mairi gasp, cry out once, quietly, as if she might disturb some sleeping animal, then fall silent. It was not till they approached the bottom of the hill that they saw her lying still and pale, dress stained and torn, the red Rose plaid tangled around her body, her hands clutching tussocks of grass and loam so tightly that the skin on her fingers was cracked and bleeding.

5

AILSA AND GENEVRA STOOD AT MAIRI'S FEET, CHEEKS flushed from exertion and the chill in the air. Lian knelt beside her limp body, one hand pressed to her heart, the other poised above her mouth and nose. The younger woman waited for a cadence that would indicate a flow of blood through Mairi's veins, a wisp of breath across her palm that would reassure her she was still alive.

The three sisters looked at one another and knew that though the mist was turning the world white and cool around them, somewhere it was dark.

Lian felt the weak flutter of Mairi's heart and sighed with relief. "She is alive."

Ailsa ran her fingers through her hair in distraction. " 'Tis no' like her to stumble, even since she's carried a stick. She's walked these paths, and forged her own, for over seventy years. She knows every hazard of the glen."

Unable to stay still, Genevra interrupted, "We should go for help."

Ailsa tilted her head back, listening, her face a mask of concentration. "No need." Her voice was oddly distant.

The three women looked up in time to see the fog part, revealing a distant figure, wavering and indistinct. They narrowed their eyes, peering into the overlapping swathes of white. They saw it again—a flicker of red-gold, a lissome stirring from side to side—before it was obscured by mist.

"What is it?" whispered Genevra.

" 'Tis Ena and Connor." Ailsa spoke stiffly, tonelessly. "They've come to help."

Lian watched, fascinated, as Ena came closer. Her hair had been tightly braided this morning, but now it hung half-unraveled to her waist, the auburn strands scattered with leaves and bits of fern and tiny twigs. She wore a battered cap that did nothing to contain her wayward curls. Her pale green skirt was smeared with the deeper green of moss and grass. She was slight, unconsciously lithe and assured as she moved. Her gray eyes flecked with green were focused on Mairi.

Lian and Genevra were surprised by Connor. Alanna had told them about her son, but not how like Ena he was. Like her, his skin was warm brown from the sun, his clothing stained with streaks of green and dark loam. Like hers, his hair was auburn and disheveled, springing out from beneath his cap in tufts that reached his shoulders.

Genevra tried to remember exactly how the two were related. Ena, of course, was Ailsa and Ian Fraser's daughter. Ian had been David Fraser's uncle, and David and Alanna were Connor's parents. Alanna and Ena were both Ailsa's daughters, which made them half-sisters. And Connor and

Ena had been born but a month apart. Genevra covered her ears to stop the confusing tangle of relationships that Mairi had called a snarled skein.

Connor regarded Ailsa's two sisters, openly curious, and though he did not share Ena's fixed stare, his eyes might otherwise have been her own.

The boy resembled Ena so much that he might have been the girl in male form, except that she glided over the ground and he walked. Her determined expression made Genevra back away, making room for the girl at Mairi's side.

"Ye can feel her heartbeat?" Ena asked Lian. She could not bear the anxious silence and tried to fill it with the sound of her voice.

"Yes, and her breath on my skin. She is unconscious after her fall down the hill."

Ena knelt. "There's swellin' in her ankle. We'll need ice to bring it down to keep it from gettin' worse."

Connor, kneeling across from his friend, began to rise, but Ena put her hand on his arm to stop him.

Genevra, Lian and Ailsa exchanged glances, before Ailsa said firmly, "She'll need him here."

"I'll go," Genevra offered. "I haven't the knack for healing as you do."

Connor began to direct her to the ice house, but Ailsa shook her head. "I'll take her. 'Twill be quicker that way."

The sisters disappeared, running swiftly.

Thoughtfully, Ena watched her mother go before returning her attention to Mairi. First she tugged free the worn, faded red plaid in which her grandmother lay tangled and tossed it over her own shoulders. Then she cupped Mairi's face in her hands, running one thumb gently along her cheekbone. She examined the color of her grandmother's skin, placed her thumbs on the closed, blue-veined eyelids, tilted her head back and to the side, listening. After she had examined the back of Mairi's head and found only a small lump where her grandmother might have struck a rock or a root, the girl began to examine her carefully, tenderly, from the neck down, searching for wounds more dangerous than the scrapes and scratches on her arms and legs.

Ena paused at Mairi's hands, carefully uncurled them from around the sod and loam, brushing the soil away. She let her grandmother's palm rest in hers and bent to contemplate the split and bleeding skin. She ached at the sight and feel of that paper-thin skin, so easily damaged. She wanted to throw back her head and shout a denial to the moon, visible in the midday sky, to release the pent-up sorrow in her chest.

"Ena," Connor whispered in concern.

She glanced at him quickly, but made no sound. From one of her pockets, she took a vial of cream and began to massage it into Mairi's gnarled fingers, softening the skin, stopping the bleeding, one finger at a time. She did not care how long it took, was hardly aware of sliding off the single ring on Mairi's hand and dropping it into her copious pocket. The sight of her grandmother's hands, so fragile, so aged, broke her heart, and she wanted to weep. "I can't," she whispered.

Connor heard. He sat back on his heels, feeling Ena's tears building behind his eyes. He knew she could not allow herself the luxury of weeping. There was work to be done.

Ena pressed her lips into a tight line as Connor crouched beside her, lending her his warmth without speaking. He had learned years ago to recognize that look of concentration, the need for stillness as she sought the weakness and pain that most needed her attention.

Ena did not find what she was seeking until she reached Mairi's right ankle, where she'd first noticed the skin beginning to swell. She barely grazed it as she slid her cupped hands cautiously around the inflammation, yet her touch was enough to make Mairi open her eyes and moan.

Through a fog of pain and confusion, she saw the people standing around, staring at her, concern in every line of their bodies. She wanted to slip back into the soft oblivion of the darkness, but she struggled to keep her eyes open, to remain conscious, so they would see she was only bruised and embarrassed and not in danger.

Ailsa and Genevra returned with the ice, and Ailsa dropped it all into her sister's hands. She felt dizzy and light-headed, as if she might be ill. Her heartbeat was labored, her body drenched in cold sweat. She gaped at her mother, battered and bruised and unnaturally pale.

Glancing up, Ena could not bear the look of dismay and terror in Ailsa's eyes. " 'Tis only a broken ankle. Connor and I'll splint it once the swellin' goes down."

Her mother nodded mutely, but her eyes were blank, her body rigid.

Ena felt Mairi move beneath her hand and, though torn, she gave her attention to the patient who needed it most. She saw at once that her grandmother was struggling, resolved to be strong for the others, as she had always been.

Leaning forward so her lips touched Mairi's ear, Ena whispered, "Let go, Gran. Your ankle's broken, I'm thinkin', and the pain must be great. 'Tis no time to worry about worryin' us. 'Tis time ye think of yourself. Let go. Let the fog envelope ye and shield ye from the pain. I'm beggin', Gran. Please." She spoke softly, rhythmically, turning the ordinary words into a spoken song as she stroked Mairi's cheek and the base of her throat, where the pulse throbbed weakly. Slowly, slowly, she mesmerized her grandmother with the sound of her voice and the touch of her hands.

With a little sigh of thankfulness, Mairi closed her eyes and surrendered to the darkness.

6

THE HALF OPEN DOOR TO MAIRI'S CROFT CREAKED ON ITS hinges and Alanna looked up. As she stared at the swath of green outside, her eyes glazed over. She went pale and her skin grew clammy as she clenched and unclenched her hands, unaware of Jenny's touch on her arm. "Something's wrong."

Jenny was frightened by Alanna's pallor and intensity, and because she believed the words she'd muttered deep and low. She had never truly understood these suspended moments in time when the Rose women became strangers, saw things invisible to others. She had seen it before, but it always made her anxious, because, to her, it was incomprehensible. "What is't?"

" 'Tis Mairi," Alanna said. She shivered as shadows closed in around her. " 'Tis comin."

Jenny went still at the dread and certainty in her tone.

A second later, mesmerized by the vivid image caught in her blind sight, Alanna heard a commotion across the clearing that shook her violently awake. Without a word, she and Jenny left the croft to see Connor carrying Mairi gingerly while Ena kept pace, holding her grandmother's hand. Lian, Genevra and Ailsa came behind, three abreast, like a protective shield.

Alanna and Jenny raced across the clearing, swift and ashen.

" 'Tis naught but a broken ankle," Connor told his mother as he moved steadily toward the threshold, ducked beneath and placed Mairi gently on the heather bed with its rough linen sheets and handwoven blanket.

While the others crowded into the cottage, clustering about Mairi, Ailsa hung back, unable to catch her breath.

Her mother's skin was translucent; the blue veins beneath were visible, the pulse of her blood so sluggish that the ends of her fingers had begun to change color. Hands clasped to stop their trembling, she forced herself closer.

Lian and Genevra, having touched Mairi's cool skin and seen her chest rise and fall regularly with each breath, turned to Ailsa, offering their hands. "She's home now," Lian said. "She's safe."

Ailsa tried three times before she forced words out of her dry throat. " 'Tis just that, in all my life, I've never," she broke off, closing her eyes to clear her mind. "I've no' seen Mairi Rose like this, not once in fifty-four years. Completely helpless." The words, once spoken, hung in the air like the shadow of a coming storm. "Broken." Ailsa shivered. Then she noticed the expression on her youngest daughter's face—the desire to comfort, the *need* to take away her mother's misery, the hopelessness.

I'd ask ye no' to mention this to your mother, Mairi'd begged her granddaughter last spring when a low stone bench defeated her. *Let her keep her illusions for a little while at least.* Ena looked away. It had been a very little while indeed.

With an effort, for Ena's sake, Ailsa fought for composure. She only wished she could take back her outburst. Her daughter's face was unusually pale, her hands clasped before her, the skin taut.

"Come," Alanna said firmly, "there're too many breathin' Gran's air. Ena'll have no room to work. Some of us must go."

Ena nodded mutely.

Without being told, Alanna began brewing rose hip tea and yew to help the pain, and blackwillow bark for a sedative, should Mairi awaken.

Ena nearly choked on the bitter smell of boiling herbs. The odors wafted over her, clung to her until she could not breathe. She was far too aware of Ailsa, Lian and Genevra watching, full of questions and doubt, swallowing the acrid taste of fear. The same fear that made her clumsy as she knelt beside her grandmother's bed with Connor across from her and cautiously unwound the bandage, revealing clumps of melting ice. First she removed the ice, which Alanna whisked away. She felt eyes boring into her and prayed they would not see what she was feeling.

Hands moving of their own volition, from memory rather than intent, she examined the bruised, puffy skin around the lacerations in Mairi's ankle. When she glanced up, Alanna handed her a steaming skunk cabbage poultice, which Ena laid gingerly around the wound to help stop swelling and infection. She was doubly grateful for Connor's presence—and his silence. "When the poultice cools," she told him, "we'll be havin' to put the splint on quickly, before the swellin' starts again."

"Aye," Connor said. "I know what to do."

The air had grown thick and warm, nearly stifling. Jenny started for the door, then saw Ailsa's pallid face, how she twined and untwined her fingers until they were pink and swollen. Jenny slipped her arm protectively around Ailsa's waist. "Ye need fresh air. Come with me now. Ye know ye can trust Ena."

Lian was skeptical. "Should not someone older, more experienced—"

"There's no such in Glen Affric," Alanna replied. "Except for Mairi. And as for experience, 'tis no' just animals she's tended to all her life." Alanna realized with a shock *she* would not choose to mend Mairi's ankle. Not with everyone watching, waiting, needing her to succeed. Only then did she know she was afraid.

She noticed Jenny guiding Ailsa outside. Disturbed by the blank look in her mother's eyes, she was glad Jenny had taken control.

Lian paced beside the kettle, hands clasped behind her. Every time she looked at Mairi, she felt a tightness in her chest, because she must stand by, helpless. Always, Lian had been the one others turned to in a crisis. Even in her anxiety and frustration, she could see how skillful the girl was, yet it did not calm her. Lian paced, counting in her head to keep her mind busy.

Concentrating fiercely, Ena removed the poultice, which Alanna carried away. Gently, she tested the wounded ankle, watching Mairi's face for any sign of waking, any hint of pain. When she saw the swelling had gone down, she emptied her two large pockets on the floor at Connor's feet, quickly picked out dried kelp and tincture of iodine, then swabbed the broken skin, moving so gently that her hand seemed to float above the cuts and abrasions.

Meanwhile, Connor methodically laid out what they would need to make a splint.

Genevra watched in fascination as Ena took a sturdy leather bag from among the jumbled vials and stones, containers of dried and fresh herbs and flowers, a carving knife and other odd utensils, along with bits and pieces of wood. She scooped out a damp brown powder speckled with green, which she sprinkled over the swollen, torn flesh. A bitter odor filled the air as she braced herself and closed her hands around the ankle with the lightest touch.

Lian opened her mouth, but before she could make a sound, Ena said, " 'Twill help keep the swellin' down."

"Are her pockets always so full of so many strange things?" Genevra whispered.

"Aye," Connor replied. "Ye never know when she might come across a wounded animal who'll no' wait for her to run home and gather her things. She picks up the herbs and flowers where she finds 'em. A storm at night could easily destroy them all. Ena's always ready—." He broke off at her nod and bent close.

They worked together, first finding the broken bones by touch, then, as carefully as he could, Connor forced them back into place. If Mairi had not already been unconscious, she would have surrendered then; the pain would have been agonizing.

Genevra was fascinated. Though they could have been reflections of one another, they were also very different. Ena moved with the fleetness of a sprite, at Mairi's ankle now, now at her head. She was never still, yet never rough or hurried. Unlike her, Connor sat heavily on the hard-packed floor, movements deliberate. He was not quicksilver or mist or motion: he was substantial; he was steady. Yet unquestionably, remarkably, they belonged together, each a necessary half of something that was more than a simple whole; it was extraordinary.

Genevra was aware of Lian's frustration, her determination to help. But unlike her half-sister, she did *not* know what to do. Even had she been allowed, she could have added nothing, suggested nothing. Genevra had always known her two half-sisters were more accomplished than she, but it had not mattered until now. She was grateful when Alanna handed her a lantern to dispel the gloom around Mairi.

Ailsa stood on the fringes, stunned, staring without seeing, listening without hearing, wrapped and protected by the mist—an invisible cloak of spider-fine gauze a screen between her and what she did not want to know.

Briskly, Ena gathered several strong lengths from the branch she'd impulsively picked up in the woods. Connor held them motionless while she took up a length of hand-woven bandage and circled the ankle again and again, until the makeshift splint was firmly in place. She moved lightly, all sleek silver and filmy speed.

Ena shifted her weight for the first time as she took Mairi's plaid from around her own shoulders and gingerly enveloped her grandmother's tangled hair and limp arms in the worn red tartan. " 'Tis your turn now," she murmured, nodding to Lian and Alanna. "Ye must keep her still and out of pain, and pray to the gods of the Celts that 'twill mend soon." She stood, and Connor rose with her, catching her as she swayed and fell.

7

THAT NIGHT THE HIGHLANDERS APPEARED TWO BY TWO ON silent feet, moving around the Rose cottage as the windless tide creeps up on the shore.

"Who are they?" Genevra whispered, startled by the soundless apparitions.

David Fraser, who had joined the others as soon as he learned of Mairi's accident, had offered to greet the guests while Jenny and Alanna rested after preparing and serving the large meal. He was grateful for Genevra's question, which gave him something to concentrate on. He had not realized, until he saw Mairi lying pale and defenseless in a drugged sleep, how even he had begun to think his mother-in-law invulnerable, how much he'd come to care for her. He'd lost his own mother when he was young, and over the years, wordlessly, unobtrusively, Mairi had filled that place in his heart that his grief had left empty. He turned to the young woman Mairi had taken under her wing. "The people have come for a *ceilidh*, and I think, to wish Mairi well." Their hands were full of restoratives and teas, fresh baked scones and bannocks and late summer flowers.

"How can they know about her fall already?"

Leaning against the cool stones of the wall, David murmured, "Mairi'd tell ye anything's possible in the mist and the moonlight. She'd say the fairies carried the news from house to house, ridin' the back of the smallest breeze."

"It happened in India, too. The news spread faster than fire. We used to blame the wind as well." As the clearing began to fill, she asked, "Has everyone come?"

"Aye, I expect so. Even if Mairi'd no' been injured, they would've come tonight. They always do when there're visitors, especially foreigners with tales of the world beyond

Glen Affric. Some're here out of curiosity, some the desire to be hospitable to strangers." He paused, watching the dark figures resolve themselves into one after another of the people he knew so well.

"Forbye, they'd no' miss the chance to see Charles Kittridge's offspring from strange, exotic lands. They've heard stories of ye and Lian for years. 'Tis a small world, our glen. No' much changes from year to year. Your arrival's excitin' enough to lure even the hermits out of their cairns." David grew somber. "Besides, to them Mairi Rose is more than a friend. She's healed them, listened to their problems, advised them, always with compassion. They come to show their affection and respect for her.

"The *ceilidh's* held in a different house each time, so all can be hosts and all guests, but everyone knew it'd be here tonight, because Mairi's mysterious 'daughters' have come home."

Genevra watched, preoccupied, pondering the many things she didn't know about this place she loved so well. Still thoughtful, she slipped inside to join her sisters.

"Be well soon. We're prayin' for ye, our Mairi Rose."

Mairi was barely conscious, and her body ached everywhere, except her ankle, where pain ate its way past blood and skin to pierce her brittle reset bone. Her daughters wanted to give her cup after cup of rosemary tea to ease the pain, an infusion of hops and blackwillow to make her sleep. They had wanted to send the people away so Mairi could rest, but she'd refused. The air in the croft eddied around her, a lacery of concern, fear, affection, doubt and unshed tears.

"I'll be easier if ye go on as we always do, my Ailsa. A *ceilidh* will distract ye, and me as well, for I can watch my daughters and granddaughters enjoyin' a tradition that's soothed and beguiled me many a night. And our neighbors're eager to meet Lian and Genevra. I'd no' have ye disappoint them."

She spoke quietly, yet the effort seemed to drain her. Ailsa sat at her mother's head, where she'd settled once the shock wore off. She'd been appalled at her behavior, though none had criticized her. Aware that Mairi needed her, and that she needed to be needed, Ailsa had seated herself on the floor and taken her mother's head in her lap. For a long while she worked the tangles out of Mairi's hair, then, holding a few strands at a time, she'd drawn a wooden comb gently through the tangles, until the long curls lay in a smooth silver fall over Ailsa's knees.

The lantern hung nearby, making her face golden and luminous, in spite of her apprehension. Connor noticed it, sitting cross-legged beside the fire, engrossed in studying the tableau in the corner. Lian knelt at Mairi's feet, patting rosemary lotion on her joints and pressing, as Cheng the alchemist had taught her, on certain spots on the uninjured foot to help the pain. Genevra was poised opposite Ailsa, placing cool compresses on Mairi's head and dried lavender in damp linen cloths on her cuts and bruises. Occasionally, Lian and Genevra changed places so Lian could apply pressure to temples and neck, and Genevra could soothe, with her lavender compresses, the cuts and bruises on thighs and legs.

Before the others began to appear, the family had eaten the meal Alanna and Jenny prepared, though the women tasted little and ate less. Now, as shadows became men, women and children, all eyes were focused on the three half-sisters around Mairi's bed. They seemed linked more tightly than ever by her need. Strand upon delicate, glistening strand united them in the quavering light of fire and candle, luminous and unmistakable. Ena wanted to run her fingers across the meshwork as she would the strings of a *clarsach*.

Then other voices were heard in the cool autumn breeze, and David offered to go greet the guests.

Now, while Ena looked on in concern, each visitor stopped briefly beside Mairi's bed, subdued by the soft light and anxious expressions, giving his or her small offering, "Tho' it can no' equal what you've given us," they said, one after another.

"Be well soon. We're prayin' for ye, our Mairi Rose."

Outside burned a large fire, bathing the old stone walls with a golden glow that competed with the silver moonlight. Tonight, after each had greeted Mairi, they slipped away, leaving unbroken the circle of yellow lamplight in which she lay, surrounded and protected by her daughters.

Curiosity would have to wait.

Nearby, the river whispered secrets in the dark—stirring, irresistible, and just beyond the hearing of those gathered around the fire. The people sat outside the tiny croft so that, in the flickering light of flame and the cool light of the moon, they looked like a sea of specters, indistinguishable one from the other. Shifting shadows bound them together, and the fine woven veil of mist that flowed around and among them. The people moved and swayed, murmured and sighed like the motion of a quiet sea. Their bodies blocked the small fire and the silver drift of moonlight, so that the faces blurred and had no features, no definition. They were all one, bound by fire and friendship and tradition and the invisible spirits of the glen.

While one man struck up a quiet tune on his fiddle, another played a finely crafted flute. The notes became a single soothing melody that calmed fast-beating hearts, and played a glimmer of hope into worried eyes.

As if this night were no different from any other, the Highlanders discussed the weather, the soon-to-be-gathered crops, those young people who had left the glen for America or Canada. They told their news and their stories in a musical cadence that drew the strangers in like the irresistible lure of a fairy's song. Then came the dancing and singing, and finally the music that shimmered over the crowd and crept into the dark, empty places in their souls.

After Mairi drifted off to sleep, Jenny and Alanna relieved the half-sisters, who reluctantly stepped out into the night, stretching their aching muscles and breathing in the clear fresh air. Ailsa and Genevra settled side by side, Genevra with her sketchbook open in her lap, while Lian sat so close to Ena that she could feel her weary breathing, see the slow, persistent pulse at the base of her throat.

Silence fell at last, and a kind of hushed expectation as the Highlanders watched Lian and Genevra and waited. Moonlight and firelight had conquered the darkness, but not the shadows; shapes and expressions shifted and changed in the flickering light. Eager now, and more at ease since Ailsa had thought it safe to leave her mother, the people asked questions of the foreigners.

Genevra let the women touch and examine the embroidered cashmere shawl she'd brought from India, and Lian offered Chinese paper lanterns, fragrant jasmine tea, as well as scrolls of poetry, written in the tiny, complex figures that did not resemble words. Genevra had brought some of the precious mementos she'd taken with her from India and stored carefully for all this time—jingling bracelets, exotic spices, a sari and the oils with which the Hindus anointed their hair and bodies.

Ena leaned forward, mesmerized. She had read books, it was true, and her mother had written of London and both its charms and squalor in her journal. The girl had known from their frequent letters that her aunts' and cousins' lives were different from hers. But now, as she heard them talk, she saw their experiences in their eyes and on their faces. They had lived through war and death, poverty and prosperity, danger and unimaginable wonders.

For the first time, Ailsa Rose's daughter began to comprehend the nature of the world beyond the lush woods and savagely beautiful mountains in the glen—a world teeming with infinite threat and infinite promise. And most of all, change. Always change.

Dazed, she met Connor's gaze across the fire; he was equally astonished and excited. But as she listened to the sighs and sadness, the laughter and amazement of those among whom she had been born, the restlessness and uncertainty crept up upon her, as it had done often since the spring, when everything had changed for her. She had guessed then, and was certain now, that her life would never be the same. She had crossed an invisible threshold and fallen, tumbling into unfamiliar shapes and feelings that caught her in a net she could not escape.

All at once, she felt a strong arm across her shoulders, catching her, holding her upright and steady.

8

ENA HAD NO CHANCE TO TURN HER HEAD BEFORE LIAN'S cheek was next to hers. "I know you are more than weary after your labors today. And that all of this," she motioned toward the objects being passed from hand to hand, "is a great shock to you. Too much to take in when already your body is exhausted and your thoughts drifting."

Unconsciously, the girl leaned gratefully into the support of her aunt's arm. "Aye, I'm a bit tired." The smooth soft satin of Lian's sleeve felt good against her skin, and her heartbeat was a soothing rhythm in Ena's ear. She'd not been aware until now that her limbs were heavy and difficult to move, her fingers raw from all the poultices and decoctions, her eyelids drooping. She sighed at the relief of leaning against someone else.

"You are worried as well, I think," Lian murmured. When Ena tried to pull away, she held her firmly. "There is no need to deny it. We are all worried about Mairi. You would not be human if you were not. I know you will give all you have to make her well; I have seen you. But it is no sin to be afraid, especially when you are a child."

Lian could not rid herself of the image of Ena Rose kneeling by Mairi's bed while everyone waited for her to make a miracle, to make what had been broken whole again.

Earlier, Lian had recovered quickly from her skepticism and frustration that she'd not been allowed to help Mairi when she'd recognized Ena's concentration and knowledge of herbs and her gentle touch. Her aunt had been impressed, then fascinated by the girl's skill and the mellifluous sound of her voice lulling her patient and observers alike. Slowly, Lian had become aware of the tension in Ena's body, of her fear, carefully concealed. The girl had appeared determined and accomplished. That was the mask she wore, because it was the one her family needed to see.

Just now she seemed separate from those around her. Lian caught a glimpse of the distance in her eyes, the turning inward, away from what, perhaps, she could not face. The same expression she'd seen the day she and Genevra arrived. That afternoon Ena might have been any age; Lian's attention had been drawn to her skill, not her features. That skill was timeless. Not once had she seen a tear or a flash of anxiety on Ena's face. Yet tonight the girl had sat huddled, arms around her knees, looking very much like a lost child.

The sight had broken Lian's heart, because she had seen it before. In some ways, Ena was a child set apart because of her lineage and abilities, as Lian had been set apart. A child expected to take on the responsibilities of an adult, because she had the skill to do so, if not the maturity. A child trying to please everyone, and thereby losing herself.

"I was like you when I was younger," Lian said, curling Ena's cold hand inside her warm one. "I did not live in a paradise like this one, but I grew up faster than a girl should have to, because there was danger in my blue English eyes, in my mother's heritage, everywhere, really. I was always afraid as my mother was always afraid, so I was never truly free."

"But I'm free," Ena objected. "I'm no' afraid of others, of the dangers in the glen, of anything. . . ." She trailed off. "I've no' had to face the things ye did. I've done what I love, is all."

"Then what is it you fear?" Lian persisted. "For I have seen my reflection in your eyes."

For a long moment, Ena was silent, staring into the wild, leaping flames. She could feel her aunt's compassion, her gentle concern in her soft touch and softer voice. "Growin' up," she said, surprising herself.

Nodding, Lian closed her eyes. The girl was changing inside and out as she began the journey to womanhood, but Ena was confused by those changes, and frightened as she had not been by cradling life and death in her nimble hands. It was just as Ailsa had said. And Lian could not suffer Ena's growing pains for her, any more than Ailsa could. "Just remember you do not have to do it all at once. Changing gradually, learning to know yourself as you go will make it easier, though I wish I could offer you more comfort than that. This I will say. You are not yet a woman grown; much of your childhood lingers. You need not hide your concern for your grandmother or anything else that disturbs you. Be a child when you feel like a child. There will be time enough to be a woman in the years to come.

"And remember this particularly. If you are lonely or afraid or tired or sad, you can come to me. I will listen, I will hold you, I will be silent if that is what you wish. But I will be here, and I will expect nothing of you but you, Ena, my long beloved niece. Do you understand?"

The girl turned, eyes suspiciously damp. "Aye, Aunt Lian, and I thank ye."

The people had begun to sing, quietly, in deference to Mairi, swaying with the words of the old songs, the old rhythms, the old blessings of music and motion and an intense awareness of and fondness for those around them.

Differences were discarded, tossed into the darkness beyond their bastion of light and heat and fellowship.

Reluctant to leave the warm cocoon of Lian's arms, Ena nevertheless rose, knowing she must check on Mairi.

As she stood, she could not help but notice Genevra, the flames as wide as a sea between them. Her aunt looked troubled. It was as if Mairi's accident had shaken her so deeply that the determination, the courage that had brought her here had drained away.

Genevra felt Ena's scrutiny; she glanced up, blinked several times, brushing away sparks and smoke, before recognition dawned in her eyes. Blue eyes flecked with gray, just as Ena's silver eyes were flecked with green. Genevra contemplated the girl who had worked on Mairi's wounds, sung her into sleep, diminished her pain.

Genevra herself had wanted to help, had come here to help, but she simply did not know how. She looked up again, sad and defenseless.

Their gazes met, held, and Ena, who was fighting to ignore her fear and doubt, her sense of impotence, felt a fragile bond with this woman whose timidity and uncertainty showed on her face. Unlike Lian, Genevra could not hide her emotions. Ena envied that freedom, that willingness to allow herself to be vulnerable, lost.

But just now, she knew she'd best turn away before her two aunts crumbled her resolve.

Fighting her way through the circle of figures without faces around the fire, Ena went to Mairi's side. "I see you're no' yet sleepin'," she whispered, "but Gran, ye need your rest." She pulled her rosewood flute from her pocket and stretched out beside her grandmother. "Let me play sleep upon ye." The last was a plea as she put the flute to her lips and began to float the silver thread of a tune on the smoky air. The notes drifted over Mairi like a warm woven blanket, like a blessing.

Ena put the flute away and inched closer till her face and her grandmother's were lit by the same light, their hands lying side by side. Jenny watched from across the room, struck by how ephemeral both appeared, with their translucent skin, Ena's auburn hair spilling over Mairi's pillow, while in the cloudy light, the red plaid that hid Mairi's hair streamed out behind her.

"They're very like one another," Jenny whispered in the shadows. Child and woman, both small and delicate, both hovering like pale fire at the heart of a flame. Jenny shook her head, but could not dislodge the image. One flame, she thought, is beginnin' to go out, while the other's just caught, is beginnin' to grow hot and bright. Ena and Mairi had met in the center, but they were moving in opposite directions.

Abruptly, she began to collect soiled wooden dishes and half empty *quachs*. What was she thinking? It was not like her to be so fanciful—or so melancholy.

Fighting off sleep for a moment more, Mairi looked at Ena apologetically.

"Don't worry for me," the girl insisted. "Your strength and spirit must be for ye now." Last spring she'd said the same. *You've cared for everyone but yourself.* " 'Tis time to stop givin' and ask for what ye need. Ask, and when 'tis offered, take it. Promise me." *I'll take care of ye when ye need me. Always.*

As she closed her eyes, Mairi breathed, "I'll try, birdeen. 'Tis all I can do."

"Aye, weel then, it'll have to be enough."

It was a long time before the last visitor left and night settled over the croft. Lian and Genevra had decided to stay at Alanna and David's large cottage, now that Mairi was injured. It would be too crowded here. Before they left to find their new beds, the two half-sisters joined Ailsa at Mairi's side. She was sleeping, but each leaned down to kiss her dry cheek; each whispered, "Good night, Mother of my heart." Ailsa and Lian lifted Mairi's hand, while Genevra rested hers gingerly on top.

"Good night, my daughters."

They gasped and looked into Mairi Rose's half-open eyes. They had not known she would hear them.

"We will leave you to rest now," Lian said, beginning to draw her hand away.

But Mairi slipped her fingers from among theirs and put hers beneath, as if to hold them all in her grasp. Outside, tawny owl and nightingale competed with the sighing song of the wind to fill the moon-washed night with music. Mairi smiled tentatively, then, as the women bent nearer, she said, "I can no' tell ye how glad I am that you've come home once more."

The tension that had held them in its grip all night relaxed at the sound of her familiar voice, the sight of her familiar smile. The sisters felt a sense of relief. Mairi had helped them when they most needed it, and they would help her now, giving of their strength and kindness, willing it to her until she was well.

"We will be back." Lian and Genevra spoke together, aware of the frailty of Mairi's hand, yet still it held theirs up. "We will always come back again."

Mairi's eyes misted over so they shimmered in the golden light. "Aye," she murmured, "but you're here now. I thank the gods for that." Her lids fluttered closed; her smile lingered for a moment, until she slipped into painless sleep.

Ailsa was the last to release her mother's hand. She pressed one palm against Genevra's, one against Lian's, while her sisters made the circle complete, impenetrable. Ailsa sighed. " 'Twill be all right now. I know it will."

GENEVRA WAS DREAMING THAT A BIRD SAT ON THE WINDOW-sill, singing in the sweetest, purest voice she had ever heard. She reached out gingerly to touch its glossy feathers, but it glided away, hovering just outside the window.

Unable to resist its lilting voice, unwilling to lose sight of the emerald and silver wings, she rose, slipped her wrapper over her nightrail and followed the brightly colored bird trailing an aria of gracefully woven notes that enticed her away from her bed and into the pale lilac light before dawn.

She moved through the mist, lifting her face to the cool, cleansing moisture, felt the dew on her bare feet and soft white gown. Genevra leaned down to brush the petals of the last wood roses, then raised her fingers to her lips and licked the dew away. It tasted sweet on her tongue, as the bird's song, turned to liquid, would have tasted.

She stopped to examine her robe and gown, noticing the dew-wet hem, feeling its chill against her skin. Her feet were very cold and uncomfortable on the rough ground. Only then did she suddenly awaken and realize she was actually standing outside in a meadow. Yet the song still spilled from the trees across the way. She had heard it in her sleep and it had become part of her dream. Her imagination had turned it into a beautiful bird. It's a good thing I was downstairs and not in the loft, she thought ruefully. Or I might have broken my neck.

The seductive lure of the music was calling. Genevra hesitated for a moment, then crept back inside and tiptoed through the large croft where her sister and the others slept, exhausted. She made no sound as she found her strongest leather slippers and lifted her hemp bag from the floor. Stepping outside, she turned without hesitation to follow the melody that had bewitched her.

The farther she walked, the softer the music became. She hurried, leaving a trail of trampled grass behind. She paused at the edge of the woods; the music had faded, softened and enfolded by the mist. What was she to do now?

She noticed a small dirt trail where the leaves had been cleared, except for a single orange oak leaf placed in the center of the path pointing south. Genevra frowned at the cleared ground and that leaf, still wet with dew, for a long time before she realized this was too carefully arranged to be natural. Nature was more hasty and scattered in her beauty.

Someone was leading her somewhere. She did not pause to wonder who; she was too charmed by the idea. Impulsively, she followed the direction of the leaf. When the path ended in a small clearing, she noticed there were two trails on the other side of the copse. She clutched her bag, considering, until she noticed the low branch of the oak in front of her. In a hollow where a bird's nest might have been, she found four pine cones in the shape of a star.

She heard a faint echo of the song from her dream, and it drew her down the path where the pine cones pointed. The air grew hushed and green and tranquil, and the duskiness of the woods, not yet penetrated by daylight, grew darker.

Next she had to choose among several paths, but only one had colored stones strung down the center like beads that had fallen from a thread. She heard the music again as she picked up a few and dropped them in her bag.

The trees were thicker here, yet she felt an openness, a sigh of relief, as if she were about to be delivered from the darkness. As the quality of light shifted, she found a crown of dried primroses, wild violets and golden celandine hanging on the knot of an ash at eye level. It was woven together with dried grasses, lovely and promising.

Genevra grinned and promptly put the crown on her head of pale blond hair, braided the night before, though many strands curled up along the weaving and around her face from the moisture in the air.

Then she heard something, stepped between the trees and found herself at the edge of the river.

Ena Rose knelt in her nightrail, the red Rose plaid hanging over her arms, a fawn-colored cap beside her on the ground. Nearby lay a rosewood flute. Genevra knew then where the music had come from. Not the brilliant colored bird she had imagined in her dream, but from this young girl's magic flute. She had no doubt it must be magic. Why else would she be here?

Ena's head was bent toward the water, and her auburn hair fell down her back, a tumble of wild curls. The girl looked up as the sun appeared through the trees on the horizon, painting the sky violet and red, tinting the water luminous pink.

When Genevra sighed and began to exclaim, Ena turned, finger to her lips. "I'd rather no' talk. Just let me show ye."

Show me what? her aunt wondered. But she did not ask. Intrigued, she crept closer, willing to be surprised.

Slowly, Ena motioned for her aunt to kneel nearby. There's something different about her, Genevra thought. Yesterday Ailsa's daughter had been what she had to be— secure, knowledgeable, skilled. Today she was merely a child.

Rising to pick up a creel she'd set among the reeds, she waded out into the water, holding her basket above the surface. Rather than following, Genevra took her own bag, found a nearby tree to lean against and discovered a tartan blanket and bladder of water awaiting her. Ena had planned ahead. Touched, Genevra sat, sketchpad in her lap. While the girl wandered, her aunt sketched her in the gossamer gown, which floated like a wedding train on the bronzed surface of the burn.

If she were not so aware of the damp, uneven ground beneath her and the scratchy bark against her back, Genevra might have thought she was dreaming again.

Then Ena cried out and fell to her knees near the bank, working her hands in the reeds and ferns. At last, with a sigh of regret, she found a supple leaf and wrapped something in it. Then she looked up meaningfully at Genevra, who had stopped, charcoal in midair, to watch.

Gathering her things, Genevra threw her bag over her shoulder and rose, tripping as she ran along the bank to keep up with Ena, who was moving downriver. She was no longer meandering where the flow of water took her, but heading with determination toward some other destination.

Genevra caught her wrapper and gown in one hand so she could run without hindrance. When Ena waded to the opposite bank and climbed out, her aunt plunged without hesitation into the shallow water and waded across, using the girl's footsteps as a guide to pull herself up onto the bank.

A few moments later, Genevra ducked beneath a swaying willow branch and doubled over, attempting to catch her breath. She was not used to running, especially not with sodden hems heavy with clinging loam slowing her progress. When she looked up, she stared openmouthed at the small clearing fringed with willows. There were row upon row of stones in the ground. Some had strange figures and symbols carved on them, some painted words, and some, apparently worn by time, were plain. A graveyard, though surely not for people. The mounds scattered with stones, grown over with moss and grass that had begun to brown from autumn's cold, were not large enough. Some were so small they made no real impression among the patterns of earth around them. Only the stones revealed their existence. And the wild roses, faded now, their petals strewn on the ground, that had been planted on each grave.

One of the larger mounds had barely a fringe of grass covering the dark, heaped earth, but there, too, roses had bloomed and died. Ena knelt beside it, using a carved, pointed stone to shovel out a narrow furrow.

Genevra crept up quietly, peering over the girl's shoulder. When the hollow was no more than six inches deep and equally wide, Ena lifted the leaf package from her basket. She opened it enough to reveal the tiny frozen bird inside, closed her eyes briefly, then hid the sad little body inside the leaf and laid both in the empty grave.

Leaning down with care and tenderness, Ena surrounded and covered the leaf and its burden with earth warmed by her hands.

Genevra moved back to the edge of the trees, fighting the sorrow Ena's grief and tenderness had kindled like the wavering flame of a candle. Clearly, to her, every life was sacred, no matter how small. The care lavished on the graveyard would have said as much, even if the simple burial had not. Genevra should have felt oppressed, as she often was by the dank, moldy smell of old death in the churchyards. But this small clearing, lit by the sun, which had reached the top branches of the trees, was not a place for lasting sadness, but a testament to the inevitable cycle of life and death. The wild roses on the ground, the intricate carvings, the moss that edged the stones with shades of green, and the soft sheen of sunlight on Ena's wild, flowing hair were silent promises to those animals that had gone and the ones who would come to be.

To her surprise, Genevra felt an intense urge to kneel again, to worship this place as she had worshipped the sweeping power of dawn and the endless pulsing flow of the river.

10

ENA ROSE, STOOD FOR A MOMENT LONGER, THEN DARTED beneath a willow at the side of the clearing. Genevra took a deep, panicked breath; she did not want to lose the girl now. Ena ducked back under the tree and paused until she saw her aunt start to move. Then in a flicker, she was gone.

They followed a narrow path, which proved a true test for Genevra's leather slippers, though Ena skipped ahead, barefoot and unencumbered. Her toes and heels did not appear to touch the rocky ground. She bent now and then, barely slackening her speed, to pick up a small piece of wood, examine it from all sides, and either drop it in her basket or discard it.

When they emerged from the woods into a long clearing by the river, Genevra almost laughed with delight. First Ena had shown her the birth of day, then the place where death lay easy; now she was showing her teeming life—its smell and sound and sight and texture.

Genevra knew the girl kept a kind of animal hospital, but she had not imagined this.

There were injured and healing animals everywhere— birds in low cages built of branches and twine, red squirrels and wood mice and badgers in low corrals meant, not to hold them prisoner, but to keep them from harming themselves further. Separate from the others was a young red deer, apparently recovered from the wound that had left a long scar on its thigh. The deer snorted and butted its head against a post and danced about restlessly.

Genevra paused, watching as Ena gave the animals fresh food and water, and scattered the ground with clean moss and straw. Each enclosure had a kind of miniature hut where the animals could hide from the icy wind or the fury of a storm.

Ena glowed as she performed these menial tasks, stopping to murmur a greeting to each animal, a trill echoing its own to each bird. Genevra could have sworn that as soon as the girl had touched each one, checking this wound, adjusting that bandage, scratching a back here, a head there, caressing the throats of the birds with a light touch of her finger, the animals grew quiet.

Her aunt had seen it happen at Ladybrooke—anyone

who fed and cared for the stray animals was welcomed. Animals seemed to know when they were likely to get food and water; they quickly came to recognize the footsteps of her daughter Elizabeth, who was the most interested in the animals from the forest, and the most responsible at remembering their needs.

But there was a subtle difference in Ena's connection to these momentarily caged wild animals. She had a way about her, an affinity and empathy for other living things, and they seemed to feel it.

Genevra sketched quickly as the shadows of bare branches made shifting patterns over the enclosure while the sun rose higher and a wind came up. Ena checked each animal, smiling over some, frowning over others, treating a few with ointments and bandages, others with herbs that she coaxed them to swallow or mixed with their food. She removed the catgut stitches she had sewn into a deep cut on a red squirrel, singing to it all the while.

Genevra tried to capture the quality of those efficient but gentle fingers, but it seemed as impossible as capturing the water sprite who had wandered in the river. She gasped when a wet nose nudged her hand, making her drop her charcoal. It was the deer, seeking attention. She stared into its liquid brown eyes, then reached out cautiously to pet it. The deer leaned farther out so she could scratch between its ears. She surprised herself by nuzzling it. She closed her eyes and lifted her face to the sun, absorbing it as she had the dew.

She did not realize how long she had stood unmoving when Ena played a few notes on her flute, and Genevra saw the dirty hem of the girl's nightrail disappearing into the shade a little way down the burn. Genevra touched her face, surprised to find her cheeks filmed with perspiration. Hurriedly, she slipped her sketchpad into her bag and made her way around the animal pens to the path Ena had followed.

She stopped abruptly when she saw a worn blanket

folded neatly beneath a tree, and beside it, a waterskin and clean white cloth. She sat down gratefully, using the cloth to wipe her face, fumbling with the stopper on the waterskin so she could take a long, cool drink. She discovered a small wooden dish covered with scones and jam, shortbread and two apples. Ena, who was nowhere in sight, seemed to think of everything. Just for a moment, Genevra leaned against the sturdy trunk of the tree and closed her eyes. The cool shadows embraced her, easing the heat in her flushed cheeks, whispering through the trees and lifting the trailing tendrils of hair off her forehead. It was so peaceful here, so cool and quiet, yet filled with the little sounds of the forest. The scratch of small animals' feet on bark and pine needles, the rustling of birds hidden in the branches overhead, the sigh of swaying limbs. It was heavenly, she thought, letting her mind drift.

When she opened her eyes, she was surprised to find Ena seated across from her, cradled by the huge old branches of an oak. Genevra brushed some pieces of bark and spruce needles from her hair, aware that Ena was watching, though her attention appeared to be fixed on an object she was carving, head bent, hair falling forward to hide her face.

Genevra felt refreshed and revitalized. She picked up an apple and bit into it, licking at the juice that ran down her chin, then took the other and tossed it to Ena, who looked up at the crunch in the stillness of this place.

The girl caught it, smiled and took a bite before she returned to her carving. She munched on the apple until she had finished it and thrown the core to a squirrel, who clutched the fruit in its mouth and was gone.

Her aunt took out her sketchpad, and for a long time, the two sat in contented silence—Genevra drawing and Ena carving. Here there were no worries, no problems, no misunderstandings. Here they were lost in a hidden sanctuary where turmoil faded, as if layer after layer of pale gauze had been draped between the world they'd left and the one Ena had created.

Genevra hadn't felt so relaxed and carefree since before the children had come down with influenza last spring. She felt no desire to speak, to break the invisible rapport with the child. Each worked at her craft leisurely; there were time enough and space enough and freedom enough.

After a while, Ena looked up, tracing the sun through the tangle of branches. She tilted her head, listening, then jumped to her feet. " 'Tis time to go home. They'll be needin' me. But ye can stay as long as ye like. I've left ye a map."

The sound of her voice was startling. Genevra dropped her pencil, astonished that the girl had spoken at all. She stared as Ena waved behind her, then disappeared, taking her knife and piece of wood. A few moments later, she reappeared, smiled once, pointing backward before she ran off. Her progress through the woods was silent, though Genevra listened carefully. Finally, with regret and more than a little curiosity, she turned in the direction the girl had indicated.

She searched for several minutes before she found the huge old oak, long past its prime, with the long, thick sweeping branch that swung out from a tall, very wide stump. As she circled the stump, she found a piece of the trunk, curved at the top, two feet high and two wide, hanging on what appeared to be leather hinges. It creaked quietly, swaying in the breeze. A door left open, she realized, seeing the dark curved hollow in the stump that, when closed, the door would make invisible.

A secret place hidden deep in the woods. Heart beating with anticipation, she knelt to look inside. A knothole in the huge branch had been popped open like a porthole on a ship, allowing sunlight to penetrate the gloom of the tiny round room inside the dead tree.

Genevra was fascinated by the table made from a small

tree stump that had been smoothed and sanded into an unusual desk. A flute lay on top of the papers, and a carved rosewood chest sat in the middle, open to reveal stacks of letters, clean parchment and some nibbed pens. Genevra could see from the handwriting on several envelopes that these were letters from herself and Lian and the children. Other drawings and poems were tacked to the wall. There were also dried flower wreaths, and here and there, in a natural indentation in the wood, sat tiny carved animals, and a wonderfully misshapen pinecone. There was a hand-built cabinet for cutting, drying and sorting herbs, and a lovely cluster of autumn leaves bound like a bouquet of flowers beside a pile of unique colored stones, worn smooth by wind and water and time. Nearby was another pile, more haphazard, made up of a strange assortment of small things—pieces of metal, broken quartz, twigs and crumpled flowers, curled leaves and something shiny. They were covered with lint, and remembering the large pockets on Ena's dresses, Genevra guessed these might be oddments dumped from those pockets at the end of the day. There was a stack of wood, obviously used for carving; two carving knives hung close by. Except for the small circle of charred stones where black and silver ash spoke of many fires, the floor was strewn with flowers and leaves.

Crouched awkwardly, Genevra grasped the top of the door to keep from falling as she took in all the treasures in this tiny place. Here was Ena's refuge where she kept the things she cherished most. Yet she had led her aunt here, invited her to see inside. It was full to the brim of energy, color, life, yet oddly intimate at the same time. Once this oak had been abandoned and common, but Ena had made it a home.

Genevra was so moved that her eyes burned and her breath gathered in her chest, pressing against her heart. She knew she would never forget this morning or this moment. The tiny, strangely shaped room revealed more about Ena than she could have written in a thousand letters or spoken in a torrent of words. The silence was part of the revelation.

Only then, just at the base of the doorway, did Genevra notice the parchment on which the girl had drawn a rough map back to Alanna's. Beside it was a piece of bark with letters tinted with dyes from plants, lichens and roots.

For Aunt Genevra

Placed above the bark was a tiny carving of a bird painted soft emerald green with silver on its head and at the tips of its wings. Genevra held it reverently in her open palm. One final gift, a fragile memento of this brief escape to a place where expectations and obligations disappeared in the mist and the pleasures, though simple, soothed and infused her spirit with new life.

11

"I THINK MAIRI IS LOOKING MUCH BETTER TODAY," LIAN declared. "There is color in her cheeks and humor in her eyes."

It had been three weeks since the accident, long enough for the sisters to be cajoled into leaving Mairi for the day. Besides, Alanna was with her grandmother and grateful for the chance to spend some time alone with Mairi. Mairi herself had practically shooed her daughters out the door like wayward chickens.

"How's a body to rest with all of ye hoverin' over me? The sun's come out for ye; 'tis a blessin' ye should thank the gods for. 'Twould be a sin to waste it."

"Are ye certain?" Ailsa had asked.

Mairi turned to her daughter with a spark of the old fire in her eyes. "Have I ever said what I didn't mean? A broken ankle's no' made me daft, ye ken. Go, all of ye. Find some pleasure and give me some peace."

"I don't blame her, you know, for insisting we go out," Genevra said. "If I were her, I should be driven quite mad by our constant fussing and worrying. I should probably go into a decline from overattention. I was glad to hear her grumble at us."

Ailsa smiled in spite of herself. "Aye, you're right. She's no' had the energy for complainin' since she was hurt."

While they walked, the sisters agreed that each day Mairi had improved in small ways, and though she could not yet walk on her injured ankle, none doubted that she would do so eventually, laughing at her own clumsiness as she used to. "She's far too stubborn to do aught else."

At that moment, they reached their destination and ducked under the trees that fringed the burn, stopping still at the scene before them.

Here the ground sloped upward, gradually at first, then sharply to the top of the hill. Just below the summit where the water disappeared into the woods, a large, flat rock protruded, a clear curtain of water pouring over it down a long, sharp drop. There the fall met the less steep, more graduated waterfalls, which descended gently from level to level, tumbling over smooth flat boulders in striated bands of color, from brown to rust to ochre. The streams met and parted and met again in rushing streams that made their way among hollows where ferns grew thick and verdant and the sunlight on the misting water made rainbows that shimmered and faded and reappeared.

Directly in front of the three women was a wide, deep *linne* where the clear golden water was tinged with green from the grasses and moss that sprouted from the rocks on the sides and the stones on the bottom.

The last time Ailsa, Lian and Genevra had been here together, Mairi had watched as they leapt one by one from the huge flat stone near the top of the hill and into the *linne*, where the rushing water grew still, though the falls continued in graduated steps below. They had forgotten how beautiful it was, how full of life and sound and motion, yet at the same time, peaceful. They had forgotten the feelings that had overwhelmed them that night, the sense of intimacy and victory.

The sun was shining through the trees, giving light, water, air a clear, sparkling brilliance. For a long while, the three stood, speechless, remembering, not wishing to diminish the memories with words.

Then they realized they were standing in the very spot where Mairi Rose had sat that night and encouraged them to take a chance. *Ye leave your mark, ye make the land remember, by takin' a risk that proves your sincerity and commitment.*

"Do ye know," Ailsa said at last, "I'm near as old now as Mam was then?"

Lian regarded her in disbelief. "Now that we are here, now that we feel the spray touch our skin and hear the sound of the river, it does not seem possible that so much time has passed since we last stood together in this place."

"I remember as vividly as if it were a fortnight past," Genevra offered.

"The feelings are as strong as the sights and sounds," Lian added. "I can hear Mairi's voice as clearly as I hear yours." *There're spirits everywhere, ye ken. In the water, in the sky, in the earth and the ever-changin' moonlight.* Lian shivered as if Mairi had touched her shoulder from her distant bed.

" 'Tis because we wondered if our father'd dreamed that night and that magic, but now 'tis our mother who's dreamin'." Ailsa took a step forward to hide the color that rushed to her cheeks then drained away. Charles Kittridge had been dead for two months when they'd last been here. But Mairi was very much alive.

Without another word, the sisters sat on a dry, flat boulder and, feeling the freedom of the place, each took down her hair and discarded her shoes. They rose together and moved toward the shallow edge of the *linne*.

Ailsa gathered the skirt of her dusty rose muslin gown, Lian the length of her green satin tunic, and Genevra the blue serge sweep of her belled skirt, and they stepped, shivering, into the burn. They gazed up at the stone and its bronze fall of water, and instinctively reached out to clasp hands.

Genevra sighed with pleasure, appreciating the setting, the moment, even more because of her journey of discovery with Ena. Since that day, she had moved decisively, with assurance, enthusiasm. It was as if she'd been reborn, as if the spark of her creativity had flared into a flame. She had been drawing, sketching, painting with watercolors in every spare moment. She had wandered off on her own several times and had not once felt lonely or afraid. "It's magic here, isn't it?" she murmured.

"Aye, and always has been." *Here earth, sky and water are close enough to touch. These things are older than we, older than memory, older than man.* Ailsa turned, looking for her mother, whose words were so lucid they seemed like a message she should learn by heart. *They remember what we never knew—every soul that's lingered here, leavin' his image in the water or his voice in the wind or his imprint in the soil.* She stepped out farther, till the water reached her thighs.

Lian stared. She had forgotten how Ailsa was transformed by the flowing water, how her body became more lithe and fluid, as if she had come home. "I am glad we chose this place today. I feel tranquil here, and welcome." *'Tis because ye were already known somewhere in the deep ancient heart of the earth, but now ye'll no' be forgotten. Not ever.* Again she felt Mairi's touch on her shoulder. "It is as if we belong, just as it seemed we belonged the first time we went to the Hill of the Hounds."

Ailsa smiled wistfully over her shoulder. "I wish ye really could buy it. 'Twould mean so much to Mam and me and Ena."

"We've written to Alex and Émile, and they think it's a grand idea."

Considering Genevra in surprise, Ailsa asked, "How do ye know?"

"The boy from Beauly brought the mail this morning," her sister said, exchanging a smile with Lian. "We wanted to surprise you." She bit her lip to keep from saying more.

"But just because your husbands agree doesn't mean ye'll find the money."

Lian grinned enigmatically. "Émile says one can always find a way if one wants something badly enough. One must merely think very hard and be very patient. I am good at being patient."

She hugged a secret to her chest with folded arms. It was not like her at all. Yet sixteen years ago, as the three prepared to climb the hill to stand on that rock, Ailsa had asked her sisters, *Should we take the chance?* And then answered her own question. *There'll be nothing to hold us back but ourselves.* It seemed Lian and Genevra had taken the words to heart. Once they'd had the idea of buying the Hill, they'd not once faltered in their resolve, no matter how impractical it might be.

I do not know if I have made my mark on the river, Lian had said that night, *but it has made its mark on me.* Apparently, she'd been right.

If there was one thing Ailsa could do, was willing and eager to do, it was believe. All at once, she found herself grinning with Lian and Genevra, full of hope and anticipation.

Alanna sat quietly at the kitchen table in her grandmother's croft, not fussing or talking much. She could see that Mairi was exhausted. So she kept her grandmother company, staying near in case she needed anything, and savoring the time alone.

"What're ye thinkin', our Alannean?"

The use of the endearment nearly unraveled Alanna's resolve to remain tranquil. Mairi had not called her Alannean—dear little Alanna—in years. She stared at the scrubbed pine table, trying to force the pattern of the grain into focus. She cleared her throat before she could speak normally. "Of the dawn when I went to the Valley of the Dead and saw that I belonged here, that though I'd not known it, the glen had always been my home."

Mairi let her eyes drift closed, smiling softly. "Aye. Ye gave me great joy that day, as you've done often since. Ye never regretted your choice?"

"No' for a single moment." Alanna wondered why they were talking about this now, why it filled her with contentment and, at the same time, a sense of alarm. "How could I regret what was my destiny? Some people never find a place like this, never find their true home. I was lucky to discover mine so young, lucky to have ye to welcome me into your croft and your heart."

"We've all been lucky in our own way," Mairi mused. "In spite of everything. Do ye no' think so?"

Alanna propped her chin up with her hand, smiling through the tears that threatened. "Aye, we've all been blessed, and mayhap I more than anyone. My woes have been small and fleetin', my joy unfalterin'. I regret only that David and I've no' had more bairns. I would've welcomed a dozen." Glancing up, she caught her grandmother's sympathetic smile.

"If any could've kept so many in hand, 'twould be ye and your David."

"Mayhap. Yet we've only Connor and I'm worried about him. We can no' seem to keep him in hand."

Reaching out for her granddaughter, Mairi winced and let her hand fall. "He'll be all right, your Connor. Have a little faith in him; he'll no' let ye down, or himself either. But ye must be patient. Ye must let things happen as they will. Your son has more common sense than ye realize. Be proud of him; 'twill mean a lot to him, your trust." She closed her eyes, exhausted from the long speech.

Frightened at how quickly contentment had turned to pain, Alanna went to the kettle and took it from the hook above the fire. It was time for Mairi's rose hip tea and decoction of yew. She puttered for a time, drawing out the task, shocked at how upset she was. She had sworn she would not let her grandmother see it. Not today, when she needed hope and warmth, not worry and dread. Yet even now, Mairi was advising her, and wisely, too. Alanna knew Connor was distressed by his parents' concern, which seemed to him a lack of faith. She'd noticed he'd been more mature, more thoughtful in the past few months. Now that she stopped to think about it, she realized he *had* begun to earn her trust. How could she let him know?

Mairi watched her oldest granddaughter secretly, observing her precise, graceful movements as well as her attempt to hide her distress. Did they think because she'd broken her foot, she had also grown blind? Did they think she did not understand the questions and doubts, love and fear that swirled through the air in this small croft? Dear Alanna. She was trying so hard.

Alanna knelt beside her grandmother, holding the cup of medicinal tea so Mairi would sip slowly. She made small talk for a time, while the herbs did their work. When she sensed the pain had gone; Mairi looked refreshed and alert. Yet Alanna hesitated before speaking. Ena had told her they must try, at least once, to get Mairi to stand. If she didn't put some weight on her ankle soon, the bones would not mend properly. Drawing a deep breath, she said, "I've been thinkin', Gran. Mayhap 'tis time ye tried out your ankle, just for a little. If ye lean on me, and I keep my arm around ye, ye might well be able to stand up, mayhap even walk a step or two?"

"Ena said the same just this mornin'." She sounded doubtful, but at Alanna's eager expression, Mairi felt a surge of obstinance. "I'll try, but just for ye."

Pleased and triumphant, Alanna lifted her grandmother

to her knees and then her feet, savoring Mairi's weight against her, Mairi's arm sliding around her waist for support. Slowly, carefully, Alanna urged her upright until she stood unsteadily, her bad foot barely touching the floor. The door was open, and for the first time in weeks, Mairi saw the world beyond her bed. The sun was shining, which was odd enough at this time of year, and the breeze that ruffled her gown was warm. Green, gold, red and yellow, the colors glowed like crushed and re-formed jewels. Mairi wanted to stand there forever, breathing in the fresh air, reminding herself how beautiful the glen was when the mist burned away and an unfamiliar brilliance settled over moor and woods. Not long ago, she would have gone out to let sun and color and warmth enfold her.

Instead, she wobbled precariously and her ankle collapsed beneath her. Alanna caught her grandmother as she fell and placed her gently back into her cocoon of sheets and blankets. Mairi was flushed and exhausted, breathing harshly, long after she lay back and closed her eyes. She winced and reached once or twice toward her ankle, as if to stop the throbbing with her gnarled fingers.

" 'Tis time to rest for the while, and to drink your tea," Alanna said without inflection. She hoped the herbs would help the pain she had caused.

"So 'tis," Mairi whispered. She could not meet her granddaughter's eyes.

Alanna struggled to hide her misgivings as she went back to preparing tea and stirring the decoction. Her grandmother should not still be so weak and frail. Alanna's hand did not tremble and she thought she did quite well at keeping her expression bland, though in her mind, over and over again, she felt Mairi's weight fall against her as her legs gave way. Panic surged through her now as it had then, draining the blood from her cheeks and making her heart race. Alanna said a silent prayer—there had been many—and arranged the steaming cups on a tray. Before she turned from the kitchen table, she took a deep breath and composed herself. Or so she thought.

Mairi's eyes were closed as her granddaughter approached, but she knew. She could taste Alanna's fear like bitter herbs on her tongue, but she did not say so. She drank her medications, and after awhile, as rose hip and yew made their way into her blood, she found her voice again.

The two women chatted about Lian and Genevra, their unexpected visit, the new life and interest the sisters had brought to the glen, the possibility of their buying the Hill of the Hounds. "They always know when they're needed," Mairi said, "when to come and when to go, even if they'd not be knowin' why 'tis they do it." Before her granddaughter could reply, she reached out to touch Alanna's hand.

"I've no' seen Jenny Fraser the while. Where's she keepin' herself? Have ye seen her?"

Startled by Mairi's wistful tone and the sudden change in subject, Alanna took a deep breath. "I've seen her many times."

"Then why has she no' been by? I miss her," Mairi insisted, as if Alanna might argue. "She's a head full of common sense on her shoulders, and a heart full of kindness and forgiveness both."

Alanna nodded in agreement. She had always liked and admired Jenny. "She said there were enough people to pester ye, Gran, that she'd only be in the way. She didn't want to cause any distress, she said."

"'Tis odd, isn't it, how others can no' see how ye feel about them, can no' guess how deeply and for how long you've cared?" She paused. "You're no' like Jenny, are ye, Alannean? Ye know your place in my heart." It was not a question.

"Aye. I know."

Mairi opened her eyes wide until her gaze locked with Alanna's. They stared at one another, openly, honestly, hiding nothing, eased by the old strands holding them together, though they saw a shadow threatening the luminous yellow lamplight in which they sat. Mairi reached up as Alanna reached down. Their palms met, fingers bent gently so they were locked together for an instant—an eternity.

Soon both were weak and shaking, and Mairi had to break the connection before each gave the other too much, or took too much away.

"Ask Jenny to come," Mairi whispered as she released her granddaughter and splintered the fine spun crystal meshwork between them. "She's earned her place in this family time and again, and I bless her for it."

Alanna's throat was choked with tears from the moment when her hands and eyes had met her grandmother's, and they'd known one another again, to the soul, as they used to know each other long ago. It was not easy, seeing so deep and so far into another; it was not gentle or kind or forgiving. And yet, it was a miracle, one she would not have asked for, and would never forget, nor could she express her exaltation and gratitude. That was part of seeing someone else's soul. There was no need for words. Indeed, they would have been a desecration. "I'll ask her, Gran. I'll tell her."

12

STANDING AT OPPOSITE ENDS OF A GRACEFUL SETTEE, LIAN and Ena lifted the linen sheet that covered it, ghostlike. The linen snapped as they undulated it between them, sending dust motes whirling into the sunlight pouring through the open French doors.

Ena sneezed violently, shaking her head to keep the dust away. She glanced at Lian, who was crinkling her nose in an effort to ward off a sneeze of her own. 'Tis a good thing she's abandoned her silk and satin tunics, Ena thought.

Already her aunt's cheek was streaked with dirt and her fingers gritty. By the end of the day, they'd both be filthy from head to foot. But the girl didn't care.

"I never thought there'd be so many bonny things hidden away at the Hill," she mused while they folded the sheet and added it to the pile. The settee they'd just revealed was made of shades of blue brocade framed by sleek rosewood.

"I told you," Lian said. "This house is full of wonders." She could barely repress her excitement, which Ena had begun to share as soon as she learned the Drouards and Kendalls were thinking of buying the house and grounds. Her aunt had asked her to come along today while she surveyed the interior more thoroughly than she had with quick glimpses on that first misty morning.

Ena had always hated the house, but now that it might belong to family, she found herself enchanted. The taint of careless English hunters and men seeking wealth by exploiting the glen had been wiped away in the wake of Lian and Genevra's enthusiasm. Now she could see its possibilities. Now she could admire the high painted and molded ceilings, the comfortable furniture and the large rooms.

Aunt and niece had spent the morning going from room to room, uncovering the furniture, flinging back the dark velvet drapes and yellowed lace beneath, attacking the flying dirt and dust with straw brooms and rags made from squares of old homespun sheets. They opened wide every window that would budge, every French door whose latch was not rusted shut, allowing the sunlight to spill in from every direction.

They'd stood motionless, considering the domed ceilings, gilded and painted with fading clouds and cherubs. "My son Vincent would be fascinated," Lian had said. "He inherited his father's love of painting. I have a suspicion that once he saw this house, his first priority would be to redo these with images of his own. I am almost afraid to guess what they might be."

In the library, they'd found yellowed and tattered pages of Celtic poetry left in a jumble on the desk. "Here is where Sebastian would settle in." Lian pulled Ena close to murmur in her ear, "He does not like to admit it, but he goes out to the old barn and writes poetry whenever he gets the chance. He hides it in his room, but once or twice he has shown a page or two to me. He is really quite good."

"Why does he hide it then?"

Lian shook her head, assuming a mock solemn expression. "He says it is not manly, that the others would laugh at him. He is very sensitive, my Sebastian. He seems to have forgotten that his father is the same, only he expresses himself on canvas instead of parchment. Besides, Sebastian is quite strong and quite intelligent. I doubt that any would dare laugh at him. Perhaps he will understand that someday."

Ena was moved by the pride with which she spoke of her sons and their accomplishments. And Lian's revelations only made the girl more eager to meet her cousins, to see the barn and the vineyard and Émile's paintings.

By mutual consent, she and Lian went to the open doors to breathe air unclouded with dust. Leaning against the frame, badly in need of painting, Ena asked shyly, "Is your house in Burgundy like this?"

Lian was surprised and pleased by her open interest. Though they had spent a few afternoons together, walking and talking, Ena had asked no questions about her aunt's life and what it was like. Lian sensed that it was sometimes on the girl's mind, but she seemed to be fighting her natural, healthy curiosity. "It is something like it, though Émile and I and the boys live in a two hundred-year-old estate with the rest of his rather large family. We have our own wing, furnished much like this, though we have added ebony tables and teak wall screens and Chinese scrolls so I feel at home there."

Hearing something in her aunt's voice, Ena turned, arms crossed over her chest. "Do ye really feel at home?"

She expected Lian to evade the question about her personal feelings, but her aunt surprised her.

"Very often I do, because Émile is there and Sebastian and Vincent and Marc. And we have large windows looking out on the vineyard and huge, very old shade trees on either side. And I enjoy working with the grapes." She met Ena's attentive gaze. "But to tell you the truth, I feel more at ease when we go to stay in the farmhouse where my husband's grandmother lived at the end of her life. We escape there as often as we can. It is much cozier, simpler, more private. Then of course sometimes Émile and I return to Chervilles to stay in the flat above Cheng's apothecary shop. That, I think, is the best of all."

Lian had talked about the old Chinese alchemist—how much he'd taught her, how he'd freed her from the constraints under which she'd lived with the family who'd taken her to France, how he'd provided her with a flat and a job she loved. "But it must seem very small after the estate and the farmhouse. How can it be best?"

Delighted by the sudden string of questions that were far more normal from a thirteen-year-old girl than Ena's usual reticence, Lian replied, "Because it is where my husband and I fell in love. We were married in the street in front of the shop. Each time I step over the threshold, I feel those awakening feelings all over again. Nothing changes in that little world, which in itself is comforting. But you know about that. It is the same in the glen, surely?"

Ena frowned, thinking. "No' much changes, aye, 'tis true. 'Tis true as well that I feel safe here." Why did the thought bother her?

"But what about falling in love? You do not seem acquainted with many children besides Connor Fraser."

"I only need one friend," the girl answered firmly. "And I've no intention of ever fallin' in love."

Lian was taken aback. "Why not?"

Without being aware of it, they'd stepped outside and

begun to wander down the flagged path toward the gardens. "It hurts too much."

Stopping in the middle of the path, her aunt regarded Ena intently. She could not exactly deny what the girl had said, but she found herself wanting to very badly. "Why do you think that? Did no one ever tell you how much joy it brings, along with the pain?"

"I've heard my mother's story and Gran's and Jenny Fraser's. They've all had a lot of sorrow." She dragged her bare toes along the old, uneven stones, watching with apparent concentration so she wouldn't have to see Lian's expression. "I'd rather be happy, is all."

Choking back the words that rose to her tongue, her aunt said cautiously, "Do you think it is easier to be happy by yourself? Do you not know about loneliness?"

"I know. But I've Mam and Mairi and Connor and the animals." She kept her head lowered, sensing Lian's probing gaze.

"When you become a woman, those things are not as satisfying as they are now. When you're older—"

"I don't want to be older, I don't want a man or children. I like things the way they are." She spoke too forcefully, revealing her yearning for something she feared, longed for and could not understand. Besides, she knew well enough that the world would not stand still for her. Mostly, she did not want to meet Lian's eyes because she did not want her aunt to see she had hit a wound Ena had not known was there.

Somehow, even with all these people who loved her, she *was* lonely. She did want something else; she just didn't know what it was. She only knew she didn't want the kind of pain Ailsa had suffered when she lost her daughter, then her husband, then the man she'd loved since childhood. Even though she'd gotten Alanna back when she returned to Glen Affric, Ailsa'd missed her for years, ached at her absence.

"I'd no' be knowin' what I want!" she cried, confused. She whirled toward the gardens and pointed dramatically. "Ye can no' force wildness into beauty or loneliness into joy. They tried it here again and again. To trim and shape and make an orderly kind of beauty that the brambles and ivy and moss and vines crept over and through, destroyin' their pretty little patterns. They never learned how daft they were. They just kept tryin' one more time. For nothing. It doesn't work, ye ken. This land was meant to grow wild, and wild it'll be, no matter how many think otherwise. Ye can no' tame it any more than ye can tame how ye feel inside."

Troubled, Lian contemplated the hedges that had obviously at one time been trimmed, the paths forced between them, the flowers planted in tidy borders and circles within marble. Ena was right; there were holly bushes and laurel and broom and heather woven into the overgrown hedges that had given up the battle long ago. The flowers had overflowed their careful boundaries, and either died or spread in all directions. The ferns and moss were soft beneath her feet, nearly covering the beautiful stone and marble placed in graceful patterns.

Ena was stumbling ahead, turning in circles, arms open in a sweeping gesture to emphasize what could not be denied. "Will you sit with me?" Lian called, wiping off a cracked stone bench with the wide hem of her trousers.

Reluctantly, the girl joined her, as suddenly silent as she was still.

"In China, the gardens in the great compounds were planned and carefully constructed by wise men who understood both nature and the nature of human emotion. Everything was measured and placed just so, to create many moods in those who looked upon this calculated beauty. Each time I wandered the gardens at my mother's house, I felt peace, then delight, then fascination, then thoughtfulness as I passed bridge after bridge, each taking me to another example of nature contained, restrained, designed so carefully that even the colors and scents of the flowers were chosen for their harmony with one another and the setting."

She paused, resting her hand lightly on her niece's shoulder. "Harmony is the word I remember most when I think of those ponds and streams and rocks and blossoming trees and flowers. I remember standing in the painted red pavilions, feeling happy only there, where order and taste and knowledge reigned. Even the disorder was planned; it, too, somehow brought peace. So it is possible to civilize nature and yet take none of its power or beauty, just as it is possible to alter the way one feels, to keep what is good and determine to leave what is unpleasant in the past. It is possible to hope, even when it seems hope must have disappeared forever."

Ena considered her aunt in disbelief, though she knew Lian would not lie. But it was difficult to imagine such a place creating such feelings. More difficult to believe that feelings that came from the deepest part of your heart could change. She did not know what she meant to say, but the words that came out were full of longing. "I would like to see those gardens."

Mairi had called, through Alanna's breathless request, and Jenny Fraser went gladly. The leather window coverings had been tied up to let fresh air into the croft, along with the gift of golden light that had come with this brief burst of clear warmth that imitated summer.

The light streamed through the windows, revealing every detail of the usually dimly lit rooms, and Jenny paused, remembering the last time she'd seen it this way, on the day Ailsa married her British barrister. She had missed this cozy croft.

The front door stood wide open, and the sunshine fell in a wide swath across the floor and Mairi on her bed.

The old woman watched, smiling slightly, for a long time before she spoke. "Come, Jenny, pull up the settle and sit ye down beside me. I've not seen your face in too long."

The affection in her voice tugged at Jenny's heart.

"Tell me what you're thinkin'. The others talk constantly. I'd hear a different voice today." She leaned up a little on her elbow, revealing that her cheeks were touched with color and her eyes with life, as they had not been since the injury. Mairi seemed animated and expectant, and she smiled the secret, intriguing smile that none had ever equaled. In the brilliance of false summer, her eyes seemed less shadowed, though her face, pale from being indoors, was webbed with new wrinkles.

"I find it a bit lonely at home, now that my grandchildren are gone for the winter," Jenny said " 'Tis far too large for just me, ye ken, and every footstep seems to echo for the longest time. At first I savored the silence, drinkin' it in like sweet wine that made me a little drunk with my freedom."

She explained how that had changed the day she'd come to Mairi's to prepare dinner in the excitement of Lian and Genevra's arrival. She had remembered that day, she mused, exactly how good a companion Alanna could be, how funny and kind and sensitive to wounds that had not yet healed.

Then the others had come, shouting and wailing, arguing and suggesting. "I was needed that night while they tried to deal with the offerin's, the river of strangers that pooled at your door, the undercurrents I sensed but couldn't understand.

"All I know," she finished, wondering what had possessed her to pour out her heart like this, "was that I felt alive that night, alive and awake and content, helpin' wherever I could."

"Then why have I no' seen ye since?" Mairi demanded.

Jenny hesitated. "I saw how many ye were, and knew I'd no' be needed after. Your daughters' wanted to take care of ye, and I'd no wish to take that pleasure from them. They'd been away so very long, ye ken." She leaned over and grew still, afraid to touch the frail woman, but Mairi took her hand and pressed it to her chest.

"You're always needed, Jenny. Surely ye must know that. You're the one who thinks a problem through quickly and acts just as quickly to solve it. You're no' torn by indecision or ghosts or visions within dreams. I thought ye understood that."

"Mayhap. But I knew as well that your little household had expanded till 'twas ready to burst at the seams, and I'd only be one more burden. Besides, I knew Ena, Ailsa, Genevra and Lian would see ye had whatever ye'd need of." She smiled wryly. "I knew they'd *insist*, one and all, on seein' to it."

Mairi let out a sigh of relief. "Och, weel, if that's it, 'tis all right then." She still held Jenny's hand, which she examined as she pondered, noticing the calluses on her fingers and palms. Most Highland women had them, but not so many or so thick.

"Ye'll think it strange, I've no doubt, when ye know why I asked ye here." Mairi paused, gathering her thoughts. "I'm askin' ye to remember your childhood friendship with Ailsa in the days to come. The years when she showed ye secrets ye'd not guessed at and miracles ye'd no' imagined. I want ye to try. My daughter needs ye."

Jenny opened her mouth, but no words came. She was too stunned. Eventually, she recovered enough to object. "But she has Lian and Genevra."

Mairi clasped her hand more tightly. "Aye, that she does. But 'tis no' the same. They didn't know her when she was a bairn, and ye beside her playin' in the grass. And they've not your particular heart or your special kind of wisdom."

Jenny wondered if she'd heard correctly. It was easy to gain Mairi's love, but difficult indeed to gain her admiration. Jenny's mouth felt dry and she shifted uncomfortably on the settle.

"Ailsa also has Alanna and Ena. But they've deep needs of their own, and 'tis no' easy to put 'em aside. Will ye promise at least to try? To be here if she needs ye? I know 'twill no' be easy, with all that's come between ye, despite your talk last spring. 'Tis why I'm askin' now. Can ye do it?"

Jenny sat for a long time, thinking, twisting the fingers of her free hand in her skirt. She thought of what she had endured, and why, of what Ailsa had faced and conquered, of the years when two small girls had not known what God could bring crashing down upon them. She remembered them holding each other, weeping at what they'd lost. Once more, she asked, "Why me?"

"You're a challenge, our Jenny, I'll give ye that. Will ye no' be convinced till I fall on my knees and turn my eyes to heaven?"

Jenny smiled. "Mayhap before then, but no' just yet."

Pleased that she'd kept her sense of humor, Mairi tried again. "You're the sensible one. 'Twill have to be ye who keeps my girls' feet on the ground. You've spent your life learnin' how. Mayhap 'tis time to teach them what ye know."

"Aye," Jenny said, flushing with pleasure. "I can. And I promise ye I will."

Once again, Mairi sighed with relief, as if Jenny had lifted a weight from her chest that had restricted her breathing. "I believe ye. You've never lied in your lifetime, so far as I know. No' even to yourself. 'Tis why you're special, Jenny Fraser, that and your givin' heart." Mairi squeezed her hand so hard that Jenny gasped.

The younger woman could not help but feel the unnatural heat in Mairi's palm. A few moments ago, her hand had been cool. "Why would ye have fever from a break in your ankle?" She leaned forward, suddenly afraid. "Is there infection?"

Mairi sobered. "No, Ena chased all the foulness away."

Only then did Jenny notice the bruises on Mairi's legs and shoulders that had not yet faded. In fact, there seemed to be more. But the warning in the woman's eye stopped her questions. "What of Ena?" she asked instead. Jenny could not think where the words had come from; she only knew she needed an answer.

"I'm no' certain yet, but the fates are sometimes kind. I know you've cared for her a long time, and I thank ye for that. It took strength of will and honor and forgiveness that few people have within them. I trust ye no' to forget *yourself* while you're busy rememberin' others. Ye deserve peace as much as they. And I thank ye. From my heart and my winterin' spirit, I thank ye. Go ye home now, for I've asked enough of ye. The gods bless ye and follow in your shadow, Jenny Fraser. Always."

Jenny was deeply shaken. Mairi sounded so certain, so final. Yet once Jenny gave her promise, she seemed more peaceful, at rest. Perhaps it was for the best.

Not until she was halfway home did Jenny stop to wonder why Ailsa would need her, and what for. It was not until then that Jenny thought of Mairi—the color in her cheeks, the glitter in her eyes. Hectic color, a feverish glitter. Not signs of improving health, but of frantic determination. Mairi's smooth, mellow voice and the crystalline light had fooled her into thinking she was better. But if that were so, she'd have no need for the promise she'd sought so doggedly.

Jenny did not understand, and could not imagine. The gift of imagination was one she had not received. For some inexplicable reason, she was glad of that just now.

13

"I CAN NO' BELIEVE YE TOOK A STRANGER TO OUR PLACE," Connor said as he and Ena sat stripping softened reeds in the vibrant afternoon light.

Ena glanced at her friend in surprise. She had not mentioned Aunt Genevra or their journey, had not, in fact, intended to speak of it at all. That morning, the shared silence and discovery was curtained in her memory by gossamer veils—protected and inviolate. Restlessly, Ena rose, pausing to contemplate Connor, who had shared all her secrets, all her specters, all her worries. Until now. She could not put into words a fear so insubstantial, a need so indefinable. "How did ye know we'd been there?"

Seeing the dark smudges under her eyes, Connor shook his head and began to trace rough figures in the dirt with a stick. "I sensed it. I helped make the place, ye ken. I know it as well as I know ye." He frowned, aggrieved. "But you've no' given me an answer. Why did ye?"

Ena collapsed onto the bench they shared, limp as a jointed wooden doll. "I think—" She paused, brow furrowed in concentration.

Impulsively, she put her hand on his as she searched for an answer that made sense. "I needed—no, I wanted—to show someone my heart, and I couldn't be passin' it around at the *ceilidh*, could I?"

Connor did not know what to make of her. That had happened often since they'd buried the wildcat last spring. Until that day, she'd never hidden anything from him, nor he from her. But she'd warned him; *Nothing'll ever be the same again*. He hadn't argued; he'd known it was the truth.

But that did not calm him. Besides her secret foray with Genevra Kendall, Ena had disappeared several times with her Aunt Lian and, most surprising, they'd spent a day together at the Hill. He'd never approached them. He knew he'd be an outsider, and that hurt. "Your aunts are no' what I expected," he said neutrally.

"Since they came, I've felt a difference in the air, and it frightens me more than anything else. Change." She shivered and stared at her hands, cracked, sore and filthy, like a bairn's or a fishwife's.

They had talked of this before. "All change is no' bad." Connor tried to think of an example. "The Hill o' the Hounds, now; your aunts are wantin' to buy it. Ye'd never again have to worry about careless hunters or tumblin' from your bed before dawn to try and outsmart 'em. The animals'll be safe. Ye can no' regret that."

I'm here and alive, and in spite of the pain, I'll never forget the thrill of the chase. "Only there'll not be another chase, another challenge." Ena hung her head, remembering her enthusiasm as she'd explored the house with her aunt. "But, aye, you're right. 'Tis the animals that matter, no' my need for adventure."

She was on her feet again, kicking up dirt with her bare toes, swinging her arms back and forth. " 'Tis just . . . so much is already changin', and I don't know why or how to stop it." She whirled. "Ye feel it, do ye no'? I've not gone daft?"

He remembered all too clearly that afternoon last spring when he'd felt her apprehension for the first time. *Make it go, Connor. Say a spell and make it yesterday.* As if she believed he had that power.

The entreaty in her eyes hurt him; he'd never seen her so shaken and confused. Always, he'd thought her wiser than he, stronger. She stared at him pleadingly and he looked away. He could not help her. He was completely powerless, and the weight of it pressed in on him like the four walls of a tiny, airless cave.

Ailsa awoke and sat up in the darkest hour of night. Ena was sitting on the edge of her boxbed, shivering, though the peat coals were warm and her plaid and wool blanket were wrapped around her. She looked as if she had been sitting there forever, feet crossed so one set of bare toes rested atop the other, making her seem young and vulnerable, though her eyes were sad and wise.

Dismayed, Ailsa thought back; she had not heard Ena leave the croft at night for a long time, not since the night

Mairi was injured. That break in a long-established habit disturbed her. Quietly, she tiptoed across the floor and sat next to her daughter.

Ena instinctively moved closer to her mother's warmth and understanding.

"Are ye sleepin' better?"

Looking up, the girl revealed eyes as green as her father's, with no trace of gray. Beneath the sadness was a spark of childlike uncertainty that flared and receded, then flared again. Her body vibrated like a coiled spring barely contained.

"Not much better, no," Ena said in strained voice. Her mother had a strange assessing look in her eye, and the girl did not want her to see too much. "I've no wish to sleep."

Ailsa took her daughter's hand, squeezing the small damp palm. At first her skin was cool, then she felt the heat beneath. "Ye must rest, *mo-run*, or ye'll burn yourself up like a candle meltin' into a pool of wax." *Your daughter shines with intelligence and curiosity*, Lian had said after their visit to the Hill. *But she seems frustrated as well. Perhaps she needs a little more freedom, a little more experience.* Ailsa had replied, *Ena's always been free; I've no wish to restrain her. I told ye, 'tis just her age—neither child nor woman—and the new unfamiliar feelin's she has.* But perhaps Lian was right.

Sagging against her mother, Ena murmured, "I wish I could rest, but it seems I've forgotten how." Without warning, she threw her arm around Ailsa's waist, hanging on as if the wind might wrench her away. "I'm so tired, Mam. So very tired."

Ailsa drew Ena's blanket about them and slipped both arms around her waist. "If ye can no' sleep, why are ye no' down by the river with the wounded creatures who need ye? At least ye find some comfort there."

"The wounded who need me are no' by the river. They're here, so here I stay."

Her mother rested her cheek on the girl's head. "Och,

Ena, there're others who care for Mairi. 'Tis no' your task alone. We need to help her as much as ye do."

"Aye, I know." The girl glanced at her grandmother, beside whom she'd knelt for a long time a few hours past, smoothing into her frail fingers the balm Lian had offered to restore the moisture to thin, dry skin. Ena enjoyed that little chore. It soothed her to run her fingertips over Mairi's skin, tracing each finger with the smooth, cool, orange-scented cream.

Sometimes, as she moved her hands rhythmically over her grandmother's, Ena's eyes would flutter closed. When she opened them, as often as not, Mairi too had drifted off, and her face had relaxed into contentment. Tonight Mairi had fallen asleep, one hand curled around her granddaughter's, her breathing light, as if it were no longer a struggle.

Ena had sat unmoving for a long time, trying to block out knowledge and thought, trying to surrender to the tranquillity, the calming weight of Mairi's hand relaxed in hers. But her mind would not stop whirling. So she waited, watching her grandmother's face, tracing with her eyes the wrinkles and lines she would have liked to trace with her fingers. When she was certain Mairi would not awaken, she'd gone to her bed and sat, elbows on knees and chin in hands, restless, ineffably sad, until her mother found her.

Massaging her daughter's tense shoulders, Ailsa murmured, "Her ankle's healin', and she's aye stronger every day. The change is slow in comin', but 'tis there." She spoke fervently, determined to believe. "You've no' call to watch over her like a sickly bairn. Your grandmother's no' helpless like your animals. She's strong, is Mairi Rose. Her strength is greater than any I've ever known. Think of all she's lived through. Think what she's survived."

"Aye, just think." Turning to her mother, Ena hesitated, but she was too exhausted to consider what she said, tired of carrying the weight alone. "Like it or no', Gran's ankle's no' healin' properly. By now she should be able to walk with a crutch, but she doesn't even try." She shook her head distractedly. "I've bound it and rebound it, used all my herbs and decoctions and made new ones; Aunt Lian's tried Chinese herbs and pressure and the things she learned from her friend the apothecary, but nothing's made a difference."

Ailsa tightened her arms around her daughter. "Ye worry overmuch. Ye always have, birdeen. Mairi's your grandmother. Of course ye feel her pain more than the others. She's seventy-two. 'Twould take her longer to progress, ye ken."

Ena sighed. Her mother honestly could not see a truth too painful to recognize. " 'Tis true, Mam. No broken bone could deplete Gran's energy or will." It was not a lie. She could not lie to Ailsa, even now. But she could remain silent, and so she did.

For once, awake and unobserved by anyone but the spirits of the air, Mairi listened. With the hush of a night slipping quickly toward dawn, she opened her eyes to the silence that had once promised rest. She fondled Charles's letters in her pocket, seeking comfort from the words she could not read, seeking guidance.

"Please," she whispered, "tell me what to do." This time there was no answer, no light in the distance, no inner sight to guide her. Alone in the darkness, she did not have to turn her head or wipe the tears from her cheeks so no one would see them, no one would know.

Mairi wept in silence, not for herself, but for her children. All of them.

14

ON A CRISP AUTUMN EVENING, EVERYONE GATHERED, AS THEY often did, at Mairi's. Lian had made her way down to the road earlier, come back with something hidden in her sleeve, and now could barely contain herself.

Alanna, David and Connor, Ailsa, Lian, Genevra and Ena felt Mairi watching them with an odd gleam in her eyes, echoing the color of gloaming at the moment when the sun glowed through the violet air, then disappeared.

Ena met Lian's gaze curiously. There were secrets in her aunt's blue eyes; they glimmered with excitement and anticipation.

"You've come far," Mairi observed, "but we've been caught up in too much drama to get to know each other properly." She looked pointedly at Lian. "I think 'tis time we do it now."

After everyone had found a cup or *quach* and filled it with cider or tea or ale, they gathered around the fire, around Mairi, who was at the center.

Ena settled in close to her grandmother, watching, perplexed, as Lian rummaged beneath a pile of woolen blankets, and with David's help, brought out a Chinese chest made of ebony and carved with winged dragons, phoenixes, clouds and other mysterious figures.

David dragged the chest over, then joined his wife, while Genevra rose to sit at one end, Lian at the other.

"My mother bequeathed me this chest when she sent the last of my belongings from China years ago," she began. "She included many things, some that had special meaning for me, some for her, and some as simple reminders of my homeland.

"When Émile and I first thought of this, we thought we were doing it only for Ena, who knew nothing of a foreign place like the Middle Kingdom. Then we realized it was for Ailsa and Mairi and Alanna and her family as well, for neither had *they* ever seen China, nor, for that matter, our vineyards, our family, our world. Photographs can tell part of the story, but not all of it."

Genevra took up where her half-sister left off. "When Lian arrived in Kent, Alex and I added treasures of our own and our childrens'. Though we farm, as you do, Ladybrooke is very different from the glen. And then there is India, where I grew up, where I met and married Alex. That's yet another world."

As Lian worked the intricate Chinese lock, she said, "I think my mother would be pleased to know she had begun a family tradition. Wan Ke-ming was all her life a woman of tradition. And some of what she has given me, which I treasure above all things, I can share with you."

Ena scooted closer, hardly aware of what she was doing, watching Lian with intense curiosity. "Are ye sayin' 'tis—"

"The very chest my mother shipped to me over so many seas that it took years to find me." She smiled poignantly, expressing without words her feelings for her dead mother. "You saw some things the night we arrived, but those were about places and progress and events. These are the treasures of our hearts."

Wearing the embroidered cashmere shawl she'd worn that first night, Genevra began taking out pieces of her life in Kent. There was a photograph of her family with she and Alex standing formally behind their two daughters and two sons. Everyone looked rigid, almost grim. "We weren't allowed to smile, you see. The photographer said it would ruin the exposure. And we had to stand still for so long that I'm sure he was right." She put down the photograph and picked up a painting of Ladybrooke.

Ena was astonished by the acres and acres of rolling land unbroken by mountains of stone or earth. She was used to abrupt changes in the landscape—jagged mountains springing out of nowhere, deep bogs beside stony ridges, lochs that glistened in the midst of dry bracken, burns that erupted from the earth, turning the land into a lush paradise of ferns and moss and tiny waterfalls.

Next Genevra brought out her daughter Anne's doll in fancy dress, whose eyes opened and closed, and a train that actually steamed around a track. David and Connor tinkered with it for a long time, determined to make it work, but the women did not wait for them. The cousins had sent brief notes scrawled in bright colors, begging Ena to come and stay with them, a reading primer, a history book and a book of simple mathematical equations. "I'm certain they weren't sorry to see these go," Genevra observed wryly. Then she produced a large, beautiful shell, curving in upon itself, pale pink with traces of gold.

Ena held it, turned it in her hands, sniffed the slight lingering smell of salt. "Where's it from?"

"The sea. There's a sandy beach just an hour's ride from our home. The children love to go there as often as they can."

Ena stared at the shell pensively. "The sea," she murmured. She knew about it, of course, the legends and myths told of gods and heroes battling the sea at every turn. But it was not a place where children went to play or discovered treasures such as this. "What's it like?"

Considering her answer, Lian glanced at Ailsa, perched protectively close to her mother, who was propped up by cushions so she could sit in bed and not be left out.

Clearly, Mairi was enjoying herself; she was smiling and her cheeks were pink with pleasure. She had not been so sociable since the accident, but tonight she watched intently, leaning forward, eyes sparkling in the firelight,—deep violet pools that absorbed all they saw, storing the images away. She listened, head tilted, mesmerized by the treasures and stories alike. She seemed to be trying to live four lifetimes in one short night—Lian's in China, Genevra's in India, Lian and Émile's in France and Alex and Genevra's after they'd returned to England. Something in her earnestness disturbed Alanna, forced her to keep watch, though she did not know what she was watching for.

Ena was also aware of her grandmother, aware, too, that Mairi wanted the girl to see, to hear, to touch and absorb all this, to come to know her family in ways she'd never thought of.

"I can show you the ocean," Genevra said, handing the girl a book from the chest.

It was about the sea, and Ena was soon completely absorbed. This was not a roiling, hissing sea of serpents and ill winds bent upon destruction; it was a quiet scene, with the blue, blue water lapping on smooth crystalline sand.

"You cannot really know the ocean from photographs and paintings," Lian insisted. "You must stand with your hair blowing about, smelling the salty water, feeling the wet sand beneath bare feet, listening to the rhythm of the waves tumbling one over the other, mesmerizing, restful. You must lift your face to the sea mist and let it settle on your skin, lick your lips lightly to taste the salt on your tongue. I believe it is something every child should experience before they lose the innocence that makes it so powerful and lovely in its simplicity. Is that not so, Alanna?"

Along with Lian, Alanna observed her young half-sister, hand resting on an image of the ocean on a balmy day, with boats against the skyline and footprints in the sand. Ena glanced up and smiled whimsically. " 'Tis aye bonny and mysterious."

Lian's eyes misted because she'd never had a daughter, and this girl was looking to her tonight, asking if it was too late, if she had missed her chance. Ena's eyes shone with hope and doubt and a faith in her aunt that touched Lian's heart.

Watching the silent interplay between the two, Alanna guessed what Lian was thinking, and an idea began to take shape. But for the moment, she was silent.

"On the way to India," Genevra intervened, "I saw more of the ocean than I ever desired. No matter how large the ship, the sea made it seem like a toy. I could see nothing but water wherever I looked." She picked through the ebony chest until she found a watercolor of a beautiful white marble palace.

"This is the house of my friend, Phoebe Quartermaine. I used to go to her for comfort when—well, I went there often. The house is built around this cool, inviting place where I used to swim and read and paint. In India, water's more precious than flowers and vines, so it's cherished and made into havens like this one."

They passed around the painting, exclaiming over the white marble columns connected by graceful arches. There were narrow coral paths winding among bright beds of flowers, rows of acacia and cypress, tamarind and date palms. "They fed the trees through underground wells so the water would stay cool," Genevra explained. There were shaded arbors, climbing roses and bougainvillea that covered the high walls, and in the midst of it all, a summerhouse, white and cool and gracefully curved.

Yet the painting held more surprises. Clear water rushed down the walls out of curved and twisted stone chutes that made it fall in angles, or propelled it into the air, where it broke into rippled waves and enchanting patterns. "The Moguls called them *Chadars*—white shawls of water." Those few words brought India back to Genevra in an instant, the part she had loved most.

There were huge pools, the sides and bottoms tiled in many colors, kept cool by latticed roofs and overhanging vines. Waterfalls gushed over stone, one above another, landing in the pools where they splintered into prismed light. Finally, there were copper fountains that flowed with fresh water.

Mairi, Ailsa, Alanna and Ena, who had been drawn to the water all their lives, who had found there solace and inspiration, thought it must be an image of the land of the fairies—seductive and bewitching.

Ena ran her fingertips over the water cascading down the canvas as if she could feel it pouring over her hand.

Genevra brought out incense and tumeric, bracelets and anklets that jingled in her hand, a mask of Ganesha, the God of Good Luck, painted red, yellow and blue; both the color and the mask's huge laughing mouth made Ena smile.

There was a deep blue sari—"I did a self-portrait wearing this, and my relatives wanted to burn it,"—sketches of strange faces and scenes, of her sisters and father and her friend Phoebe.

Ena and Alanna exclaimed when Genevra held up a sketch, half-painted, of a dark-skinned Indian girl. She had huge dark eyes, shiny black hair hanging like a rope over her shoulder, and she was beautiful. But most intriguing was her serenity, which radiated from her as heat from a candle flame. "Who is she?"

With a secret, sad smile, Genevra told them briefly about Narain. She drew Charles Kittridge's interwoven gold chain out of her bodice, revealing a strikingly beautiful amulet of gold with the Indian gods etched into the soft metal, and a large ruby at its heart. "She gave me this."

With one finger, Ena reached out to touch it gingerly.

Lian watched the girl, saw her smile of delight, then reverence for the garden of living waters in Genevra's painting. Ena had thought she knew the beauty and the blessings of all water. Twice tonight she had learned she was wrong.

"Someday I'd like to see that garden and the sea."

"Why can't ye just go? Well, mayhap no' to India, but to England and France anyway," Alanna said. "You're no' bound here, ye ken. Is she, Mam?" If Ena accepted her aunts' invitations to visit, she would meet a great many people, make new friends, learn things she'd never imagined. She felt her son's gaze and was pleased to see that he looked thoughtful, not angry or resentful. "Mam?"

Ailsa wanted to blurt out "No!" She could not envision her life without Ena, or Ena's without the security of the glen. But she was not blind; she could see the longing, the curiosity in her youngest daughter's eyes. She remembered too how actively the girl had pursued the correspondence with her aunts and cousins, how many questions she'd had, how often she'd mentioned their differing lives. "I want ye to do what ye wish, birdeen. Of course you're no' bound here."

Genevra and Lian both spoke at once, renewing their invitations. "Ena will always be welcome," Lian added.

Not yet quite finished, Genevra produced a stack of letters from Ailsa and Lian, tied with satin ribbon, and the small, flat carved box that held Charles Kittridge's letter calling her home. In a leather case, she had her father's artwork—at least a hundred sketches and etchings and half-finished paintings—which he'd left her when he died. Finally, she held two worn leather books reverently in her hands.

"This is my mother's diary, and my own. As Mairi once pointed out, I can't always express what I feel, even with my charcoal and paints, and my mother didn't know how to speak her fear out loud. So we turned to written words."

She glanced from Ena to Alanna. "Perhaps I wrote for more than myself. Perhaps you should read these someday, as I hope my daughters will."

She placed the books with her other things. "They'll be here if you want them."

15

FOR A FEW MINUTES EVERYONE STARED INTO THE FLAMES that touched them with color and shadow. Then Genevra moved her things aside and Lian bent over the chest. She, too, passed around notes from her three sons and a family portrait Emile had painted, before lifting out a tiny Chinese medicine chest and opening each drawer, explaining what her mother, and later, her friend and teacher, Cheng, had used them for. This was followed by some twists of candy stuck in slick paper, a bright pinwheel, scrolls of rice paper with the wisdom of the ancient philosophers in graceful Chinese characters. She, too, had stacks of correspondence from her sisters, and a bundle of old, yellowed letters, which she caressed lightly, explaining that her father had left them to her when he died, but never mailed them while alive. "And then, of course, there is this." She held up her arm so the intertwined white and yellow gold bracelet shimmered in the firelight. "My father gave it to my honorable mother, and she gave it to me."

Ena risked a glance at Mairi. Her eyes were filmed with tears. "At least he saw ye again," she murmured. "At least he knew you'd read the letters after all. I'm thinkin' that made him happy. Mayhap 'twas all that mattered, in the end."

A hush fell, and when Lian's throat grew tight and dry, she scattered the sad memories, resurrecting others. She took from the chest a carefully folded Chinese gown of purple satin, embroidered with plum blossoms, a sleeveless silver tunic worked in a bamboo pattern, and a clip made of sapphire and silver filigree. "I wore these things the day I married Émile."

Mairi caressed the fabric with a shaky hand. " 'Tis aye beautiful, my daughter. Would ye put it on for us? Just once?"

Lian shook her head, but Ailsa added her voice to her mother's. "Please. 'Twould be wonderful to see how ye looked that day, since we could no' be with ye."

Not until Ena held the gown draped over her arms, staring at the shimmering fabric, the intricate design, and whispered, "Please," did Lian relent. She disappeared behind a reed screen, and when she reappeared, she'd unbraided her hair and let it fall loose, except where she'd pinned it up on one side with the jeweled clip. The sleeves of the gown hung nearly to her knees, they were so wide, and they covered her hands. The silver vest only heightened the color of the gown and the carefully embroidered plum blossoms. In the golden firelight, she was beautiful.

For an instant, Ena let herself believe she was back in the time and place where such gowns had been worn and such jewelry fashioned. In a world of gardens sculpted by man to imitate nature. Peaceful gardens with shallow pools and streams scattered with healing stones just like her own. It was magic, that feeling, though it disappeared as quickly as it had come. She wanted to thank Lian for having thought of this night, having thought to share who she and Genevra were and had once been. But there were no words adequate to express her feelings. She sighed and Lian brushed her niece's shoulder as she passed. She did not speak, yet Ena thought she understood.

Lian knelt gracefully in her heavy gown and filled her hands with smooth colored stones from the garden compound in Peking, and to Ena's delight, a packet of willow bark tea. Glancing frequently at her young niece, she withdrew the last few items from the chest: a gauze curtain appliquéd with satin butterflies from her childhood bed, a silk lantern shaped like twin nightingales that Chinese revelers had hung from rooftops and trees and boats, and last, an image of the Kitchen God in red and yellow. "He must always be well fed to be appeased and agree to tell heaven only good things about the owner," Lian explained. "I must have made his stomach full and happy, because heaven has been more than kind to me." She smiled at the thought of Émile and the package he had sent.

Locking her arms around her knees, the girl was struck by the number of places she'd never seen, the things she didn't know. She caught Connor's eye and guessed he was thinking the same, though he'd been strangely silent all evening. She'd once told him everything she needed was here. He'd known even then it was not true. The restlessness she could not quite conquer returned, stronger than ever.

David was sitting beside Connor, his hand on his son's shoulder. Tonight, seeing all these wonders, Connor was curious and wanted to know more. Alanna moved closer so they sat shoulder to shoulder and shared a private smile.

For the first time in months, Ena felt a hole in her middle

where her father should have been. Stories and a mound covered in flowers were not enough. She pressed her forehead against her knees, trying to close that hole, to tell herself she had family enough, as her aunts had proved tonight.

A sigh of completion and pleasure swept the circle, but Lian raised her hand. "There is something more."

She lifted out a heavy velvet bag, untied the cord and tilted the contents onto the gauze bed curtain. Out spilled jewels so magnificent that everyone gasped. "This is my mother's legacy, which has lain hidden in the chest for too many years to count. I have no need of their value and no wish for their adornment, except for a few of Ke-ming's special pieces, which I've hidden away in my drawer at the vineyard. But I know it would break her heart that her legacy has not been used." She took a deep breath. "I have written to Émile, and this is what we propose."

All eyes were fixed on the pile of jewels that glittered and flashed and glowed on the packed dirt floor. Sapphires and pearls, white and green jade, gold bracelets, ruby earrings, a butterfly brooch made of pearls, a necklace of emeralds, gold and silver filigree hair clasps, rings and more.

Ailsa finally asked the question. "These belonged to Ke-ming, who died in a small shack in the Western Hills of China?"

"Yes," Lian replied, eyes damp. "She did not need them there; she was saving them for me. But Émile and I have been lucky.

"Now, I have saved them for you. We have chosen pieces for you, Ailsa, for Genevra and Alanna, and the most finely wrought for Mairi, our mother in all but blood."

Mairi Rose bowed her head, moved beyond words.

Struggling for composure, Lian continued, "There are enough for us to hold in trust for our children, and for Ena, who no doubt cares more for her brightly colored stones gathered from the burn and the *linne* ringed with rainbows than she does for jewels.

"We thought if we put in together, each giving a piece or two, we could buy the Hill of the Hounds outright, and then we would always have a home here."

"Ye have a home here now," Mairi whispered, just as Ailsa said the same. "You've no need for jewels and riches to make ye welcome." She smiled crookedly. "But ye know that, don't ye?"

"Yes, we know it," Genevra answered. "And we thank you. But you haven't met our children yet. Seven at once are a great drain of anyone's patience and endurance."

There were murmurs of assent. David and Alanna, in particular, knowing the difficulties as well as the benefits of wealth, were impressed that Lian and Émile had thought of such a wise way of investing these jewels that they would never wear. Mairi's face was soft with gratitude and love and something indefinable. "So be it," she said. "At last the Hill of the Hounds will belong to family."

A silence drifted over them, taking the words from their mouths and releasing them, unspoken, into the air, so that all felt and heard what could not be said properly. When smoke began to spiral in a dark curl toward the ceiling, Lian knelt once more beside the chest. "I have asked Ailsa to add her own treasures to ours; you can guess what hers will be, for you have grown up with them. One day this chest, built and carved in China, which has traveled halfway around the world, with all the possessions and offerings inside, will be our legacy to you, Alanna and Ena. Mine and Genevra's and Ailsa's. Because you are part of the story that began with Charles Kittridge in this cottage fifty-five years ago. These things are tangible; you can hold them in your hands, feel the texture, see the colors, sniff the scent and read the words. Then, perhaps, you will remember who we were, and who you are."

Ena gaped, awed and embarrassed and elated.

"But your own children, and the others—" Alanna objected.

Genevra smiled affectionately. "There's enough for everyone, much more than this. Our children have already seen the pieces and heard the stories. They won't miss a few. But you would. And as for their legacy, you can be certain we would never leave them wanting."

" 'Tis just, there're things here only ye two would understand, because ye believe in shared dreams and intuition, and the power of fate which brought us together tonight," Ailsa added. Lian and Genevra had told her about the chest, but she had not really understood until now. Her eyes filled with tears at her sisters' thoughtfulness, at the value of the treasure they would leave her daughters.

"I thank ye from my heart," Alanna said, noting that Ena was still speechless, "and I'll come to know all the things you've left us." She could not disguise the catch in her voice. "But I think, in the end, the chest should go to Ena. She's the future of this family, after all. And I've long known who I am, where I belong and the riches I already have." She looked at David, love and contentment in her eyes. "But Ena's still searchin'. 'Tis she, mayhap, who'll find herself within those ebony panels."

Ena stared at her half-sister in astonishment, though she found she was not surprised by Alanna's generosity. It was, after all, a night for giving. "Do ye really think so?"

Alanna smiled. "Aye, I believe ye'll discover much among the many facets of their spirits, hearts, souls, all linked to ours through time and blood and dreams. Ye share those inexplicable dreams. Mayhap, through theirs, ye'll come to understand yours."

"Thank ye." Ena did not argue; she sensed Alanna would not change her mind. She had never felt so close to her half-sister. She clasped her mother's hand in silence. In silence, accepted the gifts that had been offered, wishing she had something to give in return.

David and Connor felt out of place. They did not comprehend precisely what was being said, and it only emphasized the difference between them and the women. Connor watched Ena, but her attention was on her mother. She was so far away he knew he could not reach her. Again.

Unaware of the men's discomfort, Lian reached into the chest. "I have one thing more." She held up a leather folder filled with her poems. "I will leave some in the chest, for they were born of us, not me alone. But this one, written when I was young, yet content and unafraid, I would recite for you. It seems so much of this moment."

Everyone nodded and she stood in her wedding finery, holding a piece of rice paper bearing the odd Chinese ideograms that were her words and meanings and intimations.

> "This happiness is like a piece
>   of pale green jade—
>   rare, beautiful, and indestructible.
> Like the jade it can be hidden away
>   in a rosewood box for years,
> Yet lose none of its magic.
> Once the jade is carved, shaped, perfected,
>   it will never change.
> Someday a woman will open the box and hold
>   in her soft white hands—
> The jade, the stone, the memory of this night."

16

'TWAS PERFECT, MAIRI THOUGHT. I DIDN'T KNOW HOW PER-fect it would be. For awhile no one spoke, as they consumed black buns and apple pie, drank cider and ale, clinking their cups in toast after toast. When they lay back on their elbows, replete, she cleared her throat. "Now I'd ask ye to gather round me, close to the fire, for it warms my old bones." Her smile was so sweet, so beguiling, that she might have been a girl again. Even had they wanted to, no one could have refused her.

When they were seated, and the fire flickered and flared, throwing their shadows across her bed and her lap and her outstretched hands, she smiled again, sadly. "Ye must no' be interruptin', for I'm an old woman with little breath to spare."

Ailsa and Genevra sat nearest; she took their hands, mindless of her swollen joints and fragile skin. " 'Twill be difficult for ye, what I have to say. Ye must turn to one another, as ye have this night and many times before."

Ailsa stiffened, but Mairi held tight.

Ena sat in the middle, rigidly upright, gray eyes watchful. She knows, Mairi thought. Of them all, the child alone knows. Somehow that made it the smallest bit easier. And yet, far more difficult.

"You've noticed my ankle's no' healin' as it should. This break's a small thing, but no' the less a sign that the time has come." Several voices tried to interrupt, but Mairi kept her eyes on her granddaughter, and Ena's fortitude steadied her.

"I've known for a while that I'm ill deep inside where herbs and plasters can no' reach to make me better. I'll no recover from this sickness, nor will I rise again from this bed." She could not listen to their startled protests. She had practiced too long to say this in just the right way.

"I've come to accept that my time here's nearly over, yet when I close my eyes, I see dawn after painful dawn, no' the peace of gloamin', which I crave as a drunkard his whiskey. Often and often I've heard *Amadan Dhu*, the Dark Fool, laughin' at the misery to come. I've defeated him before, and he's no' a graceful loser."

The group drew closer to one another, seeking solace.

"What do ye want us to say?" Ailsa whispered.

Mairi looked sadly at her daughter. "Nothing, Ailsa-my-heart. I only want ye to listen." She looked away, unable to bear the anguish and bewilderment in her daughter's eyes. "As ye know, I've survived much and feared little in my lifetime. But one thing I do fear. Unrelentin' pain."

Knowing full well how strong Mairi Rose was, Ena regarded her closely to see if she was trying to make it easier for them by pretending fear. The girl almost fell forward when she realized that perhaps for the first time in her life, Mairi was thinking only of herself. Ena could not remember a time when Mairi hadn't been considering someone else's pain or joy or need. A chill ran down her spine and an odd satisfaction that her grandmother was a woman to be proud of, both because she had taken responsibility for helping others and because, in the end, she had realized she must help herself. It was time.

"Through seventy-two years, I've faced misfortune many times, but I'm no' strong enough to bear this particular burden. I'm too weary to fight anymore."

"I do not believe you." Lian sat on her heels, legs bent beneath her, rigid and unyielding. She had heard but not yet comprehended in her heart what Mairi was saying. "You are the most courageous woman I have ever known." She stared at her palms resting on her knees. "I once thought the same of my mother, Ke-ming, until I learned she had always been afraid. But you have never faltered."

"Thank ye for your confidence," Mairi said, "but you're wrong. Ye believe what ye wish to believe, or mayhap what ye need to."

Lian set her mouth in a stubborn line. "You were brave enough to let your husband go, though you loved him, because you knew if he stayed you would destroy one another. Brave enough to say good-bye to Ailsa without argument, when you knew argument was useless. You were constant enough to have faith in them both, and to welcome them home again, though each might well have broken your heart a second time. You were courageous enough to ask us here, knowing Charles had created us with other women, and to accept us as if we had been born of your blood. How many women could do that?"

For an eternity, Mairi could not face them. Her hands shook and her eyes burned. "Bless ye, Lian, but ye must know I didn't care for ye and Genevra out of kindness, but selfishness, for always I'd wanted many children at my feet, and ye fulfilled a need in me. Besides, I could no' take back my Charlie and love him and nurse him and hold him as he died, if I'd no' forgiven him his sins. Ye two made it easy, 'twas all, because ye needed me, and I *need* to be needed. I was a mother long before I bore a child." She brushed Ailsa's cheek softly, saying with her fingertips the things she could not put into words.

"But ye were no' ill before. I'd have known it," her daughter insisted.

Mairi regarded Ailsa with a curious look in her eyes. " 'Twas no' your weight to carry. Before I fell, I worked at weavin' an illusion of myself healthy and whole, plagued only by the small inconveniences of growin' old. But I've no' the strength to hold the threads together any more.

" 'Twas only a matter of time till ye recognized there's poison in my bones. I'm tellin' ye now so ye need no' wonder and imagine."

Slowly, she turned to her daughter with bruised, shadowed eyes. "I need ye to help me go soon, help me triumph once more over *Amadan Dhu*. I'm ready.

" 'Come unto me, O Lovely Dusk, thou that has the heart of hidden flame. Come now, come soon; take me up to the stars and into the fire.' "

Ailsa stared, face ashen. "What are ye sayin'? Surely ye'd no' ask—" Mairi stopped her with a hand on her arm and a plea in her eyes. For forgiveness or release? "Ye don't mean it!" Ailsa gasped. "You're askin' me to help ye die?" She sought vainly for words to erase her mother's, make them as though they'd never been. "Ye *might* recover."

Ailsa was closing her eyes to the truth, as Mairi had

feared she would. She turned to Genevra, who looked away, tears streaming down her cheeks, to Lian, who shook her head once, sharply. "You cannot be certain."

Each was clinging to the false thread of hope Ailsa had spun in the peat-scented air, taut now with disbelief and shock. "Ask Ena, then," Mairi said.

The girl had not moved from the moment her grandmother called them over. "Gran's right. She's very ill. I've seen it in her eyes, felt it when I lay my hands upon her body. Something's killin' her from the inside out, slowly, secretly. To destroy it is the only way to heal it."

The color had drained from Genevra, leaving her translucent, empty. She shook her head back and forth, back and forth in denial. "How can you be so sure? You've not even seen a doctor."

Ena answered quietly. "How did ye first learn of the sisters ye'd never met? How did ye know to go to one another in your dreams when ye were hurtin'? What made ye decide to come to Glen Affric now and no' before?"

Examining the stricken faces turned to Ena, the firelight burning across their skin, transforming it from moment to moment, Mairi saw how much she was asking.

She faced them fully, dropping the mask that had become her second face for so long she'd forgotten it was not real. "I'm afraid too. Can ye no' see that? Deeply afraid inside where the darkness grows and spreads. I've no wish for those I love to see my slow disintegration. I'd no' want your last memory of me to be of my shrunken body, my wanderin' mind, for 'tis the image that'll linger with ye longest."

In spite of her determination, Ena felt ill and cold and terrified of the future.

Ailsa glanced at her daughter, who was shivering. Of course Ena was afraid. They all were. Ailsa leaned toward Mairi and touched her legs, stretched out straight before her. They had lost flesh and strength and had grown flaccid. But she could not think of that now. "Mam, should we no' take ye to a hospital instead? The doctors could examine ye, tell us what ails ye, and mayhap ease your pain."

"The nearest hospital is far away in Inverness. Too far for ye to visit, too far from home. And tho' ye may no' wish to accept it, ye know as well as I the doctors could no' help me. They've painkillers, aye, and mayhap ways to keep me alive, but no way to heal me. Ailsa-my-heart, do ye honestly think they could do better than ye and Ena?"

"No. I know better." Her mother was right; they lived in an isolated glen where no advanced medical care was available. And even if they took Mairi to Inverness, no one had the power to cure what Ailsa suspected was the cancer in her mother's bones. "But still, ye ask too much of us. We can't knowin'ly end your life." She winced at the sound of the words. "To lose ye when we need ye so much. 'Tis unkind."

Ena rose to her knees, eyes sparked with anger. "Gran's been kind to others all her life, even when 'twas no' easy. 'Tis what she does and who she is. Is't not time someone did a kindness for her? Do we no' owe her that much at least?

"Many times you've needed her through the years, and she's been there, waitin'." She turned without thinking when Mairi's breathing quickened. Ena saw a ripple of pain cross her face, and the anger became a knot in her throat. "Weel, now 'tis turned the other way, and *she* needs *ye.*"

Tears dimmed Mairi's eyes at her granddaughter's furious defense. "From my heart, I ask this," she whispered, "from my spirit which has long known yours, and from my soul." She was pleading as she never had to man, woman or child. She opened her arms to encompass them all. "Think, my children. Think hard and far."

It devastated them, that plea. They heard her desperation and knew she was sincere. Ailsa, Lian, Genevra, Alanna and even David admitted that, as Ena said, Mairi had relieved and restored each of them time and again. Yet she'd never asked their help for herself. It struck them, as the flames sputtered and flashed and cast deep shadows, that it must have cost Mairi Rose a great deal to ask this now.

The half-sisters moved closer until their palms touched. It tore them apart to hear Mairi like this. They clung to one another, wondering what to do, what to say that did not sound selfish, heartless.

But in the end there was only one answer. "We cannot do as you ask," Lian said, prompted by her sisters, who had not moved or made a sound, yet all three voices spoke through her. "You are our mother, our protector, our link to our father. We could not bear to lose you too. Aside from our own loss and doubts, we do not think it right to take this decision into our own hands. We have not that power. It must be the choice of the gods. Can you not wait for that decision?"

For the first time, David spoke up. "Look around ye. There're too many gods gathered here tonight. Those who followed ye from China and your husband's Catholic god, the ones in Genevra's heart from India and her husband's Anglican deity, the ancient Celtic spirits of the glen, and the fearful god of the Kirk of Scotland. Which should decide? Which is wisest, kindest, most forgivin'?" He shrugged, but there was no nonchalance in the gesture. "Still, it does seem that, just as all the deities can no' make a single choice, neither can we."

Mairi smiled. In the midst of pain, anger and bewilderment, she smiled. "I'd have ye remember one thing. All of ye. A person knows when 'tis their time. After all, I've lived long. I'm weary and would rest. My Charlie had his chance to say good-bye in his own way on his own terms, and I would have the same. Soon enough I'll no' be able to speak, nor will I know your faces or your names when ye come near. I'd say farewell while I remember everything about ye. Before pain fills and consumes me as the sight and knowledge of your presence fills me now."

Genevra could hold back no longer. "You can't do this thing, Mairi Rose. It's a mortal sin."

Mairi bowed her head. "Are ye sayin' your God will strike me dead? 'Twould no' be much of a challenge."

Genevra was very serious. "It's wrong."

"How do ye know? Did He speak to ye in anger, forbiddin' my small death in all the world? Or do angels sit on your shoulders and whisper in your ear that Mairi Rose Kittridge must suffer long and needlessly? For what, Genevra? To have time to learn I'm no' perfect, that I've made mistakes and must now pay?"

"Not that. Never that," Genevra said.

Mairi's eyes were opaque, but she struggled to speak. "Please believe I'd no' cause ye pain simply to lessen my own. But ye too will suffer if I die slowly, wastin' away as your father did. Surely I can spare ye that, at least."

When Mairi had used up the last of her energy and Ena began to prepare her late night herbs, the others stepped outside and paused as if unable to go farther. They stood in a rough circle, a somber group, except for Connor, who hung back, wondering what all this meant and where it would end.

The sisters gravitated toward one another, fingers interlaced, sharing the turmoil of their thoughts, the chaos of their feelings through skin and rushing blood and breath. Their heartache and their need drained the air around them.

"Did it never occur to Mairi Rose how much it would hurt so many if she did this thing?" Lian murmured at last.

To everyone's surprise, it was Connor who answered. "Did it never occur to ye how much *Mairi* must be hurtin' to ask such a sacrifice of us?"

Alanna and David stared at their son. His perception and sensitivity at this difficult moment belied his youth. The Connor they knew would not have dared challenge Ailsa and her half-sisters so pointedly. David and Alanna were proud of their son, and more than a little nonplussed. He was right, after all. Why had no one else realized? Except, perhaps, for Ena?

Then they remembered Mairi's face and rationality fled.

17

IN HER DREAM, LIAN HEARD THE DISTANT NOTES OF A clarsach growing faint as they disappeared among the crags of brooding purple mountains. She tried to clutch the melody in her hand and so keep it from fading. This song, familiar, yet discordant and mysterious, crept over the moor and across the loch, winding its way among the boulders, over the foothills and into the stone mountains.

Suddenly afraid, she grasped at the receding notes, but they eluded her. She knew if she let them go, she would lose them forever. She reached out blindly when a sharp, grating sound silenced the music altogether.

Lian awoke to find herself poised on the sweet-smelling heather mattress in Alanna and David's loft. She sat still as jade, listening. It was not long before she heard the noise that had awakened her. The grating of stones against rock, the snapping of branches—the sound of an animal rushing through the woods. She was unaccountably afraid for the creature and rose, making no sound. She had learned how as a child, out of fear, but persisted as a woman, out of practicality.

Peering out the window into the chilly darkness, she saw it was nearly dawn. Concentrating, she observed the trail of something stumbling through the clearing and into the underbrush. Her pulse sang a warning in her ears. Where the brush parted a little way into the woods, she saw a flash of flowing white snag on some brambles. It was tugged briefly, urgently, then the fabric tore away, leaving a fragment hanging on the bush. Lian pushed the window open in time to hear the sound of careless footsteps. Not an animal at all. A woman fleeing something or someone, heedless of the noise she was making or the trail she left behind. The warning became a command.

With one economical motion, Lian picked up her coat and shoes, hurrying down the ladder toward the front door. By the time she reached it, her shoes were slipped haphazardly onto her feet, her coat hanging off one arm. She took a lantern from a hook on the wall, lit it with the flint nearby and slipped outside. She put on her coat and fastened the togs as she held the lantern high and followed the trail with ease. But her thoughts were not easy.

Ahead, she heard snapping branches, a thump and a sharp cry. Her prey must have fallen. That would give her a chance to catch up. The lantern light cast eerie shadows through the tangle of trees, but Lian did not notice.

Ducking beneath the branches of a willow, she caught sight of the woman, barefoot, hair flowing wildly down her back, her wrapper torn away at the heels. It could only be Ailsa. Lian had passed Genevra sleeping in Alanna's parlor, and Ena was too small and frail. She ran faster, light and quick on her feet, but Ailsa was quicker. She knew these woods too well, while Lian knew them only from memory.

Having caught her balance, Ailsa sprinted ahead. After that she stumbled rarely, rarely disturbed rocks and branches along the way.

Once she saw that Ailsa was no longer running headlong into a multitude of dangers, Lian kept her distance. She wanted to see where her half-sister was going. But she did not relax her vigilance; she could get to Ailsa in an instant if necessary. At first Lian tried to remain silent, but when she tripped on a root and cried out, Ailsa did not pause. Apparently she was so intent on her purpose she was unaware of the sights and sounds around her. Even the flickering light of the lantern and the shadows that sometimes touched her shoulders did not slow her down.

For a long time, they ran, and Lian was grateful she worked the vineyards and chased after the boys and made so many trips from the grapes to the winery to the house and back again. Her breath was labored, but that was from apprehension, not weariness. Where was Ailsa going so wildly, so late and ill-prepared?

It wasn't long before Lian realized they were heading toward the foothills where the melody in her dream had slithered from her reach. She shivered at a chill that spread through her limbs and did not come from the autumn air. She forced herself to concentrate on Ailsa's fleeing form, ghostly white against the dark mountains.

As Lian had feared, they began to climb, zigzagging through the foothills, until they came to a waterfall not much higher than a good-sized man. Ailsa closed her eyes as if in prayer and plunged into the *linne* the waterfall had created. Soaked to the waist, she climbed out on the rocks nearest the fall and picked her way over the boulders until she ducked beneath the rushing water and disappeared.

Though the light was now gray, Lian kept the lantern burning; it was more difficult to see in the dimness filled with shadows than it had been in the dark. Why am I here? she wondered. It was simple. She was worried about her sister. She could not lie in bed and wonder. She had to know.

She hesitated at the edge of the *linne*, surveying the rocky path Ailsa had taken, and knew she could not follow. She would have to wait.

A few minutes later, when her half-sister emerged, Lian moved into the shadow of a boulder, though again, Ailsa did not appear to notice her surroundings.

They were running again, climbing higher. Lian *had* to follow now; she could not find her own way home. The lantern had become useless and, eventually, she set it down. She needed both hands to pull herself up and through and around the outcroppings of stone along the intricate, invisible path Ailsa was following.

Then, abruptly, her sister stopped before a narrow passage between two tall boulders, then, breathing deeply, she slipped between them. Lian climbed up to look over and saw a lush grotto with a stream and ancient evergreens to shade it. The ground was covered in a thick, inviting carpet of pine and fir needles.

She had seen this place before, fourteen years before, in a dream where Ailsa lay bleeding until she closed her eyes, her smile achingly beautiful, and was gone. Lian had awoken, those many years ago, eyes dry and burning. The darkness that engulfed her, the bleak emptiness, had told her Ailsa was lost forever. But she had been wrong.

Why had Ailsa returned here so urgently in the darkness? Lian watched curiously as her sister picked her way through the passage and came out at the other end, a ghost with silver-streaked chestnut hair who moved in a daze toward the side of the stream.

Ailsa Rose stumbled forward, enveloped by the spot where she and Ian had last been together. She knelt, stretching out beside the spring where he'd made her lie on his warm gray cloak. The breeze ruffled her hair and the sleeves of her wrapper. Within the breeze, there was a song, and within the song, a voice she knew as she knew her own. *Ailsa,* it whispered, *you're finer than ye'd have them think. Finer and stronger and truer.*

The song faded, the wind ceased, and she cried out against the stillness. "I'm no' strong enough. No' for this."

I asked ye once to believe in me, and ye gave me that gift, the breeze sang as it rose again. *Now I give that gift to ye. I believe in ye. I know ye'll no' hold her back. Ye'll learn to let go, to have faith as ye once had faith in me, that those ye set free will return to ye, always. Do what your heart tells ye, but listen aye carefully, or ye'll hear but what ye wish. I am with ye, and so she will be with ye, for her spirit is strong, and she hears and loves the voices of the glen.*

Ailsa shook her head violently. "I can no' do it, Ian, *mo-chridhe*. I've lost too much."

So have we all. The words came from the heart of the stream, from the murmur of the water over stones and time and promises. *But 'tis no' the end,* mo-charaidh. *Ye'll go on. Always, ye go on. This I swear to ye, on my spirit and my soul.* The voice was fading, as it always did, and she reached for it, as she had reached for him so often.

"What shall I do?" She did not know if he would answer. She did not know if she could bear his silence.

Believe, my beloved. Believe in ye.

Lian crouched awkwardly, resting her head against the rock. She saw Ailsa reach out, heard her speak to no one, saw her words swept into the center of a breeze. It was cold here, and Ailsa's plea frightening. Trembling, Lian covered her eyes to shut out the image. She had once been very skilled at being blind. But somewhere in the last few years, she had lost that ability. She felt the dryness of her eyes, the grit of sand beneath her lids, and knew that, if she could have wept, she would have. But it was not wise.

Slowly, painfully, as if she had been lying so long that her body was stiff and unresponsive, Ailsa rose. Head forward so her hair hid her expression, she slipped back through the channel of rock. But she did not turn toward home. Instead, she made her way to a granite slope edged by wildly tilted stones. Kneeling, she searched the expanse of rock with both hands until she saw it. The slight stain that remained where Ian had fallen and died.

Eyes closed, she pressed warm palms against cool stone, against the last drop of Ian Fraser's blood. She raised her head, straining to feel him near again. "Ian of the Stones," she called to the day that was beginning, to the night that was ending, to the spirit of a man she had not seen for fourteen years:

> "The blessing of my love be ever with ye,
>   Over hill, over loch, over stone.
> The blessings of my heart be ever with ye,
>   Beyond earth, beyond sky, beyond death.
>   Always."

Lian guessed that, in her desperation, Ailsa was trying to hold on to those she loved, even those who had long been dead.

Hearing a sound, she saw that her sister had turned toward home. Deliberately, Lian stepped into her path so Ailsa could not help but recognize her. She was wrong.

As Ailsa passed, Lian felt her breath in her hair, yet her sister did not blink or stare or step back in shock. She was blind and deaf; she saw no one, sensed no one's presence, felt no one's pain. It was the dream Lian and Genevra had dreamed three times before they came here, only then their sister had been far away across the glen and now she stood so close that her unbound hair brushed Lian's face. But just as in the dream, she did not know her sister was there. Just like in the dream, Lian felt impotent; she could not reach Ailsa, and so she could not help her.

Hair full of pine needles, wrapper stained and torn, cheeks wet and eyes swollen, Ailsa went on her way, oblivious, caught up in a fantasy woven of moonlight.

"Why will they no' set Mairi free?" Ena asked the wind that ruffled the thin layer of grass over the grave of the wildcat she had rescued, then released last spring.

She had gone to her grandmother that morning and offered to do whatever must be done.

Touched and troubled, Mairi Rose had shaken her head. "You're only a child, Ena. Ye don't realize what you're sayin'." Before her illness she would have been able to hide the urge to weep for her thirteen-year-old granddaughter, who had made her offer so solemnly, so matter-of-factly.

"I'm a child no longer, nor have I been, except when I'm alone or with Connor by the river. The others have no', but I've done this many times. I sense in my hands and my heart when the sickness is beyond help and the pain too great to endure. I sense when peace and rest are the only medicines that'll cure." Ena's voice shook with frustration. Too often she had felt Mairi's pain in her own body, seen the yearning in her eyes.

Her grandmother had to look away from the face that so resembled both Ailsa's and Ian's. So mature and yet so very young. She knew in her heart of hearts that Ena was still a child in ways the girl could not possibly understand. " 'Tis different this time," she said firmly, skimming swollen knuckles over Ena's cheek. "I'm no' a stray bird with a broken wing or a deer brought down by a hunter's bullet. I'm your grandmother, Ena-*aghray*."

"I know it won't be easy, Gran. I'm no' a fool, or heartless either." She rolled her finger in a stray lock of auburn hair. "Besides, I promised I'd always care for ye when ye needed me. Ye'd no' break such a promise if ye'd given it to *me*." She paused, untangling her finger from her long, disheveled hair. "Can't ye see how hard 'tis for me to watch ye suffer? Do ye no' think 'tis breakin' my heart?"

"Och, my dear one, my bairn, I didn't see. Can ye forgive me for lettin' this happen, for lettin' ye too close?"

Ena leaned forward to take her grandmother's hands. Her eyes were filmed with tears, but Mairi was weeping openly. "There's nothing to forgive. I chose to try and heal ye. I wanted to." She was very earnest, very sincere. "Please, Gran, let me help ye now."

Filled with remorse, Mairi shook her head. "You've done enough and more than enough. I can't let ye destroy the last bit of your childhood. No' for me, no' for a promise, no' for anyone."

Her granddaughter had tried to make her reconsider, but Mairi would not listen.

"Please," Lian said, "allow me to treat you once more. I learned many techniques from Cheng that I was wary of attempting, but now—"

"You're more afraid of admittin' there's no cure," Mairi said softly.

Lian glanced at Ailsa and Genevra, kneeling beside the bed, and nodded. "We are all afraid, My Mother. Will you give us—give yourself—this chance to try to make you better? Will you trust me one more time?"

Wistfully, Mairi looked from face to hopeful face. "I'll always trust ye. Ye and Genevra and Ailsa. If there's a chance, I pray ye find it. 'Tis all I can promise."

"Will you try, really try to let my methods succeed? For this one night, will ye put aside your resignation?" Lian insisted.

Mairi hesitated.

"Ye know as well as we if a patient doesn't want to be cured, all the medicines in the world'll be as worthless as sugar to a starvin' deer." With a sigh, Ailsa put her hand on her mother's heart and felt the weak, irregular beat. "We're askin' ye to try, Mam. We're askin' ye to live."

Mairi could not extinguish the glimmer of faith in her daughters' faces, the optimism they could not let go of. It was all that held them upright as they gazed patiently, gently, lovingly into her eyes. "I'll try," she whispered. "I owe ye three a great deal more than that small effort."

Genevra caught a sob of sheer relief in her cupped hands. She'd not taken a breath since Lian first spoke. Now she gulped in air, filling her lungs and the hole in her chest. If Mairi had refused them, if she'd given up even the pretense of wanting to survive, Genevra would have fallen down an old, dark tunnel with no escape at the other end. Now, at least she could breathe again.

Methodically, the sisters moved the paraffin lamps closer, lighting a ring of candles that they placed near Mairi's head. They laid out the herbs and roots, powdered leaves and lotions and odd-looking objects Lian would use, just as she would use their hands when they were needed. She had not come here alone; her effort would be their effort; they would support and assist her in any way they could.

After several long, sleepless nights, this was the decision they had come to.

A chilly draught crept in the window, and Ailsa pulled the leather covering down tight, leaving a wisp of mist in the hushed, expectant air. The sound of Mairi's breathing was loud in that stillness. Barefoot, Lian, Ailsa and Genevra knelt at their mother's feet as if at a shrine.

She watched them with affection, a bittersweet smile on her slightly curved lips. They knew that smile and the strength of the woman behind it.

They spoke little as Lian bent over Mairi, doing her strange work. Ailsa and Genevra brewed the teas and the decoctions and measured out the powders as Lian had taught them, while Lian lifted Mairi's arm with great tenderness, listening to her pulse for a long while before she began to put the slightest pressure of one finger on her patient's breastbone, neck, stomach and pelvis.

She heated round glass vials that fit the curve of her hand and placed them on Mairi's back, creating heat and suction. Then she pressed on the places Cheng had shown her, bearing down with her arms, but not the weight of her body.

Through it all, Mairi made no sound, though she winced more than once.

Everyone was busy, yet everyone was waiting. It was as if they worked through a thick fog that slowed their movements, their breathing, their heartbeats. They held Mairi's head and she drank and swallowed and placed small pellets beneath her tongue, cooperating because she need do nothing on her own. Always, there were hands to hold her, lift her, turn her, draw her silver hair away from her face so it glimmered behind her, touched by the candlelight.

When Lian had completed her elaborate ritual, she sat with Mairi's head in her lap, brushing her fingers over the pallid skin of her cheeks and forehead. Genevra held one hand, Ailsa the other. Silence and contentment settled over the four of them. Mairi was weary but smiling, savoring the touch of her three daughters, their presence, their devotion, the palpable impression of their faith and hope that cloaked her as benevolently and completely as the red Rose plaid they wrapped about her shoulders.

For those few hours, as each took a turn with Mairi's head in her lap while the other two caressed her gnarled hands, she forgot her pain, the certainty that haunted her. For those few hours, she held her daughters close, and the croft was filled with golden light from lamp and fire and candle, and Mairi's ailing heart, full of elation, was encompassed by their hope, and changed and healed, if only for a moment.

She wondered if they guessed how sweetly, how tenderly, how thoroughly each was saying good-bye, without words, without thought or intention, but with instinct and the unacknowledged wisdom of their spirits.

That night Ena did not come home. Lian, Genevra and Ailsa settled Mairi for the night, staying until her eyes fluttered closed, then they stepped outside to talk, to discuss possibilities, to wonder. Mairi could not hear them, but she guessed what they were saying, and the knowledge reopened the wound from which they had staunched the flow for a little. She lay there, restless at their absence when their presence had been so strong.

She knew she would not rest, for the pain returned gradually, sweeping her into the darkness. She shivered under the wool blankets and could not bear their weight on her skin. The few hours of respite made the renewal of the struggle more difficult, though not for anything would she have given up this night, this last communion with her daughters, even had she known. They had been closer to her than ever before, and even through the fog of discomfort, she thanked the obstinance of Ailsa, Lian, Genevra, unwilling to give in, which had brought them to her.

When Ailsa crept back inside, Mairi forced her body to be still. Satisfied that she was sleeping, Ailsa put on her nightrail and slipped into bed.

Not long afterward, Mairi lost awareness of her body, racked by pain, and the covers that bound her to the bed. She did not know that for hours she tossed and turned, kicking the blankets and sheet aside each time Ailsa replaced them, that the bed was soaked with sweat, her hair clinging to her skin in long, dull tendrils.

She was not aware that Ailsa sat beside her, helpless, tortured by the sight of her mother's misery.

So it went until night crawled toward the dawn, and Mairi fell asleep at last.

Ena was caught up in a battle with a wildcat defending its lair. The girl knew one of its cubs was ill and was trying to get past the fear-crazed animal to help the mewling baby. But the cat was as big as she, and as determined. Ena cried out when a dirty paw clawed four wounds down her cheek and across her chest. She fell and the blood seeped through her torn gown, staining the fabric and the ground beneath as she tried to reach the pockets where she kept her herbs. Her arms had lost all feeling, but she flailed about, ignoring the pain, the blood, the feral golden eyes of the cat, thinking only of the dried kelp in her pocket, the tincture of iodine, the bandages.

The wildcat watched her warily, crouched to strike if she should rise, but she did not. Her wounds continued to bleed until the tall grass in which she lay was stained red, until she had no energy to reach for the relief that lay so close, tumbled in her pockets, until pain blurred her eyesight and she stopped moving. The color drained from her skin as the blood drained from her body, and at last she lay immobile, eyes glazed, heart throbbing out her life onto the deep rich loam around her.

The cat froze, head tilted, listening for danger, sniffing for deception, but hearing nothing, smelling nothing. The girl was very pale and small. She was making weak, guttural sounds of pain that began to sound like supplication. The wildcat saw she would not rise again, that she was harmless. More than harmless.

It crept closer as she stared blindly, fingers opening and closing in the blood-soaked grass. The wildcat was more powerful; it had proven its prowess. And now the girl suffered. It was not necessary. Lying beside her, giving her its warmth, it pressed its paw over her face until she was not breathing anymore. She was no longer in pain.

When the cat rose, coat matted with the girl's blood, its eyes were no longer gold, but silver flecked with green, and what it saw was not the land it knew, the lair, the cubs hidden from predators. What it saw was the sway of branches in the wind and the vastness of a sky scattered with clouds. What it saw was not the battlefield on which it lived its life, clinging by a thread as it foraged for food and crept along, trying to meld with its surroundings to avoid the threats it must avoid. What it saw was a place, a sweep of earth bound by tall, graceful trees, a kind of beauty that made it stop and drop its head and look away. It was too much. Too inviting.

The wildcat knew, too late, that in pitying its enemy's pain, in recognizing that in her weakness, she was no enemy, in taking the last breath from her body, it had taken her spirit into itself, and now, after all, would have to fight for its own survival.

Mairi woke to find the pain had diminished and that Ena's voice was in her head. *Don't ye worry, because now I'll take care of ye when ye need me. Always.*

She heard the others arrive, heard Ailsa meet them at

the door and whisper, "She's just fallen asleep. Let's no' disturb her now."

She heard the murmur of other voices, fading as the sound of footsteps faded, leaving her enveloped by the violet gray of dawn and the all too vivid colors of her dream.

18

AILSA WANTED VERY MUCH TO BE ALONE.

She'd sent Lian and Genevra off with Alanna at dawn before she glanced once more at her mother, dressed and slipped outside. She could not stay still, nor could she quiet her turbulent thoughts enough to make conversation with the daughter and sisters she knew so well. They had not sat beside Mairi for hours, as she had, seeing for the first time the depth of her distress. They had not tried time and again to wrap her mother in a safe cocoon of warm blankets, only to have her fling it away. They had not seen and felt her pain.

Now that she knew the truth, she could not bear its weight on her shoulders. How, then, had Ena, who was only thirteen, borne it?

Seeking the place where she and Mairi, Lian and Genevra had found magic and daring and a night of gilded peace, Ailsa headed for the *linne*. She hurried toward the burn that had so often given her solace and inspiration. She knelt beside the falls' uneven stair steps and filled her cupped hands with water to soothe her parched throat. But the pure, clear liquid did not quench her thirst, or the constant, growing ache in her heart. She bowed her head, ashamed because she was afraid. She was clinging to the image of her mother she wanted to remember. The Mairi Rose who was compassionate and unfaltering, who'd let nothing conquer her—not loss or sorrow or loneliness or anger. Always, she had triumphed.

But in the early morning hours before dawn, in the furrows of agony on Mairi's face, Ailsa had sensed defeat. Turning away from the memory, she looked for the sun, but its light was wrapped in clouds and did not reach the water or the spray where once had been the evanescent sheen of rainbows.

"What'll I do?" Ailsa asked the murmuring river. "What's kind or right or fair?"

Mairi's voice replied from the golden night years ago. *'Tis no' a question of proper. 'Tis a question of faith.*

She believed in her mother. Of that she was certain.

Unable to stay still, she began to climb the steep hill toward the flat stone where the great fall began. She paid no attention to her cream-colored gown as she clawed at clumps of turf and hummocks of moss and handy rocks to pull herself upward. She was breathing heavily, heart pounding, cheeks flushed with warmth as she neared the top. "Ye want me to go against my instincts, my needs, my feelin's and help ye leave me," she muttered bitterly to her absent mother.

The memory of Mairi answered softly: *'Tis your decision to make, no' mine. But I think 'twould be a fine thing to know you've conquered your fears and doubts.*

Ailsa raised her head, for the voice was so clear that she felt her mother looking up at her. Just as she'd looked up sixteen years ago when her daughter stood on that slick, flat rock, hesitating. Mairi's faith and pride in Ailsa had glowed in her eyes, and she had jumped, because she knew her mother would be waiting at the bottom.

She stood again on that boulder, hands bruised and bloody from her rash climb up the rugged autumn hillside, legs aching, dress stained and torn. The icy burn poured over her brogues as she looked down at the graduated waterfalls, the rust and brown and ochre rocks ringed in

ferns, the golden water that swirled and eddied till it settled in the *linne*. "What if I can no' think of life without
ye?" she pleaded.

And again the younger Mairi, the Mairi of sixteen years
ago, who'd lost her husband but three months past answered
gently, *I believe ye can keep the spirits of those ye love by ye if ye
choose. 'Tis no' a matter of how far they are from ye or if they
can come back again, but only how much ye believe*.

Ailsa froze at a movement on the riverbank, turned cautiously and found herself staring into the copper eyes of a
wildcat. *Never meet their eyes*, Ena had warned her. *They
take it as a threat, a challenge*. But she could not look away.

The cat seemed to want to cross the burn, but the scent
of a possible enemy had stopped it. Their gazes remained
locked and Ailsa fought for breath as the sleek cat arched
its body, then crouched low, ready to spring. Terrified, she
watched the wildcat launch itself into the air. Her heart
stopped as it glided toward her, paws extended, eyes fixed
on her face. She tried to scream, but no sound came, no
motion, no protective lunge.

The animal filled her sight for an instant that stretched
into hours, then landed on the far bank, pausing to glance
back once before it disappeared into the woods.

Why had it not struck? She'd been defenseless against it.
Then she remembered. Mairi loved wildcats—their primi-
tive, feral beauty, their power and grace. Ailsa stared at the
trail of prints the animal had left in the soft loam. She had
been warned—or perhaps—guided. Mairi would never let
her daughter suffer if she knew how to help. After all, there
was no choice to make.

She lifted her head, hearing something in the wind—a
cry of urgency, of need. She knew that sound. Without a
backward glance, Ailsa Rose began to run.

Alone among the animals, Ena felt a chill and heard
someone call. It might have been the swirling wind, moan-

ing with the pitch of a human voice. Come! I need ye. Your hands are gentle. Ena cocked her head, listening. Then she felt a pain slice through her and she cried out at its savagery. Another came on its heels, knocking her against the reed barrier she had woven, tearing the pattern down the middle as she sprawled on the moss and turf. The third took her breath, giving the wind its victory. Then there was nothing. Silence. Numbness.

She rose, guided by invisible strands that drew her inexorably forward. She found her breath and her will on the familiar winding path, and prayed for her strength. Time did not pass, but hung suspended precariously in the branches like the last autumn leaves as she made her way home. Her feet were slow and leaden, holding her back when all she wanted was to go forward. Or so she made herself believe.

Mairi looked up expectantly, though her daughter made no sound as she stepped over the threshold. "You've come," she whispered. Ailsa's gown was stained and torn, her hands scraped raw, her hair snarled and coated with a film of soil. She was breathing heavily, as if she had been running. But what caught Mairi's attention was the intense determination in her eyes, mingled with contrition and compassion.

"I want to help ye as ye asked," she told her mother. "Forgive me for takin' so long to understand."

Mairi smiled blearily. "There's no need to forgive ye. You've come." Mairi felt as if a heavy stone had been lifted from her chest.

"Surely ye knew I would, no matter what I said."

Despite her weakness, Mairi regarded her daughter with affection and compassion. "I called, but I was no' yet certain ye'd answer."

"Ye knew, Mam. I'll always come."

"Aye, so ye will. But are ye sure, my Ailsa? Once 'tis done ye can't go back."

"I'm sure. I've thought and thought. 'Twas no' easy, but I'm here."

"Even though it means forever?"

Ailsa paled but did not stumble. "Aye. Even then."

For a time, Ailsa sat beside the bed, watching the pulse at the base of Mairi's throat, counting the beats to keep herself steadfast. She was aware of the heat of her mother's body and the chill of her own. Finally, she lay down on the linen sheet and curled her fingers around Mairi's.

She felt Mairi's will flow through her like hot cider, warming away the cold. "In my soul, I know 'tis right," she murmured, "but that doesn't make it easier."

They stared at one another for a long time. "Can we do this?" Mairi breathed.

Ailsa saw how pallid her mother's skin was, how cloudy with pain her eyes. "Aye," she said with conviction. "We can."

"Come," her mother murmured, "while ye heat the water and gather the herbs, I'll tell ye what I want done with my things." She would not waver; at the very least she would try to match Ailsa's determination and faith.

Standing before the press in the kitchen, Ailsa rummaged until she found the herbs they kept hidden in the back of the cupboard. More carefully than was necessary, she laid them out on the kitchen table in tidy piles. When the kettle hung over the fire, she turned to look at Mairi. Both started to speak. Both fell silent.

Knowing she must keep moving, Ailsa began to collect the items Mairi named and placed them beside Lian's ebony chest. She stacked the tied packets of her own letters to her mother and her musical compositions, along with the letters, drawings and poems Genevra and Lian had sent over the years. She found Charles Kittridge's letters in the rosewood box where Mairi kept the gifts he'd sent from exotic lands, the drawings he'd done of her before she became his wife, the few he had done after.

"I want Ena to have the letters your father gave me."

Startled, Ailsa sat back on her heels.

"You've lived with them, read them, treasured them all your life. Ye needed them before ye met Charles, but afterward, ye'd memories of your own. But 'tis no' the only reason. Ena knows by heart the stories in your journal, Ailsa, but she needs a past apart from that. Perhaps her grandfather can give it to her, though he was gone before she was born. Can ye understand, *mo-chridhe?*"

"Aye, Mam. I see what you're tryin' to do for our girl." She tried to swallow, but there was a lump in her throat. Ena had been right. Even now, Mairi was thinking of others. Ailsa opened the Chinese chest and stored away the fragments of her mother's life, her eyes dry and burning.

"If 'tis no' one thing too many, there's something else I'd have ye do."

Nodding, Ailsa waited.

"My weddin' ring. I want to wear it once more. 'Tis too big for my finger, so Ena put it in the wee drawer in the press, where 'tis safe."

At Mairi's mention of the ring, her voice softened, her face flushed with color and her eyes filled with longing. Ailsa bowed her head, fighting tenderness and regret. She must not crumble now. It would not be fair.

She concentrated on the small task, but could not find the ring. Her fingers were clumsy as she searched the press. Her thoughts were not focused on what she was doing, but on Ena. She, above all, should be here to say good-bye to her beloved grandmother. Everyone should be here. But she knew if she tried to find them, if she waited, she might lose her resolve. And Mairi was ready, waiting.

Today for the first time, Ailsa saw what her daughter must have seen long since. Mairi looked as helpless and fragile as one of Ena's birds with a broken wing. But her wings were more than broken; they'd been torn away. Ena, *mo-run*, she thought, where are ye, child?

Mairi stared at her daughter, tears welling in her eyes. She wept for her and blessed her, prayed for Neithe, God of Waters, and Mena, Goddess of the Moon, to hold Ailsa in their thoughts and under their protection.

"I'd write a bit now," she said, "while ye look for the ring and set the tea to steeping." She wanted to give her daughter time, and she herself had some things to say to those who were absent, whose voices echoed just beyond her reach.

Awkwardly, Mairi gathered parchment and a pen that she kept by her bed. She wrote with slow, careful strokes, propping the pages on a book Alanna had lent her. She had thought writing would tire her less than speaking, but she'd been wrong. The things she had to say were not easy, nor the words to say them simple. When she was weary but satisfied, she dropped the pen, laid the parchment aside.

She drifted, letting her mind wander through the pages of her life. Scenes came into vivid focus, then dimmed and were replaced by others. She saw Charles Kittridge disappearing into the mist on the night she'd set him free. She saw herself holding Ailsa for the first time, looking into her blue-violet eyes and knowing this child was wise and strong and bonny.

She saw Ailsa's wedding day—the coach taking her daughter, her dearest friend, her living hope to London. She saw the moment years later when Charles returned and she held out her hands in welcome; the first sight of her granddaughter, Alanna, the image of herself when she was young. The appearance of each of her daughters in turn, when she'd known by the pain and confusion in their eyes that she could not help but take them in, could not help but love them.

She saw Ailsa lying on her bed, gray and without hope, until she felt the baby that was Ena move inside her. Through the haze of dreaming wakefulness, Mairi saw so much she had forgotten, so much she had thought lost.

She drifted, the hastily written pages lying nearby. When she heard footsteps, she folded them quickly and slid them under her pillow.

Ena appeared in the doorway, blinking from the sunlight, blinded by the darkness in the croft. Glancing about, the girl felt an uncomfortable prickling at the back of her neck. She shivered. "I had to come, Gran. I thought ye needed me."

"And so I do, Ena-*aghray*. Very much. Just no' mayhap the way ye think."

Facing her daughter, Ailsa looked into her wide, frightened eyes and felt again the urgent cry she had heard earlier, the need. The child was sniffing the steamy air, taking in the scent of bitter herbs. She looked from the open chest, filled neatly with her grandmother's things, to Mairi, eyes closed in relief, to Ailsa, before she stumbled forward into her mother's arms, clinging with all her strength.

"I'd decided to do this thing for Gran," Ena murmured. She'd felt no doubts until she saw her mother's face. It had turned her to ice where she stood.

Ailsa smoothed back her daughter's hair. "Surely ye didn't think I'd let ye take that weight on your narrow shoulders, especially alone. 'Tis no' your burden, my daughter, my heart. You've done so much already. 'Tis my responsibility." She gazed at Mairi over Ena's head. "And my privilege. But I didn't see that till today, till I watched ye, Mam, suffer through the night." She turned her attention back to her daughter. "Did ye no' think ye could come to me?"

Ena looked up at her, dry-eyed and speechless.

"Ye and your sisters make a formidable barrier," Mairi answered for her granddaughter.

Ailsa took Ena's face in her hands. "I was no' makin' it easy for ye, was I? But I'm here now to do what must be done."

Ena let out her breath in a rush. She was ashamed of the relief she felt. She'd not allowed herself to recognize her own reluctance. "May I stay by her?"

" 'Twould break her heart if ye left her now, and yours, I think."

Vision blurred with unshed tears, Mairi opened her arms and Ena went to her. She did not realize how much she craved her grandmother's touch until Mairi's arms closed around her, Mairi wound her fingers in her hair. The girl closed her eyes and absorbed the heat of her grandmother's body, smelled the herbs that had become part of her blood, felt the rhythm of a heartbeat echoing her own.

"Ena, ye are so dear to me." She picked a piece of bark out of the girl's hair and brushed dark loam from her cheek. "Ye must listen to me. Go where your spirit, your inner voice, leads, for your heart's too tangled in the vines of the glen, and can no' always hear the truth. Will ye promise me that? Promise it truly and no' because 'tis the last thing I ask of ye?"

Ena put her elbows on either side of Mairi's head so she could see her face. Solemnly, she considered, for she would not make a false promise. "Aye, I can promise ye truly."

Having found what she was looking for at last—the ring lying like a thread of moonlight in the darkness of the drawer—Ailsa approached the bed. She clasped it so tightly that the pattern of interwoven gold was pressed into her palm. "Ye wanted your ring, Mam." She opened her hand, displaying the thin band of gold.

Slowly, Mairi picked it up, and beginning at the tip of her ring finger, slid it over fragile skin and swollen knuckles. She was entranced by its dull gleam. She'd forgotten how beautiful it was, the white and yellow gold intertwined in a delicate pattern that had lasted fifty-five years. She turned it on her finger, once, twice, three times, remembering Charles's face when he'd given it to her. There was no object in this world she had loved more than this.

Smiling with tears on her cheeks, she slid it off and handed it to Ailsa, who stared at her in astonishment.

"I thought ye wanted to wear it again."

"Only for a little. I wanted to feel it cool against my finger, to trace its design, to remember how it felt when my husband put it there. But I've no need to take it with me, for I'll have Charlie by my side." She peered at her naked finger in the herb-scented gloom. "Besides, ye see I'll carry the mark of it forever. 'Tis enough for me." She held out her hand so her daughter and granddaughter could see the pale circle on her weathered finger—darkened by sun and soil—a band made not of gold or jewels, but of soft skin that could not be removed or lost or taken from her.

Ailsa swallowed, blinking away tears. "And now?" she asked softly.

"'Tis yours now, Ailsa-my-heart, for then the circle will be complete. Lian wears the bracelet Charles had forged for Ke-ming, Genevra the chain that belonged to her mother, and now ye'll have the first of the three, the weddin' ring that began it all. Each time ye look at it or feel its pattern or weight on your hand, you'll remember 'tis part of both your parents, no' just one, no' just the other. That's its power and its beauty. 'Tis why I want ye to have it." She dropped it into Ailsa's palm.

For an instant, Ailsa could not move, then she pressed her hand, ring and all, to her mouth. She closed her eyes and Ena moved away. She knew her mother was praying in her own way to her own gods, fighting tears with the pressure of the white and yellow gold against her lips. Then, eyes fixed on her mother, unable to make a sound, she let her hand fall, palm open, onto the woven blanket.

When she remained rigid, Ena leaned forward and took the ring, brushed it against her lips, then turned her mother's hand and slid the ring onto her finger.

"But your weddin' ring," Ailsa managed at last, turning it unconsciously in endless circles.

" 'Twill remind ye we're linked by more than accident—me and ye, Lian and Genevra," Mairi said. " 'Tis a symbol of Charlie's love, this ring, yet the two of us lived with the symbol and no' the man most of our lives. Take this symbol, wear it always and think of me together at last with the only man I've ever loved."

"How can I wear it? I've no' earned the right."

"Ye earned the right the first time ye played sleep upon me with the music of your *clarsach*, and many times since. Too many to count. Ye earned the right when ye came to offer me the gift of freedom. Take it, *mo-chridhe*. I give it freely and with love."

Finally, there was nothing more to do except deal with the well-steeped herb brew Ailsa had begun. While Ena held Mairi's hand, Ailsa added honey to cover the bitterness, took a horn cup from the press, filled it with the mixture and poured the rest outside the door, filling the kettle with water to rinse it.

She went back to the table, hands cradled around the cup, renewing her determination and her vow. The gold band glinted on her finger and she touched it lightly, grasped it firmly, turned with the cup in her hands.

"Don't be afraid," Mairi said. " 'Tis I who take the risk and the blame."

Ailsa placed one foot carefully in front of the other so she would not spill a drop. When she reached the bedside, she bent down to hand her mother the cup.

Mairi took it in one hand and patted the mattress with the other. "There are things I must say. The others'll no' be pleased when they find what you've done. They may even be angry. Remember, 'tis their pain speakin', and their envy." She shook her head. "Ye two alone were with me at the end. Ye two alone'll bid me good-bye." She looked at Ailsa and knew they were both thinking of the night before, when, as she lay in candlelight with her daughters around her, an unspoken farewell had passed among them. She wondered if they'd felt it and understood.

Ailsa squeezed her hand and nodded. "In their hearts they know."

"Remember, 'twill be difficult for ye but harder for them. Bless ye, my dear ones. Carry my blessin' with ye in all that is to come."

Quickly, she drank from the cup till it was empty, then set it aside.

" 'Twill be a while," Ena said, perching on the edge of the mattress. "But we'll be here beside ye." Ailsa and her daughter sat on either side of Mairi, clasping hands across her chest.

Mairi met her daughter's troubled gaze, again sharing her thoughts. Ena was trying to comfort her grandmother. Didn't the girl know she herself would suffer most? But perhaps she did not. She was young and could not bear to see another's pain. Always others' pain had been more difficult than her own.

Mairi drew Ailsa down to whisper, "Take care of her, *mo-ghray*. She knows so much, yet nothing at all. She thinks her heart's strong, but 'tis aye fragile."

"I know." Ailsa could not tell if her tears were for her mother's empathy or her daughter's innocence. Each was so willing to give, yet took so little. "I'll protect her."

Silence fell upon them, stealing a little of their determination. Instinctively, each clasped one of Mairi's hands as if to hold her back. No matter how they tried, they could not let go.

Mairi gazed up at them from a long distance. "Ye want to keep me here; I feel it. Ye have the power to do it. The human will's far stronger than ye think. No' only your two, but the wills of all the others are focused on keepin' me bound to this earth, this glen, this croft where I was born."

"Yet you're goin' just the same. I can feel ye slippin' away," Ailsa breathed.

" 'Tis because, no matter your doubts at this moment, our three wills would set me free; you've done me that kindness." Mairi turned her hands till she was holding them with a touch as light as the wings of a newborn bird. "Bless ye, my wild ones. May the Celtic gods keep ye safe and wise and true." Her voice began to fade like a distant echo in a valley of pines, or the song of a nightingale through billows of mist.

This time it was Mairi who tensed with fear when she felt the decoction begin to overtake her.

Ena recognized the fear; she had seen it before. She looked questioningly at Ailsa, who nodded, one hand on her mother's shoulder. The girl took Mairi's head in her lap, as she had the trembling body of the wildcat. Caressing her hair lightly, she sang her grandmother to rest.

> "Ye go home this night to your home of Winter,
> To your home of Autumn, of Spring and of Summer.
> Ye go home this night to your lastin' home,
> To your eternal bed, to your sound sleepin'."

Her voice grew hoarse and she trailed off. She took deep breaths, but could not form the words. Then she realized Ailsa had taken up where she'd left off.

> "Sleep now, sleep and so fade sorrow.
> Sleep now, sleep, and so fade pain.
> Sleep, beloved, in the strength of the earth."

They saw Mairi's face relax, felt the spirit begin to flow out of her body into the shadows beyond.

Ena could not breathe. There was a weight in her chest that crushed the air from her lungs. She wanted desperately to cry, "Don't go!"

Mairi's smile was soft and sweet. With an effort, she focused on Ailsa, then Ena. "Don't grieve for me, for I'll be with ye in the wind and the mist and the sun on the water.

Ye'll hear my voice—softly, so ye'll no' be certain, unless ye believe. There are brighter places than this dim croft. Go out and find them. As I did once. As I do now."

Then Mairi released them and was finally free.

19

INSIDE ALANNA'S COZY COTTAGE, WHERE LIAN AND GENEVRA had taken refuge when Ailsa left them at dawn, the three women heard the first rumblings of a storm far in the distance. They were seated around Alanna's loom, drinking warm cider to chase away the chill.

Just after they'd arrived, Alanna had called to David and Connor as they headed for the door. "Where're ye goin' so early, the two of ye?"

"There's a storm on the way; it'll be here before the day's out. I want to cut as much of that last field of barley as I can before it hits."

"The work'll go faster with the two of us," Connor said. He flexed his muscles, invisible beneath heavy shirt and greatcoat, in a mock show of strength. "I've grown fair quick with a scythe and bundlin' wire," he added proudly.

The boy was aware that David was watching his wife closely, more concerned by her apparent calm than he would have been by unrestrained weeping. Connor himself had been irritable since Mairi's announcement. It seemed to him that everyone was waiting, expectant. Father and son had been glad of the need for strenuous work; they would use up their excess energy in sweat and concentration.

Lian and Genevra were in greater need of distraction, haunted, as they were, by the image of Mairi lying in the candlelight, holding them close by her will, not her physical strength. Neither spoke of it, but both sensed it was the

last time they would touch her, see her tender smile, feel
the warmth and vibrancy that was Mairi Rose. Both were
still in the grip of the unexpected kinship that had bound
them closer than before. In the light of day, they were
chilled by the break in the threads that seemed to snap
when they released Mairi's hands. They were agitated,
apprehensive.

Sensing their distress, and her mother's need to be
alone, Alanna had brought them here, as she'd promised
the day they arrived, to show them how she wove the surprising things she created on her loom.

As soon as they stepped into the cottage, where a fire
blazed in the stone hearth and the glass windows kept out
the chill while letting in the thin morning light, Lian and
Genevra had felt a little better. At least they were warm
and comfortable.

Sorting through the pile of folded cloth in a basket near
the loom, Genevra had been impressed. "So many patterns
and colors and weaves. How do you manage them all?"

Alanna smiled, proud enough of her skill not to be
embarrassed. "I learned it all from Gran. She spent years
mixin' and tryin' one lichen mixed with an unusual leaf or
berry to make unique dyes. She came up with colors no
other would've attempted, and I've worked at it ever since,
sometimes cheatin' and usin' dyes from London, but 'tis
pleased I am with the result, just the same."

Lian ran the fabric through her hands, eyes closed, feeling the tautness and flow of the weave, the changes in pattern and texture. "How do you manage to make it so soft,
so close to silk?"

With little encouragement, Alanna sat at the loom and
took up the shuttle. "I've spent hours here without movin',
tryin' this and that, refinin' the thread so 'tis thin but strong.
I've made bed linens and linsey-woolsey gowns and wool
plaids, but I grew weary of the colors and rough, unvaried
weaves. I wanted to do something different. A few months

ago I started this." She showed them the cloth currently laced onto the loom. "I saw it in a dream and could no' get it from my mind. I've no memory of the rest of the dream, only this. It flowed before my eyes, streamin' like a ribbon or a path or a river, till I sat down and began to make it real."

Lian and Genevra drew in their breath at its rare beauty. It was a cloth of several thicknesses and weaves, a pattern unlike any in the basket nearby. It took them a moment to recognize the intertwined leaves of an oak in stylized colors from rust to gold to emerald to burgundy to blue, and all the shades in between. Some of the leaves were thick and sturdy, others soft and pliable as silk. Colors and patterns together made a compelling, complex, flowingly splendid cloth that echoed the feeling and vision Alanna'd described that had driven her to begin.

"It *looks* like it came from a dream," Genevra murmured, awestruck. "I've never seen so many hues blend and separate so well. It's hypnotic."

"Like the murmur of a river," Lian said, but her gaze was turned inward. "I feel I have seen it before. It is familiar to my eyes and my touch, and it is more than exquisite; it is somehow immeasurable, eternal."

Alanna was startled. " 'Tis just how I felt when I'd finished a length long enough to hold in my hand. 'Twas soothin' and felt endurin'." She blushed at the absurdity of the thought. "But 'twas how I felt. As if I'd done somethin' that'd been waitin' to be turned from chimera to reality."

The three sat side by side, their cider forgotten, each holding the fabric in both hands, running their fingers lightly over the multifaceted design as if searching for something they had not known was missing.

For a long while, mother and daughter sat unmoving, caught in a moment of unbounded time without end or origin. Their linked hands lay on Mairi's chest, but they did not look at one another. A strange, indefinable tranquillity enfolded them, delaying realization, an affinity deeper than they'd ever known—with Mairi or each other. They did not speak, for the hush was calming, and much had already been said, with and without words.

Inevitably, gradually, the harmony dissolved and time began to move again.

Gently, Ena lifted her grandmother's head from her lap and placed it on the pillow. She took a rough-hewn comb from her pocket, while Ailsa picked up another. In silent concert, they began to run them carefully through the silver strands, draped over their hands, tugging the combs through the thick mass, working out the knots, laying it smooth and untangled across her shoulders and around her head. When they were done, Mairi's hair shimmered, spread around her like skeins and filaments of moonlight, even in the murky gloom. Even though she slept and would not wake again, her thick long hair was beautiful with the vibrancy that had been Mairi Rose.

Heart heavy with resignation, Ailsa went to dip some water into a bowl from the bucket outside the door. Ena found a soft cloth to wash Mairi's face with its web of creases and furrows, closing her eyes against the light. She turned to her grandmother's hands, sliding the cloth over the fragile skin, circling each finger, one at a time, slowly, as if moving in a trance. Then, remembering how Mairi's knuckles had cracked and bled, Ena took the vial of lotion from her pocket and smoothed it into those gnarled, weathered hands until they were soft between her own.

Her mother watched, moved and mesmerized by the girl's tender care, then Ailsa too took up a cloth and washed her mother's feet. She found clean linens, and while she lifted her mother gingerly, Ena replaced the sweat-soaked sheets, unaware of the pages that fell to the floor. Together, Ailsa and Ena removed the wrinkled nightrail and slipped another over Mairi's head, straightening and smoothing it around her frail body. Finally, Ailsa folded her mother's hands across her chest, placing the one that had worn her wedding ring on top of the other, so the pale band of white was visible. Mairi would have wanted that.

That last gesture constricted Ena's chest, forcing her shoulders forward and her head down, as if to ward off a blow that had already been struck.

When she could breathe again, she followed her mother's example and began to close and tie down the leather window coverings. Then, drawn like a magnet, she went to stand beside her mother, next to the bed. Mairi lay still, smiling in contentment, her hair a silver crown, her body limp beneath her gown. Now that the burden of pain had gone, she looked younger; the beauty she had been shone through the weathered woman she'd become. She was lovely. She was happy.

"She's leavin' me behind," Ena whispered, stunned.

The girl found she could not move; her feet had become one with the well-trodden earth of the floor. She fought for each breath and stood immobile for a long, long time, listening to soft voices in the silence—the ghosts, the memories, the lingering souls of those whose feet no longer touched the ground. The whispering engulfed her, so loud it filled her head and she could hear nothing but those lovely and wrenching, heartbreaking sounds.

They began to possess her, those voices, until, abruptly, the whispers ceased and silence filled the vast and gaping emptiness. Ena looked at Mairi's motionless form and knew the voices had stopped because her grandmother's soul had slipped away. She was gone. Truly and irrevocably gone.

A wave of darkness, cold and dank, crept from the shadows and, gaining strength and speed, swept Ena into its heart. She trembled from head to toe, empty, cold, afraid. Ailsa's arm slipped around her, holding her upright, but she did not feel its weight or hear her mother's murmured consolation.

She needed Mairi's touch, her quiet compassion, the

sound of her beloved voice. The darkness whirled and spun her into a vortex where splinters of pain sliced her as she fell, knowing, now, at last, that Mairi Rose was no more. As she had not foreseen, could not have guessed, Ena could not bear her absence.

Frantic, the girl turned away from the bed. She became aware of Ailsa's hands gripping her shoulders and looked up at her mother, smoothing the turmoil from her face. "I need to walk, to breathe. Please, Mam, let me go."

Ailsa understood. She'd felt the same many times in her life, but for Ena, this was the first. "Go," she said, brushing her daughter's forehead with her lips. "But take care, our Ena. Go slow and be aware of where you're goin'. And remember, I'll be here waitin' when ye need me, as I'll be needin' ye."

Ena heard the words, but they meant nothing. She had to get away, to escape the blackness that wound itself around her heart and squeezed, cutting off the flow of blood. Blood that had come from Mairi through Ailsa and into her daughter. Mairi Rose's blood, which had ceased to run through her own veins, would not now run through Ena's. Another loss. One more that she did not know how to bear.

Only when she was certain her daughter was gone did Ailsa allow herself to collapse. She fell to her knees, running the intertwined gold bands back and forth over her lips. She wanted to cry out as it struck her fully what she had done. She wanted to feel the pain wash over her; the waiting was unendurable.

But she was numb; she could not weep.

Alanna, Lian and Genevra saw the storm creeping closer, the clouds growing darker, and their apprehension increased. The air hung heavy with moisture and the wind began to whine, then howl, when Alanna stood abruptly and her eyes glazed over. "We must go," she said. "We must hurry."

The sisters did not hesitate. Collecting coat, pelisse and plaid, the three women stepped out into the chilly wind that whipped beneath their skirts and up their sleeves.

The impulse to make haste came from inside Alanna, compelling her to leap over roots and logs and tussocks she would normally have gone around. The smell of moisture and pent-up fury permeated the air, but that only urged her to go faster.

Genevra and Lian followed without question, conscious of Alanna's panic. They fought their way through the wind toward the Rose croft, unnerved by the increasing pallor of Alanna's skin while their cheeks grew red from exertion and cold.

Suddenly, out of nowhere, David appeared. "Have ye seen Connor?"

"I thought he was with ye."

As the storm built and took on force, David knew the glen would be torn apart before it was all over. "We were workin' in the field, when all at once he froze, went pale and dropped his scythe. He ran from that field faster than I'd ever seen him run, and his face was contorted with fear or dread. 'Twas disturbin' enough, the way he left, but more bothersome that I've no' seen him since." He exchanged a bemused, troubled glance with his wife.

Alanna went white and grasped his arm. "Ena," she said. "She must've called."

David shook his head. "I heard nothing."

"No, but then, if she was callin' Connor, why would ye hear? They're aye close, those two." Her eyes were blank, her skin clammy.

When her husband saw the sheen of perspiration on her skin, he scowled to hide his dread. "You've 'seen' something?"

"Only that 'twas Ena. And there's danger. Nothing more." She took a deep breath to steady her trembling hands. "We're on our way to Mairi's. Ena's most likely to be there with all that's goin' on. Mayhap she was overwhelmed by her grandmother's illness and needed his help."

David made an effort to remain calm, but the air itself seemed determined to leave nothing undisturbed. The wind hissed, then roared so strongly that they all swayed to remain standing. "How can ye be sure?"

"I can't. I can only follow my instincts. And they lead me to Mairi's."

With no more discussion, the group set off again, moving faster, their faces set with more than concern.

Ena fled, fighting for breath. Wrapped in her own darkness, she did not notice the clouds that had begun to gather, dark and ominous, around the mountains. She did not feel the unnatural stillness or the heavy moisture that hung over the landscape like a pall.

Several times she doubled over from exhaustion and the sharp pain in her side—she who ran as far, as fast, as any in the glen. Shaken more deeply than ever before, she trembled and stumbled over ground she'd traveled hundreds of times. "I didn't know!" she cried to the heavens. "I didn't know 'twould hurt so much!" *You're only a child, Ena. Ye couldn't have known.*

She had never lost anyone before, never imagined how much it would hurt to lose her grandmother, never conceived of how deeply grief could sink into her bones, chilling her from the inside out. She had no defense against the sense of bleak barrenness that overwhelmed her.

Mairi Rose had guessed this would happen. *I'm no' a stray bird with a broken wing or a deer brought down by a hunter's bullet. I'm your grandmother, Ena-aghray. Ye can't begin to imagine how great that difference is.* She had known all along, had tried to warn the girl, but in her certainty, her arrogance, Ena had not listened or believed. *I can't let ye destroy the last bit of your childhood. Not for me, not for a promise, not for anyone.* Ena was drowning in the feelings, the doubts, the fears of everyone she cared for. She imagined her mother's dreadful grief, Alanna's, Lian's and Genevra's. Now she understood their hesitance, their denial. They'd endured this torment, each of them, while she'd been ignorant, foolish, blind. The combined weight of their sorrow—that which had been and that which was to come—nearly destroyed her.

Bent double with pain, gasping, Ena wanted to stop running, but she couldn't. The strength and determination that had allowed her to think she could end Mairi's life had drained away and left her diminished, as a tiny stream veering off from the burn drains the river and makes it less. Ena was alone and defenseless against this foe. "Connor!" she gasped. "I need ye! Connor!" There was no answer.

Ena tripped over a root and sprawled in the long grass. She grasped the grass in clumps, dug her fingers into the earth, to try to anchor herself to the ground, but she could not do that either. It was as if some unseen hand picked her up and pushed her hard, until she was running again, unable to breathe, consumed by rage and anguish.

Suddenly, out of nowhere, Connor was beside her, reaching for her hand. She twined her fingers in his as tightly as she had gripped the grass when she fell. She needed someone, something to hold onto. She closed her eyes in gratitude for the only comfort she ever thought to find again.

Connor had been working when he heard her cry inside his head, so loud it made his temples throb. He'd dropped the scythe and covered his ears with his hands to make it stop. At first he'd not known it was Ena. He had never heard her sound so desperate. He felt his father's disapproval as he turned and ran, but it had not stopped him. Ena needed him. He could no more ignore her plea than he could have stalked the wildcat alone.

He saw her face, reddened by effort and swollen with unshed tears, heard the painful rasp of her breath, and knew she could not speak and did not wish to. He sensed that her need for silence was as great as her need for the heat and weight of his hand around hers. So he remained silent, gripping her so hard, in his apprehension, that their interwoven fingers became mottled red and white.

They were headed toward the mountains and the frightful storm. He wanted to warn her, to stop her, to shake her awake. Because, though she ran as if possessed, and he beside her, she was not leading them anywhere. Connor set his jaw in determination. He had to ask. His need to know something, anything, was more important than her need for silence.

"Where are ye goin'?" he shouted over the rising wind.

"Away!" she rasped. "Just away."

When she turned to him, her eyes were wide and wild and blind. The green had disappeared, the silver turned slate gray, dark and as threatening as the storm. His heart began to pound with fear. What could have happened to change her this way? This was not the Ena he knew, had always known. This was a desperate stranger he could not abandon. Not until he found his friend again. Not until he understood. She was running from herself, from her ghosts and secret terrors, running heedlessly, crashing through the glen as if it held no danger for the unwary.

In spite of his fear, his chest ached and his eyes burned when he realized why she had called. *She* needed *him*. Usually it was he who needed her. He was as shaken by that as he was by her madness, her carelessness and the fury that drove her on and on. He did not want to let her down, could not, not only because he cared for her, but because she might never need him this way again. If he left her, she might fall apart, or fling herself into a hidden bog or fall over a twisted branch. She was completely unaware of her surroundings, completely unaware of her own danger. For once, Connor Fraser could look out for her, protect her, perhaps even calm her.

He could only pray he did not fail them both.

When David, Alanna and the half-sisters arrived, the door hung open, swinging on its hinges in the rising, bitter wind.

Lian and Genevra stumbled forward just as a gust caught the door and slammed it closed. They tugged at the latch, but the wind was their enemy today.

Then, as suddenly as it had arisen, the powerful gust died, and the door came open easily. The women ducked under the lintel and were engulfed in darkness. The leather flaps on the windows had been tied down, and what little light leaked through was murky with the coming storm. The cottage was eerily silent.

Something made David and Alanna hang back, reluctant to enter.

Lian and Genevra stopped still when they saw Ailsa kneeling in the center of the packed dirt floor, unmoving.

"Ailsa," they called, but she did not respond. "What is it? What's wrong?"

When she still did not answer, Lian found an oil lamp and lit it, holding it high, creating more shadows in the small ill-lit room. The pool of yellow light fell on their kneeling sister, moved slowly across the fire, cold ashes now, with no spark or glowing ember, to Mairi's heather mattress on the far side of the croft. She lay as motionless as her daughter, pallid and waxen.

Genevra and Lian stood beside Ailsa, trying to understand what they were seeing. For a full minute, it did not penetrate their muddled thoughts. Then, in an instant, they knew.

"She's dead." Lian's voice seemed disembodied, hollow.

The wind moaned and shrieked, expressing what they could not. Benumbed by the cold hush all around them, each heard only her heartbeat pulsing in her chest. They were numb and rigid with disbelief.

Ailsa moaned quietly and turned her head stiffly from side to side. "I helped her," she whispered hoarsely. "I had to."

Lian stiffened, Genevra clinging to her arm. "Could you not have waited for us?" The air was very close and humid, full of forming rage and shock and unexpressed grief.

Dazed from her long, silent vigil, Ailsa squinted into the lantern light, seeking the words, the explanation that eluded her. "Ye didn't approve. I thought . . ." She trailed off wanly. "I could no' wait. And Mairi couldn't."

"Not even for an hour?" Genevra's voice was piercing, betraying an edge of hysteria.

"Ye don't understand. Ye didn't see her face, the relief, the hope, the terror beneath. No matter what ye think, she was only human, ye ken. 'Twould have been cruel to keep her here one moment longer."

"Of course we don't understand," Alanna cried. "How can we when ye didn't give us the chance?"

Ailsa turned her head, startled, aware for the first time that her daughter and son-in-law had come with Lian and Genevra. Sighing in resignation, Ailsa closed her eyes and tried to think. " 'Tis complicated. So many things . . . so many feelin's, so much at stake." She hardly knew what she was saying. "I could no' let—'twas too hard." She ran out of breath, bowed her head for a moment and tried to get to her feet. She fell back, but without a pause, she tried again, collapsing again.

David stopped her from falling. "Ye can see she's no' herself," he said. "You're no' the only ones in shock. Look how stiff she is. She's strained near to breakin'." He regarded his wife, Lian and Genevra intently. "Mairi'd no' have wanted this. Have a little faith in Ailsa. Give her a little time. Surely you've known her long enough to believe she'd no' hurt ye, any of ye, if she could help it. Trust her if ye care for her. I know she'd do the same for ye." He did not know where his passionate defense had come from; he'd only known he had to speak, to protect Alanna's mother, who might well fall apart before their eyes.

"How long have ye been here on the floor, Mam?" Alanna asked, attempting conciliation. David was right. They'd not given her mother a chance.

"I don't remember. A very long time, I think."

With David helping lift her on one side and Alanna on the other, she finally stood, but there was no feeling in her feet, which dragged uselessly. They held her until she could stand on her own, and she looked at them in helpless gratitude. "I've been here since we combed Mam's hair and washed her feet, I think." She frowned. "Since Ena left."

"Ena was here as well?" Lian spoke more sharply than she intended; she tried to smooth it over. "She is so young. Should she—?" Her concern for the girl was genuine.

"No," Ailsa interrupted. "She wanted to be near, but I'd no' let her touch the cup, only sit at Mairi's side. As for me, I'd no choice, nor did I wish for one." She turned pleadingly to her sisters.

"Last night after ye left, I watched my mother and knew she was right. I saw what she'd hidden so long and so well. Ye can no' imagine her sufferin'. But little Ena could, so she wanted to release another soul from pain. For her sake, for our mother's, I did the only thing I could."

She turned to Alanna, who hovered protectively near in case Ailsa should falter again. She'd just begun to realize what all this meant to her mother, what she must be feeling—and disguising, even from herself.

"Forgive me, my daughter. I wanted ye to have a chance to say good-bye. But Ena was ready to give her the cup. I could no' let that happen, no' to them or to me. I'm sorry."

How could Alanna be angry after what Ailsa had been through? After what she'd done to protect them all. "Mam," she said softly, "it must've been the most difficult act of your life, and there've already been many. Could I have chosen, I'd have seen Gran once more. But she knew that I loved her; I knew she loved me. We spoke easily and often of things close to our hearts and kept no secrets but this one. We never doubted one another for a single moment, Gran or I. 'Tis enough to carry with me, I think. The certainty. That and the memory of all the joy she gave me through the years." Her voice broke and David went to her, supporting her with his arm across her shoulder. She turned her face to his chest and he held her close and tight.

Gathering their courage, undone by the sight of Alanna in her husband's arms, Lian and Genevra crept nearer the bed. They saw that Mairi was smiling, looking younger than she had in years. Only then did they realize she had been carrying a burden that had weighed her down, diminished her, for a very long time. But, being Mairi, she had kept it to herself.

Trying to swallow, the two half-sisters found their throats were dry and swollen, raw with the only pain they could allow themselves to feel. "She died, and we weren't with her."

Ailsa joined her sisters beside the body, tears glistening in her eyes. She reached out, and they slipped their arms around her waist, holding themselves upright as much as her. "Did ye no' tell her every day how much ye cared? Did she no' tell ye as often? And last night, when ye held her hands, did ye no' feel the affection and understanding among us? Do ye know how much she gave us in those last hours together? She gave us her trust. Knowin' 'twas hopeless, she promised to try. And try she did, for our sakes, no' her own. 'Tis a rare gift that. Is it—"

Lian interrupted, smiling with ineffable sadness. "It is more than enough. More than I ever thought to receive."

"Yes," Genevra said, weeping openly. "I only hope I gave her half as much.

20

CONNOR AND ENA REACHED THE ODDLY TILTED BOULDERS
at the foot of the mountains, but the obstacles of tortured
stone and slick black rock did not slow Ena's headlong
flight. She began to climb, hand over hand, dropping down
into narrow passages, following the sweep and jut of stone
until a wall of rock rose before her.

"Ena! Stop! Ye don't know what you're doin'. 'Tis slippery here and a storm is comin' fast over our heads. Ena!"

When she did not pause, Connor forced breath into his
aching lungs, quelling his fear the best he could, and
plunged after her. Left alone, she would surely fall; she was
moving too fast and seemed unaware of the ominous clouds
churning above her.

Reciting every prayer he could remember, he slipped
and slid, ducking when Ena's foot dislodged pebbles that
cascaded down, striking his shoulders. Connor could barely
breathe, and the moisture clung to him as the wind
shrieked past, leaving him shivering with more than cold.
Nevertheless, he climbed more quickly, forcing his bruised,
weary body to catch up with Ena, who was far more agile
than he.

She bolted along a narrow ledge, only to find herself
with one foot dangling off the edge, the other sliding on
cold, gray stone. She was gasping for breath, doubled up
with pain from running, when, suspended over a gorge far
below, she remembered Connor and turned to look for him

He limped toward her, and though his lips were moving,
she could not hear. The wind drowned out all other sound.
Ena only realized she was in peril when she saw Connor's
face, pasty with fear, and his hands grasping for her. She
froze, glancing over her shoulder into the gorge. Heart rac-

ing, she reached out, afraid to move either foot, knowing if she did, both might go out from under her.

Skin gray and face grim, Connor followed the ledge, hands flung out, both to catch Ena, if he could get to her in time, and to balance himself in the wind that pushed him from side to side, moaning as it snaked up and away. Ena reached back toward him, and though he swayed and wobbled and the footing was slick, he managed, finally, to grasp her hand and pull her away from the edge.

Shaking and chilled, Ena threw her arms around her friend and clung. He held tightly, closing his eyes in a silent prayer of thanks to the god of the mountain. "Will ye listen to me now? Ye must stop runnin'. We must go back. 'Twill rain soon, and the wind's too strong. We can no' fight both. Do ye hear me, Ena Rose?"

She nodded without looking up, and they backed carefully down the ledge until they hit the path carved into the mountain by time and weather and falling stone. They paused for a moment to catch their breath, feeling the deep cold of the mountainside creep through their clothes and beneath their skin. Hoarse from shouting, Connor drew Ena with him along the path. When they rounded a sharp corner, he could see the moor spread below, billowing like a thousand seas. He paused to examine the break in the path and, clutching her hand firmly, he started down.

But Ena held back, frightened by their precarious position. She started to fall and grasped a wide outcropping of rock desperately, letting go of Connor's hand. She tried to swing her body back onto solid stone, but her grasp slipped. Connor grabbed her around the waist and somehow they became entangled in each others' feet and slid down and down into a deep crevice in the rock, just as the rain began to pelt the jagged peaks that pierced the low, black, heavy clouds.

A layer of gloom fell like a musty blanket around the Fraser croft as storm clouds darkened and the air churned.

Jenny shivered, for the croft was chilly, but she did not move to replenish the peats and set them ablaze. She'd been overtaken by a kind of paralysis very unlike her and could not think what to do next.

A bolt of lightning split the simmering sky and Jenny stiffened. Only once before had she felt the chill that crawled up her spine as she sat restlessly listening to the rain. The chill that warned her of grief to come, invading her body, limb by limb, until she had to move, to run, to do something besides sit and wait, as she had that other time, for news she'd heard already in her heart. *Ye'll think it strange, no doubt, when ye know why I asked ye here,* Mairi Rose had said on that day not long past. She had not looked well, but had refused to discuss her health.

As Jenny stepped outside and wind threatened to take her plaid, she stopped still. Something had changed. The air was raw and somehow empty, as if the life force had been removed. *I thank ye,* Mairi had told her, grasping her hands so tightly they ached. *From my heart and my winterin' spirit I thank ye. The gods bless ye and follow in your shadow, Jenny Fraser. Always.* Almost as if she were saying goodbye.

Jenny had felt it then, but had denied what her heart and her instincts told her. But now she knew. What she was feeling in this bleak moment was the darkness created by the absence of wisdom and laughter and deep, true kindness. Mairi Rose was gone. Slow sorrow filled Jenny's veins where warm blood used to run.

She wanted to turn immediately toward the Rose croft, but she hesitated. She didn't want to intrude where she was not wanted. Then Mairi's voice came to her, wrapped in the wind and the rain. *You're always needed, Jenny. Surely ye must know that.* She could only pray Mairi was right as she began to run, ducking her head and pulling her plaid close against the merciless chill of the storm.

* * *

The door swung open, creaking on its hinges, and Jenny Fraser ducked beneath the lintel. As her gaze moved from one pallid face to another, she noticed Mairi lying on her bed, enshrouded by darkness. "I guessed she was gone, but I hoped I was wrong." She turned to Ailsa. "Can I kiss her good-bye?"

Ailsa's mouth felt dry at Jenny's beseeching expression. "Of course ye can."

She stood at the head of her mother's bed while Jenny crept closer and knelt beside the body. When she kissed the cool, waxen cheek, then leaned her own against it, Ailsa heard something rustle. She reached down for some pages of parchment covered in writing that had fallen aside. She had forgotten Mairi's last letter.

She slid the pages out, hoping to catch a breath of scent or a lingering sensation. But there was nothing. Tears stung Ailsa's eyes. Only Jenny saw them.

"What is't?" the others asked.

"Our mother left a letter." It was not easy, but Ailsa kept her voice steady.

Jenny noticed the pages rattling. *You're no' torn by indecision or ghosts or visions*, Mairi had told her. *I'm askin' ye to remember your childhood friendship with Ailsa in the days to come. Will ye promise to be here if she needs ye?*

She leaned close. "Shall I read it?" she asked simply.

Ailsa nodded. She could not yet speak her mother's words in her mother's voice. It was too soon. She handed over the letter.

"Weel then." Jenny avoided the rocking chair—only Mairi's was unoccupied—and perched on the settle. The others waited, apprehensive and expectant.

My Dear Ones,

First, I beg ye to have a care for our Ena. She doesn't recognize the gift of her innocence—which, mayhap, she'll lose today—or the rarity of that pure, untainted wisdom. She's more fragile than ye know, and she can no' guess what it is to grieve. I ask ye to teach her to feel the pain, then show her how to heal. Ye know how, every one of ye. You've healed yourselves time and again.

Please remember that this mornin' she was a child, and now she's lost between childhood and the woman she'll one day be. Don't let your grief for an old woman blind ye to a young girl's pain. She granted me the favor of wanting to release me: Grant her the favor of holdin' her close.

And please, my dear ones, forgive me for causin' ye to suffer. Know that I love ye, that I hold the image of each of ye in my hands and in my heart, and those images will no' fade, because they're part of me, of my blood, of my very bones.

Know that I hear your voices and your thoughts, as I hear the voices of the glen enfoldin' me. Ye'll hear me, too, if ye listen well, for partin' need no' mean silence among us, only a different sound, a different song to bind us.

Weep, for 'tis healin'; cry out, for 'tis release; cling together, for 'twill remind ye that you've the blessin' of each other's strength to lean on. Think kindly of me, if ye can, for bitterness will drain ye of hope. Don't let that happen, my children, my own, for 'twould break my heart, and yours.

Always,
Mairi

As the words of the letter sank in gradually, Ailsa stood, propelled by something other than sorrow. "Ena. She should be back by now. Where is she?"

"Aye," Alanna murmured. "She and Connor both."

Ailsa froze in alarm. "Connor? What do ye mean?"

"He was with David, but Ena called him and he ran," Alanna said nervously.

"And the look on his face when he turned to go," her husband added, "it frightened me. As if he'd seen a specter or heard a cry of doom. We thought they'd be here, but when we saw Mairi—"

Fear sent Ailsa toward the door. " 'Tis strange, that. Mayhap she's lost; I can feel the shadow darkenin' her path. I must find her." She prayed it was not true, that Ena was not lost so soon after Ailsa had promised Mairi to protect the girl.

"Ye can't do it alone. Let us help," David insisted.

Suddenly everyone was on their feet. "Yes, we must all go. There is so much ground to cover," Lian agreed. "How long has she been gone?"

Thunder and lightning raged outside as if mocking those within. "Far too long," Ailsa whispered. She had been wrong not to listen to the nagging voice in her head, the pain in her heart that was not Mairi. "But perhaps no' yet too late."

Stranded in the narrow confines of the crevice, unable to climb the walls of wet stone, Ena and Connor crouched in wary silence. They could see nothing, hear nothing but the wind howling above them. They clung together, at first from shock at the fall, which jarred their bodies until their teeth chattered, then as protection against the icy chill of the storm, the reverberating thunder, the rain that slashed heavily downward. In minutes, they were soaked through. Ena welcomed the cold and wet as a distraction from her chaotic emotions.

Feeling their way along the slick wall, they found a slight overhang and crept beneath it, not for a moment letting go of one another. To her horror, Ena began to shudder uncontrollably. She was no longer running, punishing her body and using up her breath, certain that if she ran far enough and fast enough, she would escape the blackness. She knew now she could never run that far or that fast; the menacing darkness had followed her here, would follow her forever.

Her linsey-woolsey gown clung to her, heavy with moisture, and she could not stop trembling. Eventually she became aware of Connor holding her, cradling her head against his shoulder, though her sodden hair dripped down his shirt. She felt his hands on her shoulders—the only warmth in this dark, cold place—felt the kindness of his silence, despite the questions that must be whirling in his head. She had led him here; because of her he was caught in the storm, in the crevice that grew darker and chillier by the moment, instead of safe and cozy beside his father's blazing fire.

Yet Connor said nothing, accused her of nothing, asked nothing from her, not even an explanation. He simply held her, rubbing her back awkwardly, bent and contorted as they were beneath the overhang. Unlike her, he had been wearing a greatcoat when the chase began. Brushing away as much moisture as he could, he wrapped it around her. Ena burrowed into the fur lining, looking for a place to hide.

Connor watched all but the top of her head disappear into the folds of his coat. She was still shuddering, gasping for air and release from whatever demons had brought her here. He simply continued to hold her. He asked nothing in return; he knew she had nothing to give. The angry storm, the menacing rocks, the icy cold and the crevice with its steep, slick sides were nothing to him. He did not fear them, only the torment consuming his friend. Connor turned away, but it did no good.

He was watching Ena fall apart before his eyes.

21

"WHERE TO BEGIN?"

"We must light the lanterns!"

"Ena knows all the places to disappear. They could be anywhere."

"Our mourning will have to wait, then," Lian said firmly. "The living come first."

Ailsa rushed about, gathering cloaks and blankets.

"We'd best break into groups to search." Genevra looked away. "It might help to concentrate on finding them. It'll fill our minds and our empty hands."

"Very wise," Lian agreed. "We must go now, soon. To be too late—" She broke off. "It must not happen. We must make certain it does not."

Jenny interrupted the babble of voices. "If ye don't mind, I'd like to help. Ye need as many as ye can get to find anyone in this storm." She could not bear the thought of being left alone with candlelight and emptiness.

Ailsa took her arm. "I'd be grateful. Ye know Ena. Mayhap even a few of her secret places we've no' seen."

Astonished at her friend's simple acceptance, Jenny took the bundle she was given and nodded when David suggested which direction she should take. She was numb and frightened, yet strangely calm. *You're the sensible one.* She only hoped Mairi was right. *'Twill have to be ye who keeps my girls' feet on the ground. You've spent your life learnin' how. Mayhap 'tis time to teach them what ye know.*

"Alanna, I think ye should stay with your grandmother," Ailsa suggested, noticing her daughter's pallor. "To leave her alone in this cold wind and rain seems cruel. Mayhap ye think me daft, but she deserves at least that much."

Alanna sagged with relief, David would find Connor.

She would not be of much help; she was feeling quite dizzy with all that had happened in the last hour. Besides, she wanted a little time alone with Mairi, even if it was too late.

"We should go!" Genevra cried. "We shouldn't waste a moment."

They left together, raincoats pulled low over their foreheads. Ailsa paused on the threshold, unable to speak, her throat was so tight. Quickly, barely making a whisper of sound as she crossed the floor, she stood beside Mairi a second time, pressing her warm palm against the crossed hands on the unmoving chest.

Alanna pretended not to notice her mother's tears as she ducked out into the roiling threat of the storm and the perils and distortions of the quickly falling darkness.

22

A LONG TIME PASSED, THOUGH HE COULD NOT JUDGE HOW long, before Ena stopped shaking and looked up at Connor. He brushed her wet, tangled hair from her cheek and murmured something, but his voice was drowned out by the thunder of boulders plunging down the hillsides, torn loose by the fury of the storm.

The children stiffened as the din echoed off the walls, deafening them. They peered upward, watching for rocks that might lodge at the top of the crevice, trapping them in this place where even the most experienced searchers would not find them. "We can shout till our voices dwindle," Connor said, full of dread, "but none'll hear us over the sound of the storm."

"No, none will hear." Ena's reckless energy had evaporated long before she began to shake in Connor's arms. She, who never lost hope, huddled, dejected and afraid, among unfriendly mountains of stone. She started when a boulder smashed into one wall of the crevice, sending shards of rock slicing downward.

They retreated as far under the overhang as they could, until the cold stone was pressing into their backs. Several large splinters missed them, but they weren't yet safe from the onslaught. One shard bounced off the opposite wall and hurtled toward them, cutting across Connor's cheek. Before the rock had hit the ground, the boy's face was half covered with blood.

Ena's hands shook as the breath she'd been holding exploded in a single word. "Connor!" He was leaning back, head braced against the rough wall, dazed by the sight of blood on his fingers when he reached up to touch his cheek.

Cramped and hampered by her trembling hands and the difficulty of moving, Ena fumbled in her pocket for the tincture of iodine, but it had shattered in the fall. She shuffled the wild herbs, seeking dried kelp to fight off infection. She found some wild alum root and knelt over her friend, sprinkling white power on the jagged gash, which was bleeding profusely. The powder did its work quickly; the blood thickened in the wound and slowed, then stopped altogether. Ena found a tiny piece of dried kelp, which she moistened with rain, then she tore off part of her shift.

Gently prodding the kelp into the cut, she tied her makeshift bandage across his cheek, over his ears and across the bridge of his nose to hold the kelp in place and make certain the bleeding did not start again. By the time she was finished, Connor was less dazed. She could see in his eyes the pain he tried valiantly to hide.

"I've some white willow bark ye can chew to ease the sting. 'Tis no as good as the teas, but I've no way to heat anything, though we've plenty of water." Ena forced herself to sound light and unconcerned, but inside, she was overwhelmed with guilt.

Connor smiled, wincing when the motion tugged at the wound. "Whatever ye have," he told her. "At least I'd the brains to be stranded with a healer."

Ena turned on him, enraged. " 'Tis no' funny, Connor Fraser. Ye could've been killed, and 'twould've been my fault." Her anger was not for him, but for herself. She'd thought of nothing but her own need when she called him, knowing he would come. Her heart pounded so hard she thought it might burst. Tossing the willow bark toward him, she looked away. She couldn't face him. Not after the danger she'd dragged him into. Now night had fallen and the storm had not abated. There was no chance they'd be found before morning. "My fault," she repeated, thinking of Mairi lying motionless forever in a dark hole in the earth. "All my fault."

Connor started to shake his head, then changed his mind when a spasm of pain shot through his wound. He remembered stalking the wildcat, the wounds and illness that had followed. Ena had blamed herself then as well. "Ye didn't force me to come with ye," he said, as he'd often said before, "any more than ye forced me to go after the wildcat last spring. I heard the disturbin' sound of your cry, and I wanted to be with ye. I could no' have left ye alone when I knew ye were in trouble. Ye'd have done the same for me. We've been friends a long time. If we don't care for one another, who will? Who else understands as ye and I understand each other?"

She kept her head turned, and he took her shoulders, forcing her to look at him. "I wanted to be here, *mocharaidh*. 'Twas my choice, and I'm no' sorry I made it."

She stared at him, transfixed, and felt he was telling the truth. "I could no' have borne it if ye'd left me alone. Yet so often when ye come to me, I've gotten ye in trouble or caused ye pain. 'Tisn't fair or right, and I'm sorry for it." She paused, smiled sadly. "But I need ye, Connor. As ye say, no one else understands."

They froze for a long moment, his hands on her shoulders, looking into each other's eyes as if gazing into a mirror. Then a fresh onslaught of rain poured down around them, and Connor felt a tremor of apprehension that had nothing to do with the storm. "Ye said 'twas all your fault," he said hastily, pushing the disquiet away. "I know ye, Ena Rose, and 'twas no' only me ye were talkin' about. 'Tis time to tell me why ye ran in the first place, what ye were runnin' from, don't ye think?"

At the tightening of his hands, Ena felt the same desire to push away the thing that wavered between them like a smoky length of gauze attached to her shoulders at one end and his at the other. She shook her head to make it go. "Aye, 'tis time." So she told him everything. When she finished and saw the compassion in his eyes, she collapsed against him. "Don't be kind to me, Connor. I can no' bear kindness now."

"Then ye'll have to forgive me, for 'tis all I can give ye. Och, Ena, I don't know how ye feel. I can't, for I've never had to make such a choice, even if, in the end, 'twas taken from your hands. But I know you're braver than I, braver than all the others. You would've broken your own heart to ease another's pain."

She wanted to deny it, to say she'd been foolish, but he didn't give her the chance. He drew her into his arms and hugged her tightly; she felt his warmth and affection like a balm that soothed her turmoil. She leaned into him, seeking more, needing it as she needed the wind and water, the moor and the woods.

She was hardly aware that he'd tilted her chin up until their faces were a breath apart. Then his lips brushed hers for an instant, for less than an indrawn breath. Both looked away, shocked and embarrassed by the sensations that assaulted them as the rain had assaulted them, striking their bodies everywhere, leaving a painful tingling in its wake. She shuddered and tried to move away, but there was nowhere to go. Though both were disturbed and shaken by the heat and need between them, they could not let go of one another. They felt they must hold on or they'd fall apart and away into loneliness and darkness.

Only then, with her damp body pressed to his and the storm roiling around them, only when she had told him things she knew she could not tell another, did Ena realize how deeply she cared for Connor Fraser, and he for her. For the first time, cramped and uncomfortable with craggy rock at their backs and above their heads, threatening and protecting them at the same time, did she understand that what she had begun to feel for her childhood friend was passion, need, a bonding of their spirits that was more than friendship. She'd thought herself incapable of such feelings, had wanted to avoid them. For a moment, she was swept up in an exultation she had never thought to know. Like her mother before her, she had found the missing piece of her soul, and, for this instant at least, she was whole.

Then she met Connor's eyes, saw her revelation reflected there; the color and emotion matched her own. His auburn hair, like hers, was dripping. The twins, the Highlanders called them. Connor, Ena's half-sister's son and Ian Fraser's great-nephew. He was nearly as close, by blood as well as spirit, as a brother.

She pulled away, hitting her head on the ledge without feeling the pain. "This can no' be," she whispered. " 'Tis wrong. 'Tis dangerous."

He did not deny it. How could he? We must part, Ena thought. 'Tis the only way. She risked a glance at his face, and could not bear what she saw, what she felt. Quickly, she looked away.

In a day of loss and painful knowledge she'd not wanted to learn, this was the hardest blow of all. Turning fully away, arms wrapped tight about her legs, Ena wanted to shriek out her fury and anguish, but she kept it inside, for Connor's sake. She rested her head on her knees, no longer worried that she might not be rescued in time, no longer intimidated by the slick stone walls rising into the black clouds. She simply didn't care. Except for Connor's sake.

Ena's shoulders slumped forward and she dug her teeth into her knee. The pain did not matter; she hardly noticed. She told herself she was a fool whose spirit, without those she loved to shape and hold it, was disappearing like smoke curling up from a dying fire.

The hours passed too slowly, while the rain fell and the wind raged and they searched for Ena like blind men reaching into unfathomable blackness.

They searched the woods, the riverbank, the stretch of the River Affric Ena had made her own. Nothing. Time and again, they saw furtive shapes in the rain that turned out to be phantoms. The glen was full of specters and false trails that night. Nevertheless, they'd have to search the lochs and braes and huge, rocky moors, and the forest beyond, unknown and menacing.

Conserving their energy, the others traded off resting and forging their way blindly through the torn and battered landscape, but Ailsa would not stop. She was bone weary; what she felt and what she dared not feel had weakened her physically, draining her energy as grieving would have drained her emotions. Lifting her sodden skirts as she prowled along the river seemed a great effort, though David held the lantern and stayed close by.

She was more disheartened with each step they took. Another crashing in the underbrush; an animal frightened by their noisy haste and their bobbing light.

"What if we don't find them?" Ailsa demanded, collapsing on a saturated stump. She clasped her hands at the back of her neck, stretching against them, trying to ease the ache in her back.

"She wasn't running toward something, but running away," David mused.

Lian and Genevra approached, heads down, the droop of their shoulders answering David's question before he asked.

"Where could she have gone?" Lian demanded, leaning gratefully against a solid oak. "She cannot have simply disappeared."

Ailsa raised her head, blue-violet eyes blazing. "No, she can't." She thought of the foothills she knew better than anyone. Better than her daughter, who was distraught, not wanting to be found. The girl might possibly go to the place where her mother was drawn, even in her sleep. "The mountains. We must go to the foothills."

Her sisters looked dubious. "But they will have gotten the worst of the storm. The stones will be slick with rain, the wind chilling and the shadows will lead us astray," Lian said.

It was true. Ena would've been foolish, half-mad to go there, fleeing without thought or wisdom. Ailsa understood that need to escape, had felt it, not only in her childhood, but in the bleak despair that pursued her when she first went to London, and most of all, after Ian died. Three times, despite the danger, because of it, she'd run into the heart of peril. And Ena was her daughter, after all.

Genevra gripped her sister's arm. "We'll find her. Hurry! Signal the others and show us the way."

The wind and thunder raged on and on, but Connor and Ena did not speak. There was nothing they could say that would not make things worse. Slowly, a little at a time, the storm abated. In the middle of the dark night, when it grew damp and still, they slumped down, exhausted, and fell asleep, back to back.

In her fevered, restless sleep, Ena dreamed of Ian and Ailsa in the shadowed cave. They were shivering, so they built a fire, and from that fire, created her, then left her to burn out. But this time, she didn't awaken when the last tendril of flame disappeared. Instead, she lay alone, caught in the cold, dark cave, unable to move, unable to escape. She knew she would lie there until she froze or starved or was crushed by a loose boulder. There was no hope or help in sight.

"Are ye goin' to give up so easily, then?" Mairi's voice drifted over her like a warm blanket. "There's still much to come for ye, my Ena. Will ye turn your back on the future and those who love ye?"

The voice faded and Ena reached for it, sobbing. Out of the stone that rose around her like a prison, she heard a voice cry, "NO!" Only when she opened her eyes did she realize the second voice had been her own. She wondered if she were answering her grandmother or calling Mairi back.

"I'll no' give up!" she shouted.

To her astonishment, Ena heard an answer. It came from high above, out of the blackness. "Don't ye move. We've ropes, but no' enough. They're bringin' more. They'll be here soon." Someone had heard her call out. They had been found at last.

She peered toward the sky as pale lantern light reached her sodden feet, which did not fit under the ledge. It was weak below, but illuminated the face above with a welcome glow. She had lied to herself when she said she did not care if she were rescued. At the sight of her mother, Lian and Genevra, faces streaked with rain, looking down at the huddled children, Ena gave a single sob of relief.

Connor would not die after all. He had been saved from her recklessness, her blindness, the consequences of her deep, wild need.

Ena did not know where the shout that brought Ailsa to the edge of the crevice had come from; she only knew she had to fight the hopelessness that had invaded her. After all, her mother, pale and shaken, hands grasping the edge of the rock till they bled, needed her.

Ena found a little courage in the knowledge that she

had a purpose, a clear, uncomplicated responsibility, an obligation to Mairi, to Ailsa, to Connor and her dead father. She simply must go on.

David and Jenny arrived with the ropes. In the flickering lantern light, they bound the heavy hemp to a thick out-cropping of rock and sent the ropes tumbling into the abyss. They began to shout instructions, but Ena did not need them. She helped Connor wrap the rope around his waist and tie it tight, tugging with all her might to signal the men above before her friend could think of something to say to try and bridge the chasm that had opened between them. Her hands shook, betraying her distress, and she refused to meet Connor's eye as he was pulled away from her.

While they hauled him up slowly, trying to keep the rope steady so he did not swing from side to side and hit the steep rock walls, Ena adjusted her own rope, closed her eyes and said a silent prayer to the gods who had always protected her. She did not know what would happen when she reached the top. Her body, numb with rain and cold, felt far too heavy to be raised out of the freezing, wet dark by a single rope.

Then she felt a tug and she was rising with agonizing slowness past the slick walls she had tumbled down so quickly. Only when she reached the top and saw the faces white with horror did she realize how bad she looked. Vaguely, she heard David and Jenny exclaim over the wound on Connor's cheek, the blood that had turned brown and icy on his shirt and in his hair. Then Ailsa took her daughter's shoulders and held on.

"Where're ye hurt, *mo-run?*"

Ena stared dully at her torn, wet, stained gown. "Don't worry for me. 'Tis Connor's blood." The words came out thick and indistinct. Vaguely, Ena wondered why. "Needs help . . . the wound . . . cleaned and . . . stitched. So many rocks. No light or room . . . to treat . . . properly." Inside her head, she spoke with perfect clarity, but Ailsa frowned, trying to understand.

"I've brought some blankets to wrap her in." Genevra's voice, echoing oddly from within a deep tunnel. "She's frozen through, no doubt. How many hours has she worn that sodden gown?"

Swaying slightly, Ena stared at herself again, wondering why they were talking so anxiously, as if holding back panic. "The . . . blanket . . . to Connor. Not cold. I'm fine." How strange her voice sounded, and how light her head felt.

"We've plenty of blankets for ye both," Ailsa said slowly and distinctly. "I'm thinkin' ye don't know how ill ye are. Connor's safe. 'Tis ye I'm worried about."

Ena shook her head from side to side, ponderously, because it was so enormous. "I'm no'. . . ." She trailed off. She could not remember what she'd meant to say.

"Thank the gods we found ye. We must get ye home now, and warm and fed."

For the second time, the girl shook her head. "Didn't . . . no' to worry . . . about me. Couldn't . . . think."

Ailsa pulled her daughter close. "I know, *mo-run*. I understand."

Voices drifted past, and the yellow glow of lanterns. She tried to hold the blankets close, but she hadn't the strength. Her eyes were bleary; the shadows of people wavered, stretched and faded. The sky began to rotate and she followed the motion with her head. There was pain somewhere, and the spinning made her want to retch. Instead, she slumped, unconscious against her mother's shoulder.

Ailsa cradled Ena protectively. This, after all, was the girl who cared for wounded animals, who rescued them from careless hunters, putting herself in danger again and again, but heedless of that danger. The child who'd treated Connor's wound in the dark and the rain, who'd stood, barely conscious, swaying, cold and weary, and insisted they take care of her friend. She did not seem aware of her own weakness. This girl who could not bear the pain of others, but ignored her own. The girl who had been willing, all alone, to fulfill Mairi's last wish.

"You've changed my life, Ena-*aghray*, in so many ways. I wonder if ye'll ever understand how much," Ailsa whispered.

23

MAIRI'S BODY WAS LAID OUT IN HER BEST WOOLEN GOWN, HER hair left unbound to flow around her shoulders. She wore the red Rose plaid like a shawl. She lay upon late roses and leaves of all color and kind—golden, red, flaming orange, yellow, rust. Around the base of the bier were other offerings of rare herbs to sweeten her journey, precious glass bottles and sketches and pieces of fabric gathered into multicolored fans, wood carvings of animals and one of Mairi's face.

The window coverings were tied back and the door wide open, so the fleeting light would illuminate her face. The floors had been swept and the furniture pushed back against the walls to make room for the mourners who streamed in to pay their respects to a woman all had trusted, many had loved, and none would likely forget.

Ailsa, Lian and Genevra had seen that Mairi's body was washed and dressed and placed on the bier, but they were reluctant to leave her. So Jenny Fraser had been the one to go search for the last fall flowers and clusters of brightly colored leaves to place around the body. The sisters had collected tiny, beautiful treasures to fill their mother's hands and lie as homage at her feet.

Jenny had cooked huge pots of stew and scotch broth and pepper soup, while Alanna baked scones and baps and black buns for those who came to honor the dead. The bier was carefully placed so Mairi was the center around which life flowed, just as she had been while she lived.

Ena sat in a corner, shivering and ill, drinking the herb decoctions Ailsa and Lian gave her, allowing them to put poultices on her chest, swallowing her hops at night. But she did not speak or moan or weep. She was numb, and glad that it was so, because she'd not escaped the void after all, but only made it darker and deeper. She was aware of the low murmur of respectful voices, the constant activity, except late at night when Jenny and Alanna left and a melancholy hush fell over Ailsa and her sisters.

Much of the time the girl drifted, half awake, half dreaming. She was swimming in murky water, each stroke slow and difficult, as if the water were pushing against her, holding her back. Her lungs ached and she needed to take a breath, but she did not rise toward the surface. She knew she might find light there; she might see. She preferred the gloom, though her chest burned from lack of air.

She changed her nightrail when a clean one was brought, but made no effort to wash or comb her hair, or to clean her hands and feet. Though Alanna and David spent more time here than at home, Connor came only once, for Mairi's sake, then slipped away without meeting Ena's gaze. She was glad of that too. Above the surface of the stagnant water was Connor, along with the air and the light.

The adults might have saved her from the storm and rocks and danger, but Ena was still lost, still trying to find her way home.

Apprehensively, Jenny knelt beside the girl. She did not care if Ena listened; she talked just the same, in a soothing voice laced with the cadence of the burn in winter, flowing slow beneath the ice.

"The women from the glen have no' stopped comin' to the door with their best mutton stew or pasties or apple pies.

Ye should see their faces, Ena. They're Scots and don't know how to feel their grief, only to show their respect with a dish of food or a blend of herbs or a bit of ribbon they can spare. Ye can see the devastation in their eyes, though."

Ena shifted uncomfortably, as Jenny leaned closer, whispering, "We're all mournin' Mairi Rose, every man, child or woman in the glen. Have ye no' seen the flowers brightenin' her bier? The people've had to search; the blooms are near all wilted, but they've brought what few they've found." She sighed at Ena's obedient nod.

"Ye and Ailsa, Lian and Genevra, at least have the memory of livin' in her croft, knowin' her as few ever did. 'Tis no' the same as havin' her alive, but 'tis a great deal, just the same. She'd want ye to remember that."

Choking back her feelings, the girl stared at her crossed ankles.

"She'd never ask for something frivolous or selfish, our Mairi," Jenny continued doggedly. "She's no' capable of such a thing. 'Tis what ye must believe, or God himself can no' be what he seems and the world is but a bad dream. And that I'll never believe. No' because I've seen God's face or felt his hand on my shoulder, but because of Mairi Rose's givin' and forgivin' heart."

Something brittle inside the girl threatened to snap, so she closed her eyes and dove into the water, far beyond the reach of the light. She had not yet wept for her grandmother. Nor did she now, as Jenny touched her matted hair and shook her head in surrender.

Just after dawn, Lian sat next to Ena, Mairi's words echoing in her head. *Take care of her; she's more fragile than ye know.*

"I am worried about you. You who were always moving are too still and too contained." *Remember that this mornin' she was a child, and now she's lost between childhood and the woman she'll one day be.* Lian said a prayer to Kwan Yin, Goddess of Mercy, and touched her niece's shoulder.

Ena glanced up, dazed. Coughing violently, she shook with the severity of her illness. Lian held the girl's feverish body and felt through her labored pulse and tissue-fine skin, the pain she was trying to quell or deny.

She can no' guess what 'tis to grieve. I ask ye to teach her to feel the pain.

Her aunt rubbed her back in slow, rhythmic circles, trying to calm her, to warm her, to wake her. "The sorrow is poisoning your blood, and will do so until you release it through your tears."

"I don't see ye cryin'," Ena said. It was a defense and a challenge.

Lian bowed her head. Though she had wept, it had been rarely and at night when she was alone. Her eyes were not red or swollen and she stood more erect than usual, because she herself could not give in completely to the ache of abandonment and grief.

Show her how to heal. Ye know how, every one of ye.

Lian had known, once. But now, this instant, she knew nothing.

The day they buried Mairi was warm and bright. The gods who had given the gift of false summer to the glen seemed to have saved this particular day, so fine that the air shimmered with clarity.

Ailsa, Alanna, David, Lian, Genevra and Jenny sat around the kitchen table, soaking in the stillness. The other mourners had stayed away; these last hours were for the family alone. Only Connor had gone, claiming he was going to the Valley of the Dead to be certain everything was ready. He had not mentioned Ena's name, and neither did his parents. The small group stared at one another, speechless, waiting for they knew not what, only that wait they must.

No one had seen Ena this morning; she'd already been gone when they rose. Now, as they sat in dull anticipation, she appeared in the doorway. The air seemed to sigh in relief and thanksgiving.

She had bathed and washed her hair, brushing it out and letting it fall loose in auburn waves to below her waist. She had cleaned her fingernails, always grimy with loam and herbs and animal dust, and wore tiny leather slippers on her feet. Her gown was deep rose, with a scooped neck and puffed sleeves trimmed in fine ribbon.

Once, long ago, Mairi Rose had fashioned a gown just like it for her young daughter Ailsa, who'd worn it for the Beltaine celebrations. For a moment, Ailsa looked away, unable to see through her tears.

Not only had Ena risen from her place in the corner, she'd transformed herself from a dusty, untidy child to a young lady. Still, she had not slept since Mairi's death; her eyes were red and irritated, and there were dark bruises beneath.

Ailsa watched her daughter, unaware that she was endlessly turning her mother's wedding ring on her finger.

The sound of voices drifted in the open door and Ena looked up eagerly, expectantly. When the sound trailed off, the girl collapsed inward, her face a mask.

Ailsa saw her daughter turn toward the door, saw her retreat once more within herself. Ena had thought she heard her grandmother's voice, had waited for Mairi to come in and join them. She had let fall, for an instant, the shield hiding her youth and vulnerability. Mairi had foreseen this moment, this struggle, this loss of innocence. *She doesn't recognize the gift of her innocence, or the rarity of that pure, untainted wisdom.* A shadow had fallen on Ena Rose, and the child did not know how to see anymore. Ailsa's heart ached for her daughter, but the girl disappeared again before her mother could comfort her.

David and Connor, Malcolm Drummond and Alistair Munro gathered to carry the bier to the valley. Connor glanced around nervously as he came in, but his father reassured him. "She's no' here, lad. Gone ahead to the valley no doubt."

The boy gaped, wondering how his father knew, but David only smiled sadly. " 'Tis no' so difficult a puzzle. You've not been near her nor spoken her name in these few days. I needed no magic to guess something was amiss."

Sighing with relief, Connor took his place beside the bier. He was doubly grateful Ena was not there in that intimate moment, not only because of his grief for Mairi, but because he did not yet know what to do about the things they had discovered in the cold, dark rain.

The men had barely bent their knees to brace the burden on their shoulders when Ailsa, Lian and Genevra were upon them. Alanna stood in the background, weeping quietly.

"Not yet!" Genevra cried.

"Give us a few moments more," Lian said softly.

"Once ye take her out that door, she'll belong to us no more," Ailsa added.

"She never truly belonged to ye. Ye were given the grace of her presence and love for a short time only. Ye can no' demand more, when already you've had so much." Jenny Fraser's hazel eyes were veiled by memory and filmed with tears. "Believe me. I learned that lesson long ago."

"Yes, but. . . ." Finding no argument, Genevra trailed off.

"Mayhap 'tis time ye accept the truth and let her go graciously, with dignity and compassion."

Ailsa shook her head. "I don't think I can."

Resting her hand on her friend's shoulder, Jenny closed the space between them. "But ye can, Ailsa Rose, because Mairi's blood runs in your veins, and her fortitude and her strength. She let go willingly, knowin' her family was gathered round her, that she'd had the chance to see ye together again. She chose to hold her loved ones close and say good-bye in her own way and her own time."

One tear, then another, trailed down Jenny's cheek. "I only hope that every one of us will be as lucky."

The boulders in the valley glittered in the clear, unclouded light of the sun. When Charles Kittridge had been laid to rest, it had been bitter cold, the wind had howled and kept his daughters teetering on the edge of his freshly dug grave. For Mairi, the wind was still, hidden among the rocks, and autumn had retreated, so the sky was dusted with thin wisps of cloud and the sunlight was a golden wash over the landscape.

Standing alone by the newly dug grave, Ena looked insubstantial, seemed to fade into the standing stones. She did not move when her family entered the valley, though her eyes followed each step.

When the small group gathered around the plain pine coffin, they felt a presence in the air. Glancing up, they saw that, though the people of the glen had chosen not to disturb this private family ceremony, they had nevertheless come to bid their Mairi Rose good-bye. They stood far back and above the rock wall at the rear of the valley, clinging to precarious footholds, crouched in caverns and on ledges and at the gaping mouths of caves. They pressed themselves against the jagged stones at the top to be as near as possible, yet not interfere. They were silent, every one of them, their faces worn by hard work and the sun and the dour mask the Highlanders wear to cover their pain.

Sixteen years ago, Ailsa, Lian and Genevra had stood hand in hand—angry, desperate, bereft, holding one another upright, afraid to fall into the darkness of their father's grave. Today they stood linked arm in arm, though they were no longer afraid of falling. They could only be grateful for the lovely day, and for David, who told them Mairi would have laughed at sun and sky and clouds, and said her Charlie was welcoming her home.

And so it seemed. Where once there had been four cairns, there were five, the last still raw and open to the pale blue sky. David Fraser had spoken to Ailsa, and together they'd chosen a long low stone, wide enough to encompass two graves. On the left, David had carved Charles Kittridge's name and dates of birth, marriage and death, on the right, Mairi's. Beneath the two names he'd carefully chipped out the words Ailsa had given him, words Mairi'd said to each of them at one time or another. Then he'd put the stone at the head of Charles and Mairi's last place of rest.

Slowly, saying each word with care, nearly succeeding at disguising the quiver in her voice, Ailsa read the inscription aloud. *"Deireadh gach comuin, sgaoileadh; Deireadh gach cogaidh, sith.* The end of all meetin's, partin'; The end of all strivin', peace." She knelt to place a luminous blue stone on the lid of the coffin. "You've earned your peace, my Mother, for your strivin' was long and stormy. Bless ye."

As Ailsa straightened, Genevra placed a deep red stone beside the blue. Though she tried to speak, no words would come, so she kissed her fingers and pressed them against the cool, smooth surface of the stone. Lian had found a stone of gilt and silver, which she put beside the others, whispering, "I will not forget the lessons you have taught me, nor the miracles you have shown me. I will try to teach my children what you would have had them know." When she rose, her cheeks were wet with tears.

Alanna lay her moss-green stone on the pine and smiled a bittersweet smile. "Thank ye, Gran, for bringin' me home."

Finally, Jenny knelt to place a wreath of autumn leaves around the small circle of treasures above Mairi's heart. "Ye had faith in me when I had none. Ye asked for my strength and my vow. Only then did I see I had both to give. Rest easy, my friend."

Reluctantly, moving without grace or lightness of foot or the assurance that had always drawn her forward, Ena crouched and slipped a tiny carved boat among the stones. "For your journey, Grandy," she managed to say. "There's room for two." She rose awkwardly, eyes fiery silver in the clear, bright sunlight. She kept her arms stiff at her sides, but could not hide the quivering of her body.

Everyone turned to her, waiting, and she glanced up at the wall of Highlanders to find strength enough to continue.

They'd asked that Ena say the blessing over her grandmother's grave. She'd been there at the end, and her blessings were strong and lingering.

"Are ye certain?" Ailsa whispered in her daughter's ear, dampening the girl's face with her tears. "Ye need no' do this simply because we asked. Ye need no' prove to us how brave ye are. We know, *mo-chridhe*. We believe." Her voice was rough from weeping, but she did not falter once.

Ena held her breath for a long moment, paled and flushed and paled again. "I can . . . I *want* to do it." She looked into her mother's eyes with thanks she could not express, started to squeeze Ailsa's hand, drew back abruptly from the thought of a compassionate human touch. She was not brave enough for that. Smiling crookedly, Ena moved to the foot of the grave.

She spoke in a small voice, which nevertheless carried around the inner circle of standing stones, so that all who'd come to honor Mairi would hear. She did not look down into the earth, but up at the distant sky. She did not realize she was shaking from head to toe. "Mairi Rose Kittridge," she said, "you're so much to so many, so much more than can be captured or expressed in words. Your heart was human, your soul better than we can understand. But we knew ye. For that alone we must thank the gods all the days of our lives, which you've touched and changed and treasured. We can but send ye on your way and wish ye well. Wish ye as much as you've given others:

> "May ye go forth under the light of the sun,
> May ye go forth with the splendor of fire,
> May ye go forth supported by the strength
>   of the earth,

May ye be surrounded,
      above, below, about,
         by the gods who have taken ye home."

She faltered on the final word, but stood up straight, unbending.

Then David reached over to rest his hand on her shoulder and squeezed just a little, in reassurance and understanding. Ena shuddered as her resolve disintegrated. Oblivious of anything but the lifeless wind and wide empty sky, Ena Rose slid from beneath David's hand and fled what she could no longer pretend to endure.

24

THERE WAS ONLY ONE PLACE TO GO, ONE PLACE THAT WAS hers, that would never change unless she changed it, one place where she'd be safe.

Ena ran blindly, lead by instinct and thirteen years of following the paths that had been forged before her feet first touched them. She ran, and the dust rose around her in clouds, coating her single lovely dress with loam dried by the full, unfiltered sun. No mist softened the sound of her flight or cleansed the dirt from her face, or made her grief less brutal.

When she reached the hollow oak, she kicked at the door, tugged it, but her fingers were numb and clumsy. When it did not open, she collapsed, grazing her arms on the rough bark, pressed her back hard against the trunk, pulled her legs up to her chest and locked her arms around them. She lay her face on her bent knees while her teeth chattered and her body trembled uncontrollably.

It was too much, too dark, too hopeless. She shook and

cried out soundlessly and blinked her dry eyes, raw from lack of sleep. But still she did not weep.

Ena disappeared so quickly that it was a moment before the others, blinded by tears, saw her running toward the entrance of the valley.

"I'll go after her," Ailsa said.

She started forward, but was kept back by one hand on each arm. Lian and Genevra held their half-sister without planning to do so. Instinct alone compelled them.

"Let her go," Genevra murmured.

"Ena has been among people for too long, I think. She needs time alone to feel her grief. Leave her for a little, Ailsa. Please."

The sisters did not notice that Connor turned, face streaked with tears, to watch his friend flee. They did not see him take a step, hesitate, reach up to run his fingers through his hair, tugging it as if, by causing himself physical pain, he could avoid the other. Finally, he looked to his mother and father.

Alanna and David recognized the indecision on their son's face—the anguish for his great-grandmother's loss, his fear of losing Ena, his fear of finding her and facing whatever he had kept inside since the day the children disappeared. His parents had once feared his connection to Ena; they feared even more his silence and sudden distance from her. They looked at each other and nodded in silent agreement.

"Go to her," Alanna said. "Ye can no' avoid her forever."

"Besides, I think she needs ye," David added. "Ye and no other."

Connor stared at them, stunned. "Ye want me to follow Ena?"

His father touched Connor's hair, rested his hand on his son's shoulder. "She's frail and vulnerable just now, and I doubt she'd let us near. Can ye comfort her?"

Shifting from foot to foot, Connor considered. "Aye," he said at last. "But—"

He was afraid, they realized. Perhaps that should have made his parents hold him back. Except they knew this time he would obey them. That, too, was disturbing. There was something amiss between their son and Ena, and only the children themselves could make it right. "But?" Alanna repeated.

Connor stood taller, straightening his slumped shoulders. "It makes no matter," he said. "She should no' be alone. I'll go." He touched his father's hand, nodded to his mother and followed the path Ena had taken. He did not need the marks of her feet in the warm earth to know where she had gone. There was only one place where she could find her childhood and clutch it close.

He ran, fleet as any deer, fleet as Ena, for he had changed as much as she.

When he found her, she sat shivering against the tree, her hideaway, her refuge. Connor stopped before he reached her, watching. She sat hunched over, her legs pulled in tight, her head against her knees, quaking as she had in the crevice, as if she could not stop. She looked small and helpless and infinitely fragile.

Connor went to her, weeping, but not for Mairi anymore. The sight of Ena, alone and devastated, undid him. Afraid as he was to touch her, aware as he was of the aching tenderness that threatened them in ways he did not wish to comprehend, he could not stay away.

Because, though he had matured, become wary, had awakened to the danger Ena represented, just now he needed her too.

Sensing his presence, she looked up, saw his tears and the compassion in his eyes. She reached out to him. "Connor." So many things she put into that single word.

He was beside her in an instant, wrapping her in his

arms, cradling her like a child that knows no comfort but the weight of gentle arms about her. Ena laid her head on Connor's shoulder, felt the damp spot where his own tears had fallen, and lost the last of her control. The tears she had denied, rejected, refused to acknowledge, built up until she could not hold them back. She slipped her arms around Connor, held him as if to let go would be to fall into the blackness, and she wept.

Shaking and shivering, she let the tears flow. Her resolve had become dust, her strength the mist that had not touched the glen since dawn, her numbness an avalanche of pain released from long confinement.

The more she wept, the tighter Connor held her. He rested his head on her hair and cried his own tears for the depth of her torment. He could not heal her, make her whole and well, as she'd done for him more than once. He could only lock his hands around her and hold tight as the tremors from her body passed into his.

They wept for a long time, while the shadows of branches shifted around them and the water flowed behind them, leaving them stranded, young, too close and too vulnerable on the bank. They wept until they were raw and withered from their sorrow for what they had lost, and what, inevitably, they must now lose.

When she stopped trembling, Ena absorbed Connor's warmth, the solid reality of his body, the thoughts, regrets and fears that passed between them, unspoken.

Connor leaned into her, eyes closed, the salt taste of tears on his tongue and the smell of soap and heather drifting up from her damp hair. This was where he belonged, where he wanted to be every moment of his life to come. To hold her when the storm had passed, to feel her fold herself inside the shelter of his body. To braid his fingers with hers and know she was clinging as tightly as he and neither wanted to let go. Not now, not in an hour, not in a lifetime. "Ena," he murmured. "Och, Ena!"

She tilted her head so she could look at his face. "Aye, Connor. Aye."

There were tears on her cheeks and he brushed them away, though more came after. When she closed her eyes and pressed the crown of her head into the curve of his throat, he sighed, then shuddered as it struck him like a boulder on his chest that they had fallen into one another as they had during that thunderous, black night.

He raised his head so his chin no longer touched her hair, though it took all the determination he had.

Ena sensed the change but did not draw away. She had no determination, no energy, no will. "I heard them talkin' one night," she said, "about maybe takin' me away from here." She wanted him to denounce them, to deny what both knew to be true.

He cleared his throat, praying for the words to come, and all the while, holding her closer, tighter. "Mayhap . . . 'twould be . . . best."

Losing her balance as she pushed away from him, Ena fell hard. "How can ye say that, Connor Fraser, when ye know—"

"Because I know. I can't be seein' ye every day, pretendin' there's no danger, that nothin's changed. We know each other too well and too long, have grown too close and care too much to be near and no' drown in our need." He stared at his hands to avoid her gaze.

"No." One word, whispered low enough to fade into the shadows.

"Aye. Think, Ena. I can no leave. My parents need me to help with the crops and cattle and sheep. But you're free; your mother told ye so. And your aunts are beggin' ye to visit. I know ye want to go. Part of ye, anyway. Mayhap 'twill even stop the nightmares."

Her utter stillness ate away at him until he looked up to see fresh tears, slow tears, silent ones, sliding down her flushed and swollen cheeks. "I'm no' strong enough to give ye up," she said.

Connor peered at her watery gray-green eyes, and felt a jolt go through him. He'd always thought her so much stronger, so much more resilient and wise. But she could not—would not—see that he was right. She knew it somewhere in her heart, of that he was certain. But the expression on her face made him equally certain she would not bend. She couldn't.

He realized in an instant that he would have to do the impossible—take on the heartbreaking burden of saving them from themselves. "This can no' go on. Ye know it can't." He could barely speak over the pounding of his heart. He'd always thought it would be she who turned him away and he who'd not accept it. He'd thought she was the leader and he the follower, but in the past few months *she* had begun to lean on *him*. He had turned to her for adventure, to follow her strange whims, to share her freedom and her courage, but she had come to him for solace, reassurance, understanding.

Why had it taken him so long to notice? Why now, when it was too late and they had come too far? " 'Tis over, what we shared. We're older now, and this must end as well." His eyes burned with tears when he'd thought himself wrung dry, and he saw the shimmer of moisture in Ena's eyes. "I'm sorry. Ye can't know how much. Ye'll never know that, though ye see what others can't."

Ena stared at her oldest friend and knew he would not relent, that she could not make him, even had she wished to. She could not keep his soul in her hand by wrenching him apart with tenderness. "I do know," she whispered. "I've always known." Known, too, the day would come when they would go their separate ways. But not now, when she needed him so much. "You're right," she forced herself to say. "We've no choice, really. I wonder if we ever did?"

She looked away so Connor would not see her break. Slowly, every part of her body aching and empty, she turned toward the river.

Connor watched her for a long time, but she did not turn back. He had won. And in winning, lost his spirit, the reflection of his soul. He didn't know if he could survive without her. As he started home, he glanced back once, and though he tried, he could not call out to her, or shout his rage to the Celtic gods. They were not listening anymore. As he disappeared into the autumn trees, the emptiness within grew until it suffocated him and broke him.

Ena did not look up; she could not watch him go. She stared at a tangle of twigs and moss circling in the river until it was sucked under and disappeared. Then there was nothing left.

Nothing at all.

Time seemed to expand and shrink before Ena's eyes, becoming one with the murmur of the burn.

Without warning, soundlessly, Lian appeared beside her to sit staring at the river—the rush and flow and sparkle, undimmed by Mairi's death. It did not seem possible. "How can this place be unchanged?" Lian wondered. "How can the wind blow without Mairi's breath to guide it? Or the burns run and the sunlight turn them glittering bronze without her vigor and her radiance? Or squirrels run up and down trees and deer cross the golden moors without Mairi's blessing to give them speed?"

Ena had intended to remain silent, refusing company or comfort. But Lian's questions made her fight back tears that burned against her eyelids. "I don't know. 'Tis true when the heart stops beatin' the body lies stiff and lifeless. Yet Mairi was our heart, and still we move and think and feel and reach." She did not look at her aunt, but at her bare feet, buried in moss.

"I know there is something to reach for still, for I have lost many in my lifetime, and always the world went on. Only today it seems wrong. I want to pull the sun down from the sky and leave us in darkness outside as deep as the darkness within. Today the wind should howl and the rain fall and clouds cut us off from the light. The glen itself should grieve for Mairi as it did the day my father was buried." Lian pressed her forehead into her knees, welcoming the discomfort, the dull ache at her temples. "Then perhaps I would hear her voice once more, and I could tell her how much—"

"She knew, Aunt Lian. She always knew."

Aware that Lian was shaking, Ena quelled a rush of fear. *Remember, no matter how difficult it is for ye, 'tis harder for them,* Mairi had warned. The girl wanted to turn away, but it was not in her nature. She could not help but examine Lian's wound and want to heal it. As she'd tried to heal Mairi's. *Can't ye see how hard 'tis for me to watch ye suffer? Do ye no' think 'tis breakin' my heart?* "Ye and my mother and Aunt Genevra, ye feel each others' pain, do ye no'? How can ye endure it when you've sorrow of your own?"

Blinking in surprise, Lian regarded her niece. "Because it is the price you pay for loving someone completely. The price is high, but you are forgetting that I also feel their joy, and that is more than worth the cost." She tilted her head in curiosity. "I thought you understood that."

Ena stood abruptly, legs tingling from disuse. Shaking her head emphatically, she began to follow the river bank.

Mairi's words came back to Lian like a sudden gust of wind. *Ena has the reckless courage of youth and a powerful faith in the rightness of the cycles of nature.* Apparently, she had lost that courage and that faith.

Lian followed her niece and the soothing whisper of the water, letting the sound flow through her, finding within it the words she sought. "Mairi was afraid to live and we to live without her. But you understood at once what we refused to see."

"Now I'm afraid." Ena caught sight of a piece of bright

green fern floating erratically down the burn. "I used to think the glen would never change nor I grow up nor people leave. I felt safe then." She reached out to catch the bit of green, but it moved beyond her reach. "But 'twas a lie. There is no safety; everything changes; we all grow old. I've no power to stop it."

They moved into the shadow of tall firs and gnarled branches that held the sun back from the water. Taken aback, Lian fell silent.

Concentrating desperately on the blurred path of moss-covered boulders and reeds and soggy loam, Ena realized her throat was closing, cutting off air and words.

"When I was a child, I lived in fear, always hiding, always wary, always waiting for danger to come devour me." Frowning at the memory, Lian avoided a muddy hole surrounded by tall grass. "I was small and impotent until the time came when I must be strong. I was nearly destroyed by political intrigues, by mistrust and fear in those who held the swords and power, by violent prejudice against anyone foreign. My isolation was my salvation." She realized Ena was ominously silent.

"For you it was different. Your isolation made you blind, your skill at healing, your compassion made you vulnerable. I think, for these things, you have suffered."

The girl veered away from the river and into the green speckled hush of the woods. "Mayhap. But I was happy too."

Lian folded her hands inside her wide sleeves, pensive and uncertain. Then she remembered Ena's face the night of the *ceilidh*, when they'd pulled her from among the rocks, when she'd stood at the foot of her grandmother's grave. *She's granted me the favor of wantin' to release me*, Mairi had written. *Grant her the favor of holding her close*. She stopped within the shadows of the woods as Ena stepped into the light of a small clearing.

Instinctively, the girl turned to find her aunt watching.

"I do not know if this is the right time or the worst I could have chosen. I only know I can keep my thoughts to myself no more."

Ena took a step forward as if to stop her, but Lian was immobile, stubborn as stone.

"For some time we have written and spoken of your visiting us in Burgundy. You would be, already *have* made yourself part of the family. You could go to school for a time with my sons, meet other children, learn a great deal. You could stay for as long as you care to, or as little. You could go to Genevra afterward, if you choose." Noticing Ena's dismay, she added, "I am not speaking of forever. The glen will be here when you return, I promise." She smiled Mairi's bittersweet smile. "I have seen in your eyes that you wish for this but are reluctant to say the words."

There'll always be change, Connor had warned her. *New possibilities and places and wonders. Surely you'll no' stay here all your life.* She'd answered him as the foolish child she'd been: *Everything I know is here.* She remembered the night Lian and Genevra had opened their magic chest and handed her beauties and mysteries more seductive than she could have imagined. They had so surprised her that she'd allowed everyone to see her frustration and longing. Ailsa had given her blessing, but it had not been easy for her.

"My mother needs me." The answer surprised her as much as Lian. "I can't leave her alone."

"Ailsa is not alone. She has Alanna and David and Connor, her grandson. She has Jenny Fraser." Her aunt paused. "I think perhaps you have tried too hard to give Ailsa joy, to make her forget her loss and sorrow. I can only tell you that it took years and a very patient man to teach me I must live for myself and not my mother, that by following my own heart I would fulfill her hopes for me. It is the same for you."

Go where your spirit, your inner voice leads, for your heart's too tangled in the vines of the glen, and can no' always hear the truth. Will ye promise me that? She'd promised Mairi faithfully. But—"I'm afraid to leave. 'Tis all I know."

"I understand," Lian murmured. "The Middle Kingdom had always been my home, and though I was always afraid, I loved it there. I loved my mother's courtyards, which lay behind high walls that kept tranquillity and peace inside. I loved the customs, the festivals, the history of what I believed to be the center of the world. China flowed through my blood, nourishing me. It was all I knew or cared to know."

She gazed back in time until her face seemed young and the passion of youth burned in her eyes. "I was forced to go to save my life, but the leaving broke my heart. I wondered what good life would be if I had no heart, no hope. Then I reached the glen and my father and Mairi Rose. And learned that I could love them too. I found sanctuary in the bleak, compelling mountains and the rushing waterfalls and a tiny, smoke-stained croft. Again, I did not wish to go. If I had stayed, here or in the Middle Kingdom, I would never have known Chervilles, never met my friend Cheng or my husband or conceived my sons. I would have missed the best, the happiest years of my life. And as Mairi pointed out, I never choose the easy way. Nor, I think, do you."

Ena shuddered when the breeze brushed her neck, ruffling her hair. In that instant she heard a voice, stronger, more enticing than the memory it was. *Ena, my heart, I'll be with ye in the wind and the mist and the sun on the water. Ye'll hear my voice, softly, so ye'll no' be certain, unless ye believe. There are brighter places than this dim croft. Go out and find them. As I did once. As I do now.*

Ena believed, would never cease to believe in Mairi and her wisdom and her vision of things to come. To stay here would be to surrender, to admit she had not the confidence, the capacity or curiosity to go forward. She was astonished to realize she was not yet ready to give up, not when the women in her family had survived so much, had persevered, had eventually prevailed. Their blood flowed in her veins, as, she hoped, did their courage and resolve. She did not want to disappear, even into paradise.

When Lian opened her arms, Ena ran to her, holding tight to what she'd only just come to know, to love, to yearn for. "Take me away," she whispered into her aunt's embroidered satin gown. "I think now I am ready."

Lian was not prepared for the feather weight of the girl's arms around her, or the heat of her body or the trust in her eyes.

Weep, for 'tis healin', Mairi Rose had commanded her daughters at the end. *Cry out, for 'tis release; cling together, for 'twill remind ye that you've the blessin' of each other's strength to lean on.*

Lian had thought only of Ailsa and Genevra, and so had been careful. And safe. But Ena was clinging to her now, and it was her youth, her changing innocence, her faith that was a blessing. When she glanced up at her aunt's rigid face and began to pull away, Lian cried, "No!" and drew her close and let her tears flow.

25

AFTER A FORTNIGHT, ENA AND HER MOTHER SAT ON THE low bench in the herb garden, plaids wrapped close about them to keep away the chill. Both wore gray out of respect, with violet ribbons at waist and wrists because Mairi Rose had abhorred the outward shows of mourning. Ailsa's hair was pinned in a crown of copper braids, Ena's caught back loosely with a violet ribbon. Mother and daughter had stayed close in the last few days, closer than usual, because they found comfort in one another, without the need for words of explanation.

Despite the consolation of Ailsa's presence and devotion, Ena rarely slept, and when she did drift off, she was plagued by poignant, vivid dreams that would not let her rest. Nor could she remember them when she woke. "I wonder if I'll ever sleep soundly, without dreams again," she murmured.

She seemed very fragile, but Ailsa knew by now that, underneath, her daughter was not easily broken. "Ye will, *mo-chridhe*, in time. But ye must take care of yourself for the now or there'll be nothing left of ye to crawl into your bed at night." She made light of it to hide her concern.

Ena half-smiled at the exaggeration, though she'd not been eating as she should, and it showed on her slender frame. In spite of it all, her body continued to mature; she could no longer deny that she'd grown taller, for her gowns were too short, and despite her lack of appetite, they'd grown too tight in the bodice. She had finally begun to try to accept what she could not stop. As Jenny Fraser had warned, she'd grow into a woman whether she would or no'.

Ena leaned against her mother and Ailsa drew her close to protect her from the thick, stinging mist. There was so little she could shield her from anymore.

"Ye saved me from myself," Ena said, reading her mother's thoughts in her eyes. "With Gran. I thought I knew what I was doin', that I was brave enough to carry it through, but I was wrong. I called out to ye without realizin' and ye came and took the cup from my hands. I ken 'twas no' easy, that sacrifice. But ye didn't hesitate." The girl's eyes shone with admiration and gratitude.

You're finer than ye'd have them think. Finer and stronger and truer. Ailsa shivered. She had not, after all, forgotten the sound of Ian Fraser's voice.

I am no' strong enough. No' for this, she'd told him in her sleep on the night her mother said that she wanted to leave them forever. And he'd replied, *I asked ye once to believe in me, and ye gave me that gift. Now I return it threefold. I believe in ye.*

Ailsa became aware of her daughter staring, her expression unreadable. "I love ye, Mam. Ye know that, don't ye?"

"I know, birdeen. And I ye." There was more, much more; she could feel it in the tautness of Ena's body, the words that hovered, unspoken, on her lips. "What is't, birdeen? What's troublin' ye?"

Ena drew a deep breath, letting it out slowly. "I want to go away for a while—I'd no' be knowin' how long—to stay with Aunt Lian and her family. And mayhap, after, with Aunt Genevra and Uncle Alex." She lifted her head into the mist, remembering Ailsa's expression the night Alanna had encouraged Ena to go after the things she yearned to know. She took her mother's hand. "If I don't go, I feel I'll sink into the earth and the sadness thick as fog in the glen. I know it'll lift one day, but just now 'tis makin' every step I take so hard."

Ailsa had expected something like this since the night when the contents of the chest had been revealed and she'd seen the look in her daughter's eyes. And that had been before Mairi's death. It made sense that the girl would want to leave behind the unhappy memories of the last months, for here they would haunt her night and day. Yet Ailsa's heart constricted at the thought of Ena's going. Just as, sixteen years before, she'd been heartsick over Alanna's choice to stay. Odd, but she could remember Mairi's wise advice quite clearly.

'Tis a mother's obligation, her heartbreak and her joy to let her children go. She must give each the gift of their own life and choices, then the gift of freedom to make of that life what they will. Ye can no' protect them from growth and change and pain.

Ena wondered at her mother's lovely, sad smile. "I only want ye to love me enough to let me go with your blessin', to wish me well."

Looking at her daughter's hopeful face, eyes wide and eager and apprehensive, Ailsa said, "I love ye that much and more." Her chest ached at the natural joy of Ena's smile. "Forbye, I'd no' have ye miss what lies beyond these hills. Even if ye stayed, ye'd always wonder and regret what ye'd never known."

"I'll be back, ye ken. I could no' stay away forever. Besides, now Lian and Genevra and Alex and Émile own the Hill and have told my cousins about it. So they can't stay away so long again." The girl frowned at a sharp memory of her last glimpse of Connor's face. She was trying to forget, though she knew it was impossible. " 'Tis no' only curiosity that calls me now. There are people, things best left behind."

There was a moment's pause. "I suspected as much. I've seen ye two together once too often. 'Tis hardest to go when ye know 'twill never be the same between ye. I can guess what's in your heart, and I know 'tis as honest as 'tis painful. But the wound will heal. 'Twill one day be but a ragged scar, and ye the stronger for bearin' it. Mayhap ye don't believe me now. Someday ye'll know it for yourself."

Ena stared, astonished and frightened by her mother's perception. Neither had had to speak the name. " 'Tis wise to leave him?" She waited, chewing her lip, looking so young, so defenseless that Ailsa wanted to take her daughter in her lap.

"Aye, and kindest as well. But 'tis no' only because of Connor that you're goin'."

Ena looked long and hard into her mother's face. "No. 'Tis for me. For the future. For all the weeks and months and years to come."

Ailsa sensed there was something her daughter was not saying, but she did not press her. Instead, she stood, drawing Ena up to face her so their plaids fell into the crooks of their elbows. Holding her daughter's flushed and trusting face, she leaned down till their foreheads touched. "I'll ask of ye one thing only. Promise me no matter how far ye travel, who ye come to know and love, how much joy ye find or how much sorrow, ye'll always keep a place protected deep inside. There should your faith abide, smolderin' low and bright and constant, so when ye do return to Glen Affric, ye can breathe the embers back to flame, be warmed by them and know that you've come home."

26

THE SKY HAD BEEN WASHED AND REWASHED IN HUES OF gold and magenta, and the sun rested red on the horizon, gathering its strength to rise through layers of color and cloud and trailing mist until it filled the morning sky. The last dawn Ena Rose would spend in the glen where she'd been born. She would be back, but she didn't know when.

A week after she'd asked her mother's blessing, Ena knelt at the foot of her grandparents' graves, a stone in each hand, dampened by her tight grasp till they shone. "I've no' much to give ye, Gran, Grandda. Just these stones, which I treasure because they're bonny and I've seen no others like them.

"Know that in goin' from here, I'll remember what I've learned from the woods, the river, the hills. Know that I'll no' forget ye, either one." Ena's throat was dry and her eyes damp. She held the two stones up to the sunlight till they glowed, then leaned down with her open palms pressed against the textured surface of the graves. When she rose, perched on her heels, she stayed unmoving for a long time, struggling with the emptiness where Mairi should have been, the two lone tears that slid down her cheeks. Finally, she murmured,

"Ancient and Enduring Ones,
   Keeper of Kindreds,
I go forth as one of your family.

"And thus," she whispered, "will I return."

* * *

The three sisters stood at the back of the Valley of the Dead. The wall riddled with crevices rose behind them, reassuringly solid and unchanging. They watched Ena kneel, saw her raise the stones skyward, then fall forward as if she would meld with them and lie at peace upon the graves of Charles Kittridge and Mairi Rose.

Ailsa, Lian and Genevra tensed as the girl leaned back and spoke softly. Too softly to hear. Yet her words brought tears to her mother's eyes.

The women waited patiently, for each had experienced such good-byes more than once in her lifetime. Lian and Genevra, with Ailsa beside them, had already placed their final stones on the one cairn made of two combined, murmured their private wishes to mother and father, body and spirit. Then they'd backed away, leaving Ena alone to say her last farewell.

"I still can't believe Mairi's gone," Genevra said, unashamed of the tears on her cheeks. "I feel her too strongly. And it's mad, but I think she feels me too."

"Of course it is not mad. She promised us, remember? I have never known Mairi Rose to break a promise." Lian did not weep, but her voice quavered. Instinctively, her sisters pressed closer, absorbing each other's warmth on this cold day.

"Listen!" Ailsa looked up at the tunneled rock above them and the wind whistled in and out, its harsh, cold cry becoming softer with each moment.

Ye'll hear me if ye listen well, for partin' need no' mean silence among us, only a different sound, a different song to bind us with its melody.

Ailsa rested her head on Lian's shoulder. "Though Ena'll be with ye when ye go from here, please know I'm thankful, for her sake and mine. 'Twas time I let her choose her own path, though I didn't want to do it. Ye made me see her new.

"I'm grateful beyond words that ye were here when . . .

that ye came in time. Mam said ye would, but I didn't know what she meant. I'm thinkin' I didn't want to know." She turned first to Lian, then to Genevra. "I dreamt it all, ye ken, your comin' and our grievin'. I thought 'twas but a memory, though Mam was dreamin' too, and she knew 'twas the future, no' the past. She saw it all. I should've listened to her fear.

"I think mayhap I guessed about Mairi long before she hurt her ankle. But I could no' admit it. 'Twas why I didn't write ye; for I can no' hide from ye even my deepest dread, and whether I will or no', all my thoughts and fears come out. I was a coward. Some part of me knew I could no' face what my instincts were sayin'. I had to stay deaf for a little longer."

"That's why we dreamed that no matter how loudly we called you couldn't hear, that you were far across the glen and we couldn't reach you, I think," Genevra mused.

"Because you were, indeed, so far away here in the Highlands, so isolated," Lian added, "we thought we were losing you. But all along, it was Mairi who was going."

Know that I love ye, that I hold the image of each of ye in my hands and in my heart, and those images will no' fade, because they're part of me, of my blood, of my very bones.

The sisters slipped their arms about each others' waists and leaned shoulder to shoulder, so different and so much the same, stricken by loss and lifted by hope as they watched Ena rise from beside the new grave, brushing the dirt and pebbles from her knees till they were clean again.

While her mother and aunts waited at the edge of the woods, Ena disappeared among the trees. She had to visit her hideaway before she left. She told herself it was only to collect a few belongings and say good-bye to her childhood, once and for all. But in her heart, she hoped she would find Connor there.

She knew long before she approached the hollow trunk

that her friend was not waiting for her. She blinked rapidly, swallowed, and knelt to swing the hidden door open.

Despite the nearby rush of the burn, the stillness overwhelmed her, along with a single blaze of anger that her friend would not even bid her farewell.

No one was there. None but the voices and images of her aunts and cousins, mother and grandmother, her fantasies and her treasures. Carefully, she collected the letters and drawings to put in the rosewood chest, which she slipped into her satchel, leaving the rest—her herbs and stones and carvings and leaves and the lopsided stump of a table—for someone else to find.

When she stepped back to duck under the curved frame of the door, she stumbled over something in the shadows. A flash of white, oddly shaped. Holding her breath, she picked up the bulky package wrapped with paper. She unfolded the rumpled parchment to find a beautiful rough piece of oak as big as her hand, swirled with hues from pale beige to brown to rust in a graceful circled pattern. Beneath it was a shiny new carving knife. She stared, afraid to move and thereby break the spell.

When she heard her mother calling, Ena spread the paper flat on the ground and read the brief scrawled message.

> Please take this with you and carve me something for when you return.
>
>   Connor

So few words to tear down easily so many new-built barriers. Shoving wood and knife and crumpled note into her bag, Ena closed the door to her refuge and fled.

By the time the women arrived in the clearing, everyone was gathered and the coachman was eager to be on his way.

The girl moved from one embrace to another, seeing a blur of familiar faces, feeling the touch of familiar hands.

She threw back her head and breathed in the chilly winter air, the damp mist, the smell of pine and fir and loam and heather, to store them inside until she returned.

Her aunts had quietly climbed into the coach, leaving Ena with the people of the glen. She caught a glimpse of Jenny with tears on her cheeks, of Alanna, who, now that all was settled, seemed reluctant to let her half-sister go, of David, who hugged her and lifted her off the ground, setting her down hard enough for her feet to sink into the soft earth.

"Don't be forgettin' that feelin', Ena Rose, for 'tis your heritage and your legacy, and I know 'twill miss the weight of your nimble feet upon the many paths you've made your own."

"Don't worry, we'll be back," Genevra called from the coach. "The children will insist on visiting the Hill soon. I don't think we could keep them away if we tried."

"We'll be waitin'!" David called back.

Ailsa drifted toward Ena and neither spoke as mother and daughter lifted one hand each and pressed them palm to palm for a long moment. It was harder than either had imagined, this parting.

When they stepped back, Ailsa saw her daughter glance about surreptitiously, and knew she would not find what she was seeking. "He ran away across the river early. I think he could no' face ye, or he could no' face good-bye." She cupped Ena's face in her hands. Her eyes were huge with dark circles of sleeplessness making them look hollow. Ailsa forced herself to concentrate on the expression in her daughter's eyes, not the tale of exhaustion they revealed without words.

"Don't hate him for it, birdeen. He's young and had no' lost anyone but a fortnight past. Now he's lost two of the people he loved most. 'Tis hard, and he's a young man now, unwillin' for others to see his tears. Forgive him. Listen for him in your heart. 'Tis where he lingers and where he'll stay."

"Are ye comin' this fortnight or should we unload again?" the driver bellowed. Beneath his rough question was compassion for the scene he turned away from for fear it would break his heart.

"I'll try," Ena whispered. She kissed Ailsa's cheek, brushed it lightly with her fingertips. "Just as I'll try to be easy without ye, though I'm thinkin' 'tis no' possible." she turned quickly and ran to the swinging door Lian held open. Before she leapt onto the step, she knelt down, took a great handful of loam and buried her nose in the feel, the scent, the spirit of the glen she loved. Feeling her throat fill with tears, she swallowed them, brushed off her hands and let her aunts lift her into the coach.

Even as the door swung closed, she stared out the window, searching in vain for a single glimpse of Connor.

As the coach lumbered down the rough track leading to the somewhat smoother dirt road out of Glen Affric, everyone but Ena looked back. Genevra and Lian grasped each other's hands beneath the warm tartan blanket.

Connor Fraser stood alone on the precipice that had once been Ailsa's secret place, where she sought solitude in the sweeping view of the glen and the knowledge that the climb up was too steep, too difficult for anyone to follow. That was partly why Connor had chosen this place; Ailsa had not been there in years. He wanted a view of the glen, though woods blended with moor and foothills and river through the thin, fine curtain of moisture in his eyes. He had been so strong, so sure the day he'd told Ena they must part. But today she was leaving him behind.

He felt brittle; the shell that had protected him was cracking slowly. His sister, his friend, his other half was going. He had sent her away. He had come here so he'd not disgrace himself or her by grabbing her hand and refusing to release her. Nor could he bear to see her face, to witness the reflection of his torment in her eyes.

Last night he'd dreamt of those eyes, but they were the golden eyes of the wildcat before it turned to flee, gracefully, swiftly, warily toward the freedom of the forest. He'd felt a fierce joy at the beauty of the sleek cat finding its way home at last.

He knew, as his gift left in the hollow oak revealed, that she'd return to the home of her heart that had forged her soul and her strength and her spirit. But the knowledge did not stop him from reaching blindly, helplessly toward the road so far below and the dust of the coach that held her now.

As he reached for the girl he'd known, the woman he would never know, his heart cried out high on the back of the wind, then low among the quivering tops of pine and fir.

The coach began to pick up speed and the occupants settled into their seats. For the moment, they left Ena to herself, giving her time to adjust to the sound of the door closing out the people of the glen. She was grateful for their restraint; her insides were in turmoil and she did not know how to stop it.

Suddenly she stiffened, tilted her head and crawled up on her knees so she could gaze out the back window. She thought she had heard something . . .

Her pulse slowed when she caught a glimpse of the red, yellow and black Fraser plaid high on a precipice where she and Connor had gone once years ago. She leaned closer to the window, but the glass was blurred by weather and age, and her eyes were swollen and gritty. She did not remember when she'd last slept through the night.

Still, she was certain she'd glimpsed Connor. She saw him reach out and down, grasping empty air, and felt as if he were squeezing her heart in his hands. Then she caught the last few fragments of his thoughts, when the wind swooped down, rattling the coach on its ancient springs.

She felt his joy and his anguish, though she could not

have heard him, and whispered, "I'm goin', Connor. I'll miss ye as the earth the trees and the trees the wind, but I'll go on. And so will ye, my friend of friends. So, I pray, will ye."

As his voice and the bright red and yellow of his plaid began to recede, Ena blinked and stared in amazement at the landscape unrolling below her. The several lochs, linked like a chain of blue stones, stretched far into the distance, sparkling as trails of mist drifted over the wind-whipped water. There were sweeping golden moors, and the vibrant green of stands of pine and spruce and fir among the skeletons of oak and birch and larch. The mist wound its way among the naked branches, blurring the sharp edges. The River Affric and several other burns made glittering patterns through the forests and fields and thickly wooded hillsides, while the jagged, slate gray mountains with their rushing silver streams loomed above it all, both treacherous and compelling.

"Oh!" she sighed, stunned by the power, the magnificence, the menace of the glen. She had never seen it like this before, laid out in one wide swathe from end to end. She'd only known it up close, bit by bit and piece by piece. She had missed this dizzying beauty all these years, she thought, as Connor blended into the landscape and she could see him no more. He was part of it now, he who, with his song of farewell, had drawn her to the window and made her look back, made her see, made her forget her sorrow in amazement. "Thank ye, my friend," she breathed, "for givin' me back my hope."

Her heart beat with excitement and anticipation. Already she had seen so much, and the journey had just begun. Suddenly, she could not wait for whatever else awaited her. She pressed her hands to the glass, as if to reach out and take hold of the pale moon suspended above the mountains in the vast morning sky.

* * *

Long after the coach had disappeared, long after the people had wandered away, Ailsa, Jenny and Alanna lingered, staring mutely at the ground, stirred into ruts of mud by the heavy wheels.

Wisely, David had taken one look at their faces and left them alone.

Alanna put her hand on her mother's shoulder and Ailsa rested her cheek upon it.

"What'll I do now?" she asked the sky, empty but for the oval of the rising moon.

It came to her then that Ian had answered that question long ago in her dream.

Ye'll learn to let go, to have faith as ye once had faith in me, that those ye set free will come back to ye, always. I am with ye, and so she will be with ye, for her spirit is strong. The answer came so quickly, so clearly, that she stumbled forward, taking Alanna with her. Ian. She'd thought he'd meant Mairi; because earlier that night her mother had asked for release. But he'd meant Ena as well. Perhaps more, because her daughter still had a long life to live. *I can no' do it,* she'd cried. "I've lost so much."

"We all have," Jenny Fraser said.

Ailsa looked up, startled, realizing she'd spoken the last words out loud. Startled too by the compassion in Jenny's gentle smile.

"But we all have a great deal, still, to be grateful for," Jenny continued, nodding imperceptibly at Alanna. "A very great deal."

Turning to her daughter, Ailsa took her hands, surprised by a sparkle of mischief beneath a sheen of tears. "What're ye no' tellin' me?" Before Alanna could answer, her mother felt a strange warmth in her daughter's hands, a movement in the center of her body—a heartbeat not her own. Ailsa looked down at Alanna's stomach and knew as certainly as she held two hands in hers, that there would be a child. She met her daughter's eyes, grinning, eyes brimming, full of joy. "You've waited so long, my wild one. Why did ye no' tell me?"

Alanna was ashamed of the truth—that she'd wanted Ailsa to "see" the baby for herself, before there was aught to prove its existence. "For ye and for Ena. I know 'twas no' easy to let her go. I wonder, if it'd been Connor, if I could've done the same. So I kept quiet, leavin' ye to one another." That, at least was true.

"Bless ye, Alannean, for thinkin' of us, but 'tis time now to think of yourself and keepin' care of this new life you've made." Ailsa placed her hand reverently on her daughter's flat belly and smiled again. "And as for Connor, ye'd no have held him back. Ye see, you're finer than me, my daughter, finer and stronger and truer." She'd heard those words before, the last time Ian had come to her. She touched her daughter's hand to her cheek.

Out of the corner of her eye, Alanna saw her son at the edge of the forest, walking, shoulders slumped, as if the will had seeped from him, and with it his hope and his strength. "I must go to him," she said.

"Aye," Jenny and Ailsa answered together. "He'll be needin' ye."

The older women smiled at one another, but Alanna barely noticed as she ran off to meet her son and lead him home.

"So now we start again," Ailsa said. "For I know you've lost as much as me in the last few weeks, Jenny. Too many endings."

'Tis no the end, mo-charaidh, Ian had told her firmly. *Ye will go on. Always ye go on. This I swear to ye, on my spirit and my soul.*

They turned away from the muddy track and automatically toward Mairi's croft. "Ye'll go on and I'll go on," Jenny said, echoing her husband's words. But he had been a dream and she was very real. "And we'll grow stronger, ye and me, as Mairi did when your father left her, as she did when she stood in this very spot and watched the coach rumble away with ye and your English husband inside. She had far less than ye that day—" She broke off as they watched Alanna and Connor talking together seriously. "Yet Mairi Rose went on learnin' every day a little more patience, learnin' how to wait and fill the waitin' no' with sorrow and bitterness, but with hope."

Ailsa watched Alanna closely, and knew her oldest daughter was her hope—she and her husband and their son, and the new child. As the pair disappeared into the woods, Ailsa revolved slowly toward Jenny as if she were a stranger newly arrived. She was pleased and dismayed and filled with awe for this woman.

"Who are ye, Jenny, that I never truly knew ye before Mam died? That I never saw ye standin' here, quiet and contained and unshakable in your faith? That I never recognized the depth of your wisdom?"

Believe, my beloved. Believe in ye.

Those had been Ian's last words to her, and now his voice was fading, fading. Ailsa smiled a bittersweet smile into the distance, and bid that voice, that ghost, that need farewell. There were too many others who lived and breathed, who she cared for so much that it surprised her.

Jenny smiled, pleased by the compliment, though she tried not to be. "Why 'tis only me, Jenny Mackensie Fraser. She who ye knew before all the others, who ye drew out of my small, dark shell and into the sunlight to show me the wonder in the world. 'Tis only me, your friend for near fifty years, but older and touched and changed by sorrow and a great deal more at peace."

While they walked, slowly, despite the brisk air, pulling their plaids over their heads, Jenny grew pensive. "Don't be thinkin' I let all my anger out that day ye challenged me. I'd raged inside too long at what ye'd taken from me. I'm no' a saint, Ailsa Rose. But I saw I was harmin' my children with my quiet fury. And 'twas no' helpin' me. So I stopped and one day ye faced me and we wept together and the rage that was poison seeped away at last."

Considering her friend through the shadow of the past, Ailsa was moved to tears. But she did not weep them; Jenny was too proud. Jenny Fraser, who had raised four children and many grandchildren and had chosen not to bequeath them the bitterness and anger that was her right and theirs.

"I finally began to understand why we were brought together—ye and me, me and Ian, Ian and ye, and in the center, Mairi, who loved and rescued each of us more than once in our lives. I've come to see that ye need no' understand the reason for every false and joyful turn ye take in life. No' understand, exactly, but ye needs must accept, my friend." She glanced at Ailsa somberly.

"Now ye can honestly call me friend without bitterness?"

Jenny took Ailsa's hands. "I can. I do. And happily, gratefully, for I'd no' lose all we've shared to the memory of a dead man. Ye were right about that. We let him guide us for too long. I must be my own strength now. Mairi told me I could do it, and I tried, and now I can stand alone at last and be glad of my freedom, rather than grievin' for my loss. Ye understand that, do ye no'?"

"Aye," Ailsa replied, "I understand." It came to her, as they stood with the wind whipping their plaids about their faces and the first snow of winter hovering just out of sight, that in falling back into the dream of what had been between her and Ian, she had been seeking not comfort, but absolution. And it seemed, miraculously, that Jenny had absolved her long ago.

Inside the coach, all three had fallen back against the uncomfortably padded seats, weary, but somehow content. Ena had slid down from the window long since and, sitting between her aunts, had been gradually lulled by the rhythm of the wheels on the road. She began to lean more and more against Lian, her eyes feeling weighed down with grains of sand. She had trouble keeping her head up, and finally, with

no battles left to fight and no strength with which to fight
them, she laid her head in Lian's lap.

Her aunt felt a rush of pleasure as the girl fell trustingly
into her arms. She reached out tentatively to caress Ena's
long, disheveled hair, her fingers, soft and full of tenderness.
She had regretted not having a daughter, and as they settled
more comfortably into one another, Lian realized Ailsa had
done more than grant Ena a chance at a new life. She had
given her half-sister a gift beyond value. If only for a while.
It was enough.

For the first time in far too long, Ena forgot her fear, confusion, restlessness, the shadows and the grief. Cradled by
her aunt's strong arms, she fell deeply, slowly, steadily, into
sleep. She uncurled her clenched hands, one finger at a time
and nestled into her heavy plaid.

She sighed softly, and slept, and no dreams came to
haunt her.

Epilogue

Glasgow, Scotland, 1997

EVA SMILED IN HER SLEEP. AN UNFAMILIAR SENSATION. SHE had been dreaming of her grandmother, Ena Rose, leaving the glen for the first time as a child. "I feel it."

"Feel what?"

Opening her eyes, surprised at how easy it was—her lids were not heavy and gritty; she did not have to concentrate to keep them from sliding shut again—Eva found herself staring at Rory Dey's face, inches away. Every feature was sharp and beautiful and clean, as if fashioned by an artist. For a moment, it did not strike her as unusual, the distinct image, unimpaired by shadows.

She had been too quick for him. He had watched her struggle toward wakefulness too often, watched the weight she tried to push away, failing at least once before she succeeded. He had lost hope of seeing her open her eyes, smiling, awake and alert. Yet today she had done just that. Rory could not take it in.

Eva stared in fascination at his tousled black hair, his parted lips, his sky blue eyes regarding her intently. Before he could adjust to her straightforward, open gaze, she caught the look of waiting, the expectation of something dreadful in Rory's eyes. He'd been watching her and worrying for a long time, she realized. Reaching out, she touched his cheek, creased by the wrinkles in his pillowcase.

Rory was startled. Eva had not touched him like that in days, had not looked *at* him but rather through him, had not smiled easily, affectionately. "Feel what?" he repeated.

Blinking, perplexed, Eva tried to remember. "Anticipation," she murmured, "amazement and delight." At his dazed expression, she raised herself onto her elbow and propped her chin up with her hand. She felt rested, refreshed. That was odd. Stranger still, there were no ghosts, no darkness lingering from her dream.

"Eva?" Rory said warily. He must have fallen back asleep and conjured this moment in his mind. It only seemed real because he wanted it so much. Her green eyes ringed in gray were clear, not puffy, red and unfocused. There was even a little color in her face, though not the hectic flush he'd seen too often in the past few days.

"I'm here," she said, brushing his lips with hers to prove it. "I think . . . it's over."

That brush of warmth had been real. He could never have imagined the riot of feelings it released in him. Instinctively, Rory caught his hand in her hair to keep her close. "How? Why?" He tried to believe but could not dismiss the disturbing image of Eva fading, being drawn into a nightmare of the past.

Except for her expression, she looked the same. Sometime while he slept, she'd cast off the dingy old-fashioned nightgown and shawl she often insisted on wearing, and he smiled at the sight of her long limbs—healthy, tan and strong from walking and swimming. She watched him with remorse, empathy—and love. His pulse slowed and he held his breath.

If he focused on her eyes, he could almost trust his own vision, the feeling in his gut that told him she was real.

"I'd not be knowing exactly why or how," she said,

responding to the questions, the doubt on his face, "but I'm thinking I took a journey with Mairi and Ailsa and Ena Rose. And they taught me that ye can survive anything if you're strong enough and determined enough. I'm here and solid and real, not fading or disappearing." She felt full of energy and ready for a challenge. And best of all, a song was forming at the back of her mind.

"You *are* back, aren't you?" No matter how he tried, he could not repress the flicker of optimism and joy that lit his eyes.

She nodded, unable to speak. They lay, faces nearly touching, elated and astonished by the sight of one another. He reached for her, kissed her deeply, released his captive breath over her forehead as he brushed it with his lips. He could taste her, see her close her eyes in pleasure, feel her tremble as he touched her shoulder lightly and trailed his fingers down her back. She did not stiffen or withdraw, and when he raised his head to look at her, she did not disappear behind the sooty veil that had become a barrier between them.

His whole body relaxed as if a great weight had been lifted off. His eyes filled with tears of relief, which he quickly blinked away.

But not quickly enough. Appalled by the things his body told her that his lips could not, by the things she had not recognized as she sank into the past, Eva went cold. Though it took more courage than she thought she possessed, she caught his face in both hands, staring directly into his eyes. "Has it been that awful for you? Did I hurt you that much?"

Sighing—with relief that she had noticed his response, with regret that she'd understood it—Rory ran his fingers through her chestnut hair. "I thought I was losing you, that you'd lost yourself somewhere in the past in someone else's pain. I watched you begin to fade, slipping away from me." He paused, wrapping a long, unwashed curl around his finger. " 'Twas the hardest thing I've ever done."

The defeat in his voice broke her heart. Noticing the bedside clock read 10:00, she sat up abruptly. " 'Tis late. Shouldn't you be at the University? What about your lectures?"

He drew her toward him. She was shaking. "It's Sunday, Eva."

"Sunday," she muttered, "Sunday." She remembered Saturday, Friday and Thursday, but vaguely, as if looking through a screen. She had gone so far away in such a short time. The thought was more than disconcerting. Closing her eyes, she swallowed dryly. "How long?"

Rory sighed. "You've not left this flat in four days."

She was silent for so long that he became anxious. "Why did you come back?" she asked. "Why did you stay? Why're you sittin' beside me now?"

"I told ye I'm a stubborn bastard, Eva Crawford. Besides, I knew if I waited about long enough you'd not be able to resist me forever. I am not, you will observe, without a good deal of charm. But I had to stay rather close to work my wiles on you. Powerful as they may be, I could hardly make you fall helplessly into my arms if I were in my bed and you in *yours*. Besides, someone had to keep you warm. Common sense, you see. Pure common sense."

Despite her perturbation, Eva could not help but smile. She felt giddy at the sound and smell and feel of the Rory she remembered. Faintly, she recalled his attempts to force her to abandon the ebony chest and the papers it held. But that was before. She met Rory's effort to distract her with an effort of her own. "Weel, at least I didn't damage your ego."

"Not a bit of it. Can't be done." Not exactly the truth; he'd been devastated to realize the words and dreams of dead ancestors held her tighter and closer than he ever could. Besides, the heat of her body, alive and awake against his, was making him think of other things. He was so grateful that Eva, *his* Eva, was here, whole and smiling.

"Nor did I lose my natural appetites. What was that you said about anticipation and delight?"

Eva's skin tingled as he gently massaged her shoulders, then her back. She wanted to close her eyes and lose herself in his touch, but she shook her head. "If you were . . . hungry . . . or lonely . . . or ready to give up, why didn't you go find yourself another woman? Someone normal, who wouldn't frighten you half to death."

Shifting his weight, he put both arms around her. "Could have, I suppose, but ye see, she wouldn't have been you. And besides—normal? Where'd the challenge be in that? I told you I can't resist a challenge, and things're never dull with you about. I'd be bored to tears by normal within two hours."

Eva stared at the rumpled covers, running her finger through the valleys and rivulets, following their meaningless course. "Wouldn't that be better than being *driven* to tears?" She knew what his answer would be, had always known, even in the darkest moment of the dream. But she wanted to hear him say it.

He stopped smiling, grasped her wandering hand and forced her to look at him. "No," he said, "it wouldn't. I love you, Eva, *you*, just as you are. I confess it's not always easy, but then, when have I ever done things the easy way? When have you, for that matter? The struggle only makes the victory sweeter. You know that as well as anyone."

Tears were sliding down her cheeks, but she seemed unaware of them. She locked her arms around his neck. "Aye, so I do." Then she added, "But I still say you should be made a saint." She gave him a stiff cock-eyed grin, but she more than half meant it. He had stayed because he refused to give up. "Sainthood and great obstinance: Aren't they the same thing?"

"Shouldn't be at all surprised. I know I protested before, but if you must canonize me to satisfy your sense of justice, I'm ready to submit." He lay flat on the bed, arms straight out from his sides, palms up. He wanted to wrap his arms around her and hold her so tightly she could never slip away again. He wanted to ask her if she loved him. He wanted to sit for hours with his cheek against her hair, feeling the warm, vital reality of her. But she was weak from lack of sleep and emotional exhaustion. He could not push her now. When she was strong again, when she'd eaten and slept and gone for a walk in the lane, *then* he'd ask again.

"At the moment, if you don't mind terribly, I'd rather you just hold me."

She was gazing at him so tenderly, with such trust and devotion that he could not speak. He had never thought to see that look again, never thought to feel her twine her fingers with his, drawing him toward her, smiling and weeping at once. Rory closed the distance between them, gripping her so tight that she gasped, then pressed her face into the hollow of his shoulder and made no other sound.

Something else was niggling at the back of his mind, something important, but he couldn't quite grasp it. Something about tomorrow.

Then it struck him, hard, and he leapt up to pace frantically beside the bed. "I lost track of the dates. Damn! Tomorrow's the twenty-first."

Rubbing her arms at the chill left by his abrupt departure, Eva watched in confusion. "And?"

"And more to the point, the beginning of my lecture series for the university. Spreading goodwill, along with a little knowledge, one hopes, through the States." He pounded his fist on the bedpost. "I'll tell them to cancel, that's all. I can't leave you."

Eva sat up straighter, and naked as she was, her dignity was impressive. "Why can't you?"

Rory recognized the danger signs, but was too distracted to heed them. "Because you seemed so . . . lost. I'd be gone for over a fortnight. I can't take the risk of leaving you alone—"

"Rory," she said, slowly, succinctly, "listen to me. I told you it's over. I'll not be in danger, for the danger's gone."

He wanted to believe her, tried to convince himself by remembering what Eva had been like before the nightmares started—independent and strong-willed, despite her imaginative, impulsive and empathetic nature. But she had changed dramatically in the past few days, become irresolute and anxious. She'd lost her appetite along with her energy. But now that he observed her closely, he saw something he'd never seen before. She'd grown increasingly insecure about herself and her career of late, and that had made her vulnerable. Now she looked confident.

Eva rose to her knees so her eyes were level with his. "I trusted ye, Rory, *mo-chridhe*, through every moment of the nightmare. I knew in my heart ye'd be here waiting for me." It was true, though she'd just now understood it. She'd felt it like a rush of heat through her cold body— luminous and irrefutable. " 'Twas daft, I'll admit, to believe such a thing when I've dragged ye through hell and couldn't even tell ye why, but somehow I knew."

She put her hands on his shoulders, staring into his blue, blue eyes. "The point is, it rather sounds as if you've cared for me like a guardian—or a parent. I'm grateful, I can no' tell ye how much, but now it's time for me to find myself again. I need to do this alone, to prove I can." She saw the doubt in his eyes.

"It's not just for me, but for both of us." Touching his forehead with hers, she murmured, "I want a lover, not a caretaker who'll always be worryin' about me."

He knew she was right, that they could never be equals if they weren't certain she could stand up without him. But what if she couldn't do it?

"I'll be all right, I promise," Eva said firmly. "You brought me through the worst, but I need to recover on my own, with my own wits and my own determination. You couldn't do that for me, even if you stayed. But I can do it, and I will."

He almost believed her. There was a new conviction in her eyes.

She took a deep breath. "I had faith in you, my heart. Now you must have faith in me."

Eva knelt on the floor beside the ebony chest that had fascinated her for so long. But she wasn't thinking of her ancestors, only of Rory. She'd been eating carefully, walking and swimming each day. She felt stronger by the hour, more herself. Tomorrow Rory would finally be home, and she'd planned a surprise. She was just gathering the last of her things; the flat was cold and empty, with only the bed, the chest and her clothes. The rest had been moved to Rory's flat by eager friends who knew how long he'd waited for Eva to overcome her doubts and take the risk of moving in.

Today, there were no doubts, just excitement and anticipation of his reaction. Rory's friends had sworn his landlady to secrecy and convinced Eva that Rory would be delighted by her decision. He did not know he'd be coming home to find her waiting nervously.

"Here, aren't ye ready yet? We're about to be on our way."

"A minute more," Eva said without looking up. In her lap lay Ailsa Rose's journal, Genevra's diary and the cashmere shawl. She'd not touched them since Rory left, had not felt the need to since she'd dreamt of little Ena in that coach, leaving the glen to find her future. If a thirteen-year-old girl could do it, so could Eva.

She shook away the dream. Or was it memory? It no longer mattered.

Eva had found her grandmother Ena's journal at the bottom of the chest, so she knew the girl from the glen had met her husband in Burgundy, that she'd had a daughter and a son, that the family returned to live in Glen Affric. Connor Fraser married a Drummond lass and lived amicably near his childhood friend. Eva needed to know no more than that.

Smiling, she placed the two journals into the trunk. She'd already wrapped the painting of the three sisters carefully and put it inside. Last of all, she laid out the shawl, still beautiful, soft and delicate, despite the passage of the years. She folded it slowly, savoring the feel of the gossamer fabric, knowing it would be a long time before she touched it again, if she ever did. Perhaps if she had a child to share it with. . . . But that was for the future.

Gingerly, she sprinkled the chest with herbs to preserve the shawl and laid it on top of the many treasures she'd discovered there. She paused, brushed her fingers over the shawl, then noticed a bit of fabric she'd not seen before. Pulling it free gently, she saw it was an intricately woven scarf in a pattern of leaves—green and gold and burgundy and blue—and the weave changed with the pattern, thicker here and thin and fine as silk there. It was beautiful; it was astonishing in its complexity. There was a small piece of linen attached to a corner. On it were the faded words: *Made by Alanna Fraser, 19th June 1896. For my daughter Kirsty on the day of her birth.* There was something about the flow of this fabric that made Eva run her hands over it again and again, until she felt that somehow she was part of the design.

There was a lesson in the weave, the pattern of leaves. Each branch represented a life, and the lives intertwined so each gave color and support to the other. Alone, Ailsa, Lian, Genevra, Jenny, Mairi and Ena would have been somehow less than what they were. Their strength had come from their faith in one another, and their profound affection.

These women had taught Eva more than strength; they had taught her it was all right to lean on Rory, that it was good to need others, if they cared for you. And Rory had made it clear that he cared for her as much as she cared for him.

Folding the scarf, she placed it inside and closed the lid. She felt no regret, only deep tenderness and relief. She pulled out the key she'd slipped into her pocket, worked it into the intricate Chinese lock and left it there, where it looked like a shining brass ornament in a field of ebony dragons and gods and winged creatures. Eva pressed her hands, palms down, against the top, feeling the imprint of those carved wonders, the patterns and hollows and graceful swells. "Sleep well," she whispered, "all of ye."

Then she rose stiffly; she'd knelt too long, unmoving. "Are you there?" she called to the men in the hall who were whiling away the time chatting up her young and pretty neighbor. "I've finished. I'm ready."

Eva tried to soothe her nervous stomach as she stopped before the bright red door and inserted the key Rory's landlady had given her. Mrs. Wallace smiled knowingly, muttering as she turned away that she loved surprises. "Surprises, surprises." Eva might have been intrigued if she weren't so anxious. The bolt slid back and she turned the knob slowly.

Taking a deep breath for courage, she pushed the door open, amazed, as always, at the light and spaciousness of the flat. Hers had been little more than a bedsit, but this was a real home, with two bedrooms, a parlor, kitchen and a study for Rory's research, besides the two baths. Every room had a skylight, but the ceiling in the large bedroom was made entirely of glass. They liked to lie on the bed and watch the clouds change shape as they moved across the sky, or the raindrops making patterns and a lovely rhythm above their heads, and sometimes, simply stare at a sky so blue it outshone Rory's eyes.

Eva paused in each room, surprised at what a difference her few possessions had made. Her guitar sat on its stand in the parlor beside her shelves of music and blank sheets for scores and several precious music books. Her brightest shawl thrown over the back of the sofa made the room seem warmer. But not warm enough.

All at once, she realized she was lonely in these big rooms, that she missed Rory coming to greet her, unwinding her muffler from around her neck while he kissed her relentlessly. The rooms were so still, so achingly empty.

She'd been too busy packing, planning and getting back her strength to notice until now, when she faced a whole night and day alone here. Unjust as it might be, she felt abandoned as she wandered through the flat. "You knew he'd not be here," she reprimanded herself. "There's plenty to keep you busy. Don't be daft."

She shrugged. "I've been told more than once that I am, you know," she answered herself, just to hear a voice in the hushed air that clung about her like fog. "That's why he loves me. Or so he says."

She stopped abruptly, frowning when she reached the bedroom. This would be the loneliest, emptiest room of all.

Except it wasn't.

Spread across the duvet were dozens of tulips and roses, as if they'd been dropped casually, haphazardly. Eva knew better. The pale roses were soft cream and white with ruffled pink edges, the tulips bright splashes of orange, red, yellow and green. There was a card propped on the pillow where she often slept. No wonder Mrs. Wallace had smiled so mysteriously, mumbling about surprises.

Eva gasped. Perhaps Rory'd come back early. Perhaps he was waiting. But she listened, felt the cool air eddy about her and knew she was alone.

At least she didn't have to worry about his reaction to her moving in. Tears came to her eyes as she reached for the card with her name scrawled in Rory's strangely elegant hand, then paused. On the night table lay a beautiful leather-bound book. Not an inexpensive reproduction, but real leather. Its fragrance was stronger than the roses. It was deep brown with burgundy silk corners and a burgundy stripe near the spine. The textured leather cried out for her to touch it, and she ran her fingers lightly over the front, holding her breath. It felt heavenly against her fingertips.

Curiously, she opened the book to find marbleized fly-leaves in wine and dove gray. She touched them admiringly, then flipped to the title page and froze.

The book was blank, but Rory had written carefully on the thick vellum page:

A Journal
by Eva Crawford
Begun this 4th day of November
in the year Nineteen hundred and Ninety-seven

The rest of the pages were untouched, waiting for the pressure of her pen. It could not be a coincidence that the journal resembled so closely the ones her ancestors had written in, except that it was new and fresh and all her own.

Rory'd made no secret of his resentment against the Rose women who'd fascinated Eva, who had drawn her away from him. Still, he'd recognized their importance to her, and this was his compromise.

He could not know that she'd sealed away those voices from the past, that she was ready now to hear her own voice, to listen to *its* songs and secrets.

She blinked back tears that blurred the words he'd written. Simple, direct, saying so much by saying so little.

The landlady must not have been able to contain her excitement. No doubt she'd phoned Rory in the States to tell him Eva was coming. He'd guessed she would be lonely in his empty flat. He'd probably asked Mrs. Wallace to bring fresh flowers up this morning, and he must have shipped the book here as well, instructing his landlady where to place it. He'd worked fast, that was clear.

And he'd done it to ease Eva's loneliness. He knew her too well. He always had.

Finally, she picked up the envelope and slipped out the single rectangular card inside. The message was brief, as she'd expected; Rory liked to get to the point when he had something important to say. There were only two words in his familiar scrawl, telling her, if she had any lingering doubts, that she'd made the right choice. Her hand shook and the tears she had been holding back defeated her, just as Rory's message, blurred and wavering as it was, restored her.

She read it aloud once, so the words would fill the room, not empty any longer.

"Welcome home."

Breathtaking romance from
New York Times **bestselling author**

KATHRYN LYNN DAVIS

All We Hold Dear

Sing to Me of Dreams

Too Deep for Tears

Pocket Books